Molôn Labé!

Molôn Labé!

by

Boston T. Party

Published by

JAVELIN PRESS

(Without any 4 USC §§ 105-110 *"Federal area"* or *"State."*)
www.javelinpress.com

Molôn Labé!   January, 2004

**Printed in the united states of America,
without any 4 USC §§ 105-110 *"Federal area"* or *"State."***

Hardcover First Edition

10 9 8 7 6 5 4   / 13 12 11 10 09

ISBN 1-888766-08-5

ACKNOWLEDGMENTS

I thank the myriad of Wyoming officials and citizens too numerous to list who variously helped with me information and advice since 1998.

Huge appreciation goes to my several local proofreaders, one of whom was also my graphic artist and produced the stunning cover. Thanks for working so hard under such a cruel holiday deadline! I'm vastly in your debt.

I'm very grateful for the help of Doug and Ancha Casey, Jim Gibbons, Lobo and Sunni, Hunter, and the many good friends of Pablo, Tony, Dr. K, and Mr. Stubbs.

My old friend "R.H." lent his special genius with details in Chapters 2009 (*e.g.*, NoClog) and 2011 (*e.g.*, strychnine). Thanks, buddy. I hope you like "The Leopard."

Muchas gracias to the two Marks (and their families) in Wyoming for their editing, and for converting bedrooms (spare and not) into "Boston T. Party Suites" during my visits. The state is in great hands with such men as you!

Science-fiction author Fran Van Cleave in particular was a huge help, and often went above and beyond the call of duty. *Molôn Labé!* became a much better story because of her invaluable assistance in training this fledgling novelist. Some of her many suggestions are personified in Chapter 2011's character Louella Davis.

Thanks, Fran, for often urging me to "show it" versus "tell it"! (Not that I still don't need gobs of work on that...)

Finally, I thank the support and interest of my dear readers and valued distributors, who waited *soooo* long for *Molôn Labé!* to come out. I hope you'll deem it worth the wait.

DEDICATION

I dedicate *Molôn Labé!* to the many freedom-loving Americans in Wyoming, present and future. See you there!

by Kenneth Royce (Boston T. Party)

You & The Police! (revised for 2005)

The definitive guide to your rights and tactics during police confrontations. When can you *refuse* to answer questions or consent to searches? Don't lose your liberty through ignorance! This 2005 edition covers the *USA PATRIOT Act* and much more.

168 pp. softcover (2005) $16 + $5 s&h (cash, please)

Bulletproof Privacy

How to Live Hidden, Happy, and Free!

Explains precisely how to lay low and be left alone by the snoops, government agents and bureaucrats. Boston shares many of his own unique methods. Now in its 10th printing!

160 pp. softcover (1997) $16 + $5 s&h (cash, please)

Hologram of Liberty

The Constitution's Shocking Alliance
with Big Government

The Convention of 1787 was the most brilliant and subtle *coup d'état* in history. The nationalist framers *designed* a strong government, guaranteed through purposely ambiguous verbiage. Many readers say this is Boston's best book. A jaw-dropper.

262 pp. softcover (1997) $20 + $5 s&h (cash, please)

Boston on Surviving Y2K

And Other Lovely Disasters

Even though Y2K was Y2¿Qué? this title remains highly useful for all preparedness planning. **Now on sale for 50% off!** (It's the same book as The Military Book Club's *Surviving Doomsday*.)

352 pp. softcover (1998) only $11 + $5 s&h (cash, please)

Boston's Gun Bible (new text for 2006)

A rousing how-to/*why*-to on our modern gun ownership. Firearms are *"liberty's teeth"* and it's time we remembered it. No other general gun book is more thorough or useful! Indispensable!

848 pp. softcover (2002-2006) $33 + $6 s&h (cash, please)

Molôn Labé! (a novel)

If you liked *Unintended Consequences* by John Ross and Ayn Rand's *Atlas Shrugged*, then Boston's novel will be a favorite. It dramatically outlines an innovative recipe for Liberty which could actually work! A thinking book for people of action; an action book for people of thought. It's getting people moving to Wyoming!

454 pp. softcover (2004) $27 + $6 s&h (cash, please)
limited edition hardcover $44 + $6 (while supplies last)

Safari Dreams (new for 2008!)

A Practical Guide To Your Hunt In Africa

Possibly the most useful "one book" for making your first safari. Thoroughly covers: rifles, calibers, bullets, insurance, health, packing and planning, trip prep, airlines, choosing your PH, shot placement, and being in the bush. Don't go to Africa without it!

220+ pp. softcover (Jan 2008) $26 + $5 s&h (cash, please)

www.javelinpress.com
www.freestatewyoming.org

FOREWORD

Nach dem Spiel
ist vor dem Spiel.
   — S. Herberger

After the game
is before the game.

The big things in life can't be seen if you're standing too nearby. The dots can't be connected if you're still seeing dots. The opthamological term for this phenomenon is *neural lateral inhibition*. Not that we seem to notice, as it's something we were born with. Unless you happen to have been born an historian.

For the historically astute, the years 1992-2020 evoked an eerie, though unmistakable, sense of *déjà vu*. For the keen mind capable of standing back from the current events swirling about him—calmly contemplating an abstract painting across the gallery floor—two dates clearly materialized from the haze. From an historian's ethereal perspective, it was, all over again, 1775 and 1929.

Both dates resembled tidal waves which left behind great swathes of destruction, forever altering the social, political, legal, and economic landscapes. Such is the nature of tidal waves, but ironically, both waves seemed to take the people of their day by nearly total surprise. Perhaps it was because they'd had so many years of gathering swell behind them. The people of 1775 had suffered a lean decade of increasing governmental rules and oppression, while the people of 1929 had rejoiced during a fat decade of swollen false prosperity and bacchanalia.

After each wave crashed, things would get worse—much worse—before they began to get better. But when you're stunned with the weight of the crash and roiling about its foam, you don't know that then.

In retrospect, the waves of 1775 and 1929 were a sort of cosmic regurgitation—timely aspirations of festering toxicity which threatened the national *corpus*. But, it didn't last. Proverbs 26:11 was amply demonstrated:

As a dog returneth to his vomit, so a fool returneth to his folly.

The fool of 1775 eventually returned to political despotism; the fool of 1929 inexorably returned to economic witchcraft. In 1992 the dog had returned to *both* strains of vomit, simultaneously. The heaving was unparalleled. By

2014 a return to political despotism had summoned economic witchcraft, and a return to economic witchcraft had beckoned political despotism.

Will 1992-2020 simply become yet another tidal wave only for future historians to recognize through their unique lack of neural lateral inhibition? Probably, not that this will make their events less surprising, less poignant, less terrifying, or less hopeful for those who lived them.

We *could* have seen all this coming, but since we could, we did not. The human blind spot is the same for rabbits—straight ahead. To see the obvious, we mustn't look *quite* at it. And this is why we miss the obvious, the looming, every time—because we're always staring right at it. The harder it runs us over, the more determined we become to *really* focus on it the next time, so that we don't miss it again.

Which is why it will keep hitting us smack in the face, forever. Unless. Unless we learn to step back and use peripheral vision.

Unless we take hockey great Wayne Gretzky's fine advice:

. . . *skate to where the puck is going to be, not where it has been.*

The Nazis lost WWII with the best mechanical computers of the mid-1940s. The Allies won WWII with the best *electronic* computers of the mid-1940s. The Nazis skated to where the puck had been. We skated to where it was going to be. The battle goes not just to the swift or the strong; it goes to whichever side first arrives at the next juncture.

Longbows trump swords. Rifles trump smoothbores. Panzers trump Maginot Lines. Dive bombers trump battleships. Atomic bombs trump TNT. Microsoft trumps IBM.

PGP trumps NSA.

(For now. Rumor is they'll soon have a working quantum computer.)

In Western films, we call the next juncture "the pass." We must, for once, "head them off at the pass."

And, finally, we will soon have our chance. We absolutely *must* catch this bus, as the next one won't be along for a very, *very* long time.

INTRODUCTION

Only a virtuous people are capable of freedom. As nations become corrupt and vicious, they have more need of masters.
— Benjamin Franklin

Molôn Labé! was postulated on several concurrent premises. While any or all of them could be unrealized in near future events, I view the chance of this as dim. Such is, evidently, my lot to write about unpleasant matters.

The first premise is that the Federal Government will—in the name of fighting the "War Against Terrorism"—unwisely continue to squeeze an increasingly incompressible core, most of whom are politically conservative (Christian, Republican, Libertarian, Independent, etc.). Most of them are gunowners, and many of *them* are "damn-the-torpedoes" Patriots. Thus, the escalating federal barbarity will eventually encounter a very resolved and highly prepared segment of the populace who will *never* docilely accept CS gas "inserted" by tanks into their homes, or FBI snipers shooting their nursing wives in the face. Once the gun confiscation raids commence, the Government will have at last crossed that "line in the sand" for 100s of thousands of Patriots. I would give up nearly everything for that day never to arrive, however, the feds apparently believe they can pull it off, so they're going for it.

The second premise requires a market and currency crash, and a subsequently very sharp recession, to which the Government grossly overreacts— causing a depression. Washington, D.C. will make things worse—on *purpose.* Government is a disease masquerading as its own cure. (The Federal Reserve did exactly this in the 1930s by the hypercontraction of credit when it *should* have relaxed things instead. But, the Insiders had to make conditions *bad* enough by 1932 for the masses to clamor for their White Knight, FDR.)

In fact, the *fear* of a crash may be enough to *cause* one. Remember, the market is primarily mass *perception.* Although the stock market has no *logical* reason to be so bullish (PE ratios of 25-to-infinity are absurd), most speculators (who imagine themselves *investors*) disagree, so they keep buying stocks. (Besides, all those IRA and 401(k) savings must go *somewhere.*) Fear, however, is three times more powerful than greed, as bear markets prove by being three times more intense than bull markets.

Another major premise, sequential to the first two, is that America will soon begin to unravel at her seams. As I wrote in *Hologram of Liberty* (pp. 9/26-33), we are no longer a workably homogenous people. Cultures, values, religions, and politics have splintered and are quickly polarizing. Great clumps of Americans no longer have *anything* significant in common with each other. We have become two (if not several) countries within an artificial whole. Just because half the country wants blue and the other half yellow, the political solution is not green. No "midway moderate" candidate can win. The 2000 Election clearly proved that future presidential elections must necessarily see-saw between fairly diametrically opposed candidates, resulting in alternating halves of voter bitterness.

The *least*-worst solution to this awful mess is a peaceful secession or a *"velvet divorce"* along the lines of 1994 Czechoslovakia (which divided into Slovakia and the Czech Republic). This idea is more and more being discussed. Even the nationally-syndicated columnist Walter E. Williams called for secession in his wonderful essay *"It's Time To Part Company"*:

> *If one group of people prefers government control and management of people's lives, and another prefers liberty and a desire to be left alone, should they be required to fight, antagonize one another, and risk bloodshed and loss of life in order to impose their preferences,* **or should they be able to peaceably part company and go their separate ways?**
>
> *Like a marriage that has gone bad, I believe there are enough irreconcilable differences between those who want to control and those want to be left alone that divorce is the only peaceable alternative. Just as in a marriage, where vows are broken, our human rights protections guaranteed by the U.S. Constitution have been grossly violated by a government instituted to protect them.* **Americans who are responsible for and support constitutional abrogation have no intention of mending their ways.**
>
> *...Americans who wish to live free have two options: We can resist, fight and risk bloodshed to force America's tyrants to respect our liberties and human rights, or we can seek a peaceful resolution of our irreconcilable differences by separating. That can be done by people in different states, say Texas and Louisiana, controlling their legislatures and then issuing a unilateral declaration of independence just as the Founders did in 1776.*
>
> *...Some independence or secessionist movements, such as our 1776 war with England and our 1861 War Between the States, have been violent, but they need not be. In 1905, Norway seceded from Sweden, Panama seceded from Colombia (1903), and West Virginia from Virginia (1863).*
>
> *The bottom line question for all of us is should we part company or continue to forcibly impose our wills on one another?*
>
> — 13 September 2000, World Net Daily

Do I believe that the USG would willingly allow a national mitosis? No, I think the Federal Government would try to crush any such attempt, as it did in the 1860s. (Note the modern antipathy towards the Confederacy and its flag.) Once, however, the Crash hits and the welfare checks become increasingly worthless through inflation, and federal troops are patrolling the streets, we will become the Yugoslavia of the Western Hemisphere. *Then*, secession will finally have its chance.

I firmly believe that the Rocky Mountain states will be *the* place to weather out this imminent "Rainy Decade." They are geographically defensible, beautiful, abundant in wildlife, and are generally populated by honest, "salt of the earth" folks. I highly recommend that you seek high ground *now*, while it's early and affordable to do so. Relocate to an area with solid, hardworking people, plenty of sunshine, and ample water. Learn a few valuable skills, such as carpentry, welding, gardening, ranching, auto repair, etc., because your "high-falutin" city skills probably will be of little worth for a while. Granted, we *will* climb our way up and out and rebuild what was lost, however, for a season, things may be pretty basic. (My book *Boston on Surviving Y2K* covered all this pretty thoroughly, and copies are available from Javelin Press for a real bargain price after Y2¿*Qué?*)

The final premise is that the Government will view this alpine convergence of self-reliant Americans as too embarrassing a contrast to the liberal urbanites who stand in soup lines. As the West becomes stronger and stronger, and the East becomes weaker and weaker, the Government will feel forced to act. Partition, much less secession, indicates to the world that Washington, D.C. has failed, and the politicians will do *whatever* they can to prevent the secession of a state. I expect they'd even call in foreign UN troops (as did the 1960s Congo Communists to forcibly regain the independent and prosperous Katanga region). This is where the "fun" begins.

So, I have written *Molôn Labé!* with these assumptions: Early 21st century will be a mess, and the feds will worsen it to the point of instituting martial law. The President will then usurp the Congress through his Executive Orders. Dr. Gary North's prescient book, *Government By Emergency*, will come to pass. *Will we win?* Will we successfully carve out an oasis of freedom in America where our lives are our own again? You'll have to read the book and find out for yourself.

Even if the feds back off and recognize the 2nd Amendment—*even if* alpine Americans are left alone to run their own lives—even if *Molôn Labé!* is destined to be pure fantasy, I'd hope that you'd nonetheless find it an intelligently crafted romp and well worth the wait.

I hope to see you in Wyoming!

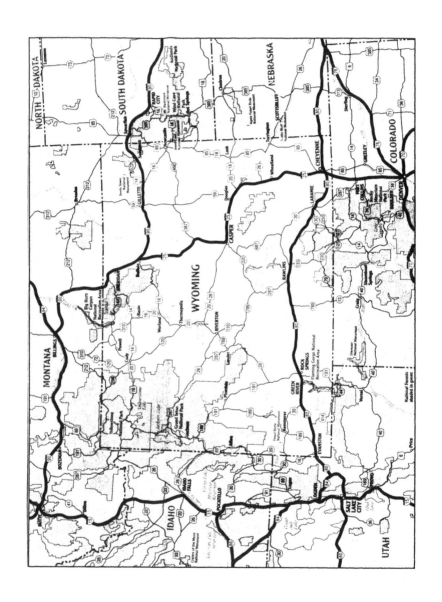

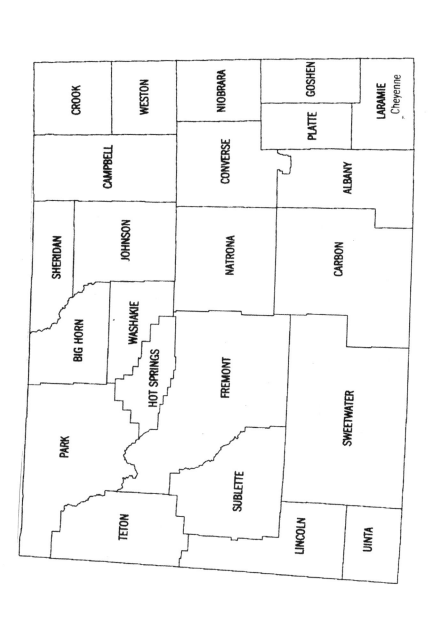

And where is that band, that so vauntingly swore
That the havoc of war and the battle's confusion,
A home and a country shall leave us no more?
Their blood has washed out their foul footsteps pollution!
No refuge could save the hireling and slave,
From the terror of flight, or the gloom of the grave.
And the star bangled banner in triumph doth wave
O'er the land of the free and the home of the brave!

Oh thus be it ever when free men shall stand,
Between their loved homes and the war's desolation!
Blest with victory and peace, may the h'ven rescued land,
Praise the Power that hath made and preserved us a nation.
Then conquer we must,
When our cause it is just,
And this be our motto: 'In God is our trust!'
And the star bangled banner in triumph shall wave
O'er the land of the free and the home of the brave!

　　　—verses 3 and 4 of the *Star Spangled Banner*

You common cry of curs, whose breath I hate
As reek o' th' rotten fens, whose loves I prize
As the dead carcasses of unburied men
That do corrupt my air — I banish you.
And here remain with your uncertainty!
Let every feeble rumour shake your hearts;
Your enemies, with nodding of their plumes,
Fan you into despair! Have the power still
To banish your defenders, till at length
Your ignorance — which finds not till it feels,
Making but reservation of yourselves
Still your own foes — deliver you
As most abated captives to some nation
That won you without blows! Despising
For you the city, thus I turn my back;
There is a world elsewhere.

　　　—*Coriolanus*, Act Three, Scene III

PROLOGUE

Americans tend to discount ideology; they do not realize that they are highly ideological themselves. Nor do they understand the true meaning of idealogy, which is "science of ideas." Such a science is legitimate and needed, and it does not contain elements that are necessarily erroneous.

In any serious conflict, a rationale of success or victory is required, together with a horizon of knowledge and of ideas that are action concepts.

...The Free World does not understand the crucial point at issue: Unless a conflict is first won spiritually, it is unlikely that it can be won materially. Ideology is the bridge to spiritual victory.

—Stefan T. Possony, *Psyops*

Natrona County, Wyoming   February 2006

"Good morning, sir. Here are last night's figures. We have sufficient numbers for five, and almost six."

The dark-haired man behind his desk nods and smiles. He is distinguished like an executive, but also tanned and rugged like a rancher. Little wonder. He's both.

"Great news, Tom. Five will work. Five is all we need for Phase 1a."

"What about the overflow from number six?" asks the assistant.

"Let's spread half into the first five and reserve the remaining half until September for any surprises."

"Yes, sir. That was my thought, too," agrees Tom.

The rancher executive turns to his computer keyboard and briskly composes a short message, which he PGP encrypts with the public key of a colleague in Phoenix. This he pastes into an email composition window. Above the encrypted message he adds some curious text which looks like a simple computer language and includes several e-remailers' addresses. The entire email is then again PGP encrypted, but with "To's" public key. An envelope within an envelope. Only the email's header (*i.e.*, From, To, Subject) is in plaintext. The Subject line reads one question.

He sits back for several moments of calm satisfaction. Then he looks up at his assistant and says, "You've put enormous work into this, Tom. We couldn't have done it without you. Would you do the honors?"

"Yes, sir! Thank you!" Tom steps behind the man's desk, places his hand on the mouse, moves the cursor to the Send icon, pauses, and clicks the mouse button. At the speed of light the email is instantly en route.

"Iacta alea est," says the man.

"The die is cast," echoes Tom.

The exclamation was attributed to Julius Caesar upon his crossing of the river Rubicon in 49 B.C. against the Senate's orders to lay down his military command. By invading central Italy from the Roman province of Cisalpine Gaul (now northern Italy), Caesar kicked off a civil war with his former ally Pompey, a Roman general whose rule extended to Syria.

"Not that you aspire to become Caesar," Tom qualifies.

"No," sighs the man, "but they will accuse me of it all the same."

* * * * * * *

Before the two men had finished speaking, the email had already crossed the Atlantic. "To" is a covert e-remailer in Berlin used by only several dozen international libertarians for urgent business. "To" picked up his web-based email from several different public terminals which required no ID or sign-up to log in. Always with Karl Heinz Kolb was his powerful laptop, loaded with virtually every encryption program in existence. It had built-in software and hardware security devices to foil any third-party attempt at usage or data downloading. His friends joked that it would probably convert any snoop into argon gas. Kolb was quietly revered for how seriously he took his computer privacy. There was none his crafty equal in all of Berlin.

Sipping his *chai* tea at the Potsdamer Platz CyberCafé, he sits down at a terminal, logs onto his Yahoo! account, opens his Inbox, and clicks on the waiting email from aglet@mail.com. Once, Kolb thought aglet was an odd name and so he looked it up. He was surprised to learn that it wasn't a name, but a thing. It is the plastic end of shoelaces that allows you to thread them through the eyeholes. Without aglets, we'd all be wearing sandals or loafers. Whoever aglet was, he evidently appreciated the small, overlooked things which made bigger things not only possible, but common.

The email is a PGP message, which he saves on a floppy. He knows that it has been encrypted with one of his public keys. The "one" in the Subject line's one question means Priority One.

Most public terminals do not have PGP installed, so the 31 year-old Berliner must use his laptop. This is really the only downside to web-based email from public computers. Kolb doesn't mind—in fact, he considers it a vital part of the process as he has no intention of *sending* email from the same terminal he receives at. Not even from different accounts, as the IP address would still be the same. Physically breaking up the email chain by using different *computers* is what makes Kolb's remailing service so solid. His laptop is the only link between them.

Analyzing his Yahoo! anonymous account would reveal only log-ons from public terminals and the receipt of encrypted remails. He never emailed anyone from that account. Thus, the *Kripos*—the *Kriminal Polizei*—could not learn from Yahoo! who he was, what he was receiving, or from whom.

Ghosts communicating with a ghost.

Kolb deletes the email from his Inbox, empties the Trash, shreds (he had installed *Eraser* on the server) Today's History from the computer, and logs out. He pays the 5€, leaves the café and disappears down the *U-Bahn* stairwell a block down the street. Twenty-three minutes later he is at a university library which also has public terminals. He boots up his laptop, inserts the floppy, and decrypts the email with his secret key. Following the enclosed forwarding instructions he prepares to send the remaining PGP message kernel down the remailing chain. The first recipient is a Copenhagen partner of the Berlin operation, so the message is encrypted on Kolb's laptop with the Dane's PGP public key. Thus, what Kolb sends is different from what he had received, in case the two emails were ever somehow compared with each other. The two remailers' public keys were known to precisely 37 people, all trusted libertarians.

From Copenhagen the kernel will skip through Helsinki, Krakow, and Tacoma before landing in Phoenix.

Four hours later the final recipient has it. Its Wyoming origin simply cannot be discerned from backtracking the IP packet flow. Physically, the trail went stone cold at Terminal #14 in the *Berlin Technische Universität* library, and that's assuming investigators could backtrack all the way to Copenhagen—and then to Berlin. Learning even that useless dead-end would require an expensive and prolonged multinational intelligence effort. The Subject line reads Lose 24lbs. In Just 5 Weeks!! Most people would have immediately deleted such an apparent spam, but the man in Phoenix had been awaiting precisely this email.

Not that he was obese. The message was a grain of sand hiding on a beach. The "24lbs." meant that he had to proceed within 24 hours. The "5" told him the scope of the operation—5 counties. Hands shaking with anticipation, he uses his PGP secret key to decrypt the message. It reads:

> *The thunderbolt falls before the noise of it is heard in the skies, prayers are said before the bell is rung for them; he receives the blow that thinks he himself is giving it, he suffers who never expected it, and he dies that look'd upon himself to be the most secure: all is done in the Night and Obscurity, amongst Storms and Confusion.*

It was a quote from Gabriel Naudé, a 17th century Paris political author.

The Phoenix man smiles, and then laughs out loud to himself. *Four years of planning and work! It was actually going to happen!* He grabs his laptop, kisses his wife good-bye and says that he'll be back in a few hours. He drives to the main downtown library on Central Avenue, walks up to the second floor where the public terminals are, signs on with an alias as a guest, and begins to work. Within an hour, the lives of 8,994 people across the Southwest are changed by an encrypted group email. The message is simple:
Solivitur ambulando. It is solved by walking.

The problem is settled by action—the theoretical by the practical.

8,994 people amongst 3,704 households already knew what to do.

2006 USA political news

The UN "Second Conference on the Illicit Trade in Small Arms and Light Weapons in All Its Aspects" meets in July. The conference votes to bind all member states to the mandatory registration of all firearms, effective by 1 January 2017.

Private gun sale activity doubles the next month.

Chelsea Clinton, graduated from Stanford even more liberal than Hillary (if such were possible), has taken up with one of Louis Farrakhan's lieutenants in Chicago. *"Mother, this is my 'village' now,"* she was rumored to have explained. Even for Hillary, this was too much and she soon after blows a gasket. During a Senate reelection campaign speech she utterly loses her temper at a heckler and is led off stage screaming profanities. The *Washington Post* laments her having been *"provoked by a white male chauvinist."* The leftist National Organization of Women gives Hillary a titular directorship and quietly backburners her with an annual salary of $180,000, which nicely covers her Prozac[®] habit.

2006 USA social news

As the cultural revolution took generations to triumph, it will take generations to roll back. And the great battles will not be political, but moral, intellectual, and spiritual. For the adversary is not another party, but another faith, another way of seeing God and man.

Needed for victory is not only a conservative spirit, to defend what is right about America and the West, but a counterrevolutionary spirit to recapture lost ground. To preserve their rights, and their right to live as they wished, the Founding Fathers had to become rebels. So shall we. (at 230)

If raw sewage is being dumped in the reservoir, buy bottled water. The rule applies to a polluted culture. (at 250)

— Pat Buchanan, *The Death of the West*

...[T]he state is best resisted by ignoring it and refusing its offers and assistance and, since the state seeks to isolate, by forging voluntary social relationships with one another to provide for our mutual needs and wants. A good and so far successful example of this is the growth of home-schooling.
— Jeffery Snyder, Interview by Carlo Stagnaro, 2/8/2001
www.lewrockwell.com/orig2/stagnaro2.html

The homeschooling movement increases by 20% per year as parents frantically rescue their children (and possibly America's future) from the government indoctrination camps. The NEA further pressures Congress to co-opt the remaining private schools under the federal net, as well as restrict homeschooling to virtual extinction. Counterpressure increases to pass some sort of voucher program to relieve alternatively schooled families from the outrageous tax burden of also supporting government schools.

A dramatic increase of criticism of the "religious right" sweeps America. Liberals castigate Christians for their "repressive beliefs."

Liberals call right-wingers "hatemongers" and conservative dialogue "hate speech." In this sense, liberals remind me of this perennially flatulent guy in my high school who was always demanding, "Who farted?!" It is the liberals who are consumed by hate; hate for all that is good, simple, pure, and decent. Conservatives generally just want to be left alone to live their own lives, and liberals quite literally hate them for it.
— James Wayne Preston, *Journals*

Illegal aliens from Mexico are increasingly diagnosed with the El Tor strain of *Vibrio cholerae*. They appreciate the free medical treatment given them in the Southwest USA.

Cheyenne, Wyoming   October 2006
Wyoming Department of Administration and Information
Division of Economic Analysis, Emerson Building

"Huh! Now, *this* is odd," observes a data analyst.

"What's odd?" asks his colleague friend in the adjoining cubicle.

"These new resident numbers. Five counties show increases of 21%."

The analysts work for the Wyoming State Data Center (WSDC) which publishes a monthly bulletin of economic conditions, housing figures, sales tax collections, cost of living indices, etc. Their second floor cubicles have a view of northern Cheyenne. It is a slate and pewter autumn day. An early storm is creeping in.

"21%? Which five counties?"

"Niobrara, Hot Springs, Johnson, Crook, and Sublette."

"Not Teton or Albany?"

"Nope, five economically mediocre counties with very low population bases and—hey, wait a minute!"

"What now?"

"They're not just sparsely populated, they're the five *least* populated counties! *That* can't be coincidence!"

"*Hmmm.* That *is* weird! Hot Springs has Thermop, Johnson has Buffalo, Crook has Sundance, and Sublette has Pinedale—and those are all nice little towns, but who the hell would move to *Lusk?* It's a tumbleweed gas stop on the way to nowhere."

"You got that right."

"Intrastate relocation?"

"Hold on, I'm accessing migration flows. Nope, very few intrastate movers. Most came from . . . California, Washington, Oregon, Colorado, Arizona, and Texas."

"That's strange. California and Colorado are typical, but we always *lose* people to Oregon, Arizona, and Texas. This makes no sense. Besides the oil boom in the early 1980s, when did we ever have a net inflow from *Texas?* What the hell is going on?"

"Hold on, lemme run some of these new addresses. I wanna see if they're urban or rural." A few mouse clicks later, he exclaims, "You wouldn't *believe* how many common addresses are popping up!"

"Common addresses? *Really?*"

"Yeah, *common.* And all of them rural. Take Crook County. I'm showing an August increase of 1,595 new residents, and guess how many of them listed their address as 2075 Highway 112?"

"How many?"

"255."

"*255!* At the *same* address?"

"Yeah. That's 16% of the county's new residents. One in six."

"What's at that address?"

"Hold on, I'm checking. A trailerpark and campground just north of Hulett. Bastiat Trailer Estates. Built this year. It's got . . . hold on . . . 70 mobile home lots."

"Four residents per trailer; that comes to a capacity of 280. So, yeah, it would easily hold 255 people."

"Hey, here's another one—384 people show their new residence as the Galtson Mobile Home Park on Highway 111 just south of Aladdin."

"Galtson? That's a funny name."

"Yeah, I thought so, too. And, hey, there's one more trailerpark, the Rothbard Trailer Court on Highway 585 south of Sundance. 316 new residents there."

"Those three trailerparks account for . . . let's see . . . 60% of the new people. Where are the rest?"

"Let's see . . . oh, there's a 'Bastiat Retirement Village' near Moorcroft with . . . 211 new residents. The balance—429 to be precise—seem spread out amongst 35 addresses. It's like 35 families just up and decided to take in a dozen people in their homes."

"This is the weirdest damn thing I've ever seen. How 'bout you?"

"Oh, by far!"

"Whaddaya bet same thing's goin' on in those other counties?"

"I'm already on it."

Within an hour, a fairly detailed abstract has been made of the numbers, which shows identical patterns in Niobrara, Hot Springs, Johnson, and Sublette counties. New community housings, trailerparks, apartment complexes, and condominiums had sprung up the past year to be filled by new residents relocating from generally six other states. The mass relocation appears to have begun in the sparsest county of Niobrara, and then in order to the next sparsest counties of Hot Springs, Sublette, Crook, and lastly Johnson—like water filling up an ice tray. This shows design, direction, and coordination.

Purpose.

"*Hey!* Guess what their voter registration is?"

"What?"

"Republican."

"*All* of them?"

"Yep. Every last adult. No Democrats. No Libertarians. No Natural Law. No Wyoming Reform. No Independents."

"Hey, then this has to be a *political* thing. Check out the Republican primary elections in those counties."

"Yeah! 15 August, right?"

"Right."

"Hold on, I gotta change screens. OK, here we go."

A furious stacatto of mouse clicks emanates from his cubicle.

"Bingo, my friend! It's *all* political! These people literally took over the Republican primaries, and elected a slate of new candidates. And get this: lots of them registered to vote at the *polls* on election day."

"How could they do *that*? I thought you had to register at least 30 days *before* the election."

"Yeah, for the *general* election. For primary elections W.S. 22-3-102 allows poll registration. They still had to be residents for 30 days, though. Look at their voter registration dates: 15 August, 15 August, 15 August."

"I'll bet the County Clerks freaked out!"

"Yeah, no shit. Probably thought it was some practical joke."

If the sudden concentration of this orchestrated immigration was suspicious, the *timing* was disturbing. Nearly nine thousand Americans—7,495 of them voters—had descended on five demographically sparse Wyoming counties just before a primary election. Come November all the political offices were up for election. Clerks, Assessors, County Attorneys, District Attorneys, Sheriffs, Commissioners, Treasurers, Coroners, Judges, everyone.

"Are you thinking what I'm thinking?"

"Who wouldn't be. Those counties are facing a, a, oh, what's it called?"

"A *coup d'état*?"

"Right! *Coup d'état*. In November those new people are planning to change every one of their county governments."

"And since those five counties are heavily Republican, the indigenous voters will likely vote the party ticket regardless of the new candidates."

"Yeah, that makes sense. By taking over the primary of the leading party, your candidates are almost guaranteed to win the general election."

The blond analyst shake his head. "Who *are* these people?"

"I guess people tired of the bullshit back in California, Texas, Oregon, and the rest. Hey, look it's 5:30. Let's get outta here and grab a few beers. Get a game plan going before we tell Jenkins about this!"

"Sounds good. We'll take all this stuff with us and work on it down at Muldoons."

"Cool. Too bad we can't write off the beers."

After several hours at their usual tavern, the two computer analysts were well and truly plastered. An early storm had hit southeast Wyoming that evening, and the roads were sheeted in black ice. Driving home, the carpooling pair careen off a mild curve in the road, go down a thirty-foot embankment and flip. One was knocked unconscious; the other had his neck broken. Their car's fuel line was ripped away by the dense underbrush, and raw gasoline spilled onto the red-hot exhaust manifold.

Only the blaze gave notice of the lonely accident, and by the time fire trucks had arrived the car was a black, smoking shell. Bits of burning computer printouts floated about like Dante's snowflakes.

The curious fattening of five Wyoming counties went unnoticed by the replacement analysts at the WSDC. The general election of 2006 was just three weeks away.

❖ 1995

When law and morality contradict each other the citizen has the cruel alternative of either losing his sense of morality or losing his respect of the law.
— Frederic Bastiat

Chaos theory maintains that the flapping of a butterfly's wings can snowball into a tropical hurricane. The theory has more than meteorological implications. A solitary and routine traffic stop can cause a legal thunderstorm.

I-25, east of Casper, Wyoming 24 May 1995

It is 2:47PM, nearly the end of Lloyd Holgate's shift. A young trooper in the Wyoming State Patrol (WSP) for two years, he has aspirations of federal law enforcement and plans to apply with the FBI next year. He has been patrolling a thirty-mile corridor of the interstate since morning. Summer tourist traffic is just beginning to trickle in the Cowboy State. While the WSP is not so notorious as the Texas DPS for ticketing speeders, the entire agency is on heightened alert after the Murrah Building bombing just five weeks ago. Troopers had been instructed to stop motorists for the pettiest of infractions and look for any probable cause (PC) of domestic terrorism. Militia members, right-wing extremists, Limbaugh Republicans, Second Amendment advocates, Constitutionalists, Patriots, and the like are all unfairly tarred with the brush of Oklahoma City.

Holgate's experienced eyes continually scan the highway for anything out of the ordinary. He has a reputation for being able to see an expired plate tag from absurd distances, as a leopard can spot a limp from across the veldt.

Predator—prey. Holgate liked the work. He looked forward to the prestige of the FBI, but would miss the daily excitement of the WSP.

Just ahead 300 yards a blue Ford Tarus brakes slightly as its driver notices Holgate's black cruiser behind him. Even though the Taurus was not speeding, most interstate drivers automatically stepped on the brake whenever they suddenly noticed a police car. Cops were used to it. Holgate would have passed the Taurus on by, but for the burnt-out left brake light. *Use any PC available to detain* his watch commander had said. *You never know what you may find.* Equipment infractions were the camel's nose under the tent for many arrests. Even if no arrest resulted, a burnt-out 30¢ bulb will net the State a $40 fine. Not that the State hasn't figured this out, of course.

Holgate closes the distance to 50 yards and radios in. "Unit 16 to Base. Request a 10-28 on a blue Ford Taurus, Wyoming plate 3-9-4-Adam-Frank-Charles. 1447."

The Taurus remains in the right lane travelling exactly 65 mph. The driver appears to be alone.

The computer check takes only twenty seconds. "Base to Unit 16. Vehicle is a 1993 Ford Taurus registered to a William Olsen Russell of Evansville. Registration current; no wants on the vehicle. 1448."

"10-4, Base. Am stopping vehicle for equipment violation. Stand by for a 10-27. 1448."

"10-4, Unit 16. 1448."

Satisfied that the car is not stolen, Holgate lights up his roof. The driver applies his right blinker and pulls over to the shoulder. Holgate stops about 25' behind and slightly to the left of the Taurus, and turns his steering wheel at full left-lock. This measure would likely save his life if his unit were rear-ended. Cops had learned this the hard way over the years.

Trooper Holgate looks in his side mirror for a break in traffic and steps out. As he approaches the Taurus he intently scans the passenger compartment for hands. Hands were dangerous; they held guns and knives. The back seat is empty, as is the front passenger seat. The driver, a white male in his late fifties, is alone. His hands are on the steering wheel, his eyes tracking Holgate in the rearview mirror.

The driver's window is down, but the car is still running. "Sir, please turn off your ignition," Holgate says firmly.

The driver does so, turns his head, and says, "Was I speeding, officer?" Not unfriendly, but not kiss-ass, either.

Cops are trained not to answer such questions until the suspect's ID has been determined. It also keeps him off-guard.

"License, registration, and proof of insurance, please," Holgate says.

The man already has them ready on the dashboard, and hands them over. He is William Olsen Russell, the registered owner of the Taurus.

"Is 3627 State Route 258 still your current address?" This is one of the first questions cops ask, for the State must always know where its Subjects reside. It also establishes a baseline for truthfulness. Any evasion or hemming and hawing will instantly alert an officer of something "hinky."

"Yep, been there nearly twenty years. What's this all about? Was I speeding?" Faintly annoyed.

Holgate says, "No, sir, you weren't speeding, but you do have a brake light out."

Russell snorts. "Brake light out, huh? Well, how could I have known *that*?" Belligerent.

"By regularly inspecting your vehicle, that's how."

"Do *you* know if *your* brake lights are working, officer?" Russell taunts. "Could one of *your* bulbs have burnt out just now?"

"Sir, we're talking about *your* vehicle, not mine, so I'm not going to argue with you. Remain in your vehicle. This won't take long." Holgate had been inclined to give a verbal warning, but no longer.

"This is frickin' great," Russell mutters, not quite under his breath.

From inside his unit Holgate radios, "16 to Base. Request a 10-27 on a William Olsen Russell, common spelling. Wyoming DL is Robert-2-7-4-5-0-3-2. DOB 6-7-38. 1449."

As Holgate writes up a ticket the dispatcher radios back. "Base to 16. Subject Russell, no wants or warrants. Status clear. 1453."

"10-4, Base, thank you. 1453."

As Holgate returns with Russell's clipboarded ticket and paperwork he notices a spent rifle shell casing on the rear passenger floorboard. He places the clipboard on the Taurus roof and his hand on his Glock 22. "Sir, do you have any weapons in the vehicle?"

"I'm not armed," Russell says.

"That wasn't my question. Do you have any weapons in the vehicle?"

Russell's eyebrows furrow. "I don't have to answer that."

Although Russell is correct, because of his noncooperation coupled with gun-related evidence and Holgate's particular fear for his safety, the trooper is now justified in performing a protective search of Russell and his *"immediate grabbable area"* according to the *Terry v. Ohio* Supreme Court case of 1968.

"Sir, you're not under arrest, but for my own safety I need to search you and the interior of this vehicle for weapons. Now, step out of the vehicle, turn around, and place your hands on the hood." Holgate pats down Russell, who is unarmed and has nothing but some coins in his pockets.

"Mr. Russell, I want you to sit there next to the guardrail in front of your vehicle, and stay there until I tell you to get up."

"Aww, this is bullshit!" Russell spits.

"It's that, or you can wait with cuffs on in the backseat of my unit until you chill out. Now sit over there!"

Russell complies, grudgingly.

Keeping him in his peripheral view, Holgate looks under the front seats and floormats, and searches the unlocked glovebox for weapons. His powers of a *Terry* frisk do not extend to sealed or locked containers, or to the trunk. He finds no weapons or contraband.

"I *told* you I wasn't armed!" Russell shouts over the traffic noise.

Holgate ignores this and finds the interior button to pop the trunk. It doesn't work. Russell disabled it months ago to prevent this very thing. He even had it keyed differently for more privacy.

Holgate walks over and says, "I need you to open your trunk."

Russell replies, "Absolutely not. A *Terry* frisk cannot include a locked trunk inaccessible without a key."

This legal knowledge surprises Holgate. Most citizens do not understand the difference between a protective frisk and a full-blown search incident to arrest.

"Sir, I am happy to radio in for a warrant, and then I *will* search your trunk—thoroughly. What do you have in there you don't want me to find?"

Russell does not fall for this. "If you already *had* probable cause to search my trunk, then you wouldn't *need* a warrant, would you? There's an automobile exception to the Fourth Amendment warrant requirement."

This surprises Holgate even more. While he considers what to do next, Russell says, "I'd like to be on my way, now. Am I free to go?"

"No, sir, you are *not* free to go. I have not returned your license and paperwork yet."

"Well, I'd like them back now. If you have a ticket for me to sign, I would like to sign it right now and be on my way."

"Why are you in such a hurry to leave?" asks Holgate.

"Why are you so determined to waste any more of my afternoon?" replies Russell. "And all for a burnt-out brake light? It's ridiculous."

"It won't take but a minute for me to look in your trunk, then you can be on your way. What's the problem with that, unless you've something to hide?"

It was always better to say "look" rather than "search."

Russell is having none of it. "The problem is that you're on some fishing expedition without any probable cause, much less my consent."

"Sir, I deal with hundreds of people every month and this is *not* the way average folks act. Most folks don't object to me having a routine look in their trunk. It's for everyone's safety. So, what do you have in the trunk that you don't want me to see?"

"Nothing but lawful, personal property."

"Well, there's no problem is there? Why not let me have a quick look?"

"Yes, there *is* a problem. I'm not a criminal. There are no warrants for my arrest, or you'd have cuffed me by now. You're unlawfully detaining me without reasonable suspicion, and I'd like to leave now."

"Your behavior *is* suspicious to me, sir. You won't let me have a look in your trunk. That gives me grounds to detain you."

"Case law has ruled exactly the opposite. Failure to consent to a search is not suspicious behavior. Just because I am exercising my rights as an American does not constitute reasonable suspicion or probable cause."

"Are you an attorney?" Holgate asks, startled.

"No. Although I am studied in the law, I haven't yet passed the bar."

It is a curious reply and Holgate doesn't know quite what to make of it. Is Russell a law student? Paralegal? Judicial scholar?

"What kind of work *are* you in?"

"That is not germane," Russell snaps.

Trying a different tack, Holgate says, "I noticed a shell casing on the floorboard and believe you have a rifle in your trunk. I need to determine that it's not stolen."

Russell snorts, "Aren't you confusing 'wants' with 'needs'? You mean you *want* to search my trunk, don't you? Well, you *can't.*"

"So, you *do* have a rifle in there?"

Russell has sparred enough. "Whether I do or not is nobody's concern since it's perfectly legal to carry a firearm locked in a trunk. It's even legal in Wyoming to openly have a firearm on the seat. You've checked me and my car interior for weapons, and I am unarmed just like I said. Any weapons in my trunk would not jeopardize your safety. You're *way* out of bounds here, Trooper Holgate. You have neither probable cause nor my consent to search, and I do not wish to answer any more questions. I'd like to sign the ticket and get home. Am I free to go?"

Holgate is at an impasse. Cajoling and stern bluffs won't work. "No, you are not free to go. Stay here. I'll be right back."

Walking to his unit he mulls over the scene. This is one of the oddest traffic stops Holgate has ever made. A middle-class, middle-aged white male with no criminal history so adamantly refusing a routine inspection. And so informed of his rights! This was really unusual.

Gotta be up to something! Probably got an AK47 in there.

Holgate has an idea. It is an old trick, but often cracks tough cases.

"16 to Base. Subject William Olsen Russell detained for possible narcotics trafficking. Request a K-9 drug unit at my 10-20; westbound I-25, two miles east of the Evansville exit. 1457."

"Base to 16, 10-4. Stand by. 1457."

A minute later he hears back, "Base to 16. WSP K-9 unavailable. DEA K-9 is on station and en route. ETA your 10-20 in six minutes. 1458." A DEA unit has just left Casper for a case in Douglas and was only a few miles away. The timing couldn't be better.

As little as Holgate wants to share with the feds, the arrival of DEA may help rattle Russell's cage. "16 to Base. 10-4, thanks. 1458."

DEA agent Arturo Gomez arrives five minutes later with his trained German shepherd, Oso. He gets out of his black Crown Victoria with some effort, weighing 320 pounds. His fellow agents snidely call him "Oilturo" for his perpetual greasy patina of sweat.

Holgate has met him a few times over the past year and knows him as an agent who gets things done. Rumor had it that Gomez supplemented his salary with "commissions" taken from seized drug cash. It was quite common amongst the Drug Warriors.

With Oso on a leash, Gomez meets the trooper behind his WSP unit. "Hey, Holgate."

"Gomez. You got here fast."

"Was just up the highway. So what's this guy's story?"

"Routine stop for equipment violation, no wants or warrants. Subject is William Olsen Russell. Evansville residence. Ring any bells?"

Gomez searches his memory. "Nah, never heard of him." His wide, pockmarked face shines like a brown mirror in the afternoon heat.

Holgate continues, "Noticed a shell casing on the floorboard, and he got uncooperative when I wanted to search his trunk. Turned into a real hard-ass and started spouting off about his constitutional rights. Knows the law pretty good; refused to open his trunk after I frisked him and the vehicle interior. Even mentioned *Terry*."

Gomez grimaces. "That's weird. What's he do for a living?" he asks, leisurely scratching a sweat-stained underarm.

"Wouldn't say. He's not an attorney, though. Maybe a paralegal. He clammed up once I insisted on going through his trunk. White guy, guns, constitutional familiarity, poor attitude towards law enforcement . . . "

"Sounds like a militia puke to me," Gomez says, finishing the train of reasoning.

"Yep, me too."

"He's your collar; how ya wanna play this?"

Holgate points to Oso. "The nose knows, right?"

Gomez chuckles. "Yep. That's why we pay him the big bucks."

* * * * * * *

Russell would never find out exactly why Oso alerted to the presence of nonexistent drugs in his trunk, but he suspects a trick. He thinks that either Holgate or Gomez transplanted the scent of marijuana from a pocket baggie to his car. All he knows is that he's never used drugs—much less driven around with a trunkload of them—and since he bought the Taurus new, no previous owner could have contaminated the car with drug scent. Holgate and Gomez concocted PC to search; it was that simple. That, or else Oso is the worst drug dog in Wyoming, giving false positives wherever he goes.

Although no drugs were found, Russell had an unloaded FAL rifle in a soft case. The FAL (*Fusil Automatique Leger*, or Light Automatic Rifle) is a Belgian military pattern rifle adopted by 93 countries since the 1950s. Russell's rifle is a civilian version without the capability of full-automatic fire.

Visually, however, it is nearly indistinguishable from its military cousin, which facilitated Congress misnaming such civilian guns as *"assault rifles."*

Its serial number was radioed in for an NCIC[1] check, and was listed in the federal database as stolen. Russell was arrested, his Ford Taurus thoroughly searched "incident to arrest," and his FAL confiscated. It was discovered the following day that Holgate had inadvertently transposed two digits of the serial number over the radio, and that Russell's rifle was indeed clean.

Although the trooper had acted in good faith and thus not jeopardized the WSP, Natrona County Attorney George Crimp had disliked Russell and his "right-wing" views for years. Russell was a persistent writer of letters to the newspaper editor and had once lambasted Crimp for his malicious prosecution of a midwife for practicing medicine without a license. The trial ended in a hung jury and Crimp declined to refile due to the public fervor.

Crimp had a golfing buddy who was a federal agent. Gordon Lorner had originally applied with the FBI but was turned down. He then applied with the Secret Service. Same result. US Marshals didn't want him either. Not even the DEA took him. Finally, Lorner found a home with the Bureau of Alcohol, Tobacco, and Firearms (ATF). A branch of the US Department of the Treasury, the ATF[2] were merely armed tax collectors, although they increasingly thought of themselves as federal police. They were infamous for malicious prosecutions of nonviolent offenses, and rarely condescended to search gang areas for armed and dangerous felons.

Crimp asked Lorner to examine Russell's FAL rifle for possible federal firearms violations. Lorner eagerly did so and came to conclude that the rifle was an illegally assembled *"assault weapon"* under Title 18 of the US Code. Section 921(30)(B)(iv) of the *1994 Public Safety and Recreational Firearms Use Protection Act* (commonly referred to as the "Crime Bill") prohibits a detachable magazine, semiautomatic rifle made in the US after 13 September 1994 to have more than one of the following features:

    a folding or telescoping stock
    a pistol grip that protrudes conspicuously beneath the action
    a bayonet mount
    a flash suppressor or threaded barrel designed to accommodate such
    a grenade launcher

---

1   **National Crime Information Center.** Through the FBI's Interstate Identification Index, the NCIC gives access to the criminal records of nearly 30 million people. Most law enforcement agencies have access. It includes information about stolen, missing, or wanted goods, such as guns, vehicles, license plates, boats, and financial instruments. It also includes information about a variety of people, such as missing and unidentified persons, foreign fugitives, and deported aliens. The NCIC also provides access to the ATF Violent Felon File, the US Secret Service Protection File, gang and terrorist organizations files, as well as state and federal criminal history records.

2   Originally a tax-enforcement agency under the Department of the Treasury, it was transferred to the Department of Justice in 2003.

Russell's rifle was an Imbel FAL receiver (made in Brazil under license by FN of Belgium) imported after September 1994, and assembled with a sufficient number of American-made parts to qualify as a domestic rifle. It originally had a pistol grip stock as its one "evil feature," and a previous owner had affixed a muzzle brake. Although muzzle brakes were not prohibited on post-ban semi-autos, a flash suppressor counted as an illegal second feature. In the opinion of ATF Agent Lorner, the muzzle brake on Russell's FAL *"significantly reduced"* the rifle's muzzle flash, and thus functioned as a flash suppressor—even though it had been sold for years as a muzzle brake.

In short, a flash suppressor was anything the ATF said it was.

This was deemed sufficient to indict Russell on felony possession of a banned "*assault weapon.*" His bail was set by the Honorable Henry T. Fleming at $25,000. Russell had to put up his home as bond.

Based on an interview with a local gun shop owner (who had been threatened with an investigation), the ATF sought and received a warrant to search Russell's home. Owning an illegally assembled "*assault weapon*" was one felony; having also *assembled* it was another. The gun shop owner thought that the FAL had been sold without the muzzle brake, but wasn't certain. Lorner wanted to search Russell's home for evidence that he had purchased and installed the brake himself, which would support a second charge of assembly. Also, with any luck, Lorner would discover other contraband during the search. He had nothing to lose by trying.

Anticipating a probable raid, Russell had days earlier moved his home computer, books, and personal records to the ranch of his boyhood friend Chet Garland. His guns (all of which were legal) he had sold to Chet for $21 in US silver coin[3]. Once he was acquitted, Chet would sell them back to Russell for the same coinage. Russell also cleaned out his two bank accounts and hid the cash with another friend.

Russell was not at home during the ATF raid, which found nothing. They were prepared to torch through his gun safe but Russell had left it open —and empty. Fuming, agents deliberately trashed his home, leaving the front door off its hinges—his tropical aquarium smashed. Russell returned home to find a soaked carpet and dead, desiccated rare fish.

A hastily scrawled note had been dropped on the living room floor. It read, "Nothing taken. ATF."

* * * * * * *

---

3   Such, in theory, activated one's 7th Amendment right to a common law trial, versus a mere maritime or equity procedure wherein few or no constitutional rights exist. Rolls of 21 junk Morgan silver dollars were sold as "7th Amendment Rolls."

Russell had been prepared to represent himself, but a Wyoming libertarian defense attorney, Juliette Kramer, offered to defend him *pro bono.* Although only twenty-nine, she was already a renowned advocate in the tradition of Gerry Spence. She had lost only her first two cases. Her courtroom brilliance was enhanced by her striking Irish/Hungarian beauty, long brown hair and flashing ice-green eyes. Her cross-examinations were piercing; her closing arguments captivating. She had a fighter's instinct for weakness and sensed precisely when to go for the kill. To underestimate "J.K." in, or out of, court was a serious mistake. Coming from a wealthy oil family, she could afford to practice for principle and specialized in Bill of Rights abuse cases. She particularly loathed the IRS, DEA, FDA, and ATF. Didn't care much for the FBI either. She once whipped the US Forest Service on a bogus firearm discharge case and they quit harassing shooters ever since.

Explaining her most recent *pro bono* charity, Miss (not "Ms.") Kramer told the local TV news, "My client Bill Russell has harmed no one. He has done no wrong. His only offense was to exercise his natural rights as a peaceable American under the Constitution. For that he has been charged with a federal felony. The US Attorney's office chose to falsely and maliciously indict Bill Russell because they knew that he could not afford an attorney. Well, now he doesn't *have* to afford one. It is my honor to defend this victim of injustice, and to accept a penny for my efforts would be a collaboration with the US Attorney's office in their goal to disenfranchise all of us from our God-given liberties protected under our Bill of Rights."

* * * * * * *

Lorner snaps off the TV. "Aww, *shit!* How'd *that* bitch hear about Russell?" turning to Assistant US Attorney (AUSA) Jack Krempler, whose office is in the Federal Building.

"Russell spread the word about his arrest to all of the gun-rights groups, and one of them must have called her," Krempler replies. "Their network has gotten pretty good these days. Our phones ring constantly."

"Yeah, thanks to the fuckin' Internet!" exclaims Lorner. "Whatever case we're working on, from Maine to Hawaii, it's as if it's happening right next door to some gun nut somewhere. Word breaks of a raid, and they're right there with their goddamned camcorders! Can't they be busted for interfering with federal officers in the performance of their duty?"

"Not unless they actually interfere. DEA got spanked pretty hard on this last year. A Circuit court ruled that since third-party recordings could be subpoenaed by the Government and defense alike they must be treated as evidence. To prevent an on-site recording is tampering with that evidence. If it happens during one of *your* raids, don't expect me to protect your dumb ass."

"Well that's great. Just fucking great."

"Watch yourself, Lorner. This case is a paper-thin beef already, and you know it. I didn't want this turd but Washington pissed and moaned that they haven't had a Wyoming ATF conviction in years and gave me the squeeze."

"Whaddaya mean 'turd'? It's a good case."

"Yeah, right. Flash suppressor, my *ass*. It's a muzzle brake."

"Hey, the law's the law, Krempler. If it *'significantly reduces'* muzzle flash, then it's a goddamn flash suppressor. Russell's probably some militia dirtbag; I mean, who else would carry an assault rifle around in their fucking *trunk*? We're the ATF and *we* don't even have .308s! Those things are only good for armed insurrection. An example's gotta be made of these anti-government nuts. *You're* the prosecutor—*you* make it stick."

"Yeah, well, easier said than done. I'll tell you right now that *voir dire* will make or break this case. Muzzle brake, flash suppressor—they look about the same to me, and they're sure as hell going to look the same to John Q. Wyoming."

"Hey, have you been *listening* to me?," Lorner demands. "It doesn't matter what the damned things *look* like, only what they *do*. I don't give a shit what they say in their *Shotgun News* ads! If they significantly reduce muzzle flash, then they're flash suppressors."

"Yeah, and the *'significantly'* part is real comforting. It's about as cut-and-dried as *'reasonable.'* What is *'significantly'*? 10%? 25%? If I move to admit into evidence your nighttime firing video of his rifle with and without the device—and that's the *only* way this case can be won—Kramer will object on several excellent grounds."

"Well, that's *your* fucking problem. I catch 'em—you clean 'em. See ya in court, Krempler."

"Yes, and without that orange and brown tie this time. You looked like a carny. Stop by my office before court for a wardrobe check."

"Yeah, right. I'll wear one of my Armanis." *Asshole.*

* * * * * * *

Man must be penetrated in order to shape such tendencies [of obedience]. *He must be made to live in a certain psychological climate.*

[Propaganda] *proceeds by psychological manipulations, by character modifications, by the creation of feelings or stereotypes useful when the time comes . . . . The two great routes that this propaganda takes are the conditioned reflex and the myth.* (at 31)

—Jacques Ellul
Propaganda: The Formation of Men's Attitudes (1965)

It is not only the juror's right, but his duty to find the verdict according to his own understanding, judgment and conscience, though in direct opposition to the instruction of the court.

—John Adams, 1771

Casper, Wyoming
Federal District Court   September 1995

The concrete Richard Cheney Federal Building loomed over downtown Casper with the personality of bomb-shelter. A gray, steady drizzle gave the four-story outpost of Occupation a particularly gloomy tone. Next week commences the trial of *The United States v. William Olsen Russell.* Middle names were apparently invented to let you know when you were thoroughly in trouble.

Some seventy jury summonses had been mailed out for the Russell trial, and 44 prospective jurors were being interviewed in what is called *voir dire.* A jury means 12 peers, and courts used to simply dragoon 12 random people off the street. One of whom could have been your mother, another a lifelong personal enemy. Twelve peers meant just that: twelve . . . peers.

Twelve seemingly average citizens.

Now Americans are no longer judged by their peers. *Voir dire* is a carefully crafted process which favors the Government by weeding out potentially sympathetic or independent-thinking jurors. Libertarian columnist Vin Suprynowicz bitterly referred to *voir dire* as "French for jury tampering." In income tax evasion cases, for example, the Government makes sure that every juror is a *"Yes, sir!"* Social Security card-carrying, Form 1040 filer who cannot fathom the proposition that the 16th Amendment was never duly ratified or that private-sector wages are not taxable *"income"* under Title 26 Internal Revenue Code.

ATF cases are notoriously weak in both law and in fact, and cannot withstand jurors who might be sympathetic, much less empathic, to the accused. The ideal juror is one who has little or no experience with guns, viewing them as unnecessary—if not vaguely frightening—objects.

AUSA Krempler and the Honorable Henry T. Fleming spent the entire morning sifting through the lives of the 44 prospective jurors. Were they members of the NRA or any other gun-rights organization? Did they agree that the Second Amendment protected only the national guard? Had they or any of their friends or relatives ever been prosecuted for a federal firearms violation? Had they ever heard of FIJA[4]? Had they ever been a member of a militia? Did they own any firearms? If so, any "assault weapons"? Did they

---

4   **Fully Informed Jury Association**, which is dedicated to informing Americans of their historic and legal right to judge the *law* as well as the facts of a case.   **www.fija.org**

have any bumper stickers on their cars? Did they homeschool? What did they read at night?

At last it was Juliette Kramer's turn to question the jury pool. After thoroughly explaining the concept and history of "presumption of innocence" and "reasonable doubt" to 44 men and women, she notices a thin, nervous fellow who seemed distracted all morning.

"Mr. Urdang, if you had to render a verdict in this case right now, before trial, what would it be?" asks Juliette.

Thomas Urdang, a life insurance salesman, ventures an answer. "Uh, well, I couldn't really say. I haven't heard the evidence yet."

"But didn't you earlier agree that a defendant is innocent until proven guilty?"

"Uh, yes, I did."

"Well, if you *believe* that, then your verdict must be 'Not Guilty,' would it not?"

Urdang squirms in his seat, his face reddening. "Uh, yes, I guess it would."

"You *guess* it would?"

"Well, no—I mean *yes*. I, I mean if I *had* to, uh, render a verdict right now, it would have to be 'Not Guilty'."

"I see. Thank you, Mr. Urdang for coming downtown this morning," Juliette says evenly. "Your Honor?"

Judge Fleming nods to Urdang and says, "You're excused, sir. Please see the court clerk on the way out to receive your juror compensation. Thank you for your service today."

Thomas Urdang self-consciously rises and stiffly walks out.

Turning to the pool of jurors, Juliette carefully explains her point. "Ladies and gentlemen, you'll recall that I earlier mentioned the danger of platitudes. Platitudes are truths which have become familiar. Too familiar. That doesn't make them any less true—just less poignant. And so they pass through the mind undigested, like a pebble through a chicken. The vital truth to remember here is that in America, one is presumed innocent unless and *until* one is *proven* guilty beyond a reasonable doubt. Sadly, that truth called 'presumption of innocence' has become a platitude. It was a platitude for Mr. Urdang, else he wouldn't have answered the way he did."

Several members unconsciously nod at this.

"Now, I did not single out Mr. Urdang to embarrass him. On the contrary. I'd have preferred that he had said, 'Why, Not Guilty, of course!' I'd have *preferred* that 'presumption of innocence' was a living, breathing *truth* to him, as it must be with all of you. Ladies and gentlemen, we cannot 'go through the motions' here, floating on platitudes. An innocent man's *future* is at stake during this trial, and you hold it in your hands. So, I will ask you all, if you had to render a verdict right now, what would it be?"

"Not Guilty," the pool answers in unison.

Juliette scans the faces for any who somehow found this difficult. She has only a few preemptory strikes left and needs to use them wisely. "Thank you, ladies and gentlemen," she beams.

"Your Honor, I have no more questions for this panel," she says.

Jack Krempler leans over to whisper in his assistant's ear. "What'd I tell you? She got the entire panel to say 'Not Guilty' and there wasn't a damn thing I could do about it."

"Pretty shrewd," admits the assistant. "How's her trial work?"

"Very solid. Excellent prep, really good use of discovery—almost intuitive."

"Sounds pretty thorough."

"Yeah, she doesn't miss much during trial."

"Where's her weakness?"

"She doesn't like curveballs thrown at her. In *Feldman* we finally located a hostile witness and got him to testify on our last day, and it really threw her for a loop. Her cross was pretty weak."

"Oh, right!" recalls the assistant. " She still got him off, though."

"Yeah . . . she did," Krempler agrees.

"Any curveballs for her this time?"

"No, just a fastball," says Krempler with a wink.

* * * * * * *

US v. Russell   Day One

"Trooper Holgate, why did you search Mr. Russell's trunk?"

"Because the DEA K-9 unit alerted to the presence of drugs."

"Were any drugs found in Mr. Russell's trunk?" asks Juliette.

"No, ma'am."

"Were any drugs found in his car at all?"

"No."

"So, the DEA's drug-sniffing dog made a mistake?"

"It happens sometimes," Holgate allows.

"Yes, I'm sure it does," Juliette says, facing the jury. "So, if Mr. Russell had no drugs in his car, then why did you arrest him?"

"Because his rifle was listed in the NCIC database as 'stolen'."

"*Had* it been stolen?"

"Uh, no, ma'am. I made a mistake on the serial number when I radioed in for the NCIC check."

"Oh, so now *you* made a mistake. I see. Well, we're all human. The dog, too, I guess."

Hearty laughter circulates through the court, causing Holgate to frown. Juliette continues, "I'm curious though—what *other* mistakes did you make that afternoon?"

"Objection!" Krempler says.

Before Fleming can respond Juliette quickly interjects, "I withdraw the question, Your Honor."

Frowning, Fleming says, "Very well. Continue, Miss Kramer."

"Trooper Holgate, did you arrest the defendant for any *other* reason besides the alleged possession of stolen property?" Juliette asks.

"No, ma'am."

"So, you did not arrest Mr. Russell for violation of federal gun laws?"

"No."

"Then—aside from your mistake on the serial number—to the best of your knowledge on the afternoon of 24 May, his rifle was perfectly *legal*, was it not?"

"To the best of my knowledge, yes," he says, shifting uncomfortably.

"So, if you *had* radioed in the *correct* serial number and properly ascertained that Mr. Russell's rifle was *not* stolen, then he wouldn't have been arrested at *all*, is that not true, Trooper Holgate?"

The young officer nervously glances at Krempler, who barely shakes his head. "Uh, that's right."

" . . . and none of us would be here today," Juliette concludes. "I've no further questions, Your Honor."

"Redirect, Mr. Krempler?" asks Fleming.

"No, Your Honor."

"Trooper Holgate, you may step down. You're excused, sir."

* * * * * * *

By the afternoon, however, things turn poorly for the defense.

Despite Juliette Kramer's objections over the video of Russell's rifle being test fired, it was shown in open court. A Technical Branch ATF agent had been flown in from Washington to explain the footage. The courtroom was darkened, and a TV/VCR was turned on. In a split screen, the rifle was fired simultaneously without and with the muzzle brake. The muzzle braked rifle had a much smaller flash plume, about half the size of the bare barrel plume. It was clearly a *"significant reduction"* of flash. When the lights came back on, Agent Lorner was wearing a very satisfied smirk.

Juliette Kramer, for the first time, looked worried.

Her cross-examination of the Washington ATF agent yielded nothing. While he admitted that individual rounds of ammunition varied slightly in powder weight, he would not allow that such was responsible for the greater muzzle flash of the bare barreled rifle. The comparison test had apparently been performed fairly, but something about the video disturbed Juliette. She sensed some kind of trick, but couldn't nail it down.

After a redirect of the witness, Krempler rests the Government's case. He sits down, confident that J.K. was going to lose this one.

* * * * * * *

Day Two

"Defense calls Mr. Harold Krassny to the stand," announces Juliette.

Harold Krassny is an spry old man, his skin weathered from seven decades of ranching life. His eyes, however, twinkle with intelligence. He is sworn in and seated.

"Mr. Krassny, are you familiar with State Exhibit A, the FAL rifle owned by Bill Russell?" asks Juliette.

"Yes, ma'am, I am."

"And how is that?"

"It used to be mine. I bought it new last November."

"What did you do with it?"

"I shot it for a while and then traded it at Natrona Sports for a really nice target pistol," answers Krassny.

"And when was that?"

"March this year."

"When you bought the rifle new did it have a muzzle brake on it?"

"No, ma'am. I ordered that from an advertiser in *The Shotgun News* and installed it myself."

"And when did you install the muzzle brake?"

"December 1994."

"Do you have a copy of the ad and receipt with you today?"

"Yes, ma'am, I do."

Turning to Judge Fleming, Juliette says, "Defense moves to enter the muzzle brake ad and receipt into evidence as Exhibits A and B." She hands them to the bailiff, who then shows them to Krempler.

Fleming asks Krempler, "Does the State have any objection?"

Frowning, Krempler replies, "No, Your Honor."

"Very well. Mark the ad and receipt as Defense Exhibits A and B. Continue Miss Kramer."

"Thank you, Your Honor. Mr. Krassny, why did you install a muzzle brake on your rifle?"

"I was trying to reduce the recoil. I weigh only 155 pounds, but at 73 years of age I'm not the 155 pounds I used to be."

The courtroom laughs at this.

"Did the muzzle brake reduce the recoil?"

"Yes, by about a third."

"Did you leave the muzzle brake on the rifle when you traded it?"

"Yes, ma'am."

Juliette walks over with the FAL pointed towards the ceiling. "Is this muzzle brake on the rifle the same one you ordered and installed?"

Krassny looks it over and nods confidently. "Yes, it is."

"How can you be sure?"

"Because I accidentally scratched it when I was installing it, and I touched it up with some cold blue. See there?"

Krempler briskly stands and says, "Your Honor, I fail to see where this is going. The owner history of the muzzle attachment is irrelevant."

Fleming slowly asks Juliette, "You are coming to a point, aren't you Miss Kramer?"

"Certainly, Your Honor. Nearly there, in fact," Juliette smiles.

"Very well. Continue. But do wrap it up." Imperious.

"Yes, Your Honor. Mr. Krassny, would you please read the ad."

"Surely. It reads 'FAL Muzzle Brake. Reduces muzzle climb and felt recoil. Blued steel. No gunsmithing required. Attaches with 4 set screws. ATF approved for post-ban rifles. $19.99.'"

Juliette turns and impales Krempler with a glare as she confirms, "'ATF approved for post-ban rifles'? Is that right, Mr. Krassny?"

"Yes, ma'am, that's what it reads."

"Mr. Krassny, did you rely in good faith upon that assertion that the purchase and installation of this accessory was in full compliance of Title 18 United States Code, section 921?"

"Why yes, *ma'am!* I didn't want to do anything *illegal!*"

A few snickers are heard at the back of the room.

Krempler sizzles, unsure if Krassny is being a smartass.

Juliette asks, "Mr. Krassny, did you ever have occasion to fire your rifle in low-light conditions whereby you could see the muzzle flash?"

"Yes, I did."

Krempler stiffens, expecting what is to come.

"Was that with or without the muzzle brake?"

"Both."

"To your recollection did the muzzle brake significantly reduce the flash signature of your rifle?"

"Objection, Your Honor!" cries Krempler. "The witness cannot render a qualified scientific opinion from objective laboratory conditions."

Juliette immediately counters, "Your Honor, the section 921 term *'significantly'* is one of subjectivity versus objectivity. Lay persons are allowed to render subjective opinions regarding pertinent adverbial issues. There is ample precedent on this point, specifically *US v.*—"

Fleming cuts her off. "I'm quite aware of the case law, Miss Kramer, thank you." He swivels his gray-maned head to Krempler and says, "Objection overruled. The witness may answer, *if* he has an opinion."

Juliette smiles. "Thank you, Your Honor. Mr. Krassny, to your recollection did the muzzle brake significantly reduce your rifle's flash signature?"

"No, ma'am. It changed the *shape* of the flash a bit because of the ports, but the overall size and brightness seemed about the same to me."

"Thank you, Mr. Krassny," Juliette smiles brightly. "No further questions, Your Honor."

"Do you wish to cross examine, Mr. Krempler?" asks Fleming.

Still sizzling, Krempler replies, "No questions." Best to get Krassny off the stand and let the ATF video do the "talking."

"Mr. Krassny, you may step down. You're dismissed."

* * * * * * *

Law is nothing unless close behind it stands a warm, living public opinion.
— Wendell Phillips

Juliette will now rest for the defense. Since the ATF video is so damaging to her case, she decides to argue against the law—always a perilous tactic, especially in federal court. Krempler has waived his right to go first. She begins her closing argument simply.

"Ladies and gentleman of the jury, why are we even *here*? To decide the fate of an honest, productive local citizen for having two ounces of steel at the end of a rifle barrel? For *that* he deserves to be punished with five years in federal prison and a $10,000 fine?"

"Objection!" cries Jack Krempler, springing to his feet.

"Sustained!" booms the Honorable Henry T. Fleming. "The jury will disregard that last remark by defense counsel. Miss Kramer, you are no doubt aware that a crime's possible sentence cannot be used to sway a jury towards acquittal! If that happens again, I will find you in contempt of court!"

"Sorry, Your Honor," Juliette intones. She knows that no remark can be truly disregarded by any jury, especially after the prosecutor and judge had made such a fuss about it. Defense attorneys had a little saying: *You can't unring a bell.* The jury would no doubt discuss the fairness of the punishment for such a technical violation.

"She's going for nullification," Krempler's assistant whispers.

"Sure she is. It's all she's *got*," gloats the AUSA. "With any luck she'll land a contempt and sour the jury."

Juliette pushes on unfazed. "Why are we even *here*? Because of a 'Simon Says' regulation which prohibits a flash suppressor on Mr. Russell's rifle. *Oooooh!* Thank God we have laws against that sort of thing—that and bayonet mounts."

The courtroom titters with laughter. Several jurors smile.

"I have here a bag of a dozen muzzle attachments. Eleven are muzzle brakes, and one is an actual, honest-to-God, flash suppressor." She dumps them on a table in front of the jury panel. Twelve black cylinders noisily roll about as she corrals them. "Can anyone spot the evil flash suppressor?"

"Objection, Your Honor!" cries Jack Krempler. "This is wholly improper! These muzz—uh, items have not been admitted into evidence!"

"Sustained!" Fleming instantly replies. "Miss Kramer, you will remove those at once! You are on very thin ice here!"

"Yes, Your Honor." Juliette begins placing them one by one back in the clear ZipLoc bag, muttering just under her breath, "Are *you* the evil one? What about you? *You* look kinda evil." Most jurors are openly snickering.

The AUSA assistant whispers, "Man, she's really pushing it!"

Jack Krempler nods stonily.

Regaining her stride, Juliette changes tack. "Folks, there is one crucial thing that Mr. Krempler from the United States Government failed to explain to all of us. It is *vital* to today's case." She pauses for a moment and stares directly at the Government's table of attorneys.

"Mr. Krempler did not explain that there are *two* kinds of crimes. A few crimes are *mala in se*, which is Latin for 'evil in themselves.' These would be crimes of violence and property, such as murder, rape, and robbery. By the way, we've all heard that saying *'Ignorance of the law is no excuse'* haven't we? Do you know where it came from? From an 18th century British legal scholar named Blackstone. His *Commentaries on the Laws of England* had an enormous influence on our jurisprudence. Blackstone wrote about ignorance of the law in this way: *'Ignorantia juris quod quisque tenetur scire, neminem excusat.'* Translation: *'Ignorance of the law, which everyone is bound to know, excuses no man.'*

"What is that law *'which everyone is bound to know'?* Why *mala in se* crimes, of course. Everyone knows that it's wrong to murder, rape, and rob. *Mala in se* crimes are recognized in every state and in every nation as crimes, and they *have* been for thousands of years.

"So, what's been keeping our lawmakers busy since at least the War of 1812? Creating new and needless *mala prohibita*—wrongs prohibited. These 'crimes' are not evil in themselves, but merely wrong because some group of politicians *said* that they're wrong. For example, that your backyard fence may not be over eight feet high, or that your home may not have rock landscaping. Or that recently imported rifles may not have muzzle attachments with a particular pattern of holes or slots. These *mala prohibita*—and there are tens of *thousands* of them—differ from city to city, from state to state, and from nation to nation. We've all heard examples of those old, silly laws still on the books, such as forbidding the whistling past a barbershop on Tuesdays. My client, Bill Russell has been tried under Title 18 of the US Code for such a 'crime.' He risks being convicted as a felon—a *felon*, ladies and gentlemen!—for a perfectly harmless metal part costing the price of lunch. 'Simon Says' that his muzzle brake cannot *'significantly reduce'* muzzle flash. Whistling past a barbershop on Tuesday . . . "

The courtroom chuckles deeply at this. Jack Krempler says nothing, his face stern.

"Mr. Krempler will tell you that the law is not on trial, that we must all obey the law—even if it's a silly one—until we have persuaded our representatives to repeal it. Now that's fine reasoning for a fifth grade social studies class, but it doesn't quite hold water in the *real* world, does it? Supreme Court Justice Douglas once wrote this about the law: *'When a legislature undertakes to proscribe the exercise of a citizen's constitutional rights it acts lawlessly, and the citizen can take matters into his own hands and proceed on the basis that such a law is no law at all.'"*

Every eye and ear in the courtroom is focused on Juliette Kramer.

"Ladies and gentlemen of the jury, the law is merely an artificial invention to promote a reasonable society. That's it. The law is no more infallible than its authors. It's nothing to worship, and it's often unworthy of respect. As with any invention, it is to be valued and respected *as long as it works*. And for a law to work, it must be *reasonable*.

"Here is the real issue in this trial. Is section 921, subsection 30, part B, subpart iv of Title 18 of the United States Code"—Juliette pauses to take an exaggerated gasp of air—"reasonable?"

The entire courtroom giggles and Juliette's heart races with hope. *Get them laughing, and they'll cease to fear. Without fear they can see the truth.* She senses a tide turning in the room against the prosecution.

"According to 250 years of Anglo-Saxon jurisprudence, is it even a law which everyone is bound to *know*? I mean, who in this courtroom besides Mr. Krempler had even *heard* of the thing? Could Mr. Krempler quote, for example, subsection *27* or subpart iii? Ladies and gentlemen, I —like any practicing attorney in federal court—have the complete set of the 50 Titles of the United States Code. They take up *nine feet* of bookshelf space! The CFR administrative regulations, which can apply criminally to any one of us here today takes up *twenty-one feet* of space! I doubt that even Mr. Krempler himself knows every one of the hundreds of thousands of laws contained in *thirty feet* of books. If *he* does not, then how can he expect you or Bill Russell to?"

The jurors are now looking at Assistant US Attorney Jack Krempler, who has suddenly become somewhat of a codefendant in the trial.

"Who on earth could possibly live long enough to read and memorize *thirty feet* of laws? But *that* is what the Government would demand from *us*, otherwise, we're 'ignorant' of the law and 'have no excuse' and should go to prison!"

The general mood is solemn as this point sinks in.

Krempler's carotid arteries are clearly pulsating from across the room. What was an open-and-shut case J.K. is turning into an indictment of federal gun laws. How he hates this woman. He hates her springy step, her insouciance, her parody of the law, her lovely musical voice. He hates the fact that she has his own initials, and uses them. And he really hates that goddamned Laura Ashley dress she had the nerve to wear in court this morning, taunting everyone—especially that old goat Fleming—with her femininity. *Why can't the little bitch wear a power suit like other women attorneys?*

Krempler tries to snap out of it, sensing that he is glowering. He considers objecting to Kramer's line of defense, but decides that it would likely come across to the jury as yelping.

The tide of Juliette's closing argument continues to swell. "Henry David Thoreau had something to say on this point in his classic work titled *On Civil Disobedience*:"

> *Must the citizen even for a moment, or in the least degree, resign his conscience to the legislator? Why has every man a conscience then? I think that we should be men first, and subjects afterward.*

"Does that sound relevant to these proceedings? It certainly does to me." Juliette pauses to gauge the jurors' mood. They are still with her. Good. Time to bring it all home.

Smoothly, she continues, "Think of it another way: If Bill Russell's muzzle brake had *fewer* holes or *smaller* holes, it might not have reduced the flash at all. It would still be the muzzle brake as advertised and all of us here —especially Bill Russell— would be at home or work. So, what we're *really* talking about is an amount of metal less in weight and less in value than . . . a couple of pennies."

From her palm, Juliette drops two pennies onto the table. They bounce on the walnut veneer Formica, surprisingly loud. One penny dies quickly but the other is made of more thespian stuff. Sensing the significance of its performance it bounces hard and sharp into a fast roll, veering to the left at the very last possible moment—as if humanly piloted—missing the table edge by an angstrom's whisker. Having achieved the court's rapt attention it then requires about a week and a half to cease languidly rolling around in infinitesimally decreasing counterclockwise circles, finally collapsing into the prolonged death diapason of a tiny manhole cover.

Even by slow-acting poison, Hamlet expired more quickly.

Juliette has the presence of mind not to move or speak until the penny has finished its brilliant cameo. By suspending the matter of *US v. Russell* for nearly half a minute—and for just two hundredths of a dollar—she has made her point. It is one of those clever courtroom tricks impossible to foresee—much less preempt—and inadvisable to interrupt once in motion.

Krempler is beside himself, a mute retaining wall of fury.

In a solemn, quiet voice, Juliette resumes the stage. "Two cents. Most of us lose more than that in the sofa every time we sit down."

Krempler angrily whispers to his assistant, "*This* is the kind of crap she's really good at. Just look at that jury. They're mesmerized."

"Two lousy cents," Juliette continues. "*That's* what Mr. Krempler and the Government think Bill Russell's reputation and freedom are worth. But they need *your* rubber stamp to do it. Don't collaborate with this, ladies and gentlemen. Bill Russell would like to go back home to his family, his job, and his community. He's been through quite enough already."

Juliette pauses briefly to let this last point sink in. Then she very quietly says, "Only *you* have the power to do the right thing here . . . and I am trusting you to do it. Thank you."

Strong applause fills the courtroom, forcing Judge Fleming to bang his gavel. Juliette delivers that blinding smile of hers, returns to her table and sits down. Bill Russell has tears in his eyes and can only nod his thanks. A buzz of whispered conversations floats up from the gallery. The controversial trial had attracted a large audience, most of it in support of Russell. The locals did not appreciate the ATF's harrassment of a long-standing citizen.

"Mr. Krempler, are you ready to close?" asks Fleming.

"I am, Your Honor," Krempler stiffly replies. He stands, clears his throat, and begins. "Ladies and gentlemen of the jury, I'm sure we all found Ms. Kramer's performance most entertaining. But it doesn't really change the issue at hand, does it? And that is the guilt or innocence of Mr. Russell. It is Mr. *Russell* who is sitting in the defendant's chair, not Title 18 of the United States Code or the ATF. Do not be deceived; what Ms. Kramer wants from you is a recipe for anarchy. Without laws, we get lawlessness. Ignore the laws you don't *like*? Well, then what's to prevent serial murderers and child rapists from ignoring laws inconvenient to *them*?"

They already do thinks Juliette as she rolls her eyes.

"Justice can be found only in a courtroom, not in the random, individual mind. *That* is why we are all here today. William Russell committed an offense under federal law. The video plainly proved that. But what about the opinion of Mr. Krassny, some may wonder? Yes, what about the opinion of an elderly man who may or may not be sympathetic with a fellow gun owner? Mr. Krassny expressed his *opinion*, but in the video we have all seen *fact*. Objective, scientific, measurable *fact*. And it is facts which must form your verdict, not mere opinion.

"We cannot, ladies and gentlemen, pick and choose which laws to uphold. We must uphold them *all*, as a house divided cannot stand. This case is one of thousands of load-bearing beams in that great house of Law and Order. As you uphold this particular law, you uphold law in general. Decent society requires it. Please do your duty as good citizens and return a verdict of Guilty."

Several hisses are heard as Krempler returns to his table. Wyomingites have never had any love for the US Government, especially when it chose to prosecute a well-liked, upstanding, long-time local citizen.

Judge Fleming turns to the jurors.

Juliette leans over and whispers to her assistant, "Here it comes."

"Ladies and gentlemen of the jury, your duty is solely to determine the guilt or innocence of the defendant based on the evidence. You do *not* have the right to consider the fairness of the law found in Title 18 of the US Code. Laws can be repealed only by the legislative branch of government, which is Congress. If you find beyond a reasonable doubt that the defendant indeed violated the federal statute in question, then you have a duty to convict—regardless of any and all other considerations which are irrelevant to your sworn duty. If, however, you have a reasonable doubt that the defendant is not guilty as charged, then you have a duty to acquit. Do you all understand the law as I've explained it to you?"

The jurors nod.

"About what I expected," whispers Juliette.

"Fine," says Judge Fleming. "The bailiff will show you to your deliberation room." With that, the jury quietly files out.

* * * * * * *

Sunlight is the best disinfectant.
   — Justice Louis Brandeis

While the jury deliberates, Krempler and his team wait in his office. He cannot contain his excitement. "I have to tell you, Lorner, that video was a winner! I was really concerned about proving a significant reduction in flash signature, but *damn*! That footage will get Russell five years!"

"Hey, counselor, the camera never lies," boasts Lorner.

Something about the way he said it makes Krempler faintly uneasy for some unknown reason, but the feeling quickly passes. The case was solid, and not even Krassny's testimony or Juliette's powerful close could subvert the video. It was in the bag.

* * * * * * *

"The muzzle brake cut down on the flash by at least half," says Dorothy Witherspoon. "That's *'significantly'* without a doubt." Ms. Witherspoon, a doughy 61 years of age, had been an elementary schoolteacher her entire life. Being the eldest juror, she was just short of throwing a tantrum for not having been chosen jury foreman.

Several jurors murmur their agreement. They had been deliberating for 50 minutes, and saw the chance to reach a Guilty verdict in time to return home for supper. The case really was clear cut.

"Shall we now poll for a verdict?" asks foreman Robert Slater.

"Not just yet," says the quiet man at the far end of the table. "Something about that video bothers me. I'd like to see it again." James Preston, a well-known rancher, is a self-described target shooter. He is the only shooter who made it past *voir dire*.

Witherspoon exasperates, "Is that *really* necessary? One flash was bigger. It seemed obvious to all of *us!*"

"Perhaps," manages Preston. "But it'll only take two minutes to watch it again. I really need to see it before I cast my verdict."

"Very well," agrees Slater, glancing at Witherspoon.

The bailiff rolls in the TV/VCR cart, and leaves the jury room to wait outside. Preston takes the remote and pushes "Play." Side by side the two muzzles fired. Clearly, the barrel with the muzzle brake had much less flash.

"Well, *now* are you satisfied?" challenges Witherspoon.

"Yes, I am satisfied," says Preston.

"Good," says Witherspoon. "Maybe *now* we can—"

Preston cuts her off. "I am satisfied that I now have irreconcilable reasonable doubt."

"*Whaaaaat?*" bellows Witherspoon. The room is instantly abuzz with the other eleven jurors all demanding an explanation.

"Not only do I believe Mr. Russell innocent, but I now believe him to have been the victim of criminal fraud. That video was rigged."

"*Rigged? Rigged how?*" demands foreman Slater.

Preston says calmly, "Let's watch it again. I'll show you."

As the video began to play, Preston pauses it during the peak of muzzle flash. The 4-head VCR still frame is magazine photo sharp.

"OK. On the left side is the bare barrel. Look at its flash plume."

"Yes, it's about twice as large—we've already seen that," chirps one of the jurors who works in the county tax assessor's office.

"I'm not talking about the size difference. Ignore that for a moment," replies Preston. "Look at the difference in *color*. The bare barreled flash is orange, but the muzzle braked flash is a bright yellow."

"Orange, yellow, bright yellow—what *difference* does it make?" blurts Witherspoon.

"It makes the difference between a guilty man and an innocent one. Those flashes are different colors because of different gunpowders. I handload for my target rifles, and I know how powders ignite differently. Gunpowder comes in three different shapes: ball, flake, and stick. Their muzzle plumes are all different. Also, if a handloader wanted to for some reason, he could load to create a huge muzzle flash, or nearly none at all."

Robert Slater ponders this carefully. Several of the jurors now regard Preston with open respect. Ms. Witherspoon simply glares at him, her arms rigidly crossed.

Finding his pace, Preston continues. "Handloaders experiment with many combinations of bullet, case, powder, and primer to discover the most efficient load for their rifle. Powders vary tremendously in burning speed. Some are extremely fast. Others are very slow. For example, ball and flake powders are usually faster burning than stick powders, which burn much more slowly to provide a longer pressure curve for heavier bullets."

"Thank you 'Mr. Science,' but this isn't conclusive at all," sneers Witherspoon.

"May I remind you that we do not have to 'conclude' that Mr. Russell is innocent—only that reasonable doubt exists. If a lab had examined the spent casings from the ATF's so-called 'comparison,' I'm convinced that different gunpowders would have been proven."

"Do the different colors of flash really mean different powders?" asks Slater, now quite concerned.

"Indeed. Those flash plumes are clouds of gunpowder still combusting past the muzzle. The slower the powder, the less is burned within the bore, and the larger the plume. The bare barrel ammo not only has a larger plume, its darker color of orange indicates far less combustion. That, and the streamers."

"Streamers? What are *streamers*?" demands Witherspoon.

"Streaming bits of unburnt powder. You see them in fireworks displays all the time. When they occur in firearms, the gunpowder burns too slowly for the barrel length. Look at the still frame. Only the bare flash has streamers. The braked flash doesn't."

Most of the jurors subconsciously nod their heads in agreement.

"Ladies and gentlemen, different powders were used to convey the false *impression* that the muzzle brake reduced the flash signature. I'm sure of it. And it could not have been done accidentally. This comparison test is a fraud designed to throw Mr. Russell in federal prison for five years. Once he got out, as a convicted felon he'd never be allowed to vote or own a gun or have a professional license. The Government doesn't seem to like this man, and after Mr. Russell was falsely arrested by the highway patrol the ATF framed him on a felony charge for something as harmless as hanging two ounces of metal on the end of his rifle barrel. With all the violent criminals on the loose, *this* is the kind of thing that should preoccupy law enforcement?"

"What if you're wrong? What if it *was* a flash suppressor?" asks a woman, an office secretary heard for the first time.

"Even if Mr. Russell *had* put a flash suppressor on his rifle, so *what*? Who here doesn't wear sunglasses to reduce daylight glare? If somebody wants to reduce nighttime flash of his rifle, that's *his* business. It's certainly not worth five years in the pen, much less *framing* somebody for it. This whole thing stinks and they want us to rubber stamp Mr. Russell as a felon. The wrong person was on trial here. It should have been ATF Agent Lorner. I'd bet that guy had something to do with this."

Several stern, contemplative nods of approval answer his argument. Few jurors liked Agent Lorner.

Joel Salazar, an accountant, says, "Let's not forget the testimony of the previous owner, Mr. Krassny. He installed an ATF-approved muzzle brake, and it's still on the rifle. That alone raises reasonable doubt in my mind."

Foreman Slater is solemn. "OK folks, let's talk about this. What are your thoughts on what Mr. Preston has just said?"

* * * * * * *

As the jurors file back into the courtroom, Krempler glances at his watch, smiles, and comments to his assistant, "An hour and ten minutes. Just about right."

The mood at the defense table is not so confident.

"Wow—that was pretty quick! Is that good?" asks Bill Russell.

"I'm not sure. We'll see," answers Juliette. She also is nervous about the jurors' early return. Such usually betokened a conviction, however, she forces herself to remain calm as one could never predict a jury.

After the jury is seated and the court is called to order, Fleming begins. "Mr. Foreman, has the jury reached a verdict?"

Robert Slater stands and replies, "We have, Your Honor."

"Very well. Will the defendant please rise."

Bill Russell and Juliette Kramer both stand. This moment was always the most exquisitely suspenseful for all present, especially for the defense. Nothing in life compared to those agonizing seconds as a defendant waited to hear the first consonant from the jury foreman's lips.

Bill Russell's future depends on that consonant. An "n" and he is vindicated and free. A hard "g" and he is a convicted felon, forbidden to ever vote, hold a professional license, or own a gun.

Focal points. They are the rudder of life. Russell had several such focal points and they flashed through his mind as the résumé of his existence. His hand-to-hand duel in a Vietnam jungle when his bayonet pierced the VC's chest barely in time. His nervous marriage proposal to Connie when he wasn't at all sure that she'd accept. At the emergency room holding his sobbing wife, waiting for the trauma surgeon to emerge with a pronouncement of life or death over their son Carl severely injured in a motorcycle accident.

So far, Bill Russell's life had not ricochetted off any unexpected hard surfaces. His trajectory had sailed on, perforating all barriers. He survived the Nam in one piece, Connie married him, and Carl not only lived but kept his damaged eye. In the courtroom Russell has time to appreciate this focal point arriving with such calenderal notice, unlike the others. He savors it, grateful for his life and family. Although death hangs not over him, a sort of amputation does. The State is poised to lop off five years of life and much of his freedom thereafter. And for what? A $20 tube of metal.

An "n" or a "g." Thumb up or thumb down. It's come to this all because of a burnt-out 30¢ bulb.

The tiny things. There's nothing bigger.

Fleming's voice snaps Russell back to the present. "Mr. Foreman, will you read the verdict."

Slater intones, "On the felony count of illegal possession of an assault weapon, we the jury, find the defendant . . . "

Over three hundred eyes and ears are locked on Slater's lips.

" . . . Not Guilty."

The courtroom erupts with cheers and applause. Krempler sits in his chair, stunned. A grapefruit can be thrown in Lorner's open mouth. Bill Russell hugs Juliette as Judge Fleming bangs and bangs his gavel, but the sound is lost amidst the furor. It takes nearly a minute for the courtroom to quiet down.

Foreman Slater continues, "Furthermore, this jury believes there is evidence of prosecutorial malfeasance in this case, and—"

The uproar is instant and deafening. Fleming's gavel pounding is a mime routine.

"—and recommends that the matter be reviewed by the Grand Jury," Slater manages to yell over the din.

Judge Fleming shouts, "Case dismissed! Court adjourned!" and flees the bench, his black robe fluttering behind him like a wake.

* * * * * * *

On the front steps of the Federal Building a large crowd gathers as the TV news crews jostle with questions for Bill Russell, Juliette Kramer, and most of the jurors, including James Preston. The afternoon rain had cleared out, leaving a bright and sunny day. It seemed fitting.

In the US Attorney's office, Krempler and Lorner are watching the live coverage. As Preston explains to the press the two different gunpowders likely used to create different flash plumes, Krempler slowly turns to Lorner. The ATF had a long and sordid history for evidence tampering such as Waco, as well as abusive raids such as in 1995 when Agent Donna Slusser stomped the Lamplugh's family kitten to death.

"What the fuck did you *do*, Lorner? Don't . . . tell . . . me . . . you—"

"Hey, you wanted a significant reduction in flash, you *got* a significant reduction in flash!" taunts Lorner. "*You're* the one who let Preston get on that jury. A target shooter? A *handloader*? Real smart, Krempler. Hey, too bad he wasn't wearing an orange and brown tie!"

"Do you know what you've *done*, genius? Michael Gartner at NBC News faked those pickup truck explosions and merely got canned. *We're* all looking at years in the federal pen!"

"Oh, *yeah*? How so? I'm not admitting to shit and they won't *find* shit 'cuz all the spent brass got thrown in the recycling barrel, so just chill out. This'll all die down."

"For the sake of your own ass, it'd better," retorts Krempler. "I didn't know a thing about this, Lorner, and I still don't. Jesus H.—what a nightmare! Just keep your mouth shut. And get the fuck out of my office!"

"Sure thing, Counselor," sneers Lorner. As he leaves, he stops, slowly turns, and says, "Hey, you didn't even compliment me on my suit!"

"Get *out*!" yells Jack Krempler. *Asshole.* He already knows what Agent Gordon Lorner would soon and forever more be called behind his back. *Flash Gordon.* Krempler lets out a mirthless chuckle.

* * * * * * *

The crowd on the Federal Building steps has not abated and is growing more festive by the minute.

Bill Russell invited Juliette Kramer and all the jurors over to his home for a backyard BBQ party on Saturday afternoon. Ms. Witherspoon stormed off, her wattles jiggling with every angry step. James Preston and Juliette Kramer manage to ease away from the crowd.

"Mr. Preston, you saved my client from prison," says Juliette. "I'd hoped to get at least one serious gun owner on the panel, but who knew how important that would be! I can't thank you enough!"

"Please, it's 'Jim.' I'm glad that I was there to help. When I reported for jury summons, I'd no idea of the adventure in store for me—for *all* of us. But there *is* one thing you could do for me."

"Certainly, Jim. What is that?" asks Juliette.

"Saving an innocent man from prison is hard work, and it's made for quite an appetite. Would you care to join me for dinner?"

Juliette smiles and laughs. To Preston it sounds like bells. "I'd love to, but only if I'm buying. What are you in the mood for?"

On a hunch, as a test, Preston replies, "Sushi. And I save it only for special occasions."

"Oooh, it's my favorite *too!* There's a new place on Midwest Avenue. Let's go!" says Juliette, laughing in that way of hers.

Yep, he thinks. *Bells.*

It is only a few blocks away, and neither of them think to drive. Without thought and in step, they turn their backs on the Federal Building and cross the street together, Juliette taking his arm as ladies do—or used to.

"I thought Fleming was about to go into cardiac arrest when he heard the verdict," Preston remarks. "He's probably up in his chambers now, chugging a bottle of bourbon!"

Juliette chuckles. "Actually, Fleming's a vodkaholic. Finlandia, if you want to buy him some. Hey, you know what a judge is, don't you?"

Grinning, Preston replies, "No, what?"

"Just a grown man wearing a dress, banging on the furniture!"

They giggle all the way to the sushi bar.

Preston could remember their dinner only through a sweet, dreamy fog. Never had he felt so instantly and so totally entranced with a woman. She was expressive, but not gushy. Brilliant, but not haughty. Her beauty she wore simply, without motive. Loveliness seemed to well from some deep, inner spring.

He had never met anyone like her. He was in very, very deep smit.

Walking her back to her green GMC Tahoe, Preston gives her a hug and thanks her for dinner.

She gets in, starts her truck, and rolls down the window. "Can I get you on my next jury? We may have to disguise you a bit. Fleming won't want you back," she says, her eyes crinkling.

"Neither would Krempler," he laughs.

Just before he turns to leave he says, "Juliette, do you know who you remind me of?"

"Hmmm. I've no idea. Who?"

There's a fond wistfulness in his smile. "Nobody."

Her face is a slow kaleidoscope of vulnerability, sweetness, and shyness. Her eyes well with tears, which she rapidly blinks back. He would never forget how she looked at him. His heart's first tattoo.

She gets out, gives him a surprisingly strong hug and lightly kisses his cheek. *Hummingbird wings.* Her long wavy brunette hair is a soft bouquet, clean and fragrant. Her ivory neck he imagines a warm cradle for his face. He suddenly feels a champagne light-headedness. *I'm actually tipsy from her.*

"Thank you," she says, softly. She slowly releases him and gets back into her truck. She still has That Look on her face. Driving away she smiles brilliantly and pantomimes *Call me!*

He smiles, nods, waves, standing there watching her taillights vanish in the dark. He can still smell her perfume wafting in the crisp night air. His feet, never touching pavement, hovercraft him back to his Suburban.

He does not recall the drive home.

* * * * * * *

James Wayne Preston is a Wyomingite in every sense of the word, an independent outdoorsman and lover of horses. Politically conservative, he is best described as a "libertarian Republican." His grandfather had made his first fortune in cattle and his second in oil. James now co-managed the ranch and family business interests with his father, Benjamin Preston.

A studious and disciplined only child, James was thin as boy and didn't really begin to fill out until he was nearly eighteen. Adventuresome and nice looking with dark brown hair and eyes, he was nonetheless a bit shy with girls in high school. Not until his junior year did he have a girlfriend, but it was a tempestuous relationship which he ended badly. He got turned down for dates for weeks afterward. Although a solid personality shielded him from most peer pressure, seventeen *is* seventeen.

His favorite grandmother had some advice which changed his life. *Jimmy, a woman will walk over, around, or through any man better looking or more wealthy if you know how to dance.* He knew it was true; Davis Bettencourt was no football star, but could he ever move a girl around on the dance floor. He was rarely without some lovely lass on his arm, including one formerly of the first-string quarterback.

So, James snuck off after school three days a week for dancing lessons across town. He even enrolled under an alias, Fred Rogers. If his dance teacher understood the pun, she never let on. James had his mother's natural rhythm and learned quickly. After just three months he could Swing, Salsa, C&W, and even Waltz. At the homecoming ball he astonished the entire school with his graceful moves. Girls all but stood in line for the next dance with him. Overnight his confidence and reputation skyrocketed. His prom was with the school's prettiest girl. His senior year ended up a huge success, academically and socially.

He planned on a military career beginning at Annapolis. Graduating fifth in his class, he proudly took on the "butter bars" of a Marine Corps second lieutenant and went off to helicopter flight school. He soon distinguished himself in the Bell AH-1W SuperCobra, and flew the sleek gunship in dozens of sorties during Desert Storm. His last had been the most interesting.

While attacking, without support, two Iraqi SA-6 "Gainful" SAM batteries he got caught in the radar of a deadly ZSU-23-4 self-propelled AA gun. The 4-barreled turreted system spewed a devastating 50-round burst of 23mm cannon shells, wounding both him and his gunner/copilot, and severely damaging his helo. Captain Preston barely limped back to base before the tail rotor sheared off. He was released from hospital nine days later on medical leave from flight duty. Desert Storm ended before he could fly again. He was happy to learn that he and his copilot had taken out two of the last SAM batteries of the war. For him it was a happy conclusion to his part of the fighting.

After the Gulf War he was offered a promotion to major if he "reupped" and switched to the MV-22 Osprey, a controversial tilt-rotor/fixed-wing assault transport. Preston seriously considered it but came to call the Osprey a "twitchy beast" and didn't much care for the hybrid craft, though he thought the tilt-rotor concept fascinating. After the MV-22's first crash in 1991 he felt his suspicions vindicated. While Preston loved being a Marine, he decided that he was too independent for military life, especially during peacetime. He left active duty as a captain with 169 combat hours. *A week and an hour* he liked to joke. He would miss the twin 1,725 horsepower GE turboshafts and the incredible nimbleness of the SuperCobra, however. Attack helos got in your blood like nothing else. He wondered if any other thrill could compare with sending Hellfire missiles into T-72 tanks. He doubted it.

Although he did not take lightly the killing of enemy soldiers, the surgical precision of his helo's weapons against the singularly evil purpose of Iraqi armor dispelled his initial qualms about combat. Saddam Hussein had had many months to withdraw from Kuwait during the Allied buildup, but refused to do so. His armored divisions could have surrendered once the air war began, but did not. Therefore, USMC Captain Preston went into, and emerged from, combat with a clean conscience.

He, like his comrades, would have preferred to continue all the way to Baghdad to finish the job. When President Bush let Saddam go with only a partial defeat, most American soldiers felt deeply let down. It helped to alienate Preston from further military service at the behest of politicians who easily lost their nerve.

Back in Wyoming he pursued several entrepreneurial projects. While his father was pleased to invest in most of his son's ventures, nothing was ever handed to James. A spoiled, indolent son was the last thing he wanted. *Wealth is the dessert of hard work* Benjamin often said. If James was ever to enjoy financial success, he would have to earn it. That suited him just fine. His innovative PERT[5] software for ranchers took off in 1991 with the advent of 386 chip personal computers. He liked the multiplication of profits inherent to the software business. *Write it once; sell it often.* It felt nice to have his own *real* money after eight years in the Marine Corps.

As a reward, he flew first-class to Rome on a hideously expensive open-jaw ticket, took delivery in Bologna of a new 1992 Ducati 900SS, and made a leisurely four month tour of East and West Europe. He had the time of his life on the stunning red and white motorcycle and came very close many times to staying overseas. The reunited and hectic Berlin was his favorite city, and a couple of business opportunities in the former East Germany nearly beguiled him. He rashly fell in love with a gorgeous art student in Budapest who quickly broke his heart after an old flame reappeared and proposed. In Switzerland he thought he'd died and gone to heaven on those endless corkscrew alpine roads, he and his V-twin Ducati merging into one thunderous carving knife of asphalt. In Portugal he almost bought a charming little beachhouse for only US$45,000, but realized that he missed his family and Wyoming too much to remain in Europe.

He and his bike flew from Paris to Montréal on an Air France 747, and returned to Casper through Canada via Thunder Bay and Banff. His wanderlust satisfied after 13,802 miles, he rolled up his sleeves to join his father on the family ranch. Although a wife and family were in the back of his busy mind, he hadn't expected to meet anyone like Juliette, much less so soon.

He was just thirty-two years old when her lightning struck in that Federal courtroom. The jury summons postcard he framed and hung on his office wall next to his *summa cum laude* diploma from the US Naval Academy. Also on the wall were many photos. Astride his Ducati above the little bay of Mykonos, Greece. Being lifted out of his smoking SuperCobra, a barely flying sieve full of ragged holes and gashes, its perspex canopy shattered and bloody. His Silver Star and Purple Heart pinned to a field medevac pillow. He and his copilot, one eye still bandaged, at Ramstein AFB Officers' Club after the war, hoisting frothy beer mugs the size of oil cans and grinning like loons because they were flying home the next day. He and his dad in the Tetons with their tenth elk together, the leaden winter sky lit by an impossibly beautiful opal sunset.

In the Bighorn National Forest with Juliette on their first camping trip.

He often gazed on that wall of momento and achievement, marveling at

---

5   **Project Evaluation and Review Technique**, a management tool and decision-making system first used during the Apollo Lunar program. It defines objectives, the sequential and interrelated steps in achieving them, and procedures for tracking progress. PERT defines the "critical path" of a project and identifies bottlenecks before they occur.

how it could so brilliantly encapsulate, like a caricature, his life. With Juliette, he would have many, many more things to add to that wall.

Casper, Wyoming

On Preston's wedding day, his father Benjamin asks him what it was like when he first met Juliette eleven months ago. He replies, "Dad, I heard bells, and she took my arm. Just like today."

Benjamin Preston looks at his son warmly. "You two are so right for each other. It's so difficult to meet the perfect woman."

"Well, it's all thanks to Gordon Lorner, Dad."

"Lorner? *Who?*"

"You remember—the Russell trial? Agent Lorner of the ATF?"

Ben Preston laughs merrily. "Oh, *yeah!* Him!"

"Juliette and I sent him a wedding invitation but he didn't show."

"Don't worry, Son. He's probably out somewhere, Doing Good."

Amidst the chuckles, Juliette smoothly sidles between her two favorite men and asks, "What's so funny, you guys?"

"I was telling Dad about us having Agent Lorner to thank."

"Really? How weird—I just saw him a few minutes ago. You can thank him yourself. Be nice, dear. Don't call him 'Flash Gordon.'"

"*What?* He's *here*? *Where?*"

"Outside in the garden talking to your cousin Amy. She seems to like him, but I think he's too old for her. She's, what, nineteen?"

The Preston men bridle instantly and begin to march off to the garden. Juliette sings out, "Just kidding, fellas!" and laughs in that way of hers as she flees the room, her wedding gown billowing like white lace exhaust.

"Cry 'Fed' will ya?" Preston laughingly bellows, picking up the chase.

"If it weren't for this dress, you couldn't catch me!" sings Juliette.

"Sweetie, in just a few hours you won't have to worry about that old wedding dress anymore!"

"That's why I had it made with Velcro," teases Juliette over her shoulder. "It'll be a real time-saver!"

"Ah, such a sensible woman I married!"

Her giggles are heard throughout the house.

❖ 2002

Liberalism is a philosophy to console the West while it commits suicide.
　— James Burnham

When a stupid man does something he knows is wrong, he always claims that it is his duty.
　— George Bernard Shaw

Logan Airport
Boston, Massachusetts   October 2002

Devin McDrung has spent the past several days training members of the Boston SWAT in clearing buildings. He is flying back home to Arizona this morning.

At the general security checkpoint he is told to turn his laptop computer on and off three times, and to remove his belt and shoes. He does all this, simmering, though without complaint. They open his bag and paw through all his belongings. Last call has just been announced for his flight.

Cleared through, his gate is literally 50' away. He is just about to give his boarding pass to the pretty blond agent when a pair of secondary security people approach him. They have a desk right at the gate.

"Sir, we need to check your things and remove your shoes," one of them says dully.

Anger rises in McDrung like throat bile. "I just *came* from security, right over there!" he points.

The second guy says, "I know, but we still need to check your stuff." He is, if this is possible, even more bovine than his partner.

McDrung feels himself beginning to snap. *Are they both afflicted with Downs Syndrome?* "Check my stuff? You're not *smart* enough to check my stuff!"

"Sir, please remove your shoes," the first one repeats.

"My shoes? They're still *untied* from the first time I removed them. You *watched* me walk over here from just fifty feet away! My flight is about leave!"

"Sir, we'll hold the plane for you. Please take your shoes off."

McDrung is glowing hot by now, throwing his lace-up tactical boots on the floor. "Do I *look* like a goddamned Arab terrorist?"

"Sir, there's no reason to get upset. Please remove your belt."

"My *belt*? How 'bout my pants, too?" McDrung drops his pants to his ankles and jigs a little 360° on his toes. "Happy *now*, you morons?"

This is too much for the pair. "Sir, sir," they implore.

"If you wanted me to board this flight in my fucking *underwear*, why didn't anybody *tell* me! I missed reading about that on my ticket! Hey, I know! Let's all fly buck *naked* with no luggage! *That* should make your jobs a *lot* easier!"

People are stopping to stare. Half are scared—half wish they could cheer him on. The cud-chewing twins in uniform now want to be rid of this guy. The pilot of his flight witnesses all this through the window and actually deplanes to see what is going on, and whether he wants to allow McDrung on his aircraft.

As he is pulling up his pants, he calmly explains to the pilot, "I am Devin McDrung. I work in conjunction with law enforcement and the military. I'm flying home after training Boston SWAT for three days. Here's my card."

The pilot looks him over, reads the card, nods. He asks the two guys, "Is this gentleman clear? We need to push back."

"Uh, yeah, he's clear."

Turning to McDrung the pilot asks, "Now, are you going to be calm, cool, and collected on my airplane?"

"No problem. Just get me out of this stupid airport."

"Then let's get aboard. We're behind schedule."

They fast walk down the jetway, followed by the boarding agent. Their steps boom in the rectangular corridor. A stewardess is standing in the plane's doorway, her hand on the door.

After the pilot, McDrung steps onto the aircraft with the stewardess closing the door behind him. Almost immediately the plane is pushed back. He turns right to face a seventy yard long tube full of eyes. Being a highly trained and experienced operator, he immediately spots the Sky Marshal, a black man in coat and tie who is eyeing McDrung sternly. Even from six rows away, McDrung can discern the shoulder holster bulge.

"Oh, do *you* want to check my shoes and underwear, too?" McDrung taunts. The Sky Marshal is fairly mortified at being outed, and snaps his head towards the window.

"I'll be in 21C, Sweetie," McDrung murmurs as he passes by.

He marches down the aisle, eyes bored straight ahead. Finding his aisle seat, he drops in, fuming—lost in the world of his disgust with air travel.

The middle seat is unoccupied. He does not bother to glance at his window seatmate to his left.

After 43 seconds of his silence, however, she can no longer contain herself. *They actually held the flight for him, and he is handsome, though in a wiry, menacing sort of way.* She assumes he may be interesting to talk to.

She puts down her magazine and with great chipperness announces, "Hi! I'm Amber Lee! And you are...?"

McDrung's head smoothly turrets on its odontoid process, inhumanly, like an owl's. His eyes are black shotgun muzzles. She knows at once that she has made a mistake.

McDrung comprehends her instantly. She is white, mid-40s wearing a violently colorful Peruvian skirt and roughly hand-knit sweater. Her dead hazel eyes are artificially animated with a concocted liveliness. She happily rattles of jewelry made by the indigenous peoples of Borneo. Her pony-tailed brunette hair is heavily streaked with gray. (No Clairol for *this* broad.) Her face might have been pretty if it hadn't been etched with those arched eyebrows one gets from walking the earth—barefoot or Birkenstocks—with that moral sanctity reserved for the racially inclusive and ecologically sensitive.

McDrung *knows* this woman. He knows without looking that her magazine is the *Mother Earth News.* He knows that her days revolve around NPR broadcasts. He knows that she goes to Yoga on Mondays and African Drumming on Thursdays. That her All-Natural toothpaste from Maine had never been tested on laboratory animals and that her car was imported from Sweden. Undoubtedly she educates the public with a few bumper stickers: *Free Tibet! I Believe Anita. Arms are for hugging.* He knows that her mountain bicycle contains more hard technology and rare metallurgy than a Saturn V moon rocket, and that its value exceeds the per capita GNP of Luxembourg. Her "life partner" is an environmental attorney who drives that *other* make of car from Sweden. She is the Sedona Chairperson for the Society Against the Keeping of Caged Birds, just like he knows that she voted for Ralph Nader because Al Gore was too conservative.

McDrung knows her instantly and hates her instantly. She is the perfect antithesis of everything McDrung believes and does.

Matter meets antimatter.

He says in a quiet, low voice, "Listen. I don't care who you are, or what you do, or how you do it. And you sure as hell don't want to know what it is that *I* do. So do us both a huge favor and don't talk to me."

Amber Lee blinks rapidly in recoil. Only out of morbid curiosity does she squeak out the obvious question. "What *do* you do?"

He is no longer looking at her, but glaring at the AirFone in the seat in front of him. "I kill things. And when I'm not killing things I teach others how to kill things."

"*Kill* . . . things?" Amber Lee is beyond shocked. *He admits it!*

McDrung has an unusually acute olfactory sense and she reeks of lavender and echinacea—mostly. *These people even smell bizarre,* he thinks. "That's right, *kill* things. Good animals. Bad people. I stay busy."

Amber Lee's mouth is working like a freshly-landed trout, though with less to say.

Then McDrung casually mentions, "You drive a Saab, don't you?"

It is not a question.

Amber Lee is speared by this. *How does this, this killer know I drive a Saab?* After a couple of seconds, some words manage to spill out. "I've, I've never believed in killing." Amazingly, she manages not to sound pious.

She is too scared. Her horror at having been cosmically provided such a seatmate has utterly overwhelmed her previous moral certitude. What a difference a single minute can make in a life.

McDrung turns once more towards her and his eyes shade yet another notch of loathing. He says with nonchalant menace, "That's why you and your kind will perish."

It is a flat statement, not a philosophical proposition.

The anthropological certainty of the remark causes Amber Lee's mouth to drop open, her mind derailed. Somehow, she believes him, and this deeply frightens her. She has never met anybody like this guy. Never wanted to, either. She begins to wonder if she will survive the flight.

McDrung has one last thing to say. "And if you have, as I suspect, the in-flight bladder control of a Betsy-Wetsy doll, then don't expect to crawl over me for the next 4½ hours. I advise that we change places *right now* so you can flitter back and forth to the lavatory from the aisle seat."

Amber Lee doesn't move, doesn't speak. She will hold it for the 4½ hours. Her urethra is already tied up in a double clove-hitch. She won't pass urine until Wednesday at the earliest.

"No? Good. Then go back to your magazine and don't say another word to me." With bored disgust he turns away.

Conversation Over.

Amber Lee apprehends that she is sitting an arm's length away from 150lbs of frothing human nitroglycerin. She can already imagine the headline: *Passenger Annoys Volatile Seatmate—Blows Up Aircraft!* She mechanically turns and buries her frozen chalk face in her little *Utne Reader*. She has developed an eye twitch, which will last eight days.

A stewardess three rows back, has heard all this and smoothly steps up to McDrung's right. "Sir, can I get you a . . . *drink*?"

With his famous evil clown grin, McDrung replies, "Jennifer, a drink is the *last* thing you'd want to give me right now." A mirthless chuckle.

After flying with United for six years, Jennifer has encountered every example of humanity grudgingly allowed on a Boeing 767. She knows he's not kidding. He is a trembling retaining wall, furious with the Iroquois gauntlet of modern airport "security." She is seeing more and more like him since 9/11. Regular people fed up with granny stripsearches, magnetometer silliness, and shoe-sniffing outrage.

Her professional instincts kick in.

Leave this man alone.

"Yes, sir."

She spreads the word to her colleagues.

Don't bother 21C. For anything. They don't.

Four hours and 33 minutes later, they touch down at SkyHarbor in Phoenix, jarring McDrung awake. He had slept through the entire flight, head-down on his tray table—even during landing.

Nobody said a word about it.

* * * * * * *

James Wayne Preston makes himself comfortable in the garden with a pen and notepad to write his father a letter.

Dear Poppa,

I've been doing a lot of thinking lately.

The proactive conservatives, meaning those who fully understand the nature of our cultural war, have had too vague a plan for future generations. They are certainly correct in having first seceded with their hearts. Then, by homeschooling their children they correctly avoided offering up their progeny to the altar of the State. But how and where will their philosophically and spiritually healthy children live?

Take an 18 year old young man who has been homeschooled with McGuffey's Readers and Maybury's "Uncle Eric" books. He knows the two basic laws: 1) Do all you have agreed to do, and 2) Do not encroach on other persons or their property. He knows that he was *born* with many fundamental rights, which cannot be taken away from him by decree. He reads five books a week because he loves reading and learning. He can count on his fingers how many hours of cable and broadcast TV he has watched. He grew up believing in heroes and in America. He is respectful of his parents and his elders. He knows that the Government is not his country, and that "law enforcement officers" are different from Peace Officers. He knows that inflation is a political phenomenon, purposely inflicted. He knows that the US dollar is doomed, as is and was all fiat currency. He knows that no law or regulation actually requires him to pay "income" taxes on his private-sector remuneration. He is an excellent woodsman and rifleman. He is more skilled with his handgun (which he wears daily) than most kids are with their skateboards. He knows that the USA is collapsing in the same way and for the same reasons as did ancient Rome—from within by decadence and apathy. He knows this has been the history of democracies.

Let's go even further. Let's add a religious component. Suppose he believes that the physical world was designed and created, versus the cumulation of accidental and beneficial mutation (which he knows to be utterly unscientific). That we are multidimensional spirit beings temporarily inhabiting physical bodies, and that there are supernatural forces acting upon, and supernatural consequences resulting from, our earthly existence. That even though much pain and suffering exists in this world (nearly all of it caused by humans), there is too much joy and beauty to ignore the lovingness behind the creation.

Now, let's tour the world in which this fine young man must live. A world in which man is his own god, and rights come from government. Where 51 voters may tyrannize 49. Where history is untaught and morals are unknown. Where heroes are mocked and decency is scoffed at. Where a young bride (assuming she chooses to marry young, much less marry at all) on her wedding night already has the sexual experience of a prostitute. Where surrogate entertainment tramples individual imagination. Where people work 45 years in jobs they hate to buy crap they don't need. Where over half their paycheck goes to interest and taxes and regulation. Where people are herded like cattle and danced like puppets by a phalanx of purposeful masters. Where their food is mixed by corporations, their public school indoctrination conducted by bureaucrats, their entertainment served by devils.

So, where does this pure young man *live*? Where is his natural habitat? He has none. He is so sane, he is *insane*.

We are, in effect, building 200mph racecars in a world without asphalt roads. We're making airplanes without their landing strips. It's one thing to rear such fine children from the laboratory of the loving home, but we need to be creating a place where they can actually *live*. Otherwise, they will die. Either they will wither up and die, or they will crash headlong into the hard world and die. Raising quality children is only the first step. Creating their habitat is the next.

Raising self-sufficient, libertarian, and Christian children in America is like raising Jewish children in 1938 Germany. What did the Jewish *Diaspora* do? What was their only choice in a world which despised them? To create their own world. Israel.

That is why we need to create a free state. Not so much for ourselves, but for our children. For James, Jr. and Hanna. Can we abandon the future entirely, calling it "our genes' problem"? Theoretically, but I am very glad that the founders of our country did not. Liberty is not a debt one pays back; it is a debt one pays *forward*. Even if liberty requires a payback, our benefactors are all dead, which leaves nobody but our posterity to receive the check.

That free state should be Wyoming. Attached is a report I've had prepared which explains the details.

Love from your son,
James

* * * * * * *

Dear James,

Your letters are always a pleasure for me. I am very blessed to have a son who is passionate about our nation's heritage of liberty. I wish that my generation did more to not leave you with this mess, but after we returned from WW2 and Korea I guess most of us just couldn't be bothered with domestic vigilance, so we wallowed in the rampant materialism of the day. I'm sorry that you and your children are paying for that now.

I've carefully read your report. Please know that I am completely behind you and your Wyoming plan.

It's the least I can do after having fallen asleep in 1953.

Your loving father

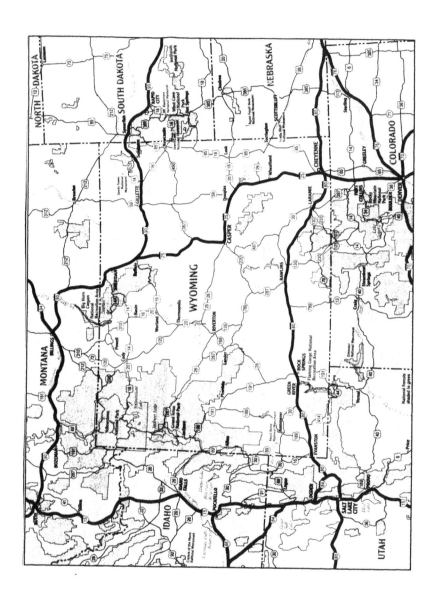

❖ 2003

I think that if you do even a cursory reading of 20th century history, you can't help but come away with a somewhat skeptical attitude towards government power. But it really doesn't have to grow out of any fundamental philosophical or political belief system. Really it's very simple—if there's a big beast that keeps running around eating people, then you can see that it ought to be caged or done away with. You don't need to base that opinion on any kind of belief system.

—Neal Stephenson, interview, *SFX* magazine #8, Jan 1996

I pitched the Wyoming plan to a renowned libertarian novelist. He did not find much with which to agree, countering that we should continue to "retake America." I replied that such simply could not be accomplished with our present numbers, nor with our likely future numbers. He opined such talk as "defeatist."

Let's say that a small child wants a cookie, but the cookie jar is on the top shelf and too high for him to reach. That cookie jar is America. We cannot reach it, but we <u>can</u> use a chair to climb onto the counter.

Wyoming is the chair.

It's time we simultaneously realize our limitations <u>and</u> our abilities. We cannot reach the cookie jar, or even the kitchen counter—but we are tall enough to climb onto that chair.

Even if we never make it to the cookie jar, there are some gummibears on the counter. So, not only will the effort prove at least somewhat worthwhile, we really have no other choice . . .

—James Wayne Preston, *Journals*

April 2003 Speech
Colorado Libertarian convention

"Look, here's the straight scoop, like it or not. The Libertarian Party has about 50,000 paid members. Even as the largest third party—or, if you prefer, the third largest party—the LP commands no more than a million votes in presidential elections, and usually less than half that. It has one US Congressman out of 435—Ron Paul of Texas—and he has to run as a Republican. It has one sheriff out of 3,100 counties, and no Senators or governors. Only billionaires like Perot or DuPont have ever hurdled the obstacles put in the way of third parties, and the LP has no billionaires on the ticket, and likely never will. The LP has never met the 15% electorate requirement to enter the presidential debates, and national media understandably carry on as if the LP isn't even a blip on the political radar screen, so the vast percentage of the electorate will never *hear* of a Libertarian candidate, and even if they ever *did*, the LP's platform of ending welfare and Social Security would end their brief interest.

"The graying Baby Boomers—who will not *begin* to die off until the year 2024, and half of them will live until 2035—will do *anything* necessary to ensure their monthly Social Security checks, including the increased wage slavery of their children and grandchildren. That means Social Security will not only remain a politically-untouchable issue for at least the next thirty years, it will also, at minimum, *double* in size during that period. And you believe that some political party will be able to reduce, privatize, or eliminate Social Security and MediCare in our lifetimes? Hah! They don't call SS a "third-rail" issue for nothing. Touch it, and you're fried.

"Point being, it is a political and social impossibility to convert the United States of America into a Libertarian nation. It'd be like trying to Christianize Iran. America simply does not want to *go* there, and since we do not believe in using force as a political instrument we cannot drag the country there kicking and screaming. Neither will we ever win by education and argument because we have no access to media and academia, and we likely never will. Perhaps after the Social Security collapse and the demise of the elderly Baby Boomers a third party may have a chance to lead from the chaos, but for the next generation or two the USA will continue to be run by some variant of the DemoPublicans. Them's the facts.

"Does that mean that libertarians, classical liberals, constitutionalists, and conservatives have no chance of some political victory in our lifetimes? No, it doesn't. All it means is that we must honestly assess our strength and pick a fight that we can actually *win* for a change. Numerically, 50,000 paid members means a good sized town. But, we are sprinkled about a nation of nearly 300 million. We have the raw numbers to win possibly a state, but we don't have the *concentration* of numbers to elect the local dogcatcher. But . . . we could *if* enough of us packed up and relocated. We *could* concentrate our numbers somewhere and become politically effective. All it would take is perspective, planning, and commitment. It's time we all got off our asses and actually inconvenienced ourselves for Liberty.

"The trouble is that most members of the national LP, sympathetic or even harmonious with a state goal, would not lend much support to the effort.

For example, why would California libertarians donate funds for a campaign in New Hampshire? As the saying goes, *All politics are local*.

"I wouldn't expect much support from the national LP. Its goal is to elect national candidates, which we have just seen is nearly impossible. Unless they snap out of their delusion and embrace our plan, we are a threat to the LP. Every campaign finance dollar we spend in our targeted state means a dollar that will not be spent trying to elect Libertarian presidents and congressmen. To them, we will be working at cross purposes.

"Accordingly, I suggest that we form a new political party in our chosen state. A party philosophically indistinguishable from the LP, but with none of the LP baggage of national aspirations.

"The LP wants to remain a national "army"? Fine. Good luck. We, however, will become the "Special Forces" of the movement. We won't fight losing wars—we will win handpicked battles, one at a time. Had the LP nominated a presidential candidate with small-unit combat experience, the LP might have figured all this out a long time ago. Instead of thinking of *strategy* like generals, they should have been thinking of unit *tactics* like noncoms and captains. But no, the LP has dreamed only of winning the war when it has not occupied even a single hill of the enemy.

"This luxurious thinking has wasted 25 years of valuable time. If we do not start making visible and dramatic gains *somewhere*, libertarians and conservatives will not be galvanized into further action. We are tired of losing across the board. Let's pick *one* winning horse and place all our bets on it. We couldn't do any worse than we already are, right?"

FREE STATE PROJECT CHOOSES ... *NEW HAMPSHIRE?*

Only 46% of FSPers participate in vote

Exclusive to *The Modern Jeffersonian*, by "Whisk E. Rebellion"
1 October 2003

The results of the September FSP vote were announced in New York City today, though not even 1 in 2 of FSP's first 5,500 members voted for their favorite state amongst the ballot's ten choices. According to FSP sources, 65-80% of the nearly 3,000 nonvoters "abstained."

Of the 2,500 members who *did* bother to vote, New Hampshire received the most 1st and 2nd votes, beating out the next favored state Wyoming by 10%. Since the Eastern USA is more populated than the West, this was reflected in the FSP's members, who naturally were inclined to stay in the East.

This was most unfortunate for the free state movement at large.

First of all, New Hampshire has 2.7 times more voters than Wyoming, which *automatically* diminishes the NH/FSP's political effectiveness by 63%.

Secondly, it is *far* too crowded back East. New Hampshire has about 140 per mile^2—twice the national average, four times that of Colorado, and *twenty-three* times Wyoming's six people/mile^2. New Hampshire is certainly a very nice state for the random newcomer, but it cannot gracefully contain a flood of 20,000+ relocators, much less the 100,000+ needed to affect politics.

Finally, even if it could, no New England state is hospitable to a thriving gun culture, a necessary feature of a modern free state (and one sadly underappreciated by the FSP). A "thriving gun culture" does not mean 4% of adults with concealed handgun permits. It does not mean more than one skeet range per county. It doesn't even mean a preponderance of hunters every deer season.

A thriving gun culture is *much* more than that. It is a culture where *all* things related to shooting are widely and passionately enjoyed. Its members would rather go to the range than bowl or golf or watch TV. They would rather go to a gun show than a football game.

New Hampshire does *not* have a thriving gun culture. With only four or five gun shows each year (the largest being just 325 tables) and little public land to shoot on, how *could* it?

Folks *already* there have few places to become 500yd Riflemen, the smallest component of Liberty. If men serious about defending their freedoms did not have the supporting terrain (and culture) to practice putting .308 FMJ into 20" circles at nearly a third of a mile, then they could not become competent with full-power semi-auto military-pattern battle rifles. They could not become Riflemen and thus have a chance of defeating a modern military which relies too much on air and artillery. Using .223 carbines within 250yds is fighting an enemy on *his* terms. We have only marksmanship and .30 caliber power on our side. Should a fight come (and I pray that it never does), then we must engage at ranges beyond our enemy's. (They have only 250yd carbines and 50yd marksmanship.)

The only advantage a militia force has are 500yd accurate rifles. Americans cannot own battle rifles and train at such distances in the East. That means FSPers in New Hampshire will not be able to, if required, effectively fight for their liberty. Libertarian philosophy is, in the end, moot if its adherents have no final resort of armed defense, and freedom has usually required the shedding of blood on battlefields. If history has taught us anything, it's that liberty is won and maintained by *Riflemen.* As Heinlein once wrote:

> *The price of freedom is the* ***willingness*** *to do sudden battle, anywhere, anytime, and with utter recklessness.*

Willingness to do sudden battle implies *capability* to do sudden battle. You must already have the tools, training, and practice to fight effectively. When you are capable and willing to fight, *then* you have options. When you are capable and willing to fight, *then* your enemy will perhaps fear and avoid you.

But not until then.

If you do not have—*right now*—an FAL, M1, M1A, or HK91, then there is something you have chosen *not* to own for your freedom.

If you *do* own such a rifle but cannot—*right now*—from offhand position hit a dinner plate at 100yds within 5 seconds on demand *without fail*, then there is a skill you have chosen *not* to earn for your freedom.

If you are not a Rifleman—*right now*—then you have announced to the world that your commitment to liberty goes only just so far. If you will not spend a summer and the price of a used jetski to become a Rifleman—to become a deadly *foe* of tyranny—then you are just mouthing platitudes, treating liberty as a hobby and expecting brave men to do your fighting *for* you.

If you're not a Rifleman—you're just a hobbyist.

By choosing to move to a state where you can't *become* a Rifleman, a hobbyist is what you'll *remain.*

The Nerf and Egghead Libertarians don't like hearing this, obviously, but facts are stubborn things.

> *The state that separates its scholars from its warriors will have its thinking done by cowards, and its fighting done by fools.*
> — Thucydides

FSPers in New Hampshire without battle rifles are like libertarians in Manhattan without handguns. All are at the mercy of any determined band of thugs. If you're not a Rifleman in the country or a Pistolero in the city, then you're merely food waiting to be eaten.

You can scream *No initiation of force!* all the way down your aggressor's gullet. Big deal. All fish wriggle when caught. Only fish with *teeth* are dangerous to anglers, and New Hampshire fish will find it very difficult to grow the teeth they need.

Also, New Hampshire is quite vulnerable to the counterresponse of a neutralizing number of East coast liberals. Vermont had been socially and politically poisoned in exactly the same way by 1988.

Most folks living *left* of the Mississippi River, however, will not move East. They understand the magic of the West and its unique suitability for a free state initiative. Thus, about 18% of original FSPers had opted out of New Hampshire, but wish the FSP every success there.

Wyoming is *our* favorite choice. It enjoys the space, the culture, and the resources to make "Free State West" work. It's also too rugged for liberals to contemplate (and Jackson is already full).

We were moving to Wyoming regardless, but had waited until today to see if the rest of our FSP comrades would be joining us. While we are sad to lose up to 4,500 of them to New Hampshire (assuming they actually move there), we've no choice but to create a second organization for our own Western purposes.

Besides, with most national attention on the FSP, a quiet Wyoming project just might succeed. As a magician misdirects audience scrutiny to hide the hare, New Hampshire may serve to misdirect the ruling powers. The rabbit could come from a Wyoming hat, versus a New Hampshire sleeve.

❖ 2004

2004 USA political news

Necessity is the plea for every infringement of human freedom. It is the argument of tyrants; it is the creed of slaves.
— William Pitt

In the classic American way, a lone gunman on Prozac® with a so-called *"assault rifle"* opens fire on a festival crowd, killing 11 and wounding 17. Although he is killed by a randomly-armed citizen, this is not reported by the national media. What *is* widely reported is that the gunman used a 30 round *"high-capacity"* magazine in his Mini14. Accordingly, the *"Crime Bill"* of 1994, due to expire on 13 September, is renewed in perpetuity by Congress, and signed by President Bush. *"In the continuing war against terrorists, we must maintain those laws which keep our cities and families safe from gun violence,"* explains the "gun-friendly" Texan President.

> *I'm not for free trade and I'm not for protection.*
> *I approve of them both, and to both have objection.*
> *In going through life I continually find*
> *It's a terrible business to make up one's mind.*
> *So in spite of all comments, reproach, and predictions,*
> *I firmly adhere to unsettled convictions.*
> — British House of Commons, 1903

2nd Amendment groups and Republican PACs who had expected Bush to veto the *"Crime Bill"* extension are stunned. Their rally cry of *"Second Term? Second Amendment!"* had not been taken up by Bush. 1.5 million NRA members switch to no-compromise RKBA groups, such as Gun Owners of America, Jews For the Preservation of Firearms Ownership, and the Second Amendment Foundation, to name a few.

In memory of Bush 1.0 in 1992, these yet-again betrayed gunowners try to deny reelection to President Bush. This time, is doesn't work. There is no spoiler third-party Perot, and the Bush machine is laden with campaign contributions. Also, the Democratic Party fields an ineffective and vacillating candidate. Finally, much of the public is nervous about "changing horses in mid-stream" during the (Forever) War on Terrorism.

2004 USA economic news

Through a classic series of cruel bear rallies and War on Terrorism panic, the Dow falls to 6,812 as increasingly nervous capital quickly moves into commodities. All the market gains since 1995 have been given back. Gold is $515/ounce, and silver $8.60. Crude oil is $34 a barrel, and pump prices $2.50/gallon.

GOING THE DISTANCE, NO MATTER WHAT

Fewer than half of libertarians armed

Exclusive to *The Modern Jeffersonian*, by "Whisk E. Rebellion"
December 2004

In his poem "The Second Coming" Yeats squarely framed the issue: *"The best lack all conviction, while the worst are full of passionate intensity."* Ayn Rand echoed that in *Atlas Shrugged* with:

> When men reduce their virtues to the approximate, then evil acquires the force of an absolute; when loyalty to an unyielding purpose is dropped by the virtuous, it's picked up by scoundrels—and you get the indecent spectacle of a cringing, bargaining, traitorous good and a self-righteously uncompromising evil.

Many Libertarians will not accept the possibility that armed struggle may become necessary to restore our freedoms, much less prepare for it with any training. They are simply too intellectually-vested in Rand and Rothbard and Rockwell.

Libertarians forgot, or never learned, that the purpose of thought is to foment and guide *action*. You've got the largest libertarian bookstore in the world selling titles on the philosophical underpinnings of gun ownership and the 2nd Amendment, but refusing to carry *Boston's Gun Bible*—arguably one of the single most useful gun books ever written—because it's *"gruesome"* and a *"blueprint for revolution."* Libertarians are too often like kids who play "Doctor" but avoid med school. On the morning of 19 April 1775, do you think the Minutemen had their noses buried in Adam Smith's *Invisible Hand*?

Absolutely not. These men had been training together for months!

How many Libertarians today do you suppose actually *own* a battle rifle, or even a hunting rifle? And I'm not talking about those who got all nervous about Y2K or urban riots and finally condescended to buy a Mini14, which has been collecting dust in the closet, unfired. I'm talking *battle rifles*: M1 Garands, M1As, FALs, HK91s. One in 50? And how many of them have actually *trained* with it? Spent days in the woods with it? One in 200?

That's one in 10,000 Libertarians whose ass is *not* a lump of cookie dough. That's one in 10,000 Libertarians who is ready, willing, and able to instantly defend home and hearth with a .30 caliber, military-pattern, battlefield-proven, Honest-to-God *rifle*.

Libertarians are like Tibetan monks facing the Red Chinese Army in 1950. Sure, they're nice, well-meaning people, but they pose absolutely no threat to armed aggressors, and that's disgraceful.

There is no excuse. Libertarians had an entire *generation* to arm and train, *and* a country in which such was legal and affordable and even socially tolerated. They chose *not* to arm, *not* to train, and now they're paying for it. *All* of us are.

In short, the real problem is good people who remain only good enough to live with themselves, and refuse to follow their philosophical, religious, and political premises to full conclusion. If Republicans had become Libertarians, if Libertarians had become Riflemen, and if conservative Christians had become *either*, we would have been enjoying limited government since the 1950s. After they had sorted out the world, the WWII vets had an epic chance to sort out America and return her to the true path. They did not. Beating the Japs and Nazis was only "half the prescription." The "full bottle" involved wiping out the Communists, both abroad and at home. Kill only half your enemies and then retire to the couch gloating about it will guarantee quite the surprise later on. To compound this error of omission, the vets raised their children in suburban A/C luxury, only to be rewarded by their revolt in the 1960s.

As in anything, the "good enough" is the enemy of the best. We must at last apply the total remedy—taking the *entire* prescription, not simply "half the bottle."

Good must boldly call evil for what it is. When Reagan did so to the USSR and pledged America to designing and building a space-based missile defense, the Soviets went nuts. They finally faced an American President who would not be placated, who would not blind himself to the brutal fact that the USSR *was* an "evil empire." Reagan's greatest asset was his adherence to basic principles. To be sure, he was a simpleton, but in the best sense. So are Americans.

Reagan appealed to that, demonstrated superb leadership, and the Soviets knew that it was Game Over. And all it took was a declaration of moral war—something FDR, Truman, Eisenhower, Kennedy, Nixon, Ford, and Carter avoided. Seven presidents cowered for *forty* years! Finally, a decent and simple man pointed a Zolan finger and said *"J'accuse."* Ten years later you could get a Big Mac in Red Square or buy surplus MiGs. It needn't have taken forty years to end the Cold War. It only took the first President to say *"Boo!"* and that entire rotting shack collapsed.

Americans could have gotten rid of Clinton had they thrown up enough fuss. Instead of asking the right questions about Vince Foster's obvious homicide and the Oklahoma City bombings, they *reelected* him in 1996! For their trouble they were dragged through still further mud of his continued scandals up until his very last day in office with those outrageous pardons.

His second term was even more putrid than his first.

That is the price of cowardice.

❖ 2005

To be GOVERNED is to be watched, inspected, spied upon, directed, law-driven, numbered, regulated, enrolled, indoctrinated, preached at, controlled, checked, estimated, valued, censured, commanded, by creatures who have neither the right nor the wisdom nor the virtue to do so. To be GOVERNED is to be at every operation, at every transaction noted, registered, counted, taxed, stamped, measured, numbered, assessed, licensed, authorized, admonished, prevented, forbidden, reformed, corrected, punished. It is, under pretext of public utility, and in the name of the general interest, to be placed under contribution, drilled, fleeced, exploited, monopolized, extorted from, squeezed, hoaxed, robbed; then, at the slightest resistance, the first word of complaint, to be repressed, fined, vilified, harassed, hunted down, abused, clubbed, disarmed, bound, choked, imprisoned, judged, condemned, shot, deported, sacrificed, sold, betrayed; and to crown all, mocked, ridiculed, derided, outraged, dishonored. That is government; that is its justice; that is its morality.

> — P.J. Proudhon, *General Idea of the Revolution in the Nineteenth Century*, translated by John Beverly Robinson (London: Freedom Press, 1923), pp. 293-294

Corruptisima republica plurimae leges.
(The more corrupt the state, the more numerous the laws.)
> — Tacitus, Anals III 27

A subtle, though vital, human dynamic is what I call "voltage." It is paramount regarding the heart of an American. Voltage. Positive or negative.

If you have a government job, if you believe that citizens "cannot take the law into their own hands," if you believe it immoral to "cheat" on your taxes, then not even conservative political beliefs will save you. Your voltage is on the side of oppression. You have the heart of a slave. You are a collaborator.

Conversely, if you don't understand why you should pay sales tax on a used car from a private seller, if you have ever acquitted a defendant charged with a harmless malum prohibitum, *if you see an obvious distinction between your country and the government, then*

you have the soul of a Patriot—even if you vote Democratic. Your voltage is on the side of freedom.
It is necessary that you daily commit acts to maintain your proper voltage. Ignore government forms, refuse to provide truthful answers to government officials, cultivate radical friendships, make undeclared income from "under the table," buy unregistered guns, circulate news about corrupt federal officials, and generally withhold your cooperation.
Done consistently, you will more likely be capable of acting valiantly and decisively when der Tag *arrives. Courage is a muscle. It must be subjected to daily use, or it will wither beyond revival.*

—James Wayne Preston, *Journals*

2005 USA political news

After he appoints two new Supreme Court Justices, President Bush wastes no time signing sweeping new legislation restricting personal freedoms in the name of the (Forever) War On Terrorism. The *USA PATRIOT Act 2* outlaws: cash transactions over $5,000; cash purchases of telephone calling cards, airline tickets, gasoline, and ammunition (and their components); and private transfers at gun shows (all go through NICS).

Restrictions on personal liberty, on the right of free expression of opinion, including freedom of the press; on the rights of assembly and associations; and violations of the privacy of postal, telegraphic, and telephonic communications and warrants for house searches, order for confiscations as well as restrictions on property, are also permissible beyond the legal limits otherwise prescribed.

— Adolf Hitler, 1933 speech calling for *"an Enabling Act"* for *"the protection of the People and the State"* in response to the Reichstag fire (which Göring's people had secretly lit but publicly blamed on the Communists)

The *Prevention of Gun Violence Act* of 2005 declares .50BMG target rifles and ammunition as *"destructive devices"* under the *National Firearms Act of 1934.* Also included are (except for a few exempted African heavy game calibers) all calibers with muzzle energies over 4,000 foot/pounds, which means the .338 Lapua Mag, .30-378 Weatherby, .408 CheyTac, etc. Also, the tax stamp fee is raised from $200 to $1,000 (which is fruitlessly challenged under the *Drexall Furniture* ruling). Prohibited for civilian possession are armor-piercing ammo, Level IIIA and IV bulletproof vests, Gen3 night vision goggles, all night vision scopes, and all infrared laser sights. A 90-day amnesty period is provided for, after which such gear is felonious contraband punishable by 10 years in federal penitentiary.

Prohibited from further domestic production or importation are detachable magazine semi-auto centerfire rifles (AR15s, Mini14s, AK47s, FALs, etc.—as well as the Rem 7400, Marlin Camp Carbine, etc.). The "handwriting is on the wall" for all but the most stubbornly blind.

near Lander, Wyoming

"Look, Honey—you got another reply from Senator Doxer."

Susan Bradford hands her husband the familiar envelope with its franked postage and blue inked return address.

Kyle Bradford, a third generation farmer near Lander, has just come in for lunch. His wife made absolutely the best lasagna, which won the Fremont County Fair "Best Meat Dish." He could smell it all the way from the barn as he hurriedly parked the tractor.

"*Oooh*, maybe I oughta save this for a special occasion," he says with sarcastic awe. Holding the envelope in his callused hands, he languidly tears it open and reads the letter aloud:

Dear Mr. Bradfurd   ,

I was very pleased to receive your letter(s). As you know, I always like to hear from concerned citizens such as yourself.

I, too, am most interested in   the Bill of Rights   .
I am also interested in your right to keep and bear arms   .

Such vital topics are very important, and it is important that we continue to think about vital topics. I think about them every day.

Thank you again for sharing your thoughts with me. I will most assuredly remember your views as I work for America in the U.S. Senate.

Very truly yours,

Dorothy Doxer

Senator Dorothy Doxer

"Another masterpiece suitable for framing," observes Susan.

"Yeah, but why upset the parrot?" Kyle replies.

Pitchforks and politicians! screams Bondo, their double yellowhead from the living room. Susan's father had taught him that phrase during the Clinton regime, and the old bird seemed to belt it out at the most uncanny moments. The Bradfords swore that their parrot was a feathered human.

"Bondo is not in the mood for Dorothy Doxer today," laughs Susan.

"Well, gee, who *would* be? I mean, who could possibly read a cheesy letter like that without throwing up?" Kyle bemoans. "'I, too, am most interested in the Bill of Rights'—we could fertilize the back 40 with that! I know we're only farmers, but do they really believe we're *that* stupid?"

Opening the oven door with a Taz potholder, Susan says over her shoulder, "*My* favorite bit was 'I will most assuredly remember your views.' Kyle, why do they even bother with this . . . this *charade* anymore?"

"This charade is all they've got left, Sweetie. It's not exactly Jefferson and Madison out there anymore," answers her husband. "Democracy is just a way of saying *Nice Doggie!* until you can find a rock."

As Susan brings the lasagna to the table she lightly pats her husband's head and says, "Nice Doggie!"

Kyle Bradford jokingly growls, then grows serious. *Why do I even bother writing them? Just to be part of the same charade? Well not anymore! Maybe it's time for the people to find a 'rock' instead of—*

"Honey, are you going to say grace?" asks Susan.

"Oh, right—sorry!" says Kyle. "Dear Lord, we thank you for—" *Pitchforks and politicians!*

"Bondo!" yell the Bradfords in unison.

Irreverent as the bird could be, he went into a fury whenever Hillary Rodham Clinton was shown on TV, so his frequent outbursts were tolerated.

As they began to eat, Susan says, "And you'd think they could have at least spelled our name right!"

"Actually, the 'u' was the *original* spelling, but Grandpa Bradfurd had to change it years ago, before I was born—after the 'unpleasantness of '59', you know," Kyle replies in mock seriousness. "Yep, the whole family was run outta town like Commie lepers, and they—"

"Oh, *hush*, you!" Susan giggles.

"—had to settle right here in Lander!" laughs Kyle.

"Gosh, that makes me the lucky one, doesn't it?" quips Susan.

"Thank you again for sharing your thoughts with me. I will most assuredly remember your views as I work for you out in the pasture," he intones.

"Yeah, you'd *better!*" Susan replies, flicking a green bean.

Bwah-hah-hah-hah-hah! A maniacal cackle.

"Bondo!"

2005 USA privacy news

The revolution [of the liberal counterculture] *will coexist until it attains hegemony. Then it will dictate.* (at 196)
— Pat Buchanan, *The Death of the West*

All state issued drivers' licenses must be biometrically numbered to your thumbprint. Police cars are equipped with fingerprint readers linked directly to NCIC. Radio jammers begin to proliferate, and relay towers are increasingly sabotaged by outraged citizens.

We are now involved in a war in this nation, a last-ditch struggle in which the other side contends only the king's men are allowed to use force or the threat of force, and that any uppity peasant finally rendered so desperate as to use the same kind of armed force routinely employed by our oppressors must surely be a "lone madman" who "snapped for no reason."
— Vin Suprynowicz, *The Ballad of Carl Drega* (2002), p. 36

The *Communications Assistance to Law Enforcement Act II* of 2005 prohibits: anonymous e-mail, cell phone, and pager accounts (which must now be linked to your biometric driver's license number), alternative Internet banking (*e.g.*, PayPal, etc.) without accompanying SSN, and coin-paid pay-phone long-distance calls (credit-card based only).

A secret requirement of *CALEA II* is that all new cell phones are manufactured to covertly transmit GPS "here-I-am" NAM (number assignment module) signals even when turned off, as long as the phone is connected to outside power (such as a 110V AC adapter/charger, or 12V DC cigarette lighter power cord). Thus, the owner's movement may be tracked even when (he thought) he had turned off his phone. Also, the phone's mike may be surreptitiously activated without the owner's knowledge. Since the battery would not be discharged, the owner would never suspect that his phone was not only a mobile tracking device, but a silent On/Off bug as well.

The government against which our ancestors took up arms was a mild and distant irritant compared to the federal scourge that rules today. Constitutional restraints on tyranny are to our masters only a hazy memory as they exercise powers beyond the dreams of history's most famous dictators. Louis the XIV never required an annual accounting of every centime every Frenchman earned. He would never have dared then to demand a third of it in yearly tribute. Ivan the Terrible never told Russian merchants whom they could or could not hire, nor, heaven help us, where they could have a smoke.
— *The Gargantuan Gunsite Gossip 2* (2001), p.611

2005 USA social news
[Treblinka's effectiveness was due to] *the moral disarmament of the victim by means of skillful doses of panic and uncertainty. This disarmament forced the victim to make a certain number of minor concessions which led to others, which in turn brought him to a third stage, and so forth, until he received a bullet in the back of the neck with head bowed and hands joined in total submission.*
— from *Treblinka* (1967), by Jean-François Steiner, p. 44

Hier ist kein "warum." (Here there is no "why.")
—a Nazi concentration guard to a bewildered prisoner,
quoted from *The Ominous Parallels*, Leonard Peikoff

A Tuscon .50 Caliber shoot scheduled three weeks before the amnesty's end is infiltrated by seven ATF agents anxious to identify possible noncompliant owners. Agent "Flash" Gordon Lorner bungles an erroneous arrest, causing a scuffle which escalates into a gunfight. Lorner loses. He takes a round of .357 SIG to the abdomen, lodging in his lower spine. The other six agents attempt to close down the event and arrest several men, but are beaten and driven off at gunpoint by a crowd of nearly 400 very angry spectators and exhibitors. President Bush exclaims, *"This is why we needed to restrict those weapons of destruction in the first place!"*

A wheelchair paraplegic with a colostomy bag, Lorner takes early retirement. He is soon drinking three fifths of Wild Turkey a week, blaming the known universe for his plight.

Lorner's shooter was later acquitted as having acted in self-defense.

The mass of men serve the state thus, not as men mainly, but as machines, with their bodies. They are the standing army, and the militia, jailers, constables, posse comitatus, etc. In most cases there is no free exercise whatever of the judgment or of the moral sense; but they put themselves on a level with wood and earth and stones... Such command no more respect than men of straw or a lump of dirt.
— Thoreau, *On the Duty of Civil Disobedience* (1849)

The US military is now fighting terrorism in a dozen countries. Islamic terrorist attacks in America increase, including a smallpox outbreak in L.A.

2005 Economic
Gold is $882/ounce, and silver is $16.39. The Dow is 5,814.

THE DEMISE OF THE U.S. MILITARY

Our volunteer Army is spent

Exclusive to *The Modern Jeffersonian*, by "Whisk E. Rebellion"
Summer 2005

For a government to project military force, its troops must be willing to kill and die. But why do troops kill and die? To serve each other. This has been true of soldiers since men have been soldiers. Read *Gates of Fire* (Pressfield), *Blackhawk Down* (Bowden), and *Band of Brothers* (Ambrose) to understand this.

Esprit de corps, comradeship, and unit cohesion are the reasons men voluntarily go into harm's way. Fighting for their county is a very distant fourth. However, to be induced to join the armed forces in the first place (assuming there is no draft) requires a love of country, and thus a willingness to fight and die for country.

Here, the United States Government and its Insiders have a problem. This isn't 1942. The Government and the country are no longer overlapping entities fighting a common foreign foe. Since the 1960s the USG (through primarily the State Department) has decreasingly supported the civic mythology of Truth, Justice, and the American Way to increasingly embrace Propaganda, Injustice, and Globalism. For the New World Order to transpire, the socialist elite (political and corporate) must first preside over the cultural and spiritual death of the USA. They must kill the heart of America and level her historic institutions. Without a national ethos we will have no choice but to accept internationalism, or so they believe.

The American people are, however, catching on. They are seeing the mitosis between their country and the Government, and are ceasing to join the military. Many of those already serving are not renewing their enlistments. The watershed administration for this was, of course, Bill Clinton's.

When Bush the Younger was narrowly elected President in 2000, the military and many Americans breathed a collective sigh. A Texan and ex-Navy reserve pilot, Bush was heir to the smoldering coals of patriotism. Here was a President who did not loathe the military. The events of 9/11 whipped that reviving blaze of patriotism into a flame . . . until the fuel ran out.

The fuel being a unified belief in country and trust in government. America had that during WWII, and even generally during the Korean War. The disaster of Vietnam and its domestic unrest emptied the bucket. The Reagan years restored a bit of it, but not even Bush the Elder's victory in Desert Storm could hold the gain. Our last patriotic fuel was spent during the Clinton regime. Americans simply gave up. George Bush and 9/11 revived the coals, but coals were all that were left to revive. Hatred of Bin Laden was not sufficient fuel. Neither was hatred of Saddam, nor of terrorism in general.

The soul of America had been burnt out and there remained nothing left to catch fire, especially after Bush so overworked our troops chasing phantoms around the world.

The politicians quickly understood this, hence their immediate clamor for a reinstituted draft. They need a draft because Americans have become unwilling cannon fodder for overseas meddling under the most silly of names: "Just Cause," "Righteous Thunder," "Iraqi Freedom," etc. Americans no longer trust the government, and feel that the American Dream has somehow, inexplicably, evaporated.

So, the United States Government and its Insiders have a problem. They have killed the goose —patriotism—which laid the golden eggs of voluntary enlistment, and they can't resuscitate it. Patriotism, like innocence or virginity, can never be reclaimed. Their reward will be an increasingly sullen and unfaithful populace.

A saturnine military with a correspondingly declining ability to project force.

In their eternal quest to absorb the country, this is what governments have never learned: if patriotism is destroyed, government will fall. Tamper with the love of country, and you've lit the fuse of revolution or devolution.

❖ 2006

2006 USA economic news

It's not Americans I find annoying; it's Americanism: a social disease of the postindustrial world that must inevitably infect each of the mercantile nations in turn, and is called "American" only because your nation is the most advanced case of the malady, much as one speaks of Spanish flu, or Japanese Type-B encephalitis. Its symptoms are a loss of work ethic, a shrinking of inner resources, and a constant need for external stimulation, followed by spiritual decay and moral narcosis.
— Trevanian, *Shibumi*, p.296

Reduction of interest rates does not stimulate the failing economy. Tax revenues suffer as profits and wages are down, so the Fed begins to again increasingly inflate the currency (*i.e.*, FRN) supply. This unlawful and immoral corruption of the price equilibrium further unhinges the economy.

The tax-free "underground" economy (and its free-market banking substitutes, such as cash, barter, e-gold, encrypted digital cash, etc.) is the only thing keeping the country from sliding into an outright depression. As much as the USG would like to crack down on the "black market," they know that the implementation of a cashless system would suffocate the economy.

Gold is $1,170/ounce. The Dow is 5,247.

Wyoming   November 2006

Eighteen of Wyoming's 23 counties saw a general maintenance of the status quo, but 5 counties had a total change of government. Four counties elected a new slate of Republican officers, and Sublette elected an avowedly libertarian sheriff to replace an incumbent who hadn't seemed to care much for the Fourth Amendment. Local reaction in the five counties was a mixture of surprise and suspicion, especially due to the victory of several write-in candidates. The Hot Springs county clerk investigated the residency qualifications of several dozen new voters, but found that they were indeed *"actually and physically . . . bona fide residents"* in accord with Wyoming Election Code provisions 22-3-102(a)(iii) and 22-3-105(b). All had local addresses and Wyoming driver's licenses, as well as employment. The modest electoral hubbub soon passed.

Natrona County, Wyoming   November 2006

James Preston saves the revisions to his PowerPoint presentation. The post-electoral review meeting will begin shortly. He can hear muffled excited voices in the next room. After years of inaction and complaining, the events of the past several months were invigorating. He smiles at the memory of how it all had started. Over dinner seven years ago a colleague had blurted the line that forever changed Preston's notions of political strategy:

> *"Libertarians could actually get somewhere if they thought less like a national political party and more like a guerrilla army."*

Preston chewed on this and came up with the idea of freedom-oriented individuals taking over Wyoming county by county. After exhaustive research he drafted the relocation plan and schedule required to pull it off.

The project was based on a known weakness of democracy: few citizens practiced it.

Of Wyoming's population, 70% were of voting age. Only about 69% register to vote in the general election, and of those only about 75% actually do—thus only about 52% of the eligible voters participate in democracy. These actual voters make up only about 36% of the general population, of whom only 50.1% are needed to win an election. What all this means is that just 1 Wyomingite in 5.5 controls politics.

This leverage was a double-edged sword: a comparatively small number of new relocators could edge out the thinly supported *status quo*. If nearly 100% of the relocators were voting eligible and registered, and if nearly 100% of them voted for their annointed candidate, then they could take the reins of government.

Concentration of numbers with a singular mission can accomplish most anything in politics. The concept was solid, and there were sufficient numbers of people keen to relocate to a freer state. All that was lacking was the planning and leadership to make it happen.

Preston understood the shrewd organization the Wyoming project required and recalled his MBA program study scheme. Taking 15 credit hours per semester, he endeavored to pull a 4.0 which meant A's in every class. But not all A's were alike. A for A, a 90 was the same as a 100. Thus, it made no strategic sense to make high 90s in four courses but allow the fifth course to be dragged down to a B+. Better to spread out the semester effort in order to make low 90s in all five courses. So, Preston kept a running weekly account of his grades so that he could calculate just how much or little effort each course required in order to land a low 90. For example, if he had a 96 in Managerial Finance before going into the final exam (which was 25% of the course grade), he knew that he could make as low as a 72 on the final and still get an A for the class. Thus, he could use some of that study time for another class which needed a higher grade on its final exam.

So, his study load was spread exactly as needed—neither too thick nor too thin in any course. After two semesters he had perfected his system, and began to take 18 credits. The faculty and students thought him crazy for shouldering six courses (and all on Tuesdays and Thursdays, so as to give him 4-day weekends), but he managed the burden just fine. Privately, he thought such a heavy course load was the best way to keep him fully interested in his studies. Only challenges kept him interested.

Wyoming was such a challenge.

He would need fresh and accurate county data regarding population, percentage of eligible voters, percentage of registered voters, historical vs. expected voter turnout, absentee voting numbers, etc.

The relocators had to be coordinated and then "posted" wherever they were most needed. He was under no illusion as to the difficulty of directing the immigration of thousands of freethinking and independent Americans. Having once chaired a libertarian conference, he likened it to "herding stray cats." To command staunch individualists as a collective had never been done, but that was precisely what the project depended on: loyal allied troops under a General Eisenhower. Some soldiers would have to drop behind enemy lines before D-Day, others would have to hit the beach under fire, and still others would land only after the beachheads had been won.

It was a monumental undertaking. It had never been attempted, much less accomplished. The stakes were grand, but so was the prize—a free state.

Preston's dozen key people had assembled in the game room. Trophy heads from Wyoming, Montana, and Botswana covered much of the north wall. A rifle rack stretching across the entire 24' length of the west wall was filled with historical, military, and hunting long guns. Preston was especially proud of his chronological collection of semi-auto battle rifles. Not carbines, but full-power rifles. Beginning on the left with a Model 1890 7mm Mexican Mondragon, it extended to a 6.5mm Cei-Rigotti, a .276 Pedersen T2E1, a 1939 gas-trap M1 Garand, an M1941 Johnson smuggled back by a WW2 USMC paratrooper, an SVT40 Tokarev with Finnish capture stamp, an AG42B Ljungman, Walther G41(W) and G43, an FN49 with Luxembourg crest, a MAS 49/56, a TRW M14 with welded selector switch, a Spanish CETME 7.62, a BM62, a SIG 510-4 and SG542, a 50.63 para FAL, an HK91, a 1961 Portuguese variant AR10 with an American TELKO semi-auto lower, and even a 1980s HAC7 from the defunct Holloway Arms Corp. Most unique was a 1954 Brazilian copy of the G43 in .30-06, one of just 300 made.

Most of them had their original sling and bayonet, as well as other accessories when available. All were in at least 90%, if not 95% condition.

Many gun collectors thought Preston's wall a more complete collection of battle rifles than even the Buffalo Bill Firearms Museum in Cody.

One gap left to be filled was a .308 Ljungman, the FM59. Only ten were converted in 1959, and just three made it to the USA. The other seven were in Europe. The last known price for one was $8,650 in 2002.

Also, he very much wanted an FG42 but they were Class III full-auto guns, and Preston didn't want to go through the ATF hassle. (Some relocated Canadians with money and CNC mills were toying with the idea of making a semi-auto version, and Preston had lined up to buy one of their first guns.)

Some rifles were duplicate models just for shooting, like the .308 Korean War Tanker M1 Garand converted by Smith Enterprise.

Preston's favorite medium game rifle is a .308 Savage Scout, which the factory had totally redesigned in 2006 with a custom Hogue stock and a Burris 2-7x Scout Ballistic Plex scope in a Leupold Quick-Release mount. The package was so good that even some Steyr Scout purists bought them.

The first rifle he took to Africa, now relegated as a loaner for friends, was a Winchester Model 70 Classic Super Express in .416 Rem Mag topped with a Burris 1.75-5x20mm (3P#4 reticle) in Talley QD rings.

His favorite big game rifle (a gift from father) is a Dakota 76 African Traveler in .450 Dakota (including a second takedown barrel in .338 Lapua) topped with an illuminated 1½-6x Schmidt & Bender. A custom rifle case in Cape buffalo hide was a gift of his wife Juliette. His best friend and hunting partner chimed in with a hundred handloaded 500gr Woodleigh softs. His son and daughter had a handsome buffalo hide sling made. The rifle was Preston's most prized possession. He was found admiring it at least weekly.

Preston smiles as he enters the game room, it being full of his favorite rifles, hunting memories, and friends.

"OK, we've got excellent footholds so far. Five sleepy counties which nobody paid much attention to. We also have Senate District 1 and House Districts 2, 20, 27, and 40. Excellent work, people!"

Heads nod as soft applause fills the room. The election had gone precisely to plan, and everyone has a happy glow of satisfaction about them.

Preston continues. "Now, let's discuss what we need in January's general session. First, our proposed constitutional amendment. Second, . . . "

❖ 2007

The masses have always been as if one person, and this has further intensified since the advent of mass media (and our inevitable control). Our data proves that the homogeneity of Americans approximately doubled from the years 1950-2000. Accordingly, we can now quantify within 95.44% certainty (i.e., 2 standard deviations, $\pm 2\sigma$, from the mean comprised by Bell Curve distribution) the range of typical American activity. Undesirable activities outside that 2 sigma can safely be (from a political standpoint) targeted for gradual regulatory restriction and, ultimately, prohibition.

Activities outside of 3 sigma ($\pm 3\sigma$, which is 99.72% of Bell Curve distribution) are considered (by their very rarity) extremist in nature, and can be immediately targeted for prohibition (regardless of whether they are innocuous or patently undesirable).

The point is this: extremist behavior in any guise is not long to be tolerated. The public must be constantly shown that their safety lies only within 2 sigma of the sociological mean. Stray too far from the collective norm—whether you collect cars, guns, or wives—and society will suddenly disown you.

Evidence has shown that anything participated in by less than 5% of the population has very little political support, and such participated in by less than 0.3% has none at all. Without a significant sociological base, any undesirable activity or belief can easily be eradicated by legislative decree. Britain's leaders understood this perfectly as they have succeeded in disarming the marginal gun-owning population, who by 2000 constituted only 4% of households, thus outside 2 sigma of the sociological mean.

If, for example, rockclimbing were outlawed, less than 1% of the people would be affected and the remaining 99+% would have little knowledge of the prohibition. Even if they were aware of the prohibition, that 99+% would not understand or empathize with the rockclimbers. They could not even sympathize conceptually as fellow oppressed, since the masses have little or no conscious feeling of being oppressed.

To prove the matter from another direction, if the viewing of professional sports or the drinking of cheap beer were severely restricted by regulation, there would be a revolution the next morning. We ride a rough, simple beast, and we must take care not to interfere with its coarse (and largely harmless) prerogatives. Yet

*we must also continuously herd the beast within its allowed pasture,
all the while shrinking the boundaries inch by inch, day by day.
How far can it be shrunk? To zero. As the Nazi concentration
camp technicians scientifically proved, the human spirit can be
squeezed right out of its fleshy host. Whether or not this is desirable
is a political question, but the science of doing so is well understood
and completely reproducible.*
　　　—Julius N. Harquist, *The Gaian Convergence*, p.146
　　　River Lethe Press (2007)

*A voice murmured, "Let's run away." But other voices answered,
"Where to? Wait and see! There will always be time later." Nobody
wanted to revolt. You don't revolt against the unknown.*
　　　— from *Treblinka* (1967), by Jean-François Steiner, p. 22

Wyoming   January 2007
　　　The new county government officers are sworn in, and life pretty much
goes on as usual. It soon becomes apparent that the new folks in office possess
an unusually high degree of competence and integrity. They seem likely to do
their jobs well, so their odd rise to power is quickly forgotten.

Cheyenne Sentinel   February 2007
　　　In its biennial general session the 59th Legislature today proposed that
Article 20, Section 1 of the Wyoming Constitution be amended with the
following language (new text in bold):

*Any amendment or amendments to this constitution may be
proposed in either branch of the legislature..., and it shall be the duty
of the legislature to submit such amendment or amendments to the
electors of the state at the next general election, **or at the next
special election convened by the governor, which shall in any
event take place within one hundred and eighty (180) days of
passage by both houses.***

The speaker of the house explained, *'This proposed amendment will allow our
constitution to be improved by the voters more quickly in case of extraordinary events or unforeseen pressures."* The governor hailed the proposal as,
*"A necessary amendment to keep government responsive to the people during
these dynamic times."*
　　　Voters are expected to ratify the proposed amendment in the next general election in November 2008.

Washington, D.C.
J. Edgar Hoover FBI Building   **March 2007**

The FBI Headquarters was completed in 1975 just before Hoover's death. A massive tetrahedron concrete bunker, its 2.5 million square feet filled the entire block from 9th to 10th Streets and north to E Street.

Because of Pennsylvania Avenue height restrictions (so as not to block the Capitol) it was only seven stories on that side, but four stories higher at the rear northern face. Visually, it looked like gargantuan toaster with two slices of bread sticking out. It was, by all accounts, a brutal and hideous edifice posing as an impregnable fortress, dispensing with any Art Deco touches enjoyed by the Department of Justice Building across the Avenue. Rows of trees did no more to soften the FBIHQ's image than a dress on Janet Reno.

The interior was no less unattractive. A drab rabbit warren of white corridors and anonymous doors, teeming with almost 8,000 employees. Agents generally loathed the building.

The public knew only of the large E Street entrance near Ford's theater, used by the tri-hourly tour groups. After tramping through the building past the third-floor glass-walled Crime Lab (the "Fish Bowl") and Firearms Exhibit (featuring over 5,000 guns), the tour highlight was an MP5 submachine gun demo straight out of the movie *Brazil*.

Your FBI At Work—that sort of thing.

The public was never shown anything really sensitive, such as the Strategic Information and Operations Center (SIOC). SIOC is the FBIHQ's command post on the 5th floor, a large windowless room full of computer terminals. Agents called it "the submarine." When any large or multiple ops were running, SIOC was a very busy place. Headed up by a Criminal Investigations Division (CID) unit chief, the post was one of the most dreaded in the FBI. Lots of responsibility, but little real authority.

Special Agents and expected visitors used the Penn Avenue entrance on the opposite side of the building. To prevent drive-through attacks, the entrance was guarded by three sturdy reinforced-concrete planters. Just inside is a comfortable reception lobby with couches, coffee tables, and stuffed chairs. Facing the entrance behind the sign-in desk is a large one-way mirror. Hanging on the wall are three portraits: Hoover, the President, and the AG. Only Hoover's portrait is screwed into the wall; the other two are hung by wire. Hoover is eternal; politicians come and go. In the left wall are two elevators. The right wall is plate glass looking onto a small brick courtyard with park benches and a fountain. It was apparently just for show, as nobody had ever been seen using it.

Special Agent Douglas Bleth walks west on Penn past the red-roofed newsstand and enters the building. He is to brief the Director at 9AM, who had been phoned by the Wyoming Secretary of State to look into the odd and possibly alarming sudden influx of new residents. A plainclothes guard at the desk checks his badge and plastic smart-card ID as Bleth signs in. The guard nods and presses a hidden button under the desk. One of the elevator doors swishes open. Again, just like *Brazil.*

Bleth steps inside and presses "7." The FBI top brass—"sultans of the 7th floor"—commanded sweeping views of Penn Avenue. But of course.

After a brief wait, Bleth is shown into the Director's office.

"So, who's behind all this?" asks the Director without preamble. Such pleasantries as "Good morning" were usually a waste of his time.

Bleth says, "We have yet to learn the personalities of their C^3I."

C^3I stands for Command, Control, Communication, Intelligence.

"Analysis of new residents' email traffic shows that their instructions likely came from encrypted messages forwarded in bulk by foreign emailers. 'Remailers' they're called."

The Director parries, "If these Wyoming people are receiving encrypted foreign email, then how do you know this isn't a foreign operation?"

Bleth has already considered this. "Technically, we don't, but what would any foreign country have to gain by any of this? It seems like a domestic operation, probably from the right-wing element given the conservative nature of Wyoming."

"Good point," the Director says, nods—satisfied. "What are these nine thousand people up to?"

"We think that they are part of, or somehow connected to, the Free State Project. You know, that group which—"

The Director harumphs. "Yes, I've heard of them. Just another libertarian pipe dream, like colonizing space on personal rocket ships. It's a last gasp effort of people who just can't get along in society. Desperate kooks."

"I agree, sir, it is farfetched, but the FSP make no secret of desiring to take over a state through the electoral process, even though their membership officially chose New Hampshire back in 2003. The new residents of Wyoming already have five counties. That's nearly a fourth of the state. And it's all been legal as far as we can tell."

"Right—as far as we can *tell*," says the Director. He is silent for a moment and then asks, "How are these people in communication?"

"Through PGP encryption, but with a twist. Let's say that you want to send a group message to a thousand people, but encrypted. Not only is the message identical, the encryption is identical, or else you would have to encrypt it a thousand different ways—one way for each recipient according their unique public key half. For large group comm, this is far too cumbersome. So, public key encryption is not the answer unless everyone had the *secret* key, allowing the sender to encrypt the message with the public key. Although this could be done, it's needless extra work."

"Why is that?" asks the Director.

"Because of the way PGP operates, secret keys are not added to third party keyrings—only public keys are. Secret keys are added to the secret key ring only during a key pair's generation by the creator. I don't think PGP will allow an outside secret key to be added to the ring, and even if it can be done I'd bet it's really tricky. Too tricky for most users. The other way to do it would be to send out a file secring.pgp containing this group secret key and have the users substitute it for their own PGP secret keyring file when decrypting group email. Either way, it's a lot of extra work."

"And the 'needless' part?"

"PGP users who want to encrypt something solely for *themselves* don't have to use the RSA public key algorithm since they're not sending it to anybody else. As the sender and the recipients are all of the same group, it's like they're the same person for the purposes of this encrypted message. Therefore, *single* key, or symmetric, encryption is what you'd use. Meaning, the passphrase both encrypts and decrypts the message.

"As far as the algorithms go, asymmetric encryption is no stronger than symmetric. All asymmetric encryption does is allow two people to exchange encrypted messages without having first shared a passphrase. If a secure channel exists for communicating a common passphrase, then there is no problem using symmetric encryption. The key bit lengths are not equal, however. A 128-bit symmetric IDEA key is about the same as a 1024-bit asymmetric RSA key."

The Director looks lost. "What exactly are 'bits'?" The Director, a former federal judge, is notoriously ignorant of technical matters. Science, mathematics, computers—all of it is beyond him.

Bleth groans inwardly. "A binary digit, b-, -it. Computers are just a collection of switches and can only read ON/OFF, 1 or 0. Humans use a base 10 numeric system, and computers use base 2. Although any of our numbers can be translated in base 2 bits, it takes many more bits to do so."

Bleth pauses to see if the Director is following him.

"I understand. Go on."

"Given equal encryption strength, an asymmetric key is longer than a symmetric key because asymmetric algorithms are not as efficient."

"I'm with you. Continue."

"So, for these thousand people to individually decrypt your email, they must all know the common passphrase, right? But here's the problem, how do you secretly tell all of them in advance what the passphrase is? You need a secure prior channel to them. What the NSA believes is that each of the Wyoming people were, before they moved, initially contacted through their *own* key pair and told of the group passphrases to be used in the future. While it would be sweaty work, you'd only have to do it once. After everyone was on board with the passphrases, encrypted group emailings would be easy."

The Director is looking off into space, thinking. "Any success decrypting those emails?"

"None, sir. The NSA is working on them now."

"But hasn't the RSA algorithm been broken before?"

"Yes and no."

"What do you mean?"

"RSA is considered a very strong algorithm; it has no glaring weaknesses. Same for IDEA, Blowfish, Twofish, MARS, RIJNDAEL, and many others. A cryptological attack on such is actually an attack on the *key* itself, and a short key will compromise an impregnable algorithm. In symmetric encryption the key length decides the number of possible permutations, or "keyspace.' However, in asymmetric encryption like RSA, key length determines the size of the product of two huge parent prime numbers. The two encryptions are attacked differently. Symmetric by dictionary brute force, and asymmetric by factoring.

"The alleged cracking of RSA was merely a successful factoring attack on a 425-bit key, which is about like a 50-bit DES symmetric key. *'Fisher Price encryption,'* one analyst called it. Nobody serious about their privacy uses anything less than a 1024-bit RSA key, if not 4096 or more. Nevertheless, it took six months and 1,600 PCs to break that 425-bit key in a distributed Internet attack. The combined effort equaled about 5,000 computer years, or what the techs call MIPS."

"Goodness. What if the key is longer?"

"If a key is at least 128-bit symmetric, or 1024-bit asymmetric, it is considered unbreakable by brute force."

"Come on! *'Unbreakable?'* The NSA has *26 acres* of computers!"

"Yes, sir, unbreakable. And the NSA could have 26 *million* acres of computers. A 128-bit IDEA key has 2^{128} permutations, which is 3.4 times 10 to the 38th power. That's an ungodly number; the keyspace is astronomical. Every bit is like a fork in the road, and every single one of them must be guessed correctly. The trouble is, you have to make up to 3.4×10^{38} guesses before you're told if you guessed them correctly. It's like a giant labyrinth, except that you're never told which turns were wrong. Every attempt is a failure but one, and there are no shortcuts. All the computers on the planet working in tandem couldn't crack it in a million years."

"*Really?* That sounds like wild hyperbole, Bleth."

Patiently, Bleth explains, "The Japanese have an array of computers in Osaka used to track and simulate global environmental conditions. The array is huge; the size of four tennis courts. Their Earth Simulator is capable of 35 *trillion* instructions per second, and is as powerful as the twelve next fastest computers *combined*. It could have cracked that 50-bit DES key in a max time of just 75 minutes. A 60-bit key would need 53 days. A 70-bit key about 64,000 years. A 128-bit key would take them up to $2x10^{19}$ *years* to crack. That's 2 followed by 19 zeroes, which is a billion times longer than the age of the universe."

The magnitude of the problem is beginning to sink in. The Director is now fairly aghast. "A *billion years* longer than the age of the universe?"

"No, sir, a billion *times* longer than the universe's 20 billion years."

"*Jesus*. But computers are getting faster every day—isn't it just a matter of time before they bridge the gap?"

"Except for older encrypted files, no sir. In fact, it's just the opposite. Faster computers help encryption far more than decryption."

"*What?* How can *that* be?"

"Because it's easier to *generate* a key than it is to crack it, increases in computational horsepower help encryption far more than decryption. Adding just one more bit to a key *doubles* the number of permutations, and thus computer time. A 256-bit key isn't merely twice as tough as a 128-bit key, it's as many *times* tougher than the 128-bit key is on its own."

The Director brightens with understanding. "Because it's 2 to the 256th power? It's like two 128-bit keys multiplied against each other."

He's beginning to get it thinks Bleth. "Yes, sir! So, no matter how fast our computers become, it's an effortless thing for encryption technology to stay ahead by increasing key bit length. Not even just stay ahead, but *increase* the gap. Think of it this way: for every penny decryption gains, encryption gains a billion dollars. Forever. Ever since PCs became powerful enough to run Phil Zimmermann's PGP that's been a foregone conclusion. It was Game Over the moment the game began."

"*Shit!* It's *that* bad?"

"Actually, sir, it's far, far worse, especially with factoring attacks on asymmetric encryption. It is a million million quadrillion times more difficult to factor a product than to generate one. That's 10 to the 27th power. So, for every penny that decryption gains due to computational increases in processing power, asymmetric encryption gains a stack of $100 bills about 1,074 light years in length. Or, 33,941,566 round trips to the sun."

"A stack? Not laid end-to-end?" the Director asks, facetiously.

Bleth smiles thinly. "Yes, sir. Right now, there is encryption software which support huge key lengths, like 4096 and bigger. A 4096-bit key couldn't be broken if every atom in the universe were used to construct a giant computer and it chewed on it for 20 billion years. That's why the NSA fought so long and hard to prevent civilian encryption software from becoming ubiquitous. *'Every day the dike doesn't break is a victory'* is how one NSA official put it back in 1992. When that proved unstoppable, they then tried to force

56-bit DES as the standard because they could break DES. When that didn't work, they tried to implement key-escrow[1] under Clipper. Director Freeh was a tireless supporter of it, as you may recall."

"Yes, but Clipper went nowhere and the civilian encryption cat is out of the bag. What is the NSA doing about it?"

"Short of some miraculous mathematical advance in factoring[2] to crack RSA keys, or the construction of a quantum computer in the next five years, there is little they *can* do about it."

"So, I take it the NSA is . . . less than hopeful in our case?"

"They say that several things will likely make decryption impossible. One, they have no plaintext to work from; two, the message lengths are short, under 500 bytes; three, the symmetric key length is a robust 128 bits; and four, we may be seeing a regular change in keys."

"What do you mean by a 'regular change in keys'?" The Director braces himself for yet another avalanche of new information.

"NSA believes that these new Wyoming residents were given several different passphrases in advance, which have so far been used only once. The email Subjects contain prefixes such as 'Adam' and 'Brian,' which likely signify which key was used. These keys are, in effect, 'single session' keys which makes them virtually impossible to crack, especially without any plaintext. Since 'Edward' is so far the highest letter name used, NSA hopes that a short stack of only five different keys—'A' through 'E'—were provided and that the email receivers will at some point begin to reuse the earlier keys. Remember, these people are neither trained agents nor computer experts. They're just average folks so their comm network cannot be overly complex. I think the NSA is right, that they'll start reusing old keys for simplicity's sake. Their superiors are not likely to repeat the trouble of individually PGPing each of their new residents with new key passphrases.

"So, when they begin to reuse old keys the cumulative message length per key will increase, which will slightly ease decryption efforts. Even if the NSA does crack one of the keys, the messages encrypted with the remaining keys will remain unsolved."

The Director interrupts with a question. "What if the original stack of keys was not a short stack? What if the stack is twenty-six passphrases high from A to Z and we never see anything past 'J'?"

---

1   A scheme whereby a government agency holds copies of everybody's encryption keys to use when allowed by a court. Imagine if the police had copies of everybody's housekeys. Same thing. The potential for abuse is staggering, which is why the public shouted it down in the early-mid 1990s.

2   In the equation AB = C, factoring is trying to figure out the factors A and B from the product C. Factoring is extremely difficult when the factors are very large prime numbers. It's like trying to learn which shade of blue and yellow paint were mixed to make a particular green. This mathematical phenomenon of a "one-way street" is what public key encryption depends on. No new techniques for factoring large primes are expected, not that the NSA isn't trying.

Good question! thinks Bleth. *There may be hope for the man.* "If there is no reiteration of key usage and message length is kept short, then brute force cryptanalysis will be unavailing. Especially if the passphrases were unusually robust."

"Explain."

"Let's say the recipient sees 'David' in the subject line, and thus knows to use the passphrase called 'David' from his list. If he cuts-and-pastes the passphrase instead of typing it in, then he bypasses the keyboard altogether, thus defeating keysniffing programs. We are quite concerned about that possibility. Use of the RAM buffer can sometimes defeat Magic Lantern[3].

"The NSA also pointed out that if the cut-and-paste method of passphrase entry were used, then the passphrases could be *very* long strings of typographical gibberish, including the metacharacters. Such passphrases could not possibly be remembered, or even typed in perfectly. They would *have* to be cut-and-pasted. So, if metacharacters such as $ and % and * were used, that's a possible total of 95 characters including the numerals and upper and lower case letters. Even early versions of PGP support 79 character passphrases, which is a keyspace of 95^{79}, or 1.7 times 10^{156}. That's many times larger than the number of atoms in the entire universe."

"My God!" gasps the Director.

"And it could be even worse. They could be using more than just 95 characters in their passphrases. The total number of keyboard accessible characters is actually *256*. By holding the Alt button and typing in certain numbers up to 256, characters such as ¢ and © can be used. A 256 ASCII passphrase of 79 characters would contain 256^{79} possible permutations, which is 1.78 followed by 190 zeroes. That number is 10^{34} times larger than using the 95 character field, which was huge enough by itself."

"Bleth, these numbers are incomprehensible. Who can grasp them?" says the Director, nearly whining.

Consulting his notes, Bleth replies, "I completely understand, sir. Think of it this way. Imagine the keyspace of 95^{79} to be a square inch, roughly the area of a postage stamp."

"OK. I can see where you're going with this. The keyspace of 256^{79} is the size of Texas or something, right?"

"Much larger, Director."

"North America?"

"Larger."

Taking a wild stab the Director ventures, "The surface area of the entire planet Earth?"

"Yes, sir. Times 3 *trillion* planet Earths."

---

3   "Magic Lantern" is an FBI program to learn passphrases by methods outside of computational attack, such as planting key sniffers on target computers or installing tiny video cameras to record user keystrokes.

The Director is speechless.

"Let's *really* put this in perspective. There are about 8.69×10^{69} atoms in the Earth. If the visible universe, which is a cube roughly 1.5 billion light years per side, were 100% filled with matter instead of its far less than a billionth of 1%, there *still* would be fewer atoms than 1.78×10^{190}. *That's* how big a PGP keyspace can be if the user goes 256 ASCII and uses the PGP maximum length passphrase of 79 characters."

"Good God, I had no idea," says the Director wearily.

"The NSA analyst told me, *'If they're using long passphrases with 256 field ASCII characters, forget it; not in a trillion lifetimes.'* Quite frankly, the NSA has very little optimism in a successful decryption effort. They feel that much more can be gained from the human element."

"For example?"

"The technical security of PGP and how it has been used through foreign remailers in this case was quite sophisticated. We are advised to probe what is always the weakest link in the chain, human beings. For example, the World War Two Ultra program to crack the Germans' Enigma encoding machine would not have been successful without the sloppy techniques of too many German operators. The Gestapo's *Sicherheitsdienst* in particular were quite helpful to the British as they usually used profanities in choosing their three letter key settings."

"So what do you have in mind?"

"Remember, IDEA passphrases perform both encryption and decryption functions. Conversely, the members could just as easily and securely send message *up* the chain of command with the same passphrases. Symmetric encryption is a two-way street, and that's what we exploit."

"You're about to lose me here. What does this all mean?"

"It means that their scheme, though clever, has a *flaw*. All we have to do is a bit of DCS1000[4] traffic analysis of these new Wyoming residents. What they are looking for are emails encrypted with a symmetric key, versus with the much more common asymmetric method employed by nearly all PGP users. Asymmetric encryption is the *raison d'etre* of PGP. It is *very* unusual for somebody to send a PGP email that was encrypted merely with the IDEA algorithm—a conventional symmetric algorithm, which means that the recipient knows the same passphrase as the sender. Such just isn't done these days; it dismisses the whole point of public key encryption. So, we merely look for IDEA-encrypted emails. Easy."

"Can DCS1000 differentiate between the two different encryptions?"

"Not directly. All encryption software packages append their file names with a unique extension, such as .asc or .two or .enc. After searching

---

4   Originally called "Carnivore" until public outrage forced its name-change in February 2001, it is an email vacuuming system at the ISP level. It flags for key words and names.

for key words in plaintext, these known file extensions are the next search priority. A shrewd user knows this and either renames the files with an innocuous extension, or simply ZIP compresses the files which take on the extension .zip.

"Even if the file extension has been renamed, there is the matter of plaintext software headers. Abi-Coder and Twofish have none, but all PGP files have a plaintext header reading 'BEGIN PGP MESSAGE' with a version designation, and a footer reading 'END PGP MESSAGE.' It's one of the few faults of PGP. A few other encryption software packages also have plaintext labels, such as VGP, Kryptel Lite, and Diamond PC-1. Unless these files have been ZIP compressed—which garbles plaintext in the process of compression—DCS1000 easily flags them."

"Then why didn't these people use, what was it, Twofish? Then there would be no plaintext labels telling us that they used PGP."

"Probably because PGP is universal. Even though Twofish is easy to install and use, it's one more step for everyone to do and whoever planned this figured it just wasn't worth the bother. Personally, I doubt those folks in Wyoming bother renaming PGP files or compressing them or removing headers. I'd bet we'll find them sent as is. When they do, DCS1000 will try to open them up in PGP. If the file was encrypted with asymmetric RSA, then the PGP dialogue box will read that we do not have that particular secret key."

"Will the secret key have a name?" asks the Director.

"It must have *some* name; the key pair generation process demands it. This is so the PGP user can differentiate between keys on his secret keyring. But what the user names the pair is up to him. If these people are smart then they will not have given their key pair any identifying name. They could simply use alphabet letters or numbers."

"But you're not expecting this RSA encryption, are you?"

"No, sir. If the file was encrypted with conventional symmetric IDEA, then the PGP dialogue box will say so and ask for the password.

"It'll go down like this: Smith, a new resident in Wyoming, sends one of these unusually encrypted emails. While we won't know the content, we *will* have a brand new piece of information—the IP[5] address of the *recipient*. This will prove invaluable because the recipient is almost guaranteed to be *higher* in the chain of command than Smith. Smith is a buck private in the organization; he was induced to move to Wyoming. He won't be using this encrypted channel to chat with his enlisted men buddies. No, he will use it only to ask his sergeant for orders. Once we have the sergeant, we'll wait for him to query his lieutenant, and then the lieutenant his captain, and so on. Over time through traffic analysis, we'll roll up this group all the way to their general staff."

---

5   Internet Protocol, which can be linked to the telephone number of a computer's modem.

"Excellent. Fine work, Bleth. I suggest that for each area of immigration—there are, what, five counties?—we focus on the *first* people to arrive. They likely work in some coordinating capacity for the later people, and so they'll be in more frequent contact with their command."

"That's a great idea, sir. We'll get right on it."

Bleth had already thought of this.

"Let me know the moment you get a break. I don't like the idea of 9,000 people all being part of some scheme directed by God knows who through encrypted email. Even if they haven't yet broken the law. The size and secrecy of this whole thing bothers me. Have you ever seen anything like it, Bleth?"

"No, sir, not outside the service. It resembles a military operation; a wartime invasion, actually."

"It does, doesn't it? We know who the troops are—all 8,994 of them. Find their general, Bleth."

"Yes, sir. We will."

Natrona County, Wyoming
Preston Ranch   Spring 2007

"Folks, we have achieved our first legislative goal, a bit of constitutional 'prepositioning.' This will speed the passage of proposed amendments by virtue of a special election instead of waiting up to nearly two years for the next general election."

"Any expected opposition to ratification in 2008?" asks a white-haired jurist-looking fellow.

Preston answers, "No organized opposition, no. Perhaps 20 to 30% may oppose on the general principle of not tampering with their state constitution, but they will be insufficient to block ratification. As you well know, it is critical that such be in place by January 2015 of the 63rd Legislature, else our plan will have been mired in the mud of time, allowing opposition many months to organize. Little does this current government realize that they have been hoisted by their own petard."

The room chuckles heartily at this.

Preston then laid out the project's three sequential goals[6] ...

* * * * * * *

---

6   These are fully discussed in the Appendix "Wyoming Report" pages 389-391.

❶ Acquire political control of 16 of the 23 counties by 11/2014.

This is home turf, where Life is lived. Over half the battle of Freedom is in controlling one's county government by electing the sheriff and county commissioners (who could effectively limit state and federal intrusion, as did Sheriff Mattis of Big Horn in the late 1990's). If you are free in your county, then you are generally free indeed.

The team recognized how vital employment would be to the project's success. As a successful entrepreneur, Preston understood the necessity of revitalizing depressed counties with an influx of new businesses. Such not only brought in hundreds of needed relocators, but gained them instant grace with the community. But they had to be carefully chosen businesses, *i.e.,* noncontroversial industries which did not siphon away indigenous jobs and capital. Industries which made the best use of the counties' features. Niobrara County, for example, was a vast and empty prairie with over 500 acres/person. It was thus ideal for an aviation engineering and design firm, Maxwell Aviation, which produced homebuilt and production composite aircraft. They also made target drones for the US military, which were tested at nearby Camp Guernsey. Employing over 300 people, both the state and county governments did somersalts to lure Maxwell's relocation. Niobrara County also had the oldest median age (41.4) and the smallest average household (2.21). It was literally dying out. The influx of dozens of new families brought a desperately needed vitality to the entire county. Maxwell Aviation threw an Open House, and all of Niobrara showed up. Locals joked that it was the most interesting thing that had happened there since the western *The Lawless Men* was shot near Lusk back in 1923.

Similarly, Preston and his team analyzed what existed and what was needed in the other target counties, and packaged the relocation of people and businesses accordingly. Crook County saw the relocation of a midwest sporting goods factory, Johnson enjoyed two new firearm manufacturers, Sublette an alpine training academy for international athletes, and Hot Springs a national HQ for an insurance company serving retired military.

The calculated synergy was a Win-Win for everyone, which explained why things were working out so well. The success of the 2006 county elections had proven the concept. Wyoming was the contiguous 48's least explored, utilized, and industrialized state, and it was simply a matter of time before others would have figured that out. It had already begun to boom in its own right, but in that typical liberal fashion which had long ago ruined much of Oregon, Colorado, and Arizona. One Aspen or Sedona was enough.

❷   Acquire a majority in both the House and Senate by 11/2014.

Such could see through the repeal of oppressive legislation and the introduction of beneficial constitutional amendments.

The Wyoming legislature is made up of 30 Senators and 60 Congressmen. All serve single-member districts which are reshaped every ten years from US Census data. Each Senate district had about 15,000 people and comprised two House districts of about 7,500 each. These districts spilled over county and even city lines. Fremont county, for example, was in five Senate districts and six House districts. Senate District 1 comprised all of Crook, Weston, and Niobrara counties, as well as 20% of Converse and Goshen. The larger cities of Casper, Rock Springs, Laramie, Gillette, and Cheyenne comprised their own Senate districts, as well as multiple House districts. Medium-sized cities such as Evanston, Green River, and Sheridan had their own House districts.

Therefore, it required a precise coordination of relocators. It was very tricky work, especially in conjunction with saturating the counties.

❸   Elect the state executive officers in 11/2014.

This was, obviously, the plan's *coup de grâce*. A state governor backed by an allied legislature and judiciary could accomplish far-reaching reforms affecting all but the most federal of oppression.

Although it was a most ambitious project, it wasn't "all or nothing." If ❸ did not happen, then at least they had most of the counties and the majority of the legislature. If ❷ and ❸ did not transpire, then at least most of the counties were in their hands.

Even if not all 16 counties were taken, at least *several* would have been. Accomplishing only "2½" of their 3 goals still would have created several thousand square miles of freedom in America. Aim at the horizon, and you'll just clear your feet. However, aim at the stars and you'll reach at least the horizon, maybe farther. In short, the project could not *utterly* fail. Acquiring even just *one* county was one county more than they had.

The whole thing suited Preston perfectly. He was a superb planner and organizer, one of those rare people who could zoom in and out of a concept. He neither got lost in the big picture nor mired in the details. His mind worked like a spreadsheet: change one value and he would instantly understand how it affected everything else. After three years of planning sessions, his colleagues grew in awe of his talents and called him "The Wizard."

But how to "herd stray cats"? First, Preston and his team had to learn more about their relocators. Many questions were asked of them:

In which election year could they move? 2006, 2008, etc.?

How many voting age family members would they total?

Are they financially independent (business, investments, etc.)? If a business owner, how many jobs could they supply?

If not financially independent, what employment would they need?

Rural or urban preference of living? If rural, which first 3 choices of counties? Last 3 choices? If urban, which first 3 choices of cities? Last 3 choices?

What monthly rent/mortgage could they afford?

Home: hacienda, house, cabin, apartment, trailer, community?

Willing to take in renters? If so, how many and for how long?

So that the relocators could choose amongst the Wyoming counties and cities, detailed information was supplied. They got not only statistical abstracts, but digital videos of walking tours and even overhead flights, as well as interviews of residents explaining what they liked best and least about their area. Unpleasant facts were not glossed over—folks got the whole picture, warts and all. For example, everyone knew that Niobrara county was Nebraska's topographical twin and used logging chains for windsocks—which sort of helped to explain why fewer than 3,000 people lived there.

Some relocators liked the quaint little town of Buffalo, some chose Hot Springs and its therapeutic waters, while others preferred the quiet wooded terrain of Crook county.   Some relocators even liked the wind-swept desolation of Niobrara.

Their mosaic answers formed the initial rough image of what Preston and his team had to work with.   Naturally, not every relocator preference could be met (*e.g.,* far too many wanted to live in Sheridan or Casper), but probably 70% of a relocator's overall desire was assuaged.

Business owners were given first priority, then those with large families or contingencies, and then those who were financially independent.

Single employees had the least bargaining power, which was fair as they had the least to offer. Those who preferred a rural life had more clout over urbanites, as filling up the county around the larger cities of Gillette, Casper, Sheridan, Riverton, and Lander (all of which comprised at least one House District) was more difficult than relocating people to those cities.

Granted, any liberty-minded American was free to move to Wyoming whenever and wherever he wanted, and thus not be subject to any relocation restrictions. However, he would be outside the "fraternity" and thus not privy to the many co-ops and business opportunities available to those within the project.

Intra-state relocation flexibility was somewhat limited. The issue was not just to get relocators to Wyoming, but to place them within the proper counties and legislative districts needed to progressively win the state. For example, it would accomplish little to install 2,000 relocators in Weston county in 2010, only for most of them to move to Sheridan and Cody the next year. They needed to *stay* in Weston county long enough to keep it under political control until a statewide victory was won.

Relocators voluntarily obliged themselves to being "posted" (almost like being in the military) and they had to commit themselves to at least two election cycles—meaning, a minimum 25 month "enlistment." After that, they could relocate elsewhere in Wyoming, or even leave the state. For example, one could arrive in October 2006 just in time to register for the November election, and move after voting in the November 2008 election.

People differ wildly in their personalities. Some can "delay gratification" in exchange for a larger payoff later (in business this is called the "back-end"), while most others must Enjoy-Now/Pay-Later ("front end"). Still others will exchange a theoretical ideal for the security of the middle. So, for their 25 month hitch, several arrangements were offered:

1)   Guaranteed *arrival* in one of your top 3 counties/cities, but only if you agreed to move (if deemed necessary) after 12 months to wherever posted (including one of your 3 least favorite choices). Thus, you could arrive in Jackson and be posted to Lusk the next year, but it was also possible that that you might not be reposted anywhere, much less to one of your bottom 3 choices. This appealed to 30% of relocators. Gamblers.

2)   Guaranteed later posting to one of your top 3 choices of counties/cities after your first 12 months, but only if you agreed to *arrive* wherever posted (including one of your least 3 favorite choices). Many single relocators chose this option, likening their first year as a sort of "boot camp." After that, they'd be living in a preferred area and ready to start a family there. 40% chose this Pay-Once-Now/Enjoy-Later-Forever option.

3)   Guaranteed not to be reposted within your 25 months in exchange for not arriving in one of your least 3 favorite counties/cities. Thus, you arrived somewhere in the middle of relocation choices and never had to move. 30% of relocators chose the security of the middle.

The relocators' picks for/against certain counties/cities were on file *before* they were told of Options 1-3. That way, they could not skew relocation to their advantage by fudging on their choices.

Options #1 and #2 (mirror images of each other) comprised 70% of relocators, all of whom were available for the less popular areas. Thus, they experienced the highs and lows of Wyoming life.

Option #3 comprised 30% of relocators, who "fattened the middle" of the county/city choice. They wouldn't enjoy the Big Horn or Teton mountains, but they also wouldn't have to endure the Thunder Basin National Grassland of Campbell and Converse counties, either.

Every relocator "paid their dues," whether by cover charge, balloon payment or monthly installments. It was at least tolerable to everyone.

Not all of the counties were included in the project. It had been decided at the outset that such would be a pointless attempt to saturate the staunchly democratic counties of Sweetwater, Carbon, Albany, and Laramie. Uinta was still up in the air until after the 2010 election.

Those remaining counties (*i.e.,* those as much or more Republican than the state average) are available for relocation only on a staggered schedule. The project goal was not simply to move a bunch of people into Wyoming, but to fill up particular counties in a particular order. In 2006, just five counties could be saturated with the number of available relocators: Nibrara, Hot Springs, Sublette, Crook, and Johnson. Relocators wanting to end up in Jackson, Cody, or Sheridan had to bide their time as the respective counties of Teton, Park, and Sheridan were not available until 2010 and 2014.

The smart relocators chose Option #2 and moved to Wyoming early, thus assuring their place in a top location when the time came later. This incentive to early migration was built into the plan by Preston and his team. The more relocators who arrived early, the better chance of success the project would have. Early relocators also made data projection much easier.

* * * * * * *

Preston continues with the business at hand. "Now, let's talk about Phase 1b in 2008 and Phase 2a in 2010. With our five counties, we have, as planned, checkerboarded the counties of Fremont, Washakie, Campbell, and Weston. They are next for 'contagion' in 2010."

Preston often employed viral metaphors, and emphasized the value of picking counties for their "opportunistic infections" of neighboring counties. Although a low population base was critical, the number of contiguous counties with a high Republican percentage was a vital criterion. Once a particular county had been taken in 2006, holding it in 2010 under an incumbent government would not require as many voters (because many of the indigenous voters would support reelection). So, for example, Crook County could spare in 2010 some of its relocators to neighboring Weston.

The notion was military in theory: holding a hill required fewer soldiers than taking it in the first place. Fight, win, hold, move to the next hill.

Repeat until victory.

"In the 2008 elections, we plan to win Senate Districts 2, 18, 20, and 22, as well as House Districts 1, 26, 27, 28, 30, and 50. Such will prepare us for winning the related counties of Weston, Big Horn, Washakie, Park, Converse, and Lincoln in 2010.

"A successful election sweep in 2008 will give us a running total of 5 Senators and 10 Congressmen—a 16.7% block in the legislature. Then we can control most swing vote issues. That will very likely wake up the powers that be, even though the counties and districts of capital and minerals are still in their hands. So, from November 2008 on, we should expect increased scrutiny. It may get a little dicey after that."

"You never promised us green lights and blue skies, Jim," says a handsome woman in her fifties.

Preston smiles. "Just remember that in about four years, Margaret."

A balding accountant-type asks, "What about the districts in 2010?"

Preston replies, "Ah, Phase 2a. In the 2010 elections, we plan to take Senate Districts 3, 16, 19, and 23, as well as House Districts 4, 6, 21, 24, 25, 51, and 54. A successful 2010 election will give us a total of 9 Senators and 17 Congressmen—a near 30% block in the legislature. We will also have 11 of the 23 counties, which will then include Weston, Big Horn, Washakie, Park, and Converse. Goshen may also be within our grasp by 2010. At that point, having doubled our geographical and political power since 2006, we will have become an entrenched force in Wyoming.

"This is when the political climb grows increasingly uphill. From 2011 on, we will need to court national capital and expertise to see us to 2014. Remember your Revolutionary War history? Louis XVI let the Continental Army fight on its own for nearly three years before deciding that they had proven themselves worthy of support. Only after they had defeated Burgoyne at Saratoga in October 1777, taking 3,000 prisoners, did the French sign a pact with them the next February. So, ladies and gentlemen, for the first half of this struggle we're mostly on our own. After the 2010 elections, however, we'll need some OPM.

"Capital is the biggest skeptic and the petroleum and cattle money will need convincing that we are here to stay. Only then can we take on Sheridan, Campbell, and Natrona counties in order to win the state in 2014.

"Nevertheless, by 2010 we expect to have the upper half of Wyoming. Geographically and politically, that will be quite a stronghold. Even if we cannot take the state in 2014, we *will* be able to significantly direct, if not control, its politics.

"Personally, however, I believe that we'll pull it off."

2007 USA political news

[T]*he* (Supreme) *Court is the battering ram of revolution.*
— Pat Buchanan, *The Death of the West* (2002), p.253

When words lose their meaning, people lose their liberty.
— Confucius

The famous 2nd Amendment case *Emerson v. US* is at last heard by the US
Supreme Court, which in a 7-2 decision partially affirms the 2002 5th Circuit
Court ruling that to keep and bear arms is indeed an individual right, but not a
fundamental one because of modern police protection and the national
guards. Justices Scalia and Thomas bitterly dissent, arguing that the 2nd
Amendment *is* a fundament right. All nine Justices, however, ignore the
pesky *"shall not be infringed"* verbiage.

> *Once alienated, an "unalienable right" is apt to be forever lost, in
> which case we are no longer even remotely the last best hope of
> earth but merely a seedy imperial state whose citizens are kept in
> line by SWAT teams and whose way of death, not life, is universally
> imitated.*
> — Gore Vidal, *Perpetual War for Perpetual Peace* (2002), p.20

Reaction from gunowners is resoundingly acrimonious. *"The gloves are off!"*
is the common sentiment in the Rural South and Inland West.

> *Perhaps an elected official will one day simply refuse to comply with
> a Supreme Court decision.*
> *That suggestion will be regarded as shocking, but it should not
> be. To the objection that a rejection of a court's authority would be
> civil disobedience, the answer is that a Supreme Court that issues
> orders without authority engages in an equally dangerous form of
> civil disobedience.*
> — Robert Bork, 1997

Congress and President immediately reply with the *Dangerous Weapons Act*
of 2007, which requires the federal registration of all currently owned centerfire, semiautomatic rifles and their ammunition. (Handguns, shotguns, and
rimfires are, for the moment, exempt.) The NICS apparatus is modified to act
as the registry. Again, the amnesty period is just 90 days. Failure to register
affected firearms means an automatic 5-year felony prison term.

> *It has, after all, been explained to us that the heart of the matter is
> not personal guilt, but social danger. One can imprison an innocent*

person if he is socially hostile. And one can release a guilty man if he is socially friendly....

And it must be kept in mind that it was not what he had done that constituted the defendant's burden, but what he might do if he were not shot now. "We protect ourselves not only against the past but also against the future." (quoting the organizer of the Department of Exceptional Courts of the People's Commissariat of Justice, N.V. Krylenko)

— Alexandr Solzhenitsyn, *The Gulag Archipelago,* Vol. 1

Plumbing supply houses are within a week cleaned out of large diameter (8"+) PVC pipe and end caps, purchased mostly with cash. Enrollment in the shooting academies plummets as students don't want to risk travelling with unregistered firearms.

President Bush insists that the *DWA* is not a stepping stone to confiscation, that handguns and sporting long guns are not next, and that lawful owners should have no qualms about mere registration. Gunowners do not believe him. Even the NRA joins in the hoots and hollers.

To implement a popular (i.e., not actively resisted) tyranny, discover through constant polling the general shape and dimension of your target people's activities and simply erect your wall just slightly outside such. A wall is not a wall if one never bumps into it...

For those who do encounter the regulatory boundary, their first reaction is to retract, rather than to circumvent or smash through. This retraction readjusts their active area to that of the masses, which is precisely the point. De Tocqueville's term "compresses" is particularly apt here. Circumferential regulation compresses those who otherwise would "live large outside the box" or "color outside the lines."

Often, in moments of waggish humor, our legislators have proscribed many harmless activities, for the simple reason that they could do so without fear of consequence. For example, the 1994 prohibition of bayonet lugs on assault weapons. There had hardly been an historic criminal issue of bayonets, much less a recent rash of drive-by bayonetings—but that was not the point, obviously. Watching the henceforth frantic removal by gun importers of tiny bits of steel from rifle barrels was responsible for gales of laughter within many marbled halls.

If such mocking legislation can compress even an armed and informed citizenry, then it can compress anyone. We have built a wall around the very people most equipped (both psychologically and materially) to reduce it to rubble. Their lack of resistance has served to embolden our more craven colleagues, and thus has increased general regulatory velocity.

What are holistic healthnuts and privacy paranoids to gunowners? If riflemen ranchers did not dare open fire, then what will homeschoolers do—pelt us with their phonics workbooks? The war has been won. All that remains is the mopping up. By the year 2020 we will declare as felonious contraband all semi-automatic rifles and shotguns and require their confiscation. (Superposed trap shotguns will not be affected, so as not to alienate the cultured man with a Perazzi.) Lines will form around the block as assault weapons owners queue up for their own castration.

What is vital to apprehend is that this castration is merely a formality, for we have long ago castrated that most important organ. Their spirit.

We may have to throw them a bit of constitutional "just compensation" in order to appease the Republicans and the NRA, but this nominal sum will easily be absorbed by the federal budget.

— Julius N. Harquist, *The Gaian Convergence*, p.89
River Lethe Press (2007)

To consider the judges as the ultimate arbiters of all constitutional questions is a very dangerous doctrine indeed, and one which would place us under the despotism of an oligarchy.

— Thomas Jefferson

Les tyrannies d'aujourd' hui	Today's tyrannies
se sont perfectionnées;	have perfected themselves:
Elles n'admettent plus	they tolerate neither
le silence, ni la neutralité.	silence nor neutrality.
Il faut se prononcer,	One must proclaim oneself,
être pour ou contre.	For or against.
Bon, dans ce cas,	Well, in that case,
Je suis contre.	I am against.

— Camus

2007 USA social news

The summer's record heat and drought sparks racial tensions in several metro areas. L.A. experiences riots more intense than in 1992, and this time white neighborhoods suffer widespread damage. It takes National Guard troops a week of fighting to quell the disturbances. 386 people are killed, and property damage is in the tens of billions of dollars. Martial law is kept in force until November.

A multi-drug resistant (MDR) strain of *Salmonella typhi* sweeps southern California. The etiologic agent (*i.e.,* origin) is illegal aliens from Mexico. L.A. County (with a population greater than Georgia) is particularly hard hit. The percentage of Hispanics in southern California exceeds 50%, resulting in a stampede of white flight to Oregon, Washington, Arizona, Utah, and Colorado. Property values crash in L.A. Rural mountain properties in the Rockies increase by 40% in value within a year.

2007 USA economic news

Gold is $1,429/ounce. The stock market, at 4,823, is in its seventh year of decline. Bonds have been performing well, however, inflation is beginning to take off.

Virginia   Summer 2007

Katherine Jessup was a cancer patient on a heavy regimen of chemotherapy. The powerful drug Cis-Plat nauseated her and she couldn't keep it down. She needed another drug to relieve the nausea so that she could tolerate her chemo. This other drug, tetrahydrocannabinol, was very affordable, easy to administer, and had decades of clinical trials and common usage with few or no side effects.

It was, however, illegal.

$C_{21}H_{30}O_2$—or THC—is a phenol derived from hemp resin. It is more commonly known as *cannabis*. Marijuana.

While prohibiting marijuana, the federal government allows the pharmaceutical industry to sell a synthesized form of THC as an oral medication—Marinol. Real genius at work here. Since the issue is nausea, patients can't keep oral medication—including Marinol—in their stomachs long enough to work. That is why THC must be ingested through the lungs.

Katherine Jessup had never been a drug user. She had never smoked marijuana, or even cigarettes. Only after lengthy studying which proved the medicinal value of marijuana for alleviating severe nausea did she try it. It worked very well, and reduced some of the pain from cancer. Since she and her husband did not want to buy marijuana on the retail market and support a criminal drug culture, they decided to grow what she needed in their basement. The process was surprisingly easy, just like the instructional DVD from Loompanics Press promised. A few grow lights on a timer and some fertilizer were the basic supplies. After seven months of homegrown medical marijuana, Katherine Jessup began to recover. She and Tom even resumed their lovemaking. Her doctors thought that she would go into remission soon.

She never had the chance to find out.

Acting on a tip, the DEA raided the Jessups and found several marijuana plants growing in their basement. The tipster was later learned to have been a "friend" who staunchly supported the War on Some Drugs. The irony of her daily vodka martini habit was lost on most everybody.

The feds charged the Jessups with cultivation with intent to sell. Judge Gray instructed the jury to ignore Katherine Jessup's "medical cannabis" defense, opining that it was just a ruse to justify their "pot habit." The jury reluctantly found her guilty, and several jurors later wept when Judge Gray sentenced her to the custody of the Bureau of Prisons for a term of five years. The jurors hadn't heard of the Fully Informed Jury Amendment (FIJA) and didn't know of their 1,000-year-old right to judge both the facts and the *law* and acquit nonviolent offenders of harmful and unconstitutional legislation.

At the Federal Prison Camp in Allentown, Pennsylvania Katherine Jessup lasted only five weeks. Denied the one drug which would have allowed her chemotherapy, she was found dead in her cell one morning having choked on her own vomit during the night. Her case and subsequent death caused howls of protest, but, like most protest, it went nowhere.

Judge Gray, who tried to justify his actions by federal drug case sentencing guidelines, got a few death threats, but nothing came of them. It was typical American outrage: high heat, low Btu's. Emotionally satisfying, but ineffective.

Katherine's husband, Tom, sentenced to three years probation for cultivation, went into an emotional spiral, lost his business, became an alcoholic and killed himself in a one-car crash. Only the Internet press carried the story of his tragic death.

Washington, D.C.   FBIHQ   September 2007

Special Agent Douglas Bleth is not looking forward to his follow-up meeting with the Director. He has not yet identified the Wyoming "general."

The Director rises and smiles. "Ah, Bleth, good to see you again. What do you have for me today?"

Bleth says, "We've made some progress, though not as much as we'd have liked."

Frowning, the Director says, "*Hmmm.* Go on."

"Two things we *are* sure of. One, that the Wyoming relocation is expanding to other counties."

"*Really?*"

"Yes, sir. We have access to weekly aggregates from the Wyoming SecState's office. New relocators are concentrating in several other counties along last year's model."

"So," the Director says, "they're marching onwards, eh?"

Bleth nods and says, "We've identified five, and maybe seven, new counties that they're moving into."

This surprises the Director. "*Seven?* Plus the five they already have?"

"Yes, sir. Assuming their 2010 electoral success, that would make up to twelve of Wyoming's twenty-three counties. Half the state."

"Half the state . . ." the Director echoes.

"Yes, sir, but something else we've learned is even more disturbing. Their numbers are also increasing within particular congressional districts overlapping the first five counties they saturated last year. Take Senate District 16, for example. While much of it is in Sublette County, which they already have, the rest extends into neighboring Lincoln County. New people are pouring into Lincoln. But here's the interesting thing. When they took over Sublette in 2006, they only moved to the *southern* part of the county, the part that's within Senate District 16. The northern half of Sublette is in SD 17, which also extends into Fremont and Teton Counties."

"Bleth, I'm not following you," the Director exasperates. "What are you telling me?"

"That this mass relocation is a *movement* not merely about certain counties, but to influence, if not control, *state* politics. That the Wyoming relocation of those now 11,000 people was and is coordinated by some hierarchy. It can't be happening any other way."

The Director looks skeptical.

"Sir, maybe it would help if I drew out a simple diagram. It helped us when we were figuring this thing out."

"OK, go ahead."

Bleth reaches in his folder and takes out a clean sheet of copy paper. Moving to the Director's desk, he draws two vertically contiguous squares and says, "These are two neighboring counties, Lincoln and Sublette."

"OK, I'm with you so far," the Director jokes.

Smiling as he labels them, Bleth continues, "Now, Sublette's election was in 2006. Sheriff, coroner, county commissioners, dogcatcher—the whole county government. Lincoln's election is in 2010."

Bleth then takes a yellow highlighter and fills in all of Lincoln County and the lower half of Sublette. "This yellow area is Senate District 16. Its senator is up for reelection next year in November.

"Now, if you only wanted to take over Sublette, it wouldn't matter *where* your people landed inside the county, right?"

The Director nods. "Correct."

Bleth continues, "And if you wanted to take over Lincoln, same thing. Your people could land in any part of the county. *But*, if you also wanted to take over Senate District 16 which overlaps both counties, you would coordinate your people in a very *specific* way.

"Basically, you'd numerically saturate Sublette to win in 2006, but you'd have them only in the *south*—in that portion *within* SD 16. Then, after your 2006 Sublette victory you concentrate on winning SD 16 in 2008 and start putting new people into *Lincoln* County. Adding more to Sublette would be pointless since you've already got *that* county and they wouldn't help saturate Lincoln, which is what you're trying to win in 2010."

The Director understands. "Yes, that follows. It's the only way of maximizing a limited resource. The southern Sublette County people are like a '2-for-1' deal which helps to win Senate District 16. And the people you put in Lincoln for this year's SD 16 election will help you get Lincoln in 2010."

"Precisely, sir. If we hadn't analyzed their relocation geographics, we wouldn't have wondered why people *hadn't* moved to *northern* Sublette in the Pinedale area, which is very desirable. Because they concentrated only in Marbleton and Big Piney, and then began to populate Lincoln County was the clue we needed. And they're still not moving to Pinedale."

"Why not?"

"Probably because they don't have the numbers for Senate District 17 and its Teton and Fremont Counties. Not for the general election in 2010, anyway. Both have a higher percentage of Democratic voters and would take more conservative newcomers to saturate. That's the other thing, sir. They've picked the most conservative counties for their first two waves. They've yet to touch Sheridan, Campbell, and Natrona. They're going where, one, they're likely to win, and two, to counties with strategically overlapping congressional districts with the correct election cycle sequence. County A, then a legislative district common to County B, and then County B. It's a very clever and workable formula."

The Director is lost in thought.

Bleth offers, "We're also seeing them use it in Weston County for House District 1, as well as in Converse County for HD 2."

Finally the Director says, "It almost reminds me of a board game. Somebody put a great deal of thought and planning into this, Bleth. The elegance of the scheme shows that."

"Yes, sir, I agree. And so far it's been successful. The details required must be considerable. We estimate that their margin for error is *very* thin, under 5%. It's like having $1,000 to bid on several objects which will sell for a total of $951 to $999. If you bid too high on one then you're forced to bid too low on another, losing it. A very challenging process. Your board game analogy is right on. Whoever's orchestrating this must have daily accurate figures and some great software to crunch it all."

"You're forgetting the most important element, Bleth."

"Sir?"

"The theory behind all this is useless without the leadership to find, collect, and direct thousands of people to actually become a *part* of this. Remember, we're talking about human beings here, and apparently of a strong independent nature. I mean, how do you cordon off certain counties and even areas *within* those counties and get *individualists* to move there? To *stay* there for at least two election cycles, county and congressional district?"

"The leverage or incentive would have to be pretty strong," Bleth says.

"True, but it still all finally boils down to the leadership of one man," explains the Director. "One general. Have you found him yet?"

"No, sir. To tell the truth, until we unraveled their relocation scheme, I wasn't totally convinced that there even *was* a general. We have, however, identified several of their senior noncoms and a lieutenant or two."

"Well, if you've breached their officer corps why can't you chase it up to their general staff?"

Bleth says, "Because the higher ranking coordinators are using much more sophisticated communication techniques. Encrypted remails from public terminals, I'd bet. Nothing incriminating is done over any phone lines. We've learned nothing from their computers from the several 'sneak and peaks,' either."

"What would you need to penetrate their techniques?"

"Three dozen agents for thirty days of man-on-man surveillance of six subjects," Bleth says firmly. "We'd surely learn more about their contacts, meeting places, other modes of communication, etc."

The Director ponders this. Such would be expensive and it might even tip off the subjects, but some risks are worth taking.

"Then," Bleth says, "we use our arrest powers under *Patriot Act II* and squeeze them to talk. Though it'd be a stretch, we could get warrants under section 404 for their illegal use of encryption in the commission of a federal crime. All we'd need to do is decide on *which* federal crime. Income tax evasion, money laundering, gun violations, even terrorism if we're lucky."

"The same idea crossed my mind, too. Look into that, Bleth. You'll have my approval for the surveillance manpower you need. Let's start digging in these people's lives. Everybody has *some* dirt on them, whether they know it or not."

Bleth nods happily. "Yes, sir. We'll get right on it."

Wyoming   Fall 2007

Life for the relocators in the five counties of Niobrara, Crook, Johnson, Sublette, and Hot Springs is prosperous and pleasant. The locals were at first wary of all the newcomers, but that quickly passed once they proved themselves to be productive, respectful, and likeable.

Highly intelligent, too. The newcomers sparked something of an intellectual revival. Political debates, scientific discussions, travel experience, computer expertise, and chess clubs were like a fresh breeze for the mind.

Housing had been tight at first, and new mobile home parks were only a temporary expedient for most. New home construction was booming, which did much for the local economies, as did the new companies founded in or transplanted to the five counties.

The new county government officials (libertarians generally in Republican clothing) strove not to alienate the old-timers with sudden radical changes. The political ships of state were kept on even keel, but with a course slowly increasing towards liberty. Any new proposals smacking of do-gooder origins were canned by the freedom-oriented county councils. Several older laws restricting individual liberty were quietly hunted down and repealed.

A major county-level goal was the eradication of building permits and zoning requirements. It would take some time to accomplish the necessary social inroads (people first needed convincing that "architectural anarchy" would not result), but the process was already well under way.

So as to acquaint newcomers to Wyoming life, a flyer was circulated.

Wyoming Rules and Etiquette for You New Folks

Consider very carefully whom you invite to join us: Are they rugged and hard-working, or are they soft and lazy? Will they adapt and fit in, or will they pine for their metropolitan condo? Do they revel in freedom, or are they busybodies who "know what's best" for everyone else? Do they honor their word even to their own hurt, or do they justify ways to renege on obligations which become inconvenient to keep? Are they willing to take chances and boldly try new things, or do risks frighten them?

Only when you are convinced (preferably after years of association) that they are quality people should you confide our Wyoming venture. If they are not hardy, industrious, generally libertarian, honest, and courageous, then we do not want them. (They wouldn't like it there, anyway.)

When you discuss Wyoming and your move there, be discreet. While you're welcome to extol its free-market climate and honest people, please do not hail Wyoming as some sort of "promised land."

We have no guarantee of what we will accomplish politically. We may simply saturate a county or two, or we may end up electing the state government, or something in between. Whatever we achieve, we will enjoy more freedom than we do now, and this is what makes our efforts worthwhile. Besides, we really have no other choice, do we?

OK, now to the "rules."

❶ Leave behind most of your old ways of doing things.

You moved to Wyoming for a different pace of life. Allow that to happen. Embrace Wyoming's way of doing things, and gracefully accept the fact that you're no longer in Denver, Dallas, or Des Moines.

❷   Don't try to change Wyoming into something it's not.

Can't get *The New York Times* at the newsstand? No Mercedes dealership in your town? Lousy espresso at the local coffee shop? We coulda told ya. Learn to live with the *Cheyenne Sentinel*, American cars, and black coffee. If you must have big city amenities, then choose Casper, Jackson, Sheridan, or Cheyenne. Everyplace else is a small town, and folks *like* it that way.

❸   The locals know more about Wyoming life than you do.

Don't be too quick to assert that your way is a better way. Give the locals a fair chance to prove that they know their business. They likely do.

❹   Arrive ready to work and eager to lend a hand.

Wyoming is a hardy place, and life can be arduous. Nobody is despised more than a goldbricker, or a shirker. So, get some calluses. Be willing to help out instantly, and you'll quickly gain the favor of your neighbors.

❺   Don't whine. Don't bitch.

You've nothing to complain about. 98% of the world would gladly trade places with you. You're living in what is still one of the world's freest countries, and you're living in America's freest state. Wyoming is soon to be the freest place on the planet, and you are a part of that.

Yes, it can be cold and windy and provincial in Wyoming—but you *knew* that before you came out. (It was in all the brochures.)

Don't grouse about it.

❻   Don't try to convert everyone into becoming a Libertarian.

Most Wyomingites are already politically conservative. Libertarianism is the logical conclusion for many Republicans, if they will spend the time and effort to examine their beliefs.

If they do not—if they stubbornly stick to a comfortable, lazy, and unchallenging dogma—then there is little you can do:

> *A false conclusion once arrived at and widely accepted is not easily dislodged, and the less it is understood the more tenaciously it is held.*
> — George Contor's *Law of Conservation of Ignorance*

❼   Concentrate on being a good example.

What you do speaks louder than what you say. You are missionaries in a new land. Will the locals want what you have?

❖ 2008

A really efficient totalitarian state would be one in which the all-powerful executive of political bosses and their army of managers control a population of slaves who do not have to be coerced, because they love their servitude.
— Aldous Huxley, *Brave New World*

2008 USA privacy news

All measures foment countermeasures, and *CALEA II* was no different. The "sneak and peak" warrants of 2002 (whereby "key-sniffing" programs and devices were installed on subjects' computers without their knowledge) had been often thwarted by keeping encryption passphrases on one's PDA to be link-downloaded when needed (bypassing the computer's keyboard).

To thwart *CALEA II*'s "Give up your passphrase, or else!" threat, a new software called *Bye-Bye* incorporated tamperguards to automatically shred a raided hard drive's encryption keys, making the passphrase useless. It was activated by the user within any OS through a hotkey (*e.g.,* Shift + F12). If the computer was connected to an APS, *Bye-Bye* could, should the owner be away, be triggered by the home-security system, auto-boot from a very simple DOS floppy (which the owner left in the drive when not using the computer), shred the PGP keys, shred itself and all traces of its installation, and then shut down (which required only 25 seconds in all). *Bye-Bye* used the Gutmann shredding standard of 35 random overwrite passes, and was thought 100% effective. Once shredded, the keys were *gone*. Bye-bye. If one could not be proven the owner or user of a key pair, then one could not be pressured to disclose the passphrase. (Besides, how would the court know if *correct* one had been given? No keys existed to find out.)

Very careful folks simply keep spare keys hidden elsewhere (*e.g.,* on secreted floppies, within obscure Internet files, etc.), and never left them on the hard drive at all.

The most shrewd of all keep their keys (active and spare) *encrypted* through PGP's IDEA algorithm (which was symmetric encryption that did not generate its own key pair). After all, possession of an open key pair is *prima facie* evidence of having encrypted a particular file. By encrypting the key pair, the owner forced the government to first break through that IDEA "envelope" before it could ascertain the PGP key pair necessary to connect them with encrypted files.   This sly tactic maddens the NSA and FBI computer techs, which in turn drive the US Attorneys into a frenzy as they cannot even *begin* to make a case based on the subject's raided computer. Measure—countermeasure.

Man has continued to evolve by acts of disobedience.
—Erich Fromm, "On Disobedience"

Casper, Wyoming   February 2008

Life for Bill Russell had pretty much returned to normal since his 1995 ATF trial. A defendant's acquital in such cases had one of two long-term results: increased hassle by the feds, or near immunity from it. Russell had been left alone these past thirteen years. He considered suing ATF Agent Lorner for criminal fraud and obstruction of justice, but Juliette convinced him that it was likely futile. *Lorner's on very thin ice, Bill, so why don't we just let him keep hopping about. He'll plung through someday*, she had said.

He reluctantly agreed, Agent Lorner being a very bitter pill to swallow. It seemed as though nothing ever happened to rogue federal agents, no matter who they worked for or what they did. They were truly above justice. All a federal judge had to say was "sovereign immunity."

Case closed.

FBI HRT sniper/murderer Lon Horiuchi had proven that. At least the FBI had felt enough pressure by 1995 to take away his rifle. Rumor had it that that was a more severe punishment to "Hooch" than prison. *They might as well have cut his balls off,* his team colleague Chris Whitcomb remarked. Having to live on a military base under constant guard—rarely venturing out in public—was a consequence for blatantly shooting a nursing mother in the face with a .308 and then committing perjury over it.

Poor "Hooch." No more freedom. No more sniper rifle.

Maybe a bit of justice *had* seeped in after all.

Russell, however, still enjoyed both his freedom *and* his FAL rifle. Juliette's vigorous motions got it returned in 1996, though somewhat worse for wear from vindictive federal hands. He has stayed in regular contact with the Prestons, having dinner with them several times a year. He is an enthusiastic helper of the Wyoming migration since his retirement.

Russell holds the small UPS package, puzzled. He hadn't ordered anything from Denver, much less had it sent Red Label. He looks at the sender's name. Harold Krassny. *Krassny? The man who owned my FAL and testified at my trial?* With his Mad Dog "Bearcat" knife he slits open the tape and opens the box. Wrapped in a towel is a WW2-era Colt 1911A1 .45 pistol in its issue holster. *Whaaat?* There is also neat handwritten note.

Dear Bill,
*   I hope you will enjoy this, which served me well in Europe over sixty years ago. For reasons soon to become clear, I won't be needing it any more. Think of it as some long overdue compensation for the crap the ATF put you through back in 1995, and as my gratitude for having the opportunity to help a fellow shooter in time of trouble. It will go well with your FAL during the interesting times ahead.*
*   I hope that you will remember me then.*

*   Warm regards,*
*   Harold*

Russell is bowled over by the unexpected gift. He reverently takes the Colt out of its brown leather flap holster. It shows signs of honest wear, but no abuse. He grins, relishing the smells of the manganese phosphate finish, gun oil, and leather. He removes the magazine and checks the chamber, which is empty. The trigger is pretty decent for an issue .45, and the bore is still sharp. He can't stop grinning. He's never had a WW2 1911A1—much less one from a combat vet he knows. *What a treasure!* He reads over the note again, and then notices a postscript at the very bottom.

P.S. Since I illegally sent/transferred a gun to you across state lines outside of the required NICS background check, paperwork, blah, blah, blah, you should probably burn the box and this P.S. No use having evidence around. You can always say that I gave the Colt to you years ago, when private transfers were still legal.

Russell smiles as he tears off the postscript. *What a fine man!* As he lights the box and postscript ablaze in his backyard burn barrel, an uncomfortable notion intrudes on his happy reverie. *I hope Harold's not in any trouble.*

Colorado
Boulder County Sheriff's Office

Detective Luther Thompkins groans when he sees 36 unread emails in his Inbox. He reads the subject lines first. There is a lot of spam:

Reduce your mortgage payments NOW!
Luther Thompkins, enlarge your penis safely and reliably!!!
Hot babes show it all for you!!

Et cetera. Thompkins laughs to himself. *So, I'm undersexed, got a little dick, and am paying too much interest on my house! How do they know all this?* Cleaned of spam, the Inbox is now manageable. He then searches for important emails and his eyes stop at:

An urgent message from Harold Krassny!

Harold Krassny? he ponders. It's a vaguely familiar name and Thompkins needs a few seconds to dredge up the memory. *That rancher from Wyoming who was my childhood camp counselor?* It's curious enough to hear from Krassny, but even more so because it's marked "urgent." Thompkins clicks on the blue text and a new box opens:

The following message is encrypted.
To decrypt, click on the question box below:

Thompkins moves the cursor and clicks on the box. It changes into:

What was the name of your 4th-grade summer camp?

What the hell is this? he wonders. He types in "Camp Flaming River" and hits <Enter>. After a couple of seconds the message scrolls out.

From: Harold Krassny

Dear Luther,
I was your camp counselor, if you'll recall. You had a bit of diffi-culty there at first, but not for long.

Thompkins bitterly recalls that summer, being called *"our token nigger"* by the older boys. Krassny took him under his wing and taught him how to box. How to stand up like a man for himself. How not to take shit. Several days later Thompkins treated the largest of his tormentors to a *"token ass-kicking."* Nobody at camp ever called him "nigger" after that. As his single mother would often later say *"Luther may be scrawny, but he's savin' up to be wiry!"*

Thompkins subconsciously smiles at hearing from Krassny after so many years, and reads on.

I sincerely apologize for adding to your already crushing caseload, but it was for good reason. I thought you would like to know where to find my body, dead by my own hand.
Please do not rush over with paramedics, as this email was sent seven hours ago—purposely delayed by a forwarding service. At this reading, I am by now at room temperature. No hurry.
I am in Suite 1602 of the Excelsior Hotel west of Boulder in the mountains. So as not to disturb the hotel staff (who have been su-perb), an envelope has been left for you at the front desk. In it is my room cardkey. You will find my body in tidy condition in the bathtub, expired by an overdose of sleeping pills and alcohol.
Although I have "checked out" without having checked out, my hotel bill has been prepaid, along with a nice gratuity for the staff.
Please do everything you can not to inconvenience or embar-rass the Excelsior. Perhaps I could have chosen the Motel 7 for this disembarkation, but there is such a lovely Yamaha baby grand

piano in my suite, and the room service is incomparable. I've had a fine last 48 hours here.

My public farewell note is attached to this email, encrypted with the same password. A handwritten copy of that note will be found in my suite. It will soon have very wide publication on the Net.

Again, I apologize for this intrusion. You turned out to be a good man, and a good detective. Perhaps we will meet again. Meanwhile, I wish you every joy in life.

Best regards,
Harold Krassny

Detective Thompkins immediately grabs the phonebook, looks up the number for the Excelsior, and stabs at the phone.

It is answered on the third ring by a pleasant female voice. "Good evening, the Excelsior Hotel. How may I direct your call?"

"Suite 1602," Thompkins barks.

If the operator is offended by his brusqueness, she doesn't show it. "Certainly, sir. Have a pleasant evening."

Seconds later he hears the phone ringing. It rings for well over a minute without answer. The operator comes back on the line. Thomkins tells her, "I need to speak to your night manager immediately." He is put through at once.

Thomkins explains that he is enroute because the hotel has a dead or dying man in Suite 1602, and gives the night manager his cell phone number.

"We're en route with paramedics. Call me immediately from Mr. Krassny's suite."

Thompkins hangs up and tells his assistant, "Charlie, have the ME and EMTs meet us at the Excelsior. Have them park someplace discreet."

Thompkins decrypts Krassny's suicide note and prints it out. Skimming it over, he tells Charlie, "You're driving us out to the mountains."

During the 20 minute trip, Thompkins reads.

From Harold Krassny,
To Whom It May Concern:

I never understood the point of a suicide note. To the author it is invariably redundant. To the readers, eternally incomplete. Whether or not the self-deceased "left a note" is always the third question asked (after "When?" and "How?", of course). If a note cannot explain the author's decision, then how much more inexplicable is its lack?

So, to fully play the part expected of this role—and not wanting to add to the grief, sorrow, and confusion amongst my living friends and loved ones—I shall "leave a note." My literary skills aside, the answers found herein will remain superficial. Such is the unavoidable nature of the missive.

Some of you may ask yourselves if there was anything you could have done to prevent my act. Grieve not, dear ones, there was nothing anyone could have done. If there had been, I would have asked. Shy I was not.

They say that to voluntarily forfeit one's life is an act of depression and loneliness. That's often true, I'm sure. However, it's only partly true in my case. I packed up before checkout-time because I finally faced a conclusion long ago suspected: that this is a sick, cruel joke of a world—increasingly uninhabitable for anyone with 35¢ worth of integrity, honor, intelligence, compassion, or decency.

I did not kill myself.

I merely preempted the terminal toxicity of our environment.

I do not blame the Creator. His love for us and His creation remains quite evident through the persistent beauty and wonder we cannot quite manage to completely smother.

No, this earthly putrescence we've made ourselves.

Cowardice (and its first cousin, Apathy) creates the same hell on earth as does Evil. It just takes a bit longer, that's all. Edmund Burke said it best, "All that is necessary for the triumph of evil is that good men do nothing." You see, evil is the default of humanity. It is a spiritual force of gravity. It is always present, and it is always to be resisted. Good people, through rare effort, can and have resisted the gravity of evil. America always had powerful legs for jumping, but never developed wings to stay aloft.

I couldn't tolerate it any longer. The trouble with cynicism these days is that you just can't keep up.

I had a good run. I served my country during WWII when the government still served America. I enjoyed the undeserved love and companionship of my dear wife, Delores, for 55 years, and the gift of our two perfect children, Michael and Rachel. I experienced what Mark Twain perfectly described as a "thunderclap of grief." Its suddenness was terrifying; its intensity deafening; its effect devastating.

Their death in a small plane crash last year extinguished my last three reasons to carry on past the age of 85. I might as well have been in that plane with them, for we all died in that smoking scar left on a Utah mountainside.

My beautiful America is gone. My beloved wife and children are gone. The rest of my family are gone. Most of my friends are gone. After months of slogging through the endless sludge of mourning, it dawned on me that my life was effectively over.

Not, however, without a little "account balancing" before I went; before my health was irretrievably affected.

Our cultural and economic masters have (through the gradual assent of the people, to be sure) created an impenetrable, soul-sucking web of regulation and oppression. They control our diets, our money, our education, our political institutions, our travel, our *communications, and our recreation. The rural sanctuary of ranch and farm are being assaulted. There is nowhere to hide. We have been transformed into cogs of a great machine, all within my lifetime. There will not be, within the next decade or two, any escape from this. After a generation, perhaps, though I never would have seen it.*

Our rulers left one crucial element out of their vast equation. Desperation. They disregarded Sun Tzu's wise counsel of leaving a way of escape to a surrounded enemy. Average people sentenced to what is effectually life imprisonment will begin to realize they have nothing to lose. A few of them will, as I did, "connect the dots"—forming a line leading to their jailers.

I once read, "Wisdom is knowing what to do next. Courage is doing it."

If that's true, then integrity is caring to know what to do next.

I was a warrior. I flew fighters six miles high over Nazi Germany. 343rd Fighter Squadron, 55th Fighter Group, 8th Air Force. I had eleven confirmed aerial kills, and five probables.

When I arrived at the 55th's first base in Nuthampstead in the fall of 1943, I flew a P-38 Lightning, arguably the world's coldest airplane. It had basically no cockpit heat, and no combination of cold weather gear ever really worked. (Once we switched over to P-51s we gave our leather fleece-lined suits and boots to the Red Cross girls for their winter wear. They looked like little brown bears.)

Great instruments and an excellent shooting platform with lovely handling and no torque, but the P-38 was far too fussy. The Curtiss electric props were very complicated and twitchy, and maintenance on those tightly-cowled twin Allisons was a nightmare. There was always some coolant leak to chase. The turbosuperchargers were controlled by an oil regulator which often froze at high altitude, giving the pilot only two throttle settings: 10 or 80 inches of mercury—too little to sustain flight or too much for the supercharger. Finally, the plane's stab elevator and twin booms looked like nothing else in the sky, making us easily recognizable to the enemy. P-38 pilots got only 1.5 Germans per loss, the worst record of the ETO (though they did much better in the Pacific). I had only two kills and one probable in mine.

The P-38 did, however, make me a lot of money. We used to bet on who would first get from our hardstands to the taxi strip, and I would always win. How'd I do it? I had learned to contort my arms, hands, and fingers in such a way so that I could start both engines at once. I spent many a fine weekend in London on that trick!

Just when I'd nearly pulled off a transfer to "Hub" Zemke's P-47 squadron in the 56th FG, we got our P-51D Mustangs. About the same time (this was spring of 1944) our 55th FG transferred to its new base at Wormingford, about six miles from Colchester. No more quagmire mud of Nuthampstead; no more P-38s! Our 343rd FS Mustangs ($51,572 in 1944 dollars!) had a distinctive paint *scheme: yellow/green nose and spinner, OD rear fuselage, and yellow rudder. The P-51D was a nearly perfect fighter. The liquid-cooled V-12 Merlin was a joy, it handled like a sports car, and with those drop tanks it had legs for Berlin and back. Good guns, too. If you could get a shot inside 300yds with less than 20 degrees of deflection, those six .50s really did the the job. The Mustang wasn't as robust as the Thunderbolt, but it had a much greater range. Most of our missions were long-range escorts of B-17Gs. Bomber crews had to do 25 missions for their tour, but fighter pilots had to do 50. At the end, you got a 50 mission "crush" hat. That and your white silk scarf just drove the ladies wild.*

I'll never forget 1944 Wormingford. The Tannoy public address system constantly droning on. All of us (officers, too) painting invasion stripes on our planes for D-Day. The stray dogs we quickly adopted once threatened with extermination. That day in early August when a horde of G.I.s hopped the fence behind the work line and shocked the entire wheat field because the English farmers were doing it too slowly. Red Cross girls with doughnuts on their fingers like a dozen rings. That lone V1 buzz bomb. The old ruined windmill just below the propellor shop. My ground crew waiting like puppies for my return, and then giving me smiles and thumbs up when they saw that the red gun tape had been shot off. The huge Christmas Eve air armada with 2,046 bombers and 853 fighters.

In December 1944 I was hit by flak over Dortmund. My wingman was also hit and went down. While trying to limp back to base alone a Focke-Wulf 190A-8 hammered me at 900 yards with his four 20mm cannons. I tried to split-S for the deck, but my damaged Mustang just wasn't up to it. I bailed out in the Dutch clouds to fight my way to the Allied lines 50km away. In getting there, however, three Germans died from my Colt .45. I took one of their Lugers, which was easier to scrounge up ammo for, just in case.

Thompkins' cell phone rudely interrupts. It is the night manager. He found Harold Krassny in the bathtub, quite dead. Thompkins tells him that he is enroute and will cancel the EMT. He grudgingly disconnects the call, as if the action somehow makes Krassny's death a certainty.

He turns to his assistant and says, "You can slow it down a bit, Charlie. We're not in any hurry now."

After two days in southern Holland I found the Canadian lines west of Nijmegen and caught a C-47 right back to Wormingford. My ground crew wept openly and unashamedly. They'd heard I went down with my wingman. They were mighty relieved when I assured them of no mechanical failure. I was issued another P-51D just in time for the Battle of the Bulge. I flew that plane, tail number 472138, for the rest of the war, including a few weeks from our Occupation base in Kaufbeuren, Germany.

Sorry to blab on about this. Delores often urged me to write my wartime memoirs, but since the USAAF trained about 35,000 fighter pilots I didn't figure I had all that much unique to say.

Anyway, I was a warrior once again, sixty years later. I discovered a new enemy of America and went to make war upon him before I died. Now, I have a total of sixteen confirmed kills. Fourteen during WWII, and two this week. Back in the 1940s, the government trained me to kill national socialists. I simply used that training to kill two international socialists six decades later.

The first was a modern reincarnation of Josef Goebbels, the Nazi Propaganda Minister. His lifetime work in Hollywood to debase and putrefy all that was decent for the sake of "entertainment" was well known. When the man became a US Senator with his eye on the presidency, I felt that I could no longer turn a blind eye. Easier to get him before he announced his candidacy and got Secret Service protection. It was my honor to cleave his vile corporeal self from his eternally damned soul. You will find his body in the boathouse of his cabin in the Sierras.

Thompkins rereads the paragraph. He'd no idea Krassny was so . . . so *intense.* Especially for a guy in his eighties!

The second was an avowed globalist, and a quite famous one, at that. American only in the geographical sense, the man was consumed with creating a one-world government to rule over deflated nations (and thus powerless peoples). He has actively conspired to deliver us over to jurisdiction of the UN. The arrogant evil of the man was quite insufferable to me. His body will never be found. It will probably take several days for anyone to be sure of whom it is I have described.

So, meanwhile, please do a bed-check.

One of your globalists is missing.

Thompkins laughs out loud. Charlie looks at him, questioning. Thompkins says, "Man, is the shit ever gonna fly!"

But that's not quite all. After WWII I was trained for intelligence. Donovan of the OSS liked how I had fought my way out of Occupied Territory. "We want shooters and looters!" he once told me. They taught us that merely killing the enemy was not enough. We had to know the enemy and his plans as well as he did. Before I was mustered out of the Army as a lieutenant colonel, I spent three years in postwar Germany gathering intelligence on the Soviets.

But enough about me.

Before they died by my hand several days ago, I squeezed much useful information from that rotten pair. (It is easy to get to such people. Their smugness leads to gaping holes in their per-

sonal security. Cats don't fear mice. Maybe they will now.) Meetings, key players, upcoming events to expect, timetables, addresses, phone numbers, etc.

I got both of their laptops, too. Before they died, I "persuaded" them to reveal all the necessary passphrases. My old OSS training came in handy there . . .

The hard drives I copied onto CDs and sent to whom I am sure would be interested parties. A transcript digest of our "interviews" was emailed to several dozen freedom-oriented individuals and organizations all over the world. It is my hope that this information will be stepping stones for further action against our would-be enslavers.

Thompkins suddenly realizes that he will be given a harsh grilling about Krassny. A *"What-did-you-know-and-when-did-you-know-it?"* type of thing. He'd better keep his wits about him. He can't look like he's rooting for Krassny's one-man cleanup act.

I had several other enemy targets on my list, but the financial expense and physical stress of the first two ops have drained me. I could not manage a third, much less a thirteenth. To attempt it would risk capture, trial, etc., and I won't be made a public spectacle anymore than I have to. Thus, I will have to be satisfied with just the two. Still, not bad for an octogenarian!

My assets have already been liquidated. My home sold, my possessions distributed. All incriminating records destroyed. All they can do now is call me names and pee on my grave.

None of us is immortal; none of us is free. We really have nothing to lose by at last going on the offensive. Claire Wolfe once wrote, "America is at that awkward stage. It's too late to work within the system, but too early to shoot the bastards."

Obviously, I think it's high time we shoot the bastards, but everyone runs on a different calender. My fight was over, and I was pleased to get in a few good punches before I left the ring. Who knows what it will take to knock out the giant? Let's find out! Get in there and do him some damage!

I have proved, twice, that it can be done. Pick targets who are truly deserving of your attention, but be sure that nothing personally links you with them. Do not, for example, choose the prosecutor who sent your brother up the river for tax evasion. No, choose a public figure whose treason to America and to the Bill of Rights is well-known, but unconnected with you and yours.

The most important thing is to act totally on your own. Three may keep a secret if two are dead, as Ben Franklin once wrote. Do your own research and planning, be extremely thorough, leave as little to chance as you possibly can, and act alone. Destroy all notes and keep no "trophies" (this especially includes newspaper articles). Finally, keep your mouth shut! Do all this, and there will be practi-

cally zero chance of your ever being investigated, arrested, prosecuted, and convicted of action.

If you are ever questioned, you should say something like, "I've done nothing wrong, and I believe that you are trying to mix me up in something I had nothing to do with. I have nothing at all to say to you. Please contact my attorney." Never try to spar with detectives; that is what they do for a living. Anything you tell them increases their knowledge about you. They will reply that you can help them find the guilty party by eliminating yourself as a suspect. You should counter by saying that it is not your place to help the police in their investigation, especially when they suspect you.

Don't offer or provide an alibi. The longer it takes for them to learn of it, the less time they have to disprove it.

Utter silence cannot be used against you, nor can it be misconstrued. You can always say something later (not that I recommend it), but you can never take back something you stupidly said.

If they argue that they merely need information about somebody else, tell them to get a material witness warrant. If that occurs (which is unlikely in routine police fishing expeditions), your attorney will negotiate proper immunity for your testimony. (By the way, "transactional" immunity is superior to " derivative use" immunity.)

Never consent to a search of your property. If they taunt you with "If you're innocent then you have nothing to hide," reply that they wouldn't be talking to you if they thought you were innocent.

You have nothing to lose by fighting. Irony of ironies, that's the greatest freedom. That odd freedom is the end result of our oppression. Slavery truly is freedom, but not the way our masters intended. And that's why they will lose this war. I only wish that I were around to see it. But you will be.

Good luck!   God bless!
Harold Krassny

Thompkins finishes reading just as Charlie brakes to a stop in front of the Excelsior. *Feisty old guy. If you're gonna go, be organized, tidy, and useful.* Thompkins has to restrain himself from laughing out loud again. The very solemn and dignified Excelsior Hotel night manager standing at the bottom of the marble steps simply wouldn't understand.

* * * * * * *

Krassny's note spreads like a wildfire over the Net. Public reaction is vigorous, both for and against. Depending on whom you asked, Krassny was a great man or an ice-cold murderer. The major networks refuse to cover Krassny's actions, fearing to air his reasons and thus egg on imitators.

Imitators sprung into action within a week. Nearly a dozen politicians, and liberal elite were killed in a surprising variety of methods. About half of the actors were arrested, but this only warned others to be more careful.

Denver FBI Field Office

Given the "domestic terrorism" and interstate aspects of the two homicides, the FBI is lead agency for the Krassny investigation. A senior Assistant Special Agent in Charge (ASAC) briefs his boss.

"We've analyzed twelve months of his banking, phone, email, and credit card records. There is not one whit of evidence linking him to the murders, much less to any accomplices. No incriminating library activity. We can only presume that he drove to California and Connecticut, as there is no record of his using any of the common carriers. He must have had a second car, as his oil change history shows only average mileage. There are no hotel records within 400 miles of either victim. By all accounts, Krassny was highly intelligent and methodical. And he *was* trained by Army Intelligence and OSS. If we haven't found anything by now, we're not likely to."

The Denver special agent in charge (SAC) says, "You've found *nothing*? Nothing at *all*?"

"Nothing. If it weren't for his confession, there would be absolutely no evidence connecting Krassny with his victims. California authorities found Mr. Lowenstein's body only because of Krassny's boathouse tip. That suggests that Krassny either committed the murder or knew who did."

The Denver SAC sighs deeply. "The Seat of Government[1] is screaming about this, Hendricks. The Director is convinced of a conspiracy."

"If there is, sir, we have no leads. Krassny was a typical Wyoming conservative, a rancher suspicious of government. That description could apply to most of the inland Western population."

"I tend to agree," says the SAC, "but none of the sultans of the 7th floor can believe that some 85 year old pulled this off alone. If we don't find some accomplices, we're running a shoddy investigation. Find *something*. What's the Casper FO[2] learned? That's where Krassny lived, for Christ's sake!"

"Nothing conclusive from Casper, sir. One thing was kind of interesting, though. Krassny testified in 1995 as a defense witness in an ATF case, so they checked into his relationship with the defendant, one William Russell. Russell immediately clammed up, and his attorney is demanding transactional immunity. Casper agents don't think Russell is involved, but just being a pain in the ass. They're still investigating, however. They report that the locals are not being very cooperative, and seem to applaud what Krassny did."

---
1   "Seat of Government" was J. Edgar Hoover's magisterial term for Washington, D.C.
2   Field Office, one of 93 FBI FOs across the USA.

"Why am I not surprised?" says the SAC. "What about Krassny's contact with anti-government groups? What do we have on that?"

"Very little. We don't know whom or from where he emailed, but several groups and individuals already being monitored may have received the so-called 'transcript digest.'"

"Well if you have some possible recipients then why don't you have the IP address of Krassny's email? Backtrack from there?"

"Because he used remailers, sir. There's no easy way to backtrack through the entire daisy-chain. We're working with several foreign agencies to get the email history of the remailers. It'll take weeks to process the data. Longer if he used different terminals."

The SAC nods, frowning, as if he anticipated this. "OK, then what about those CDs Krassny mailed? You wouldn't believe the pressure I'm getting from On High to locate them, as well as the hard drives from those laptops. Whatever they contained is apparently highly sensitive."

"Nothing on those, either. We don't know who received the CDs. Neither FedEx, UPS, nor the USPS have any records. A CD and its packaging weighs less than 16 ounces, so he wasn't required to have a postal clerk stamp them. He could have simply dropped them in a mailbox. Anonymous, reliable, and untraceable."

"And the hard drives?"

"A search of Krassny's former ranch failed to find them. He may have destroyed them."

"Spilt milk. The CDs are our priority. Whatever's on them is very important and will foment more terrorist activity, if we are to believe Krassny. We need to think about this whole thing from *his* perspective. If you were Harold Krassny, who would *you* send them to? Who is radical enough and competent enough to make violent use of them?"

The ASAC thinks for a moment and then ventures, "How about the Libertarian Party?"

The SAC snorts with laughter. "The LP doesn't believe in conspiracies, much less violence. If they got a CD they'd piss their hemp pants. Even the NRA has more guts than the LP. No, let's think more towards the anarchists and militia-types. People itching for action, not more talk."

"What about APIM, American Patriots In Motion?"

"*Now* you're thinking! I'd bet my right nut they got a CD in the mail! And they're in Aurora, right in our backyard. Get on them, Hendricks."

"Yes, sir."

The SAC wraps up the meeting. "Learn more about Krassny and who he regularly corresponded with. Who was he on email or fax alerts with? What magazine subscriptions did he take? There are people and organizations that he thought highly enough of to send them those CDs. Put together a list of possible recipients and I'll ask HQ for surveillance. Then we just might get lucky and catch one of them in the act. These people aren't the KGB or even LCN[3]—they're anti-government extremist losers. Have something for me by Thursday. We need a break on this fast, or we'll all be transferred to some RA[4] in Moosejaw, North Dakota."

Wyoming life   Summer 2008

The relocators quickly came to absolutely love their new state. The locals are rugged and honest, who enjoy a robust and rural living. Wyoming is an outdoorsman's paradise, with superb fishing and hunting, as well as several beautiful mountain ranges in which to hike, camp, and horseback.

The new entrepreneurs quickly take advantage of Wyoming's excellent business climate and incorporation laws, and start up hundreds of new companies, many with a national customer base. Paying little to no state taxes, they enjoy a comparative advantage over most other states.

2008 USA economic news

Gold is $1,867/ounce. The Dow is 4,309. Annual inflation is 17%. Taiwan's formal secession from China just before the Beijing Olympics causes great nervousness in the world markets.

Wyoming   November 2008

Between the general elections of 2006 and 2010 are the 2008 congressional elections for all of the House and half of the Senate. Just as FBI Special Agent Bleth had outlined to the Director, nearly 6,000 new relocators saturated and won HDs 1, 26, 27, 28, 30, and 50, as well as SDs 2, 18, 20, 22. They are now poised to achieve their 2010 goal of winning the counties of Lincoln, Park, Big Horn, Washakie, Converse, and Weston.

Also, the proposed Constitutional Amendment A from February 2007 was ratified, which allows the governor to call for special *ad hoc* elections.

*   *   *   *   *   *   *

Throughout our purposeful accretions of control were many nervous moments when just one recalcitrant state governor could have successfully called our bluff. (Amongst ourselves, we called them "Rhineland gambles.") Some post-Vietnam gambles, for example, were the 55mph national speed limit, Waco, the Brady bill, and the Gun-Free School Zones Act. If one governor had had the courage to stand up to the U.S. Congress and declare his state's intransigence on the matter, we'd have been set back a decade.

---

3   Bureau shorthand for *La Cosa Nostra*—*i.e.*, the Mafia.
4   Resident Agency, which is much smaller than a Field Office. There are 128 RAs in the USA.

In a larger sense, two presidential administrations caused us great concern: those of Carter and Clinton.

The utter failure of the Carter administration and its Federal Reserve Board had us very deeply worried. His economic and social malaise fomented the rise of the first survival movement replete with guns, gold, freeze-dried food, and dedicated literature. More ominously, it created the first modern tax revolt since the Whiskey Rebellion of 1794. (One of my colleagues, who had often safaried in Tanzania, opined that the Carter years had wounded the American "Cape Buffalo," which was poised for a classic 270° deadly counterattack. He remarked that if you could not finish off a wounded buffalo, the only alternative was to run back to the Land Rover and drive like hell to camp.)

What is not widely understood about movements (regardless of their politics) is that they are phenomena specifically related to a particular swath of people of the moment. The timing for such is actually quite narrow, analogous to lighting a match between gusts of wind. A man is generally incendiary during only two periods of his life: from 20-30 years old when he is ablaze with freshly imbued knowledge yet unburdened with responsibilities, and from 50-60 years old when his children have become self-sufficient and he still has one last roar left in him and little to risk in using it.

The maturity of the vast crop of Baby Boomers into college age in the 1960s is the most poignant example of the volatility of youth. The phenomenon of the Hippie Movement was not at all surprising. (What would have been astounding is if it had not occurred.) In fact, it was sublimely easy for us to anticipate. Their parents had just survived the Depression and won WWII; they were ready for "The Good Life." Their children, however, had none of the tempering that comes with struggle. Not having participated in their parents' victory, they subconsciously felt uneasy and guilty about sharing in the spoils. This has occurred many times throughout history. Predictably, they rejected their parents' culture for one of their own, but this time (with the convergence of quality recreational drugs, worryfree sex through The Pill, and an entirely-owned music which was individually reproducible through modern electronics) Youth had somewhere to go—its very own culture. This had never before happened in history. A tidal wave hit the mother culture and washed it out to sea. Even those of us who had anticipated this counterculture occasionally found its bottomless nihilism harrowing. When Nixon pulled out of Vietnam, the Hippies hated him for it as it negated their reason for rebellion, leaving them without a visible cause.

But, I digress.

The second incendiary period of a man's life is from 50-60. (Although a few men may indeed remain incendiary from 30-50 years of age, they are quite rare and sociologically insignificant.) Patriotic men are like an opponent's chess pieces which offer only two decades of danger, and macro events must be timed to interleave

that pair of decades. Men between 30 and 50 are temporarily neutralized by the domestic demands their own lives, and men past 60
can be considered "off the board."

During the Carter years of the late 1970s, the WWII and Korean
War vets were greatly disturbed by macro events, and still young
enough (i.e., in their 50s and 60s) to resist. This swath of men were
the last true "God & Country" folks and very much still "on the
board," so their deep convictions could not be too overtly ridiculed.

Simultaneously we also had Vietnam vets (84% of whom under
30 years old) with recent military training and experience, coupled
with fresh resentment towards Government. The movement had the
patriotism and venerable wisdom of the WWII vets (i.e., leadership)
coupled with the youthful rage of the Vietnam vets (i.e., troops).
This was a highly flammable sociological brew. I argued vigorously
that the anti-Carter/tax revolt/survival movement would—without
some variety of pressure release—metastasize by 1982 as outright
insurrection. We had overreached ourselves. History has taught us
that we could apply heat, or we could apply pressure, but not both.
Thus, we elected to slow cook, with less pressure.

Our data suggested that a temporary and artificial period of
calm, economic prosperity, and good old-fashioned patriotism would
avert disaster. If such could be maintained for ten to fifteen years,
the WWII vets would be in their 70s and thus too old for mass resistance (especially since over 25% of them suffered from increasingly
debilitating combat wounds). If we could be patient, a bit of time
would march these good soldiers "off the board." During that period,
the Vietnam vets, being between 30 and 50 years old, would be
temporarily dormant.

So, we ran back to the Land Rover and drove like hell to
Ronald Reagan's home to persuade him to seek the Presidency.
(Incidentally, Reagan's candidacy was initially fiercely resisted by
some in our circle, who were finally mollified by the choice of our
man George Bush, Sr. as Vice President.) The twelve tranquil years
of Reagan and Bush released the pressure most satisfactorily. By
the early 1990s, the fiercely patriotic veterans of WWII were chronologically "off the board" (with the Korea War veterans five to eight
years behind). Their "going away" party was the putative collapse of
the Soviet Empire, a mass sedative of great efficacy. The Depres-
sion-era generation had beat the Nazis and the Nips, and then
buried the Soviet Commies for good measure.

Job well done. Time for bed.

The next general period of alarm for us was the public uproar
over the Clinton administration, the first Baby Boomer President.
(Notice here the changing of the generational guard.) The WWII/Ko-
rea War vets were naturally horrified at Clinton's public policies and
private actions, but were unable (as we predicted) to do much from
the nursing home other than grouse with Rush Limbaugh. (It was
often noted by my colleagues that Limbaugh could have single-

handedly toppled the Clinton administration if he had stoutly defended the Branch Davidians, or hammered away on the obviously suspicious Vince Foster death. However, there was never any danger of that, as Rush had been judiciously installed as the conservatives' pressure-release valve, just as Reagan had been. It's not as though this were any huge secret; Limbaugh's boss was none other than arch-liberal Phil Donahue.)

The Vietnam vets, however, remained a dangerous force. Being in their 50s, they were clearly "still on the board." They formed the backbone of the militia movement, which was amply fueled by mass anger over Waco. By 1994, much of the public had galvanized against Clinton, as demonstrated by the so-called "Republican Revolution" in November. Unless dramatic action was taken, he was destined to be ousted in 1996.

The 19 April 1995 timing of the Murrah Building bombing by right-wing extremists could not have been more perfect. (We jokingly referred to the event as the "second Reichstag fire.") After a wonderfully suspenseful two days, Americans had a new face of evil —Timothy McVeigh. (Americans always need a name and a face to hate: Adolf Hitler, Saddam Hussein, McVeigh, Osama bin Laden, etc.) Once the militia tiger was defanged by Oklahoma City, Clinton was reelected in 1996 (thanks in great part to the helpful non-candidacy of Bob Dole) and brazenly forged ahead—often farther and faster than we counseled. His coarse sense of the people (and their moral vacuity) was proven correct time and time again. Just when we were convinced that he had really gone too far, he would land on his feet, grinning. As much as we loathed the crudeness of the man, his political sense truly was superb. (Clinton also benefitted incalculably from the deft helmsmanship of Fed Chairman Greenspan, who forestalled the inevitable economic collapse until Bush Jr.'s term.)

So, by 2010 we will have come to fear no public reaction to our policies. Without an effective leader, public discontent is destined to remain as ineffective as the mewling of a small child (albeit just as annoying). For several reasons, no effective leader can emerge from the legislative or judicial branches of Government. Leaders are executive by definition. Regarding the presidency, we control all Democratic and Republican party nominations and sufficiently influence all elections.

One small potential concern is, however, an effective and charismatic governor, especially from one of the lesser states wherein we have less control. The surprise victory of Jesse Ventura in Minnesota, for example, is precisely the sort of thing which must be prevented from regular occurrence. Americans have always been followers who require a strong leader, and we must ensure that no such leader arises out of the states independently from our sphere.

— Julius N. Harquist, *The Gaian Convergence*, pp.62-64
River Lethe Press (2007)

It never troubles the wolf how many the sheep may be.
— Sir Francis Bacon

Washington, D.C.   FBIHQ   November 2008

The Director is grimly pleased. "Well, Bleth, you were right about the Wyoming thing. They took those legislative districts just like you predicted. Nice work."

"Thank you, sir"

"What counties are they trying for in 2010?"

Bleth consults a colored map and says, "Lincoln, Park, Big Horn Washakie, Converse, Weston, and maybe Goshen."

"*Seven* counties, huh? That's two more than in 2006."

"Yes, sir. They've probably ironed out many of the wrinkles and now feel more confident."

The Director nods and says, "That makes sense. Still no idea who's running this thing?"

Bleth shakes his head. "No, sir, not yet. We're beginning to think that some old Wyoming money is behind this—that the leadership is probably business rather than political. Casper rather than Cheyenne. Our surveillance was largely unsuccessful, but we did learn of a 'TW' in Natrona County. No leads, however, in the Capitol."

"Natrona County? Oil?"

"Unknown at this time. Since nothing seems to be emanating from the mining areas of the southwest, it's likely petrol money. Ranching, perhaps."

"What about Jackson Hole money?"

"No evidence suggesting that. Besides, the last thing the Teton billionaires want are new people filling up 'their' state. They look down on even the millionaires. They wouldn't support such a populist phenomenon as tens of thousands of new people taking over a dozen conservative counties."

"Probably not," says the Director. "So, how far do you think this thing will go? Will it end with twelve counties in 2010, or are they trying for a statewide majority after that?"

"What we'll be looking for from 2010 to November 2012 are newcomers in congressional districts overlapping counties they *already* have. That's been the clue that contiguous counties are slated for the following general election. So, two years before we'll know which new counties they plan to saturate. It's not much, but it *is* a glimpse into their future."

The Director ponders this. "So, the general elections of 2006 and 2010 can tell us only what they've accomplished, but the congressional elections of 2008 and 2012 illuminate two years forward."

"Correct, sir. By November 2012 we'll know if there is to be a *third* wave of counties in 2014. Certainly the infrastructure exists for it. Their momentum is really picking up, their organization is very good, their security excellent. Funding is apparently not an issue. As long as they can find the bodies, I see no reason why they won't repeat 2006 and 2008 for 2010 and 2012. It's likely just a matter of continuing the numbers."

"Yeah, that's precisely what bothers me; the numbers involved. How and where are they *finding* thousands of these people?"

"We've asked ourselves that same question. Some undoubtedly came from the Free State Project organization. Many of them did not move to New Hampshire because they'd opted out of all but the western state choices."

"OK, some came from the FSP, but not all. What about the rest?"

"They're likely using the commercial databases," Bleth says. "Perhaps they've even tapped into the State of Wyoming tourism website and download the IPs and email address of every contact."

The Director brightens with an idea. "Have you considered salting these databases with an alias, somebody who seems to be interested in traveling or relocating to Wyoming? See if you get contacted by these people?"

Bleth considers this. "That's an interesting idea, sir. It'd be easy enough to try."

The Director smiles. "You can't catch fish without a line in the water."

Natrona County, Wyoming   November 2008

Preston smiles. He was blessed to have onboard a statistical genius in his assistant Tom Parks. The elections had gone quite well. They had moved the right number of relocators into the legislative districts; just enough to get the desired ballot results. It was a matter of calculating indigenous voter behavior through regression analysis of past registrations and elections.

On top of that, they had to keep track of the *unaffiliated* newcomers and their likely voting patterns. By using sophisticated software which analyzed their previous ZIP codes and spending habits (information easily and legally available from commercial databases), they can narrowly forecast their votes on election day.

Preston's margin for error was very tight, about 3%. Senate District 20 was a real squeaker; the libertarian candidate had won by just 83 votes. A couple of HDs were also nail-biters.

Preston loved the tension. What were video games to this? Juliette put her legal career on hold to run the family businesses, leaving Preston free to play "The Wizard" (or "TW" as his family and friends jokingly called him).

Five counties and 16.7% of the legislature. It was working. The relocators were generally very pleased with their move, and enthusiastically encouraged kindred spirits to join them. At this rate, the 16,328 quota between now and October 2010 would be met.

2010's Phase 2a was crucial. If the wave did not crash on *that* sandbar, the movement would have critical mass and be unstopable for 2014.

Preston had heard from his D.C. sources that the US Government (USG) was keenly interested in Wyoming's sudden popularity, but didn't quite know what to make of it. Good. By the time they did, it would be too late. It was likely already too late now, but Preston would feel much more comfortable after the elections in 2010.

After that the machine would be mostly running itself, and Preston could finally turn his attention to attracting the capital needed for 2012 and 2014. His father, who knew simply everyone of means in Wyoming, would be a huge help there. Extremely wealthy businessmen were generally not very philosophical and would have little interest in the vaunted goals of a Free Wyoming, but they all spoke the language of Money.

As a workforce, the relocators have much to offer. The nation's best and brightest are swarming to the Cowboy State, many of them entrepreneurs. Over 75% are under the age of 50, and 40% between 18 and 34. Nearly half of them currently earn at least $70,000. Over half have college degrees, and one-fifth have done post-graduate work. A largely young, well-educated, up-wardly mobile group which honors their contractual obligations would be welcome anywhere.

Old Wyoming Money would listen. Oil and gas and cattle and minerals can only go so far. The 21st Century was already 8% over, and Wyoming had to grow with the rest of the world. Few states had Wyoming's natural resources. Soon, few states would have her human resources. Combining the two would make Wyoming as powerful as Texas was in the 1960s.

It was a paradigm begging to happen. Preston was happy to oblige.

Washington, D.C.
FBIHQ, Counter-Terrorism Unit   December 2008

"What's the body count now?" asks the CT Chief.

"Nineteen. Mostly federal judges and prosecutors. Fewer VIPs as they have better security."

"Do you think these Krassnyites are connected to that crackpot 'Assassination Politics' scheme?"

"No, sir, not really. While Harold Krassny was undoubtedly familiar with AP, he probably recognized that it wouldn't work, just as we did."

"Why wouldn't AP have worked? The Bureau was at one time very concerned, you know."

"It's main fault was the payment operation."

"Really? I thought encrypted digital cash was a proven technology. Isn't the anonymity of payors and payees assured, not only from each other but from any third party including law enforcement?"

"Yes, sir, that part is true. The technology *does* guarantee anonymity. But I was referring to the *human* element of the payment operation. Here's how AP was supposed to work. A website, probably based offshore, would list the names of politicians and judges for assassination and collect, as a clearinghouse, anonymous e-cash donations for anyone who successfully 'predicted' the date of their deaths. Obviously, only the murderers themselves could know that in advance."

"Yes, I'm familiar with the overall scheme. Where's the problem?"

"Let's say that the average politically-motivated killer required at least $500,000 to offset his risk. Then, let's say that the average politically-motivated donor would chip in a max of $100. That means a *minimum* of 5,000 donors, and realistically three to five times that. Remember, the donors are forsaking money for a murder that might *never* take place, and if it doesn't, there's no way to get a refund."

The CT Chief asks, "Where would the money be in the meantime?"

"Presumably in a website e-cash account waiting for a 'predictor.'"

"Just sitting there for years?"

"Potentially, yes, sir."

"Hmmm. That doesn't seem like an attractive plan to the donors."

"No, sir. Anonymity is also a double-edged sword because the website people cannot know the donors' identities. So, the donors and the killers cannot *quite* touch. The killers won't act unless the money is there, and the donors won't sufficiently chip in on blind faith of action which may never happen."

"What if donors instead *pledged* to donate X amount upon a death? That removes the blind faith issue."

"For the donors, but not the *killers*. They are already taking a huge risk in the act; they certainly wouldn't take on the secondary risk of nonpayment. For a contract killing to happen, people have to donate money *before* the murder. Very few killers would act based on a promise of *ex post facto* donations, so the money has to be in the hands of the website coordinators first. No, the pledge scenario just couldn't work. The faith component has to be splintered into thousands of little donor pieces, not singularly shouldered by the killer. If AP was to work, the money must be waiting for the killer in advance.

"Another aspect of the funding dilemma bears mentioning. To donate anonymously would require a *very* high degree of internet and computer sophistication. Although the encrypted digital cash technology is well-proven, there are still many secondary avenues of detection, such as email history. Nipping this in the bud was, as you know, one of the main reasons of the DCS1000 'Carnivore' program. By monitoring all email traffic at the *ISP* level, we can get some hooks into many anonymous e-cash transactions, and it takes an above-average level of computer privacy technique to circumvent that. To fund an AP murder, you'd have to: first, be online; second, be very familiar with encrypted e-cash; third, have almost hacker-quality computer skills to completely cover your tracks; and fourth, be willing to forego some hard cash in the *hope* of a death. There probably just aren't the numbers of people out there to sufficiently fund a murder. Not very often, anyway."

The CT Chief ponders this, nodding.

"Besides, we thought of a way to foil any real-world AP scheme."

"How's that?" asks the Chief.

"The entire idea is hinged upon the killer *proving* that his 'prediction' was the correct one. Let's say that John Q. Senator is a website target and the actual donations total $500,000. Such would be public information to us as well as to every potential donor and killer. Now let's say that a very serious individual who personally hates John Q. Senator has decided to commit the murder and knows that the Senator will be vulnerable on, oh, 3 March 2009. He emails his encrypted 'prediction' of the Senator's death. On 3 March 2009 he successfully commits the murder.

"But here's the catch nobody considered: there is no guarantee that the Senator's death will be *reported* as having occurred on 3 March 2009. Remember, all of law enforcement knew that the Senator was not only on the target list, but that donations for his death had reached a viable level. So, are we going to dutifully report the correct time, place, and manner of his death? Of course not. That would assure his killer of untraceable payment, turning law enforcement into a sort of collaboration. The catch to AP is that it often depends upon our cooperation—cooperation which we can withhold.

"No, what the Bureau *would* have done as soon as an AP website listed its targets was this: Publicly declare that any death of such persons will be concealed by government authorities for at least several days, thus negating any sufficiently accurate 'prediction' by the perpetrator. Unless a target were killed in a very public manner—which dramatically increases the perp's risk—the details of his death could be kept foggy enough to thwart payment. The 'prediction' has to be verified to the satisfaction of the website coordinators, and we could introduce enough doubt in the matter. Plenty to dissuade an ongoing series of murders."

The CT Chief asks, "What if the killer can provide proof of his deed to the website in addition to his 'prediction'?"

"That would *enhance* the website's complicity, which they would be very reluctant to do."

"Well, what about the highly public murders? The Senator's head is blown apart by a sniper's bullet during an outdoor speech?"

"Since the killer's risk is *much* higher in such a scenario so would his required payment, and this magnifies the funding problem I described earlier. Instead of $500,000, now *$1,000,000* becomes the new equilibrium. Maybe even more. I suspect that most targets worth a million dollars or more in donations would have sufficient security to neutralize an AP threat.

"Furthermore, an executive order could be signed that would offer any website target Secret Service protection. That would increase a perp's risk many times more, raising the stakes beyond the wallet of a populist scheme.

"So far, I have discussed only the donors and the killers. Their link is the website, and that's the *real* Achille's heel of AP. The website could easily be discredited by the spread of rumors. We could claim that it had been compromised, or that it was stealing the donor funds, or that it had no intention of ever paying off any 'predictors.' We could easily destroy any trust the participants had in the website."

The CT Chief nods in admiration. "Yes, that *would* work."

"But let's assume that an AP website *does* manage to survive long enough to foment a few murders. Websites are run by people, and *anybody* is subject to arrest, prosecution, conviction, and imprisonment. AP's inventor James Bell found that out personally. His argument that website personnel have no knowledge of or complicity in a crime just won't wash. Holding money for killers and then effecting disbursement of that money *is* complicity.

"Since judges would be on a target list, they could not allow an AP scheme to operate unmolested. All judges in the land would have a vested interest in shutting down AP websites immediately. Judges can rule any way they desire if the daisy chain remains intact to the Supreme Court, which it would once we educated the judiciary of the threat which AP poses to them.

"In short, such a site could simply not be allowed to legally exist for very long in the U.S. Justice would shut it down almost immediately."

"What if it's based offshore?"

"Not a problem. We would pressure whatever foreign government had jurisdiction in shutting it down.

"What if that foreign government approves of the AP website and refuses to shut it down?"

"Then we'd fight fire with fire. AP can go both ways. We'd simply create a *competing* AP website targeting *their* officials."

"Gee, you *have* given all this some thought, haven't you?"

A tight smile. "Yes, sir, a bit."

"So, give me the takeaway here on AP and the Krassnyites."

"In our opinion, 'Assassination Politics', while a very frightening notion, is too vulnerable a scheme to succeed. What Harold Krassny did, however, is far more disturbing. By example he agitated random individuals. He basically said, 'There are bad people out there who deserve to be killed, and you can kill them with little risk. So what are you waiting for?'

"Now *that* is a very difficult proposition to counter, especially since Krassny's dead. There is no website; there are no donors. These perps are linked only by a common idea, one they've all thought of before Krassny's example. Krassny was a bolt of lightning into a parched forest, and the resulting fire is, or soon will be, out of our control. We can protect a few trees in particular, but many acres will burn and there's nothing we can do about it. Gentlemen, we're facing a force of Nature here. The conflagration will end only by a lack of heat, or by a lack of fuel. It either rains or the fire runs out of forest."

"Since the potential 'forest' is so large, how about making it rain?"

"That's probably our best hope, but at the moment I have no ideas on how to create a deluge. Many Americans have felt pushed around long enough, and they've reached a level of desperation that overwhelms all moral sense. In fact, their moral sense is what's *energizing* this thing. Because of its considerable public support it is a phenomenon many times worse than Islamic terrorism. There's a lot of pent-up rage that is becoming unbound. Most of the victims are seen by many average Americans as evil powermongers, and few tears have been shed over their deaths.

"Although Bell's AP scheme has not transpired, he *did* get a lot of normally peaceable Americans thinking about retribution, and that was a larger contribution than even the technical details of AP. Here's a James Bell quote: *'With my essay, I simply proposed that we libertarians begin to treat aggression by government as being essentially equivalent to aggression by muggers, rapists, robbers, and murderers, and view their acts as a continuing series of aggressions. Seen this way, it should not be necessary to wait for their next aggression; they will . . . always be aggressing, again and again, until they are stopped for good.'"*

The room erupts. "Shit!" "Good Lord!"

"Bell fertilized the soil—not for himself because the AP sprout could never take root—but for Krassny. His example *has* taken root. What we're facing is a vicarious bloodlust focused on government leaders and political figures. It's likely to become our newest national specator sport. We're staring at the French Revolution here, and Harold Krassny is the ghost of Robespierre. I think that heads have only just *begun* to roll."

2008 USA social news

Hearing media people describe liberals is like listening to a fish characterize water: Water? What water? (at 63)

Postulating the existence of the ghosts of liberal imaginations and pursuing the logic of their paranoia, what is the threat posed by the "religious right" precisely? Is the nation in imminent danger of having its coarseness removed? When anal sex, oral sex, premarital sex are all gleefully laughed about on prime-time TV, the peril of religious values infecting the culture would seem to be somewhat overrated. (at 180)

— Ann Coulter,
Slander: Liberal Lies About the American Right

A tidal wave of "political correctness" crashes over the land. Hollywood stars try to outdo each other in moral sanctity and in blaming the "religious right" for the nation's economic woes. It is all Bush's fault.

Our principal trouble today in this country seems to be that too many people have too much time on their hands.
— Justice Clarence Thomas, 1998

2008 political news

The Canadian province of Quebec finally secedes after a referendum passes at 53%. Though hardly a popular mandate, the other 47% seem poised to take the looming secession in stride. Democratic equanimity is, after all, the Canadian way. Separatist movements in Alberta and B.C. double in strength nearly overnight. Canada, historically a rather purposeless nation formed largely by default, is splitting at her tenuous seams.

After eight years, the Democratic Party is finally back in the White House. McBlane and Wiedermann are elected. Liberals across the country are dizzy with joy to have finally seen the last of Bush, Inc.—determined to make the Republicans pay for their Orwellian regime.

The federal gun registration under the *DWA* is amended to include semiautomatic shotguns and handguns, as well as manually-loaded centerfire rifles. (Rimfires remain exempt.) Also affected for the first time are the pre-1899 *"antique"* firearms (*e.g.,* Mauser bolt-actions, Winchester lever-actions, etc.), which were formerly exempt from nearly all federal gun regulation. National compliance is estimated to be an average of only 12%, and less than 5% in the rural South and inland West.

A police state is a self-perpetuating system that will grow until it collapses under its own weight, or until people have reached the limits of their endurance. (at 17)
— Claire Wolfe and Aaron Zelman, *The State vs. The People*

The dispensing of injustice is always in the right hands.
— Stanislaw J. Lem

* * * * * *

Harold Krassny's dissemination of the laptop data began to bear fruit. A well-known libertarian pseudonymic columnist writes a devastating story about the Oklahoma City bombings, bringing to light unmistakable Government complicity. The more federal officials deny the allegations, the worse they look. The faith of American public slips drastically.

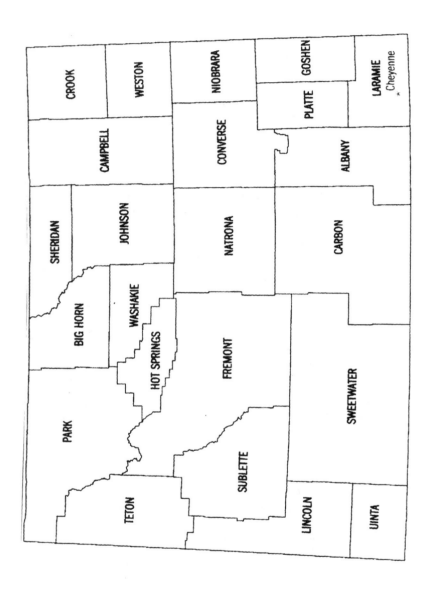

A REPORT ON THE BOMBINGS AT OKLAHOMA CITY

Exclusive to *The Modern Jeffersonian*, by "Whisk E. Rebellion"
Fall 2008

*When federal intelligence agencies in the United States decide to move in a particular direction—**or when a faction of them** decides to move in a particular direction—they do so when to move in that direction would scratch a number of different itches at different levels simultaneously.*

> — intelligence analyst Dave Emory, from *The Oklahoma City Bombing and the Politics of Terror*, by David Hoffman, p. 327

As many of you already know, a Wyoming WW2 vet named Harold Krassny distributed over the Internet the laptop files of his two victims. Without divulging how I received excerpts of these files, they contained a virtual treasure trove of incriminating information on Government "black ops."

Topping the list of these was the Murrah Building bombings. As this report will prove, that horrible event was planned and executed by individuals serving the Federal Government.

Creation/evolution of the "covert cadre"

Independent and interlinked officials, agents, and operatives of several federal intelligence (*e.g.*, CIA, NSA, NRO, ONI, Army CID, etc.) and law enforcement agencies (*e.g.*, FBI, DEA, ATF, Secret Service, etc.) had, by the mid-1980s, coalesced into a covert cadre. They are often referred to as a "rogue element" within the US Government. (Most metropolitan police departments have such "rogue elements", such as the LAPD Rampart Division.)

They are not under the direction of the president or Congress. Rather, they are directed by the same people (*i.e.*, the "shadow government") who direct the president and much of the Congress. The purpose of this covert cadre is to accomplish highly sensitive and clandestine operations to indirectly further the scope of federal powers. Generally, the president and Congress are "not in the loop" for these ops.

The need for more regulation restricting freedom

In 1993 the FBI directly supplied Islamic terrorists with the explosive materials and expertise necessary to topple the World Trade Center. When the Bureau's *agent saboteur* was never told why real explosives were being provided in what was supposedly a sting operation, he became suspicious and tape-recorded further contacts with his FBI handler. The text of such, unmistakenly proving active federal collusion, was reported by many papers, including the *New York Times*.

The *Anti-Terrorism* bill had been introduced just after the February 1993 bombing of the Word Trade Center, and Clinton just couldn't seem to push it through. The controllers of the covert cadre had long believed that an act of domestic terrorism was required to shock the public into accepting new stringent regulations reducing their individual rights.

Oklahoma City

On 30 August 1994 ATF agent Angela Finley sent a status report of Elohim City (EC) in eastern Oklahoma near Muldrow, which was classified *Sensitive and Significant* (vs. *Routine*). It went to the heads of ATF, Treasury, Justice, and the NSC. Through the lengthy infiltration of Confidential Informant (CI) Carol Howe it described the paramilitary activities of the EC 1,100 acre white supremacist compound and its often expressed interest in bombing federal facilities.

This report caught the attention of certain government people.

The ATF did not want to wait; they wanted to be proactive. Still stinging after their Waco fiasco, they planned a 25 March 1995 series of nationwide paramilitary raids on many militia groups. Concerned ATF agents leaked the plan to Congressman Steve Stockman (R-TX), who immediately fired off a letter to AG Janet Reno that such action would "run the risk of an irreparable breach between the Federal Government and the public." Although his letter went unanswered, the raids were quietly called off.

The ATF were mollified with the promise that they would soon be instrumental in thwarting a terrorist bombing of a federal facility. By early April the ATF were included in an ongoing FBI undercover sting operation concerning an Iraqi terrorist ring based in Oklahoma City. Several of the key Iraqis had ties to individuals at EC.

What came out later was that Timothy McVeigh was actively working with these Iraqis, who were plotting to blow up a federal building. Terry Nichols was likely the initial contact with fundamentalist muslims during his many trips to the Philippines. What McVeigh and Nichols did not know, however, was that the Iraqis were also planning to dump the bombing in their laps as a right-wing act.

Many eyewitnesses have said that McVeigh, a decorated Gulf War sergeant, was an ATF informant paid to infiltrate the Islamic terrorist group. (Another possible taskmaster was the US Army Special Forces Covert Tactical Unit.) What is known is that at least one federal infiltrator/saboteur *was* placed in the group. He would soon become famous as "John Doe #2."

It was decided by the covert cadre that a bombing could then be easily blamed on either the Iraqi Hezbollah or the Elohim City white-supremacists, whichever was later deemed more useful.

18-19 April 1995

On midnight of 18 April 1995 the front of the Oklahoma City Murrah Building was placed under surveillance by ATF agents. The building's security staff, Federal Protective Services, was to leave at 0200 hours and return at 0600. The Ryder truck, driven by McVeigh and John Doe #2, was to park in front at 0300. The truck was packed with 1,000lbs. of ammonium nitrate/fuel oil (ANFO). It was—like the 1993 WTC bombing—never meant to go off.

In OKC, however, the relatively small amount of low-explosive would *seem* to the public sufficiently large to destroy the Murrah Building, when all it could do was merely blow out a few windows. ANFO is a very ineffective explosive for air blasts. At less than half the velocity of detonation (VOD) of C-4, ANFO is simply just too slow to bring down a reinforced concrete building forty feet away.

John Doe #2, an FBI agent saboteur, was to have disarmed the bomb before it was supposed to detonate at 0330, leaving a surprised "Lee Harvey McVeigh" (who possibly thought that he was helping to set up the Iraqis by driving the truck) to be arrested "in the nick of time." John Doe #2 would then be placed on the FBI's Most Wanted list in the hopes of establishing his bona fides with neo-Nazi groups or militias—whom he could then easily infiltrate. That was, at least, the official plan.

The covert team, however, had another plan which would serve much larger interests. They successfully passed themselves off as federal agents to McVeigh and John Doe #2, and convinced the pair that the truck's delivery had been postponed to 0900 for greater drama (since the building would be full of people then) and arrest publicity (shown live on morning TV news).

Thus, the Ryder truck did not show at 0300. On-site federal agents became very worried. By 0330 an FBI team near the State Fairgrounds with radio-tracking equipment was searching for the truck. By 0400 they had relocated downtown, though without success. Unbeknownst to the ATF and

FBI, the transmitter beacon on the truck had been disabled by operatives. When the truck had not arrived by 0600, on-site agents naturally assumed that the staged arrest had been postponed until the following evening. The op was called off at 0630 because the truck was to have been driven to the *unoccupied* Murrah Building in order to safely arrest McVeigh and regain control of the truck bomb.

At 0215, covert operatives secretly entered the Murrah Building on foot from the underground parking garage. (Hours earlier they had left a van containing all their necessary gear.) Concealed behind decorative planters, they placed 10lb. C-4 high-explosive charges with radio-controlled detonators on six reinforced concrete columns at their 3rd floor junctions: A3, A5, A7, B3, B4, and B5. (Columns A4 and A6 were expected to fall on their own from the collapsing cantilever floors.) They quickly finished their work and left on foot through the garage at 0257. (An agent would return by 0530 to retrieve the van.) They had not been seen by the ATF/FBI surveillance agents on the other side of the building.

The OCPD Bomb Squad arrived at 0630, searched the first two floors, and left by 0830. Unfortunately, they did not search the 3rd floor.

At 0704 a group alphanumeric page was sent by the covert cadre to all OKC ATF agents. Of the thirteen agents, five had been out all night on the sting operation. The pager message read "UNODIR NO-GO OFFICE." "UNODIR" means "unless otherwise directed." ATF clerical staff did not receive this group page, and showed up for work as usual. The purpose of the page was to prevent ATF agents from interfering with the Murrah Building 0900 delivery of the Ryder truck. Ironically, their absence would create suspicsion that the ATF had prior knowledge of the bomb plot.

Several neighborhood security cameras across the street from the Murrah Building clearly recorded the arrival of the Ryder truck at 0859 hours. Timothy McVeigh, the driver, exited the truck, crossed NW 5th Street and walked east to Robinson Avenue, where he turned north towards the YMCA building and a parking garage.

The passenger, swarthy, black-haired John Doe #2, was seen by one witness to have walked to the rear of the truck. He then noticed with alarm that the door's padlock had been changed, thus he could not deactivate the truck bomb as planned. In great haste he fast-walked east on 5th Street and turned south on Broadway to his getaway driver and vehicle, a brown Chevy pickup truck with tinted windows. Several witnesses soon after identified Hussain al-Hussaini as the driver, leaving downtown at a high rate of speed over the Walnut Street Bridge. The FBI put out an APB on the truck, which it inexplicably cancelled hours later.

The ATF and FBI agents who had been on-station hours earlier got word that the Ryder truck, which had been hidden overnight in plain sight at the Remington Park Race Track parking lot, was spotted at the intersection of Reno and M.L.K. By the time agents arrived downtown it was 0901 hours and the truck was already parked in front of the Murrah Building.

At 0902 hours an encrypted radio signal was sent by the covert team from five blocks away on 5th Street to set off the diversionary truck bomb. The triggering of the interior charges did not occur until several seconds later, probably because of a faulty ignition system. (Whether it was a timer, radio, pressure, or seismic device is unknown.) This delay sufficiently separated the explosions to be noticeable by dozens of witnesses and victims, as well as by two seismogram stations 4.34 and 16.25 miles away.

Four of the six interior charges detonated. (For some unknown reason, the C-4 charges on columns B4 and B5 did not detonate.) Pieces of the Murrah Building were blown *into* the Athenian restaurant 150' across the street. The sequence of truck and then building explosions was even caught on videotape by Southwestern Bell employees. No videos from any buildings were shown at the trials, and none have been publicly aired.

If McVeigh was an ATF informant then he would have been utterly surprised by the explosions, feeling like Lee Harvey Oswald inside the Dallas Schoolbook Depository just after John F. Kennedy had been assassinated by triangulated rifle fire. McVeigh reached his yellow Mercury Marquis at 0905, which he had parked behind a vacant house several blocks northeast. Unbeknownst to him, covert operatives had not only removed its rear license plate, but installed a GPS tracking beacon. It was a fairly simply matter to arrange for his detention and arrest ninety minutes later on northbound I-35 near Perry, Oklahoma. Though armed with a .45 Glock 21, McVeigh did not shoot OHP Trooper Hanger—possibly because he thought he was protected by his work with the ATF and would be released shortly after his arrest.

At first, most experts—from former FBI chief Oliver "Buck" Revell to former CIA CT director Vince Cannistraro to former Israeli Defense Intelligence specialist Avi Lipkin—blamed Islamic terrorists. So did major media.

A few hours later a Jordanian named Abraham Ahmed (observed by American Airlines staff as "acting nervous") was detained in Chicago by FBI during his flight from Oklahoma City to Jordan. After a six-hour interrogation he was released and allowed to continue his trip. The next day the British interrogated him for five hours in London and then returned him to the U.S. His check-through luggage contained tools, electrical components, a timing device, and a photo album of weapons and missiles.

This same Abraham Ahmed would later serve on 15 June as the interpreter of the Iraqi Hussain al-Hussaini, the man identified by several witnesses as the driver of the brown Chevy pickup. Al-Hussaini worked for a Sam Khalid, who had been investigated by the FBI for PLO ties.

Suffice to say that there was much evidence supporting the Islamic terrorist theory. Yet, less than 48 hours later on 21 April, the FBI announced their arrest of McVeigh, an angry white guy. The public was intentionally kept waiting for two days in order to enhance the drama of the FBI arresting him just one hour before he was to be released from the Noble County Jail. Meanwhile, his yellow Mercury had been planted with "right-wing extremist" literature while it sat abandoned on the highway.

The Islamic angle was immediately discarded and the Oklahoma City bombing was the fault of the militias and Rush Limbaugh.

Shortly after McVeighs's arrest, FBIHQ was informed through highly discreet channels of the interior C-4 charges, which had shattered four reinforced concrete columns and caused the building's north face collapse. The FBI were now in a quandry. They had locked themselves on McVeigh and the Patriot Movement as the perpertrators, but could not suddenly purport that he and Nichols had also placed sophisticated C-4 charges *inside* the building. They also could not float the theory that the Iraqis and McVeigh had colluded in the bombings, for that would raise embarrassing questions.

So, the FBI were forced to keep increasing the size of the ANFO truck bomb to "explain" the interior devastation. First, 2,000lbs, then 4,000, then 4,800, and finally *7,000* lbs. This desperate tactic was, however, replete with problems. Government officials quickly became alarmed at the instantaneous barrage of professional and military skepticism over the alleged ANFO bomb. Demolition experts around the world, including British experts on IRA bombings, bitterly scoffed at the truck bomb story (even though nitromethane was allegedly used instead of mere diesel fuel).

Two independent Pentagon experts concluded that the destruction was caused by five seperate bombs. In the spring of 1997, explosives experts at Eglin AFB's Wright Laboratory Armament Directorate released a 56 page report of their reproductive blast test. It said, *"It must be concluded that the damage at the Murrah Federal Building is not the result of the truck-bomb itself, but rather due to other factors such as locally placed charges within the building itself..."* Even FEMA was forced to admit that 4,800lbs of ANFO could not have caused the crater (allegedly 30' in diameter, but which was quickly covered from public view due to its small size).

The explosive power of ANFO does not increase in proportion to its amount, since large quantities do not ignite efficiently even with precisely controlled triggers. In fact, a 7,000lb ANFO device built along the alleged model would scatter up to nearly half its prills without having detonated at all.

Retired US Air Force General Benton K. Partin, an engineer and weapons expert, assembled a devasting report. It thoroughly dismissed the possibility of an ANFO truck bomb having shattered four reinforced concrete pillars with only 10% of the blast pressure required to do so. The destruction of column B3, Partin explained, was the "smoking gun" of supplementing contact demolition charges placed inside the building.

In a panic, and against a formal request by concerned Americans and members of Congress, the USG had—for alleged "health hazards" and humanitarian concerns"—the Murray Building demolished (*i.e.*, blown up a third and final time) on 23 May, just four weeks after 19 April. The debris was trucked to a remote area and guarded until buried.

The impossible 7,000lb ANFO bomb

In *American Terrorist* (pp.214-220), McVeigh allegedly told the authors quite an amazing tale. He and Nichols supposedly drove to a public lake, mixed 108 bags of 50lb ammonium nitrate (5,400lbs total) with three 55 gal drums of liquid nitromethane (1,200lbs total), poured this into thirteen barrels (nine by funnel through bung holes), arranged the filled barrels weighing about 500lbs each, installed a dual-ignition system through the cab wall, wiped down the cab interior, washed up and changed clothes—*all in the time span of under four hours inside the confines of a 20' truck.*

Assuming a full four hours with nothing to do but mix and pour the components, the two men had to process 1,350lbs of ammonium nitrate with 41 gallons of liquid *every hour*. Or, 22½lbs with about three quarts *every minute*. Every minute nonstop, without interruption, for nearly 240 minutes.

Also, the required very thorough mixing of the ANFO should not be overlooked. Ammonium nitrate prills (1-2mm in diameter) have a coating to protect against moisture. Liquid fuel must be *very* evenly mixed to coat most of the prills and dissolve their external coating. Dry prills will not detonate easily, if at all. This mixing process is very tedious and time consuming. Professionals use motorized mixers. It's not something easily done by hand in the back of a 20' box truck under time pressure with witnesses just outside.

And yet McVeigh and Nichols supposedly accomplished all this in *less* than four hours (69% of the barrels to be filled by *funnel*), plus arrange the barrels, build the ignition system, clean up, and change clothes.

Try to fill a 55 gal barrel by funnel through the bung hole with sand sometime. It takes about 20 minutes. And that's nicely flowing sand, versus soggy, clumpy ANFO. Assuming sand, however, the funnel filling of 9 barrels would take 2.7 hours, leaving less than 78 minutes (*i.e.*, 1.3 hours) for mixing, arranging, building, cleaning, etc.—and, oh, filling the other 4 barrels.

Then, there is the matter of insufficient space within the truck. A 20' box truck would not have had the working room for the job. Go rent one sometime, cart in 108 50lb bags, three full 55 gal. drums, and 13 empty plastic 55 gal. drums. Imagine two men trying to mix and pour all of this within that very small space—much less within four hours. It truly defies belief.

An ex-rocket-scientist was asked if McVeigh's schedule were possible. He laughed, replying that even if such could have been accomplished within four hours (which was *"impossible"*), there were the deadly nitromethane fumes inside such a confined space. *"Without breathers and a fuel-compatible pump? No way! Nitromethane is incredibly toxic. In 30 minutes they'd have been incoherent; in an hour their faces would have slid off!"*

Yet we are expected to believe that 165 gallons of nitromethane were *"poured...into the five-gallon plastic buckets,weighing out the measurements on* [a] *bathroom scale."* I suppose that we are also to believe that the deadly fuel was siphoned by sucking on a length of garden hose.

So, the "official" story of McVeigh and Nichols building this alleged bomb within 4 hours inside a 20' Ryder truck parked at a lake, on high alert for over an hour because of people fishing 25yds away is absurd fiction.

Why did McVeigh tell such a tale?

Regardless of McVeigh's level of bombing guilt versus any federal collusion as an informant, he may have been offered a cruel bargain. Keep his mouth shut about what happened, parrot the ridiculous story of building a 7,000lb ANFO bomb in the confines of a 20' box truck, and his family would not be harmed. Playing the "good soldier" would guarantee their safety. Also, McVeigh might have been promised that the lethal injection would be only a deep sedative, and that he would be revived later for plastic surgery and supervised freedom abroad. (Not that McVeigh would have been allowed to live in any case, but he may have been convinced otherwise.) McVeigh, already convicted to a death sentence with no chance of reversal, had nothing to gain but his family's continued safety. An intelligent man, he'd have agreed.

According to Clinton, the OKC bombing(s) *"broke the spell"* of the increasing anti-government sentiment and its "Republican Revolution" of November 1994. The growing inertia of conservative politics evaporated. Accordingly, Clinton signed his beloved *Anti-Terrorism Act* on 20 April 1996 (Adolf Hitler's 107th birthday), which created a 2,500 man Rapid Deployment Force under the Attorney General.

Only the Federal Government benefitted from the OKC bombings.

❖ 2009

Own a small business?
Then what are you doing in _California?_

Like to conceal-carry your defensive handgun?
Then what are you doing in _Missouri?_

Own a .308 battle rifle?
Then what are you doing in _Chicago?_

Care enough about your children to home-school them?
Then what are you doing in _Manhattan?_

Like to vote Libertarian?
Then what are you doing in _Newark?_

Believe in the Bill of Rights?
Then what are you doing in _Massachusetts?_

Tired of inner-city ghetto crime?
Then what are you doing in _Detroit?_

Really—what . . . on . . . earth . . . are . . . you . . . _doing?_

You don't have to live this way any longer! You don't have to feel like some hermit, surrounded by people you've nothing in common with. Your environment won't change, so why not alter your environment? Why not join us in what is becoming the world's freest place?

Want to start a small business without restrictive licenses and a lot of red tape? Fine—we have the state for you. Want to continue home-schooling your children but aren't that solid in chemistry? No problem, the retired professor across the street will teach them in trade for piano lessons. Want to set up a pistol range in your back yard? Marvelous—a guy down the road already makes the steel targets. Want to shoot your dad's Korean War M1 Garand off the deck every weekend?

Excellent—your neighbor will let you shoot his G43 in exchange. Like organic vegetables and medicinal herbs, but don't have time to garden? No sweat— folks just outside town already grow them. Want to live amongst people who will help you fulfill your dreams and not envy your success? Super—they're waiting to meet you . . . in Wyoming!

Want a local government that will leave you alone?
Come to *Wyoming!*
Want friendly neighbors who also believe in freedom?
They're in *Wyoming!*
Want to finally enjoy life without needless hassle?
Join us in *Wyoming!*

Oh, moving across the country is too inconvenient for you? Don't want to pull up roots? Fine. Stay home. Alone.

Home-schoolers in Maryland.	*Isolated.*
Gun owners in Illinois.	*Vulnerable.*
Conservatives in California.	*Ineffective.*
Libertarians in New Jersey.	*Outnumbered.*
Constitutionalists in Massachusetts.	*Alone.*

Stay home in Occupied Territory like a fish in a barrel, while your "family" and "friends" and "neighbors" make hushed phone calls to 1-800 fink lines and report you for *"suspicious"* behavior.

Stay home, waiting for the knock on the door—*your* door—to roundup your children from the *"inadequacies"* of homeschooling, to cart off your *"subversive"* books, to collect your *"dangerous and illegal"* firearms, to confiscate your home computer for evidence of *"terrorist"* activity, to excavate your backyard for buried *"cash and contraband."*

Stay home, like a dead man waiting for the coroner. Your corpse has already been measured, your coffin has already been built, your burial plot already dug. Stay home, like a Jew in 1937 Germany, thinking they'll leave you in peace as long as you don't make trouble.

You threaten them simply by being who you are—off-beat and independent-thinking. They'll get around to you when your cattle car is ready; they'll kick your door down on their schedule.

And gee, all you have to do is . . . just . . . stay . . . home.

Or . . . you can join thousands of other folks just like you and live the American dream. Life. Liberty. The pursuit of happiness.

Join us and learn what freedom you've been missing! In *Wyoming!*

Washington, D.C.   FBIHQ   January 2009

The Director finishes reading the Wyoming flyer and rubs his eyes. "My God, what a bunch of *nuts*! How did you get a copy of this, Bleth?"

"I salted enough libertarian chat rooms and websites, apparently. Since I haven't heard anything more from them, they may have figured out that I used an alias."

"Where did you get this thing?"

"It was a .pdf file emailed from a remailer. No leads on its origin."

The Director sighs. "Well, keep on it. Try to get to the next level and be invited to move to Bear Dropping, Wyoming."

* * * * * * *

[T]he tax-gatherer is the very man I have to deal with—for it is, after all, with men and not with parchment that I quarrel—and he has voluntarily chosen to be an agent of the government.
— Thoreau, *On the Duty of Civil Disobedience* (1849)

After the first death, there is no other.
— Dylan Thomas

Montgomery County, Maryland   February 2009

The dawn air was frigid, and a sheet of thin ice covered the wealthy suburban neighborhood. Very little was stirring but the paperboy on his moped and a few early commuters groggily leaving their homes to get a jump on the morning Beltway traffic.

Precisely at 5:45AM Jonathan Douglas Gray stepped onto the porch of his two-story Tudor, locked the front door behind him, and eased into a loping jog towards the park six blocks away. His morning runs were always 45 minutes. It's how he remained in such good physical condition into his late-50s even after a lifetime of government service.

He looked back on his career as a federal district court judge with great pride. Congressional laws deserve to be upheld, and vigorously so. The magnificent system of federalism was not as ambiguous as those "states rights" whiners claimed. Through the constitutional clauses of *"interstate and foreign commerce"* and *"necessary and proper"* and *"supreme law of the land"* the Congress and the President have the power to set public policy. This necessarily touched on many areas of common life thought by libertarians to be sacrosanct—not so! While on the bench, Judge Gray eagerly gave the harshest punishments to those who would dare violate federal laws controlling guns, drugs, education, and small business.

Some defendants in court actually floated arguments that the Constitution protected some "right" to own assault weapons, or use marijuana for allegedly "medical" purposes. The very idea! As if that venerable document were written so millions of Americans could shoot up with heroin and then fire machineguns into schoolyards! To operate unlicensed and unregulated companies. To have children off the tax roles—birthed by black market midwives, no less!—and then evade public education through the sham of "homeschooling." To willfully circumvent the National ID Card, a device vital for corralling terrorists, shadow criminals, money launderers, and tax cheats.

No, that was *anarchy*. Judge Gray was well served by a single, overriding premise: What is not in control is *out* of control. Yes, America is a free country, but freedom is not unlimited. We enjoy our liberties *because* of laws—every one of them part of the vast bulwark against anarchy.

To Judge Gray there were no bad laws, only underappreciated ones.

He upheld them all. If he did not, who *would*? Laws were conceived and passed for good reason by professional legislators elected to office by a citizenry generally incapable of running their own lives. Gray understood that people are unfit for self-rule. They always have been, and always will be. Gray also understood that a small, select class of men were born to wisely rule. Such had always been the case. One never has to ask if one is among the ruling class any more than a fish ever questions its innate ability to swim. People are who they *should* be.

Jonathan Douglas Gray had been a federal judge and faithful protector of the law because it was his particular fate. The thousands of criminals who yearly clogged his beautiful court with the stink of their insolence were also playing out their part. Gray realized long ago that a man of his position must cultivate a garden of calm perspective: without the great unwashed there could be no laws, no court, no judgeship.

Rulers needed subjects just as subjects needed rulers.

Still, the notion often rankled. When it did, Gray "threw the book" at the latest would-be anarchist. Asymmetrical punishment, he called it. An eye for a tooth. The Government could not afford to appear weak, not for a second. Yes, stern measures were best. One had to shock *das Volk* with regular harsh sentences in order to keep them in line.

One also had to rule one's body to keep *it* in line. Gray's flesh was always pleading for a "day off" from its morning jogs. He never gave in. His body was subject to his iron will every minute of every day. Being called a "Health Nazi" by the *lumpenproletariat* was a jealous compliment.

Gray would return home at 6:30, take a cold shower of distilled water, rub himself down with coconut oil, and eat a light breakfast of organic bran, yogurt, and precisely measured Brewer's yeast. He would leave for his law firm at 7:15. Regularity of schedule had served him well.

Until today.

He reaches the park a few minutes later. On the familiar jogging path he feels his muscles warm and loosen up, his stride relaxing. His exhalations are bursts of steam, as if from a mighty train. The image always invigorates him. Powerful. In control. Exercising while sluggards slept.

The morning is silent but for his rhythmic breathing and crunchy footfalls on the frozen gravel trail. His normal route through the park is a figure-eight, with the middle deep inside the woods and the top and bottom ends near the streets. As he nears the top of the park he notices the gray-blue dawning light through the thinning trees.

Gray sees another jogger up ahead on the left. Tall and muscular, with blonde hair under his knit watch cap. Gray instantly seethes inside. Few people ran in "his" park this early and it always irked him when they did. Especially if they were in good shape. He overtakes the jogger in a blue sweatsuit and passes by on the right without even condescending to look at him.

The tall jogger slightly picks up his pace, keeping one step behind. He raises his right arm, its hand grasping a leather sap filled with 16 ounces of fine lead shot. Gray feels a sense of vague alarm and begins to turn his head, but the jogger is too quick for him. He smashes the sap on the back of Gray's head, causing his brain's frontal lobe to bounce off the inside of his forehead. He is unconscious before he even hits the ground in a sprawl. He will not wake up for hours, and when he does he will not recall being struck.

As he bags the sap in a ZipLoc and pockets it, the jogger forces his breathing to slow as he intently scans the park. *Alone.* He then hoists the 165 pound Gray as if a bag of dogfood and trudges the twenty yards up a knoll to the treeline by the street. He puts Gray down behind some shrubbery, takes out a pair of compact Steiner 8x22 binoculars from underneath his sweatshirt and carefully surveys the street. *Be thorough. Don't be in a hurry to move.*

The neighorbood is still sleepy and quiet.

His parked car is just thirty feet away, beckoning as his escape. He had carefully chosen something fitting for the area—a white, late 1990s Lincoln. He picked white because it was the most common color. Nearly 60% of rental cars were white. It also had a large trunk. A van, although roomier, was subjected to much more police scrutiny.

A Lincoln would raise no attention and was instantly forgettable.

The preparation of the car had been paramount. The registration must be valid in case he were stopped, but not linkable to him. He bought it with cash from a private owner last week. The title had not been transferred, but he signed a bill of sale made out to a fictitious company. He even printed up business cards to show any officer during a traffic stop. Once this mission was completed, he would simply resell the Lincoln on the previous owner's title (being careful not to leave fingerprints on it), never having registered it himself. No paper or financial records tied him to the car, and he had disguised himself to thwart recognition by the seller. He could even dump the car. The only thing more untraceable would have been to use a stolen car, but the risks were too great. One random license check would catch him. Interim ownership was best.

He had left the trunk just slightly open so he doesn't have to use a key. *This is my moment of greatest risk* the man reminds himself. From shrubbery to trunk is only thirty feet and five seconds, but they are the most important five seconds of his life. The quality of his future depends upon nobody driving around the corner, or leaving their house, or looking out their front window during that brief time. He could explain being discovered next to the downed jogger, but there was simply no plausible explanation for putting an unconscious man in a car trunk.

A thought flashes through his mind. *Still time to quit and just walk away. I can snap the bastard's neck and leave him here. Easy!* He rejects the craven idea. *No, that's the chickenshit way out, and it's too good for Gray! Stick with the plan!* He will go through with it.

The man is on fire with acuity, too excited to be nervous. He scans the neighborhood one last time. Nobody is stirring. The longer he waits, the riskier it becomes. *Time to just go for it!* He picks up Gray and walks briskly, but smoothly, to the rear of the white Lincoln, lifts the lid and gently places him inside. He forces himself not to look around, which would look suspicious if somebody were watching him.

The trunk is completely and carefully lined with 6mil heavy plastic, taped securely around all edges. On top of that is a second sheet of the same plastic to prevent any transfer of hair or fiber residue Gray to trunk, or vice versa. The spare tire and jack had been moved to the rear floorboard so that he does not have to open the trunk in the event of a flat.

He needs to bind up Gray so that he cannot free himself or pound on the trunk lid to attract attention. He has an overwhelming desire to drive away *now*, to leave the area immediately, but he knows that's just panic talking. *Stick with the plan!* He quickly covers Gray's head with a cotton hood and then cable-ties his feet and hands together. He had considered using tape but tape picks up *lots* of tell-tale debris. Modern crime labs can even lift prints from the adhesive side with dye staining or lasers.

He bags his Microflex Diamond Grip latex gloves and tosses them inside with the sap. Then he covers the jogger with the second plastic sheet and closes the trunk lid.

The electric latch sound is immensely reassuring. *I am 80% homefree.*

He takes one last casual look around the neighborhood. Still alone. He gets in the car, carefully placing his size 12 running shoes in a plastic bag on the floorboard. He bought them for a dollar at a garage sale months prior in another state. Although he is a size 10, he wanted larger mission shoes in order to leave contradictory evidence. With two extra pairs of heavy socks, they fit fine. His shaved calves and feet left no hairs in the shoes.

He bags his $1.00 bargain footwear and slips on another used pair— size 10—unsoiled from his jog. Nothing from the Lincoln is in the park, and nothing from the park is in the Lincoln.

Nothing besides Jonathan Douglas Gray, that is.

He then dumps out two lipstick-stained cigarette butts he found in a mall ashtray. The man neither smoked nor wore lipstick, but these two false clues may cause the FBI to search for a woman driver. Having been a cop after Desert Storm while he got his Chemical Engineering B.S. on the GI Bill, the man knew police work. He understood that investigators' time was, like anybody else's, finite, and the more time you caused them to waste, the better your chances of success. Forensic crime labs with DNA analysis could identify subjects from their saliva left in payphone mouthpieces, but the finer the tool the easier it is to blunt its edge. A bag full of cigarette butts, hair clippings, used tissues, and the like dumped at a crime scene will overwhelm any forensic lab, including the FBI's. A powerful floodlight negates $4,000 night vision devices. And so on.

Technology only has advantages when kept on its own terms. Where it magnifies, give it a boxcar load. The FBI cannot keep up with its Carnivore DCS1000 analysis of email traffic any more than the Treasury Department can filter through the millions of annual Currency Transaction Reports. Like finding a needle in a needlestack.

It was all about the signal-to-noise ratio.

The man smiles at his reflection on all this as he inserts the ignition key. The Lincoln starts immediately, fully warmed up by the 150 mile trip to the park. He had arrived precisely at 5:30AM so it hadn't cooled down. He leisurely drives towards the highway. Removing his watch cap and blonde wig, and bagging them both, he is glad to see his short, brown hair again in the mirror. A few miles later he pulls next to a trashcan, tosses in his bagged shoes, cap, wig, and drives on.

I am 85% homefree.

Several minutes later he is on I-270 South heading towards D.C. He checks his rearview mirror for a break in traffic behind him, and when he sees one he flips a toggle switch on the console. A rectangular piece of metal falls from behind his car and skitters to the shoulder. *Worked perfectly!* He had installed a powerful electromagnet behind his car's license plate and bracket. An hour earlier he stuck on an old, expired steel license plate (which he found at a flea market) over his own. It was his homage to "Q" and James Bond.

I am 90% homefree.

The most dangerous part has passed. Now, he must play the part of a commuter who has a perfectly good reason to be where he was at six in the morning, along with a mundane, believable, and verifiable destination. He obeys all traffic laws and drives at 2mph under the speed limits. He has mug of steaming coffee fresh brewed from a 12VDC machine. Hanging in the back is a business suit.

Just another commuter.

The man revels in the rich coffee aroma, taking a first sip. He glances again at himself in the mirror. Although his face is calm, his eyes glow with accomplishment. He never felt more alive, and allows himself a chuckle. Turning over his shoulder he asks, "You all right back there, Judge?"

Gray had, for all practical purposes, sent an innocent and harmless woman to her death. Today comes the bill.

The man recalls the horrible account of Katherine Jessup's needless death as he takes the Beltway to I-66 West. He'd never met Katherine Jessup. Didn't know anyone who had, either. But when he read her story and saw her picture he thought *That could have been my daughter. Jenny had those same wistful eyes before she died of breast cancer in college her sophomore year.*

Actually, the naseau that Jenny suffered from Adriamycin—better known as "Red Death" to its miserable patients—was more responsible for her demise than the cancer itself. The man had to watch his beautiful daughter waste away to a Dachau-wisp before death mercifully took her. The tragedy spun his wife into a chronic depression. She soon after ODed on barbituates.

He only learned of medical marijuana later through the Katherine Jessup story, but this was months after Jenny's funeral on that sullen, drizzly Tuesday morning. *Medical marijuana should not only be legal, but it should have been on 60 Minutes years ago! I might still have my wife and daughter!*

Not surprisingly, the man focused on the medical rights issue. Every FDA incursion against vitamin sellers, every DEA raid of holistic health practitioners, every natural herb shop stormed by submachine-gun wielding US Postal Inspectors in federal black ratcheted the man's anger one more notch. Peaceable Americans were being hounded out of business and into prison over some useful flower, stem, tree bark, or root. He stewed for years over Judge Gray, who seemed the epitome of every senseless and montrous invasion of medical privacy.

Gray had returned to private law practice shortly after being hounded off the federal bench for his draconian rulings, which he blamed on mandatory sentencing guidelines. The old Nuremberg defense of "just following orders" excused no perpetrator of evil. Not then, and not now.

When Harold Krassny publicized the reasons for his actions, something clicked within the man. *About time! The federal government long ago declared war on us, and we're only now just waking up to it.*

After Krassny's example, the rudiments of a plan soon hatched in the man's mind. It wouldn't bring Jenny or the Jessups back, but it was The Next Best Thing.

Alexandria, Virginia
Law Offices of Schwartz, Williams, and Gray   8:24AM

Senior partner Ira Schwartz buzzes his secretary. "Apparently Jon's running a little late. Have him drop by my office when he gets in. We need to discuss *McFarland*."

"Yes, sir."

northern Virginia   8:24AM

The man exits the highway onto a small county road and drives southwest about twenty miles. He then turns onto an overgrown dirt road which winds its way into the George Washington National Forest. After several miles he stops just past a pair of trees flanking the road. He dons a new pair of rubber surgical gloves, gets out, and retrieves a small bag hidden behind an old rotten log. In it are a heavy chain, combination padlock, and sign. He strings the chain between the trees across the road and padlocks it. The sign reads *Closed for public use. By order of US Forest Service.* It is an authentic sign, "borrowed" from a gate miles away.

He studies the road in front of him. It is a rarely used forest road hardly more than a trail, its ruts nearly overgrown with lush grass. By the dirt he can tell that nobody but himself had driven on it since yesterday. The man drives two more miles down the road, turns around, and parks. It is 8:55AM. The sun strains through the leaden winter sky, and all is quiet.

He gets out and surveys the area with a hand-held milspec thermal device capable of detecting human presence within 600 yards. He is quite alone. He walks about fifty yards through the trees, and removes a large, weighted-down tarp. The pit he dug yesterday is undisturbed, as is the covered shovel and several 5-gallon plastic cans.

He returns to the car, opens the trunk, and dons new gloves. Gray is half awake, groggily straining at his cableties. The man lifts Gray out, still hooded, and carries him near the pit.

"Who, who *are* you? Where *am* I?" Gray manages to sputter through his hood.

The man says, "We've never met, but I know who *you* are."

"Well, if you know who *I* am, then you must realize what colossal trouble you have gotten yourself into!" Gray snaps.

"It seems only *one* of us is in any trouble," the man says evenly. "I'm not the one bound up and blindfolded miles from home, now am I?"

Gray is only momentarily fazed by this. "You are in much more trouble, whoever you are. You should have kidnapped a wealthy man, not an influential one. Release me at once! I have important business to attend to, and my people in Washington already know that I'm missing. Furthermore, I can assure you that the FBI will—"

The man gives Gray a brutal slap across his left cheek. "You're a very important guy—noted for the record, Judge. Now shut up."

The full terror of his predicament falls on Gray. *Nobody knows I'm missing! Nobody is coming to help!* Gray knows that he is going to die—horribly—and begins to panic. "Y-you're g-g-going to *kill* me!"

"Calm down, calm down. You're only upsetting yourself," the man soothes. "And you're not making that headache any better. That was a nasty fall you took."

This confuses Gray. He doesn't remember falling, but even if he did fall he doesn't understand why he's been abducted. "You're, you're *not* going to *kill* me?"

The man chuckles. "If I were going to kill you, would you still be blindfolded? Listen, I'm going to give you something for your headache, and then we'll talk. I'm sure you've got a lot of questions."

The man lifts the cotton hood over Gray's mouth, opens a small plastic bottle of Evian drinking water and allows him a long swig before he swallows a gel capsule. Strangely, Gray seems to trust the man and his calm voice.

"Good. Your discomfort will be gone soon. You're not going to start shouting for help now, are you?"

Gray shakes his head. "No, but I demand some answers. Just who in the hell do you think you—"

Slap! Spittle is flung several feet.

"Stimulus—response, Judge. Are you getting the idea here?"

Gray nods vigorously.

"That's better. Just to be on the safe side, I can't risk you shouting for help. I'll let you go later, but right now I need to tape your mouth. Besides, I'm tired of hearing your voice. Just cooperate and everything'll be fine, OK?"

Without waiting for a reply the man yanks off Gray's cotton hood and seals his mouth with duct-tape. With heavy scissors he cuts off Gray's shoes, socks, and all of his clothes except for his underwear.

Gray blinks rapidly from the sunlight and strains to make out his kidnapper's face. Seeing it, he knows, seals his death. He begins to tremble.

While Gray is wriggling in his boxer shorts, the man goes to the 4'x6' pit and removes a sheet of plywood from an interior earthen shelf, exposing an empty smaller hole below. It is lined with 10mil black landscaping plastic, forming a water-holding pit 3' deep and 3'x5' in dimension.

"Hey, did you know that Evian spelled backwards is 'naive'?" He then kicks the cabletied Gray into the pit, who lands in a bruised heap.

"I've two words for you, Judge: *Katherine . . . Jessup!*"

Gray frantically searches his terrified mind for the familiar name. A burble of queasiness interrupts his thoughts.

The man continues, "Well, J.D., I lied. I couldn't find any headache medicine. But I did bring some concentrated powdered ipecac."

Cephaelis ipecacuanha is a creeping plant of tropical South America. Its dried rhizome and roots are used to prepare a very powerful emetic. An emetic, from the Greek *emetikos*, is something that induces vomiting. Taken raw it works immediately and cannot be resisted. The capsule has delayed reaction by a minute or so. Every drugstore sells it, and it requires no prescription. First aid kits have ipecac in case a victim has been poisoned.

Gray feels himself growing increasingly nauseous as the homemade capsule dissolves. Having dropped out of med school to become a lawyer, he knows full well what ipecac is. His fall only accentuates its effect. From the pit bottom he can see his captor standing at the edge, his arms crossed.

The man's voice is calm, but brittle with anger. "You remember *her* don't you, Your Honor? An innocent woman just trying to deal with her cancer? You sent her to prison where she died! Her husband, Tom, became an alcoholic and soon after killed himself in a car crash. Didn't the Justice Department update you on *that* little detail?"

Gray is groaning loudly through the duct tape, trying to say something.

"Just like somebody in Florida CS-gassed that hideous, lantern-jawed woman 'for the children,' you're going to die in the same horrible way Katherine Jessup did. And I promise you that nobody will *ever* find your decomposed body, Judge."

Gray is now shaking with fear as his gut churns. He had not eaten anything since dinner and his stomach is void of all food. The human physiology has a wonderful cadence of circadian rhythms, and the empty stomach of Jonathan Douglas Gray had prepared itself for the regular 6:55AM intake of breakfast with a full complement of digestive acids. The more he struggles the sicker he becomes. His nausea then passes that Point Of No Return and Gray knows he can no longer fight it.

Alexandria, Virginia
Law Offices of Schwartz, Williams, and Gray   9:07AM

"Did you try his cell phone?"

"Yes, sir, right after I called his home. I only got his voice mail. No response from his pager, either."

Ira Schwartz frowns. "This isn't like him. He has court at 2:00PM. I'd better drive up to Montgomery County and see if something happened to him at home. Meanwhile, try and reach a neighbor to knock on his door."

northern Virginia   9:07AM

"You knew this day had to come, Judge," the man says evenly.

As Gray contemplates his death sentence a full pint of vomitus suddenly boils up, unstoppable as a train. His cheeks actually bulge out Dizzy Gillespie-like from the impact of the tidal wave—his nostrils spew twin jets of thin, yellow puke. He thrashes violently; his sinus cavity ablaze with 1.0pH juices ten times the strength of battery acid. Successive waves of nausea fill his lungs with with the corrosive fluid, putting Gray in a Panic beyond anything ever called the name, increasing exponentially with every second.

As Gray writhes in the damp, cold earth the man intones over and over, "Katherine Jessup. Katherine Jessup. Katherine Jessup."

The seconds tick off like millennia for Gray as his own body kills itself in a grostesque spectacle. He is a gurgling mass of agony. The woman's name reverberates within his mind. *Katherine Jessup? Katherine Jessup!* In his last coherent memory, Gray finally recalls the sunken face belonging to the emaciated frame of that druggie. *Pothead bitch! The law's the law!* Her image recedes to a phosphene-studded blackness as Gray ceases to struggle, his eyes wrenched wide open, unseeing.

There is no longer any movement from the pit. The man feels no remorse, and a strange calm falls on him. *Dogma creates karma, Judge Gray.* He only wishes that husband Tom Jessup, rather than a stranger, had settled the account, but life's double-entry bookkeeping is an imperfect process.

The man waits another minute and then begins uncapping the eight 5-gallon plastic jugs of NoClog drain cleaner. Bought with cash months ago from a janitorial supply house in South Carolina, no incriminating purchase records will ever surface. He carefully empties the 40 gallons over Gray's body, completely filling the plastic-lined pit. The highly caustic solution will make mulch of Gray in a matter of days. He will be heavy slurry in two weeks. In a month all physical and DNA evidence, including teeth and bones, will be destroyed. Even if the pit were discovered, forensics would not be able to determine what, much less *who*, had been buried there.

He wipes the NoClog jug spouts with one of Gray's socks. Then he hangs the sock and the rest of Gray's clothes on a dead twig and lights them on fire. He drops the ashes in the pool of NoClog, along with Gray's shoes. He cuts up the empty jugs with the scissors and drops the pieces in the pool. Retrieving the second plastic sheet from the trunk, he cuts it into small squares and drops them in the pit, along with the leather sap, empty bottle of water, and scissors. Finally, he turns his gloves inside-out and burns them.

Everything that had come in direct or indirect contact with Judge Gray during the morning is now being dissolved by 40 gallons of NoClog. There is zero physical evidence that Gray was ever in the Lincoln trunk.

The man blows on his sweaty palms for a few seconds, and then dons a new pair of surgical gloves. He wraps the 4'x6' sheet of plywood with the ground tarp and places it on the 6' long dirt shelf. It rests just inches over the pool of NoClog and will act as a roof for the dirt above. He chose exterior plywood, which is chemically treated to resist decay and rot. The wood roof should last at least a year.

He begins to fill the upper pit from the adjacent dirtpile. Bodies buried deeper than four feet will not be disturbed by animal and insect activity.

The man knows these things because he spent months in research. *Measure twice, cut once— measure once, cut twice* as his carpenter grandpa used to say. He knows that the grave will not likely be discovered by hikers, and that the police technology of ground radar enhancement and aerial infrared photography would be greatly hampered by the dense forest—assuming the police ever learned where to look in the first place.

Tamping the earth with a broken log, the pit is filled in 40 minutes. The man knows that a slight depression from settling is inevitable, which increases long-term risk of discovery. It is a fair bargain as the NoClog will have done its work by then. It is more important that Gray's pit not be found for at least a month. The excess dirt he flings about in a 360° pattern. He scatters twigs and leaves over the grave to match the surrounding terrain, then brushes clear his tracks as he steps backwards to his car.

No trace of the pit or his path can be seen.

He listens intently but the woods are peaceful.

Still wearing his gloves, he then bags the shovel. Next he carefully strips the trunk and floorboard of the plastic sheeting and bags it. Finally, he changes clothes and burns his jogging suit. There is little black smoke from the suit as he had chosen cotton over polyester after testing both. The gloves make a bit of smoke as they melt into an indistinct blob. He starts the Lincoln and heads back down the road.

Just a few last errands to do after he leaves the forest. First, he stops behind a grocery store dumpster near the highway, dons yet a new pair of gloves, and throws away the large bag containing the morning's evidence.

All soil evidence from the park and the woods is gone. Once the man gets home he will painstakingly wash and vacuum the car. He feels confident that no trace evidence remained, but thoroughness pays off.

I am 95% homefree.

He resumes his southbound highway travel.

Sixty miles down the road is an abandoned gas station in North Carolina, behind which the man parks. He puts on today's last pair of gloves. From the rear floorboard he gets a 4-ton floor jack and two pairs of jack stands. He jacks up the car front and rear, suspending it on the stands. Underneath an old faded canvas are the Lincoln's original wheels and hubcaps, which he swaps for the flea market truck tires and rims he has been driving on for two days. He returns the spare tire and jack to the trunk. It takes only 24 minutes. If investigators found any tire tracks by the Maryland park or in the Virginia woods, such would clue them to a ½-ton pickup. A luxury car is the last thing they'd be looking for.

Details. Planning. Success.

I am 98% homefree.

After a quick sponge bath and final change of clothes, he drives away feeling incredibly refreshed and relaxed. The digital clock reads 11:56. *Got it all done before noon!* the man thinks to himself as he reviews the entire morning in his mind. Something a detective once wrote occurs to him:

> *In every crime the perpetrator leaves something behind and takes something with him.*

He is confident that nobody saw him at the park or in the woods, that he did not leave behind any linkable forensic evidence, and that nothing of Jonathan Douglas Gray remains in his car or on his person. Having tanked up yesterday, there is no gas station video of him between Maryland and his home in North Carolina. Since he had slept in his car in the woods, there is no hotel record. During his trip he made no phone calls.

He ghosted into Montgomery County and ghosted out.

He reviews his intricate planning. He had made no previous contact with Gray, nor had he sent any angry letters to the editor about the Jessup case. His operation notes he never put to paper. He did his planning on computer and saved the encrypted Notepad files only to floppy diskette, not the hard drive. After he had flawlessly memorized the details, he software shredded the files before burning the internal mylar disk and flushing its ashes down a public toilet.

The interstate aspect of the operation will greatly complicate matters for investigators. The abduction took place in Maryland, the burial in Virginia, and he lives in North Carolina. The man knew firsthand that the more agencies involved in a case, the greater odds of interdepartmental foot-dragging and disinterest. As the FBI had jurisdiction over kidnapping, the turf-war between the Bureau and any state authorities wouldn't help, either.

There was simply nothing to link him with Gray, much less indicate his involvement in the abduction. The only thing that could hang him was his own tongue, and the man would carry this secret to the grave.

I am 99.9999% homefree.

There are no absolute certainties in life but somethings are practically 100%. His remaining uncaught was one of them. He knew he had only a 1 in 1,000,000 chance of apprehension. After the FBI had knocked their heads against the wall for weeks, they'd know it too.

He silently congratulated himself on his fine planning and execution. It was just as Sun-Tzu had written—every battle is won *before* it is fought.

The state calls its own violence law, but that of the individual crime.
— Max Stirner

Montgomery County, Maryland   7:41PM

To William Almond, a junior FBI Assistant Special Agent in Charge (ASAC) of the Baltimore FO, the Gray disappearance has all the hallmarks of a kidnapping. Gray's term on the bench had seen many controversial cases. He was a prime target for the rash of retribution fomented by Harold Krassny last year.

After searching Gray's home, agents learned that his car was still garaged and that he had not made any phone calls or emails which indicated travel plans. He neither boarded an airplane or train, nor rented a car. His credit card records showed no activity since the previous evening. The morning paper still lay on the sidewalk. Since Gray had phoned a colleague from home after a late dinner, everything pointed to a morning abduction.

His friends all say that Gray jogged religiously in his nearby park, so the agents cordon off the park and canvass the neighborhood for witnesses. They soon get lucky.

A pretty redhead agent had been transferred from Utah to the Alexandria branch of the WFO[1]. (All agents had to do a mandatory five years in a top-ten FO.) She liked the area and requested to remain there. Personnel Branch sent her to the Baltimore FO. Because of her outrigger ears she had been nicknamed "Wingnut" years ago. A good agent, she hit paydirt.

One resident across the park thinks she might have seen a white domestic sedan (*"it was boxy"*) parked around dawn, but can't be totally sure.

Now we're getting somewhere Almond thinks to himself. *The park. That's where I would have snatched him.* He directs his agents to focus on that area of the park and street. The earlier drizzle compounds the difficulty of searching for clues in the dark. They find some large footprints leading from the jogging path to the street, but nothing else. In the street they find the two cigarette butts, but aren't sure if they're connected to the case.

The FBI has a vehicle description which could be anything from a Buick to a Cadillac, and a few footprints—neither of which necessarily had anything whatever to do with Gray. The vehicle description is too vague for an APB (All Points Bulletin) or even a BOLO (Be On The Lookout). Besides, after fourteen hours it could be in Florida by now.

The Asian forensics tech is very good, even though he is only thirty. Lou has been with the Baltimore FO for two years. Almond likes him.

---

1   Washington Field Office

Lou describes the scene. "The plaster casts of the size 12 footprints are too indistinct to identify but they were from running shoes, and very worn ones. The depth of the prints indicate a weight of 350 to 400 pounds."

Almond nods appreciatively. "Either a really fat guy had just taken up jogging or one man was toting something heavy, such as a body."

Lou grins. "Just so."

"What else?"

"OK, Gray came from his home and would have been running north up the path there. Now, look behind this tree. See how the grass has been bedded down? Perfect place of concealment for an ambush."

Almond asks, "Any litter or markings on the tree?"

"No, nothing."

"One perp or two?"

Lou says, "Almost definitely one. There's not enough trampling for two, and very little even for one. He wasn't here long."

Almond thinks for a moment. "That suggests he knew Gray's jogging routine, which means prior surveillance. It was a well-planned abduction, not something spontaneous and opportunistic. This was no park goblin."

"Agreed," says Lou.

Almond asks, "How do you think he took him down?"

"Can't say for sure. Since nobody heard any gunshots we can probably rule out a firearm. He could have used a suppressor but we both know that's pretty rare. If you want a SWAG[2], I'd say that he either tasered or sapped him. Quiet, leaving no blood and the fewest clues. It's got plausible deniability, too. If anyone came across them the assailant could say that he found some jogger who collapsed from a heart attack. 'Wait here while I go for help'—that sort of thing."

Almond slowly nods and says, "Yeah, that makes sense. How do you think he got him out of the park?"

"He carried him up there," Lou says. They both walk up the knoll, being careful to flank the flagged footprints.

"Look behind these bushes. See how there's more trampling of the grass? He carried Gray here, set him down briefly to see if the street was clear. Then he either signals his smoking female driver or he carries Gray to his parked vehicle. No discernible tire tracks. Remember, it happened nearly fourteen hours ago, and it's been sleeting off and on all day. Big, white, domestic four-door the lady said?"

"Yeah, but didn't know the make. Didn't notice which state the plate was, either. Our only witness so far. Wingnut's writing up the 302[3] now."

---

2   Scientific Wild Ass Guess
3   FBI Document-302 reports are FBI witness statements.

Lou is mildly disgusted. "No make, no state? Typical zero situational awareness. People have no eye for details these days."

"If they did, we wouldn't need *you*, now would we?" Almond counters with a grin. "So, got any ideas on this?"

Lou thinks for a bit and answers, "Well, something like a Caprice or a Sedan deVille would have been smart. Common, innocuous, and with a trunk plenty big enough for a body. Worst thing in this wealthy hood would have been a van or a pickup with a camper. That'd have stood out like denim shorts at the opera. Use a clean, white OldsmoBuick and nobody will ever see you. Toss in Gray and drive away. From taking him down to starting the car meant less than sixty seconds. Two minutes, tops."

Almond is staring far away, pondering this.

Lou continues, "He chose a spot in the park closest to the street, yet with perfect terrain for surprise. And he did it just before dawn when everyone's still asleep and it's too dark to see anything anyway. Very slick. Textbook snatch."

Almond says, "And the weather. I wouldn't be surprised if he even waited for a nasty day like this to obscure any clues."

"Yeah, I was thinking that, too," Lou agrees.

They are both silent for a moment and then Lou says, "Bill, I don't think we're gonna find much more than we already have. We've got no real witness, and the only thing that ties him to this park is the soil on his shoes. I'd be sort of astonished if he's still wearing them. They're probably at the bottom of the Chesapeake Bay by now. This guy doesn't seem to be the type who makes many mistakes."

"No, he doesn't, does he?" Almond echoes. Something occurs to him. "You know, he's so meticulous and organized—I'll bet he's a loner."

"You think so?"

"Yeah, I do. I don't think those Virginia Slims have anything to do with this, not that they shouldn't be analyzed. *Female* getaway driver? You know how rare that is."

"Yeah, I see your point," Lou agrees.

Almond continues, "Planned and executed the whole thing himself, including doing his own driving. He's quiet and thorough. He wouldn't trust anybody else. And he won't blab about it down at the Rusty Udder, either."

"What mistakes would you say he *did* make?" asks the tech.

"You mean besides having done it in the first place?" Almond mulls this over for a bit and says, "Well, as far as the op itself, it was damn clean. Although he left footprints and his car was likely seen by at least one witness, I can't see how either were avoidable. But if it were me, I'd have done things differently. Waited for Gray at or in his home, done him inside for privacy, and then driven him away in his own BMW. That way, no suspicious vehicle would have been seen in the neighborhood. It also would have increased his time line by at least a day or two since we wouldn't have known if Gray simply took off on some secret *rendezvous* to shack up with a woman."

Lou says, "Yeah, that'd make my job even tougher."

Almond smirks. "Hell, to *really* muddy the trail, send an email from Gray's computer to his office telling them to cancel his week's appointments because some urgent personal matter came up. Dump the car later, with or without Gray, depending on how you wanted it to look. Get him drunk and put him in it over a cliff, whatever. Yeah, that's the way a *pro* would have done it, if only to enhance the time line and case confusion. So, maybe this guy isn't actually a working hitter. I'm thinking he's an amateur who now has some valuable experience at Judge Gray's expense."

The tech nods in agreement. "*Hmmm*, that makes sense. Hey, you know I once testified in Gray's court about five years ago? Seemed like a high-handed ass to me. Was a real bulldog for Justice, I heard. Hated anti-government types. I saw him send a guy away for three years—just some average Joe who had an AR15 with an M16 hammer and didn't know it."

Almond frowns with recollection. "Oh, *right!* What a shitty deal."

"Yeah, lost his business. Wife left him. Everyone but ATF and IRS thought it was pretty fucked. Hell, F-Troop[4] probably switched the parts."

"Wouldn't be the first time," Almond snorts.

Lou is suddenly animated. "Oh, *shit!*—remember that cancer woman who grew pot for the nausea? The one who died in FPC? Geez, what a flap *that* caused! That was Gray, too. Hey, you think this could be another KK? The prick was a perfect candidate, you know."

KK was Bureau slang for "Krassny Krime." Some waggish agent in the WFO came up with the acronym and it stuck.

Almond had been wondering the same thing since he first arrived. *Is this KK34?* He decides to be noncommittal. "Too early to tell. We'll look into any threats made on Gray."

"Yeah, and I'll bet you find a bunch, too. The guy was *un*loved, even for a federal judge."

Special Agent Almond has a bad feeling about the case. Somehow he senses—knows, even—that Jonathan Douglas Gray is probably very, very dead, and will likely never, never be found.

He's done what he can for the evening. "OK, thanks, Lou. Good work. Let's call it a night here. We'll keep the park cordoned off and interview any joggers who show up tomorrow morning. Maybe they saw or heard something. I'm going back to the office to see if there were any morning NCIC requests on any vehicles which could be our man's. Maybe a clean, white OldsmoBuick got stopped for speeding or something."

---

4   A disparaging name used by many federal agents for the ATF.

Lou is skeptical. "Yeah . . . maybe."

"Hey, they caught the Son of Sam through a parking ticket."

"True. I'll call if I come up with anything more, but I'm not hopeful. I'll do some impression tests around dawn to get a better estimate of the guy's weight at the same soil temperature. Gray weighed 165 according to his DL, so I may be able to narrow the abductor's weight to within 20 or 30 pounds. And, we may find some trace evidence during the day—when we can *see*."

"Right. Talk to you in the morning. Tomorrow I'll look for any security cameras between here and the highway. That's paid off before."

Lou grins. "Big Brother is watching. Hey, speaking of which, you got flags on all his credit cards?"

"Yeah, but I doubt anything'll hook. Wallet was found on his dresser intact. No credit cards missing. You dusted the place and came up with *nada*. I'm sure the guy never entered the residence."

"Yeah. Got his package in the park and hauled ass."

"Yep, that's about it. Grab-n-go."

"Oh, well. We'll keep at it. We could get lucky, you know. You find Gray and the guy who took him, you're senior ASAC for sure. Then you can finally get a Bucar and leave your crappy POV at home."

Almond grins. "Gee, thanks. Then I'll get to be your boss someday. Were you planning on a *lengthy* career with the Bureau?"

2009 USA political news

There are more instances of the abridgement of the freedom of the people by gradual and silent encroachment of those in power than by violent and sudden usurpations.
—James Madison

To say that a government that serves the people is allowed to disarm the people is a simple contradiction in terms and a legal impossibility.
—Donald M. Smith

On the 75th anniversary of the *National Firearms Act* of 1934, Congress passes the *Assault Weapons Registration Act* of 2009 which declares all *"assault weapons"* to be *"destructive devices"* under the *NFA34*. Those owners (who had already complied with *DWA 2007*) unwilling or unable to meet the registration criteria and pay the now $1,000 tax must surrender their weapons within 90 days. Companies selling gun parts and accessories are raided for their customer lists. Many firms (having been tipped off by sympathetic cops) shred their hard drives beforehand, thwarting the raids. Dozens of ATF raids on gunowners result in bloody shootouts.

Vice President Wiedermann is investigated for income tax fraud.

After wisely waiting until after its hosting of the 2008 Olympics, China goads Taiwan into declaring independence and then invades the *"renegade province."* The Western nations pout furiously, just as they did in response to Hitler during the 1930s.

2009 USA privacy news

It will soon be possible to assert almost continuous control over every citizen and to maintain up-to-date files containing even the most personal details about health and personal behavior of every citizen, in addition to the more customary data. These files will be subject to instantaneous retrieval by the authorities. Power will gravitate into the hands of those who control information.
        —Zbigniew Brzezinski, "The Technotronic Era"

Since the encryption cat was long out of the bag, Congress copied the British *Regulation of Investigatory Powers Act of 2000* (R.I.P.) which allows the courts to demand from defendants (at the threat of contempt of court for noncompliance) their encryption passphrases. In response to Americans destroying their hard drive encryption keys before seizure, Congress passes *CALEA III* which makes a federal felony of failure to willfully provide functioning keys and passphrase pursuant to a court order. Although this is in direct conflict with 5th Amendment protection against compelled self-testimony, the ACLU and other alleged civil liberty organizations are curiously muted in their opposition to *CALEA III.* Burden of proof for willfulness is now on the defendant, just as in Britain. Britain never had a pesky 5th Amendment, and now neither does America.

CALEA III also requires in every new vehicle RFID (Radio Frequency Identification) VIN chips, which are trackable by satellite.

A police state is a small price to pay for living in the freest country on earth!
        —C. Montgomery Burns

2009 USA economic news

The OPEC nations, including Russia, formally adopt the *Euro* as their account currency—dumping the US dollar. Since nearly two-thirds of all dollars circulated overseas (giving the US Government interest-free credit), these former Eurodollars have no choice but to "come home," thus wrecking the price/goods equilibrium.

People rush into gold, which rockets to $2,278/ounce. All other commodities The Dow falls to 3,721. Annual inflation is 21%.

Washington, D.C.   **FBIHQ**   **July 2009**

The FBI is comprised of Divisions, which have Sections, which have Units. Divisions are headed by Assistant Directors (ADs), Sections by Deputy Assistant Directors (DADs), and Units by Chiefs.

The Assistant Director of the Criminal Investigations Division (CID) heads up the Bureau's most important division, with 70% of its agents. He had called a meeting of his Section Deputy Assistant Directors to discuss the KKs for his briefing of the Director and the rest of the FBI brass before they leave for vacation in August. Present are the DADs of General Crimes (GC), Counter-Terrorism (CT), Terrorism Section (TS), and the Chief of Terrorist Research and Analysis Center (TRAC), a Unit of TS.

Also in attendance is the Chief of the Special Operations and Research Unit (SOARU) from the FBI National Academy, a unit which began as the Terrorist Research and Management Staff under chain-smoking, ex-Marine Conrad "Connie" Hassel. The unit, informally known as "the wild bunch," originally had to make do in the basement—between the gun-cleaning room and Hoover's old fallout shelter. SOARU, a sort of SWAT think-tank, is known for its superb CT-planning and support.

The Homeland Security liaison was also present.

The Assistant Director's 7th floor office has a panoramic view of Pennsylvania Avenue and the Mall, although the optical quality of several inches of bulletproof glass is less than crystal-clear. It is a typically muggy July day. He begins the meeting by asking the TRAC Chief, "Have you uncovered any organization, any links?"

"No, sir. Harold Krassny acted alone—just as he wrote in his suicide note—and had no accomplices. The copycat murders and abductions against VIPs are apparently being committed by lone, sporadic perpetrators, all UNSUBs[5]. It's like a multi-headed serial killer. Their only link so far seems to be Krassny's publicized idea. It's the Bureau's worst nightmare: a solitary crazed individual who, by his warped example, foments a string of action by like individuals, none of whom know each other. If a single-person 'cell' can conceive, plot, and execute a deadly crime, leaving little or no evidence, and then manage not to brag about it to a friend or bartender, then there is less than a 2% chance of his apprehension. Such a perpetrator has only 1 in 63 odds of capture. This is not widely known by the public."

The AD nods. "And let's keep it that way. Disclosure would only encourage the unstable. Go on."

"Since the victims are particularly chosen by their assailants for purposes of retribution, we have been analyzing any threatening correspondence, emails, and letters to newspaper editors. The smart perps, however, would never have threatened their targets or complained in a public forum."

---

5   UNknown SUBjects

To the DAD of Terrorism Section, the AD asks, "Who have we identified as potentially at risk?"

"Based on the characteristics of the thirty nine victims so far, we've constructed a list of VIPs whom we believe are at heightened risk. Predictably, it reads like a *Who's Who*. The list includes virtually everyone of any prominence in the Democratic National Party, liberal Republicans, TV and film production, media, and radical environmental organizations. At the top of the list are those who have what Krassnyites would consider extremely liberal credentials. Since eight of the victims were, or had been, federal judges, we've paid close attention to the judiciary. Judges and U.S. Attorneys who've been involved in controversial tax and gun cases, as well as everyone involved with Ruby Ridge and Waco, have all been notified to take precautions. Many of them have hired armed security. As you know, the Bureau has offered anyone on the risk list firearms training at Quantico."

"Any takers?" the AD asks, mostly out of general curiosity.

"Yes, sir. Several, however the shooting instructors tell me that judges are even worse students than doctors. Their God-complex inhibits learning and subordination."

Several in the room chuckle at this.

"Did Judge Gray go through the course? He was a friend of mine, you know," the AD says.

"No, sir, he declined the course. Said he wouldn't live in fear."

"A pity. He might have had a chance in that park. Any progress in his investigation? Any ransom note?"

The DAD of Terrorism Section answers, "No, sir, no note. No progress. It's gone completely stale these past five months. No witnesses, no video evidence, and no useful forensic evidence. We fear that Judge Gray is probably dead. At this point, the only leads we'll likely get are when we find his body, which may be never. The case agents are not optimistic—sorry."

The AD is solemn, pensive.

The Deputy Assistant Director of Counter-Terrorism speaks up. "Sir, we think we may have learned something interesting."

"Yes? Go on, Cliff," says the AD.

"Although the phenomenon originated from the right-wing, the eco-extremists and corporate-bashers seem to be chiming in. It's surprising to see that both sides have many common enemies, such as those in international banking and multinational corporations benefitting from GATT and NAFTA. We recommend expanding the general investigation to suspected left-wing domestic terrorists. We could see some proactive success there."

The AD comments, "Good idea, Cliff. Go with it. You know, I'm still amazed that this whole thing hasn't broken in the news."

"I don't think they'd ever touch it, sir. Remember that guy in Washington state back in 1995 who posted that Internet essay 'Assassination Politics'? It described the idea of awarding anonymous cash prizes to those who 'predicted' the death of government employees who violated the Bill of Rights. It was nothing less than a call for a wave of assassinations. The media barely reported it."

The DAD of Terrorism Section retorts, "You're comparing fruits to nuts, Cliff. James Dalton Bell was nipped in the bud. IRS took him down two years later. Bell was a crackpot, but Krassny was a *successful* crackpot who got away with two murders has so far engendered nearly two-dozen copycat crimes that we *know* of. The *only* thing that will prevent this story from breaking is if we persuade the TV execs that they are *personally* at risk from the Krassnyites, and that publicizing their successes will only embolden them. The KK perps are Internet savvy, and so far it's only an Internet locus of origin. That works to our favor because it's a community and it can be tracked. Even in 2009 over half the American public does not surf the Net, thank God. Broadcast stories on network TV about abducted and murdered VIPs—and the Bureau's inability to do anything about it—and this thing would go from epidemic to *pandemic*. Instead of 39 cases, how about 1,039? It'd turn into a shooting gallery. We'd never catch up. Remember the D.C. sniper back in 2002? We all worked on that for weeks; everything else was back-burnered. This Krassny thing breaks on national TV and the entire Bureau will be slammed with new cases. Sir, I recommend that we ask for a media blackout under *USA PATRIOT* Act II."

"I understand your feelings, Fred, but the Director will deal with that when the time comes," the AD replies. "Now, who can tell me more about the kidnappings?"

The DAD of General Crimes is heard for the first time. "The abductions are causing the most concern amongst case agents. From an investigative standpoint, finding bodies would be preferable. And, the victims' families would have closure. But when a former Deputy Commerce Secretary simply vanishes with no warning or ransom note, we must establish that he didn't merely run off with his mistress. Before that, we must first establish if he even *had* a mistress to run off *with*. Inexplicable disappearances cost us nearly a week of time interviewing family and acquaintances, and analyzing phone and email records, airline reservation and credit-card data, security-camera tapes, and so forth.

"Then, once we've established that he is not *willfully* missing, we must then rule out the possibility of a solitary accident. Did he drive into a ravine? Have a boating accident? Get lost hiking in the Rockies and fall down a mine-shaft? All of these possibilities must be eliminated before we can finally conclude foul play, and even then we're never *really* quite certain until we get a break. So, by *not* leaving a body the perpetrators automatically gain a week head start."

"It's like we get hit with a seven-day handicap right from the beginning," the AD observes.

"Exactly, sir. And after a week, any clues they might have left are likely stale, contaminated, or destroyed."

"Have any bodies of the abductees been discovered?" asks the AD.

"No, sir. Of the twenty-three we have classified as likely Krassnyite victims, only six were found at the crime scene. None of the other seventeen have so far been found. We do, however, expect some of them to start turning up. It is quite tedious and time-consuming to totally dispose of a body, especially without witnesses. Short of incineration or chemical decomposition through acids or alkalies, human remains have a stubborn habit of surfacing. Hunters and hikers are constantly discovering buried remains. We believe that the perpetrators are inexperienced, even though they have so far managed to avoid apprehension. As amateurs, they are bound to have made *some* errors, so it's just a matter of time before we get forensic leads. From there we may get DNA, tire tracks, fingerprints, cigarette-butts, witnesses, security-camera evidence, etc.

"At the moment, however, we see no breakthroughs on the horizon, and five of these cases are over four months old. The agents must move on to fresher cases after that much time."

The AD nods. He had been a Philadelphia Special Agent and SAC, and well understood case work. "What about the six murders?"

"We may soon have a break there. Four of the murders have similar MOs, suggesting two serial actors. One pair were stabbed; the other shot. Analysis of ballistic evidence looks promising. Spent shell cases were found at both crime scenes. An identical H&K .45 USP was used. We're comparing the cases to our database[6]. If the handgun was made after 2000 and if it hasn't been stolen or altered, we should be able to identify the owner through NICS[7] data. We're cautiously optimistic on this."

"Glad to hear that. What about the stabbing victims? Any success there?" asks the AD.

"Not yet, sir. But unless lots of hydrogen peroxide is used it is very difficult to totally remove all blood residue from surfaces, and we'll likely be

---

6   Since 2000, several manufacturers such as H&K, Glock, Ruger, and S&W have been providing fired-rounds from their new handguns to the FBI before delivering them to market. Although such ballistic evidence is of dubious crime-fighting value, it provides a pretext for the eventual owner registration of handguns.

7   **National Instant Check System**, an unconstitutional computerized background screening program for people who buy firearms through federally licensed dealers on ATF Form 4473. Immediately after the purchaser has been cleared for the transaction, the NICS data is by law supposed to be destroyed in order to prevent the formation of a database of gun owners. As is typical of government's *"Do as I say, not as I do"* attitude, NICS data is never destroyed.

able to tie the knife to the two victims once we locate their assailant. His knife won't help us catch him, but it will help us convict him."

The AD says, "OK, what about backtracking this whole thing? Working from the point of contagion, so to speak. We know that Krassny posted his deeds on the Internet via several dozen websites, chat rooms, and forums. What about traffic analysis of log-ons? We learn of these people the same way they learned of Krassny. That'd give us an initial lead base to work with."

The Counter-Terrorism DAD picks up the baton. "Yes, sir, we're already on it. Many of those sites are visited through secondary browsers, such as anonymizer.com. This muddies the trail considerably. What has been more profitable is to DCS1000 search for all emails which contained URL links to Krassny posts. Let's say that Smith originally happens upon such a post. Though he declines Krassny's example, he forwards the link to Jones, who is made of more volatile stuff. And Jones to Brown, and so forth.

"We are concentrating on individuals who sent and/or received the most number of Krassny posts. From there, we compare them to rosters of known hate criminals, militia members, illegal tax protestors, sovereign citizen types, patriot agitators, etc. Within this list, we focus on males under 35 and those over 60, meaning males likely without families. Given the intellectual and physical demands of committing these crimes, we tend to dismiss the very young and the very old, such as under 25 and over 70."

"But Krassny was in his—what?—mid-80s, and he successfully killed two men," observes the AD.

"Yes sir, but we think he was the exception that will prove the rule. An octogenarian may have started this, but we doubt it's the elderly who are keeping it going. Another filter we are developing will flag those who have suffered recent psychological triggers, such as death of a loved one, divorce, bankruptcy, or loss of job. For example, Krassny had recently lost his wife and two grown children. TRAC is helping us to define other search parameters, such as prior military service—especially combat experience. Commercial and government databases are 98% linked today, fortunately. We couldn't have done this ten, or even five, years ago."

The AD seems impressed. "And who have you come up with?"

"At the moment, we are interested in eleven possibles and are analyzing their travel, phone, and email records to see if we can place them near the time and location of any these deaths and abductions. It's a long shot, but four of these men have suspicious travel patterns and two of them are good friends."

"Do you think these two were accomplices in some of these crimes?"

"We can't say. We do know that they didn't travel together, but they may have compared tactics with each other. Both are well-known 'patriot' agitator-types. Both gun-nuts. Both Marine Corps vets. Bradford is a farmer in

Lander, Wyoming, and Swan is a diesel mechanic in Logan, Utah. They're
four hours apart by car, and their wives are second cousins. They stay in regular touch by PGP encrypted email, which we have yet to break."

"Farmers and mechanics using PGP. That's just great," the AD sighs.
"NSA had their chance to nip all that in the bud twenty years ago and now we
have to deal with common terrorists using unbreakable encryption."

The Counter-Terrorism DAD ignores this and continues, "It was the
farmer who emailed the mechanic the Krassny posts. Within weeks—"

The TRAC Chief interrupts with, "How do you know *that* if they're
both using PGP?"

"Good question. Although Bradford's email text was encrypted, sub-
ject lines are not. One read 'check out this link!!!' Once Swan decrypted
Bradford's email, he then clicked on an enclosed URL which had posted
Krassny's suicide letter. We know this from analyzing Swan's surf history."

"Good work. Go on," the AD says.

"Thank you, sir. Within weeks both of them took independent trips to
Denver according to their gas card and hotel receipts. From what we can tell,
neither of them had any business or family reason for their travel."

The AD says, "Denver. Those three abductions?"

"Yes, sir. The dates show some correlation to their travel. Furthermore, email traffic analysis shows a flurry of communication just prior to and
after all three Denver crimes."

The Assistant Director looks skeptical.

"It's thin but it's the only thing with any promise," the Counter-Terrorism DAD allows.

"Do you have PC for a search warrant?"

"We're a long way from that. We *are* monitoring their phones and
email, however. First bit of incriminating evidence we hear, we'll get warrants. The judges are very interested in some resolution here."

"No doubt. I'm assuming you've yet to question these two."

"Correct. We don't want to alarm them this early. We installed GPS
tracking beacons in their vehicles. Their names are flagged in all travel computers. With any luck, they will act again. If they drive or fly within one hundred miles of any VIP on our list, we'll be alerted immediately."

The AD says, "We don't have that kind of time. The Director demands
a break in this before he goes on vacation in August. So do I. I want their
computers key-sniffed for passphrases. On my authority, go proactive with
Magic Lantern and DIRT[8]. I'm scheduling another meeting for next week,
same time. Have something new for me then."

---

8   **Data Interception by Remote Transmission**, a computer monitoring program that can be unde-
tectably installed on a target computer by email. It transmits a record of user keystrokes to authorities each time
the user goes online.

* * * * * * *

"Good afternoon, Director. It's a pleasure to meet you. May I say that I was personally very pleased with your nomination, and feel very confident that the Bureau is under excellent helmsmanship."

"Thank you, Agent Bleth, I appreciate your sentiments. I'm looking forward to the next ten years. Now, I've read your reports on the Wyoming newcomers and their growing control of the counties and legislature. You've been on this since 2007?"

"Yes, Director. Since just a few months after their first election when they took over five counties out of the blue. During these past two years, I've learned much more about them and their agenda."

"Good. Let's hear it."

The White House, Oval Office   July 2009

The President looks up from his desk as his new FBI Director Paul Klein is ushered in. "Hi, Paul. Thanks for coming over. So, what do you have on this Wyoming election thing?"

"It took a little over two years to piece it together, but the Bureau is confident of its conclusions," the Director answers.

"Five months ago the Bureau *had* no conclusions. What was the breakthrough here?"

"Email traffic, Mr. President. Their imperfect security measures and occasionally unencrypted email. We learn more through email analysis than most people realize. DCS1000 gives us tremendous leverage in communication surveillance. Over 95% of the work is completely automated. Also, the NSA finally gave us the help we needed with their quantum computer. Once we had assembled a useful list of target names, words, phrases, and addresses, the picture more or less painted itself."

"It's those Free State Project people, right?"

"In part, yes, sir. It began as a splinter group from the FSP's October 2003 vote for New Hampshire. Nearly 20% of their 5,500 membership were split between New England and the Rocky Mountains. We've suspected from the start that the Western membership had probably struck out on their own. Now we have more of an understanding of their schedule, key players, etc."

"Do they have anything to do with this wave of kidnapping and assassination brought on by that Krassny fellow?"

"We've uncovered no links to the Krassnyites so far, Mr. President. We do, however, expect two search warrants regarding the Denver crimes."

"Are these subjects Wyoming newcomers?"

"No, sir. In fact, only one is from Wyoming and he was born there."

The President frowns. "OK. So, what's the newcomer agenda?"

"The recent libertarians plan to progressively take over the political structure of the state—probably over the course of eight years and three election cycles: 2006, 2010, and 2014."

The President's mouth slightly drops open. "Can that even be done?"

"Theoretically, yes. It's just a matter of the right numbers moving into the state on a coordinated basis. They have already elected and installed five county governments and about 17% of the state legislators. Federal agencies such as the FBI, DEA, ATF, and IRS report extremely diminished cooperation in those counties. Justice is looking into what can be done about that. Next November is their second general election cycle, and they will try to add another five to seven counties to give them nearly half the state geographically, and about 30% of the legislature."

The President says, "I know it's a 'free country' and all, but something about this makes me uneasy. It's just so . . . so *unprecedented*."

"I completely agree, Mr. President. We'll keep on top of it."

Although we are certainly correct to wail about the metastasization of the modern Police State, we are forgetting its crucial prerequisite: our prior abandonment of a countervailing culture. Laws can only advance into the previously occupied territory of culture. When culture shrinks, laws are soon passed to fill the vacuum.

The 2nd Amendment and your right to own and carry tools for self-defense is obviously the prime example here. One hundred years ago, it would have been wholly unthinkable to propose, much less pass, a bill restricting—much less prohibiting outright— the open carry of a personal handgun. Or the purchase of one. Or the shooting of verminous prairie dogs. Or the hunting of wild game. The shooting and hunting culture was far too deep and widespread.

By 2000, however, our culture had shrunk considerably which of course invited its residual elimination by a vast network of laws. We had gradually acquiesced to the most outrageous of 'Simon Says' regulations and ridiculous restrictions. The gun industry pretzeled itself into every contortion demanded by Congress, to the ridiculous point of making pump-action AR15s and AK47s to avoid the 'assault weapons' ban on military-pattern semi-autos.

We barely caught on in time to have saved ourselves. In order to regain our lost ground, we organized more gun shows and transformed them into almost community-wide events, with games, competitions, prizes, celebrities, and delicious new foods. The .50 caliber shoots were an example.

We embarked on a serious drive to introduce youngsters to the fun of shooting. Culturally, we were soon to die off if we didn't. We "adopted" sons of single moms and took them regularly to the gun range or ranch for an afternoon of plinking. Then, after a few years, to their first deer hunt. In short, we made a conscious and calculated effort to transfer manhood to boys in the manner done for thousands of years. A grown male who had somehow not become a man is a sickening spectacle and makes eventually for an untenable society. We taught boys by the thousands how to shoot, how to box, how to hunt (and why), how to speak the truth firmly and without equivocation, how to recognize and properly court a decent young lady (assuming he could find one), how to stand up for his rights and dignity, and how to honor his own integrity above all things. This was only possible by getting the poor boys away from

that infernal TV set, which will over time reduce mind and morals to mush—precisely as it was designed to.
We began to take back cultural ground, leaving the laws with less and less fertile soil in which to flourish. Truth and manliness once again began to be respected. All this, however, has only been the beginning of the beginning. We are still quite far from yet being out of the woods, but at least now we have some breathing room before the pressing of the grapes of wrath.
— James Wayne Preston, *Journals*

Logan, Utah   January 2010

Frank Edwin Swan is a gun owner. Federal NICS records (that is, the ones which by law are to be destroyed after the purchaser's background check has been approved) show that Swan had purchased a Bushmaster AR15 and Beretta 92 in 1999. Thus, he is know to have only a .223 and 9mm. However, in 2003 Swan bought a thick green paperback book which changed his life. He sold his AR and Beretta at a large Salt Lake City gunshow and traded up to a Springfield Armory® Squad Scout M1A™ .308 battle rifle and a .45 Glock 21. These guns he legally bought from private sellers with cash, thus creating no NICS records at all.

The .308 is over twice as powerful as the .223, and can perforate much more cover. One round from a .308 will drop a man for good, whereas two to five rounds are required from a .223. Similarly, the .45ACP is a significantly better stopper than the 9mm, especially when using FMJ.

Swan's Glock 21 needed nothing but tritium night sights. Before retiring for the night, he always attached to the frame rail a powerful tactical white light. Over 70% of defensive gunfire happens at night, so being able to illuminate your threat was paramount. Legally, morally, and tactically you cannot shoot at anything you haven't first positively identified as a legitimate threat.

Because it was an American-made rifle with no pistol grip, a post-ban M1A could (under the 1994 *"Crime Bill"*) have a flash suppressor. Swan replaced the stock part for a Smith Enterprise Vortex. Made of forged 8620 hardened steel (just like the M1 and M14), the Vortex was brutally strong and totally eliminated muzzle flash from the 18" barrel. Thus, Swan would not blind himself during a nighttime gunfight.

With a hunting 5 round magazine, his defensive M1A even doubled as a deer rifle if necessary. Finally, he mounted an Aimpoint CompM2 red-dot sight, and a SureFire tactical light.

Next, Swan experimented with different surplus ammo until he found that Portuguese FMJ was the most accurate in his rifle. Sold by mail order in 1,000 round lots for only 15¢/round delivered, Swan bought several thousand rounds. He could not even begin to reload his own ammo for 15¢/round, especially for what his time was worth. His friends kidded him for buying so much, but Swan had learned from that big green book that *"ammo turns money into skill"* and that it was preferable to have 900 rounds of skill and 100rds of ammo, versus 1,000 rounds of ammo and no skill.

Possibly being in a gunfight means risking incoming fire, so Swan thought it prudent to buy a bulletproof vest. He learned to avoid any vest made of Zylon or Goldflex (which permanently degrade from humidity and light over time, and got several cops killed or injured before being recalled). Kevlar aramid was the only way to go. Level IIIA protection (which will stop nearly all handgun rounds) was the best balance between cost, protection, and wearability. He picked a US Armor IIIA with a Level IV (rifle protection) titanium shock plate.

The vest carrier was also important. For home defense, he chose a police tactical model which had a built-in holster and several utility pouches. The garment hung on his bedpost by his nightstand. Also on the bedpost were a pair of Peltor electronic shooting muffs which amplified inaudible sounds but blocked out gunfire. Wearing his Peltors, Swan could clearly hear a whispered conversation in another part of the house. (He proved this with friends one evening, to their stunned amazement. They then all bought their own.)

His final item of apparel was a bedside pair of slip-on boots.

If ever woken up in the middle of the night by something suspicious, Swan required less than fifteen seconds to put on his boots, vest, and ears to investigate matters. His M1A was under the bed if he ever needed it quickly.

Although his child support and alimony payments took much of Swan's income, he worked overtime for many months in order to afford training back in 2004 at the world-renowned defensive shooting academies of Gunsite in Arizona and Thunder Ranch of Texas. The handgun and rifle courses cost nearly $1,000 each in tuition, not including travel, ammo, lodging, etc. Swan considered the money well spent—the training invaluable. He felt confident that he could defend himself during a lethal emergency.

Unbeknownst to him, he would soon have his chance to find out.

Washington, D.C.
J. Edgar Hoover FBI Building   January 2010

The Assistant Director of the Criminal Investigation Division grimaces at the mountain of folders on his walnut desk. Violent Census 2010 protests, attacks on Federal Reserve officials and buildings, and civil unrest. *It never ends!* Jerome Devereaux oversees all intrusive techniques, such as wiretaps, Magic Lantern insertions, "sneak and peek" warrants, long-term undercover ops, stings, etc. He picks up two folders from the top of the stack. The proposed joint raids in Utah and Wyoming. He's been under tremendous pressure for over a year to produce an arrest in the Krassnyite phenomenon.

Finally, western agents are ready to search and question two suspects. They are both gun owners and members of 2nd Amendment groups. Both harbor anti-government views.

Both had been to Denver near the time of the three abductions.

Devereaux knows that the probable cause is based only on weak circumstantial evidence, but the Bureau cannot continue to be accused of "doing nothing." Not when judges, congressmen, and VIPs are being kidnapped and murdered at the rate of two a month.

The AD signs off on the two raids as Active SCI (Sensitive Compartmented Information). US Attorneys in Casper and Salt Lake City would strictly curtail dissemination of the case details.

Maybe we'll get a break.

Then the American people will see the Bureau taking action.

Positive public perception is the FBI's greatest asset. The Bureau learned this most poignantly as it had been gradually lost during years of scandals of Ruby Ridge, Waco, Whitewater-gate, Jewell-gate, Foster-gate, Laptop-gate, Missing MP5s-gate, 9/11-gate, Crime Lab-gate, etc.

It all began with Ruby Ridge. Back in the mid-1990s, Director Louis Freeh personally deemed HRT SWAT sniper Lon Horiuchi's second shot (which struck Vicki Weaver in the face and killed her) as *"unconstitutional"* but did not censure him.

It would have greatly dampened HRT morale.

No, the FBI must stand by its own. If it didn't, who would?

Freeh put great pressure on the Justice Department to kill the manslaughter charge filed by the state of Idaho. It worked. The matter was moved to federal court against Idaho's wishes, where it died by judicial decree. Federal agents have *"sovereign immunity"* while enforcing federal law and cannot be held responsible by the states or the people.

All who were paying attention got the message.

The Republic is dead. The gloves are off.

2010 USA social news

Only a mass reconversion of Western women to an idea that they seem to have given up—that the good life lies in bearing and raising children and sending them out into the world to continue the family and nation—can prevent the Death of the West.

— Pat Buchanan, *The Death of the West* (2002), p.24

White America was dying out. Just to maintain current population levels, families must have 2.5 children. That means for every family with only 2, another must have 3. For every family with only one child, another must have 4. For each family with no children at all, other families must have 5.

The family unit—the spawning ground of lies, betrayals, mediocrity, hypocrisy, and violence—will be abolished. The family unit, which only dampens imagination and curbs free will, must be eliminated.
— Michael Swift, "Towards a Homoerotic Order,"
Gay Community News, 7 November 1987

Great civilizations and animal standards of behavior coexist for short periods.
— Jenkin Lloyd Jones

California is steadily depopulating of white middle-class. The Hispanics rejoice in "taking back" the state via their *Reconquista.* Given the increased crime, poverty, and taxes, many whites are glad to let them have it. One typical newspaper ad reads:

Will trade beautiful 4/3 in Orange County for mobile home or cabin on acreage in Rockies. Serious offers only, please.

The applicant has no takers.

Logan, Utah   February 2010   4:28AM

FBI agents from Salt Lake City, Boise, and Pocatello have descended upon the sleepy neighborhood of Frank Edwin Swan. The FBI for weeks had surveilled the diesel mechanic, who lived alone since his divorce eight years ago. Intelligence showed that he awoke regularly at 0530 on weekdays. Accordingly, the FBI chose to execute the raid when he was most likely at the bottom of his longest and deepest REM cycle of delta sleep. Swan would be groggiest then. That meant 0430.

Salt Lake FBI SWAT "got the ticket" for the dynamic entry. They are "jocked out" and "on line" at Phase Line Yellow, the forward rallying point. They will not bother to knock.

"No knock" warrants were originally authorized by the Supreme Court only to: prevent the easy destruction of evidence, protect lives (*e.g.,* hostages), or prevent the escape of a dangerous suspect. Additionally, police are not required to knock/announce if the suspect already knows that the police are present.

None of these factors apply to Swan, but federal judges generally give the FBI whatever they request. Utah authorities were especially cooperative with the Government since the 2002 Winter Olympics. When the Salt Lake FBI SAC made the point that Swan was wanted for questioning in the abduction of three Denver men (one of them a sitting judge), the Federal District Court judge immediately approved a no-knock search warrant.

The softly snoring Frank Swan is aware of none of this.

Eighty-six yards away FBI SWAT commander Raymond Wilcox switches his encrypted Motorola headset radio to the channel used by the entry teams. "TOC to all units. You have compromise authority and permission to move to Green."

The SWAT operators begin to surround Swan's small home. Phase Line Green is their final position before dynamic entry. Team White will enter the front and Team Black the back. Simultaneously. (They don't call it "dynamic entry" for nothing.) Team Green will cover the left side and Team Red the right. These color codes for target buildings are standard SWAT jargon. The area is cordoned off for two blocks by over twenty FBI agents, sheriff's deputies, and police. Two ambulances are standing by. So many men and vehicles are bound to rile up the neighborhood dogs.

near Lander, Wyoming   4:29AM

FBI agents from Casper, Rock Springs, Laramie, Cheyenne, and Lander have converged on the small farm of Kyle and Susan Bradford. They timed the raid with Swan's so that the subjects could not warn each other. The Bradfords live at the end of a remote county road, and their nearest neighbor is several hundred yards away behind a small knoll.

For the FBI, it was ideal. Seclusion was preferred for such raids. It not only limited risk of collateral damage, but the subjects could be isolated from interfering third parties such as friends, media, etc. As the Weaver family learned at Ruby Ridge, a remote homestead is a mixed blessing.

Logan, Utah   4:30AM

Several dogs up and down the street begin to bark from all the activity, waking a blue heeler at the foot of Swan's bed. His intelligent brown eyes are alert, his ears radar dishes swiveling about. The dog jumps to the floor and runs to the bedroom window. He sees several dark shadows moving stealthily by his master's house. His low, soft growl snaps Swan instantly awake from a very deep sleep. After seven years he knew every nuance of every bark and growl. This growl meant *Danger!*

"What is it, Otto?" Swan whispers hoarsely. Otto is still on point, softly growling at the window. Still in sweatpants, Swan gets up and peeks slightly through the top of the drapes. *Shit! Burglars!* He forces himself to take deep breaths as he dons his emergency gear. He is dressed in seconds.

He unholsters his Glock and does a blind system check of mag and chamber. Holding the .45 in his right hand, he removes the magazine with his left and touches the top round with his index finger. Loaded. The ISMI chrome-silicon mag spring would last years fully depressed. He reinserts the magazine with a *Tap-Tug*. Fully seated. Then he grabs the middle of the slide with his left hand and pulls it back about a half inch. With his middle finger he feels the partially chambered round. He pushes the slide forward, feeling the flush barrel lockup to ensure that it's in battery. A man should be able to load, unload, check, and clear his weapons by tactile feel only. During a gunfight you cannot risk taking your eyes off your threats.

Swan easily sees his tritium sights as the decaying hydrogen isotope H_3 glows reassuringly inside its hardened sapphire vials. Swan reholsters the Glock. Fourteen rounds of Triton 200 grain hollowpoints. Night sights. Tactical light. Bulletproof vest. Peltors. Boots.

All Swan needs now is the proper *mindset*—the most important ingredient for victory. Without a fighting spirit the best gear is irrelevant. *With a fighting spirit you can defend yourself with a rolled-up newspaper.*

Always Cheat. Always Win. The only unfair fight is the one you lose.

He is halfway down the hall before he recalls something his Thunder Ranch instructor Clint Smith once said. From Swan's memory a small piece calves off: *There is a big difference in being in a fight and going to a fight. You get caught in a fight with a handgun. You go to a fight with a rifle.*

Why fight with 14 rounds of .45 when you can fight with 20 rounds of .308? Besides, rifles are much easier to hit with during great stress.

Swan stops in mid-stride, returns to his bed, holsters his Glock, and grabs his M1A. Again, he does a blind system check of mag and chamber. He keeps the rifle in Condition One, meaning cocked and locked. His instructors taught him that he may not have the luxury of time or silence to chamber a first round. Thus, a home defensive rifle should be kept in Condition One. Very few gunowners know to do this and the ones who do are often uncomfortable with the "danger" of keeping a cocked and locked rifle in the house. Swan knows better because he has been trained better.

With the 11½ pounds of stock and steel in his hands he feels immensely more prepared. What a difference a *rifle* makes. He walks down the hall with his M1A shouldered in the High Ready position, safety off, trigger finger straight. His left hand is underneath the forestock—thumb on the flashlight's momentary ON/OFF rubber button.

near Lander, Wyoming   4:30AM

Raid leader Scott Malone checks his watch and nods to his men. An entry man with a battering ram steps forward on the front porch. There will be no knocking at the Bradford farm, either.

Logan, Utah

Commander Wilcox makes a radio call to his men. All silently click in to communicate that they are standing by at Green.

The White Team leader hand signals "breacher up!" and an operator moves forward with a sawed-off 12 gauge Remington 870 pump shotgun loaded with Hatton rounds. The powdered lead shells were specifically designed for safely blowing apart door hinges.

Wilcox checks his watch. It is precisely 0430. He looks at his Special Agent in Charge, who nods. Wilcox presses the transmit button and speaks. *TOC to all units. I have control. Stand by. Five. Four. Three.*

near Lander, Wyoming

Five agents are "stacked" just beside the door's left jamb. Malone holds up his non-gun hand and counts down from five to one. Their tension doubles as they anticipate being released in seconds, like a coiled spring.

Logan, Utah

Two. One. Execute! Execute! Execute!

Swan suddenly remembers to switch on the Aimpoint, and its small orange-red dot comes immediately to life. Battery life of the CompM2 is literally thousands of hours, and the unit is quite rugged. Even if the device failed he could still use his iron sights.

Swan is just twenty feet from the kitchen back door when his home explodes from both ends with a stereophonic crash. His Peltors blank out from nearly a second of sonic overpressure. Both front and rear doors blow off the jambs and fly inside in a shower of splinters.

Home invasion!

Gruff voices are screaming but Swan cannot make out the words amidst the smoke and confusion. The front doorway is blocked by the heavy sofa which Swan had pushed aside earlier that evening for vacuuming. It is his great fortune that he'd been too tired to move it back. Because of the sofa, the armed men in front are delayed entry.

Cover! Swan ducks in a left-side bathroom doorway, keeping his rifle pointed down the hall towards the kitchen. He has a nearly overwhelming urge to begin shooting at the burglars he knows are just a split-second away, but forces himself to wait for visibly armed and hostile threats.

Through the kitchen door several dark gun-carrying forms in black ski masks pour inside. Swan lights up the one in front, quickly takes up the first stage of the M1A trigger, focuses on the glowing dot, and squeezes out the rest of the trigger pull. *Front sight! Press! Front sight!* What happens in an eyeblink seems to take hours, but time distortions usually occur when you are fighting for your life. After a mini-eternity his rifle finally *Booms!* Swan sees and hears his assailant hit in the lower chest with the 2,500 foot pound impact of a rifle bullet at nearly point-blank range. As he falls, Swan visually picks up Aimpoint dot the following shots he knew would come.

Front sight! Press! Front sight!

near Lander, Wyoming

The Bradfords' front door is bashed in and federal agents immediately pour through the house. *FBI! FBI!* They approach the master bedroom in an urgent tangle of flashlight beams as Kyle Bradford groggily reaches for his Ed Brown Kobra .45 on the nightstand.

Freeze! Don't move!

Logan, Utah

Two other intruders become instantly visible and Swan shoots them both in the head within .52 seconds of each other. He notes that he saw his Aimpoint dot before and after each shot, just like he was trained. The terminal ballistics of a .308 round to the human cranial cavity are stupefying. Their heads literally burst with loud *Thwhops!* and the men collapse like string-cut puppets. The kitchen walls are instantly painted in gore.

Swan hears much barking, pistol fire, and shouting from the front of his home and is suddenly aware of his dog attacking intruders in the living room. *Otto is buying me time!* He swats down the impulse to save his dog and instead rushes down the hall towards the kitchen, muzzle leading the way.

A fourth invader suddenly appears through the kitchen doorway, his Oakley goggles covered with the blood and brain matter of his colleagues. Screaming something unintelligible at the top of his lungs, he muzzles a black subgun at the homeowner. The FBI are not accustomed to being shot at during raids, and this agent, shocked at the deaths of his comrades, has forgotten to identify himself.

Swan marvels at burglars who can afford Heckler & Koch MP5s while centering the red dot on the invader's chest as he presses out the trigger. The impact makes an dull clanging sound, but the man drops instantly. Swan steps over the four bodies and stops next to the doorway. He has a difficult time not slipping on the tile. The kitchen floor is slick with blood, its copper stench heavy in the air with the smell of burnt gunpowder and hot brass.

The magnitude of events presses upon Swan's consciousness but he is too busy. *The answer to fear is preoccupation. Solve your problem!* He is more than preoccupied, he is furious. *They started this party, but I am going to finish it for them!*

He flips a wall switch, and a porchlight illuminates two other men partially concealed behind small trees. They immediately pour bursts of 9mm subgun fire at the rear of the house, shooting out the light. Through his Peltors Swan hears raspy chirps of the suppressed MP5s, their winking muzzles strangely captivating. 147 grain slugs shatter the kitchen window, raining glass on the besieged homeowner. *May your enemies be on full-auto!* as Jeff Cooper said. Single well-placed shots are what win battles.

Swan crouches, pies out slightly past the right door jamb, quickly lights up the kneeling man on the left and fires three aimed rounds through the tree. FMJ zip through the small tree as if it were balsa wood, striking the man behind and causing him to expose more of himself. *Shoot what is available, while it is available, until something else becomes available.* Swan fires twice more, knocking the man over in a lifeless sprawl.

Five down, one to go.

near Lander, Wyoming

FBI! Hands up, now! scream three agents more or less in unison. As the Bradfords are blinded by the powerful tac lights, Kyle slowly withdraws his hand from the .45 and pulls Susan to him. Agents yank away the down comforter and plaid flannel sheets to expose the terrified, naked couple, and roughly drag them from their warm bed. They are handcuffed and herded to separate areas of the house.

"Susan, say nothing to them!" Kyle yells from the hallway.

"Shut the fuck up, you!" snarls an agent as he shoves Kyle along.

In the background, Bondo the parrot is squawking at full volume.

Logan, Utah

From behind Swan a raking burst just over his head showers him with shards of dishes. *They're making their way from the front!* Swan understands at once that he will be overcome by the men coming down the hall. His world is violent chaos and it's getting worse by the second. He must flee and find cover *now*. He can take the remaining guy in the yard, but not the several in the house. There is Danger in front, but Death is clearly behind him. No choice but to charge the Danger. This clarity is oddly comforting.

His life is about to *really* suck, so he takes a deep breath. Another burst of fire from behind rakes the wall above him, digging out chunks of white plaster. Although he does not know it, White and Black Teams are now being very cautious in their shooting for fear of hitting each other in the crossfire. Swan turns and fires three rounds at the living room in hopes of suppressing their fire, the .308 concussion pounding his mastoid bones. He wills himself to ignore this sudden headache. *When you don't have time for the pain.*

Swan thinks that the several rounds in his rifle and the fourteen in his Glock will be enough to get him to safety until the police arrive. With all this pre-dawn gunfire they should be here any minute. He is surprised not to hear any sirens yet. He notes that he is incredibly thirsty, though calm. His mouth is tomb dry but his nose drips from excitement.

The suddenness of this violence has dumped a keg of adrenaline into Swan's endocrinology. He finds it difficult to think clearly. His 11½ pound rifle feels like 50. His shoulders burn, his head throbs. His hand and arm movements have become coarse, which would have greatly compromised handgun accuracy. He notices the onset of tunnel vision and counteracts it by moving his head and eyes about, scanning for new threats. Lessons from his instructors playback surreally—like old movies—reminding him to breathe, think, move, fight. *So much to remember!*

Move! he commands himself. Swan leaps through the kitchen doorway onto the concrete steps, then drops over to the left side. Here he has kneeling cover to engage the last man in the backyard.

Although Swan could have no way of knowing it, the time from Otto's growl until his first shot was 46 seconds. From his first shot until now was just 11 seconds. An incredible vehemence has engulfed him in under a minute. Less than two minutes ago Swan was deep asleep. Within the time slice of a TV commercial break he has shot and probably killed five intruders by rifle-fire, and is fleeing his home in fear of his life.

From his house he hears the pounding footsteps of several men booming like thunderclaps in his electronic earmuffs. Shouts of *Lear!—Lear!* are an odd thing for burglars to yell. *Maybe it's a name.* He cannot imagine what valuables they think he owns to justify such a massive home invasion.

He no longer hears Otto barking. *Bastards shot my dog, too! Can't think about him now—time to move!*

Sure wish I had another mag for my rifle! He meant to order a butt-stock magazine pouch, but it was one of those unperformed details which comprise modern Life. That old poem flashes through his mind: *For want of a nail, the shoe was lost . . .* He shakes himself back into focus.

Swan lights up the last dark hooded form and fires three rounds, hitting the intruder's left shoulder and arm. The man goes down screaming. Relief floods Swan as he is now free to escape. *I'm sure glad my rifle has a light!* He figures he has five or six rounds left in his M1A but is unsure. *Whoever said "count your rounds" probably never traded gunfire with anyone!* He lights up the writhing man one last time to make sure that he is out of the fight, and notices the large white letters on the intruder's vest, letters which he did not see earlier. His heart stops at the familiar abbreviation:

FBI

Swan's concentration is instantly erased by this new, horrible reality. *Oh, shit! What the hell do the feds want with me? I didn't know they were FBI, but they'll never believe me! They'll gun me down because of this!* He frantically grasps at the stillborn hope that it has all been a dream, but the illuminated cloud of hanging gunsmoke tells him otherwise. *I am screwed!*

near Lander, Wyoming

" . . . and have a warrant to search these premises," lead FBI agent Malone says.

"Search for *what?*" Kyle demands. "What's going *on?*"

"I'll ask the questions here. Just sit tight and do not interfere. If you need to go to the bathroom, one of the agents will accompany you. Now, do you have any other weapons in the house?"

Logan, Utah

Why did they break into my home? What do they want? Why are the FBI wearing masks? Aren't they proud of what they do? Only criminals wear masks! He forces himself to continue deep, regular breathing as his body desperately needs dirigible volumes of oxygen. *Must press on and escape! They will kill me rather than let me surrender! I might as well go down like a man, fighting! The bastards have left me with nothing to lose!*

The FBI has discovered the (admittedly rare) flip-side to dynamic entry raids: causing such desperation in a subject can backfire. In a "fight or flight" scenario, some men fought, even against overwhelming odds. A man with "no way out" just may create one. And you don't want to be in his way when he does.

Swan hears the agents coming down the hall. They will be through the kitchen in seconds . . . after having stepped over four of their buddies. And they will be very, very pissed.

near Lander, Wyoming

An agent leers at a naked Susan Bradford on the living room sofa. "Got any concealed weapons on you, Honey?"

Susan glares at the agent in black tactical garb. "You're a creep!"

"And you're really sexy when you're angry, didya know that?"

Logan, Utah

A solid plan crystallizes in Swan's mind. Run to the fence on his left, hop over and take cover behind the neighbor's woodpile. From there, the alley. *A good plan now is better than a perfect plan later.*

Agents are in the kitchen now and he is still outside by the steps.

Move or die!

Swan springs up and runs to the fence. In his eagerness to escape he neglects to pie out and clear the left corner of his house. Given his limited training and practice, it is an understandable lapse. He has done extremely well to have gotten even this far against highly-trained multiple assailants. Five for five is pretty good.

But, a mistake is a mistake, and not clearing your last corner is one of the worst ones to make. *You have the rest of your life to solve your problem. How long you live depends on how well you do it.* Swan does not notice a member of Green Team against the wall, behind his peripheral vision.

As Swan runs towards the fence and safety, already imagining how he will bound over and land, the agent draws a careful bead on the running man and squeezes the trigger of his 9mm MP5.

Five rapid tubercular coughs are heard from the AWC suppressor, echoed by five sickening thuds of impact.

near Lander, Wyoming
"My wife and I are both naked and *handcuffed!* Why are you worried about weapons in the house? Still feeling a bit inferior? Are we not defenseless enough for you?"

Logan, Utah
Swan is stitched across the back with a ragged diagonal line. The impacts feel like hammer blows but the US Armor Level IIIA vest does its job, stopping rounds #2, #3, #4, and #5. Although a 9mm subgun is not a rifle, being hit in the back with four rounds within a half second will drop a man. Swan falls facedown and is immediately swarmed by Green Team. His M1A is kicked away and gloved hands yank the Glock from its holster.

near Lander, Wyoming
"Shut up, Bradford," commands Malone. "We know you and Swan had something to do with Denver. The Bureau may be slow, but—"

"*Swan?* What does *Frank* have to do with this?" Kyle demands.

"You tell us, farmboy. What were you two doing in Denver?" sneers the agent. Since the Bradfords are not under arrest—only detained—no *Miranda* reading of their rights is required.

Kyle Bradford never placed much stock in ESP but he suddenly has a sense almost strong enough to pass for actual knowledge: his boyhood buddy Frank Swan is in very bad trouble.

Logan, Utah
No bulletproof vest, however, can protect what it doesn't cover. Swan is bleeding profusely from the first round, which shattered his left thigh bone and severed the femoral artery. From just below his groin, hot oil of life spurts out regular bursts, soaking his sweatpants and the cold ground beneath him. In the moonlight it looks black. Because he is shivering he must be cold, though he is too numb to feel it. *Wounded! How bad?*

His lungs howl for air, but gasping for breath is a difficult task with angry men pinning him down. His consciousness begins to evaporate, gently, like a fading dream.

near Lander, Wyoming

"Susan! They're raiding Frank's place right now!" Kyle shouts.

"*Frank?* What's *happening?*" Susan yells from the living room.

Logan, Utah

"*Where the fuck are they?!*" screams a White Team agent. "*What did you do with them?!*" He presumes that Swan will, under such pressure, reveal where he had taken the three Denver abductees.

Swan hears the words through a thickening fog but does not understand. He thinks he means the dead guys in the kitchen and backyard, but that doesn't make sense. Nothing about any of this makes sense.

"Wh—*who*?" Swan manages to ask.

While an agent has a knee to Swan's neck and a Springfield Armory .45 to his head, another agent is wrenching his hands behind his back and cuffing him. Two other agents are holding Swan down by his legs.

"*You know goddamn well who, asshole!*"

One of the Red Team agents looks up and says, "Scrote's wearing a *vest*! He knew we were coming, Dennis!"

"Yeah, no shit!" the White Team agent says. "He blocked his front door, too! Took us forever to get through!"

The urgent flurry of radio chatter and the icy handcuffs on his wrists remind Swan that he is police custody. He has never been arrested in his life. He is terribly confused. *Police!* He vaguely recalls something from a thin yellow book about keeping silent and demanding to speak with your attorney.

"C—call my *lawyer*," Swan says barely, but with clear umbrage. He takes several more labored breaths, accepting the sudden realization that he would never see the inside of a courtroom. He is dying, and knows it.

A feathery swooshing sensation engulfs him as *animus* detaches from *corpus,* all 65 trillion cells being evacuated of spirit. *Going home.* In a giddy state of shock he confuses the steam from his blood soaking the frozen earth as his soul floating into the starry night.

Hello!

Swan giggles softly.

"Fucker's laughing at us!" the White Team agent spits.

Before his bloodpressure fades out, Swan's forty-three years of life muster one last defiant tug. It is his final thought and emotion—a parting shot of anger.

Otto!

The thread breaks and he is untethered. *So it was a dream after all!* Swan floats away, unweighted, toward a beautiful, loving light. He hears singing, soft and lovely. Water in water, spirit in spirit, he is gone. Only the barest suggestion of a smile is left on his face.

SWAT commander Wilcox coldly stares down at the deceased mechanic. "Little late for your lawyer, Mr. Swan."

There is much shouting as EMT personnel rush into the house and backyard for the wounded agents. Three in the kitchen are dead, but the fourth took his hit to the ceramic trauma plate and is only winded. The agent shot through the tree is critically injured to the head, and not expected to make it to the hospital. The other agent would live but the .308 wounds are devastating. His arm will require amputation just below the shoulder.

Wilcox abruptly turns to the White Team agent. "And *you*, Señor *Dumbfuck!* You really dropped your pack on this one! You *know* better than to question a subject *before* he's been Mirandized! What if he *told* you something? It could have got tossed out because he wasn't aware of his rights! Do I need to send you back to Quantico for a refresher?"

"Sorry, sir. Wasn't thinking," the agent replies, eyes down, chastised.

The neighborhood is now alive with dozens of frightened—though unquenchably curious—residents in bathrobes. A multitude of dogs are barking. Squad cars are screeching up in front of Swan's home with lights flashing, and more police and EMT are pouring onto the property.

A Green Team member implores, "Sir, Swan *had* to know we were coming. Look at his gear! Vest, Peltors—who's ever seen such a thing? And who uses a *rifle* in his house?"

Wilcox considers this. "Somebody who doesn't fuck around, that's who. Probably militia. He nearly escaped, too. He may have a car and driver waiting. I want a grid search of the surrounding ten blocks. *Now!*"

"Yes, sir!"

Wilcox seems to decide something else. "Yeah, I think he knew we were coming. Probably got tipped off by someone in the PD or SO just before we got on line. And now six of my men are dead or wounded! If this thing was leaked I'm gonna have somebody's Logan, Utah ass on a spit, I swear to God!"

near Lander, Wyoming

After twenty minutes the Bradfords are finally allowed to cover themselves with their own bed sheets. Their farmhouse is ransacked over the course of five hours. Agents confiscate all firearms, paper records, disks, as well as the computer.

Malone's cell phone rings. It is Wilcox, calling from Utah with the bad news. Moods blacken as word spreads to the agents.

Bondo is still screaming his little lungs out. The leering FBI agent says to Susan, "Will you shut up that fucking bird?"

Susan coldly replies, "You've broken into his home and he's upset. As long as you're here, he'll keep screaming."

The agent counters, "If you don't shut him up *right now*, I will!"

"Oh, are you going to *shoot* our parrot? Federal agents seem to have a thing against family pets. Let's see, the ATF hates cats, the US Marshals hate dogs—I guess the FBI hates parrots," Susan taunts. "What do US Customs hate, *ferrets*?"

The scene is getting ugly so another agent interrupts with, "Mike, just put his cage in a closet or something!"

Special Agent Michael Tipton has an idea. "How about *outside*?"

"It's below freezing out there!" Susan vehemently objects. "He's a *tropical* bird; he can't handle the cold!"

"Tough shit, lady. You had your chance," Tipton sneers. "Maybe if he quiets down I'll remember to bring him back inside before he turns into a parrotsicle." He chuckles at his new word.

Tipton picks up Bondo's cage and carries it outside. On the way he says to the bird, "You have the right to remain silent. Anything you say can and will—"

* * * * * * *

Later that day a Salt Lake City spokesman for the FBI announces with thinly concealed pride the twin raids in connection with the Denver kidnappings. "Although we cannot comment on any evidence so far uncovered, our investigations are continuing."

An Internet reporter pipes up. "How do you explain the bloodshed in the Logan raid? We hear from a neighbor that the SWAT team did not identify themselves and were fired upon by Mr. Swan as intruders."

The FBI spokesman replies with an indignant wave of dismissal. "That is simply not true. The raid was executed according by law and Mr. Swan knew that law enforcement were present. He blocked his front door in order to delay entry, and then chose to fire upon federal agents with a deadly assault rifle rather than peaceably surrender. It was a bloody and unsolicited attack on law enforcement officers legitimately performing their sworn duties."

"How did Swan manage to kill four agents and wound two others?" asks another reporter.

Just like the FBI at Rosebud, North Dakota and Miami, just like the US Marshals at Ruby Ridge, and just like the ATF at Waco, whenever any federal agency takes a licking, two old excuses are always trotted out.

They knew we were coming. We were outgunned.

"Do you mean to say that the FBI suspects a leak from local law enforcement in Logan?"

"We are investigating that possibility, yes," replies the Bureau suit.

* * * * * * *

The Bradfords are not charged with any crime, and their case becomes a new cause *célèbre* amongst the civil rights groups. At a national press conference with their attorney, they speak for the first time.

In a steady, acidic voice, Kyle explains, "Without any provocation or probable cause, the *Waffen* FBI surrounded the home of my childhood friend Frank Swan—who was asleep. They never called him on the phone. They chose not to wait until he was driving to work. No, they surrounded a harmless, slumbering man at 4:30 in the morning—like hyenas. As the FBI burst into his home, Frank woke up and began to defend himself from what he no doubt thought was a pre-dawn home invasion by assailants.

"While his dog, Otto, was dying on the living room floor after protecting his master, Frank fought his way out of the house and nearly made it to safety when FBI Special Agent Donald Hoyt shot him five times in the back with a submachine gun. The FBI have expressed no apology for their obscene display of naked power. The FBI have expressed no remorse over my friend's needless death. Instead, they remain defensive and arrogant over the public outrage, and insist that the four agents 'died for their country.' I profoundly disagree. These agents are the type of government thugs that Americans fought over two hundred years ago on the road between Concord and Boston. Every 'dynamic entry' raid is meant to say, 'We are all powerful; you are nothing.' How many more innocent people must be cut down by machinegun fire in the middle of the night before we admit that federal law enforcement are at war with the American people?!

"At precisely the same time, my wife and I were also raided by the FBI, though fortunately by agents less trigger-happy than those who killed Frank. In that raid we lost a member of our family. My wife Susan would like to tell you about it. Honey?"

Susan Bradford steps up to the microphone. She is a trim, fresh-faced brunette about 35 years old. "During their search of our farmhouse, one of the Cheyenne FBI agents, Michael Tipton, intentionally put our tame, caged parrot outside to freeze to death. We raised Bondo from a chick, taught him to sing, do chin-ups with his beak, and many other cute tricks. Agent Tipton killed a harmless family pet in a cowardly and despicable act. When we demanded that the FBI buy us another bird out of simple decency, they laughed in our face! So, if you have a dog, cat, hamster, parrot, or goldfish, beware agencies of federal law enforcement!"

Their press conference revives the story with new life. They repeatedly air a video of Bondo singing "I Left My Heart in San Francisco," and his cruel death strikes a chord with the public.

* * * * * * *

The Cheyenne FBI SAC is furious. "Tipton, you killed their *parrot*?"

"Uh, well, not on purpose, sir. We just forgot to bring it back in."

"*'We'*? What's this 'we' shit? You mean 'you'! *You* forgot to bring it back in! Hell, 'forgot' my *ass*! 'Parrotsicle'? You just had to teach Mrs. Bradford a lesson, didn't you?"

"No, sir! I was busy conducting a search of the premises and forgot to return the bird indoors."

"Aww, *bullshit*! Look, I don't give a fuck about their parrot, either, but the damn bird has become some kind of *martyr*. The entire country is talking about it and we look like assholes. Even Leno made a joke about it last night. The audience actually *booed!* Booed the FBI! You remember the first commandment from the Academy, don't you, Tipton?"

"Uh, don't embarrass the Bureau?" Tipton ventures.

"That's right, don't embarrass the Bureau! You stepped in shit and now we *all* stink! Devereaux himself called me about this."

Tipton blanches. "The AD of CID?"

"The same. And the Director's *pissed.* So, guess what, my bird-hating friend—you're buying the Bradfords a new parrot. And try to act real sorry in front of the media. Get out; go home!"

Tipton leaves the SAC in a huff and stalks through the office to the elevators. A lone voice from a cubicle sings out in mock-parrot style, "Go get 'em, Feathers! *Bwarrk!* " The room erupts in laughter.

Special Agent Michael Tipton groans. He now has his Bureau nickname, and it's nothing as macho as "Speed" or "Hammer." The more he resists being called "Feathers" the more his colleagues will use it. He'll never live it down. He knows FBI culture well enough to understand that tatoos are less permanent.

He pictures his future clearly: He will come to work and find his desk drawers filled with goose down. He will get anonymous Tweety Bird cards in the mail. Fellow agents will learn the Monty Python "Dead Parrot" sketch by heart and recite it just within earshot. An application to the Audubon Society will be filled out in Tipton's name.

It will never end. No humor was as vicious as cop humor.

Fucking parrot! He stabs the elevator button with sufficient force to fold his fingernail painfully in half. He swears loudly.

A fellow agent walks past and tosses out, "Going . . . *down*, Tipton?"

Just before the elevator doors close, from deep within the Cheyenne FBI offices comes a raucous *Bwarrk!* As he descends Tipton can still hear the laughter a floor and a half above through the elevator shaft.

* * * * * * *

After nine weeks of investigations of the Swan and Bradford raids, several things finally became known. First, Frank Swan and Kyle Bradford *did* independently travel through Denver, but the purpose of their trips was to look at a fishing cabin near Fairplay that they were considering buying. Second, all attempts to link the two men to terrorist activity failed. They weren't even members of any militias. Finally, no evidence could be found that the men had anything to do with the Denver kidnappings. Although they had read the Krassny posts online, so had hundreds of thousands of other Americans.

The FBI had barked up the wrong pair of trees, resulting in the death of five men, a dog, and a parrot. It is an unmitigated public relations disaster. Howls of protest rain on the Bureau, and Gore Vidal comes out of retirement in Italy to pen a scorching article on the *"eerie and persistent incompetence"* of the FBI. Animal rights groups make a particularly ugly stink. There is even talk in Congress of merging the FBI with the Department of Homeland Security, and that *really* gets the Bureau's attention.

The brother and parents of Frank Swan sued, as did the Bradfords. The Justice Department quickly settled out of court as a *"humanitarian gesture"*—though without admitting any fault. They had done the same thing regarding Ruby Ridge, tossing out $3.1 million to the surviving Weaver family to shut down their $200 million civil suit.

2010 USA political news

Vice President Wiedermann heads off possible impeachment and resigns. Melvin Connor is sworn as the new VP.

The 2010 Census has nearly 150 questions and is met with massive noncompliance. Hundreds of censustakers are roughed up. Despite dire threats of imprisonment, many Americans learn that they are not required to answer the questionnaire beyond the number of citizens in their household.

2010 USA economic news

Gold is $2,573 and the Dow is 3409.

Wyoming General Election   November 2010

The US Government and most states had, through their increasingly draconian actions, boosted the "market" for freedom. Hence, many Americans were fleeing Kalifornia, Neu Jersey, Taxachusetts, Maryland, etc. This migration was like the electrical potential of voltage; it was looking for somewhere to go. Only one state was an "closed circuit" with little impedance. Libertarian-leaning Americans continued to pour into Wyoming, especially when they heard good reports from friends and family who had been there since 2006.

Freedom there was maintaining itself and not shrinking.

Much had been learned about relocation logistics from the "dress rehearsal" of 2006, and 2010 went more smoothly. Besides the counties of Weston, Big Horn, Washakie, Park, Converse, and Lincoln, a hoped-for overflow made Goshen County possible as well. Twelve of Wyoming's 23 counties were to be under *laissez-faire* government in January. Except for the counties of Sheridan and Campbell (slated for 2014), the entire northern band of the state was in libertarian hands.

Continued advances in the legislature had been planned and achieved. Senate Districts 3, 16, 19, and 23, and House Districts 4, 6, 21, 24, 25, 51, and 54 were won by new candidates embracing liberty.

Washington, D.C.   FBIHQ   November 2010

"Bleth, nice to see you again," Director Klein says.

"Thank you, sir."

"Lots of news from Wyoming, I hear."

"Yes, sir. It was a very successful election for the newcomers. I'm now positive that they'll be going for the entire state government in 2014."

"Really? What makes you so sure?"

"It's pretty simple: why have only *half* a state? Especially when their formula and their organization have been so effective for the past four years? It'd be like Hitler satisfied with Poland after the success of blitzkrieg."

Director Klein nods and says, "Yes, that makes sense. Only at the state level would they have any *real* power. How much are those Free State Project people involved in this?"

"Back in 2006, perhaps a bit as a splinter faction. Today, not at all. I've concluded that the FSP has nothing to do with the Wyoming operation. They're still trying to make a go of their New Hampshire choice up in Coos County, though the Quebec secession two years ago increased FSP numbers. However, since the Wyoming operation has given libertarians a *second* choice of state, it seems to have drawn a lot of interest away from New Hampshire. There are some grumblings about that among the original FSP cadre. Several discussion groups have called the Wyoming faction 'splitters.' I find that amusing coming from people supposedly dedicated to competition and free choice."

"Why has a splinter Wyoming group been more successful than the chosen New Hampshire?"

"Primarily because Wyoming has 40% the population and twenty-five times less density. Any large group of newcomers risks being alienated by the indigenous citizens, but that hasn't happened in Wyoming because there is *so* much room. New Hampshire, however, is one of the oldest and most established states. And New Englanders aren't well-known for being overly gregarious to outsiders. They've an entrenched nativist attitude.

"So, for the purposes of a free state idea, I think that Wyoming was clearly the better choice. It's surrounded by sympathetic allies versus antagonists. It has 23 counties versus 10. Its people are western and independent and naturally distrustful of government. Its energy resources are fourth only to Alaska, Texas, and California. And, finally, whoever is behind the Wyoming operation is *really* marshalling his people. I'd bet he is or was either a military officer or a CEO of a fairly large corporation. The efficiency of their progress is remarkable."

"Well why did the FSP choose New Hampshire then?"

"For several faulty reasons. They overemphasized the importance of a coastline, as if 18 miles of seashore truly increases New Hampshire autonomy. A half-dozen Coast Guard cutters could blockade the entire stretch. They focused too much on a state's current reality rather than its *potential*. Wyoming was a shirt they could grow into, but they chose New Hampshire because they thought the shirt already fit. And they got all gooey when the 2003 governor said 'Come on up; we'd be glad to have you!' In my view, the FSP got suckered in by too many superficialities. Wyoming always had the *real* potential and somebody else clearly figured that out.

"If populations had been equal, then New Hampshire would have been tenable. But a free state initiative is, first and foremost, a *numbers* game. FSPers must maximize their voting leverage to push through their political agenda, so they require a sparsely populated state. That's Wyoming, but they instead chose the *third most* populated state on their list, with the second most voters. As I said, they got suckered in by the superficial advantages of New Hampshire and forgot all about the most *important* criterion—low county population. It's the key factor to electoral success. Once in office, they can *change* the political environment to their liking—but only once they're *in*. They must *first* win elections, and it's 5 to 15 times more difficult in New Hampshire even with fusion candidates."

"How's it going with the FSP up there?"

"Sir, the FSP married a beautiful, mature divorcée who is set in her ways and difficult, instead of a pretty Wyoming college girl who would become the better wife. They had, in my opinion, a shortage of *vision*. They chose a picked fruit versus one that was still ripening on the vine. The error of their decision is becoming clear. In New Hampshire they've hardly saturated even the least populated county of Coos. Elsewhere they've dribbled in with little or no regard to any statewide effectiveness, such as the southern counties of Hillsborough and Rockingham for the Boston job market."

"You mean they moved to New Hampshire just so they could commute to *Massachusetts*?" the Director asks with a stunned look on his face.

"Yes, sir, if you can believe it. It's greatly diminished the Coos County effort. Nearly split the New Hampshire movement in half, actually."

The Director harumphs with bland glee. "These people can't even agree on what part of New Hampshire to take over. Sorry, go on, Bleth."

"There are several main differences between the two groups of free staters. One, the Wyoming group seems much more resolute. Remember, of the original 5,500 FSP members, only *46%* took the time to send in their one page ballot. And the envelope was even pre-addressed."

"Why did nearly 3,000 members not vote?"

"At least two-thirds allegedly 'abstained' because they had no strong preference between the ten state choices."

"*Abstained?* They didn't vote but were relied upon by the FSP to actually move to a state chosen by *others*?"

"It was a contradiction, I agree.

"OK, let's get back to Wyoming."

"Yes, sir. The second difference is that the Wyoming people are predominantly rural, while the New Hampshire people are urban. They are 80/20 inverse images of each other. Because so many Wyoming counties had less than 15,000 or even 8,000 people, they were ripe for takeover by newcomers not adverse to rural life. Several of those counties are extremely desolate. Imagine central Kansas but without the charm. This is a hardy bunch.

"In New Hampshire only the northern county of Coos is sparsely populated, but it's still five times denser than the Wyoming average. The FSPers are facing a somewhat chilly reception there. In Coos County a man named Carl Drega went on a 1997 shooting rampage and killed two state troopers. Libertarians claimed that Drega had been pushed over the edge by environmental regulations, and one notorious columnist even titled a book *The Ballad of Carl Drega*. So, many locals in Coos County aren't very happy with an invasion of libertarians whom they suspect of applauding the nut Drega.

"The third difference I've seen is that the Wyoming people are uprooting and transplanting many more businesses. They're not relying on local jobs, they're *bringing* jobs with them in their companies. There's almost none of that in New Hampshire.

"In conclusion, New Hampshire was a much steeper hill than Wyoming to climb—socially, demographically, industrially, and politically. And they're trying to do it with far less organization and absolutely zero operational security. They chat freely online and over the phone about their people, plans, problems, etc.

"Taking over a state can only be done through a succession of *county* victories to hone political skills and also to showcase the alleged virtues of a libertarian society. That's why the Wyoming newcomers have gone so much further. Their coordinators are treating the state like an archipelago nation to be conquered island by island, and they're doing it. New Hampshire, with only 10 counties, is a different model and one far less suited for the FSP."

"Anything new on the Wyoming methodology?"

"Yes, sir, and this is interesting," Bleth says. "RV and mobile home parks and co-housing communities are built in preparation for the newcomers. Looking at county building permits is another way I've learned to forecast where people are moving to next in Wyoming."

"Have you investigated who's doing all this building?"

"It's a pretty diversified group of folks. No one particular corporation, unfortunately. We're still on top of it, though. The day a new permit is filed, we look into it."

"I'm sure you do, Bleth. You've been very thorough so far."

"Thank you, sir. Oh, and you'll like this. Some of these newcomers are mobile residents in RVs who seem to be posted in successive areas as needed. They'll move from one Wyoming county or legislative district to another in late September, dock at one of their RV parks, declare a change of address and register in the new locale just in time to vote there. These people *must* be directly controlled by whoever's crunching the electoral data, so we're investigating communication links. We suspect cell phones or pagers owned through intermediaries. They get a new posting and they can be on the road in the morning. Most are retirees. They probably love the 'action.' After the November elections, many of them avoid the snows and head south to Texas and Arizona for the winter. But they always return to Wyoming every May, almost like some kind of military TDY. They're a very effective and efficient voting block. And nobody resents them. They have their own retirement income, so they don't stress the local job market. They bring their own homes, so they don't burden the local housing supply. They arrive, spend outside income, and cause no trouble. It's perfect. Since they love the RV life anyway, *somebody* thought to put them to good use. What do they care if they change locales a few times a year? Wyoming residency gives them great tax advantages, and fuel's cheap there."

Director Klein laughs suddenly.

"*Sir?*"

"Sorry, but they remind me of Gallagher's quip that Jehovah's Witnesses should deliver the mail and deaf people should live near the airports."

"Oh, right. Maybe Gallagher is in charge out there."

They both chuckle at this.

Klein ruminates, "RVers as a mobile voting strike force. That's damn clever. You get the feeling that we're playing a bad game of catch-up here?"

"Only several times a month, sir."

"Anything new on the Wyoming organizers?" asks Klein.

Bleth says, "Not really. It's a very tight-knit group, however. Since they have been elected to 12 counties, we are focusing our investigation on their sheriffs and county commissioners. Those leaders will almost certainly be in regular communication with their hierarchy. Also, we've managed to obtain—and please don't ask me how—a list of the FSPers who voted in October 2003 for Wyoming, but so far we haven't been able to make any leadership connections. Who ever is behind this may not have even signed up under the FSP back when they were looking for their first 5,000 members for the vote."

"*Hmmm.* That'd be curious, wouldn't it?"

"Yes, sir. It would suggest that *their* plan preceded the July 2001 founding of the FSP—that there always *was* a splinter group."

The Director chuckles. "If their plan *preceded* the FSP, then the *FSP* is the splinter group, not the Wyoming people." Klein shakes his head. "We could be looking at this whole thing *backwards.* We may have to investigate further back than 2001."

"I'm beginning to think so, yes, sir."

"Good, I'm glad you agree. How would you feel about a Wyoming transfer? SAC of Casper, perhaps? I know that might seem like a demotion from HQ, but I hope you know that's not the case. I need somebody in Wyoming to crack this thing. Who else better than you?"

Bleth doesn't even pause to answer. "I serve the Bureau, sir. I'd be pleased to transfer wherever you think best."

"Thank you, Bleth. I knew I could count on you. Will 90 days be enough time?"

"Yes, sir. I rent, and as you probably know I'm not married. I can leave even sooner than that."

"Good, but I've got to smooth this over with what will be a very unhappy Casper ASAC who was expecting the slot. While I figure out where to send *him*, start packing your bags. I'll see that nothing new gets put on your plate here in the meantime."

"Thank you, sir."

"Oh, and start thinking about how you'll infiltrate those people."

"Yes, sir, I have. I think the Bureau should buy me an RV. A really nice one. I brought a Winnebago brochure with me to show you."

Klein is stunned for a second, and then says, "You're kidding, right?"

Bleth tries not to, but laughs. "It was worth a try. If you don't ask, the answer's always 'No.' Good day, Director."

THE 2010 CENSUS & *YOU*
WHAT ARE YOUR *RIGHTS?*

In order to apportion Representatives and direct taxes to the States, the decennial census was authorized by the Constitution in Article 1, Section 3:

The actual enumeration shall be made . . . every . . . ten years, in a manner as they (Congress) *shall by law direct.*

Nothing in the Constitution requires Americans to answer any Census question beyond the number of people in one's household. This is *all* the Federal Government needs to fulfill its constitutional duty of apportionment.

Unfortunately, the Government has transformed the Census into an unconstitutional invasion of our privacy. The 1870 Census asked only five questions. The 2010 Census will pose *hundreds* of questions ranging from your ethnic background, religious preference, education, and how many flush toilets you have.

Contrary to popular belief and Government propaganda, **you do *not* have to answer anything on the form beyond how many people are living in your household.** Do not let the Government try to intimidate you; there are *no* legal penalties if you reserve your right to privacy. Congress may have unlawfully expanded the Census, but they have not required you to waive your rights to privacy. Just because the Government asks doesn't mean that you have to *answer.*

Recall the law-abiding 110,000 Japanese-Americans who were rounded up during World War 2 and herded into concentration camps? Most of them lost their homes and businesses. (Many thousands of German- and Italian-Americans were also rounded up, though this is not widely known.) How did the Government know their ancestry?

From the 1940 Census!
Knowledge is *power!*

This unlawful roundup was permitted by the US Supreme Court in 1944 *Korematsu.* Only a half century later was the Government forced to apologize and offer some minuscule reparations for the Japanese-Americans' loss of freedom and property. Most of those harmed had died long before.

Over 90% of what the Government knows about you and your family is information that came directly, or indirectly, from *you.* From warranty card info to credit applications, Americans snitch on *themselves* daily and this information (*i.e.,* power) is used against us!

You are *not* required by law to answer intrusive Census questions.
You are *not* required by law to speak with Census-takers.
You are *not* required by law to allow Census-takers in your home.

Census technology and Nazi Germany misuse of it

*Satan rose up against Israel and incited [King] David to take a census of Israel... **This command was also evil in the sight of God**... Then David said to God, "I have sinned greatly by doing this. Now I beg you to take away the guilt of your servant. I have done a very foolish thing."*
—I Chronicles 21:1,8

In 2001 a groundbreaking book was published which proved the partnership between IBM Germany and the Nazi government. *IBM and the Holocaust* by Edwin Black fully describes how IBM punch card technology was designed and employed to identify German Jews and other "undesirables."

*After decades of documentation by the best minds, the most studied among them would confess that they never really understood the Holocaust process . . . How could it happen? How were they selected? **How did the Nazis get the names? They always had the names.***

What seemingly magical scheduling process could have allowed millions of Nazi victims to step onto train platforms in Germany or nineteen other Nazi-occupied countries, travel for two and three days by rail, and then step onto a ramp at Auschwitz or Treblinka—and within an hour be marched into gas chambers. Hour after hour. Day after day. Timetable after timetable. Like clockwork, and always with blitzkrieg efficiency.

The survivors would never know. The liberators would never know. The politicians who made speeches would never know. The prosecutors who prosecuted would never know. The debaters would never know.

The question was barely even raised.
—Edwin Black, *IBM and the Holocaust* (2001), p. 425-426

The process of genocide goes like this: First, the government desires the technology. Once it has that, then come the laws. After the laws comes action. IBM took governments (US and Nazi Germany) into the information age back in the 1930s. Today, Microsoft, Oracle, and other amoral computer companies are taking the Government into the next generation of omniscience.

In using statistics, the government now has the road map to switch from knowledge to deeds.
— Friedrich Zahn, German Statistical Archive (1936)

*Theoretically, the collection of data for each person can be so abundant and complete, **that we can finally speak of a paper human representing the natural human.** (op. cit., p.304)*
— 1936 journal of the German Statistical Society

*We are no longer dealing with general censuses, **but we are really following individuals.** (op. cit., p.323)*
— René Carmille of the National Statistical Service of 1941 Occupied France

*It possessed the technology to scrutinize an entire nation.
...No one would escape. This was something new for mankind. Never before had so many people been identified so precisely, so silently, so quickly, and with such far-reaching consequences.
The dawn of the Information Age began at the sunset of human decency. (op. cit., p.104)*
— regarding IBM in Nazi Germany (Dehomag)

A special envelope containing a so-called Supplemental Card was created. This all-important card recorded the individual's bloodline data and functioned as the racial linchpin of the operation. Each head of household was to fill out his name and address and then document his family's ancestral lines. Jews understandably feared the newest identification. Census takers were cautioned to overcome any distrust by assuring families that the information would not be released to the financial authorities. (op. cit., p.170)
— regarding Nazi Germany's 1939 census

*Another sign that bodes ill: Today, notices informed the Jewish population of Warsaw that next Saturday there will be a census of the Jewish inhabitants . . . **Our hearts tell us of evil; some catastrophe for the Jews of Warsaw lies in this census. Otherwise there would be no need for it.**
The order for the census stated that it is being held to gather data for administrative purposes. That's a neat phrase, but it contains catastrophe . . . We are certain that this census is being taken for the purpose of expelling "nonproductive elements" . . . **We are all caught in a net, doomed to destruction.***
— October 1939 diary of Warsaw Jew Chaim Kaplan

> *The evacuation* (i.e., deportation to concentration camps for disposal) *of Poles and Jews in the new Eastern Provinces will be conducted by Security Police* . . . **The census documents provide the basis for evacuation.**
> — Reinhard Heydrich's 1939 memo
> *Evacuation of the New Eastern Provinces*

Without the intimate collaboration between IBM and the Nazi government, the Holocaust could never have happened. If the Jews had not obeyed the command to register themselves during the census process, the Nazis simply would not have known whom to roundup, or where.

The Census of 2010 is of an unconstitutional scope, and with an evil purpose—to register the characteristics, assets, and habits of Americans for the purpose of selection, ostracization, and confiscation. We are told that the information collected will not be shared or misused, that our privacy will be protected.

This is a *lie!*
This has always *been* a lie!

Ask the Japanese-Americans of the 1940s. Ask the Jews under Hitler.

We are poised for a Holocaust to rid America of *"extremists"* and *"religious fanatics"* and *"survivalists"* and *"gun nuts"* and other groups of concerned peaceable folk.

The Jews of 20th century Europe may not have had any warning of what was in store for them. It had never before happened, and to contemplate systematic genocide was unimaginable.

But, 21st century Americans will have no excuse to be surprised.

Registering yourself during the 2010 Census is like sending a list of your household valuables to a burglars' guild. Do not invite—no, *guarantee* trouble for yourself. Do not participate with oppression!

Tyranny cannot succeed without its victims' cooperation.

Tyranny cannot succeed without *your* cooperation.

❖ 2011

North Carolina   8 February 2011

It has been two years since the man's op in Maryland. Not to his surprise, the remains of Judge Gray have not been found. Even if they had, the FBI would not be able to identify them after all this time. The investigation of Gray's disappearance had quickly stalled for utter lack of evidence, leaving the FBI with no choice but to move on to newer cases.

The man was keen to oblige. A new case is exactly what he is about to give them. He had taken a year to decompress from the Gray op as he chose his next subject, and then another year to plan for the second op. Although he knew he could still likely succeed within a narrower time window, the man believed in giving himself every possible advantage before action.

There was nothing bigger than the tiny things, but the dozens of tiny things always took months to tease out. Traffic and weather patterns, security cameras, garbage pickups, store business hours, personal habits and schedule of the subject, etc. He envisioned a balance scale with the police and the FBI and Murphy on one side, and his planning on the other. Each tiny thing he anticipated and neutralized was like a grain of sand on his side. Only when they had accumulated into an overwhelming disparity of weight would the man even consider committing to an op.

At that point he would query his most reliable implement: his gut hunch. Scientists approximated it with a branch of mathematics called "fuzzy logic" which very accurately measured hitherto subconscious intangibles. If the man's gut hunch said "Go" then he finally went into action.

That moment had come last week after a good night's sleep.

Privy to a great secret, only he knows what is in store for a thoroughly depraved and perfidious public figure. He signals left as he enters northbound I-95—an arrow in flight towards its unsuspecting target.

Washington, D.C.

Senator Clayton Hengel (D-CA) hangs up the phone, smug and satisfied. His wife had just bought yet another "Honey-I'll-be-quite-late-tonight-so-don't-wait-up" call, and at 6:25PM no less. *Did she even care anymore? Well, who could blame her?*

D.C. was hard on marriages, even when spouses *were* faithful.

He pours himself a generous bourbon, slopping over the rim of the rocks glass. Yes, he *would* be quite late tonight. He reaches for his hybrid wireless PDA with its own IP address. The small, powerful device replaced his cell phone a few years back. As he punches in a familiar number his groin begins to tingle. The call answers on its fourth ring, "Is that you, darling?"

Hengel chuckles merrily. "Either you're a mind reader or you looked at the Caller ID."

A lusty giggle. "Oh, I'm a mind reader all right, and I know just what's on *your* mind!"

Hengel takes a quick gulp of bourbon and blurts, "How can I help it? You give me the naughtiest thoughts."

Another giggle. "When will you be over? I just bought some new lingerie, but you'd better hurry."

"Be there at seven," Hengel says. "Oh, I'll bring our favorite Shiraz."

"Sweetie, you think of everything. I love you, Claytie."

The Senator smiles. "I love you too, Brian. See you soon."

* * * * * * *

Months ago the man learned the IP address of Hengel's PDA and regularly accessed its billing history. From there he discovered the Senator's lobbyist lover in Georgetown. Nearly every member of Congress had a dirty secret or two. Hengel's would do nicely.

Several blocks away from the Hart Senate Office Building, the man listens in on the two lovebirds over his customized scanner. Its many features included a frequency sniffer, digital decryption module, and voiceprint analysis. For the past two hours it had dutifully searched several hundred nearby active PDA frequencies per second for Hengel's voiceprint. Tuesday evenings Hengel usually went to Brian's condo for two or three hours.

The man starts up the black Lexus and smoothly enters the winter evening traffic. *Yes, Senator—you're going to be quite late tonight.*

* * * * * * *

Senator Hengel parks a block away from Brian Ostergaard's condo two minutes before seven. He used to be nervous almost to the point of paranoia during such rendezvous, even wearing a wig and glasses from his car to the condo. Fourteen months of the affair without being "outed" have pretty much eliminated his earlier anxiety. He is United States Senator Clayton Douglas Hengel, a powerful and important man.

And an excited one, at that. Energized with anticipation, he springs out with a bottle of wine in hand, and clicks the automatic lock on his keychain. The alarm chirp of his Mercedes seems abnormally loud, startling Hengel. The sidewalk has patches of ice so he steps carefully.

He looks up from the icy concrete and he sees walking toward him a man in a beautifully cut Armani. Hengel grows nervous. As they close distance the stranger's face brightens with apparent recognition and friendliness.

"Senator Hengel! How are you tonight?"

The paranoia returns instantly. Fear flutters inside his chest like a trapped bat. Then he remembers that he is a powerful and important man. The stranger seems friendly, respectful, and wealthy. *Just another admirer. Nice looking, too.*

Hengel forces himself to relax. "Fine, fine! Mister . . . ?"

"West, Senator. Please call me Victor."

"How are you this evening, Victor?" Hengel asks in a smooth baritone.

"Quite well, Senator, thank you. I know you're a very busy man but I'd just like to shake the hand that sponsored the *Deadly Weapons Act*. I appreciate your clear stand on the gun issue. It can be hard to distinguish between one's true friends and enemies on the Hill."

Hengel's relief is complete. He removes his leather glove and happily obliges West with a hearty handshake. "It was my pleasure. Anything to make America's streets safer. And what do *you* do here in Washington, Victor?" *So handsome! I wonder if he's . . .*

"Oh, I work at Justice," West says with a steady gaze.

"Really?" *What luck! He actually works in the Beltway!*

"Yes. Field assignments, mainly."

Field assignments! A man of action! Be still my beating heart! He slyly appraises West's obvious fitness. *Even if Brian still went to Bally's, he'd never look this good! Oh, right—Brian is upstairs, waiting.*

"Glad to hear it, Victor. Keep up the fine work! I'm expected at a conference shortly, but it was a pleasure meeting you. Please call my office if I can ever be of help. I'm always happy to hear from my friends at Justice."

"Thank you, Senator. I'll keep that in mind. Good night, sir."

"Yes, you too, Victor."

Hengel walks away with that happy glow about him whenever he meets an enthusiastic member of the public, especially one who also happens to be such a beautiful guy. *He shook my hand with such care! And the way he stared into my eyes! Too bad he doesn't work at State. He'd be gay for sure!*

Hengel sneaks an over-the-shoulder look at West in his butch stride, evidently unconcerned with the ice. *I must conjure a way to meet him again sometime. Under the guise of government business, of course!*

His musings are interrupted as he feels a cool sensation on the back of his right hand. He stops underneath the lighted alcove, looks at his hand and sees some kind of clear residue. *Did that come from Victor?* He sniffs at it. Vaguely medicinal. Muttering, he wipes it off on the wine bottle's brown paper bag. The cool sensation—though not unpleasant—remains, like an invigorating conditioner on the scalp.

He looks down the sidewalk but West is gone. As Hengel goes through the building's front door, he wonders how such a clean-cut and gorgeous man could be so untidy.

* * * * * * *

"Victor West" turns the corner at a steady walk, smiling. The puns of his alias and employment were surely lost on the Senator. He carefully peels off his rubber thumb sachet, satisfied that most of its liquid is gone—smeared on Hengel's hand. He bags it in a little ZipLoc containing an ounce of powdered charcoal. To further protect himself he had coated most of his hand with NuSkin, which was tested for impermeability with a harmless compound. During and after Hengel the man had to concentrate on not touching himself with his own right thumb.

The NuSkin he would peel off later. The man could have easily poisoned Hengel from a distance with a dart, but then he wouldn't have had the satisfaction of meeting the treacherous old bastard face-to-face.

He also wouldn't have gotten the creeps from Hengel checking him out like a side of beef, either. *And what do you do here in Washington, Victor?*

In retrospect he wishes he'd replied "Sanitation."

To sponsor congressional legislation which plainly violated the Bill of Rights was traitorous. By deputing the use of force to disarm peaceable citizens, Hengel had initiated aggression and could—even under libertarian principles—be resisted with force. Although many libertarians would disagree with this strict scrutiny, he had no time for intellectual pantywaists. This was a *war* and too few Americans realized it. That's why they were losing their freedom. The war wasn't really even about politics, but for the right of individuals to enjoy sovereign and productive lives. It had been a unilateral war for decades, the government "shooting fish in a barrel" and the fish not even sensing that they were in a barrel, much less being shot.

No longer, however, thanks to the example of Krassny. Freedom may not survive this generation, but at least it would not expire without a fight.

The USG is astonished by the Krassnyite phenomenon, just as the Nazis were astonished by the Warsaw ghetto uprising of April 1943, and just as the Romans were astonished by the slave revolt under gladiator Spartacus. Bullies are always amazed when their victims resist.

Their first thought is *No fair!* They actually believe their violent control is a right. When aggression is left unchecked—challenged evil is indignant. Serial murderers winking at bereaved families during trial is what happens when good people, out of cowardice, refuse to defend themselves against street punks. *SS* death camp commandants shouting *Heil Hitler!* before their execution is what happens when citizens, out of cowardice, refuse to resist thugs hiding behind uniforms and politicians.

The man reaches his car parked two blocks over. *I wonder how the Senator is feeling right about now* he muses as he drives off into the frigid February night.

* * * * * * *

By the time Hengel steps out of the elevator, his sudden wheezing frightens him. He tells himself it's just chemical sensitivity to the freshly painted hallway, but he's never had a reaction this severe. The tightening of his chest worsens with each passing second. *Heart attack? Impossible! Not after a lifetime of jogging and healthy diet!*

Down the hall from Ostergaard's door Hengel staggers, dropping the wine bottle and vomiting onto his Gucci loafers. He can see nothing but the fuzzy-edged door . . . suddenly hard and reassuring beneath his pounding fists. "Br—*Brian!*"

* * * * * * *

The secondhand chair squeaks noisily as Louella Davis leans forward to place the black Jack on the red Queen. She should be reading that lovely new mystery novel instead of playing Canfield, but she can't concentrate.

If only the Senior Center were open tonight! She could play Bridge with her girlfriends, nattering about their lost youth—anything to forget about her cramped condo and a widow's loneliness. She knew that her nights at the Senior Center were just a temporary fix, but as she completed her "final lap" they sufficed to push away the drabs.

A hallway noise makes her jump. *Someone yelling for help outside?*

Heart pounding, Louella pushes herself stiffly upright. Though she lived in a comparatively safe Georgetown, violent crime often seeped in from outside. *Damn politicians! Can't keep the Center open, or the streets safe in the nation's capital . . .*

The shriek sounds like it's *right* outside.

Louella scurries to the door and peers through the peephole. Through her milky cataracts she can make out a man crumpled in the hallway. Heart attack, or maybe a stroke like Jerry, dying in the bathroom without so much as a chance to say good-bye after 46 years of marriage.

She takes a deep breath, unlocks the door, and flings it open, her mouth agape in shock. She sees her creepy-nice neighbor in whory Marlene Dietrich drag. At first, Louella thinks that Mr. Ostergaard is kissing the fallen man, but then she realizes that it's lugubrious CPR.

"Ms. Davis, the Senator's stopped breathing! Call 9-1-1!" screeches Ostergaard, his mint-green nightgown splayed open.

Dear God! Louella bolts back inside her apartment for the phone. As she dials the three-digit number for the second time in her life, she somehow knows that it's a waste of time. Death she has seen before.

* * * * * * *

Junior EMT Nick Booker quickly ascertains that their unresponsive DOA with the Hill haircut and expensive shoes is an important senator.

They'd arrived within minutes of the call to find pupils fixed and dilated. Defibbed him three times anyway with the screaming queen boyfriend in full freakout mode, and for what? Damn doc tells them to hang a bag of lido and keep him on Code A on their way back to the hospital.

Even the D.C. Metro cops, who have seen it all, are pretty stunned by the senator's lousy timing. Dying on the doorstep of your lingerie-clad gay lover was no way to go.

Being on cash retainer with *National Enquirer* hardly makes up for the worry about accidental needle sticks from these patients. Still, the call Booker was about to make was worth an easy two or three grand.

* * * * * * *

The man switches his scanner to the EMT frequencies and soon hears the DOA call on Hengel. Cardiac arrest, a paramedic says. Barring a detailed toxicology screen, his death will be ruled as natural causes.

He signals right and pulls over. Leaving the engine running, he gets out and walks around to the rear passenger side. A storm grate is next to the curb. The man squats down and reaches inside his shirt pocket. From a little metal tin he produces something about the size of a marble.

It is a clear capsule full of purple crystals. Potassium permanganate ($KMnO_4$) makes a mildly astringent antiseptic when dissolved in water, sometimes used by hospitals as a douche for fungal conditions. The capsule is tightly nested in a half capsule filled with clear liquid—glycerine ($C_3H_8O_3$). The half capsule is secured by a piece of tape around the circumference. Sticking halfway through the purple capsule is a straight pin.

The man pushes the pin through the crystals and into the glycerine, then withdraws it. The glycerine slowly seeps among the purple crystals, turning them a muddy brown. He places the capsule in the ZipLoc containing the rubber sachet and powdered charcoal, and then drops the baggie through the grate onto a concrete shelf four feet below. Instinctively he steps back.

For a few seconds nothing happens. Then, a small *pop!* A plume of hissing white smoke pours from the punctured capsule. The hissing grows louder—echoing within the concrete chamber—and suddenly the capsule turns blindingly white hot. The chamber is uncannily lit as if by magnesium flare. He can actually feel the heat and turns his head. It burns like rocket fuel for about ten seconds and then abruptly dies out. The whole package is nothing but a smoking black pea. *Bye-bye Hengel. Bye-bye evidence.*

Just as the man is walking around the Lexus—just as he is about to drive away—a D.C. Metro cop turns a corner and slowly approaches.

Shit! The man forces himself not to react to this random bad timing. *Stay cool and everything will be fine.* He is just reaching for the door handle as the cop pulls up and asks from an open window, "Everything all right, sir?" His breath is a vapor in the cold evening air.

In a luxury automobile and tailored suit, the man is well protected during a routine police encounter. D.C. Metro avoided stepping on powerful toes. He waves and smiles pleasantly as he opens his door to get in. "Everything's fine, officer. One of my tires felt a bit low on air and I wanted to check it out. But thank you for stopping. Good night, officer."

Reassurance. Respect. Reason. Gratitude. Closure.

Control.

The cop nods. "Good night, sir." His patrol car is already moving.

As the man drives away he grins tightly. He had parked so that the tailpipe was just behind the storm grate, thus hiding any escaping capsule smoke with his car's exhaust. The cop hadn't seen a thing.

Hengel had gone quite smoothly, and was certainly much less work than Gray. He'd considered abducting the Senator, but the discovery of his homosexual affair provided far too tempting an opportunity. The media will have fresh meat for many days of story.

And, with any luck, Brian Ostergaard's firm, the rabidly anti-self defense Policy Center on Violence, will be tar-babied with the scandal. Let *them* swat a few flies for a change. The PCV was a noisome bunch using concocted statistics, phony polls, and specious arguments to stampede the public into supporting unconstitutional and ineffective "gun control." The sexual and political collusion between a PCV lobbyist and the senatorial sponsor of the *DWA* would be too outrageous for even the national media to ignore.

It's always better to scratch two itches at once, the man thinks.

* * * * * * *

The FBI Special Agents on site at Brian Ostergaard's condo are taking special care. Although no foul play seems evident, Senator Hengel ranked #18 on the KK risk list. His Mercedes was already being taken to the crime lab. His body would shortly be autopsied by one of the FBI's best forensic pathologists. The condo building's front door, stairwell, elevator, and third floor hallway have been dusted for fingerprints. There had been no doorman on duty and no witnesses of the Senator's movement from car to hallway.

Mrs. Davis was of little help. She hadn't seen Hengel until opening her door. She thought that he was arriving rather than leaving, but wasn't sure.

Ostergaard had wisely changed his attire before the FBI had arrived, but neglected to remove every last trace of his makeup. A bit of eye shadow could still be seen.

A junior agent is taking Ostergaard's statement for an FD-302. "Sir, was Senator Hengel carrying anything when you found him in the hallway?"

"No, no, I don't think so. Not that I saw, at least."

"What about the bottle of wine we found in the hall?"

Ostergaard then recalls the Shiraz. "Oh, well, that could have been his. I didn't see it, though. I found him unconscious on the floor and tried to revive him with CPR. I wasn't paying attention to what he may have been carrying."

"Was the Senator a frequent guest in your home, Mr. Ostergaard?"

"Uh, no, I wouldn't say 'frequent'." Nervous.

"Then tonight was some sort of special occasion?" Setting him up.

"Uh, uh, no—no special occasion," says Ostergaard, rattled.

"So, then he *usually* arrived with an expensive bottle of red wine during his *infrequent* visits?" Skewered.

"Look, I don't know if it was even his, or if it was why he brought it."

Senior agent Paul Kinney has been listening in and is suspicious. He locates the wine which has already been bagged and tagged. He gingerly picks it up and looks through the thick polyethylene ZipLoc. The wine hadn't been opened and was in a brown paper bag. He notices an oily smear on the otherwise unsoiled and crisp bag. *Probably purchased this evening.*

The oily smear bothers him, however. On a hunch, he opens the evidence ZipLoc and ventures a sniff. Frowning, he sniffs again. Looking up, he asks Ostergaard, "Did you at any time handle this?"

Ostergaard is puzzled by all this sudden attention to the wine. "No, no I didn't. I didn't even *see* it until one of your agents found it in the hall."

"Sir, have you washed your hands since Senator Hengel was here?"

"Washed my *hands?* I can't see what—"

Kinney cuts him off. "Just answer my question. Have you washed your hands tonight?"

Ostergaard senses the mood change and it unnerves him. He replies a bit too forcefully, "No, I *haven't* washed my hands tonight. *Why?*"

"Good. Don't. We'll need to get some hand residue samples right now. Agent Ferris will take care of it."

Kinney turns and motions to another of his junior agents and quietly says, "Call Lloyd Moss down at CTU. I need the composition of that oily stain on the brown paper bag. Tonight. And get samples from all sinks and P-traps, as well as the bathtub drain."

The junior agent's eyes bulge. "Poison?"

"Very possibly," Kinney allows.

"Really? *Him?*" junior says, eyes darting to Ostergaard.

"Can't say for sure. If we can place Hengel here before seven, then, yeah, maybe. If we can't, then it might not have been Ostergaard."

* * * * * * *

The next day, Kinney, Ferris, and two junior agents meet in a conference room to discuss Hengel with Lloyd Moss from the CTU.

The Chemistry and Toxicology Unit of the FBI Crime Lab handles drug analysis, poison identification, arson evidence, and explosive composition. It enjoys some of the world's most sophisticated equipment, such as mass spectrometers, liquid chromatographs, and electron microscopes.

Not that such equipment assures fair and quality work.

The vaunted FBI Crime Lab was the subject of much scandal in the 1990s. Its reputation was shattered in 1997 by an 18-month government investigation which upheld allegations of serious malpractice. Lab examiners often worked backwards from the evidence to prove guilt, following no protocols, and ignoring precautions against contamination of evidence (*e.g.,* from carpeted floors and unfiltered air). Reports were altered or destroyed to enhance federal trial cases. The book exposé *Tainting Evidence* caused shockwaves throughout the Justice Department.

Little had been done since then to patch up the Lab's poor rep. Filters were installed and the carpeting removed, but not much else. Still, within the FBI, the Crime Lab examiners are cardinals of the Bureau vatican and highly regarded by field agents.

Lloyd Moss begins. "An identical solution was found on the brown paper bag, on the back of Hengel's right hand, and in his bloodstream. It was primarily CH_3SO, dimethyl sulfoxide. DMSO for short. No license is needed for purchase. It's an anti-inflammatory and pain reliever used as a liniment for arthritic animals. Available at all vet supply stores. Cheap, too."

"Is DMSO fatal?"

"Not in such a small quantity. But what it carried was. Strychnine."

"*Strychnine?*" the junior agents ask in unison.

"Yep, one of the most lethal natural poisons around. Quick, too. $C_{21}H_{22}N_2O_2$ to us chemists, strychnine is a deadly crystalline alkaloid. It's extracted from the seed of the *Strychnos nux-vomica*, an East Indian tree."

"So, our guy grows some of these East Indian trees in his backyard?" asks a junior agent known for his wisecracks.

Kinney and Ferris both glare at Smartass. So does the second junior agent after watching their reaction.

Moss takes the facetiousness in stride. Shaking his head he says, "Not likely. He probably bought some rodent bait and leeched out the crystals. Cheap, easy, and untraceable."

"Could he have bought strychnine from a medical supply house?"

"No, not in this concentration. In *very* dilute form it's sometimes used as a stimulant, but nobody stocks it full strength. No, our guy bought a $10 box of rat poison and boiled off the inert ingredients himself. Any chemistry student could have done it."

"How much strychnine is fatal?"

"LD_{50} is just 1 milligram per kilo of body weight[1]. LD_{100} is only about 20% higher, so no more than 100mg. would've been needed for the 180 pound Hengel. A fat drop is all it took. The DMSO transdermal carrier did the rest."

"How'd the perp apply it to Hengel?" asks the second junior agent.

"Very simply. From his gloved right thumb as he shook Hengel's hand. Politicians love to meet admirers." The room is momentarily quiet as everyone contemplates how easy it would have been.

"Any traces of DMSO or strychnine at Ostergaard's place?"

"No, none."

Kinney says, "Well, that fits. We got a liquor store hit on Hengel's VISA. He bought that bottle of Shiraz at 6:47PM. He died *arriving* on Ostergaard's doorstep, not leaving. Ostergaard's in the clear."

"Any liquor store camera footage?"

"Yeah, including the parking lot. Hengel had no contact with anyone but the clerk. We checked him and the store for poison. Nada. This wasn't a random act. Hengel was targeted."

Moss says, "He couldn't have been poisoned then, anyway. *Way* too early. Though not instantaneous, pure strychnine is still pretty fast. It wouldn't have taken fifteen minutes. He'd never've made it to Ostergaard's."

"How long *would* it have taken?" Kinney asks.

"Oh, say, three minutes. Since Hengel wiped off some of it, five, tops."

Kinney says, "So, backtracking Hengel's movements and assuming it wasn't Ostergaard, a third party could have made contact only in the third-

---

1   LD_{50} is standard toxicity measure of median lethal dosage, *i.e.* mortality for 50% of subjects.

floor hallway, the elevator, the ground floor, sidewalk, or street out in front. And not before then since Hegel's car was clean."

"That's seems to follow, yes," Moss replies.

Kinney says, "So, logically, where did he met Hengel?"

Ferris offers, "Not in the elevator or on the third floor. And probably not even on the ground floor. Too much possible exposure to witnesses."

Kinney is pleased. "Exactly."

Ferris brightens. "Then it was outside the building on the sidewalk or street. Simply walked up, said hello, shook his hand, and strolled off. He'd have been a couple of miles away when Hengel collapsed in the hall."

Kinney nods his head. "Very good. But why even take the risk of *any* exposure? He didn't *have* to contact Hengel at all. Why not just drug his car door handle or something?"

Moss understands why not. "Because that wouldn't have fulfilled his needs. Because Hengel was somehow *personal*."

Heads nod. This makes sense to all in the room.

"Jilted boyfriend?" poses the serious junior agent.

Kinney says, "That was my first thought, but since Hengel was #18 on the KK risk list, let's eliminate the political motive before the sexual."

Moss keeps the ball rolling. "OK, it's probable that the perp knew his concoction's kill time, which means he planned on death occurring within three to five minutes of a handshake. He *could* have chosen another poison, one that acted faster like nicotine, or slower like ricin, but didn't. So, what does his choice of strychnine tell us?"

"That he needed sufficient delay in order to escape," says Smartass, coming out of his shell.

"Correct. But why not a poison that caused death in several *hours* versus several minutes?" prods Kinney.

Ferris jumps in. "Because death had to occur while Hengel was still at Ostergaard's. To cause a scandal—maybe even cast suspicion!"

"Bingo!" says Kinney. "Our man likely has strong political feelings about Hengel and the gun-control PCV."

Lloyd Moss speaks what is on everyone's mind. "Guys, I'd say we have ourselves another KK. And I'd bet Hengel wasn't his first."

Kinney mulls this over and says, "And *I'd* bet Hengel won't be his *last*. Our man has found a hobby."

The room turns silent as everybody ponders this.

Something suddenly occurs to Moss. "I wonder why he didn't plant some strychnine or DMSO at Ostergaard's, especially in a container with his prints already on it? That'd have *really* caused him some trouble."

Kinney frowns at this. "Yeah, you're right Lloyd, that *is* baffling. Our guy is certainly sophisticated enough to have thought of this, and skilled enough to have done it. It would have cooked Ostergaard's goose unless we figured it out."

"Maybe he has some principles. Didn't want to send an innocent man to prison for homicide."

It's Smartass, but he's serious now. This time nobody glares. His comments actually make an odd kind of sense.

Kinney remarks out loud, almost to himself, "A principled killer. Shit, just what we need."

* * * * * * *

The next day FBI Director Klein phones the White House. Hengel and the President had gone to Georgetown together.

"Sir, we've established several facts about the Senator's death. He was definitely murdered." Klein then fully explains the poison and its delivery.

The President is silent for several seconds. He pales visibily as he says, "So, anybody with high school chemistry, $20 of feed store supplies, and a rubber glove can kill politicians with a handshake?"

"That's about it, sir. One last thing. The Bureau now believes that the same man also abducted and probably killed Judge Gray two years ago."

The President's eyebrows arch in skepticism. "A serial killer? There have been over two dozen KKs in or around the Beltway, Paul. And Clayton wasn't abducted like Jon Gray."

"Yes, sir, that's true, but the other KK perpetrators all left at least *some* evidence behind, though nothing conclusive. The Gray and Hengel acts were different. Both in adverse weather, and both on an early February Tuesday. Both committed absolutely clean, unlike the other KKs."

"But they were two years apart," challenges the President.

"Yes, sir, but to us that may indicate the depth of his planning. He takes all the time he needs to execute his deed perfectly. He attacks suddenly, decisively, and leaves no trail. He operates in low-light conditions. He's patient and highly intelligent. Strongly motivated, but he has a rein on his emotions. My SOARU boys call him 'The Leopard.' He's likely between 40 and 55. A younger man would act more rashly. An older man wouldn't have the drive."

"'The Leopard,' huh? Jesus, Paul, don't let the media hear that."

"Certainly not, sir. I've sent strict instructions that the moniker is not to be used in any internal memoranda."

"Good. What else?"

Klein hesitates, and then says it. "Well, sir, we're thinking that he could even be law enforcement. It would explain why we've no leads so far."

The President drops his pen in surprise. "Paul, are you serious?"

"Yes, sir. We both know that it's happened before. Right now we're compiling a list of LE officers, active duty or not, who have expressed strong right-wing political opinions. As you know, we've been correlating NRA membership lists for years. In particular we're focussing on dismissed tri-state officers who harbor a grudge against the Government and who may have seen Judge Gray and Senator Hengel as appropriate targets."

"Hmmm. Well, his long planning period works in our favor. You've got until February 2013 to catch him," concludes the President, bitterly.

* * * * * * *

FBI Special Agent Kinney barges into his superior's office. The SAC of the Washington FO looks up in surprise, indignation, and curiosity.

"Sir, we have a break in Hengel."

"Really?"

"Yes, sir. Two witnesses, and now some physical evidence."

"Witnesses? It's been four days. Who piped up now?"

"The first was a neighbor across the street from Ostergaard's condo. He was walking his dog around 1900 hours and saw a man briefly talking to the Senator. He was about six feet tall, mid-forties, medium-length blonde hair, wearing a suit and tie, carrying a briefcase."

The SAC perks up. "Did he see this man shake Hengel's hand?"

"No, sir. They were in the middle of a conversation when he left his residence. The witness continued walking north for a block and then turned right. About a minute later this same well-dressed man had also taken the same route. While the dog stopped to pee, the witness turned and saw the man get into a black or dark blue, four-door sedan. He thinks it was a Lexus or an Infinity."

The SAC is silent, his fingers steepled in front of his face. After a moment he says, "Did he notice any other person in the vicinity?"

"Negative."

"Well, then it seems he saw our man. Did he see his face clearly?"

"Unfortunately not. Said he seemed handsome, but average. Couldn't offer anything more than that. The witness is 63 years old and wears glasses."

"You said witnesses, plural. Who else do we have?"

Kinney grins. "A Metro cop."

The SAC's eyes widen. "No shit? A cop?"

Still grinning, Kinney says, "Yes, sir. He saw a well-dressed man alone in a black 2006 Lexus stopped at about 1915 hours on N and 25th, by the south end of Rock Creek Park. Said he'd stopped to check a tire."

"This cop get his DL and run a 27?"

"No, he had no reasonable suspicion to detain him. Cop never even got out of his unit. They spoke only a few words as he drove by on patrol. Said he wasn't acting nervous or suspicious in any way. Was polite and confident. The cop didn't think anything about it until we tickled Metro for any contacts with a dark-colored Lexus. The encounter was so brief and nonchalant that the cop hardly remembered it."

"Physical description of the suspect?"

"Virtually the same as the dog-walker, though he thought he might be able to recognize him again. He's working with an FIC artist now, but the face they have so far could be nearly anyone of that archetype."

The SAC grimaces. "I've never trusted the Facial Identification Catalog images, Kinney. I know I'm 'old school' but all experienced sketch artists agree that the 'Chinese menu' of 960 facial features is dangerously manipulative. Remember the original OKBomb John Doe #2? The frontal bareheaded view of a man? That was from the FIC! The witness had only seen him in *profile,* and wearing a baseball cap! No wonder we never caught him, even after we had to replace the FIC image with a hand-drawn sketch. Kinney, get an *artist* on this. See if Jeanne Boylan is available."

Kinney is making notes. "Yes, sir."

"Did your witness get a plate?"

"Not the number, but he thought it might be a Virginia plate. Not D.C. The year and make he's positive on; his uncle has the same car but in silver. We're compiling a database on all black 2006 Lexuses registered in Virginia, West Virginia, Maryland, Delaware."

The SAC is pensive. He offers a final idea. "Computer time is cheap. Extend the database to include D.C., Pennsylvania, Ohio, and North Carolina. If we miss this guy, it won't be because he lives in Philly or Canton."

"Yes, sir," Kinney says while making notes.

"You'll still correlate the list of Lexus owners with disgruntled LE officers, right?"

"Yes, sir, active, dismissed, and retired."

"Good. I know it's a long shot, but we've got to start somewhere."

"I agree, sir. And the physical evidence looks encouraging."

The SAC had almost forgotten. "Yeah, what's the story on that?"

"The Metro cop took us to the spot on N where the Lexus had stopped. I had a team scour the area within a 100 yard radius. Nothing conclusive on the street, sidewalk, or grass, but below a storm grate they saw scorched concrete. They pulled the grate and collected samples of some charred material. Materials says it's the remains of a small chemical self-destruct device contained in clear polyethylene, like a ZipLoc bag."

"Chemical self-destruct device? What the hell?" exclaims the SAC.

"Yes, sir, it is. Glycerine, potassium permanganate, and charcoal. According to the ATF, this sort of thing has been used by arsonists. Through spectroscopic analysis, the PE's dictation says that some of the burned material is consistent with incinerated strychnine."

"Only 'consistent with', not 'identified as'?" asks the SAC, disappointed. The term "consistent with" is forensic science shorthand for "may" and allows for reasonable doubt in trial proceedings, while "identified as" does not.

"Yes, sir."

"Well, it's still something. Juries can always be led to believe that 'consistent with' means guilty. Find our Lexus owner, Kinney."

* * * * * * *

North Carolina   25 February 2011

Two weeks later FBI Special Agents Malmberg and Swingle from the Raleigh FO pull up to a tidy split-level home outside Wake Forest. They've been interviewing all owners of dark colored 2006 Lexuses. This is their last stop, though it was first on their list. The registered owner of this Lexus was an LLC shell. The agents had to screen the insurance company databases for its VIN to find a policy tied to a driver. This alone made them suspicious.

Then, they had to find his actual residence. That, and the background investigation, took two days. His DL address was a mail drop, and no property or phone was listed in his name. They made several phone calls to his former superiors, which yielded little. Looked at his credit card records for the past year. A new electric stove delivered to his home, paid for by his VISA card, was all it took.

The Bureau was buzzing all the way to D.C. He *so* fit the case profile. Traps and traces on his phone had been activated this morning. Four supporting agents are standing by one block over.

Walking up the driveway, Swingle ventures around the left garage corner and looks through a window.

Rejoining Malmberg, he says, "Yep, it's parked inside."

Malmberg nods as he pushes the doorbell.

Within seconds the door is opened by a fit and handsome man in his mid-forties with medium-length blonde hair, about six feet tall.

"Raymond Foster?"

The homeowner coolly sizes up the agents, instantly pegging them for feds. "Yes. Who are you?"

"Mr. Foster, I'm Special Agent Malmberg with the FBI, and this is Special Agent Swingle." They flash their leather wallet shields. "May we—"

"Gentlemen, I'd like to inspect your credentials," says Foster. "And a business card from each of you, too."

Malmberg glances at Swingle. Most people went into a flutter at a surprise interview by the FBI. That Foster did not was unusual. The agents also weren't used to having their creds inspected, but if they refused Foster could claim that he didn't believe they were FBI and close the door.

As Foster pockets their cards, Malmberg tries again. "May we come in and talk with you?"

It's not a question. It never really is.

Foster returns their badges after a thorough scrutiny. "Here is fine. What do you want?"

Malmberg notices Foster's hawklike alertness. This would not be easy.

"Sir, it's probably less embarrassing if we did this inside. It'll only take a minute," says Swingle.

"What can I possibly have to be embarrassed about standing in my own front doorway?" Foster calmly replies. "We talk here, or not at all. Your choice."

"As you wish, Mr. Foster," says Malmberg. *What an asshole!* "Do you own a black 2006 Lexus?"

"Why do you ask?"

"Sir, please answer the question," Swingle says firmly.

Foster doesn't quite roll his eyes, but almost. He says in a clear voice, "Are you here to detain or arrest me under lawful due process?"

Malmberg senses that he's struck paydirt.

"No, sir, and don't overreact," Swingle retorts. "This is just routine questioning as part of a general inquiry. Now, do you own such a vehicle?"

Malmberg winces inside at Swingle's line. After eight years in the Durham PD, Foster knows that "routine questioning" is never routine.

Foster parries, "You need to tell me what this is all about and why you're really here."

Malmberg watches his partner bridle and say, "Sir, we're not obliged to discuss the nature of our investigation with the public."

"Oh, so an 'inquiry' has just been elevated to an *investigation*?" Foster retorts with a challenging stare. "Well, as *you* know, *I'm* not obliged to discuss my possessions with strangers who drop by unannounced."

He begins to shut the door.

Malmberg sees his fish getting away and can't stop himself from blurting, "Sir, we *know* you own a black 2006 Lexus."

"Most impressive," Foster says blandly. "Good day, Agents Malmberg and Swingle. Do call for an appointment if you must come by again."

Malmberg is now very anxious. Nobody they've interviewed over the past three days has been so blatantly uncooperative. Foster is definitely hiding something. Just before the door closes Malmberg takes a final gamble, trying to provoke any reaction to confirm his suspicions. A twitch of the eye. A stammer. A dropped jaw. A nervous scratching of the nose. A cough.

Anything, and Malmberg would have him.

"Sir, do you recall your whereabouts on Tuesday, February 8th?"

The door stops. Only half of Foster's face can be seen. He stares at the feds for one long second, a hard glint shining in his eye.

"Good-bye, gentlemen," Foster says, almost bored sounding.

Malmberg sees no chink in Foster's armor, which to Malmberg is the biggest chink of all. *Think you're a pro, eh? Too much of pro is amateur!*

The door closes, leaving the two agents standing on his porch, their department store suit jackets luffing in the breeze.

They walk back to their Bucar without a word and drive away. Around the block they pull up next to their colleagues.

Through his open window Malmberg says, "Did you copy all that?" *These idiots probably fucked up the radio link.*

"Loud and clear, George. What a hard-ass. If it's him, we won't get him the easy way."

"Yeah, no shit, Frank," Malmberg spits. *As if you could get him at all!* "See ya back at the ranch." *Dork!*

Malmberg peels away with authority. As they drive south on Highway 1 to the Raleigh FO, Swingle says, "Real smart. You tipped off Foster."

Malmberg hates to be criticized; it reminds him of his worthless, drunk old man. He fights a bilious surge of anger. *Just keep your cool, George.*

"Well worth it," Malmberg snaps. "*You* saw the way he glared at us."

Swingle turns away and shakes his head.

"Fucker's dirty, Lyle," Malmberg mutters.

"Yeah, probably, but now he knows he's under glass."

"So, what? According to the guys in the Durham FO he had a rep for hating the Bureau and feds in general. Rattling his cage may trip him up."

Swingle considers this. "Decorated combat vet? Former cop? Three victorious gunfights—all headshots?"

Malmberg is silent, fuming.

"Somehow I don't think Foster's cage is so easily rattled, George."

"We'll see, Lyle. We'll see. I wonder who he called once we left?"

* * * * * * *

Fifteen minutes later at their Raleigh FO, Malmberg and Swingle barge in a technician's office. He looks up through his thick glasses and says, "You here about Foster, right?"

"No duh. Whaddaya got?" says Malmberg. "He make any calls?"

The tech shakes his head. "No calls, but one email. Wanna read it?"

Malmberg just stares at him. *Dorito crumb punk!*

"Okay, *okay*—here's a printout."

Malmberg looks at it, his face a grimace as if trying to focus. Swingle cranes his head over to read it and then frowns.

"Hey, what the fuck is this?" Malmberg says. "It's all gibberish!"

The tech applies his best shit-eating grin. "In our biz, it's called 'encryption,' not 'gibberish.' Anyway, he emailed his attorney. Maybe you've heard of him: Solomon Rothstein?"

Malmberg has had enough for the day. "Awww, fuck!"

"Oh, this is Not Good," Swingle moans. "I give it about 10 minutes before the SAC hauls us in to ask if we *really* know what the hell we're doing."

The tech says, "Yeah, I hear that Rothstein is the Prince of Darkness. Before you bag Foster, you better make sure you got about a dozen witnesses and a truck full of surveillance video. His fingerprints in blood would help. And then, *maybe* ... "

10 minutes later

"Do you guys *really* know what the hell you're doing?" demands the SAC. "I just got off the phone with the US Attorney. This Foster 'person of interest' called his lawyer just after your contact interview. Talk about a 'Red Alert'! And you didn't even arrest the guy!"

Swingle says, "Yes, sir, we've heard. We're not exposed on this, I promise. Since we had no PC to arrest, we weren't required to Mirandize him. And we didn't force our way into his home. Everything was done by the Manual. Frank has the interview audio."

The SAC calms down a bit and says, "Yeah, I've listened to it. The interview was kosher, I agree. We just have to step carefully from now on, especially when you interview Foster's friends and associates. Rothstein is gonna stay on top of us on this."

"Yes, sir."

"Don't look so glum," says the SAC. "This'll cheer you up. A warrant for Foster's bank records. Since he didn't buy any gopher poison on his credit cards during the past year, maybe he wrote a check at some feed store."

Malmberg replies, "I wouldn't bet on it, sir. Probably paid cash. He works pretty damn clean."

The SAC smiles. "Not clean enough. Dumbshit used his own car, didn't he? Keep digging, boys. Don't screw up so I can keep Rothstein off our asses."

Snow Hill, North Carolina   March 2011

Malmberg hates this part of the job. Endless field interview and 302s.

"Lyle, if I smell another bag of grain, I'm gonna puke!"

"Not unless I puke first. What is this, George, our 27th ag supply we've been to?" Swingle whines.

Malmberg replies with a bitter chuckle. "127th, it feels like. OK, this is it. 'Snow Hill Farm and Ranch.'"

FBI agents always got people's attention in the hinterlands. They couldn't believe G-men in their little towns. This feed store manager was no different.

"Yes, sir, Agent Malmberg. Anything I can do to help. Let's ask Jenny. She's here most of the time."

Malmberg loves this kind of fawning. *Fuckin A you'll do anything to help! Maybe this Jenny isn't a cow like the others.*

Jenny is called into the Mr. Brunton's office, its walls adorned with years of outdated calenders featuring Tractors Of The Month and so forth.

After introducing themselves, Agent Swingle asks, "Jenny do you recall having seen the man in this photo in your store?"

She carefully looks at the reproduced driver's license photo. "He looks kinda familiar. Maybe he's been here once before. He's not a regular, that's for sure."

Malmberg thinks Jenny is good looking, for a country chick. *Nice ass.* He says, "Maybe once before? The man we're looking may have bought some gopher bait or horse liniment. Does that ring any bells?"

This is borderline tainting a witnesses. Swingle shoots Malmberg a hard glance. Neither Jenny nor her manager notice; they're still looking at Foster's photo.

She looks up with a growing smile. "Yeah, gopher bait! I *do* remember a guy who bought some. Just a few months ago. December, yeah. That's why he stood out in my mind."

"Why was that?" Malmberg says.

Jenny looks at him like he's the silliest man on earth.

"Because gophers hibernate in winter."

Smartass little bitch!

Brunton adds, "Most rodents do," trying to be helpful.

Malmberg thinks he comes across like the *Jeopardy* know-it-all Alex Trebek. *Ooh, I'm sorry, George, but the answer we were looking for was "hi-ber-nate." Hibernate. Most rodents hi-ber-nate in winter.*

Swingle asks, "Now Jenny, was *that* the man who bought the gopher bait in December?"

Her smile fades as she looks back at the photo. Time slows to a virtual standstill. The agents are hungry for the meat of confirmation, and she knows it. She wants to help the FBI, but doesn't want to get the wrong man into trouble, either. She finally looks up. "I couldn't say for sure."

Malmberg moves a few inches closer and says, "Jenny, now this is very important. Just answer us this: *could* it have been the same man?" His very proximity is almost sexual, though she doesn't notice him trying to peek down her plaid flannel blouse.

Jenny's eyes fall back to the grainy color photo. He's handsome, but cold and distant. He *does* look familiar, though, and the FBI seems to already know who he is and what he purchased at her store. The two agents obviously want him very badly. She's flattered they think she can help.

He could even be a terrorist.

She makes a decision.

"Well, now that I look at it again, yes, it *could* have been him."

Malmberg's glance at Swingle hums with triumph.

"I'm not positive, sir, but yes, it could have been him," Jenny says.

Malmberg turns to the manager. "Mr. Brunton, we'll need to drive Jenny to Raleigh for a statement. We'll have her back in a few hours." *Maybe.*

Nobody asks Jenny. She is now just a commodity to be transported and inventoried in the commerce of law enforcement, a subcorporation of Justice.

Brunton is delighted to have been of help. "Yes, fine, fine. I'll cover for her in the meantime."

Jenny looks over her shoulder on the way out, suddenly having second thoughts. She feels as though she's fallen in a rushing river which is rapidly taking her downstream. And she realizes she can't swim, but it's too late.

* * * * * * *

When she began equivocating during the car trip to Raleigh, they gently steered her back on course. Malmberg knows they are cutting things too closely, but they are desperate to keep Jenny onboard. By the time she made her statement, she was "90% sure" that Raymond Scott Foster was the man who purchased with cash a box of Gopher BeGone on or about Saturday, 18 December 2010. Her deposition, along with the D.C. evidence, constituted probable cause for a Federal District Judge to sign a search warrant.

* * * * * * *

Raleigh FBI waits to execute the warrant at 10:03AM when Foster is en route downtown to meet a friend, have lunch, and then go to the gym. He won't be home until after three. Agents tail Foster, waiting for a call from the forensics team. At 2:48PM, it comes. The senior ASAC answers, listens for about 30 seconds, mutters "Thanks" and hangs up.

His face grim, he says to his fellow agents, "Nada. Not in the house, not in the car. No strychnine, no DMSO, no potassium permanganate, no glycerine, no Senator Hengel dartboard. They went through his place for nearly five hours and found nada. Fucking *nada*."

* * * * * * *

At 3:16PM Raymond Foster pulls up in his driveway. He senses something is wrong as a neighbor saunters over, frowning.

"Hey, Ray, the feds were in your house all day. What's up?"

Foster replies with steely calm, "May I use your telephone, Ed?"

* * * * * * *

"Whaddaya mean he's got a fucking *alibi*?" yells Malmberg. "How could he be in goddamn *Durham* when he was up in D.C. offing Hengel?"

The SAC says in his most soothing voice, "George, calm down. Foster could have *told* you that he was attending his daughter's play at Duke and that he took half the cast out for dinner afterwards, but he's never liked the Bureau. I guess he hoped we'd act on bad info and embarrass ourselves."

The SAC then turns arctic. "And that's exactly what *happened*. Did you know that Foster was in Jacksonville—*Florida*, by the way—with his brother's family from December 17th until January 2nd?"

Swingle and Malmberg just stand there, blinking.

"Yeah, I know what's going through your minds: no airline travel during that time on his credit cards. Well, there wouldn't be. He *drove*."

Malmberg coughs. *Oh shit!*

"Sir, we couldn't have known about his Christmas vacation or his daughter's play. Foster clammed up on us from the start!"

The SAC turns red. "And just when did we rely solely on *subjects'* testimony to make our cases? Hell, if they always *talked*, half of us would be looking for other careers! This was damn sloppy work! Actually, it was even worse than sloppy. You've exposed the Bureau!"

"*S-sir?*" Swingle manages to blurt.

"Oh, yeah, here's the best part," says the SAC, taking a deep breath to force his heart rate down. "The US Attorney just heard from Rothstein. Seems our favorite shyster had a little chat with your feed store witness Jenny Collins. She told him that you and Malmberg convinced her to finger Foster when she repeatedly told you that she was nowhere near certain about him. Now, tell me there's absolutely *no* truth whatsoever to *that*."

Swingle glances at Malmberg and swallows, hard.

Malmberg returns the glance with a stare. *Don't fade on me now, Lyle!*

* * * * * * *

Durants Neck, North Carolina   March 2011

A tea kettle whistle rises in tone, peaking at a high D#. It's hard to tear himself away from his living room view of the Albemarle Sound cypress trees, but he pads to the kitchen, removes the kettle, and makes his Chinese herbal tea. He hears a low rumbling *boom* from across the Perquimans River to the west. Harvey Point is the CIA's secretive 1,600 acre paramilitary training base. Locals are accustomed to helicopters and blacked-out transports coming and going at all hours. Plus the random, incessant explosions.

He returns to his reading chair by the window, settles in, and spreads out the morning newspaper. He's been looking forward to reading the top story for nearly an hour, but forced himself to leisurely get around to it.

It's an article about the FBI, featuring the fruitless search of an innocent man's home. Unnamed sources described the quest for owners of 2006 Lexus automobiles, and how one Raymond Foster evidently fit the vague description of Senator Hengel's killer. The main thread of the story was how the FBI case agents failed to clear Foster as a possible suspect and then apparently manipulated a young female witness into making an inaccurate statement. The botched Swan and Bradford raids out West were also mentioned.

The man puts down the paper and takes a sip of hot tea. He smiles faintly as he remembers that night in D.C. It was very bad fortune to have been seen by *two* witnesses, and one of them a cop. That bad fortune was compounded by the fact that the Metro cop had recalled the year, make, and color of the car. Nevertheless, the trail had ended there.

The Lexus wasn't his. Never was. He "borrowed" it from a Falls Church, Virginia woman he knew of through a mutual friend. She would be in Spain the entire month of February, and was storing her car at their friend's house. When the man learned that this friend would be in Seattle on business, he simply drove to Fairfax, parked a quarter mile away, and walked with his electronics briefcase to his friend's home. He had the house keys and alarm combo. The Lexus was parked in the garage, with the keys. He swapped out its plates and drove across the Potomac into D.C. wearing a movie-quality blonde wig. He returned by 7:45PM, reinstalled the original plates, wiped off his prints, walked back to his car, and drove home.

If the Lexus owner or their mutual friend were ever questioned, they enjoyed the unassailable alibi of having been out of town. They had zero risk. That was paramount, for the man would not jeopardize innocent third parties.

And, there was nearly zero risk for him. The mutual friend would never know that he'd used the Lexus for a few hours.

It was just about perfect.

The man smiles at the FBI's resources wasted on tracking down and questioning all those blonde-haired male Lexus owners.

Only a dumbshit would ever use his own car!

2011 USA economic news

Cast your whole vote, not a strip of paper merely, but your whole influence. A minority is powerless while it conforms to the majority; it is not even a minority then; but it is irresistible when it clogs by its whole weight. If the alternative is to keep all just men in prison, or give up war and slavery, the State will not hesitate which to choose. If a thousand men were not to pay their tax bills this year, that would not be as violent and bloody a measure as it would be to pay them, and enable the State to commit violence and shed innocent blood. This is, in fact, the definition of a peaceable revolution, if any such is possible.
— Henry David Thoreau, *Civil Disobedience*

The first Baby Boomers (*i.e.,* those born in 1946) begin to turn 65 years old in the spring and permanently leave the workforce. The retirement has two macro effects. The first is that they no longer buy new stocks with their paychecks. The market infusion from their IRAs, 401(k)s and Keoghs is over.

Economists call the 79 million Baby Boomers "the rat in the snake" for their post-WW2 demographic swell. As a percentage of the population, nothing like it in history had ever happened.

By December the Dow has tumbled 18% from 3,409 to 3,024. Gold is $3,067/ounce. A 1:1 ratio of gold and the Dow has not been seen since January 1980 when both were at 800. Annual inflation is 24%.

The second effect is the great (and final) drain on the "Social Security" system, which comes under unpreventable actuarial attack. It quickly becomes obvious that the so-called "trust fund" was never actually there—just like all those anti-government whackos had been claiming since the mid-1970s. President McBlane signs an SS tax hike which nearly doubles FICA withholding from wages.

Colleges erupt. *"Why pay it—we'll never see it!"* students chant. The fabric of America, already badly frayed at its edges, begins to unravel.

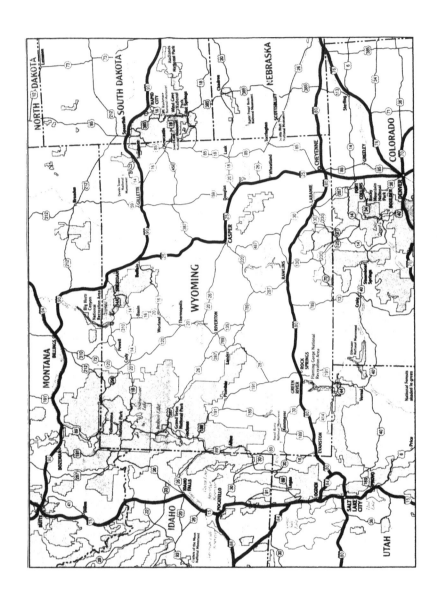

❖ 2012

Casper, Wyoming
Preston Ranch   **Summer 2012**

James, Jr. and Hanna were away at church camp, and have turned into quite the little letter writers. Father and son are enjoying the exchange of thoughts, ideas, and advice. Juliette teased her husband for "stalking the mailbox," waiting for his son's next missive. The latest one contained a question: "Hey Dad, which is worse in a friend, weakness or selfishness?"

Dear #1 Son,

Your mom and I were very happy to read that you'd won the .22 rifle competition last week! And with a camp's "ratty old Marlin", too! I'm sure it wasn't much of a contest because you've been a great shot since you were eight. If they'd let you use your own .22 Ruger, nobody would have had a chance!

You raise an interesting question. I would have to say that weakness is worse in a friend than selfishness.

Selfishness is more reliable; it can be plugged into your equation and planned for. Weakness, however, springs up erratically and is usually more difficult to envision than selfishness.

I'll tell you *exactly* what weakness in a friend is like. It's like buying a mediocre quality rifle scope, such as a Tasco. Remember that BLR .308 we bought last year with the Tasco? Remember how quickly it broke at the range after just 47 rounds?

Oh, it'll look nice and give OK service—as long as it doesn't get used *too* much or knocked around or have to endure huge environmental swings. *However,* on the day when you *really* need it to perform, when all is riding on that moment, after you've come to rely on it because it's never let you down before, it will daisy on you.

And when that happens, you're presented with the balloon payment. See, you hadn't truly *paid* for your Tasco when you bought it, like a Leupold. Oh, no—the final bill for mediocre quality always comes later, and far enough into the future that you got suckered into believing that you'd bought great quality for much less.

You don't buy mediocre quality, you only lease it. There's always a final payment due at the end. (We've talked about leasing, right?)

Ironically, you'd have been better off having bought *low* quality. It would have failed on you almost instantly, and you'd have learned right then to invest in only the best. But when you buy mediocre quality and it eventually fails on you, you're tempted to think that you merely got a lemon and then you go out and replace it with another Tasco. When the second one fails on you again, you're faced with owning up to a pair of very unpleasant facts: one, you mistakenly bought cheap, and two, you repeated the error. Many people cannot admit this to themselves, so what do they do? Yep, they buy their *third* Tasco. Pride locked them into circular behavior. After the money spent on three Tascos they could have bought a Leupold in the first place.

So, friends are like scopes. Invest in the best, and any failures you suffer in them you will know are rare. Avoid weak people and you avoid the sneaking suspicion that they will someday let you down. Because they will. They won't be able to help it, no matter their devotion to you.

How I wished I learned this at your age! Aren't you blessed to have such a wise dad? Heh! (Actually, I am the blessed one, with a son keen enough to have asked the question.) Anyway, I hope this was helpful to you. (Are there any "Leupold" quality kids there?) Till next time,

Your loving father

P.S. Hanna writes your mother that "her big brother" has been sticking up for her. Good boy! That's what big brothers do.

2012 USA economic and social news

The stock market continues to slide, despite Fed intervention with cheap money. The housing market, long stagnant, begins to contract. Suburban homes are dumped for 30¢ on the dollar. Gold is over $3,200/ounce.

The Gray Outrage begins. "Golden Years" have turned to pewter. *"We didn't work for 45 years to live in a mobile home and eat cat-food!"* Their outrage is countered by a youth revolt over the SS tax hike. Blaming the *"old farts"* for their high taxes, assaults on the elderly increase. Nursing homes install metal detectors, and retirement villages bristle with barbed wire and rifle-toting guards.

Casper FBI Field Office   November 2012

Special Agent Bleth picks up the phone, disconnecting the speaker. Director Klein's familiar voice says, "Doug, how are you this morning?"

"Fine, sir, thank you. And you?"

He hears Klein's tinny laugh in reply. "D.C. was and always will be a swamp. Only the alligators have changed. So, bring me up to speed on the Wyoming election yesterday."

Bleth gathers his notes and says, "Just about what we expected, sir. They've won SDs 26, 28, and 30. Meaning, they're targeting Fremont and Natrona counties. HD victories were 3, 5, 22, 29, 31, 32, 34, 38, and 52. Affected counties were also Platte, Campbell, and Sheridan."

"So, in the 2014 general election you're expecting, what, five new counties?"

"That's correct, sir. For a total of 17 of 23 counties. Libertarians now control 40% of the Senate and 43% of the House. If they are successful in 2014, their block in the legislature will be about 55%. Then they will be able to table and pass all majority vote bills."

Director Klein observes, "But they won't have a two-thirds majority to override vetoes, right?"

Bleth sighs. "True, but if they elect their candidate for governor, there won't be anything *to* veto. The governor and 50.1% of the legislature will be all they need to pass any bill they desire."

"Oh, right, I forgot about their executive branch. Any leads on their likely gubernatorial candidate?"

"Not yet, sir, but he should surface next year to begin his campaign."

Klein harumphs. "Well, he's sure taking his time, isn't he?"

2012 USA political news

But we are in the age of the mediocre man. He is dull, colorless, boring—but inevitably victorious. The amoeba outlives the tiger because it divides and continues in its immortal monotony. The masses are the final tyrants....

The roar of the plodders is inarticulate, but deafening. They have no brain, but they have a thousand arms to grasp and clutch at you, drag you down.

— Trevanian, *Shibumi*, p.106

Even though SS is a "third rail issue" the Republican presidential candidate truthfully warns the public that the current SS program is *"doomed by long overdue reality"* and that an immediate reduction in benefits is the only way to prevent collapse. The Libertarian candidate is even more stern on SS, stating that the elderly have *"bought into a false retirement that will soon evaporate before their eyes."*

McBlane declares that SS benefits will remain in force regardless of the taxes required. This is precisely what the Gray Lobby wants to hear, and the McBlane/Connor Democratic ticket is elected by their vast support.

> The two party system...is a triumph of the dialectic. It showed that two could be one and one could be two and had probably been fabricated by Hegel for the American market on a subcontract from General Dynamics.
> — I.F. Stone

Evanston, Wyoming   December 2012
To the Editor of the *Evanston Herald*

Dear Sir,

Your article on the tax dilemma was most appreciated. Here is the *dignus vindice nodus*. Here is the core problem. The American people *finance* their own oppression through federal taxes. Let's say that a state got uppity and tried to assert its rightful domain in the matter of traffic laws, such as speed limits, seat-belts, helmets, open-containers, insurance, etc. Technically, these are not federal laws but state laws enacted under the federal blackmail of withholding highway funding. Who collects that federal highway tax money in the first place? The states do, at the gas pump!

It's one thing to endure the withholding of federal highway funds, but it's yet another to make their withholding irrelevant by refusing to collect federal excise taxes at the gas pump and increase the state tax to cover the shortfall. Coldly analyzed, the states really don't *need* the USG involved in their highway programs. Knocking the feds out of the loop is conceptually the most simple and elegant solution, but the one fraught with the most risk.

Another example: the so-called "income" tax applied to simple wages. How free can a people hope to become while they allow a *third* of their paycheck to be withheld? *Half* of their inheritance to be stolen?

So, until the issue of locally-collected federal taxes is taken head-on, no real reduction in federal tyranny can ever occur. As long as victims continue to finance their oppressors, they will remain victims.

The first rule of warfare is to not support your enemy. In fact, giving aid or comfort to your enemy is the very definition of treason. The word derives from the Latin *trans*, give + *dare*, over. Isn't paying taxes to an oppressive government "giving over" to your enemy?

It was a shame that your article was published *after* the elections instead of before. A month ago, it might have woken up some voters.

For Truth, Justice, and the American Way,
Barbara Adams
Bear River, Wyoming

* * * * * * *

To the Editor of the *Evanston Herald*

Dear Sir,

I read your feature story on IRS abuses with detached interest.

I don't pay income taxes for the same reason I don't bowl or golf. It's simply not in my nature. *"But you can reduce your taxes to zero if you have a home office and write off blah, blah, blah!"* folks tell me. Yeah? So what? Taxation is theft, and income taxation is the worst form of it. I will not jump through the IRS hoops of deductions and allowances in order to reduce this theft. If they insist on stealing, fine, let them steal with no illusions—just like any highway robber. But to insist that we also play some game culminating on every April 15th is obscene. If the IRS can find somebody sufficiently dishonest or cowardly to withhold 30% of my earnings, well goodie for them. But I will not rent a warehouse to store years of receipts; I will not ruin my eyesight by reading their mountain of regulations in 8-point type; I will not squander dozens of sun-filled hours every year filling out their damned forms. Whatever percentage I could reduce my income taxes by "playing the game" just isn't worth it.

The IRS is a rapist promising to be "gentle" in exchange for your monthly love letters.

While I may not be able to make the IRS irrelevant financially, I *can* make them irrelevant in every other area of my life. I absolutely *refuse* to keep track of mileage, cell phone usage, or T&E expenses. I will not plan my vacations around business opportunities for the tax write-off. My life exists for me to *enjoy*, and playing the deduction game is like trying to enjoy a fine restaurant dinner with a calorie counter.

I live by the *calendar* year, not the fiscal.

The IRS wants to be the thief? Fine, they can steal what they want and then piss off. Take "their" 30% and go away, leaving me free not to have to think about the IRS until next year. That 30% I will simply consider A Cost To Living On This Planet. With the other 70% remaining, I will live fully—completely unsullied by thoughts of thieves and parasites.

Let's say the IRS comes after me, steals all I own, and sends me to prison. OK, they get to take care of me for five years before they let me go. What then? I would live the rest of my life in a tent in some National Forest rather than sign onto their feudalism.

Government has an invisible gun to all our heads, and that's just the problem. The gun is invisible, yet we still pay as if a muzzle ring of barrel steel is pressed to our temples. Why are we giving up over half our lives to taxes, inflation, and regulation because of an *invisible* gun? The mugger armed with a revolver can shoot only six people, so why is a seventh threatened? Or a hundredth? Because of leverage. His leverage of our fear. Nobody wants to take bullet one through six. Nobody has the balls to confront his assailant. Yet if enough of us *do*, he will run out of ammunition and the rest of us will be free.

All we must do is call his bluff to neutralize his leverage. It is not the six bullets in his gun which give him power over a crowd, it is our unanimous cowardice. Truly, it is the slave which makes slavery possible. You cannot tame a badger or a wolverine for they are implacably ferocious. There are no Cape Buffalo in yoke, no mustangs in harness. We, however, have allowed ourselves to become domesticated sheep by our fear of invisible—and hence increasingly imaginary—threats.

It is time to realize that all this is a *war* and the frontline is daily life. There is no rear. There is no safety. It is Total War and all of us are soldiers under barrage. All of us will die, so why are we squandering away our lives as if we're immortal—fooling ourselves with some implicit infinity when a measly century is about all we'll get? It's not how we die that's important, but how we have lived. I'll take 40 years of full-bore, no-compromise living over 100 years of surrender and cowardice. I'd rather live 100% for 40 years than 40% for 100 years.

I'll suffer what taxation theft I can endure, but I am not infinitely compressible. At some point, I may just "go Drega" on them, and won't they be surprised! But until then, I consciously make these parasites irrelevant. They can steal that 30% from me, but not a single moment of joy for being alive.

Yours for a free Republic!
David Furr
Evanston, Wyoming

Casper, Wyoming   December 2012

There were several gun shows in Casper each year, which the Prestons never missed. James, Jr. loved to chat with the veterans, especially a 92-year-old Marine who is Casper's last survivor of Guadacanal.

As they walk out to their truck, they can't help but notice that every windshield in the parking lot has a flyer under the wiper. They take one and huddle together to read it. Within seconds, they are howling with laughter.

"Dad, is this thing a *joke?*" asks James, Jr.

"It sure is, my boy—but whoever wrote it didn't know that."

Juliette smiles at Preston. "It's going on your office wall, isn't it?"

Preston is still laughing. "How could it *not?*"

"The author," Juliette wisecracks, "just *has* to be from Boulder."

"Where's *Boulder?*" asks Hanna.

Preston squeezes her hand. "We'll take a field trip there sometime."

Submissive Inviting the Sharing of Suppressed Yearnings (SISSY)

Our goal is to expose once and for all the real cause of criminal violence. Crimes are violent only because the "victim" might resist. If the initiator could *peaceably* get what he wanted, he would *forsake* any violence in doing so. Makes sense, doesn't it?

The root of "coercion" is one party not willing to *share*.

Let us therefore go directly to the heart of the matter. We must simply *outlaw resistance.* Those who "defend" themselves are *willing partners* in the deadly dance of violence. It takes *two* to Tango! Turn him down!

Self defense has no defense!

By mandating submission, we remove the reason for violence. Do you see the elegant simplicity of this? Eliminate resistance and you eliminate violence!

Make a fist—Go to jail!

We propose the registration of all Carnally-Generous men ("rapists"). Thereafter, all Carnal Gifts shall take place by random selection. The Carnally-Generous simply chooses his preferred Receptor, who reports for Submission Duty. (This is scheduled at *mutual* convenience—fair is fair.) No fuss, no muss. "Rape" without violence is merely sex, and any woman's reluctance to accept a Carnal Gift is *elitism*, pure and simple.

No more "rapist." No more "victim." *No more violence!*

The Submission Program can also be applied to "muggings" and all other so-called "crimes of violence."

A nonviolent society through submission!

Imagine the tax savings from closing down all the unnecessary "Sex Crimes" police units. This would free up law enforcement to investigate *real* crimes such as: hate speech, homophobic discrimination, unregistered gun trafficking, suspicious cash transactions, underground home-schooling, spanking, vaccination evasion, sedition, and hooliganism.

There can be no peace until we embrace the will of others.
The only real evil is *not sharing*.

Join SISSY today!

Wyoming life

DSA, Inc. (the FAL battle rifle manufacturer) had enough of Illinois and was enticed by the economic freedom and shooting culture of Wyoming. By next year, the superb rifles will be made in a new plant outside Douglas.

Ron Smith of Smith Enterprise (formerly of Tempe, Arizona) relocated his forging operations and machine shop to Guernsey in May. Catering to *serious* users of the M14 system, Ron has brought the venerable rifle into the 21st century. His forged receiver 18" barrel gun with gas-block front sight and direct-connect Vortex flash suppressor is lightweight, reliable, and 1¼MOA accurate with quality FMJ. Special Forces operators love it, and have made kills on the enemy out to 800 meters.

Wyoming now has two battle rifle systems manufacturers. Perhaps an HK91 firm would "complete the set" by relocating to the Riflemen's state.

❖ 2013

Washington, D.C.   FBIHQ   January 2013

The Bureau assembled a special task force solely for "The Leopard" in anticipation of his next biennial February homicide. Agents are focusing on a roster of all surviving VIPs and politicians within a 200 mile radius of D.C. still on the KK risk list. Extra security has been provided to these potential targets, in the hope of catching the elusive killer in the act.

Wyoming   2013

By now the Cowboy State migration was a fairly open secret. What had been a surprise in 2006 and half-known in 2010 was now the subject of national discussion. Nothing in conservative or libertarian politics had ever been so proactive, and it was causing quite a stir. The freedom-loving American had chafed at his restraints for decades. He was tired of liberals taxing him for something he would have done anyway, and then doing it poorly or not at all. Worse still was taxing him for something he *never* would have done, and then actually doing it.

Now he had somewhere to *go*. Everyone did. Instead of banging their heads against a wall in New Jersey and Missouri, instead of slowly being crushed by the regulatory grindstone of California, instead of seeing their beloved Arizona and Colorado and Oregon being taken over by socialist yuppies, they simply moved.

The exodus to Wyoming had reached "critical mass" in 2008 and was growing rapidly on its own. The last general election in 2010 garnered the libertarians seven more counties, for a total of 12 of 23. After the congressional election of 2012, they controlled 40% of the legislature. Libertarians had grafted themselves onto Wyoming's "DNA" and were enjoying the increased freedom for which they had worked so hard.

The free state initiative was a virtual reality in half of Wyoming. 2014 is the year to finally accomplish phase 3a: electing the executive branch and a majority of the legislature. Recruiting new relocators for this last push has been comparatively easy, for nothing succeeds like success.

Getting the first 9,000 to Wyoming in 2006 had been a monumental task. Only the truly committed packed their bags. The rest stayed home, biding their time. There are few liberties in large cities, and all the sunny states had been taken, so if you could handle a bit of wind and cold and isolation, then Wyoming would work for you. The "Mayflower folks" also had the most work to do, for they had to iron out the relocation wrinkles and assuage the concerns of the locals. Pioneering is exhausting effort, but extremely rewarding. They proved that Wyoming was a surprisingly palatable state to live.

The second wave in 2010 had the benefit of a proven operation which enjoyed a fourth of the state and one-sixth of the legislature. Though a full statewide victory was not assured, at least the "10ers" were confident that they could not be socially or politically dislodged.

The third wave of 2014 would have the easiest work. Simply show up for a raging party already in progress. They wouldn't have the first choices of areas, but that's the price of arriving late.

West Palm Beach, Florida   February 2013
UN Ambassador Vincent Coleman and Treasury Secretary Jared Spriggs are old Yale grad student buddies. They've enjoyed yachting together for over 20 years, and get down to Florida twice a year. Anything to be free of Manhattan and the Beltway for a few days.

They prefer to bareboat their co-owned 42' ketch rig to the Bahamas for the local cuisine, beaches, and women. The pair were quite well-known amongst the Nassau crowd.

After being overdue by 3 hours, the US Coast Guard began a search. Charred flotsam was found 30 miles off the Floridian shore. A propane explosion was suspected, but certain FBI agents of the WFO had their doubts. The deceased Coleman and Spriggs were at the near top of the KK risk list, but since "The Leopard" had never seemed to strike far from D.C., the yachting pair had not been assigned a security detail for their Bahamas trip.

2013 USA political news
I live in the Managerial Age, in a world of "Admin." The greatest evil is not now done in those sordid "dens of crime" that Dickens loved to paint. It is not done even in concentration camps and labor camps. In those we see its final result. But it is conceived and ordered, (moved, seconded, carried, and minuted) in clean, carpeted, warmed, and well-lighted offices, by quiet men with white collars and cut fingernails and smooth-shaven cheeks who do not need to raise their voice. Hence, naturally enough, my symbol for Hell is something like the bureaucracy of a police state or the offices of a thoroughly nasty business concern.
—C.S. Lewis, *The Screwtape Letters* (preface to 1961 edition)

President McBlane dies suddenly in July of an aneurysm. Vice President Melvin Connor is sworn in office. He vows to continue his predecessor's policies, though privately he resents the political obligation.

The income and SS tax revolt is fully ablaze, with the participation of many employers who are horrified at the FICA matching burden. The IRS issues many harsh proclamations, but the people have become more desperate than afraid. In response to ageism crimes, Congress passes the death penalty for *"assaults against the aged."*

Washington, D.C.
The White House   July 2013

After becoming acquainted with the FBI's current cases and issues, President Connor asks, "So, Paul, what do you have on this Wyoming thing?"

The two had gone to Georgetown together.

Director Klein says, "Quite a lot, sir. At least all the big pieces. After 2014, they will attempt to repeal legislation they deem 'oppressive' while amending the state constitution to solidify their scheme. By focusing on several hot issues in the West, such as land and water rights, gun rights, parental rights, and the free market, they aim to garner vast public support. Our data indicate that at least 60% of Wyomingites would back a charismatic governor embracing these issues. Also, much of the West would be highly sympathetic to such an administration."

"Any idea of their likely candidate for next year?"

"Possibly a rancher from Casper named James Preston. Annapolis. Marine helo pilot in the first Gulf War. Silver Star. Wyoming businessman. He's been involved in libertarian politics for over a decade. Both he and his defense attorney wife come from money, and both have been very successful."

The President nods. "Go on."

"Operating virtually unopposed, the administration will seek and likely win sweeping changes in Wyoming, with increasing public support. The success of these issues will tempt Montana, Idaho, and possibly other conservative western states into mimicry.

"A league with Montana and Idaho would create a common border with Alberta and British Columbia, the two western Canadian provinces most susceptible to secessionist pressures. Canada already split at her *Québécois* seam and there's little to stave off an eventual western secession. A successful confederation there could then also lure in a portion of the Pacific Northwest, the so-called 'Ecotopia.'

"Beginning with Wyoming, we believe that at some point one or more of the western states will directly challenge the Government for their political autonomy. We do not know if they plan to actually secede *de jure* as did the South in 1861, or *de facto* as did Taiwan in 1949."

The President is furious. "*De jure* or *de facto*, I will not preside over a dismembered United States of America! The Union is inviolate! The Civil War decided that!" Turning to the AG, he demands, "Isn't that so, Janet?"

All eyes swivel on her, and she squirms at this direct question. "Uh, well, yes and no, sir."

"Yes and *no*?" challenges the President. "How is there any *doubt* in the matter? You're telling me that secession is still legal for a state—a century and a half after Appomattox?"

"In the strictest sense of the law, possibly," Vorn says.

"Explain that," snaps Connor.

"In short, secession can be construed as one of the powers reserved to the states and the people by the Tenth Amendment, especially since it is nowhere prohibited in the Constitution. Furthermore, secession is a reciprocal right of *accession*, which the states exercised when they ratified the Constitution. Since the states joined the federal union as sovereign bodies, they have a legal right to quit the union, and this was not successfully disputed by the North in 1861. That's why the Confederate President Jefferson Davis was never tried for treason after the Civil War. By declaring his allegiance to a new country, the Confederate States of America, he had renounced his US citizenship. The same with General Robert E. Lee. When his beloved Virginia seceded, a change of citizenship occurred for Virginians. Hence, Lee did not commit Article III, Section 3 *'treason'* against the United States. He had become a foreigner *vis-à-vis* the US prior to his levying war."

The room is sepulchral in its silence.

"Not that secession could ever likely transpire," Vorn hurriedly qualifies.

"Nevertheless, a state so inclined *could* make a legal case, right?" asks the President.

"Yes, sir, it could, although making a case is not the same as proving one. Whatever legal merits a secessionist state may advance, their position would be overshadowed by its political impossibility. I've no doubt that the Supreme Court would have ample grounds to rule against such a challenge."

"Well, *that's* reassuring," Connor says sarcastically. "But that's a future matter to worry about. We've got more pressing issues such as this nationwide rash of VIP murders. For God's sake, not even our UN Ambassador or SecTres were safe! Blown up in the Atlantic! Paul, has the FBI yet connected these Krassnyite sickos to this Wyoming thing? And since Krassny was from Casper, is there any link to Preston?"

"Negative on both accounts so far, sir. Except for general philosophical alignment, the Bureau has yet to find any connection. We're still investigating, however."

"Well, find *something!* I can't believe that seven dozen federal officials and business elite have all been murdered by unconnected individuals. *Somebody* is orchestrating this, this rampage, and I'll bet he's in Wyoming."

Klein says, "Mr. President, we are closely watching all known activists in Wyoming, including James Preston. Through MDES[1] we are monitoring their Internet activity, email, phone calls, credit card usage, and travel. Short of surveilling these people man-on-man, the Bureau is doing all it can."

The President seems unpersuaded. "I hear you Paul, but did MDES and the CIA's computers foresee 9/11?"

The FBI director blandly replies, "Sir, no system is perfect and sometimes suspects simply 'fall through the cracks' and you don't find out until it's too late."

"'Cracks?' What *'cracks?'* The bombers, nearly *half* of them on the terrorist watch list, bought airline tickets through *credit cards* under their *own names!* What else could they have done to get noticed, run newspaper ads? But did your expensive computers pick up on them? No. Were there any agents at the boarding gates to intercept those bastards? No. So, you'll understand why I am less than impressed with your MDES."

Klein is visibly affected by this, coming not only from the President but from a friend. "Sir, I can't answer for the failure of my predecessor, nor am I a computer expert. But I *have* been assured that our system today *will* alert us to a similar attempt. The linkage of national databases has been greatly improved since 2001. I completely understand your skepticism, sir, but it truly *is* a different ball game today."

"Yeah, well we'll see." Connor is barely mollified. "There just *has* to be a connection between these Krassnyite murders and the Wyoming people. You haven't found it because it's not there—you haven't found it because these people have been anticipating our technology and techniques. Do you think they've been emailing each other in the clear from their homes? No, I'd bet they're using encryption from public terminals. The email privacy loophole."

Klein says, "We realize that that's a probability, and we're monitoring dozens of library and cyberchat terminals. Sir, I assure you, we're on top of it. As soon as we discover anything, we'll put some agents on the ground."

The President nods reluctantly. "When you do, just make sure you actually have some probable cause. If the Bureau steps in shit again like the Swan and Bradford raids—or that ex-cop Foster in North Carolina—Congress

---

1   **Multidomain Expert System**, an FBI computer array which uses "fuzzy logic" to mimic inferential judgments about the possible meaning of discrete events collected by the national databases. For example, if a person books a flight and a hotel reservation, and another person is also reserved at the same hotel, and both of these persons are criminal suspects, then they probably have a criminal relationship. Only MDES would pick up on the two seemingly unrelated persons and postulate a relationship. MDES has three knowledge bases: terrorism, counterintelligence, and organized crime. The FBI has nearly a dozen operational MDES workstations throughout the US, the main ones being in D.C., New York City, and Houston. The MDES computer cursor is shaped like a tiny pistol, with its barrel always pointing at a particular piece of data.

will roll you over into Homeland Security. I want *results,* Paul. Solid, clean, useful *results.* I want this Krassnyite thing stopped dead in its tracks. It's affecting the operation of Government. Good people are resigning in droves. If it's found out later that Preston was Krassny's nephew or something, I'm going to have some Bureau ass. Do you read me?"

Stung and bitter, FBI Director Klein simply says, "Yes, sir."

2013 USA economic news

Tax revenues have plummeted from both the retiring Baby Boomers and the tax revolt. Annual inflation is now 25%, and rising. Unemployment is over 15%. At 40+%, this recalls the "Misery Index" of the Carter years.

How can we account for our present situation unless we believe that men high in this government are concerting to deliver us to disaster? This must be the product of a great conspiracy, a conspiracy on a scale so immense as to dwarf any previous such venture in the history of man. A conspiracy of infamy so black that, when it is finally exposed, its principals shall be forever deserving of the maledictions of all honest men.

— Congressional Record, 82nd Congress, page 6,602

* * * * * * *

Under a government which imprisons unjustly, the true place for a just man is also a prison.
— Thoreau, *On the Duty of Civil Disobedience* (1849)

Evanston, Wyoming

To Whom It May Concern:

My anti-IRS letter to the *Evanston Herald* editor last December did not go without Government notice. I'd heard that federal agents scoured the newspapers for dissident letters.

Well, it's true. They do. (Consider using an alias, folks.)

The Government wasted no time in charging me with "failure to file" and "income tax evasion." Evidently, the future of the nation required it. I could find no lawyer to defend me on the real merits (*i.e.,* lack of jurisdiction and cause). My trial was convened in record time, and the US Attorney's office steamrollered over my *pro se* defense.

All with the help of twelve very carefully picked juror puppets who "did their duty" in putting away for 10 years an evil "tax cheat."

I wanted only to live apart from "society." Ironically, the feeling was mutual, but how dare I live apart on my *own* terms! How *dare* my wife and I retire to a secluded farm with our loving family, generating our own electricity, growing our own food, teaching our own children! How dare we make society irrelevant! Yes, you wanted me gone, but on *your* terms. I could not be permitted to leave society—your wounded pride demanded my *expulsion* from it, on criminal grounds. *"You can't quit—you're fired!"*

The so-called "Justice Department" honors me with incarceration. Under tyrannical government, the only place for a free man is behind bars. My conscience is clean; my honor intact. Within heart and mind my liberty soars untethered. Those on the outside remain bound by their own illusions; trussed up by mythology. I enjoy the vast peace of a man who never compromised his integrity, who never betrayed first principles. Having never harmed nor cheated anyone, for my treason to universal corruption I am to be separated from the loving bosom of my family, and banished to the company of thieves and murderers.

With great and deliberate effort "The People" have sifted me from their putrid brine of collusion and cast me out. For that, I thank them, as the stench really was just this side of unbearable.

Even though my prison cell mirror will be stainless steel and bolted to a concrete wall, I'll look myself squarely in the face. How you all can do so, transmogrified by shame and sellout, I cannot imagine. My principles were a daily indictment to you, so I was sent away for *mala prohibita*.

What you all would *like* to do—and let's be honest about it—is to cleave my soul from my body. What you all would *like* to do is kill me, publicly and violently. Mere incarceration just isn't *quite* enough, is it? Ten years in prison is only vaguely satisfying—like half a sandwich. You're still hungry for my death! And why don't you simply kill me? Why *can't* you? Because you are still chained to those echoes of "decent society" and "justice." You are like a married man who sneaks off to the whorehouse on Friday nights, yet dutifully shows up in church on Sunday mornings with his sweet wife and children. What you'd *really* like to do is to abandon your family and dive headlong into sin. The surreptitious wallowing is pure frustration. What you *want* is to slough off this chafing pretense of "society" and regress to mob status, appeasing every coarse appetite with the blood of innocents.

Not to worry; you're quickly getting there.

I go to prison a free man. It is the *rest* of you who are behind barbed wire. Don't wrestle with the paradox. It's beyond your understanding, else you would not wield depravity against the decent, perjury against the peaceful, coercion against the honest. You steaming herds can't help but embrace wickedness.

"Thy sin's not accidental, but a trade."

With contempt,
David Furr
(formerly of) Evanston, Wyoming

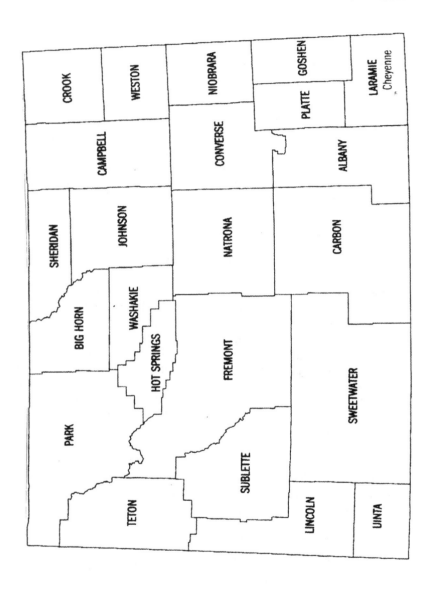

❖ 2014

Casper, Wyoming   January 2014

With the crucial general election just eleven months away, a fork in the political road awaits James Preston. Whether to compete in the Republican primary against Michael Dowling (a strong though not unbeatable GOP favorite), or run under the county-successful Laissez-Faire Party banner (which is already supported by many Republican voters). Running the numbers was up to Preston's assistant, Tom Parks. After a week and a half of data crunching, Parks arrived at his opinion.

"If we win the Republican primary, we will certainly win in November, but the primary will be a tougher race than an LFP 3rd party ticket."

"Why is that?" asks Preston.

"Because about 25% of Democrats would vote for your LFP candidacy, increasing your edge over Dowling. In the GOP primary, however, you'd have to battle it out solely amongst Republicans. While that's worked out for many of our county candidates, primaries are much tougher at the state level. Dowling is a real veteran at them, too. He holds a lot of sway behind closed doors. My data suggests pretty much a dead heat for you there."

Preston nods absentmindedly, gazing out the study window at the snow-capped Medicine Bow peaks. "So, I should run under the LFP?"

"Yes, sir, that's my recommendation. By avoiding the GOP primary battle you can win the war with the defection of enough Democrats."

Preston laughs. "How ironic, Tom. Wyoming gets its first libertarian governor because of the Democrats!"

Parks smiles. "Well, you've heard that a libertarian is a liberal who understands economics."

"Or a conservative who's had his ass kicked by the cops," replies Preston, finishing the famous line by professor Richard Boddy, a black libertarian who taught in southern California.

"Exactly," says Parks. "And since Wyoming has so far generally resisted the police state trend, not enough conservatives have yet been rousted by the cops to shock them into libertarianism."

"But in this depression," Preston says, "plenty of Democrats are beginning to understand economics."

Parks slowly nods with obvious satisfaction. Preston gets it.

"Tom, we'll win this thing on the *economics*. That's the *key*. You've just crystallized my campaign for me! Call the Laissez-Faire Party people over for a meeting next week. We need to coordinate my announcement that I'm running in the LFP primary this August."

Parks says, "Yes, sir," chuckling.

"What is it?"

"Dowling will never know what hit him come November. He'll have thought that your LFP candidacy was a critical mistake, that you should have tried to beat him in the primary as a Republican."

Preston thinks for a moment and then quotes Sun Tzu:

"Fight downhill; do not ascend to attack."

"Tom, Dowling doesn't know that, as of today, *he* will be the one ascending to attack."

Parks grins, "And that's why he's already lost. Only we could choose the battle, and we chose to avoid the one which favored him."

"Every battle is won before it's even fought, eh, Tom?"

Wyoming   Spring 2014

Freedom-hungry Americans continue to pour in, mostly under the auspices of the Free State Wyoming, which offers several county choices. While no relocator is required to join the FSW, the organization's benefits were too plentiful to resist. A newcomer would be instantly tied into a network to assist with moving, as well as finding housing, employment, and friends. Also, FSW people and companies transact with each other first, thus nonmembers miss out on many lucrative dealings. Being "posted" to the FSW's choice of county was a small temporary price to pay.

Wyoming Laissez-Faire Party primary   August 2014

Several Wyoming relocators tossed their hat in the ring, but most of the delegates already had their man in mind, without whom the party wouldn't even exist. Preston easily wins the LFP nomination for governor. He will be running against Republican Michael Dowling and Democrat Evan Landers. The three-way race sparks a marked increase in voter interest.

Washington, D.C.   FBIHQ   August 2014

"Director, I have SAC Bleth on the line from Casper."

"Yes, I'll take it," says Klein. "Doug, how are you?"

"Fine, Director, thank you. You told me to call as soon as I returned from the LFP convention."

"Did they try to draft you?" Klein asks with a laugh.

"No, sir. I just kept my mouth shut and nobody really noticed me. Anyway, sir, it's James Preston."

"Well, we've expected that for a while. Keep digging in the man's past, Doug. Everyone's dirty."

Wyoming   September-October 2014

Because of its rural population, Wyoming is a tough state to campaign. Only Cheyenne, Casper, Laramie, Gillette, and Rock Springs had over 25,000 people (though nearly half the state lived in one of the five cities). To meet the other half of Wyoming, a candidate had to visit dozens of very small towns. And since there were no shuttle flights, driving is the only option. Preston had briefly considered a helicopter tour (*e.g.,* LBJ's 1948 Texas campaign for the US Senate), but decided that it smacked of a gaucherie to be avoided.

Juliette, as was often the case, had the answer. "Why not do what Jesse Ventura did in Minnesota in 1998? Use a caravan of RVs? Our mobile home would be the rolling HQ, and we'd save a fortune in hotel bills. We could have a live Internet feed, and do radio show interviews by cell phone over the Wyoming News Network. Besides, it'd be fun! The children would love it. We could stop for malts at Yellowstone Drugs in Shoshoni."

"I like it!" Preston said. "I haven't been on an RV vacation since my parents took the family on a three week Colorado ski trip. We hit at least a dozen mountains. An RV campaign, huh? Yeah, let's do it!"

Back in 1998 the Wyoming Libertarian Party had a gaily painted red, white, and blue *Freedom Xpress*. Dave Dawson and Steve Richardson campaigned in it, thoroughly covering the state in just six days, Monday through Saturday. (Presumably they rested on the seventh day.)

The Prestons decided on two RV campaign tours: the first a 12 day tour in September, and then a blazing four day push ending in Cheyenne on election day, 4 November. The first tour would be very business-like, with many interviews, luncheons, media spots, and speeches.

The second tour would be a party.

Washington, D.C.   FBIHQ   October 2014

"So, anything new on this Preston?" asks Director Klein.

"Yes, sir. After the Marines he spent time in Europe. We've learned something interesting about his stay in Hungary. In Budapest, he met—"

Cheyenne, Wyoming
Republican Party campaign HQ   October 2014

Ted Swanson, campaign chairman, rereads the anonymous letter postmarked Casper. *This is just what we need on that snooty moralist!* he thinks.

James Preston Fathered Illegitimate Budapest Son
Exclusive to the *Rawlins Gazette*, by Alfred Walsh

Reliable sources in the Hungarian capital report that James Preston, the Laissez-Faire Party gubernatorial candidate, fathered a child from a 1992 romance with a 20 year old college student. The son, now an engineering student and air force reservist, was apparently unaware of his American parent.

The mother said that she and Preston had planned to marry until he learned of the pregnancy, which caused him to break the engagement and return to the United States. She stated that Preston has refused to visit or have any contact with his 22 year old son, whom she has raised alone.

James Preston, husband and father of two (Wyoming) children, was unavailable for comment.

Preston responds to the furor several days later with an Open Letter.

"If Mr. Walsh or his editor at the *Rawlins Gazette* had bothered to ask me, they could have easily learned the truth about my son, Istvan. His mother broke up with me because her previous boyfriend proposed. I still have her letter to that fact. When her fiancé discovered that she was three months pregnant by another man, he left her. She wrote to tell me that, and unless I contributed to the costs of her raising the baby alone (she no longer wanted to marry), she threatened to have an abortion.

"I have that letter as well, along with 18 years of cancelled checks for child support.

"I repeatedly asked to be a part of Istvan's life on whatever terms she would allow, and even flew to Budapest in 1994 to press my case. She denied my requests (claiming that meeting me would "confuse" him), and consequently I have yet to see my first born child who grew up thinking that his father had been killed in a traffic accident.

"All of this I explained to Juliette before our engagement, but we had not told our children. There seemed no point in telling them since I had never even met Istvan, although my family would very much like to. He is an innocent victim of, in part, the youthful carelessness of his father.

"I did as much as I was allowed to, but I wish that I could have done and been much more. Given the highly suspicious political timing of Mr. Walsh's article, the bright side is that I and my family may finally get to meet Istvan. That would be worth far more than this week's turmoil."

The GOP smear tactic backfires. The public sees Preston as a victim of duplicity, just like Istvan. His approval rating shoots up by 15 points.

Michael Dowling nearly fires Ted Swanson over it, but the election is too close to find another campaign manager.

Wyoming General Election   Tuesday, 4 November 2014

I miss civilization—and I want it back.
   —Marylynne Robinson

Preston's second tour was a four day, nonstop, madcap, rolling party with lots of horn-honking and banner waving. The weather was glorious; rare fall days of brilliant cornflower-blue skies.

The main RV, the *Prestonian*, towed a 26' flatbed trailer made up like a parade float. The thing was jumping with music and singing and dancing, and Preston gave impromptu speeches from a little bandstand. Locals hitched rides for several blocks or a couple of miles, while others joined the caravan in their cars. Just before getting onto a highway the caravan stopped so all the people on the flatbed trailer could pile in the RVs, and then the convoy would take off. The music/dance trailer was Juliette's idea. She wished it to be as rowdy as the "Twist and Shout" parade scene in *Ferris Bueller's Day Off*.

She wasn't disappointed.

At times the tour had over thirty vehicles in tow going down the road. Two carloads of Campus Libertarians from Laramie actually followed the entire way. Even the media got caught up in the thing, and began a running commentary of the tour. Folks learned over the radio and TV when the caravan would be passing through their town and made a point of getting a glimpse of it. When the trail of RVs got to Jackson at midnight on Sunday, hundreds of people were waiting for them at Town Square, cheering.

Live Internet TV carried it all.

Monday and Tuesday they went eastward on I-80 to cover the lower portion of Wyoming, catching the major populations of Evanston, Green River, Rock Springs, Rawlins, Laramie, and Cheyenne. The tour had gained huge attention by then, totally stealing the limelight from the other campaigns. Politics were rarely *fun* and the Prestons were determined to wrap up their bid for the governor's mansion on a lighthearted note.

Cheyenne, Wyoming   8:09PM
Michael Dowling Republican Party campaign HQ

"Given that none of the candidates are up against an incumbent, this will probably be a very close race with Preston, sir," Ted Swanson says. "Within 3%, I'd say."

Dowling's jaw is set and angry. "Yeah, thanks to that damned Laissez-Faire Party! If they spoil this election and throw it to Landers, Republicans will never forgive them."

"Sir, I urged you to coopt some of the LFP's platform to luff Preston's sails, but you wouldn't have it. The GOP is getting left behind in this recent surge of libertarianism."

"Ted, I will not placate anarchy! If that's what the Wyoming people want, then I will not be the one to ruin this state!"

Cheyenne, Wyoming   8:12PM
James Preston Laissez-Faire Party campaign HQ

"Dad, what are the numbers? Are we winning?" asks James, Jr.

"The polls just closed a little over an hour ago, son. Dowling and I are still neck and neck, but there's a lot of vote counting left to do. We won't know for two or three hours. Hang tight, kiddo."

Dowling Republican Party campaign HQ   8:58PM

"Where the hell is Mallory? Where are the state troopers?" demands Dowling. Captain David Mallory, head of the capitol security detail, is designated to drive the new governor-elect.

"I don't know," replies Swanson, "but I'll find out." After a short cell phone call, he says, "Mallory's over at Preston's. The troopers too. They've been there for twenty minutes and don't seem to be leaving."

"Shit!" exclaims Dowling. "What do the cops know that we don't?"

Although only 30% of the precincts have reported in, Preston has taken the lead over Dowling by two points. The Democrat Landers is five points behind Dowling.

Preston Laissez-Faire Party campaign HQ   9:32PM

Over half of the precincts have reported in. Preston is leading the pack at 39%, Dowling at 35%, and Landers at 26%—and his gain is still increasing. Juliette looks at her husband and says, "Honey, I think we're going to win!"

Preston nods with a wary grin. "You've always had a nose for things. You just may be right."

The buzz around the HQ has been growing for the past half hour. Like a charge of static electricity, the mounting excitement is thick in the air.

Landers Democratic Party campaign HQ   9:35PM

Evan Landers had little expectation of winning, and he now has no chance of beating Preston or even Dowling. He feels almost relieved. He would have had to battle a Republican legislature, like Clinton in 1995. That would've been more work than Landers really wanted.

Dowling Republican Party campaign HQ   11:08PM

Dowling hangs up the phone with Governor-elect James Preston, and fumes, "Well, Ted, you didn't quite call this thing, did you? *Six* points! Not

'within 3%' but *six* points!   In a three-way race that's nearly a mandate!
Thanks a lot, Ted! And now, for my goddamned concession speech!"
    Dowling leaves the back office for the large conference room.

*"Friends and supporters! I thank you for your hard work and sacrifice
these past months. We tried our best, but Wyoming has decided against us.
(groaning and mild wailing) Yes, it's true. I've just seen the election data. Of
the 91% of precincts having tallied their ballots, James Preston has received
41% of the popular vote. Just moments ago I spoke with him to concede the
election and (more wailing), and to congratulate him for not only his victory,
but also for his honorably-run campaign. As hard as we worked, we simply
didn't have the numbers.   While James Preston and I have significant
differences of political opinion, I do believe that he is a good man who will
assemble a competent administration. The election is over and decided, so let
us all work together in these difficult times. Good night, and thank you all
again for your hard work and support."*

    As his supporters mill about in clumps of commiseration, Dowling
smoothly makes his way through them, pausing here and there to share a
personal word of thanks. There is nothing more doleful than a campaign HQ
on the night of their losing, and Landers has no desire to wallow in the mood.
    Wyomingans made a startlingly bold choice with Preston and his
Laissez-Faire Party's agenda. A perilous gamble, if anyone asked Dowling.
*It's a goddamned four year blind date! They've unmade their bed; now let
them lie in it!* muses the defeated Republican candidate as he anticipated the
night's drunken stupor awaiting him. He walks past his campaign manager
without a word and leaves the building.
    Stung and disgusted, Ted Swanson just shakes his head.

*   *   *   *   *   *   *

    The final vote was 41% Preston, 35% Dowling, and 24% Landers.
James Wayne Preston had beat Dowling by exactly 17,750 votes of the
295,833 cast. The irony is that 17,750 is ten times 1,775—the year of Concord
and Lexington which sparked the Revolution. Much talk is made about the
"eerie coincidence."
    A columnist would remind Wyoming of another: the deaths of Thomas
Jefferson and John Adams within hours of each other on 4 July 1826—on the
Declaration of Independence 50th Anniversary.

A man may conduct himself well in both adversity and good fortune, but if you want to test his character, give him power.
— Abraham Lincoln

Cheyenne, Wyoming   11:16PM
Laissez-Faire Party Headquarters

Governor-Elect James Wayne Preston and his stunning wife Juliette make their way hand-in-hand to the speaker's platform amidst deafening applause. Wyomingans are rejoicing this election night for the Prestons.

Seeing Juliette to her chair, Preston then softly waves the audience to a hush. Without notes, he begins in a clear, baritone voice.

"Good evening! I am honored that you have today chosen me as your new Governor, and I thank you for your trust in me. I will not let you down. Having never before been a politician, forgive me if that promise seems a bit shopworn, but, (interrupted by laughter) *but, I just don't know any better.* (more laughter)

"Many of you are quite new to Wyoming, however, the simple and rugged values of the Western Frontier were written on your hearts long before your move here. You escaped the less-free states in our American Union and got here as soon as you could! (laughter) *I thank you for your support, and welcome you as productive and respectable Citizens.*

"To those of you longer acquainted with our state's quality of life, I thank you for your many years of friendship. It was you who urged me to run for office, and here I am, so you've nobody to blame but yourselves. (laughter) *First generation or fifth, we are all Wyomingites—and I shoulder our modern dilemmas with each of you.*

"I don't have to tell you that the American West is a precious place, populated with the 'salt of the earth.' Here, life is not complicated with lawyerly evasions and bureaucratic nonsense. Here, a man's word is his bond. Here, our women and children are safe in their homes and on their streets. Here, we respect hard work and business accomplishment. We practice personal charity. Here, we raise our children by the family's values—not by the State's dictates. (strong applause) *Here, we love and cherish our beautiful land and do not need Washington, D.C's 'help' on environmental issues. We know how to keep our water clean and our soil healthy. We live here!* (strong applause)

"If the Potomac Parasites continue to try to run our lives, they may find out that we can do without them ... entirely!" (even stronger applause)

"Here, in the American West, we believe in the sacred right of self-defense. Adults are presumed responsible enough to own and carry weapons until found otherwise by a jury of their peers. (great applause) *We know that arms are the badge of free people, and that disarmament is the shame of*

slaves. I will see to it that your Wyoming government does everything it can to protect and support your right to keep and bear arms. Consequently, my *friend Representative Margaret Haskins from Laramie will introduce a constitutional amendment protecting your right to own and carry guns without any possible infringement from any Wyoming official.* (wild applause)

"Thank you. Thank you for that. By the way, my father-in-law gave me a new .338 Win Mag for elk season, and if any of you have a pet handload for it, please call my office. (laughter and applause)

"Here in Wyoming, we don't care where you came from. Nor do we care about your skin or your religion. Here in Wyoming, we have only these three questions: 'Will you keep your word, even to your own hurt?' (The Governor waits several seconds for an answer to his non-rhetorical question) *I asked you, 'Will you keep your word, even to your own hurt?'* (Yes!) *'Will you respect your neighbor's property and stay out of his way?'* (Yes!) *And finally, 'Will you pull your own weight?'* (Yes!)

"A long time ago, America would have agreed with you, but no more. **Beginning tonight, that America will live again—in *Wyoming!*"**

Springing to their feet as one man, the crowd shakes the auditorium with a happy roar lasting minutes, waving the three-fingered "W-for-Wyoming" salute. Preston leisurely makes his way through the cheering throng, stopping often to shake hands and briefly converse with individuals.

"We're behind you, Gov!" a woman exclaims.

A leathery old rancher gets Preston's attention to recommend his favorite .338WM load of a 225 grain Barnes X bullet atop 71 grains of Viht N160, with Winchester case and primer.

"It's powerful and real accurate, Governor."

"Thanks a lot—I'll let you know how it shoots," replies Preston.

"Governor, you're welcome to hunt on my ranch *any* time!" gushes the old rancher.

Preston responds with an impish grin, "Are there enough elk for *both* of us?" They laughingly part, and Preston's aide writes down the rancher's phone number and handload information.

The Preston family is ushered outside by three state troopers, followed by a throng of supporters. Captain Mallory is waiting by a limo, holding open the door. "Congratulations, Governor. My men and I are looking forward to serving under you."

Preston smiles. "Thank you, Captain. I wish you all a placid term!"

The Prestons wave good-night one last time, are seated inside the limo, and driven away. During their short trip to the hotel, Juliette gently asks her pensive husband, "What are you thinking about, dear? Affairs of State?"

Chuckling, Preston gently squeezes his wife's hand and replies, "No, not exactly, Dove. I just never would have figured that old fellow for something as exotic as VihtaVuori powder. It's from Finland, you know. Would've bet he was an IMR-4831 man."

"Yeah, me *too*," Juliette deadpans. Although the Prestons had been married for 18 years, it still takes the Governor-Elect a few seconds to decide that his lovely wife, an excellent rifle shot in her own right, was joshing him.

Exiting the limo several minutes later, they were still giggling about it.

*   *   *   *   *   *   *

The next day the election results were published. Seven new counties were added to the libertarian orbit : Platte, Campbell, Sheridan, Natrona, Fremont, Teton, and surprisingly Uinta. All but the southern Democratic counties of Sweetwater, Carbon, Albany, and Laramie are in Laissez-Faire hands.

The Senate is now 56.7% controlled by freedom-supporting delegates, having added SDs 5, 17, 21, 24, 25, and 29.

The House is 61.7% in the hands of Preston's people, having added HDs 14, 16, 19, 23, 33, 36, 37, 55, 56, and 57.

The Wyoming Supreme Court is also in the libertarian camp. Of the five justices, two are already pro-freedom. One is retiring early and another had died of lung cancer. Preston would nominate their replacements. The remaining justice, an intractable Democrat from Rock Springs, would be pretty much on his own.

Both houses of the legislature, the supreme court, and the entire executive branch are now controlled by liberty-loving men and women. The hard work of eleven years by thousands of people has finally paid off. All totaled, about 38,000 new folks have moved into Wyoming as organized relocators.

America was about to have its first free state since 1789.

*   *   *   *   *   *   *

Members and front organizations must continually embarrass, discredit and degrade our critics. When obstructionists become too irritating, label them as fascist, or Nazi or anti-Semitic... The [erroneous] *association will, after enough repetition, become "fact" in the public mind.*
— Moscow Central Committee, 1943

Washington, D.C.
The White House   Wednesday, 5 November 2014

"Well, shit, they *did* it!" Watching the taped speech after a Cabinet meeting, President Connor continues to the room, "Either Preston's the greatest orator since William Jennings Bryan, or he actually *believes* that crap!"

Secretary of State Julius Harquist respectfully offers, "Perhaps, Mr. President, *both* assessments are accurate." Most of those present nodded at the SecState's reasoning.

Chewing on that for a moment, the President then intercoms his appointment secretary and quietly says, "Doris, have FBI Director Klein and the Attorney General join me for a private breakfast tomorrow morning at 7:30. All may not be 'quiet on the Western Front.'"

Dismissing the room, Connor asks his Deputy Chief of Staff Phillip Miles to remain. The Chief of Staff, Robert Hackett, was undergoing chemotherapy for bone cancer at Walter Reed and was not expected to return to work for some time, if ever. Miles, a relative newcomer to Washington, was filling in.

After the office had cleared, Miles delicately inquires, "Is it not just a *bit* premature to release the dogs, Mr. President? It's only *Wyoming*."

"Ever held an acorn in your hand, Phil?" the President asks in reply. Seeing the blank look on Miles's face, the President elaborates, "What you can hold in your hand today grows too large to embrace with your arms tomorrow. This Wyoming thing will become a damned oak tree, with Montana and maybe Idaho following Preston's lead. You *heard* the man, Phil—he called us traitorous parasites, and all but advocated a western secession—and that was his *victory* speech! Who the hell knows *what* he'll be urging at his *inauguration*! A militia tractor assault on Washington, I'll bet. A year from now it'll be some Patriot redoubt in the Rockies. *Jesus*."

"I rather doubt *that*, Mr. President. Still, he *does* exude a remarkable populist charm. Case in point, asking for advice on his rifle was *especially* deft, I must admit," observes Miles.

"Yeah, *wasn't* it though?" the President savagely agrees. "Who ever *heard* of such a thing? Next, we'll see him having a beer with 'the people' at some truck stop on I-25. How any multimillionaire can be such a proletarian gun-nut is utterly beyond me!"

Pouring a deep Scotch, Connor warms further to the subject. "And that crowd! Waving that 3-fingered "W" like at some Bolivian political rally. They *love* him! What's *with* those people out west—is their ground water contaminated or something?

Miles is already familiar with Connor's well-known presidential rant, so he steels himself for a long evening.

"Oh, and how about his lawyer *wife*? Just our luck she's brilliant *and* beautiful. *You* remember how far that shrewd cow Hillary took her cokehead, whorebait husband. Well, Juliette Preston could pass for Gabrielle Anwar—*plus*, she's *twice* as bright as Hillary *ever* was. Hell, *how* many languages do they speak? They probably play Scrabble in Portuguese!"

"Nevertheless, Mr. President . . . ," as Miles tries to calm his mood.

"He doesn't *play* anything, does he?" asks Connor, not hearing.

"Play? *Sir?*"

"*Musical instruments*, Phil. Christ help us if he shows up on the *Tonight Show* playing blues with the band. Clinton practically got elected by that saxophone gig on *Letterman*, remember?"

"I believe it was *Arsenio*, sir," Miles offers.

"Right, Arsenio. Hell, he and Clinton are both gone, aren't they!"

Miles says, "Anyway, Preston is only the Governor-Elect of *Wyoming*; you're the President of the United States. He's not after *your* job, sir."

VP when President McBlane had died last July, Connor was eligible for his own first election in 2016. It would also have to be his *only* election according the 22nd Amendment to the Constitution, which read, *"and no person who has held the office of President, or acted as President, for more than two years of a term to which some other person was elected President shall be elected to the office of President more than once."* The only thing more frustrating than a two-term presidency is a one-term presidency. Even though Connor would serve out nearly all of McBlane's second term, the fact that it was *McBlane's* term, not Connor's was most irksome of all as he was politically bound to his predecessor's agenda. Connor could not totally pursue his own policies unless and until he had been elected in his own right.

That was still two full years away, and it rankled Connor to no end.

"Yeah, well, 2016 is gonna be a goddamned free-for-all. You've seen the projections on probable third party strength, Phil. That pious coalition of Libertarians and Republicans and Conservative Christians could actually take 20% of the House. The *Laissez-Faire* Party—good God! A bunch of health-nut homeschoolers! Unless Preston steps on his dick, we could see him running for *this* office in 2020."

Miles counters, "Mr. President, that's *then*, and this is now. And I *still* think that putting the AG and Klein on Preston is prema—"

"'Premature' my *ass*, Phil. I've got a bad feeling about this. The West is a damned tinderbox just *waiting* for some spark like Preston. As if the water rights issue weren't bad enough, word's *already* out about the UN's 're-wilding' Biosphere plan to redistribute most of our rural population to the metros. You're from Topeka, Phil—*you* know what that means to Preston's ranching voters. Why those people can't be content in nice apartments, I just can't fathom. Oh, and you *know* that the western states in particular are going to absolutely *shit* when next spring's assault rifle confiscation bill is introduced. I can't have some modern-day Patrick Henry fanning the flames. Preston's got to *go*."

"Sir, what are you going to *do*?" asks Miles.

"I'm going to crush that acorn before we need the chainsaws. The AG's a vicious bitch—that's why I *chose* her. She'll have some ideas. And

Klein—Klein's been her lapdog for years ever since she was a DC judge. We're having a 'power breakfast' tomorrow morning to hash out how to put that hick state back in its pissant place. We'll *see* who wins this thing, Phil—Jefferson or *Machiavelli*."

"You're absolutely right, Mr. President," answers Miles.

"Well, that's what they *pay* me for. Get some sleep, Phil. Tomorrow's a long day," says the President, wickedly flashing the "W" sign.

"Yes, sir. Good night, Mr. President."

As Phillip Miles silently pads out, Connor returns to his desk, a gift to Rutherford B. Hayes from Her Majesty Queen Victoria in 1880. Hewn from oak timbers of the H.M.S. *Resolute*, the desk is actually smaller than one might suspect, though quite dense at 350 pounds. Relentlessly moved about since 1902 from the residence to the Broadcast Room to the Smithsonian, it had been returned to the Oval Office by Bill Clinton in 1993.

Connor chuckles at the debauchery likely performed on the desktop by *"Zippy"*—Clinton's nickname amongst the Presidential Protection Division of the Secret Service. *The dumbshit's mistake was <u>perjuring</u> himself over it. Imagine getting impeached over a piece of tail!* The whole Monica Lewinsky flap was like Dillinger getting caught for shoplifting.

Connor was smarter—much smarter than that.

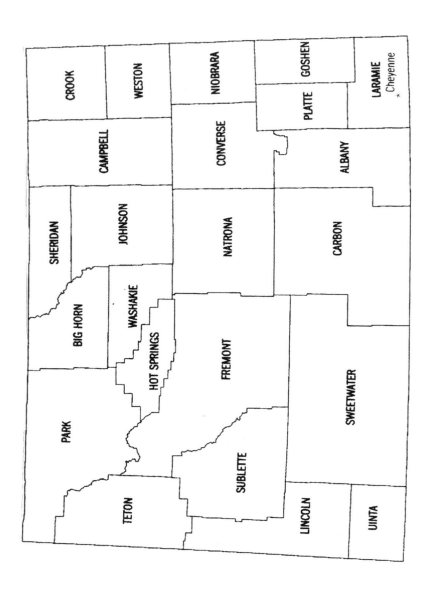

❖ 2015

Sometimes it is said that man cannot be entrusted with the government of himself. Can he, then, be trusted with the government of others? Or have we found angels in the form of kings to govern him? Let history answer this question.
I know no safe depository of the ultimate powers of the society but the people themselves; and if we think them not enlightened enough to exercise their control with a wholesome discretion, the remedy is not to take it from them, but to inform their discretion.
— Thomas Jefferson

Liberty is always dangerous, but it is the safest thing we have.
— Harry Emerson Fosdick

Cheyenne, Wyoming   Monday, 6 January 2015

Hand in hand with Juliette, Preston steps up to the rostrum in front of the Corinthian columns of the sandstone capitol. Its 24k gold leaf dome gleams in bleak winter sun. Their two teenagers James, Jr. and Hanna stand beside them, beaming. Although an icy, blustery day, 24,000 Wyomingans had enthusiastically assembled—nearly half of Cheyenne.

Chief Justice Pollard, an old friend of Benjamin Preston, smiles warmly at Ben's son as he prepares to lead Preston in the oath of office. In his sonorous voice, Preston intones the oath of 1889, with one wispy alteration.

"I do solemnly swear that I will support, obey and defend the Constitution for the United States of America, and the constitution of Wyoming, and that I will discharge the duties of my office with fidelity; that I have not paid or contributed, or promised to pay or contribute, either directly or indirectly, any money or other valuable thing, to procure my nomination or election, except for necessary and proper expenses authorized by law; that I have not, knowingly, violated any election law of the state, or procured it to be done by others in my behalf; that I will not knowingly receive, directly or indirectly, any money or other valuable thing for the performance or nonperformance of any act or duty pertaining to my office, other than the compensation allowed by law."

"Congratulations, Governor."

"Thank you, Mister Chief Justice," replies Preston. He gives Juliette a discreet kiss, holding her emerald eyes in his for that extra second which conveys volumes. Preston then squares himself to the rostrum and looks out on the cheering crowd with its breathy condensation.

"Thank you, ladies and gentlemen. I cannot describe the honor I feel for you having chosen me as your governor. Mindful of my own limited abilities, I also cannot describe my trepidations as I enter this office. It is one thing to captain the course of a business or of a family, but yet another to take the helm of a ship of state. As I took the oath of office, I felt the weight of power and responsibility fall on my shoulders.

"Power and responsibility. They are inseparable, for power without responsibility is madness, and responsibility without power is futility. They must be exercised jointly as they are a curse without each other. You, the people of Wyoming, are the sovereigns. I, and the entire Wyoming government, are your servants. I pray that I and your government will always exercise this stewardship with wisdom, grace, and courage.

"As I mentioned in my victory speech last November, we face difficult times as Americans. We have become foreigners within our own country. Jefferson once wrote that the Federal Government was not 'the exclusive or final judge of the extent of the powers delegated to itself.' Somewhere along the way, we forgot that. But never again. You needed the governor's office on your side, and now you have it! (applause)

"I am committed to recreating at least a small piece of America for us, here in Wyoming. So are you, or else you wouldn't have elected me. I cannot accomplish this goal alone. I am only in office to help you *all accomplish this. I can't do this thing alone; I can't do anything, truly, but to stay out of your way. And isn't that* really *the only thing Americans ever wanted from Government—to stay out of our way?* (great applause)

"I'm firmly convinced that Wyoming is destined to be a beacon of freedom to our fellow western states. Because of our particular spirit and hardiness, we have prospered in the face of great adversities. We have even done so under burdensome government. While we can't do much about our fierce winters, we don't *have to lug around oppressive government on our backs, like a sack of cement!* **What has the Federal Government ever attempted for us that we couldn't have done ourselves?** *Truly, government is a disease masquerading as its own cure!* (laughter) *Well, 'to cure the patient would kill the doctor.'* (laughter) *Beginning today, we 'check ourselves out of the hospital' and Wyoming will be the leader in America's rediscovering of Freedom.* (great applause and cheers)

I can't help it if the rest of the country isn't interested in living free and responsible lives, but here in Wyoming, beginning today, *we aim to take our lives* back! (thunderous applause) *We invite our western neighbors to join us* in this Second American Renaissance. We challenge our western neighbors to create for liberty-loving people a happier home than even Wyoming.

"This 'Wyoming Experiment' will be carefully monitored by our faraway puppetmasters in Washington, D.C. In the Kentucky Resolutions of 1798, Thomas Jefferson wrote that the States 'are not united on the principle of unlimited submission to their general government,. . . and that whensoever the general government assumes undelegated powers, its acts are unauthoritative, void, and of no force.' (great applause) I think that the country is fed up with five Supreme Court Justices ruling 300 million Americans with ridiculous rulings based on the overextended interstate commerce clause. (applause) Americans are sick and tired of the President and a handful of traitorous Senators binding us all to poisonous treaties and UN resolutions which conspire to remove us from our farms and homes. (continuing applause) And we have had it with Executive Orders trying to disarm us. (great applause) I say this to the Potomac Parasites, **'Mind the nation's business and stay out of ours!'** (wild applause) Even though the Tenth Amendment doesn't read 'expressly delegated'—that's how the people of the 1790s interpreted it, that's how Thomas Jefferson interpreted it, **and, by God, that's how I will interpret it!** (uproarious applause)

"Thank you. Here in Wyoming, we are still committed to the once-orthodox proposition that peaceful, productive, and respectable folks are entitled to live their own lives as they see fit. As your Governor, I solemnly pledge to you my life, my fortune, and my sacred honor that my office will always be used to protect your Liberty—no matter the threat. In the words of a French libertarian long ago, I pledge to you that the Wyoming government will 'Laissez vous faire'—**We will leave you alone!** (wild applause)

"Wyoming has a history of giving first and taking last. We were the first government on earth to politically emancipate women in 1869, but the last state to ask for federal aid during the Great Depression. We have prostrated ourselves for the nation, only to be used as a milk cow for our minerals, energy, land, and water. From here on out, we will be the nation's milk cow only for freedom and prosperity. If anybody wants our coal, helium, bentonite, oil, natural gas, or water, they'll have to pay us a fair market price and respect our Western ways during the deal! (more applause)

"From today on, we will live the Golden Rule and demand the Bill of Rights, especially the Second and Tenth Amendments. We will live as decent Citizens. Citizens—not slaves. Our rights were not given to us by the Constitution; they were merely codified by the Constitution. The Federal Government may indeed ignore that codification, but it cannot erase our rights themselves. In Wyoming we are free people, and from this day on we will act like it! We will run honest and productive businesses, we will raise our families as we see fit, and we will bear arms as free people used to do.

"Thank you again for the honor of this office. Now, you've got freer lives to live and I've got a lot of government to remove from your way. Shall we get to work? Good day to you all. God bless!"

24,000 hands went up with the "W" sign.

* * * * * * *

People are "free" or not solely according to their perceptions. Freedom is relative to whom one questions. To the recent emigrant from North Korea, the U.S. is more free than he could ever have imagined. Similarly, most Americans believe themselves to be free, primarily because that's what they've been taught. (The echoic freedom of our nation's early history has naturally been indispensable in this regard.)

Thus, in their own minds, they are free—and so are all other Americans. Egocentrism fuels such a general psychological projection. The masses cannot understand what the extremists are all upset about. "Buying assault weapons to someday wield against the government? Why, it's outrageous! Don't they know that America is the freest nation on earth?"

However, to the home-schooling, pot-smoking, gun-toting, seatbelt-shunning, tax-evading, SSN-eschewing entrepreneurial libertarian, the U.S. is a very stifling regulatory atmosphere. Such an extremist not only perceives himself to be under "tyranny" (his most favored term), he also imagines (through the neutral mechanism of egocentrism) the rest of the country to be under tyranny as well. He is thus at a loss to explain why the masses are not consciously hostile to this situation, as he is.

The masses do not feel oppressed because, by their own reckoning, they are not oppressed. They can largely do whatever they please, whenever they desire. This leaves the extremist complaining about his clipped wings to people whose wings have long since atrophied—an indignant eagle screeching to dodos.

Flight had been bred out of the dodo eons ago. His withered wings were the result, not the cause. Although we can take the eagle from the sky, we cannot take the sky from the eagle. We cannot directly breed flight from him. No matter. We will indirectly attentuate his urge to fly by eliminating his means to fly.

Wings clipped, he will have no choice but to hop around in the dirt with the dodos. The dodos will take the sky from him...

—Julius N. Harquist, *The Gaian Convergence*, p.31
River Lethe Press (2007)

Washington, D.C.   The White House

Snide comments float about the Oval Office.

"Could he have mentioned Thomas Jefferson just *one* more time?"

"'Foreigners within our own country'—*jeez!*"

"That Tenth Amendment comment was a shot across our bow."

Attorney General Janet Vorn exclaims, "Did you hear that, Mr. President? He altered the oath's language!" Having gained the room's attention, the AG continues, "Instead of swearing to defend 'the Constitution *of* the *United States*,' as is required of all state governors, Preston said 'the Constitution *for* the United States *of America*'!"

Warming to the subject, the AG elaborates, "You see, in the Preamble, the Constitution refers to itself as *'the Constitution for the United States of America'* whereas the presidential oath mandates allegiance to *'the Constitution of the United States'*—a different matter altogether."

"Janet, you're 'lecturing to the faculty,' not to some freshman law class —we *know* all this already," the President admonishes.

"Yes, sir, but *this* is truly unprecedented in American history. Not only does Preston *know* about it, but he actually *recited* his *own* 'corrected' oath to embrace the *'for the U.S.A.'* Constitution!"

"So what if he did?" asks Deputy Chief of Staff Phillip Miles. Heads swivel towards his befuddlement.

Patiently, though with a hint of exasperation, the AG explains, "Phil, our 'First Federalist' Alexander Hamilton had the presidential oath altered while serving in Committee of Style during the final days of the 1787 Philadelphia Convention. If not for him, we'd all be bound to the publicly known Constitution—the *'for the U.S.A.'* version."

Dark, intelligent eyes about the Oval Office glow at her reminder of this. For Miles, it is no reminder—it is apparent to all present that he never knew any of this in the first place.

Exultant in her windfall student, Vorn eagerly presses forward. "The Constitution in Article 6, Section 3 requires all officers to support *'this Constitution'*—meaning the Constitution *'for the U.S.A.'* and any amendments, which includes the Bill of Rights. Clearly, this would not do. Given the Article 2, Section 1, Clause 7 presidential oath reference to the *'Constitution of the United States'* it seems that Article 6, Section 3 was a tragic oversight. Congress happily circumvented that error with a 1789 act requiring allegiance to the *'of the United States'* Constitution. The state constitutions were thereafter all written, or rewritten, with the *'of the United States'* language.

"We all appreciate how important the Civil War was, especially with its Reconstruction era 14th Amendment. All of this finally began to be capitalized on in 1940 with the *Buck* Act, and later with the various UN conventions. The arduous work to achieve the nationalist dreams of the Hamiltonian Framers by eliminating the stubborn vestiges of state autonomy *was* within just several years of completion. Until now. Until *Preston.* By changing a few words in his oath of office, he has chopped many invisible control wires the Federal Government has enjoyed over the so-called 'sovereign' states. He has threatened the brilliant work of some 230 years."

Clearly confused, Miles interrupts with, "What 'control wires,'" Ms. Vorn? And what is this *'of the United States'* constitution?"

Seeing the AG's *Should I tell him?* raised eyebrows, President Connor answers, "I'm sorry that you weren't brought onboard earlier, Phil, but I saw no need to add to your busy workload."

With the President's implicit approval, the AG explains with her typical air of pedantry. "The American people and their state politicians have lived under the propagated delusion that sovereignty originates with *'the People'* and that what was not *specifically* delegated by the Constitution to the Federal Government remains with the people and their states. Had the Tenth Amendment read *'expressly delegated'* that notion would indeed be fact and not delusion. However, our onetime friend James Madison—thankfully still under Hamilton's wing in 1789—removed the word *'expressly'* which left *'delegated'* without any adverbial restriction, as it had suffered under in the Articles of Confederation. That one tiny bit of clever Madisonian syntax turned the seemingly Jeffersonian constitutional republic on its head. You see, instead of the Government being limited to only that which it was explicitly *authorized* to do in the Constitution, the Government can actually do anything not expressly *prohibited*."

Noticing Miles's furrowed brow, AG Vorn offers, "Think of it *this* way. You're an ambitious federal 'butler' with dreams of grandeur. Which national household would you prefer: one in which your freedom of action is confined *to* ABC; *or*, one in which you may do anything *except* XYZ?"

Basking in the gradual understanding on Miles's face, the AG milks the analogy still further. "The bulter's constitutional contract was skimpy, *by design*. His prohibitory XYZs are very basic and not terribly inconvenient. Because of the *'general welfare'* and *'interstate commerce'* clauses, our lucky butler can—because the contract *doesn't* specifically that say he can *not*—raid the refrigerator, borrow the family car, and even sleep with the master's daughter. Oh, sure, the 'master' is complaining, but he is bound by his own hastily made contract. And, best yet, any changes in that contract can be proposed only by the congressional *maids*!"

A phlegmy wave of laughter sweeps the Oval Office, which Miles nervously joins. *Don't blow it, Phil. Hear this witch out.*

Amidst the residual chuckles, Miles says, "Yes, I follow you so far, but what about the 'control wires' and this other constitution?"

The AG plows on. "The 10th Amendment was merely built upon the foundation of the presidential oath. Remember, except for three or four fools, nobody at 1787 Philadelphia wanted a *limited* Federal Government. Nobody there *wanted* some Jeffersonian republic of yeoman farmers each under their own vine and fig tree[1]. Why do you think the increasingly federalist Congress sent Jefferson to *Europe* during the crucial years of the mid-1780s? He would have single-handedly compromised our plans in Philadelphia and probably stolen Madison away from us several years earlier than he did. Only *after* the Constitution had been ratified and our Government had been on-line for six months was Jefferson allowed to return home in 1789. Then, he was given the cozy post of Secretary of State where he could be watched and overruled by Hamilton, our first Secretary of the Treasury.

"Anyway, back to the presidential oath. Even though the Constitution *for* the United States of America was contrived, written, and ratified by our political ancestors, it was not perfect for our purposes. You see, the substantial Jeffersonian sentiment of the day had to be assuaged with a Bill of Rights, else the Constitution could never have been ratified. Thus, the scrappy bone of freedom thrown to the people of the late 18th century has traveled full circle to become a bone in *our* throats. The Framers foresaw this would happen someday, so they wrote the presidential oath in such a way that *we* have a quiet, legal means for crushing that bone.

"Since you do not hold an actual office under the political trust of the people, you were not required to swear an oath, therefore you were not told of our 'Constitution *of* the United States.'"

"So, what *is* its meaning and purpose?" asks Miles tautly.

"It is only because of two factors that you may learn of it. First, its secret was blown in 1997 by a book called *Hologram of Liberty*. While its author had no *direct* proof of our Constitution, he did, quite amazingly, point to its *likely* existence through a succinct interweaving of historically circumstantial evidence. To use a physics analogy, he postulated the nature of electricity *before* the existence of electrons could be confirmed by scientific equipment. It probably had to happen eventually. Our activities had become *so* 'unconstitutional' that somebody was bound to suggest that there must be another batch of 'programming' other than the visible '*Constitution for the United States of America.*' Move enough chairs around in an old house and someone's gonna cry '*Ghost!*' The author finally did that and Preston must have read his book, even though it was generally ignored by the conservatives. The President's trust in you is the second." At this, the AG simply stopped talking, preferring to drink in Miles's suspense.

With visible restraint, Miles quietly asks, "Ms. Vorn, what *is* this so-called '*Constitution of the United States*'?"

"It's our private, hidden charter, Phil. To use a computer analogy, it's like a UNIX shell, or a hidden 'device driver'—a TSR, or Terminate and Stay Resident program, if you will.

---

1   Refers to King Solomon's 40 year peaceful and prosperous reign from 972-932 B.C. at 1 Kings 4:25: "*And Judah and Israel dwelt safely, every man under his vine and under his fig tree.*"

"Most of us here are not computer programmers like you, Janet," the President gently chides.

"Right—sorry, sir. Before 1997, before *Hologram*, the masses had no idea that it even existed. In a nutshell, our little Constitution mandates our prime directive, which is the continuance and growth of the Federal Government over any and all other considerations. It mandates our allegiance to the federal 'U.S.' over the national U.S.A. It requires that Federal needs crowd out state concerns, that public policy shall precede individual rights, that corporate economics stand above employees and entrepreneurs, that powers of national emergency override the democratic process, and, most importantly, that political power is restored to its *rightful* place in the *Government.* *We* are the sovereigns, Phil, not 'the People' and certainly not the states. The nation of the United States of America was always meant to be a *business,* and the corporate federal entity called the 'United States' is simply the board of directors for 'USA, Inc.' Through that nimble verbiage in the presidential oath, the U.S. runs the U.S.A."

Pausing for effect as this sunk in, Vorn summarizes this last point. "Did you *really* imagine that we'd allow the political and economic reality of this country to be dictated by some old piece of parchment kept in a nitrogen-filled case at the National Archives? No, we simply embrace Hamilton's view of the *'for the U.S.A.'* Constitution as *'a frail and worthless fabric . . . merely a stepping stone to something better.'* Phil, *everything* has been a 'stepping stone to something better.' The 1780s Annapolis and Philadelphia conventions, the Constitutions—both *'for the U.S.A.'* and *'of the U.S.'*—the *GATT*s and *NAFTA*s, even the UN charter. All stepping stones."

To the room Miles abruptly asks, "What is this 'something better'?"

At a nod from President Connor, Secretary of State Harquist replies, "Why, the Godhood of mankind, of course."

"*Sir*?" says Miles.

"The unity of man necessary to reach our Godhood was interrupted at the Tower of Babel. Oh, yes; that corny Bible story was *quite* accurate, but our shattered unity has painstakingly been reassembled over the last six thousand years. Yes, Mr. Miles, we *are* gods—gods kept locked inside prison cells of flesh by that Cosmic Jailkeeper, the so-called 'Lord Almighty' who hoards the Light and punishes the Lightgiver, Lucifer. Americans prattle about political conspiracies to enslave *man*kind when the vilest conspiracy of all is right under their bovine noses—the Cosmic Conspiracy to enslave *God*kind."

Miles just sits there, skewered by the shock of it all.

FBI Director Klein studies him intently.

Uncorked, Harquist—that bow-tied, blinking gnome—continues in his reedy voice, "For centuries we endeavored to, so to speak, 'pick the lock' to our cell. We're far too advanced for that now. Five thousand years ago, we didn't understand the God Power—now we *do*. Our scientists and mystics have pierced the astral veil. That old miser holds no secrets from us anymore. We now know that we can simply walk *through* our prison walls, and believe me when I tell you, Mr. Miles, that we are on the verge of doing so. The Enlightened Ones in our midst have already pushed through, and we are poised to gather up our Select for the Transformation."

Miles's façade of rapt interest is but a retaining wall for the mounting black horror he feels inside. Looking about the room, he sees nothing but sly camaraderie. Devils all around him, he dares not risk even a syllable. *If I can just stay calm long enough to hear the rest and make a smooth exit.*

Noticing Miles unconsciously fidgeting with his tie, Klein makes a mental note to himself.

Harquist drones on. "None of us here relishes the dirty work of politics, but it is necessary preparation for our Transformation. Since not all mankind may join us, we must ensure that those destined to remain behind as hairless apes cannot hinder us. The Constitutions, the Civil War, the World Wars, this Oval Office, the UN, *all of it*, is simply prelaunch activity. Have no illusions, Mr. Miles, we *rule* this world, and all other worlds out there we will rule also."

In spite of his emotional nausea, Miles manages to conjure up a credible visage of awe.

"Well said, Julius, thank you," the President smoothly interjects, signaling the end to any further galactic musings.

The man always admitted far too much, which is why River Lethe Press pulled Harquist's book shortly after publication. Another similarly candid book suffered the same fate: Carroll Quigley's *On Tragedy and Hope*, which frankly outlined the Insiders' plan to rule the masses through police state technology. It wasn't wise policy for Big Brother to brag *before* having first achieved all of his goals.

"So, Phil, now you know 'the rest of the story.' We can't make an issue of Preston's 'corrected' oath as it would publicize the matter and invite questions. I'm sure you understand."

Miles replies with a solemn nod. "Yes, sir, I do."

"Shall we return now to Governor Preston?" the President asks.

Ending for the day Miles's education, the congregated demigods agree that the Wyoming Governor should not be permitted to complete a successful term of office.

"Have you any thoughts on that, Janet?" inquire the President.

The AG greedily resumes center stage. "Yes, sir, I do. Preston is like some blind man groping around in the dark with one hand on our ankle. While he'll probably never realize *what* he's actually got, nevertheless the damage he can do will delay us, and we can brook no more delays. All of you know that we're at least six years behind schedule as it is. If those people weren't so well armed we could have dealt with them under Clinton. If Preston succeeds in leading Wyoming and other western states to *de facto* secession, we will lose our golden opportunity for decades.

"So, you see, it's not about just Wyoming. It's not even about just the country. It's about us realizing our Transformation. No man, no state, and no country is worth our failure. Preston has stumbled onto something and the rest is merely sequential association. He's a smart man, but what's more disturbing, he's also *lucky*. Smart *and* lucky usually spell disaster. We simply cannot allow him to grope around for much longer, else he might begin to recognize the shapes he feels."

"Just so," Connor grants, as the rest nod in agreement.

"Maybe some infidelity scandal here would suit our purpose?" the Secretary of State suggests.

A rude thought crosses Connor's mind. *Harquist should talk. He's not even faithful to his own wife, much less his mistress!*

"The public would never believe it, Julius," answers Vorn. "That's Ward and June Cleaver you're talking about. You saw how he handled that exposé on his illegitimate Hungarian son. Dowling looked like shit."

"Janet's right, Julius. Besides, the Bureau has already examined the man from teeth to toenails, and he's absolutely clean. A real Boy Scout," muses Klein.

"We've got over five million federal laws on the books, Paul. You can't tell me that Preston has abided by every *one* of them!" Harquist counters. "I mean, what else are those laws *for*?"

"We all take your point, Julius, but this administration cannot be seen as attacking a popular governor—especially one hypercritical of the Government—with some obscure regulation," explains the President.

AG Vorn says, "What a shame there's been no link so far to Krassny."

"If Preston's were Krassny's nephew or something," says Miles, "the media would shred him to bits." Miles figured he had to offer *something*, and this remark was generic enough to be safe.

Aaron Stanford, Secretary of the Treasury, enters the discussion. "Mr. President, I've already asked IRS Commissioner Belton to review Preston's business affairs. I'm confident that some kind of case could be assembled in time. Income tax evasion is a very pliable tool."

"It would have to go way beyond mere evasion, Aaron. We'd need outright tax *fraud* to sink his ship," the President asserts. *Just like Joseph Wiedermann, the prick.*

"Maybe even some RICO[2] charges as well," says Klein.

"Ah, *RICO*. I've always thought that was such a mellifluous word," purs AG Vorn. The room chuckles at this.

Phillip Miles stares about the Oval Office, neither seeing nor hearing, his mind swimming.

The meeting continues in that vein for several more minutes with a firm resolve to deal with Preston at the soonest viable opportunity.

* * * * * * *

Back at his office, Miles aimlessly shuffles some papers about, giving up at just after 5PM. *What have I gotten myself involved in?*

Feigning a headache, he collected his briefcase, left the White House through the East Entrance and drove northwest on Pennsylvania Avenue towards his Georgetown condo on Avon Place NW near R Street. He never noticed Washington Circle's snarled traffic with its miasma of honking and profanity. Fortunately, he missed getting delayed by one of the random but ubiquitous US Army mobile checkpoints.

After a brisk shower, he dressed for a quiet dinner out. Even though a light snow had begun to fall, Miles elected to walk. Leisurely moving down the steps, Miles turned left and walked south to Cambridge Place on his way to 30th Street. He glanced at 3027, what used to be the home of Vince Foster, Clinton's first Deputy White House Counsel. The highly suspicious death (and its subsequent cover-up) of the highest level federal official since JFK had quite the chilling effect on 1993 Washington. Clinton simply brought his "Arkansas Mafia" tactics to the nation's capital, and Foster's homicide (to cover-up Clinton's murder of the Branch Davidians by illegally using Delta Force) was a sharp lesson to the Beltway political machine.

Just in case anybody needed a reminder, they had only to wait three years. On 3 April 1996, Commerce Secretary Ron Brown's Air Force jet crashed into a Croatian mountainside, and the Air Force killed the safety investigation. Brown was only months away from prison for his rat's nest of criminal deals, including accepting $700,000 from Communist Vietnam to cancel our trade embargo. When Brown's mess became too vast even for Clinton to call off the dogs (the DOJ, the FDIC, the Congressional Reform and Oversight Committee, the FBI, the DOE, the IRS, etc.), Brown vowed in February 1996 not to take the rap alone by fingering the Clintons and McDougal.

From then on, Ron Brown was a dead man holding interim air.

---

2   **Racketeer Influenced and Corrupt Organization** laws designed to investigate, control, and prosecute organized crime. Originally relating to extortion and coercion, the term "racketeering" (like the USSR's "hooliganism") has come to mean just about anything the DOJ wants it to mean, such as interfering with interstate or foreign commerce.

While "Billary" were long gone, one nevertheless didn't tweak Washington's tail foolishly. *Hairless apes indeed,* as Miles recalled Harquist's choice phrase. Rough politics might be excused, but not this ugly conspiracy for some gilded global slavery. He would have to very carefully consider his actions from here on.

Fifteen minutes later he arrives in a dark mood at his favorite Chinese restaurant on Wisconsin Avenue and Prospect Street, is warmly greeted as a regular and quickly seated. While waiting for his meal, he fishes out his cell phone, but the battery is dead. Miles finds the payphone, digs out a calling card, and dials the San Diego number of his Harvard roommate and best friend, Steve Dunbar. Dunbar was from Jackson, Wyoming, where his parents had opened a ski lodge in the 1970s. An old Republican family, his parents were friends of the Prestons.

"Hey, it's P.R., howya been? Ah, same old crap—it's *Washington*, Steve-o. Listen, I know it's short notice, but I could use a break for a few days. You up for some fishing off Cabo this weekend? Boat's on me. Really? Great! I'll email you tomorrow about my flight. I sound kinda funny? Yeah, well, I can't get into it right now. We'll talk about it this weekend. All I can say is that for the first time in my life I feel like I'm in *way* over my head. I need some help on this, buddy, and you're the only one I think I can trust with it. No, I'm not trying to keep you in suspense—I just can't go into it right now. Thanks. We'll talk Friday. OK, see you then."

Returning to his table, his meal is waiting for him. Scraping his chopsticks against each other as the spicy peanut sauce scent of his *kung-pao* chicken wafts, Miles suddenly feels much better. He's very glad he called his friend. *Steve will have some ideas.*

Engrossed in thought, Phillip Miles did not notice the inconspicuous carpet cleaning van parked cater-corner across the street. Equipped with the very best telcom technology, the men inside were also engrossed in the thoughts of the Deputy Chief of Staff. Thanks to the eager help of Lucent Technologies and the Bell companies years ago, any phone's conversation could be routed through the FBI's digital recording banks within 15 seconds. This was legal without a search warrant under the *USA PATRIOT Act*[3] of 2001 and the *Communications Assistance for Law Enforcement Act III* of 2009 (one of President McBlane's first bills to sign—which he did gladly).

Civil libertarians had argued, fruitlessly, that *CALEA III* would actually *"create an Orwellian Thought Police."* Senator Kennedy (D-MA) blasted this as *"shrill and baseless melodrama."*

While Miles was walking south on 30th Street NW, his credit card records were being analyzed by the gray men in the gray van, who correctly

---

3   "Uniting and Strengthening America by Providing Appropriate Tools Required to Intercept and Obstruct Terrorism" The acronymania is getting pretty ridiculous.

surmised that he was enroute to the Peking Palace. A telephone database was immediately accessed which listed the restaurant's payphone number. As Miles was entering his calling card number, his payphone was "touched," as the Thought Police called it. Once Miles had entered his friend's number, Steve Dunbar's name and address filled a small window on the screen. Their call was not only recorded but automatically transcribed by the finest AI voice recognition software in existence, which used contextual analysis to virtually eliminate transliteration error. The conversation was also fed through a sophisticated lie-detection software which analyzed micro-tremors.

Miles and Dunbar had no inkling of all this, for the real-time splice was absolutely silent. In fact, only the phone company and the Government knew, or *could* know. *"A sufficiently advanced technology is indistinguishable from magic,"* as the science-fiction author Arthur C. Clarke once observed.

FBI Special Agent Nowlin has heard enough. "Sounds hinky. And he used a payphone to bypass his cell. Compile a full doss on this Steven Joseph Dunbar by 0800. Route both of their comms from Dixie-Cups-and-string to sat phone through the Box. California, D.C., Baja, *wherever*, I want airtight coverage—*got it?* Put a six-man tag team on Miles by 2200 and we'll hand off to them. Get me the SAC, *now.*"

Deep sea fishing off Cabo San Lucas? Well, Phillip Roland Miles, I'm a fisher of men, and my fish bait their own hooks.

* * * * * * *

The secret of good government is to let man alone.
— Lao Tze, 270 A.D.

There is nothing more difficult to take in hand, more perilous to conduct, or more uncertain in its success than to take the lead in the introduction of a new order of things.
— Machiavelli, 1513

Cheyenne, Wyoming   February 2015

During its 40 days of general session, the Wyoming legislature worked fast. Most of the desired changes had been drafted by Preston's people months before the election and it was just a matter of the final wording. To streamline a government took careful planning. Political power—like energy—could not be eliminated, only changed in *form*. What was taken back from government had to be returned to its source, the People. Since they had relinquished their sovereignty slowly, it could be returned only slowly, at a rate they could absorb—as well as appreciate. The fate of the 14th century Italian politician di Rienzo was a poignant lesson.

Cola di Rienzo was a young Roman lawyer in his mid-30s. He went to Avignon in the year 1343 to ask Pope Clement VI for his support against the feuding aristocracy who dominated the capital. Clement agreed, and sent di Rienzo back to Rome with money and encouragement.

Filled with dreams of returning the glory that was Rome, di Rienzo dressed in the white toga of an ancient senator and challenged the people to seize the government, restore the popular assembly, and elect a tribune strong enough to protect them from the nobility. Backed by the poor, the merchants, and the papacy, di Rienzo was first elected dictator and later allowed the old popular title of tribune. When the nobles protested, his armed revolutionaries ran them out of the city to their country estates.

Di Rienzo brought impartial justice and stable prices back to Rome. A court of conciliation ended nearly 2,000 feuds. Crooked judges were exposed and punished. Peasants tilled their fields in peace and security. All became tranquil and prosperous in Rome, and the entire penisula marveled.

The mantle of power, however, proved too heady for di Rienzo. He became increasingly extravagant and megalomanic. Then, he tried to enlarge his reign by inviting all of Italy to join his federation. This frightened Pope Clement VI. A unified Italy—much less, a reconstituted Roman empire— would make the Italian Church a prisoner of the state. Clement abandoned di Rienzo on 3 December 1347 as a heretic and criminal, and called upon all Romans to banish him. If this were not done, the Pope threatened, then the Jubilee of 1350 would be cancelled, a devastating economic impact.

Suddenly, di Rienzo lost support from the poor, the merchants, and the Church. The nobles raised an army against him and marched on Rome. Di Rienzo frantically called the people to arms, but they refused, preferring the Jubilee's profits over paying taxes and military service. The army of the nobles arrived unchallenged two weeks later, and the triumphant aristocracy reentered their city palaces. Clement named two of them as senators over Rome. Di Rienzo fled to Naples.

Six years later, di Rienzo, now a broken man from flight and imprisonment, was returned by the Church to Rome as senator and local governor. (Meanwhile, a brutal tribune named Baroncelli had arisen, so di Rienzo's old supporters desired his return following a successful uprising against Baroncelli.) The old fire and dreams of his youth were gone; di Rienzo toed the papal line. The nobles still hated him, and the proletariat (after initial excitement) grew to see him as disloyal. Two months after his return, di Rienzo was seized by a street mob shouting *Long live the people! Death to the traitor Cola di Rienzo!* He was taken to the steps of the Capitol and stabbed by over a hundred people. His body was dragged through the streets to be hung up at a butcher's stall for two days, spat upon and disgraced.

The moral was multifaceted: Finances are often more valued than freedom, alliances will shift, and the people are eternally fickle. Preston understood that radical politics were a very risky business.

The trick was to pour through a funnel, consistently yet gradually. Post-1991 Russia was the now-classic example of what happened when too much freedom was returned too quickly. Unaccustomed to liberty, the former USSR (except for the Czech Republic) begged for Communism's return after the mafia chaos, and got it in 2009.

Still, what the legislators accomplished in only six weeks astounded the nation (and much of Wyoming). The *Cheyenne Sentinel* quoted Governor Preston's summary of the first 40 days:

"Point One. We applaud the inherent value of an armed citizenry. Armed Citizens kill three times more violent criminals than do the police. They also injure far fewer innocent bystanders than do the police: 1 in 50 vs. 1 in 9. Accordingly, as self-protection is a communal good and an individual *right*—not a privilege—the state sales tax on firearms, ammunition, and shooting gear is today repealed. We ask the Federal Government to follow our lead and repeal their own excise taxes on these articles.

"Point Two. Furthermore, the Wyoming legislature follows the lead of Vermont and Alaska, and hereby recognizes the right of any sane, non-felon adult to own and carry weapons without requirement of license or permit. As the cities and counties are creatures of the state, there shall be no local infringement of this cornerstone right. Carry what you want, how you want, where you want, and we won't bother you unless you mess up. If you're unhappy about seeing armed Citizens on your street, then there are dozens of other states which welcome you. So would their *criminals*!

Accordingly, the legislature proposes that Article 1, Section 24 of the Wyoming Constitution be replaced with the following language:

No state, county, or city representative, officer, agent, employee, or functionary, may deny, infringe, regulate, or tax the absolute right of the people, in either their individual or collective militia capacities, to purchase, own, convey, carry, train with, and use weapons and their accoutrements. Any act or order which would, directly or indirectly, or under any guise or pretense, deny, infringe, regulate, or tax this cornerstone right is null and void at moment of passage, and may lawfully be, without pain of prosecution, ignored, or, if deemed necessary by the people or any of them, forcibly resisted.

"Point Three. The legislature proposes that Article 1, Section 28 of the Wyoming Constitution be replaced with the following language: *"No tax shall be imposed or increased without the consent of a three-fourths majority of electors in a preceding general election."* This means that you the people must overwhelmingly approve any new tax or rate hike. No longer will representatives be able to impose or increase taxes at their whim.

"Point Four. No longer will we be the first generation to drive slower than our parents. We follow the one-time lead of our neighbor state Montana in the matter of daytime highway speed limits—*'Reasonable and prudent.'* While the enforcement judgment of what is *'reasonable and prudent'* will be up to the police officer, as long as the road and traffic conditions allow, a competent driver should have no problem enjoying a capable machine at triple-digit speeds in good weather. It used to be done in Germany, before the EC became too powerful.

"Point Five. We fully recognize your Sixth Amendment right to a speedy and public jury trial in *'all criminal prosecutions.'* In our view, *'all'* means exactly that—all. Therefore, we heartily repudiate the Supreme Court's *Blanton* doctrine[4], which is classic *Animal Farm* 'except-for' jurisprudence. In Wyoming, your right in *any* criminal case to a jury trial by twelve peers is guaranteed in full, including a unanimous verdict to convict. Accordingly, the legislature has proposed that Article 1, Section 9 of the Wyoming Constitution be so amended.

"Point Six. The real purpose of a *jury* trial is to try the *law* before the community. The Fully Informed Jury Amendment simply codifies what Americans well understood before the War Between the States and reinstitutes the most important 'check and balance' on the government. FIJA is hereby passed by the legislature not only as a bill, but as a proposed constitutional amendment. It reads:

> *An accused or aggrieved party's rights to trial by jury, in all instances where the government or any of its agencies is an opposing party, includes the right to inform the jurors of their power to judge the law as well as the evidence, and to vote on the verdict according to conscience.*
>
> *This right shall not be infringed by any statute, juror oath, court order, or procedure or practice of the court, including the use of any method of jury selection which could preclude or limit the impanelment of jurors willing to exercise this power.*
>
> *Nor shall this right be infringed by preventing any party to the trial, once the jurors have been informed of their powers, from presenting arguments to the jury which may pertain to issues of law and conscience, including (1) the merit, intent, constitutionality or applicability of the law in the instant case; (2) the motives, moral*

---

4   *Blanton v. North Las Vegas* 489 US 541, whereby the Supreme Court ruled that the 6th Amendment meant only *"capital"* crimes, and offenses punishable by less than six months imprisonment are *"petty"* in which you have no constitutional right to a jury trial. For more information, visit **www.fija.org**.

perspective, or circumstances of the accused or aggrieved party; (3) the degree and direction of guilt or actual harm done; or (4) the sanctions which may be applied to the losing party.

Failure to allow the accused or aggrieved party or counsel for that party to so inform the jury shall be grounds for mistrial and another trial by jury.

"Point Seven. We repudiate the Socialist doctrine of the State owning our children. We believe that you the *parents* own your children. Therefore, the legislature has proposed the Parental Rights Amendment:

The right of parents to direct the upbringing and education of their children shall not be infringed.

The legislature shall have power to enforce, by appropriate legislation, the provisions of this article.

"Point Eight. Most countries have a 'loser pays' civil court system, and Wyoming will lead the way in America. In our state civil courts regarding cases exceeding $1,000, the petitioner shall be required, if duly demanded by the defendant, to post a bond for the defendant's reasonably expected costs and attorney's fees. No more 'contingency fee' nuisance lawsuits in Wyoming!

"Point Nine. No purpose of government—state, local, or federal—is so compelling as to justify the homelessness of its Citizens over tax bills. The *ad valorem* property tax has become a disguised form of cruel tenancy to extort endless bond issues by threat of eviction. Accordingly, the legislature has proposed to amend the Article 19, Section 9 of Wyoming Constitution by striking out the text *'for taxes'* regarding forced sales. Meanwhile, I have halted all evictions from, and forced sales of, homesteads for nonpayment of state taxes.

"Finally, Point Ten. The legislature proposes that Article 20, Section 1 of the Wyoming Constitution be amended with the following language (new text in bold):

Any amendment or amendments to this constitution may be proposed **by either a popular referendum signed by at least twenty thousand (20,000) electors, or** *in either branch of the legislature..., and it shall be the duty of the legislature to submit such amendment or amendments to the electors of the state at the next general election, or at the next special election convened by the governor, which shall in any event take place within one hundred and eighty (180) days of* **the referendum or** *passage by both houses.*

"This will allow the people to *directly* propose constitutional amendments beneficial to their liberty, and thus no longer be held constitutional hostage by a legislature loath to relinquish its power.

"With these Ten Points we are well on our way to restoring some of your many rights long ago eroded by government. All responsible adults are now free to: be armed anywhere and anyhow without permission, travel in their car as fast as is reasonable and prudent, enjoy full rights of a jury trial with twelve fully informed jurors, directly control all proposed new taxes, no longer be subjected to nuisance lawsuits, raise and educate their children as they see fit, be free from eviction for unpaid taxes, and directly propose new constitutional amendments without approval of the legislature.

"Let me and your representatives hear from you on what you would like us to consider next. Folks, the only valid purpose of government is to uphold the rights of its Citizens. Anything else is *your* affair!

"And this is only a beginning! Remember, Freedom is always unfinished business."

Washington, D.C.   FBIHQ   February 2015

In a macabre amalgam of professionalism and morbid curiosity, the Bureau braces itself for news of the "The Leopard's" next victim. They do not have long to wait.

* * * * * * *

The fact is that the average man's love of liberty is nine-tenths imaginary, exactly like his love of sense, justice and truth. He is not actually happy when free; he is uncomfortable, a bit alarmed, and intolerably lonely. Liberty is not a thing for the great masses of men. It is the exclusive possession of a small and disreputable minority, like knowledge, courage and honor. It takes a special sort of man to understand and enjoy liberty—and he is usually an outlaw in democratic societies.
— H.L. Mencken, 12 February 1923, *Baltimore Evening Sun*

All progress has resulted from people who took unpopular positions.
— Adlai Stevenson

Wyoming   February 2015

James Preston quickly becomes known for his particular style and schedule. Much of it he gleaned from maverick Minnesota Governor Jesse Ventura, such as his monthly bus tours to different parts of the state and his

11AM-1PM Thursday radio show "Lunch With the Governor" (91.9FM from Laramie with statewide repeaters).

Preston reserves Sundays totally for his family, enjoying afternoon outings following church, and taking no official phone calls or visits.

With the media Preston discusses only policy, and avoids all personal questions (except during his radio show). He is a man of clear demarcations, rigorously enforced. After a few weeks, everyone understands this and works around it. The Wyoming people have regular access to their governor, and the Prestons never feel as though they've lost their father to a political vortex.

Washington, D.C.   FBIHQ   February 2015

Director Klein does not want to make this call to the President. "The Leopard" has struck for the fourth time—right on schedule on the second Tuesday in February of an odd-numbered year—as if to mock the world's most prestigious law enforcement agency.

"Mr. President, I'm afraid we have some bad news," ventures Klein.

He hears Connor sigh heavily, then say, "What is it, Paul?"

The Director pauses involuntarily. "Julius Harquist was just found dead. I'm very sorry, sir."

Klein can actually feel the silent rage over the secure phone line. "*When? How?*" demands the President.

"He failed to check in with his Secret Service protection detail this morning. They just called me five minutes ago."

Connor says, "Julius always did find personal security beneath him. I heard that Henry Kissinger felt the same way. What *is* it about Secretaries of State? Paul, what happened?"

"Sir, we're almost positive that it was the same man who first acted back in 2009. Judge Gray's abductor."

The President says in a steely tone, "Paul—what . . . *happened?*"

Klein closes his eyes as he grimaces. "Secretary Harquist was choked to death. With his own book."

"*What? Choked?*"

"Yes, sir. A dozen pages were torn out of *The Gaian Convergence*, crumpled, and then crammed down his throat. It wasn't pretty."

Annual Governor's Association Conference
Washington, D.C.   February 2015

Of the 50 states, only Wyoming had anything interesting to report. Preston's *10 Points* were the talk of the town. Few believed that the seven proposed constitutional amendments would be ratified by Wyomingites, even though popular support seemed strong. They were simply too radical to be taken "seriously."

At the White House dinner President Connor condescended to make a personal remark, and a very dry one at that. "Governor, you're in the 'driver's seat' now. Good luck keeping out of the ditches."

Preston whispered his wife, winking, "See? I *told* you he'd like me!"

New York Governor Conan O'Brien sought out his Wyoming counterpart to offer some advice: *"If you stand on principle, you don't go anywhere!"*

Preston retorted, "Conan, when you stand on principle, you don't *have* to go anywhere because you're always where you *should* be."

The famous O'Brien wit had no snappy comeback for this.

Preston particularly enjoyed discussing politics with Governor Louis Drake of Alaska, a libertarianesque Republican.

"Liberal Democrats are not the problem," Preston declares.

"They're not?" says Drake.

"No, not really. In any political society you'll find two general camps: those who work for a living and those who would rather *vote* for a living. Apparently it's human nature. So, we will always have Liberal Democrats, or some ghastly equivalent. But they are not *truly* the problem."

"Why not, if they're opposed to free-markets, honest politics, and personal responsibility?"

"Because political animals and their supporters are a human constant. They're an eternal force to be resisted, like gravity or atmospheric pressure. Givens are not worth fretting over. Just transcend them and go on with life."

"I don't understand . . . Then who are the problem?"

"Our friends and colleagues and fellow travelers, of course."

Drake is stunned. "*What?* "

"Look, enemies are a given. One can make solid calculations about them and render them moot, if not defeat them. Bad people are not the trouble. *Allies,* however, are the real unknown variable. The reason why mankind never enjoys any lasting freedom is because good people refuse to remain effective. They avoid the courage and vigilance demanded by the struggle. They remain merely 'good enough' to get by in life without sinking to outright theft and murder. While any display of goodness is welcome, diluted goodness is not sufficient to displace evil."

Drake slowly nods and says, "It's a stringent position, but I can't see much to disagree with."

"Think of it this way," Preston says. "If you've ever had an infection and were prescribed an antibiotic, what did your doctor impress upon you?"

Drake thinks for a moment and replies, "To take the entire prescription? Not to stop after you're feeling better?"

"Exactly! Or, in other words, to see the battle *through.* If you don't, the remaining bacterial colonies increase their immunity. They will lay dormant as they gather strength to return twice as powerful. Conservatives never finished the war against domestic socialism. They only wanted to relieve themselves of the *symptoms*. They merely took aspirin for the brain tumor of liberalism. The Reagan years were the prime example. Four years later they got Clinton. So, evil people aren't the problem. Wimpy good people *are*. Republicans who 'settle for looser chains' and won't go whole hog by embracing libertarianism."

"How so?" Drake says.

Here's the secret to Republicans: they are not comfortable with more than half the story or huge amounts of freedom. They never have been. Republicans quote the *Federalist* papers, but rarely the *Antifederalist Papers*. Republicans tolerate handguns—*if* they're worn concealed like some embarrassing family secret—but battle rifles and their historical purpose for controlling bad government make them nervous."

"Boy, that's true!" Drake says.

"Republicans support conceal-carry permits but not Vermont-style carry where no permit is required. You personally know about this when you were in the Alaskan legislature back in 2003 during the passage of your own Vermont-style carry."

"Yeah, I sure do, Jim. Con Bunde, a Republican from Anchorage, just couldn't see his way into trusting the common folk. He was more worried about the so-called 'court of public opinion' than our constitutional rights!"

"A pretty typical response," Preston says. "Republicans back the NRA, but not the 'radical' GOA or JPFO. Republicans want school vouchers, but not the dismantling of government education. Republicans send their children to private schools rather than homeschool. Republicans have no problem with their own coffee, alcohol, and tobacco, but pot is evil—hence they eagerly back the War on Some Drugs. Republicans seek to partially privatize Social Security, but they will not admit that the entire program was a fraud from the beginning and close it down. Republicans don't demand that income taxes be eliminated, but merely replaced with a flat tax. Or if eliminated, then replaced with a 'revenue-equivalent' national sales tax."

Drake is nodding stonily, deep in thought.

Preston wraps it up. "All these things aren't even *half* measures, they're more like *tenth* measures. They're not even enough to postpone totalitarianism for their grandchildren. Gutless. They know better, but they just don't have the courage to take freedom to its logical conclusion, and that is the primary trouble with conservatives."

"Well, Jim, now I'm ashamed to have run under the GOP!" Drake says.

Preston smiles at the Alaskan governor and replies, "Louis, I know you're a better man than to sell out your principles to the party machine. If you lead, the Alaskan people will follow. It's why they elected you, regardless of the GOP banner. Just do what you know is right and you'll never cheat the man in the glass."

Drake guffaws loudly, surprising Preston. "You know that poem too! It's one of my favorites!"

With a laughing start, they recite it in unison:

When you get what you want in your struggle for self
And the world makes you king for a day,
Just go to a mirror and look at yourself
And see what that man has to say.

For it isn't your father or mother or wife
Whose judgment upon you must pass,
The fellow whose verdict counts most in your life
Is the one staring back from the glass.

Some people might think you're a straight-shootin' chum
And call you a wonderful guy.
But the man in the glass says you're only a bum
If you can't look him straight in the eye.

He's the fellow to please, never mind all the rest
For he's the one with you clear to the end.
And you have passed your most dangerous test
If the guy in the glass is your friend.

You may fool the whole world down the pathway of years
And get pats on the back as you pass,
But your final reward will be heartache and tears
If you've cheated the man in the glass.

When they finish, they become acutely aware of the silence at their table. Drake looks around and says, "Heard *that* one before?" Preston has to turn away to keep from laughing. He knows he has a comrade in Juneau. Meeting Drake was about the only bright spot in a rather dreary, perfunctory trip.

Wyoming   March-April 2015

The Fully Informed Jury Amendment required the most effort to educate the public. Preston devoted much time to FIJA on his Thursday two-hour radio shows. He patiently explained that fully informed jurors had been the norm during the beginning of the American Republic, but that this right had been whittled away by judges and prosecutors. It was Preston's intention to bring it back in an overall process he called "reverse gradualism."

Fortunately, many Wyomingites had at least heard of the concept because of publicity from neighboring South Dakota where it had been on the ballot since 2002:

Laws are meant to promote harmony in society. When laws make sense, they do promote harmony.

Sometimes, though, a law or its application strikes a sour note. When someone is unjustly accused by our justice system, it does more damage than a thousand appropriate convictions and punishments can repair.

Legislators try to do good things when they make laws. Occasionally, however, even well-intended laws cause disasters for peaceful, honest people: an elderly man convicted of "cruelty to animals" after using his cane in defense of an attacking dog; parents convicted of "child pornography" after taking family photos of their toddler in the tub; a lady convicted under the "open container" law after collecting empty beer cans along the road to use in making novelty hats.

Verdicts like these create hardship, discord, and cynicism. Not harmony. Not justice.

For justice to be served, an accused person must be allowed to present a complete defense. If he's barred from arguing that applying the letter of the law will not make common sense, an unjust verdict can easily result. Such arguments are presently denied to accused persons.

Amendment A's critics have been implying that South Dakota's citizen jurors aren't bright enough to tell a good explanation from a bad one, and don't have enough common sense to deliver justice. Interestingly, these arrogant, unfounded slurs have come almost entirely from lawyers.

True, asking the legislature to improve a faulty law is an option —but only for those with time and money to burn. It's not much help to someone already being wrongly prosecuted. "A" will provide for those who need it most, when and where it counts.

In sum, Amendment A will reinforce our right as Americans to a fair trial. If ever accused of breaking a law that we feel is flawed, or wrongly applied, or carries too harsh a punishment, we should be able to say so in court. It just makes common sense.

— Proponent's Argument, South Dakota 2002 General Election Question Pamphlet

Finally ratified there in 2010 thanks to the tireless work of www.fija.org and www.commonsensejustice.us, FIJA had a head start in Wyoming.

Opponents of juror rights were legion. Government officials and the ABA hated it, and their arguments stretched the limits of silliness. A former state AG called FIJA *"a goofy idea."* A lobbyist for the Wyoming Trial Lawyers' Association assserted that *"FIJA would allow juries to be arbitrary, unreasonable, vindictive, mean-spirited, ignorant, and unpatriotic. A jury could ignore treason. It could impose a trivial fine for murder."* (As if juries impose sentences. Only judges can.) A rep from the Unified Justice System (the legislative-peddling arm of judges and prosecutors) said *"This will clog up the system."* Tim Barnett chimed in from the Wyoming Bar: *"If FIJA passes, I could get arrested for driving while intoxicated and say, 'You can't convict me. I'm Irish. I have a God-given right to drive drunk.'"* An AP story had hysterically claimed that *"Advocates of FIJA want juries to be able to ignore the law"* and that thousands of violent criminals would be set free. When nobody could provide even *one* example of this ever having happened (besides, perhaps O.J. Simpson), their silly agitation was exposed to all.

Several dozen criminal defense lawyers privately supported FIJA but would not go public because *"The Bar would look for a way to punish me, and judges would punish my clients for years."* The WTLA sent lawyers to meetings of many special-interest organizations, such as the Chamber of Commerce and Industry, Retailers' Association, Bankers' Association, Municipal League, Association of County Commissioners, Sheriffs' Association, State Attorneys' Association, Trial Lawyers' Association, and the Criminal Defense Lawyers' Association. Since every one of these organizations had a vested interest in the law enforcement/prison/industrial complex, they all published resolutions opposing FIJA.

> *It always takes an enormous exertion just to ascertain what liberals are so damn upset about. Once you figure out what has propelled the tolerant crowd into frenzies of demonic rage, it invariably turns out to be a perfectly ordinary view held by many good-hearted Americans.* (p.199)
> — Ann Coulter, *Slander*

Nevertheless, FIJA opponents were wary of *too* much public campaigning. They worried that advertising would backfire since voters tend to be suspicious of attorneys (*"If the state bar opposes FIJA, then it must be good!"*). They were right. FIJA advocates hammered on the fact that *"only lawyers and government officials oppose FIJA."*

Ted Nugent and Al "Grandpa Munster" Lewis graciously cut some radio spot ads, which ran on every station in Wyoming. The *Wall Street Journal* did a nice feature story, as did the *New York Times*. A well-known libertarian financial newsletter author kicked in $100,000 for the war chest.

Wyoming became the second government on earth to protect the rights of parents, jurors, homeowners, small businessmen, farmers, ranchers, gunowners, and civil court defendants.

Wyoming Special Election   April 2015

Constitutional Amendments A through G are ratified by the voters with an average approval of 71%. A return of real freedom had been offered to the people, and they eagerly took it. Most could not recall the time when elections added to their quality of life.

The fact is that political liberty is so rare in the history of the human race as to be regarded an aberration more than an achievement.
— Jeff Cooper, *The Gargantuan Gunsite Gossip 2*

Wyoming   June 2015
On earth there is no heaven, but there are places of it.
— Jules Renard

The "Preston Experiment" is by all objective accounts wildly succeeding. There is a marked and steady decline in taxes, petty lawsuits, crime, and unemployment. New businesses spring up almost overnight. Several large multinational corporations are relocating their American headquarters to the favorable climate of tax-free Wyoming. (Even though these corporate socialists are not advocates of a truly free market, tax-free *was* tax-free. They're moving to Wyoming for the same reason their cleaning staff is hired from certain religious groups known for their honesty. Use 'em, but don't join 'em.) Even tourism shows a 40% increase, reflecting many Americans' desire to see for themselves if Wyoming should be their next home.

For many thousands, it is.

New York City, D.C., L.A., San Francisco, Aspen, etc.
Thomas Sowell, who is one of our favorite commentators, points out three things that make the collectivists uneasy. These are cars, guns, and home schooling, all of which grant to the individual a degree of independence of action which terrifies the champions of the super state. Cars, guns and home schooling reduce the need for the statism so prized by the socialists. They do not wish you freedom to move around. They do not wish you to be able to protect yourself. And they do not wish you to decide what your children should be taught. Such things reduce the power of the state over the citizen. (at 915)
— Jeff Cooper, *The Gargantuan Gunsite Gossip 2*

The Liberazzi were beside themselves to explain the *"phenomenon."* They accused Preston's staff of falsifying the statistics. When independent researchers confirmed the numbers, government supremacists then claimed that *"all new brooms sweep clean"* and that the whole thing was a fluke, an unnatural freak of politics, *"a cheap card trick."* Deep in their envious heart-of-hearts, they knew better.

Moral indignation is a technique used to endow the idiot with dignity.
— McLuhan

A man will occasionally stumble over the truth, but most of the time he will pick himself up and continue on.
— Winston Churchill

Likening the Wyomingans to bacteria, the liberals made noises of overwhelming the state with a vast "T-cell" immigration of themselves. *"We'll retake the state in the same way they stole it in 2014!"* they exclaimed. *"This is America and they can't prevent us from moving there!"*

Cheyenne, Wyoming   June 2015

Preston gets wind of this and convenes a meeting with his staff and others. "They're right, you know. It's a free country. We can't *prevent* them from moving here, nor can we evict them once they've arrived."

Heads nod in agreement.

"But we may, as the French would say, *chasse-cousins*. We may "chase away cousins" by making Wyoming *so* utterly unpalatable that they couldn't *stand* the place and don't bother coming!"

"Why not? New Jersey and Massachusetts did it to *us*!" quips Chief Justice Pollard. The room breaks up laughing.

"How do we accomplish *that*?" asks Attorney General Warner.

"Simple," replies Preston with a sly grin.

"Jim, *are you thinking . . .* ," asks Juliette with a growing smile.

"My wife knows me *too* well," Preston says with mock resignation.

Seeing the questioning looks about his office, the Governor smiles and explains, "Because of our cold climate, Wyoming has no roaches or fleas. A pest is a pest. It's all about creating the proper environment. So, what do liberals fear and hate the *most*?"

After a few seconds of pondering this riddle, the room begins to chuckle as each person" saw the light." Preston then fans the chuckles into roaring laughter as he describs what he had in mind.

To his personal secretary, Preston says, "Carol, I need to meet with Senator Haskins tomorrow morning. Tell her that I have an idea for a bill that the legislature should enjoy passing. Also, inform the Legislative Service Office that I will convene a special session for Monday 6 July."

"In the summer? Right after the weekend of the 4th? Are you certain, Governor?" asks his secretary.

"Carol, you're forgetting that Wyoming has an anniversary that week and there's already a celebration planned. Most of the legislators will be in Cheyenne on that Friday, anyway. Might as well put them to work while they're in town. Besides, they'll all get their *per diems*, so that'll help."

Cheyenne, Wyoming   Friday, 10 July 2015

The bill sailed through a special session in just one week. Since there was concurrence on the language, the Joint Conference Committee was avoided. The bill was enrolled by the LSO and given a number, read by the Presiding Officers of both houses, signed in the presence of a quorum, and sent to Governor Preston. He signed it at once and presented it to the people precisely on the day of Wyoming's 125 year statehood anniversary.

The concept was elegantly simple, just as Preston said.

It worked like this: Taxation discourages the object, which affects personal habits. When personal habits are altered, people themselves are changed. Change a people and one changes a *nation*—all through taxation. A simple 357 member majority of the US Congress can change an entire nation simply through taxation policy.

Congress had learned this quite well from taxing the interest on personal savings, thus discouraging savings and encouraging hand-to-mouth consumption which shortened the time horizon of the electorate, not to mention destroying their self-reliance and ability to delay gratification. A proud, independent nation of hardy savers was transformed into a now-oriented, *Gimme!* flock of buzzards feeding on the public's rotting carcass. Since no citizen can be outside of the citizenry, America was, in effect, feeding on herself. Through taxation policy, we had been reduced to an indirect cannibalism.

Preston's idea was to use taxation policy, but in *reverse*.

Effective immediately, anybody openly wearing a functional and loaded sidearm in a store was *exempt* from paying the sales tax of that particular transaction. Since the legislature had planned to cut sales taxes anyway, this indirect method seemed a good first step. With an expected further reduction in crime it was reasoned that the commensurately shrinking police force neatly matched the loss of sales tax revenue. Besides, it is the *unarmed* who need police protection, so let *them* pay for the cops.

Overnight, the entire state strapped on their pistols and revolvers. 21st Century Wyoming was now more widely-armed than it had been even in the 19th Century. In fact, it was the most well-armed region on the planet as far as actual gun-*bearing* went.

Some business owners and managers, however, found the notion of armed customers abhorrent and made a fairly big stink. They put large "No Guns!" signs in their front windows, but immediately found themselves losing business. Also, their stores were favored by the dwindling population of criminals. So, by a brutal combination of sales loss and increased crime, these stores quickly reversed their gun-phobic policy or went out of business.

Washington, D.C.   Friday, 10 July 2015

As to the abuses I meet with, I number them among my honors. One cannot behave so as to obtain the esteem of the wise and the good without drawing on oneself at the same time the envy and malice of the foolish and wicked, and the latter is testimony of the former. The best men have always had their share of this treatment, the more of it in proportion to their different and greater degree of

merit. A man, therefore, has some reason to be ashamed of himself when he meets none of it.
— Benjamin Franklin, 1767

To be a liberal you have to be able to believe two contradictory things at the same time.
— Vin Suprynowicz, *The Ballad of Carl Drega* (2002), p. 669

Already chewing their elbows over Preston's *10 Points* of February, the liberal Democrats went nova.

Legal authorities were heatedly consulted in the hopes of learning of some constitutional recourse through the Department of Justice (DOJ), but the preliminary consensus was that no violation of civil rights had occurred. The 50 states still enjoyed, surprisingly enough, wide latitude in their domestic taxation policies and it was opined that Wyoming's sales tax exemption for gun-bearers was not unconstitutional—especially when this issue was contrasted with some of the more outrageous provisions of the Internal Revenue Code. The Federal Government was the master of pursuing "public policy" through selective taxation and regulation, so to accuse Wyoming of taxation favoritism was like the ocean calling the pond "wet."

Except for the unconstitutional "school-zone" prohibition (which had been overturned by the 1991 Supreme Court case *U.S. v. Lopez*), there was no congressional ban on the *intra*state bearing of arms, nor did such seem constitutionally possible. When it was suggested that the ATF enforce the school-zone ban, Attorney General Vorn exclaimed, "There's no point in shutting an empty barn after the horses ran off!"

President Connor tried to mollify the despair by offering, "Why not just let them all wipe themselves *out*? Maybe they will come to their senses when blood up to their ankles is running in the streets!"

To D.C.'s stunned amazement, this did not occur.

Cheyenne Frontier Days   September 2015
For ten days Cheyenne is home to the largest rodeo on earth. Over 300,000 visitors from all 50 states enjoy professional displays of bronc riding, calf roping, and steer wrestling, as well as four parades.

Vegetarian and animal rights advocates from Colorado's front range drive up to protest the *"cruel and inhuman treatment of animal citizens solely for the purpose of sport."* They blanket pickup windshields with their flyers. James Preston, Jr. snags one and exclaims, "Hey, Dad! It's from *Boulder!*"

Life Isn't For Eating (LIFE)

So called "vegetarians" hide behind their proclaimed love for animals yet kill beautiful, helpless plants. This is like Axe Murderers for Gun Control—what hypocrites! Our organization LIFE has a slogan:

If meat is murder, then salad is slaughter!

Life is Life, and to consume Life for "food" is nothing less than Cosmic Cannibalism. (We were, until informed of its teeming Nutrient citizenry, eating soil.) We must ban "harvesting"—which is nothing more than the wanton, systematic killing of plants for food. Many of these "vegetarians" even cultivate plots of carnage (which they call "gardens") in their own backyards! Cut down in their prime, plant butchers rip and shred Nature's most delicate and vulnerable of citizens, only to "toss" the dismembered bits in the air for their "salads." End the madness!

Think we're being hysterical? Well, have you ever noticed the violence inherent to the names of many "foods"? For example:

black-eyed peas	arti*choke*
crushed red pepper	chopped sirloin
mashed potatoes	bruised bananas
scrambled eggs	battered shrimp

We propose the immediate registration of all:

pruning shears	paring knives
hedge clippers	apple corers
lawnmowers	potato peelers
salad shredders, spinners, and tongs	

Some would say that registration of these "garden" and "kitchen" implements of death is but a stepping stone to their eventual confiscation, but this is just not true. We merely want to know where they are.

There is much you can do, such as the boycotting of "popcorn." Take the moral high ground and refuse to heat our Kernel Brethren to 500° until they *explode!* For *snacks!* Orville Redenbacker is the Dr. Mengele of Corn—General Mills the Auschwitz. The caring substitute for "popcorn" are styrofoam packing "peanuts"—beautifully inert—if you have the strength to lift them.

Before you prepare your dinner, look for **LIFE**'s Seal of Inertness. Remember, start your day with a **LIFE** breakfast—a fresh, heaping bowl of steam! *Mmmm, good!*

Wyoming   October 2015

G.K. Chesterton is much more concerned that children are being deprived from developing riches of nobility. For Chesterton, all boys must play games—cops and robbers, Robin Hood, the Sheriff of Nottingham, and cowboys and indians. Boys must play at being the knight or the soldier in order to develop the noble virtues of courage, justice, discipline and self-sacrifice. If boys are not allowed to develop these virtues when they are young, they will not develop them later. To deprive children of bows and arrows is to form men and women without courage, conviction or commitment. For Chesterton, possessing bows and arrows, in fact, weaponry of all kinds, is not some sort of an eccentric, aberrant or deviant behavior, It is rooted in a most precious human attribute, the inspiration to act nobly. Chesterton admits that bows and arrows can be instruments of destruction, but the good they do is greater by far than their potential harm, because they are instruments by which children are naturally inclined to reach a higher human potential.
— Dr. Andrew Tadie

As to the species of exercise I advise the gun. While this gives a moderate exercise to the body, it gives boldness, enterprise, and independence to the mind.
— Thomas Jefferson, 19 August 1785

An unforeseen new industry arose. Simply owning and wearing a sidearm did not mean that you knew how to use it, and Wyomingans enrolled themselves by the thousands in the many new defensive shooting schools. Their quality was generally very good, as most of these schools were taught by graduates of Thunder Ranch, Gunsite, and other prestigious firearm academies. Depending on the training, expertise, and teaching skill of the instructors, the schools offered everything from Basic Handgun to Team Tactics to Urban Battle Rifle to Precision Rifle. One school, jokingly called "Half-Inch Harvard," specialized only in training students with their .50BMG target rifles at ranges up to 1500yds. Thousands of gunowners began to learn the extent of what they *assumed* they knew, and it was a rather humbling experience to confront one's own ignorance. As a result, negligent discharges (called "accidents" by the uninformed) became uncommon, and the safety of gunhandling increased dramatically.

The *"rash of gunfire"* predicted by *TIME* magazine never happened, nor did *Newsweek*'s forecasted *"daily Main Street shootouts."* Conservative political pundits reminded the public that such wild and unfounded predictions previously had been made about those 39 States which enacted *"shall issue"* concealed carry legislation.

Street crime, always low in Wyoming, is vanishing. Each recently armed Wyomingite created his/her own new "crime-free zone," and criminals, for once in their wretched lives, just didn't feel "safe" anymore. As Wyoming became (to paraphrase Robert Heinlein) *"an armed and polite society"* the demand for local police and sheriffs' deputies fell by about 2% per month. Law enforcement personnel began looking for other work as the armed Citizens became, in a sense, *de facto* peace officers.

Preston's "proper environment" worked. The Eastern Fascists and California Commies stayed put. They simply could not fathom mixing in some "Wild West" society. Many lost their moving company deposits when they cancelled their relocation plans. Thousands already at sail in socialist junks came about and returned to their liberal ports of call.

Of the several hundred who actually made it to Wyoming and gave the place a fair chance, over half had a profound philosophical and political conversion, and stayed on. Here, one didn't live by smarmy platitudes or backhanded tributes to Truth and Justice. Here, there *was* Truth and Justice for every Citizen, regardless of one's melatonin or wallet girth.

Many of them increasingly embraced the shooting culture with great vigor. One of their favorite new hobbies was to email lurid jpgs of themselves shooting Colt 1911s, Glocks, AR15s, AK47s, M1As, and FALs to their old pinko friends. This caused quite an uproar back East.

One self-described "former inmate of Greenwich Village" was *really* bitten by the gunbug. CBS *60 Minutes* included him in their story on Wyoming, filming him at "Half-Inch Harvard" in camo fatigues firing .50BMG API from a Barrett M99 at a 500yd steel plate. *"When the target needs just a bit more than API, it's time for a Raufoss[5]! It goes to 11!"* The CBS cameraman, also a fan of the comedy film *Spinal Tap*, immediately got the joke and barely stifled a guffaw. "Raufoss Ralph" made sure that his NY relatives tuned in for the segment's airing. Predictably, they were outraged and tried to have him declared insane, but nobody had much interest in going out to Gillette to fetch him for the hearing. *"That entire state is already a loony bin, so let's just leave him there!"* reasoned his sister.

The few gunphobes still living in Wyoming, however, now faced the Hobson's choice of wearing a handgun (which they did not and would not own, much less wear), or bearing the brunt of the state's sales tax. Dozens tried to circumvent this by wearing realistic airsoft pistols in leather holsters, but they were quickly caught and convicted of fraud and sales tax evasion. Cornered by their own mealy politics and personal irresponsibility (they

---

5   An exotic and expensive High-Explosive Armor-Piercing round. Known as "Greentip" to the US military. It contains a small quantity of RDX Comp A-4 explosive (less than ¼oz., thus legal for civilians) which, upon impact, sets off the incendiary and zirconium compounds to enhance the target penetration of the tungsten carbide core. Very zappy stuff. Standard M2 HB ammo for the US Navy. It costs the USG $9/round, and fetches over $40 at gun shows.

wanted the *police* to protect them, but *didn't* want to single-handedly fund them), they began to move out—a hidden benefit not contemplated by Preston.

Wyoming   November 2015

Until this fearful mommified welfare state is replaced by a restored nation of self-sufficient households led by men—note the word is not "persons," but "men"—willing to sling a loaded M14 or M1 Garand over their shoulder (engage the safety), stride down down the busiest street in town, walk up to the first armed policeman they see, and fearlessly declare, "I am an armed citizen and member of the militia; I am teaching my sons to safely and effectively keep and bear arms; are you going to congratulate me and thank me, or do we shoot it out right here?" we are well on our way to becoming a nation of armed overseers and peasant slaves.

— Vin Suprynowicz, *The Ballad of Carl Drega* (2002), p. 387

Wyoming had called the bluff of enforcement. People simply went about armed everywhere. It was too late for federal roadblocks and checkpoints. The armed Citizens, not the fedgoons, now had the superior numbers. If ATF agents began unconstitutionally enforcing the *"school zone"* gun ban overturned by *Lopez*, if they tried to arrest anybody selling a privately owned gun outside of the federal NICS registration system, they'd be resisted—and they knew it. More importantly, Wyomingites knew it.

To circumvent the unlawful federal ban on private transfers at gun shows, folks simply created "collectors clubs" and put on "private exhibits" for the club members (who all knew each other). You walked in with a rifle case, and left with a rifle case. Whether the case had been full and then empty, or empty and then full, no outside ATF observer could discern. Besides, all the local ATF agents had been identified long ago, and flyers circulated with pictures of their faces and cars. The idea caught on across the West and catalogs were being compiled of agents in Montana, South Dakota, Idaho, Nevada, and western Colorado. No longer could, for example, a Billings-based ATF agent spy on Wyoming gun shows in anonymity. Doormen at shows checked the drivers' licenses of suspected agents, and those caught were hounded out of the building.

There hadn't been an ATF arrest in Wyoming since the summer of 2012. Agents had little choice but to move on to more docile pastures such as northern Utah and eastern Colorado.

* * * * * * *

President Connor remained deeply disturbed about Wyoming's sales tax exemption for armed customers. "Wear a gun and pay no sales tax? It's *obscene*! What's *next*, tax breaks for snipers?"

Cheyenne, Wyoming   November 2015

No person will be enlisted who cannot when firing at the distance of 200 yards, at a rest, put ten consecutive shots in a target, the average distance not to exceed five inches from the centre of the bull's eye to the center of the ball. (Note: This is 5MOA.)

—Vermont qualifications for enlistment, 1861

The lessons that ought to be learned [from the Boer War], *I think, are three. First, men fight their very best when they fight to defend their homelands against a foreign invader. Second, when it comes to imparting of skill the public sector can never equal the private. Third, marksmanship is an art to be cultivated rather than a commodity to be issued.* (at 367)

I have gradually come round to the conclusion, over the several decades of endeavor, that marksmanship cannot be taught "in bulk."
. . . no training system designed for departments or armies can hope to develop artists—and marksmanship is definitely an art.

The study of history shows us that really good combat riflemen come from a cultural base in which rifle shooting is practiced both as a sport and a means of subsistence.

As our civilization decays, we have lessening opportunity to acquire young men for our public defense who know anything about guns or fighting. Our consolation may be that our prospective enemies are no better off. (at 720)

—Jeff Cooper, *The Gargantuan Gunsite Gossip 2* (2001)

On hearing of the President's frustrated remark from Phillip Miles, Preston smiled. "Tax breaks for snipers. *Hmmm.* I think Connor's *on* to something! What about this: why not give a, let's see . . . biennial $500 tax credit to those who can shoot a tight group at long range? I mean, wouldn't *you* pay just $250 a year to maintain a competent rifleman? Sounds like a *bargain* to me! Aren't the states *supposed* to cultivate riflery for citizen militiamen?"

After much public debate, 4MOA at 300yds became the criterion.

MOA means "minute of angle" and describes the ever widening cone of bullet impact over distance. There are 360° in a circle, and each degree has 60 minutes. Thus, a circle has 21,400 minute "slices." 1MOA is a very thin slice: at a mile it is just 18" in width.

1MOA at 100yds roughly equals a 1" diameter circle; 4MOA equals 4". At 200yds, 4MOA is an 8" circle. At 300yds, 4MOA is a 12" circle—the diameter of a large dinner plate.

4MOA was considered demanding enough to demonstrate true talent (*i.e.,* being able to hit a stationary clay pigeon at 100yds), yet not so stringent as to unfairly exclude capable riflemen. Most of the debate centered on whether or not to handicap the more accurate rifles (*i.e.,* bolt-actions with scopes) by requiring of them a smaller group. After input from the entire state, it was decided that the same 4MOA would be required from all guns, but that a 45 second time limit would be imposed. Such would indirectly handicap the manual repeaters and thus make them pay for their superior accuracy—sort of like actual combat.

Some folks wanted to toughen things up by mandating "Mexican Match" (where all shooters use not only a common caliber such as the .308, but common *ammunition*, such as Federal Premium or M118 FMJ), but this was viewed as too stringent. (Besides, it would have taken far too long for everyone to zero on Election Day.) So, the choice of rifle, caliber, sights, ammo, and accoutrement was left to the "Potential Voter" (the "PV").

The other main area for debate was whether or not to require a minimum caliber. While all were agreed that only centerfire rifle cartridges could be used, many wanted to see .243 as the minimum caliber—which would have effectively eliminated all .223 carbines, such as the AR15, etc. *"A .223 gives only 750 foot pounds of energy at 300 yards!"* was the cry. This was not "real" rifle-like power, they argued, as the .308 gave over 1600fpe. The .223 had been proven lacking in actual combat since the 1960s.

Moderation prevailed when it was mentioned that most ladies, and many men, just would not (or could not) afford and/or train with a .308 battle rifle. Besides, 4MOA with an AR15 meant head-shot accuracy at 100yds while delivering over 1100fpe—certainly useful performance. The entire point of a rifle is to accurately deliver incapacitating energy at a distance, and within its parameters the .223 was effective (especially with a 64gr. softpoint bullet). Better to keep as many Wyomingites involved and proficient in riflery, rather than try to create some elite force of "he-men" wielding .308 battle rifles. Moreover, the "he-men" would stick to their .308s regardless, so little point was seen in alienating those who favored the .223.

So, a democratic and egalitarian spirit prevailed: Bring any rifle chambered for a centerfire *rifle* cartridge (*i.e.,* at least 1200fpe of muzzle energy, and thus not a pistol cartridge such as the .30 Carbine, 9mm, .45ACP, etc.), and you'd be allowed to compete for your tax credit.

A major problem with the 300yd requirement quickly became obvious: there were insufficient long-distance shooting ranges. Even if Wyoming had enough rifle ranges to handle the demand, the verification of 300yd targets required downrange personnel or televised targets, all of which was simply too expensive. An M1A rifleman offered an ingenious solution he had learned from a company that sold parts and targets, Fred's (in Buffalo).

Before moving to Wyoming, Fred was heavily involved in one of the most battle rifle oriented shooting ranges of the country, the Riverside Gun Club in Ramseur, North Carolina. Realizing that a nation's liberty was ultimately protected by the quality of its riflemen, the RGC ran a unique match every month in which dozens of riflemen competed in very challenging and realistic drills.

What was not shot at distance on steel was shot at 25yds on paper. The RGC used 2¼" and 1½" wide silhouettes which approximated 18" targets at 200 and 300yds. (Remember, it's an MOA thing. Shooting within 1" at 25yds equals 4" at 100yds or 12" at 300yds—meaning 4MOA.) Granted, such work at 25yds couldn't train one for doping range, declination, and wind, but it was a fine way of training target acquisition, sight picture, and trigger work, thus getting a shooter 75% of the way there to becoming a Rifleman.

The paper 25yd targets were also the answer to Wyoming's needs. Each paper contained five B-27 silhouette targets at an apparent distance of 300yds. Shooters downloaded practice targets from the state website.

Constructing dozens of 25yd ranges across Wyoming was infinitely easier than long-distance ranges. In fact, a 25yd range could be built on private property, as long as it was certified by the county clerk and operated by a judge of election. All he needed was a laser rangefinder, PACT timer, and centerline opter to measure questionable hits. Each target paper was backed with a carbonless copy, which acted as the receipt. The top paper was the official target to be scored and certified, and the yellow paper behind was kept by the rifleman.

It was agreed that five hits on five targets was preferable to five hits on only one target, for two reasons: Five separate targets would test a rifleman's target acquisition, and it would also eliminate any argument over whether or not a single target group contained four vs. five shots.

The battle rifle folks had demanded two hits per target (thus ten shots total for the paper) as the standard, but such would have required those shooting lever and bolt guns to reload. It was decided to keep the contest purely at the accuracy level, however, it was conceded that as riflery skill increased, contests in the future could possibly incorporate other factors such as reloading and even malfunction clearing. It was best to start simply.

Each of the five targets required one hit apiece, all within 60 seconds. This time would be reduced in successive election years by 5 seconds, bottoming out at 45 seconds by the year 2022.

Any shooting position was allowed, including prone, but the line began in the standing position with rifles shouldered in Low Ready. While remaining standing was the fastest way to shoot, it was obviously the least accurate. Most riflemen favored either to sit or squat (a.k.a. "rice paddy prone"), and gladly spent the extra time it took to assume for the increased accuracy. Kneeling was not considered as stable as sitting or squatting.

A hit was recorded when the hole touched the edge of the target. Any rifleman making a shot after the 60 second *Beep!* was disqualified. If your rifle or ammo failed to fire during the contest, too bad. If you made all five hits, you got the full $500 tax credit.

Fail to make all five hits and Wyoming kept your $100 entry fee.

Finally, you were allowed only five rounds in your rifle, and you had to bring your *own* rifle. No borrowing of rifles on the range was allowed.

For those too frail, old, or infirm to accurately shoot their rifles, their $100 fee would allow them to choose a minor rifleman as their proxy under the same terms. (Adults were presumed to shoot for themselves.) A youth could proxy only once per year. This would keep the elderly in the loop, plus help to train the next generation of riflemen.

New target ranges were quickly built and soon crackled with gunfire. A 4MOA group at 300yds was standard accuracy for antelope and deer, which abounded in Wyoming. Many hunters already had the skill to make grade.

The cartridge requirement inevitably included those which were clearly not a great choice at 300yds, such as the .30-30 and the .45-70, but were fairly effective out to 200yds. These were allowed under general principle, as had been the .223. Granted, nobody buying his first rifle for a tax-credit shoot would likely *choose* a .30-30, but for many PVs a lever-action .30-30 was all they had. Thus, why break up a man and his rifle? One Olde Duffer, for example, had a well-worn .45-70 Marlin which very accurately (*i.e.,* 1MOA at 100yds) threw his handloaded 350gr Hornady JHPs.

Regarding battle rifles and carbines, while the .223 was satisfactory within 200yds, the .308 was much better suited for Wyoming's open spaces, making it the battle cartridge of the realm. The .223 was relegated to smaller framed shooters.

There were several viable battle rifle choices.

Fred's primarily sold stocks for the M14/M1A, which Fred considered the best battle rifle ever made. He had a point. The M14, a "product-improved" M1 Garand, had positive chambering (which the AR10, FAL, and HK91, with their non-reciprocating charging handles, did not), excellent sights and whopping 27" radius, ambidextrous safety and mag release, a quickly replaceable trigger group, and buttstock storage which contained a cleaning rod (vital to tap out a stuck bullet or case). Semi-auto versions of the M14, called the M1A, had been manufactured by Springfield Armory® since the 1980s and were generally regarded as very fine rifles. (Many M14 riflemen viewed Springfield Armory's cast receiver quality as spotty, and preferred a forged receiver gun custom built by Ron Smith of Smith Enterprises in Guernsey, formerly of Tempe, Arizona.)

M14s were accurate and robust, and a fine choice for one's battle rifle. They easily make the 4MOA/300yds grade with iron sights. One Viet Nam vet, a Navy riverboatman, carried an M14 back in 1966 and thus preferred an M1A as his battle rifle. M14 owners were a very organized group, and shared with each other many tips and sources.

Speaking of AR10s, they were considered too fussy and exotic, and too often suffered from quality control problems. Still, those who carried AR10s usually shot them very well (when they functioned reliably). One of the AR10's biggest champions, a software engineer, lived in Worland.

Those who chose the FAL remained a noisy group, and much good-natured joshing was heard back and forth between them and the M14 folks. The FAL is a very fine and proven battle rifle, but the M14 people don't care for its lack of positive feeding, mediocre sights, and poor trigger. Still, the FAL is quite accurate and reliable.

The HK91 is a very rugged battle rifle, but whose poor trigger and coarse rear sight severely hamper long-range accuracy. The 91 has substantially more recoil than the M14 or FAL, which reduced its popularity. Their fans, however, seem a somewhat pompous lot (as is often the case with owners of any expensive German product), grandly extolling the 91's engineering and ruggedness over all other rifles. (They did, however, give the M1A and FAL their due.)

Still, most people didn't make a cult out of equipment. A western rancher explained why over a century earlier:

> *The truth is that any good modern rifle is good enough. The determining factor is the man behind the gun.*
> — Theodore Roosevelt, 1910

Regardless of one's rifle, the shoots became very congenial occasions.

One 15 year old young man was to be his Grandpa's proxy using his antelope rifle, a four-digit (*i.e., circa* 1937) Winchester Model 70 in .270 with a Shepherd 310-P1 scope. A young wife was keen to shoot with her first rifle (a gift from her husband), a Browning BLR in .308. A college freshman in Laramie bought her first AR15 (a pre-ban Bushmaster Dissipator with 16" barrel) and shot 100rds of 55gr FMJ every Sunday afternoon following church in preparation for her tax credit shoot in 2016.

It was the proliferation of stories like these which further knitted together Wyoming society around the issue of riflery and common defense. People all across the state really felt like they were part of an important, shared destiny. Wyoming was fast creating a citizen militia which trained itself at private expense.

Even the Swiss began to take notice and sent over a couple of observers with their SIG550s. Everyone loved their fine carbines, but lamented that they weren't made in .308. Now *that* would be a rifle.

Cheyenne, Wyoming   December 2015

"Hey, Gov! I heard you're in this month's *Playboy!*" a radio show caller says.

Preston laughs, "Yeah, but not the centerfold. It was just an interview. I think it turned out pretty well. They even quoted me accurately[6]."

---

[6]   This is reproduced in the Appendix, at pages 405-431. Most of the lengthy interview covers the thoughts and beliefs of Gov. Preston, and is largely incidental to the Wyoming story. Hence, reading it before going on to the next chapter is recommended, though not absolutely required.

❖ 2016

Cheyenne, Wyoming
Budget Session   **January 2016**

The Laissez-Faire Party and libertarian Republicans now has 19 of 30 Senators, and 40 of 60 Congressmen. The remaining minority of old-guard Republicans and Democrats are reduced to titular legislators, as they haven't introduced and passed any bills of their own in two years. They now watch in a mixture of awe, sanguinity, grudging approval, and bitterness at the "Preston Revolution" taking place. Barring some unforeseen political disaster, the Democrats have been locked out of Wyoming state politics for the next several election cycles. The people had finally tasted some real freedom (and its subsequent economic boom). What could the old mainline parties offer in response? Less freedom and more taxes?

The business of the legislature included three proposed constitutional amendments. They read as follows:

"Proposed Constitutional Amendment A: To replace Article 1, Section 17 of the Wyoming Constitution with:

The right of the writ of habeas corpus shall not be suspended unless, when in case of invasion, the public safety may require it.

"Proposed Constitutional Amendment B: To eliminate the state power of 'eminent domain' by replacing Article 1, Sections 32 and 33 with:

Private property shall not be taken, damaged, reduced in value or enjoyment for private or public use unless by voluntary and informed consent of the owner in a fair and free market transaction.

"Proposed Constitutional Amendment C: To eliminate the government requirement for professional licenses:

The government shall not require from any individual, as a prerequisite for, or condition of, private employment or commercial enterprise, any license or permit.

As was his wont, Governor Preston explained the proposed amendments in a televised speech.

"The writ of habeas corpus is your natural right, not a mere privilege which is constitutionally revokable during insurrections. Habeas corpus is Latin for "you have the body," meaning a judge who compels the court appearance of a prisoner claiming unlawful imprisonment due to restraint of liberty and due process. The English jurist Blackstone wrote that the writ of habeas corpus was a 'cornerstone' right. Thomas Jefferson was particularly upset when the framers of the US Constitution referred to this right as a mere privilege in Article I, Section 9—language which our own constitution unfortunately copied. Our proposed amendment will correct that error.

"Amendment B. If your government desires a privately owned property, then it can bid for it like any potential buyer. Some have criticized this proposed amendment for not including a war or insurrection exception. Any property so necessary to Wyoming would likely be recognized as such by its owner and willingly sold at a fair price. If not, then he has to live with his irate community thereafter. If the owner's intransigence to sell comes during war or insurrection, then his community will undoubtedly bring great pressure upon him to act sensibly. Such pressure, if warranted, should come from a local community rather than from distant government officials exercising force majeure through power of eminent domain.

"Amendment C. It is this administration's goal to eliminate the requirement for professional licenses, and your legislature has passed a bill and proposed constitutional amendment to do just that. We believe that it is the proper place of the private sector to accredit the professions, and the responsibility of the buyer to ascertain the expected quality of services to be rendered. Guilds and consumer organizations will be of great help there. Several tiers of quality within each profession will emerge, each stratum receiving the level of income it deserves. The shoddy practitioners will become infamous soon enough. If you want a house built cheaply, then hire an unaccredited company. Or, if you take no chances, then hire the expensive services of a bonded contracting firm. Either way, it's going to be your choice. Caveat emptor. Choose wisely and contract thoroughly. We're all adults here, and it's time we started acting like it."

Amendment A was fairly uncontroversial. Amendment B had most government extremacists howling, naturally. Amendment C awoke those in bed with the government/corporate complex. The corporate capitalists had long used licensing requirements to restrict, if not prevent, nascent competition from developing. For the first time in the Preston administration, Big Money was threatened. Most unions, leagues, associations, brotherhoods, orders, guilds, lodges, and fraternities vowed to fight C.

Big Horn County, Wyoming   **February 2016**

The county seat of Greybull is home to the Aerial Firefighting Museum, which has five of the six WW2 PB4Y-2 Catalinas still flying. One relocator, a retired USAF colonel toured the museum back in 2009 when he was checking out the county. The people were pleasant and the flying conditions were very good, so he returned the next year and built north of town an airpark country club, complete with taxiways to each property's own hangar.

The thirty lots sold out in four months. Locals called the subdivision the "Big Horn County Air Force."

* * * * * * *

We want one class to have a liberal education. We want another class, a much larger class of necessity, to forgo the privilege of a liberal education and fit themselves to perform specific, difficult, manual tasks.
— Woodrow Wilson, to a group of businessmen just prior World War I

After 30-odd years of "progressive" government schooling, America has raised two whole generations of emotionally hollow automatons whose "political opinions" are based on what teacher said and which opinions get applauded or booed on Oprah Winfrey and Jerry Springer and Dan Rather's CBS Liberal News.
How did the pod people take over while you weren't looking?
It's the government schools, stupid.
— Vin Suprynowicz, *The Ballad of Carl Drega* (2002), p. 532

Cheyenne, Wyoming   **March 2016**

Tom Parks briefs Governor Preston on the success of the Ten Points.

"Violent crime, which was already low in 2014, is down by 82%. Property crime, including cold burglaries, are down 56%. Wyoming now enjoys the lowest crime rate in the nation."

The Governor laughs. "Then maybe they'll stop calling it the 'Preston Experiment.' If our Ten Points were ever an 'experiment' the results are conclusive by now. What else?"

"After the removal of daytime highway speed limits, fatalities increased slightly for several months and then dropped down to 2014 levels."

Preston nods grimly. "Sounds like a few irresponsible drivers weeded themselves out. Well, we expected that, though I'm sorry that they sometimes hurt or killed innocent people. Go on."

"Finally, there is extremely widespread approval of the amendments regarding jury trials, parental rights, and taxation. We knocked it out of the park with those, Governor."

Preston smiles. "I hear that people in other states are getting jealous. All this country needed was one bold example to remind them of the freedom they started out with in the early 18th century. Wyomingites will never go back to the way it was. The liberty genie is out of the bottle."

"Yes, sir. It's very exciting."

"OK, we've gotten past the base of our mountain. Now for the first real ascent. Abolishing public education." Turning to his Attorney General, Preston asks, "So, what have you got?"

"Governor, we've researched the legal history of public education in America all the way back to mid 19th century Massachusetts. We specifically scrutinized the redistributive court orders of the 1980s, particularly in Texas which mandated bilingual education. We have arrived at the proverbial good news and bad news. It makes sense to outline the bad news first."

Preston is listening intently, ready to make notes. "OK then. Let's hear the bad news."

"Yes, sir. First, your administration's goal is to, by some point and through some means, transform all Wyoming public education into privately-funded schools supported by free-market forces, isn't that correct."

"Perfectly correct. Free-market forces meaning the parents."

"Understood, Governor. The parents, yes."

Preston smiles at his formality. The terminologies of attorneys and economists are necessarily rigid and precise, but they often obscure the fact that law and money are human institutions, affecting real people.

The AG continues. "Furthermore, to achieve privatization would seem to first require a parental discretionary funding of private schools, such as a voucher system, would it not?"

"It would seem so, yes."

"And once mar—, uh, parents begin to send their children to private schools without the previous double burden of supporting the public schools, an increasing emigration from the public schools would ensue. In effect, you propose that the free-market effectively close down government education in Wyoming."

"That was the idea, yes." Preston frowns, not seeing where this is going. "So what's the bad news?"

"The bad news is that, in our opinion, we cannot legally accomplish this. Not under current case law. The courts would almost certainly rule it unconstitutional on First Amendment grounds, as well as others."

Preston is quiet for several moments. Then, with great deliberation he asks, "How can this *be*? Didn't that 2002 Supreme Court case *Zelman v. Simmons-Harris* uphold voucher programs?"

The AG replies, "Only partially, and that was largely due to the financial disincentives created by the Ohio Pilot Project Scholarship Program. Private schools received only half the government assistance given to community schools and one-third given to the so-called 'magnet' schools. Families still had to copay a portion of private school tuition. In the name of 'neutrality to religion,' the Ohio program went out of its way to favor government schools, which is why the Court did not strike it down. Even still, it was only a 5-4 decision, with Breyer, Stevens, Ginsburg, and Souter dissenting. Breyer dissented on the dubious, if not ridiculous, grounds that the program would foment 'divisiveness' and 'religious strife.'"

"That's pretty overblown," Preston says.

"Yes, sir. The majority of the Court thought so, too."

"Sorry, go on, " Preston urges.

"What we have in mind for Wyoming goes far beyond a mere supplementation of public education. We propose to *supplant* public education when such will not have been seen by the Court as a failure in the first place. Because we propose to return 100% of school tax funds to parents in voucher form to be spent at their sole discretion, there are no financial *dis*incentives to private schools. In fact, it's quite the opposite. Even though the *Mueller* line of cases requires true private choice amongst a broad class of citizens, and even though religious schools directly benefit by their choice, the post-Rehnquist Court would bend over backwards to declare that our scheme is not neutral to religion."

"How so? The purpose is not to benefit religious schools, but only to provide full choice of education to the parents," says Preston.

"Because over 50% of Wyoming's private schools are religious. The dissenters in *Zelman* tried to use the statistical argument that since over 80% of Ohio's private schools were parochial, there was no true free choice —only a 'Hobson's choice.' Private spending of transferable vouchers would tend to favor religious schools, which they'll say offends the Establishment Clause. I think the modern Court would so rule even if the Wyoming percentage of religious schools was far *less* than 50% because the average amount of the voucher would at least equal the average parochial school tuition, which in their minds would be 'advancing religious education.' In fact, if only *one* sectarian school received voucher funds, the Court would probably ban the program. That's how strict they are about this."

Preston is astonished. "You're kidding!"

"No, sir. They will employ the *Nyquist* argument against our voucher program, claiming that the 'effect of the aid is unmistakenly to provide desired financial support for nonpublic, sectarian institutions,' even though such is not our goal. They could revive the strict construction posed by dissenters in the 1947 *Everson* case who claimed that bus fare rebates for parochial students offended the Constitution. They could take that line of 'reasoning' so far as to exclude roads, sanitation services, and police and fire protection to churches. Even a policeman helping a child across the street to a religious school is conceivably unconstitutional. This Court would love to reverse *Mueller* and *Zelman*, especially since veterans' and welfare benefits may be spent by recipients at religious institutions and schools."

Preston considers this, frowning, and then asks, "You mentioned other grounds that the courts could overturn our program?"

"Yes, sir. Due process and Fourteenth Amendment concerns."

"Explain."

"Case law on the subject has basically concluded that public education must be evenly provided. In San Antonio, Texas, for example, there is a very wide property value disparity between the wealthy white northern Alamo Heights hamlet and Hispanic neighborhoods. Hence, per student property taxes varied by over 10 to 1, causing an inequality in education. Alamo Heights was spending more on their sports departments than were entire schools in the Hispanic districts, which sued in federal court. Alamo Heights parents argued that they merely wanted to receive the quality of education that they paid for in taxes. A free-market notion, to be sure, but it did not prevail. The court ruled that children in Texas public schools had a constitutional right to a substantially equal education, regardless of where they lived or how much their parents paid in property taxes. The ruling enjoined an adjustment of property tax disbursements for education. The wealthier districts were made to kick in funds to the poorer districts. It caused quite a stir there."

"So what are you telling me?" Preston asks.

"Governor, our conclusion is this: the Supreme Court will not likely allow a student exodus into private schools at the funding loss to public education. Since the public education infrastructure already exists, it has a fixed cost to sustain. Every $1,000 in taxes which is lost to private schools does not *ipso facto* translate into a $1,000 of expenses which the public schools can cut from their budget. They'd first fire teachers, which would raise class sizes and thus lower quality.

"Sure, public schools would, over time, stair-step reduce their fixed costs due to fewer and fewer students, but between the steps would be much dislocation. Downsizing always happens in increments and the quality of education would suffer as successive equilibriums are reached. Organizations need time to adjust to changes in size, but meanwhile the downsizing of public education would naturally foment inequality, which would be successfully challenged in federal court on 14th Amendment grounds."

"Hmmm. Yes, I see your point."

"That is the bad news: public education must be substantially equal across the state. A voucher program would have different local effect on public schools, depending on how many parents opted for private education. The resulting quality disparity of public schools would be unconstitutional under current Supreme Court rulings."

Preston asks, "You mentioned something about *good* news?"

"Yes, sir, the good news is that the Supreme Court has never ruled that a state must even provide public education." The AG permits himself a thin smile in triumph.

"*What?*" Preston can't quite believe where this is leading.

"Think of it like a game of baseball. If you play, then you have to play by the rules—rules made by others. Arguing about school vouchers is like arguing that you'd like to run from first to third base and skip second. It's just not going to happen. *But* . . . nobody . . . can . . . force . . . us . . . to play the game in the first place!"

"You're joking!" Preston blurts.

"No, sir! Not at all. For all the damaging constitutional revisionism, this is still America, sir. There are actually very few internal duties commanded of the states by the Constitution and case law. Although a French province, for example, could not do this, one of the United States can. We don't yet quite have a true national government. The states still retain, amazingly enough, some powerful prerogatives. Where does it say that a state has to provide public education at all? It was the states which usurped education because they wanted to control their citizens. We can get *out* for the opposite reason, because we *don't* want to control our citizens."

Preston stands and begins to wander about his office, his mind reeling from the implications. "Unbelievable . . . unbelievable."

The AG continues, "Some things can be ended by gradual reduction, like quitting smoking by the wearing of a nicotine patch. In our opinion, public education is not one of them. It's a matter of going 'cold turkey.' We see no impassible barrier to quitting public education by September 2018."

Preston is still generally speechless.

"Sir, if England could sell off British TeleCom, then why can't a state sell off its government schools? Libertarians were all looking at some *gradual* way to return to private education, and nobody thought to consider the simplest solution: if you want separation of school and state, then *separate*. Just have the state totally divest from the education business. Overnight."

Preston remains stunned. "My . . . God, you're right! All those gradual measures were predicated on expected political resistance. Nobody ever thought through the issue assuming a *cooperative* state government! For that matter, neither did I. We've all been so conditioned to accept certain boundaries and impossibilities because of government. That includes me and I'm the *governor!* Now we must all reshape our perspectives. This . . . this slices the Gordian knot right in half!"

The AG nods. "That's the good news, sir. No vouchers, no tax rebates, no gradual divestment—no nicotine patch. We simply get out of the education industry by declaring it and issuing quit claim deeds of school property to private corporations owned by the locals. The buildings don't go away, the teachers aren't fired, the books don't vanish. All that happens is a change of ownership. The local parents simply pay tuition instead of property taxes. This transfer could take place over a summer vacation. All we need to do is draft the legal template."

Preston laughs merrily. "It's brilliant! We simply step off the playing field; we quit the game. For decades we've been haggling over the rules, when all this time we never had to play ball in the first place! The NEA and the AFT will absolutely *shit!*"

The AG deadpans, "Well, it's about time they shat, sir."

The room breaks up with hearty laughter.

During a lull, Preston asks, "If we pull this off, how many other states do you imagine would follow our lead?"

"Oh, I'd think at least a dozen, Governor," the AG chuckles.

"A *dozen* states!" Preston pratically dances a jig. "That would be the deathknell of public education! *Millions* of families would relocate to those states. Much of California and the East Coast would be depopulated of its best people. It'd be tantamount to a revolution! No more federal control of education. No more socialist indoctrination. No more desecration of our American heroes and history. No more drug-sniffing dogs and random locker searches. No more UNESCO hovering over our schools. No more 'citizens of the world' bullshit. No more Ritalin and Prozac pumped into our children! No more residential property taxes! We wouldn't be producing a nation of drugged-out dummies! There really could be a future for America!"

"There's just one problem, Governor. Well, two, actually."

Preston's eyes narrow. "And what would those be?"

"First, this is prevented by Article 7, and much of Article 15."

"So, we need constitutional amendments. Of course! What was I thinking? Sorry, I got a little excited there."

"That's understandable, sir. So did we."

Preston says, "I'll need a draft of proposals by Monday so that—"

The AG gently interrupts, "Sir, we've already put them together. They're still a bit rough, but they're not the real problem. We've a much taller hurdle to clear."

"You mean the second problem?"

"Yes, sir. And it's formidable. I have here a copy of the Wyoming

Constitution. Let me show you something in Article 21. We didn't see this at first, but when we did it added a level of complexity to the plan."

When the AG read aloud the relevant sections the entire room took in a collective gasp.

Preston is stunned. "My God, Paul, can this even be *done*? I mean, it sounds like catching birds by sprinkling salt on their tails."

"I really couldn't say for sure, Governor. To be honest, my first reaction was negative. It was like learning how to crack a safe and then discovering that the safe itself is in a deep cave protected by an army."

Preston nods bitterly. "That's sounds about right. What were they *thinking* back in 1889? To lock something up is one thing, but to throw away the *key*?"

"Section 28 is an obvious roadblock, but it is the final sentence of section 23 which, as you aptly put it, 'threw away the key.' Repealing section 28 is pointless without first repealing the problematic language in section 23."

"Which it expressly forbids," points out Preston.

"Yes, sir. However, I have an idea. And it's one that our supreme court may embrace, especially when they understand the broader implications involved for the future."

The AG spends several minutes outlining what he has in mind.

Preston is silent for a moment and then says, "When I told my wife that I felt I should run for Governor she asked me if I *really* knew what I was getting into. I thought I did, but now I can see what she meant. Paul, this is absolutely huge—*atomic*, really. Even if the Wyoming supreme court goes along, what kind of federal challenge can we expect? Can it go all the way to the US Supreme Court?"

The AG replies, "That's very likely, Governor. The broader implications wouldn't be lost on them. The way I see it, there are three possible outcomes: Jeffersonian, Madisonian, and Hamiltonian."

Everyone present was well-versed in the history of the late 1780s and constitutional debates.

"Let's just pray it's not Hamiltonian," Preston observes. "OK, people, there's going to be quite an uproar about this and a lot of scared people to calm. Politically speaking, this is equivalent to tampering with constitutional DNA. It will be our biggest fight. We win this, we find that 'key' they tried to throw away and we use it."

The AG nods and summarizes, "It will break the back of renegade federalism."

Preston says, "You may just be right, Paul. Gosh, I'd love to read the history books thirty years from now! We'll either be patriots or scoundrels."

Reply to my Atheist and Agnostic Friends by Wyoming Gov. James W. Preston

Thank you all for your well-constructed letters in response to my interview in PLAYBOY. In short, my Christian worldview has variously been described as "primitive, superstitious, and irrational." Assuming, arguendo, that you are correct—how are you harmed?

Where is the tort?

In 1963 William F. Buckley wrote about the conservative mix of Christians and atheists: "The freeway remains large, large enough to accommodate very different players with highly different prejudices and techniques. The differences are now tonal, now substantive, but they do not appear to be choking each other off. The symbiosis may yet be a general consensus on the proper balance between freedom, order, and tradition."

I hope that the "choking each other off" has not begun.

In discussing morality and crime in the interview, I tried to demonstrate that Christianity and libertarianism are much more compatible than often believed. They are not mutually exclusive.

To reiterate, I did not, and never will, propose to criminalize certain actions held dear by libertarians. I only pointed out that they were arguably unprofitable to the individual, if not detrimental. And you must concede that a people generally drunk, high, or strung-out is no credible model for a free and healthy society.

Because of any political system's inability to embrace and further a comprehensive moral code (i.e., regarding the intrapersonal, vs. the interpersonal, which is the easy part), I have long believed that a purely secular libertarian society would not last beyond its founding generation. Galt's Gulch was and is a fantasy. There is more—much more—to a successful society than its members merely keeping their word and not initiating violence.

I've studied nearly everything by Rand, Rothbard, Friedman et al, and there is almost nothing about love, humility, kindness, forgiveness, chastity (when did anyone last hear that word!), honor, mercy, propriety, integrity, or decency.

Faith is a four-letter word, practiced only by "mystics."

Rand's social clique would not have exploded if she, as the elder party, had been wise enough to forgive Nathaniel Branden and also to own up to her primary responsibility in the matter. The Objectivist movement might have gone further if its cosmology had not been so saturated with such stifling arrogance. (Look at 1960s pictures of Rand's "Collective"— haughtiness drips from every pixel.)

Being a libertarian is not internally sufficient for good citizenship. I know far too many who are breathtakingly sloven, lazy, lewd, rude, petty, wimpy, and even mean-spirited. I would not live among them even though it were a society free of fraud and violence.

So if you truly believe that a free and healthy society can easily dispense with such "outdated affectations" without obvious harm, then please offer just one example. Will Durant, the famous (secular) historian, wrote that "There is no significant example in history, before our time, of a society successfully maintaining moral life without the aid of religion." That was in 1968. Nearly a half century later his observation is all the more poignant.

The West has fully entered the post-Christian age and it shows. By all indices it is not "successfully maintaining moral life." While the decline has not been instantaneous, it has been rapid enough to notice within a lifetime. The decency and wholesomeness of the 1950s, for example, seem almost extraterrestrial to us now. The Boy Scout Association is relentlessly attacked for their explicit morality and their right as a private organization to set standards for membership which exclude practicing homosexuals.

Where is the harm of citizens being cheerful, thrifty, clean, kind, helpful, brave, reverent, etc.? How would libertarian principles be violated? When the Boy Scout Code of Honor is a source of derision and legal action, the social implications are ominous indeed.

Because I am championing essentially spiritual values, the hardcore evangelical atheists (i.e., the God-haters vs. the casual atheists and mere agnostics) couldn't help but incant their nonbelief. The God-haters cannot subscribe to spiritual values, so Christian libertarians must be denounced as heretics of a secular humanism.

Beware, however, if you are tempted of this. For are you not at a total loss as to what to criticize in the society which I would, if I had the unilateral power, establish in Wyoming? Remember, I would not intrude upon your freedom to poison or degrade yourself any more than I would coerce you to attend church.

So, what, precisely, is your gripe? Since it does not reside in the physical, it must be metaphysical. As you do not believe in the preternatural, this poses a knotty dilemma—an unscratchable itch.

To an atheist colleague withdrawing from the National Review, WFB wrote: " [I] should hate for you to think that the distance between atheism and Christianity is any greater than the distance between Christianity and atheism. And so if you are correct, that our coadjutorship was incongruous, I...should have been the first to spot it and act on it...because my faith imposes upon me more rigorous standards of association than yours does."

My generic thoughts on the matter cannot be better expressed than that. Those atheist friends and colleagues who profess difficulty with my Christianity should keep in mind that their atheism can be similarly difficult for me. However, "the freeway remains large, large enough to accommodate very different players..."

I will close with a final question: Why is the "threat" of a chaste, judicious, and decent society—arrived at without the use of force— so alarming to you? When you have that figured out, please reply. I am most curious in your answer.

Sincerely,
James W. Preston

Lander, Wyoming   April 2016

Kyle and Susan Bradford were delighted to help out with the great migration. They portioned off 20 acres of their ranch and built a dozen 1,400 square foot cabins on an acre each, with a common storage barn, rec hall, gun range, and fishing pond. One young couple from Colorado knew the Bradfords and brought eleven other couples with them. Each pair had all the privacy they wanted, but they could also blend in and out of their small community whenever it suited them. Some were highly social, and some were more reserved. Some traveled frequently, while others rarely left the valley.

It was the best of all worlds. Most vowed they'd never move again.

As a gift they pooled their money for a beautiful macaw chick named Caesar. Only four months old, he was already hand-tamed and allowed even strangers to tickle his gorgeous purple and gold belly. Susan fell for the friendly bird and vowed deadly woe upon anybody who ever harmed him.

The Bradfords had made homes for two dozen libertarian relocators. Kyle and Susan considered it payback for the cruel death of Bondo.

Cheyenne, Wyoming   May 2016

"Paul, how are we doing on that constitutional issue you raised? Where are we with the legislature and supreme court?" Preston asks.

"Governor, I think we can weather the domestic squall until we arrive at the federal storm. Wyoming congressmen and justices won't be the problem. Federal courts *will* be."

"That was my read, too," Preston agrees. "Well, first we have to *get* to federal court. We must demonstrate that Wyoming is serious about controlling her own internal matters, which certainly includes education."

"Yes, sir. We will. Who knows, Governor, we could see a lot of national support for us in this. America loves an underdog."

Preston smiles and says, "Almost as much as they hate a traitor. We've got to show that education home-rule is an American right and tradition that was stolen from us in the 19th century."

Preston walks over to a window and gazes at the cobalt blue sky, thinking deeply. Then he turns and says, "One last thing, folks. We can't allow a word of this to leak out until we have a comprehensive, turn-key plan to offer. Otherwise, the Democrats will peck the concept to death. Factually and organizationally this must be a slam-dunk. Recall how the Federalists wrote the Constitution in secret and surprised the nation with a *fait accompli*? How the *Federalist* papers convinced New York? How they outmaneuvered their opponents and rammed through ratification? We'll need a consolidated effort like that. It must so bold and so complete that the opposition is paralyzed, fractious, and ineffective. Just like the antifederalists were. We'll have only one chance at this, so let's make it happen!"

"Yes, sir! I have some ideas regarding the timing, if I may."

"Certainly," says Preston.

"We should wait until after the general election before we publicize this. Let the voters first ratify the *habeas corpus*, eminent domain, and professional license amendments. Let the people first digest what they've been given. Then, they will be ready for more. Ratification of those amendments will also strengthen our hand in the Capitol. Also, we should gain two more Senators and three more Congressmen in November. That will give us a 63% majority in the Senate and a two-thirds majority in the House. With those numbers, you will fully be in the driver's seat, Governor. Our Ten Points have been a raging success, and four-fifths of Wyoming is behind you."

"It *has* all gone very well, hasn't it? You raise an excellent point about timing, Paul. All right, the initiative will not be publicized until the general session in January. Can we hash out all the details before then?"

"Yes, sir!" the room says in unison.

"Good. Then let's get cracking. I think we've worked out the legal aspects as best we can for now, but there are still financial details of divestiture. There are taxes and mineral royalties and funds intertwined with public education. And what about the University? Privatizing *that* will be a tough sell. All right, who do we need for our team? First, can we get John Taylor Gatto? He's been looking for this chance the past twenty years. Next,—"

Wyoming life   2016

The robust Wyoming economy was enhanced by the state's own airline, *Flyoming*. A fleet of modern twin turboprops (manufactured in Lusk by Maxwell Aviation) knitted the ninth largest state together, specializing in flights such Green River/Sheridan, Cheyenne/Worland, and Cody/Rawlins. The U of W in Laramie was directly served by flights from eight cities. No longer did students have to brave icy highways going home for Christmas.

The FAA and TSA tried to regulate *Flyoming*, but the Wyoming AG kept them legally at bay because of the strict *intra*state nature of the airline, which was outside of the Government's interstate commerce clause powers under the Constitution at I:8:3. The issue was headed to the Supreme Court, not that many Wyomingites cared.

Passengers with diplomas from recognized shooting academies received a 10% discount and were allowed to fly armed. Other passengers could carry onboard unloaded firearms with their actions cable-tied shut (just like at gun shows). This measure encouraged nonaccredited gunowners to go through school, which many of them did.

* * * * * * *

For their 20th wedding anniversary, James and Juliette Preston take a three week trip, beginning at her mother country of Ireland. To protest the purposely humiliating searches at airport "security", they arrive at Denver's DIA in bathing suits. Juliette's toned body in a Hawaiian one-piece nearly shuts down Concourse B. At first threatened with arrest, the Preston's tenacious stance (and notoriety) gets them onboard. The captain personally greets them into First Class and thanks them for their protest.

Their point made, the Prestons change midflight into dinner attire, as was once considered appropriate for airline travel, especially international. Pilot-to-pilot, James is invited up to the Boeing 797 cockpit for coffee.

From Ireland, they travel to Hungary to meet Juliette's distant relatives and James's son Istvan. They all spend a week camping on Lake Balaton.

The White House   September 2016
"Mr. President, we have just heard something interesting from Cheyenne. The Preston administration is working on some kind of school privatization scheme. It could be slated for their January session."

"*Now* what the hell are they up to?" Connor exasperates.

"We don't know any details now, but apparently it's pretty radical. Our source heard about it accidentally and doesn't have a reliable feed of information. We learned about it by a rather odd coincidence."

Connor snorts. "There's no such thing as coincidence. Coincidence is only something unexplainable at a superficial level. We only call it that to persuade ourselves we're in still control. What else did you learn?"

"He says that Preston's running it pretty tightly and that his staff are very excited about it, whatever it is."

"Well find out, damn it! If they spring something popular, it could spread like wildfire across the West. We lose public education, we lose our grasp on the nation. The NEA and AFT will just *shit!*"

Connor thinks for a moment and then says, "It's probably some new wrinkle on the voucher program. Get me some hard facts on what they're up to out there. If it's, as you say, 'radical' then it's sensitive. Maybe we can leak it and ruin their timing with a lot of preemptive bad press. Kill the thing before it ever gets to the legislative starting gate in January. Hell, if we can get a reactionary campaign going before their November elections, we may even derail ratification of those fucking amendments. Right of *habeas corpus*, my ass. Get moving on this, and I mean yesterday! I want details in two weeks, no excuses."

"Yes, Mr. President. Right away."

Cheyenne, Wyoming

"Governor, we just got an encrypted email from P.R. Something's come up you should know about."

Preston swivels his leather chair around. "Do tell."

"We've got a leak. Or, more accurately, somebody trying to become one. At State. A carry-over from the last administration. He used to work in Washington. He doesn't know about our privatization initiative, but he's become very curious in what we've been working on."

Preston frowns and asks, "At State, you say? Thank God it wasn't at the Treasurer's. That'd be much harder to plug."

The Governor stands and walks about the room as he always does when he is chewing on a problem. "Can we feed him something without it being suspicious?"

"I don't see why not, Governor. He's pretty hungry."

"Good. OK, here's what I have in mind. Suppose we—"

The White House   November 2016

Phillip Miles enters the Oval Office, clears his throat, and says, "Mr. President, we just heard from our man in Cheyenne. He managed to glance at a cover sheet on a secretary's desk. It was entitled 'A Proposed 2017 General Session Bill regarding Tax Credits and Vouchers for Private Schools.' It seems that may have we overconstrued this."

Connor shakes his head in disgust. "Tax credits and vouchers—same old horseshit. Preston's lost his nerve. Shot his wad with those 'Ten Points' last year."

"It looks that way, Mr. President."

"Yep. Aw, hell, now I've gotta meet with the Prime Minister Ben Moshe. He wants Stealth fighters again. Fat chance! As if we haven't done enough for Israel over the past seventy years. Oh—good work, Phil, thanks."

"Certainly, Mr. President. And congratulations on your election."

"Yeah, and the only one I'll ever get thanks to the 22nd Amendment."

Wyoming General Election   November 2016

The libertarian tide now covers two-thirds of the Capitol by taking House Districts 15, 35, and 58 and Senate Districts 4 and 10.

Amendment A on the writ of *habeas corpus* passed by 66%.

Amendment B on eliminating eminent domain passed by 73%.

Amendment C on eliminating the requirement of professional licenses was not ratified. Only 42% of the voters supported C. The scare tactics and huge treasury of the unions paid off. The amendment was proposed too soon for most people, who were still digesting the past two years of change.

Liberation was often a slow and painful process.

* * * * * * *

In 1215, the wealthy barons of England collectively challenged the power of King John I, forcing him to sign the Magna Carta on 17 June at the meadow of Runnymeade.

Today, only two classes of entities have the clout to take on the USG. The first are large corporations. Will they grow tired of the federal regulatory game or have our rulers been partners with Feudal, Inc. since WW2? Most probably the latter.

The second class are the 50 states. Will any of them finally grow indignant of the powers filched by Washington, D.C. and act to reclaim them?

—James Wayne Preston, *Journals*

Cheyenne, Wyoming   December 2016

"So, gentlemen, what do you have for me today?" asks Preston.

"Sir, we've completed the preliminary report on federal commerce clause powers over the states, and what Wyoming's options might be."

Preston smiles. "Ah, yes, the Phase V. Good. We've got to keep thinking ahead. Make Washington play catch-up for a change. Let's see it."

Preston quickly devours the four-page report at his renowned 900 wpm reading speed. In just over two minutes, he puts it down, smiles, and says, "Well, as if we haven't stirred up enough dust!"

"In for a penny, in for a pound, right Governor?" quips his aide.

Preston laughs. "Apparently so, Tom. Apparently so."

Federal Interstate Commerce Power vs. Wyoming Intrastate Activities

History of US interstate commerce power

The alleged rationale for the Constitution—the stated exigency that caused the 1787 Convention at Philadelphia—was the "crisis" of commerce between the States. Every American history book agrees on this. As the mythology goes, the States were squabbling sovereigns which got into tariff wars with each other and prevented the emergence of a true nation, and thus was at risk from England, France, Spain, and the Indians. Although tariff wars certainly occurred they were hardly a "crisis." They could have been solved by incorporating into the Articles of Confederation the following clause which was later written into the Constitution:

> *No state shall, without the consent of the Congress, lay any imposts or duties on imports or exports, except what may be **absolutely necessary** for executing its inspection laws; . . .*
> — Article 1, Section 10, Clause 2 of the US Constitution

If the point of the Constitution was to eliminate tariff issues, that clause alone would have easily sufficed. However, this was not all what Hamilton and Madison had in mind. They wanted the new government to *"regulate commerce"*—a power that extends (as time would prove) *far* beyond mere nationalization of tariffs.

To that end, the authors also included a clause that *should* have been seen as unnecessary to I:10:2:

> *[The Congress shall have power] to regulate commerce with foreign nations, and among the several states, . . .*
> — Article 1, Section 8, Clause 3 of the U.S. Constitution

The unnecessary clause of I:8:3 is "Smoking Gun #1." It is the DNA of the future behemoth. Not even the antifederalists of the day suspected this camel's nose under the tent. It was generally a dormant power until activated in the 1930s. Today, the commerce clause energizes over half of all federal legislation, most of it antithetical to the Bill of Rights. For example, nearly all of the anti-2nd Amendment gun laws stem from I:8:3.

Now, to "Smoking Gun #2." In order to allow for what would later be termed "elastic" or "implied" powers of the federal government, the following clause was inserted:

> *To make all laws which shall be **necessary** and proper for carrying into execution the foregoing powers, . . .*
> — Article 1, Section 8, Clause 18 of the U.S. Constitution

During the 1791 battle over the first Bank of the US, Jefferson and Hamilton argued ferociously over the meaning of *"necessary."* Both correctly discerned that the future of America rested, by implication, on the outcome. Since the Bank was neither explicitly nor implicitly authorized in the Constitution, Jefferson rightly declared it to be unconstitutional. He argued that *"necessary"* of I:8:18 meant "necessary" and not, as Hamilton asserted in a 15,000 word rebuttal, "expedient" or "helpful." Hamilton wrote that Jefferson's definition *"would be to give it same force as if...absolutely ... had been prefixed to it."*

Naturally, the States had *not* been informed of this looming ambiguity during the ratification debates. In fact, *The Federalist* went out of its way to calm the people that the proposed system was not injurious to State sovereignty or their rights. For example, Madison, in #39, promised that:

> The powers delegated to the proposed Constitution are few and defined. Those which are to remain in the State governments are numerous and indefinite . . .
>
> [Federal] jurisdiction extends to certain enumerated subjects only, and leaves to the several States a residuary and inviolable sovereignty over all other subjects.

Two centuries later we are the debauched virgin who sobs the morning after, *"But he said he loved me!"*

The clue that *Federalist* assurances were disingenuous is found in the language difference between I:10:2 restricting the States with *"**absolutely** necessary"* and I:8:18 allegedly restricting Congress with *"necessary."* This is "Smoking Gun #2" that the Founding Lawyers of 1787 never meant to create a perpetual republic.

What they *really* desired was a mercantilistic state protected by a national government in full power of both purse and sword, but since about 50% of the people did not share that goal, the Founding Lawyers could only achieve their scheme over time through constitutional artifice with the collusion of federal judges. By successfully designing the "rules of the game" they were destined to win, eventually.

And every bit of it was and is "constitutional."

The whole thing was a fraud from the very beginning.

Post-1789 awakening of interstate commerce power

Article I, Section 8, Clause 3 of the US Constitution delegates to Congress the power to *"regulate commerce with foreign nations, and among the several states, and with the Indian tribes."* One of its first usages was a 1790 trade embargo on Rhode Island in punishment for being the only colony to boycott the Philadelphia convention and for not joining the new United States (due to a 1788 referendum 11-1 *against* statehood).

This I:8:3 clause is the direct source of the most important peacetime powers of the USG. The Government's war on (some) drugs, guns, privacy, cash, alternative medicine, etc. stems from I:8:3. So does the discredited scheme of "affirmative action." Any random federal intrusion of your life, such as the National ID Card, is likely powered by the commerce clause.

Until FDR's New Deal, the commerce clause was rarely used to interfere with the internal commerce and activities of the states. Since the 1930s, however, the Supreme Court has declared that the clause embraces anything which *"affects interstate commerce"*—a phrase of limitless scope. According to this rationale, the cumulative effect of minor intrastate transactions affects interstate commerce. Under the "aggregation principle" even a farmer consuming 100% of his own wheat falls under I:8:3 because if millions of farmers did so it would suppress the wheat market.

All of this was foreseen, if not planned, by Alexander Hamilton. In 1788 he assured America in *The Federalist* #17 that:

> *The administration of private justice between the citizens of the same State, the supervision of agriculture and of other concerns of a similar nature, all those things, in short, which are proper to be provided for by local legislation, **can never be desirable cares of a general jurisdiction.***

Three years later he divulged the hidden, though inexorable, truth about the I:8:3 clause:

> *What regulation of* [interstate] *commerce does not* [theoretically] *extend to the internal commerce of every state?*
> — Alexander Hamilton, *Report on Manufacturers* (1791)

Wyoming intrastate commerce

Phase V of our plan is to directly challenge the unconstitutionally excessive *"affects"* scope of I:8:3 by starting or supporting several new *intra*state industries. We have several concurrent goals—legal, commercial, and sociological:

❶ Drive a legal wedge in the expanded commerce clause power.
❷ Augment the commercial self-sufficiency of Wyoming.
❸ Increase the unified spirit of Wyomingites.

Even if ❶ legal and ❷ commercial fail, we still achieve ❸ sociological. We've nothing to lose by trying, and it's high time at least *one* of the states begins to *directly* challenge the USG for its constitutional prerogatives. Our own *Flyoming* airline is a perfect example. Here are two others.

intra-Wyoming CyberGold

Although the US Constitution (in I:10:1) prohibits the states from coining money or emitting bills of credit, individuals are free to do so. A Wyoming electronic scrip would help strengthen the state's economy by giving its people the easy opportunity of supporting each other first.

Transactions would be allowed only between Wyoming IP addresses on our own Intranet. Electronic credits would not be exportable outside Wyoming's borders. This would negate most of the nexus with I:8:3.

A substantially insular Wyoming economy based on its own encrypted digital gold would break the state's dependence and vulnerability on the failing "US dollar" (*i.e.*, Federal Reserve Note) and US economy.

Imagine Wyomingites sitting in a lifeboat onboard the *Titanic*. If the mothership does not sink, fine—our situation is improved without us having to do a thing. If the mothership finally goes under, we survive . . . *without us having to do a thing.* The lifeboat's buoyancy provides for an inevitable detachment from the mothership. As long as those in the lifeboat boarded their vessel to capacity *prior* to any emergency, it will remain *their* lifeboat during the ensuing panic.

Time is quickly running out, however. Wyoming must become watertight and capacious *before* the rush begins. Very soon it will be "any port in a storm" and Wyoming must have achieved near full occupancy before then, else we'll be swamped by the desperate who have little to offer.

intra-Wyoming gun manufacturers

Here, the plan is *extremely* bold and will attract the most attention. Is a wholly intrastate gun making industry possible in the 21st century? Perhaps, especially if we tie it into Wyoming's constitutional right of a militia.

USG response vs. Wyoming counterresponse

First, the Government will enjoin through federal court the cessation of these lawful intrastate industries.

Wyoming will not comply. Her message to the other 49 states will be, *"Why does Washington, D.C. care if we operate industries solely within our own state borders? What is harmful or unconstitutional about that?"*

Then come the US Marshals, FBI, etc. The Governor will block them with personnel from local police, sheriff's deputies and *posse comitatus*, the Wyoming State Patrol, and, if need be, the state militia.

After that, it is up to the Congress and the President to declare Wyoming in *"insurrection"* under I:8:15 of the US Constitution and attempt to occupy the state with federal troops under martial law. It is time to force the Government's hand and demonstrate to the country that America has been under quiet Occupation by an internal foreign government since WWI. The time for meek acquiescence is over. We will at last withdraw the leverage of our putrid cooperation and give the feds no option but to physically occupy (versus virtually through intimidation).

If we are a free people, then we should *act* like free people.

If we are an occupied people, then *they* should act like occupiers.

No more whitewash of freedom! No more façades! No more Potemkin villages of American liberty!

Unless we are brave we will never be free. It has been generations since we have been brave, and thus generations since we have been free. It's time to quit resting on the laurels of 1776. It's time to quit coasting on the momentum given us by the blood of 18th century patriots.

We either roll over like puppies with urine-soaked pink bellies, or we stand up and fight like Americans once did.

There is no middle ground.

There never was.

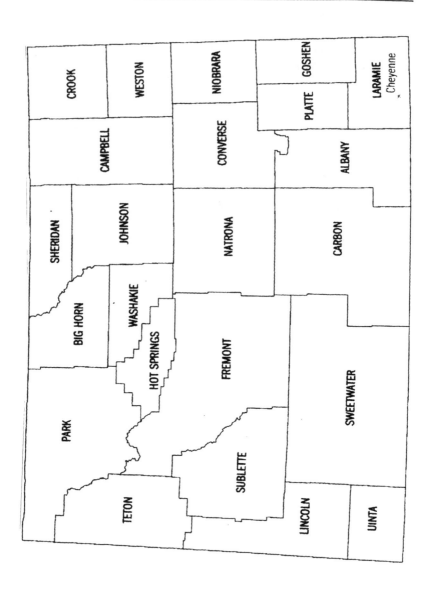

❖ 2017

2017 USA political news

In accordance with the UN's July 2006 conference on "light weapons", mandatory gun registration for all member nations goes in effect on 1 January. Only in America is there any significant popular outcry and resistance. US Congressmen claim frustration at the UN directive, saying that their "hands were tied" by the VI:2 treaty power clause of the Constitution which makes UN "gun control" our *"supreme law of the land."* Privately, these same politicians gloat at the long-last arrival of national gun registration.

Confiscation was only a matter of time.

Washington, D.C.   January 2017

White House chief of staff Phillip Miles has been uneasy for several months. He is now almost positive that he is under surveillance. On three separate occasions he was convinced that he was followed. Some of his letters appeared opened, while others never arrived. The White House Communications Agency inexplicably requested that he swap his pager and cell phone for "newer" models, but no other colleague had to turn in theirs.

He tried to persuade himself that his two years of, well, spying for Governor Preston had inculcated a natural sense of paranoia. But when he came home last week to discover some of his computer DVDs missing, he owned up to the fact that the feds were on to him. Though he had steeled himself over the past months for this likelihood, accepting it was difficult for Miles.

He begins to make plans to resign and move far away from the East coast. Even Wyoming might not be far enough. New Zealand, maybe.

* * * * * * *

As long as the child breathes the poisoned air of nationalism (patriotism), education in world-mindedness can produce only rather precarious results. As we have pointed out, it is frequently the family that infects the child with extreme nationalism. The (public) school should therefore...combat family attitudes that favor jingoism .... We shall presently recognize in nationalism the major obstacle to the development of world mindedness.... [E]ach member nation

...has a duty to see to it that nothing in its curriculum, course of study and textbooks is contrary to UNESCO's aims.
— UNESCO, Publication 356

Cheyenne, Wyoming
State Capitol, General Session   January 2017

"Point One. Waste water. Regarding the environmental concerns over the private use of our water, we have a simple solution: Waste water shall outflow upstream from your fresh water intake. You will intake your own effluvia before anybody else does. If you can live with it, then most likely your downstream neighbors can, too. Think of it as a mandatory Golden Rule.

"Point Two: Taxes. Several states have managed to do without sales and/or income taxes[1]. Wyoming, however, will set a new example. We propose to eliminate and prohibit all property taxes on homesteads[2] in conjunction with the privatization of all Wyoming public schools.
"Which brings us to Point Three: education . . .

...he who overcomes his enemies by stratagem, is as much to be praised as he who overcomes them by force.
— Machiavelli

Washington, D.C.
The White House   January 2017

"What in the fuck *happened*?!" spits President Connor. "They want to dump their entire public education program! Next year! All of it, including the U of W!"

"Mr. President, according to our source in Cheyenne—"

"Your *'source'*? Fuck him! *Fuck* your 'source'! Tax credits and vouchers my ass! We got D-Day'ed! God*damn!*"

"*D*-day'ed? Sir?" Miles asks, flummoxed.

"Yes, Miles, D-Day'ed! You know, June 6, 1944? It's like we were staring at Calais because of all the bogus intel about Patton's phantom army in East Anglia, and 'Dwight D. Prestonhower' lands at fucking Normandy Beach

---

[1]   States without sales tax are: Alaska, Delaware, Montana, New Hampshire, and Oregon.
    States without income tax are: Alaska, Florida, New Hampshire, Nevada, South Dakota, Tennessee, Texas, Washington, and Wyoming.
    Alaska and New Hampshire have no sales or income tax, but a very high property tax.
    Thus, it makes implicit sense to live in South Dakota or Wyoming and shop in Montana, or to live in Washington or Nevada and shop in Oregon. New Hampshire is fine for employment and shopping, but live in Vermont or Maine for their lower property taxes.

[2]   Although several states have very *low* property taxes (*e.g.*, Arkansas, Kentucky, West Virginia, New Mexico, and Mississippi), no state has ever dispensed with residential property taxes altogether.

Still stomping about, President Connor says, "Well, they may propose this, but let's see if they can wade through the shitstorm the country sends their way. Abolishing public education! It's *unAmerican!*"

Attorney General Janet Vorn speaks up. "Mr. President, we just looked into their education reform. They can't dump the public schools."

Connor freezes in mid-grimace. "What do you mean?"

"Sir, their own constitution *requires* public education:"

The legislature shall make laws for the establishment and mainte-nance of systems of public schools which shall be open to all children of the state and free from sectarian control.
— Wyoming Constitution, Article 21, section 28

"But they *can't* repeal it because of a previous section which is controlling:"

...The following article [sections] shall be irrevocable without the consent of the United States and the people of this state:
— Wyoming Constitution, Article 21, section 23

Vorn continues, "Mr. President, they're 'locked in.' They'd need the consent of Congress to repeal section 23. They're *stuck* with public schools. In fact, they can't even go very far with a voucher or tax credit scheme because of unavoidable 1st Amendment conflict. If their supreme court doesn't enforce section 23, the federal judiciary will. I've spoken with the Solicitor General about this, and he's prepared to take it all the way to the Supreme Court."

"That's great news! Preston's libertarian wave will crash on the sand bar of their own constitution—I love it! With any luck it'll drown 'em all."

Cheyenne Sentinel **February 2017**

"Yesterday the Wyoming legislature passed several proposed constitutional amendments that would fully divest the State of Wyoming from public education by the beginning of the school year next September. A concurrent proposal would eliminate all residential property taxes, which are levied specifically for public schools. Mineral royalties and other taxes earmarked for education would continue to go into a general education fund, to be drawn upon by the parents on a per student capita basis.

"Voters will decide during a special election set for this August. Reaction around the country is strong and mixed. This is apparently an issue with little room for fence-sitting. The National Education Association and the American Federation of Teachers have announced that they will file suit in federal court if the Wyoming constitutional amendments are ratified."

* * * * * * *

The national outcry was deafening and blistering. Wyoming was accused by the East Coast liberals of "exchanging education for ignorance." A nationwide boycott of Wyoming goods and toursim was threatened, and a swelling uproar demanded that the Federal Government step in to prevent Wyoming's proposals.

Far too few people acknowledged the long since buried fact that public education had been created by the *states*, and what the states created they could also abolish. The simple logic of this argument was drowned out by nothing less than mass hysteria. Americans had long forgotten that they were supposedly given a *republic* where local and state prerogatives exceeded all but the most explicit and urgent of federal concerns.

Taxation is far greater an evil than theft. It is a form of slavery. If you cannot choose the disposition of your property, you are a slave. If you must ask permission to work, and/or pay involuntary tribute to anyone from your wages, you are a slave....

How is it that so many have so much difficulty with this?

And spare me the arguments that begin with, "But how could we (whatever) if there was no taxation?" If a person will not concede the moral wrongness of forcible confiscation of property, no fruitful discussion of this subject is possible. Without first getting an understanding that taxation is wrong, no serious effort will be made to find an ethical and moral way to do "whatever."

Furthermore, those who want to enjoy the "benefits" of taxation (a "free" school, a "free" highway) generally prefer to do so without acknowledging the uncomfortable fact that they supported the underlying convenient theft. Thus, the taxmen and their supporters inevitably drag us into a culture of lies and deceit, which must in the end corrode and destroy all that is good in any culture, finally rendering the language so twisted and full of euphemism and misnomer that it becomes almost impossible to even <u>describe</u> a moral system of exchange and equity, let alone claw our way out of the pit to rediscover one. (at 98-99)

If you have ever voted in favor of a school bond—taking money from your neighbor on the threat of the government seizure of his or her house, in order to school your own kids—then you are a socialist. And as with alcoholism, you are not going to get cured until you admit it....

But if we haven't established anything else by now, surely it's clear that the kind of vested interests who now fatten at the trough of "public education" will run us in gleeful circles and never allow us to get there through any "gradual transition." The rule of nature and of history is that the new seeds sprout in the sun only after the old tree has finally toppled in ruin.

So: Why prop up this rotting hulk any longer? Why? (at 203)

— Vin Suprynowicz, *The Ballad of Carl Drega*

* * * * * *

To further explain the admittedly dramatic initiatives, Governor Preston makes a televised speech.

"Let me discuss the privatization of Wyoming's education. This is not a vote of no-confidence against our public school teachers or administrators. They have done the best they can given all the restrictions the federal government has placed upon them. But since we do have government schools, it is the equivalent of our children being taught with an effectiveness similar to Amtrak or the US Postal Service. Our children deserve better!

This is our chance—our one chance—to return control of our children's education to the people of Wyoming. We can give our children better and more responsive schools for less money.

"The buildings, teachers, and students will be no different from the previous year. Only the landlord will change. Ladies and gentlemen, here is your chance to own and control your local schools. You already have been paying for them through property taxes and bond issues. You will still pay for your local schools, but without the needless middleman of government. Here is your chance to improve your children's education, to experiment and to learn from other schools. To cut or increase budgets wherever and whenever you deem necessary. To enjoy a choice of schools for a change. This has always been the right of parents, but it was taken from you over a hundred years ago. And now, your government would like to return to you that stolen property. It is your choice whether to accept it.

"Government education is not consistent with any free country, much less with America. Since the states unlawfully took over the education and indoctrination of our children, have they produced any more Jeffersons? Any more Madisons? Any more Hamiltons? No. These brilliant men—these Founding Fathers—were all products of home-schooling, private education, and parochial universities. Somehow, America flourished for over a hundred years without government schools.

"Since public education, however, only those with enough money could afford private schools. Only those with enough time had the option of homeschooling. Everyone else with average time and money had no choice but public schools, which have been declining in quality for fifty years. Their "product"—our children— cannot compete against the Germans and the Japanese, or even against the British. High-school exams of 1917 cannot be passed by college graduates of 2017. Students are taught less and less each year and graduate without the skills needed to survive, much less succeed, in the real world. Nearly a third are functionally illiterate. This is absolutely criminal! And we will no longer tolerate it in Wyoming!

"If we don't embrace a separation of school and state today, our children will be fully indoctrinated by the socialist bureaucrats of Washington, D.C. and the UN. They've gradually been doing so for over thirty years as it is. Upon ratification, Wyomingites will no longer be coerced into educating the children of strangers. We believe in the simple right of people to fully receive the local quality of life they pay to enjoy. Perfect economic equality is not possible, not even by stealing from the more wealthy to give to the less wealthy. Let's concentrate on increasing the size of the pie instead of squabbling over ever-shrinking slices.

"Upon ratification, we expect a proliferation of privately-funded scholarships to make up the gap for families temporarily unable to afford the quality of education they desire for their children. Mrs. Preston and I have started such a fund ourselves, in which we welcome fellow donors.

"In closing, let me remind us all of something long since forgotten. These recent initiatives are fully within the prerogative of any state in the Union. The states created drivers licences, vehicle registration, and public schools. And by the same token, the states may amend or abolish their own systems whenever their citizens so choose. And Wyomingites have chosen to return to the heritage of our once free nation and shun the shackles of licenses, permits, and prior restraint. Behave responsibly and nobody will bother you unless you mess up.

"If the rest of the country does not agree, then they do not have to come here. Neither the states nor the Federal Government have any right to interfere with the internal matters of Wyoming. We mind our own business and expect others to do the same. In five years, we'll see who has the brightest students!

"Thank you, and may God continue to bless Wyoming and her people."

Cheyenne, Wyoming   March 2017

"If we lose in district court, we will appeal to the 10th Circuit Court of Appeals. If we win in district court, the Government will appeal."

"So, either way this is destined to be heard in the Appellate Court in Denver?" Preston asks.

"Yes, sir."

"Do you still think it will go as far as the US Supreme Court?"

"Very likely. The Government will want to nip this in the bud, not only to maintain public education, but to forestall secession in violation of section 24 which declares Wyoming an *'inseparable part of the federal union.'* Also, the Government must convince those other states with similar clauses to our section 23 that, as the Borg in *Star Trek* would say, *'Resistance is futile.'* So, yes sir, it will probably go to the Supreme Court. If we are the petitioner, they will most certainly deny *certiorari* and let the 10th Circuit Court ruling stand. What we do about *that* will be your decision."

Preston sighs with a grin. "That's why they pay me the big bucks."

Wyoming   Spring 2017

Since most of the nation's shooting academies had been squeezed out of business by regulation stopping just shy of prohibition, many of them simply relocated to Wyoming's ample space and supporting gun culture. Consequently, Wyoming enjoyed the highest quality of shooting instruction in the world. Thousands of annual students from across the country and globe enrolled, especially ex-gunowners from England, Australia, and Canada. Attending a 1000yd .50BMG rifle course at "Half-Inch Harvard" became the newest sport of the wealthy. The gun-free Japanese flocked in by the hundreds to shoot Winchester .30-30s and single-action Colt .45s. Germans, forbidden to own *any* military-pattern rifle, loved to rent HK91s, FALs, M14s, and M1 Garands.

Schools blatantly serving outsiders tended to be located near Cheyenne (just 2 hours from Denver's DIA), or Evanston (an hour from SLC). The "domestic" schools were sprinkled about Wyoming, many of them in the Big Horn Basin for its good year-round weather.

In a phenomenon not seen in America since the 1770s, thousands of statewide riflemen are training together in the form of citizens' militias. Many drill as 4-man teams—popularly called "knots"—for their flexibility (*e.g.,* as a .50BMG countersniper team, or battle rifle patrol), divisibility (*e.g.,* a pair of sniper/observer teams, or four recon scouts), and blendability (2 per squad, 8 per platoon). Four-man knots offer good concentration of force, yet can move with stealth. As most knots are composed of men who have known each other for years (and thus nearly impossible to infiltrate), their unit integrity—one of the main keys to effectiveness—is superb. Their comsec and opsec is tight, and improving.

They generally practice fieldcraft, fire-and-maneuver drills, and target recognition out to 600yds. Specially constructed "jungle lanes" are used by competing knots to test their skills. Also, shooting competitions open to the public attract much local weekend interest and further enhance popular support of the gun culture (as was common in Switzerland until the 1990s).

In most of rural Wyoming, a man going about his daily business with a slung rifle is rarely cause for concern, or even comment (except perhaps to ask about sights, trigger, stock, etc.). In the towns and cities, nearly half the adults openly wear sidearms, and another 20% or so carry them concealed. This was not an affectation, but a badge of citizenship. Nearly every Wyomingite was, in effect, his or her own Gadsden flag—calmly but implacably warning others *Don't Tread On Me.*

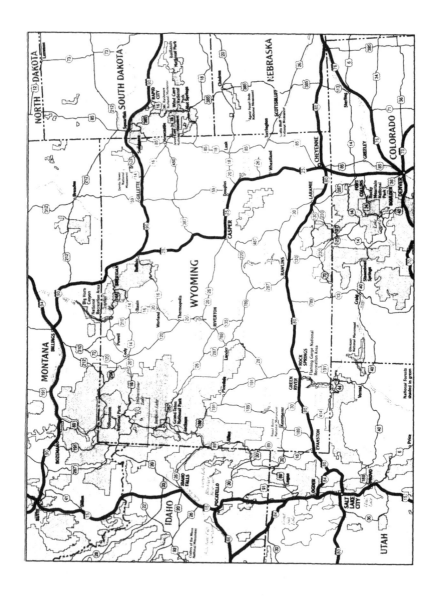

PLAYBOY INTERVIEW:

JAMES PRESTON

a second candid conversation with
Wyoming's Laissez-Faire Party Governor

James Preston's administration, with the enthusiastic support of the Wyoming legislature, proposes to divest the government of public education and turn it completely over to local, private concerns. Senator Schumer went so far as to call his goal "cannon fire on Fort Sumter."

Even though 57% of Wyoming voters favored the privatization of education in a recent constitutional amendment election, several law-suits have been filed in federal court to prevent it. Plaintiffs include the NEA, AFT, and other teachers' unions, as well as a consortium of Wyoming parents.

Two years following our first interview, we spoke with Governor James Preston about his "separation of education and state."

Governor Preston, PLAYBOY is very pleased to have you back for a second interview.

Thank you, Tom. I certainly enjoyed the first one.

Wyoming is the first state ever to propose dismantling its public education system. Much of the country seems horrified by this.

Horrified, eh? Perhaps they wouldn't be so shocked if they'd asked themselves why any government on these shores is involved in education in the *first* place. If one lives with a malignant tumor long enough it acquires the status of a vital organ.

But to address your question, education is a matter of parental, not state,

concern. We in Wyoming are reclaiming our right to eliminate the forcible government indoctrination of our children. The Special Election will be held in August, and we are confident that the proposed constitutional amendments will be ratified.

The shrieking from the NEA about this is just amazing. They apparently believe that education is not possible without government schools. Well, they're half right, at least.

How so?

Government education *does* require *government* schools. (laughs)

You have been consistently and intensely critical of public

schools, calling them *"training camps for future slaves."* **How can you justify that claim when this country still enjoys the greatest amount of personal freedom in the world?**

First of all, to compare our level of freedom to that of other countries is not accurate or even helpful. As I've long been fond of saying, *"America is merely the healthiest patient in the cancer ward."* The comparison should be made against (1) the theoretical ideal, and (2) against the greater freedom America once had until the 1920s. To compare our freedom to the rest of the world only serves to slyly misdirect us from the freedom we ourselves have already *lost.* It's a way of shrinking the yardstick of measurement. Contrasted to other nations—sure, we're still six feet tall. However, contrasted to ourself—which is the only *proper* standard, in both the philosophic and historic senses—we have become a midget.

And, I am convinced that the government indoctrination of our schoolchildren has been largely to blame for this unnecessary decline.

Really? How so?

Well, because it was the stated and published goals of the public educators in the early 19th century. Their object was not quality education, but docile citizens. Not independent thought, but conformity. Intellectuals of every era have distrusted the common man, likening him to a coarse beast of burden which must be kept under yoke. They greatly feared popular uprisings. Shay's Rebellion in 1786 Massachusetts—which sparked

the Annapolis and Philadelphia constitutional conventions—was still fresh on Bostonians' minds in 1818 where the first public school movement began in America. Then, many educators traveled to Prussia to learn their methods.

Why Prussia?

Gatto's fine book *Dumbing Us Down* outlined the whole sordid story. When Napoleon trounced Prussia in 1806 at the Battle of Jena, intellectuals decided that the reason for their defeat was a failure of the troops versus their commanders. They concluded that Prussian soldiers were too independent and thought too much for themselves.

As if soldiers would fall into philosophical debates over Kant in the field?

(laughs) Pretty much! No commander wants an army of deeply contemplative troops. (laughs) This reminds me of a story about Henry Kissinger. He was once asked if he feared assassination. He thought for a moment and replied, *"No, because only an intellectual would ever choose me, and even then he couldn't decide to pull the trigger!"* (laughs)

But seriously, the Prussian intellectuals believed that their citizens simply were not obedient enough and hesitated to fire on the enemy. The US Army noticed the same thing during World War Two when researchers discovered that only 20% of American soldiers would fire on an exposed enemy. The Army addressed this, and by the Korean War some 55% of soldiers would fire to kill. By Vietnam it was 90%. With the conditioning from violent films, video games, and military simulators, the percentage today is about 100%.

This has spilled over into our police, who have donned an alarmingly military guise. Federal law enforcement is now predominantly composed of agents with little onsite conscience. For example, a very high percentage of FBI agents for the past 50 years have been Mormons and/or ex-Marines.

Why is that?

Because their members are naturally "Yes, sir!" type of folks, which explains why the FBI wants them. They are what Erich Hoffer calls "true believers." They will obey even the most ghastly orders if there is a sufficient gloss of God and Country.

As an ex-Marine myself, I got only as far as captain since everybody knew that there was only so much crap I'd take! (laughs)

Anyway, the Prussians' goal of education was to create pliable students to be molded into compliant citizens. Meaning, those who work and fight at the behest of the government, and never have to decide to pull the trigger. This was accomplished by purposely *not* training the students how to *think*.

How did Prussian schools teach students not to *think*? Teaching not to think sounds like an oxymoron. Mustn't education, *any* education, awaken minds and activate the thought process?

No, not at all. Teaching by rote a series of disconnected facts is not the same as teaching one to actually think.

What the Prussians did was unequivocally premeditated. They rearranged their school system into three tiers, as a very broad pyramid. About 1% of students *were* taught to think in the *Academie*. These would be the future leaders, doctors, lawyers, business chairmen, etc. About 5% were *somewhat* taught to think in the *Realshulen*. They would become the middle managers and politicians. Some mental faculty was required, but not *too* much! (laughs)

The rest, 94% of students were left in the *Volkschulen* to learn harmony, obedience, and docility. Cooks, mechanics, laborers, and, most importantly, soldiers. Reading was very much discouraged, as it tended to provoke dissent amongst the proletariat. It still does.

How were these Prussian *Volkschulen* different?

Their most telling trait was severe regimentation. The very word *Kindergarten* means "garden of children." Think about that. The Prussian educators not only had to get their indoctrinating paws on children as young as four years old, but they had the *nerve* to refer to them with a horticultural analogy. "Sorry, Inge, you're not a unique person, you're just one plant in the garden." Children are *not* a bunch of plants to be grown and harvested!

I never thought of it quite like that, but the analogy *is* inherently dehumanizing.

Absolutely. The battle for the metaphor is the most important, as it pre-structures thought, and thus action. In fact, we could continue their farming analogy even further. The testing which placed students in their "proper tier" of schooling were like threshers separating the *Academie* wheat from the *Volkschulen* chaff.

Yes, that follows. So, how were things taught in the *Volkschulen*?

They took the grand subject of Life and chopped it up into little subsets. Instead of illuminating the mysteries of living as a holistic system—as it most certainly is—they cleaved mathematics from music, philosophy from language, and so on. They taught the pixels, but not the *picture* formed by the pixels. In doing so, they created adults who could not *see*.

Could you elaborate on that?

Of course. Thinking really is all about *seeing*. Our brains are wired to receive information mostly by sight, about 80%. In fact, PET scans of the brain have proven that *visualizing* an object stimulates the same area of the brain as actually *seeing* the object. The eye is merely the camera for the recording tape of the brain. We only know what we have seen. That's why dreams often seem so real. The taped version is just as vivid to the mind as the live version. Physiologically, there's almost no difference. That's why sports trainers stress the repetitive visualization of movement—constant mental rehearsals. It actually imprints athletic memory, as the mind cannot distinguish between mental versus physical rehearsal.

It's no coincidence that when one has a eureka moment, one says, *"Oh, I see!"* What Prussian *Volkschulen* did was intentionally prevent the child from ever opening its mind's eye. The goal was to keep the people at large mentally blind. Sure, the masses stumble about fairly well in the *pretense* of seeing—just as a blind person with a cane can walk across town—but make no mistake; they *are* stumbling about in the dark by feel.

By segregating subjects and teaching them out of order, the mind's eye is never trained to see the "big picture." Vision, I tell you, is the key to nearly everything in life. If you can't see it, you can't know it or do it.

I understand your point, but I'm not convinced that merely teaching by subject necessarily stunts mental growth.

OK, let's take mathematics for example. It is without dispute that the USA scores lowest in math amongst the Western world. I recall we may have beaten Portugal once, but not by much. (laughs) The most exciting thing about math is not the numbers, but the *theory*. Mathematics is a way of understanding particular kinds of relationships. Numbers are simply the alphabet of expression.

For example, what is, oh, 7 times 19? It's 133. Now, did I multiply 7 times 10, which is 70, and then 7 times 9, adding the 63 to the 70? No! I took a shortcut. Why go through all of that when 7 times 20 is 140, and 7 times 19 is merely 140 minus 7? But kids aren't being taught to take shortcuts, because they can't *see* the numerical landscape and recognize shortcuts when they exist. They're taught to literally go by the numbers, like a blind man tapping with his cane.

What is not seen is not understood. See? (laughs)

Yes, I do. But does your analogy hold for higher mathematics?

Well, if we know that A has a specific relation to C, and that A also has a specific relation to B, then we can figure out what B is to C.

That's algebra. To use what you know to learn what you don't. Calculus is even *more* fascinating, because it explains relationships at an even deeper level.

Physics, especially quantum physics, gets *really* hairy. Either Life has the possibility for many states and is forced by observation to be in one particular state, *or* Life is many worlds in simultaneous coexistence which *appear* to us as a single state. Whichever it is, the math of quantum physics contends that Life is much more surreal and inexplicable than imagined under Newtonian physics.

But instead of firing up students about the marvel of math, "teachers" immediately bog them down in quadratic equations and log tables. It's like trying to teach dancing by steps but without the rhythm.

My point is this: mathematics are merely one tool for understanding and enjoying Life. Art is another. So is science. Music, *et cetera*. The mind—the *awakened* mind—uses all of these rays of light in its "lens" to *see*, to understand. The more rays of light, the more chromatic your picture. This was the avowed purpose of the long-lost classical education.

On a related note, it constantly amazes me how much of Life can be grasped by analogy. We learn about Life analogously through nature, through human relationships, and through science. It's all grist for the mill.

So, back to the Prussian system of education.

Yes, the *Volkschulen*.

They broke up Life into pieces. By dividing Life, they conquered free inquisition. They conquered thought itself. Then, they broke up the pieces into units, and units into small blocks of classtime lasting 50 minutes.

First, regiment the entire student body by artificial age groups. No more one-room schoolhouse. This separates older students from younger ones, which reduces socialization and nullifies any generational continuity. I mean, do you work or vacation solely with 34 year olds? It's ridiculous, but accepted without a thought in government schools.

You're right...no where else are you placed in a strict age group.

If you really dwell on it, it seems quite odd. I don't think that we even remotely understand the sociological damage it's done.

So, children are clumped together by age—their first experience at being a part of a collective. Then, get them accustomed to moving by a series of ringing bells. The bell commands when to sit down and stay, when to stand up and leave, when to eat, when to play, and when to go home. Pavlov's bell—day in and day out—for 12 years! Class starts and then ends 50 minutes later. Who can possibly learn *anything* during these cruel and artificial blocks of time? Just when you've become interested in a lesson, it's time to rush off with the herd to the next class. The whole arrangement is little more than moving cattle from field to field. Hey, another analogy!

No problem! PLAYBOY interviews are known for free-form digressions.

Yes, well I'll try not to abuse the privilege. So, *what* were we talking about? (laughs)

Anyway, the New England educators of the 19th century studied Prussian education and imported it to America. Massachusetts passed the first compulsory attendance law in 1852. Parents who resisted had their children taken from them by the state militia. Barnstable on Cape Cod held out until the 1880s. By 1900 compulsory attendance laws were universal. It is vital to understand that none of this was necessary, as basic literacy was 98% *before* government schools, after which it never exceeded 91%. Just as in Prussia, reading was discouraged. After all, illiteracy is the first and the most effective form of censorship.

Basic literacy had to be maintained until the advent of auditory mass propaganda, the common household radio of the 1930s. After the 1950s, TV did all the speaking, and literacy was thereafter shot to hell.

Anyway, the school year grew longer and longer, from 12 weeks to 10 months. When I was a child, we weren't in school after Memorial Day or before Labor Day. We'll probably see it grow to 11 months if the current bill in Congress passes. As if 10 months of crappy schooling isn't enough! The State has increasingly asserted that your child belongs to them, not to you. This is undiluted Communist and Nazi doctrine.

Tell us something about your own education. Did you go to public or private schools?

I went to both about 50/50. By law the Prussian model still serves as the basis for our schools today, including most of the private ones if they want to receive government money.

Even though my private education was engineered on Prussian lines, it was nonetheless at least twice the quality as the government schools I attended. I give credit to several particular teachers and professors of mine who conscientiously taught me how to think. Fortunately, they appeared in a rather relay form, and I was not long without my next mentor.

So, whatever auspicious mental faculty I am accused to possess (laughs), I owe to these dedicated men and women, most of whom I encountered in private schools. And, because of the perception and finances of my parents, I was not only allowed to, but encouraged to attend private school.

If your private education was nonetheless structured along the Prussian model, and you survived, then how can the same structure really be so detrimental for public school children? I mean, you don't seem visibly harmed by your education.

(laughs) Well, I survived in *spite* of the system, not because of it. Actually, my mother had homeschooled me before *Kindergarten* and I already knew how to read at a second grade level. Both of my parents were avid readers, which sort of rubbed off on me. (laughs) My *Kindergarten* teacher in private school, by the way, was superb—almost Montessorian. I now see what a difference she made.

Had I gone exclusively to government schools, I might not have made it. Too many children don't.

What do you mean "too many children don't"?

Think about it, Tom: You march off to school with your chronological peers, with whom you'll graduate 12 years later. "Class of 2018" is merely Orwellian NewSpeak for "Herd of 2018." If you fail to keep up to the statistical mean, you get sent to "remedial" or "special-ed" classes. You open your books when you're told, you eat when you're told, you pee when you're told, you go home when you're told.

You do everything as a group, and nothing as an individual. You even *shower* together, which is calculated to strip away a child's sense of self and dignity. Even in 7th Grade I thought it was weird. I mean, where else is one forced to bathe in *public*?

Well, in the military, of course.

Right, that *other* bastion of individualism. (laughs) So, are you seeing the bigger picture here, Tom? Government schools are kiddie boot camps designed by one of the most militaristic races in modern history. The parallels are profound. Can you imagine army basic training without the preconditioning of grade school? Wouldn't work. Draftees would be too independent. So, you've got to "sand 'em down" while they're schoolchildren.

You go through metal detectors at the door, and suffer obtrusive searches by the dog-handling drug cops. You're encouraged to snitch on your fellow students, as well as on your own family. Doodle a third

grade picture of a rifle-toting soldier or fighter plane with missiles, and you'll get expelled for "violent tendencies." Same thing if you defend yourself against the schoolyard bully. Fail to intimately describe your dreams, your fears, your aspirations, and they'll call in the school shrink. Become bored or fidgety in class—and who *wouldn't*—and you're sent to Nurse Ritalin or Doctor Prozac.

So, what have you learned after 12 years? That there is no such thing as personal privacy, and that the Bill of Rights died long ago. That private property is whatever the authorities allow. You've learned to "go with the flow" and "not rock the boat" and that you "can't fight City Hall." You've learned that "the needs of the many take precedence over the needs of the few, or the one." You've learned to shut up and do what you're *told*. And if you encounter somebody who *hasn't* learned these things, you turn him in for "suspicious" or "antisocial" behavior.

In short, you have learned to be a slave within a Police State.

Oh, come on now..."slave within a Police State"? Isn't that tilting at hyperbole?

I'll let *you* answer that yourself.

So you believe that we *do* have personal privacy? That the Bill of Rights *is* in effect? That your private property *is* off limits to bureaucrats? That you have a *right* to the fruits of your own labor, and take home 100% of your paycheck? That your individual opinion is heard and respected by the high-thinking throng? That you actually have a *say* in national government? That you can speak your mind without fear of retribution? That nobody will shun you as an "extremist" or turn you in as a "terrorist"? That you're a free man in a free country? Do you actually believe *any* of that? And if you don't, then how can I be "tilting at hyperbole"?

Hmmm. You touch on many issues inherent to the eternal balancing of public and private concerns.

It sounds like you attended government schools! (laughs) Did you?

Well...yes, I did.

It shows. I don't say that to insult you, but since my suspicion was correct, it rather proves my point, doesn't it?

How so?

Because your natural response to my challenge was to defend governmental intrusiveness.

I did not defend governmental intrusiveness.

You did, in two ways. First, by not attacking it, and second by implying that it should exist in counterbalance to private interests.

You did not unreservedly defend an individual's right to his or her own life, which tells me one of two things: Either you don't believe in such a right, or if you do, you feel that you have too much to risk by freely admitting it. So, which is it?

I do not believe that those issues are as clear-cut as you describe, is what I believe. There are many shades of gray.

Gray is more deadly than black or white. Extremism has never killed as well as moderateness.

Please explain.

Black or white opinions are emphatic, and demand an emphatic response. Gray opinions do not, which in turn allows bad gray opinions to flourish when they should be challenged. Sometimes, moderation is called for, but generally it's just chickenshit.

Do you have children, Tom?

Yes, two daughters, 7 and 10.

Where do they go to school?

Uh, at a private school.

Oh, and you placed them there because you believe in *government* schools, right?

Well, ah, the gov—, uh, public schools in our district are not great.

I'm not surprised. They're not really great *anywhere.* They were not designed to educate, but to *indoctrinate.* You can't reform a system which was designed to wither the human mind and spirit. The government schools are doing exactly what they're *supposed* to do.

But you and your wife feel so strongly about quality education for your little girls that you choose to pay *twice* for it since you pay school taxes that you don't use?

I guess that's true.

Gee, Tom, you could move to Wyoming and pay just *once*, not twice.

Do you actually believe that the United States is ready, much less eager, for the kind of sweeping educational reform you propose?

I can't speak for the U.S. Nobody can. We're too large of a country for one opinion on the matter, or on *any* matter for that fact. That is precisely why the 50 States must be allowed to once again run their own affairs. I have never declared that what we have chosen in Wyoming should be *de rigueur* for Massachusetts. But, unfortunately, Massachusetts believes their system to be *de rigueur* for all of us. And, we got it. We have a Prussian Massachusetts system of government schools which mandates conformity at the expense of thinking. That's over with in Wyoming, and we'll put our literacy rates and SAT scores up against any slave school in the nation. Especially those in Massachusetts. (laughs)

I still have difficulty in believing public schools to be as poor as you suggest.

If one judges the tree by its fruit, then public education collapsed about 30 years ago. Clerks cannot count change without the register doing it for them, a third of people today do not know who won World War Two, and *nobody* can properly diagram a sentence. Why, the average *Ph.D.* cannot pass a college entrance exam from 1906! How much more evidence do you need?

Still, aren't you being too harsh on the public schools? They do the best they can with the student material they're given. It's not their fault we have drugs and gang violence.

Bullshit, Tom. It is *precisely* their fault! The socialist government schools don't *reflect* the problems of the outside world—they are *causing* these problems. Why are children into drugs, gangs, and self-mutilation? Why are children exhibiting the social pathologies of prison inmates? Because they *are* prison inmates! There's more freedom at a low-security federal work camp than there is at the local government high school. Children get kidnapped at the age of 5 and sentenced to 12 years of excruciatingly dull and damaging programming. It's a sham, and kids know it. And we're shocked when they *rebel*? Compare Columbine to Attica, and the murderous rampage of Harris and Klebold becomes more understandable.

After 12 years of indoctrination at the obscene expense of awakened minds, most kids have no job prospects beyond McDonalds. Who else can afford to pay a totally unskilled and unthinking employee the current minimum wage of $12.65 an hour? While they're pushing a colorful icon of french fries on the register —because they can't do the math— their *gangsta* pals are laughing at them for even working at all. Running drugs can make more money in a single day than a month of flipping burgers.

The entire socialist agenda has created an unnatural America where children cannot work, and do not want to if they could. And who pays for it? Mom, with her two jobs. She works just to pay the family's *tax* bill, much of it for the local government youth propaganda camp. That's assuming she works. Often she's a ward of the State on food stamps, AFDC, public housing, etc. If the father actually tries to support her and his children, she loses her welfare checks. All this has transformed and ruined our society.

So, don't defend the government schools as being blameless. They're not, not by a long shot. If they had actually *educated* children, we'd today have grown adults with real minds and real futures. If you had taken the children of 1890s parents and put them in today's schools and society, they'd have been horrified and livid with the result.

Even the liberals are finally getting concerned.

How so?

Well, I have a comic actor friend in Hollywood who is quite well known through his stand-up and movie career. Although we vastly differ on political and religious matters, he once commented that it was absolutely criminal that public schools were such cesspools of gang violence, drugs, and apathy. He said that the issue totally transcended any political sensitivities, and that our schools were not tranquil havens for real learning was a national outrage. I was quite stunned by Rick's intense opinion, and wholeheartedly agreed with him.

We are currently digging the grave of government education in Wyoming. Within two years we will have achieved separation of school and state. Education will at last revert to being a family matter, not a government one.

The government teachers, however, are howling like scalded banshees. You never heard such caterwauling! I ask them why they are worried about private sector competition if their government schools are so good? They've no answer for that. They're like Yugo salesmen squealing about the new VW dealership going in across the street. Yugo salesmen who secretly drive VWs.

What do you mean?

That many government teachers send *their* children to private schools. In Chicago 40% do, and in D.C. 90% do. It's just like Congress having exempted themselves from their own Social Security creature and enjoying a fully-funded private scheme. Government employees should be required to live under their *own* programs.

Private schools are well and good for those families who can afford them, but what about poor families? Is it fair that they have no option but public education?

I don't buy that, Tom. People have an amazing knack for affording that which is important to them. I've seen so-called "poor" people with a DVD collection to rival my own. Satellite dishes and big-screen TVs in every mobile home. Poor people in America drive better cars than do wealthy people in many countries. If education is important, they will find a way to pay for it.

But what about those living on a fixed income?

Yes, well, who *fixed* it? Money comes from other people, who spend it only for perceived value. Why have a *fixed* perceived value? *Anybody* can increase their value to others. Instead of spending over 30 hours a week watching TV as a sedative, why not find some productive work? Learn a foreign language from library teaching tapes? Learn a skill?

But why should innocent children be denied the best education just because they were born to low-income parents?

And children born to wealthy parents have an *unfair* advantage? It's an advantage, but not an unfair one. Is it fair that low-income parents were born in America? Go visit the Third World and you'll see some *really* low-income families. It's not a matter of "fairness." Look, as human beings who can learn from history, we are capable of not making the mistakes of others, if we choose not to. This has been the backdrop of Western culture. Observe, learn, progress, *ad infinitum.*

My parents and my wife's parents worked hard, and they worked smart. They taught us to do the same, and we did. My wife and I looked for a mate with the same values and work ethics in order to further that through our children. A family's history—wealth or poverty—is not accidental, it is cumulative. It is mostly a result of choice, of sequential programming.

How much of all this is Nature and how much is Nurture? Nobody knows exactly, however *both* can be skewed in a family's favor. Over time, enough quality Nurture will improve Nature. It takes conscious effort and constant work, because the default is to remain lazy and stupid. Those who

work hard and smart deserve to reap the benefits, which pass on to their children. That is not "unfair." That is Life.

If low-income families are not spending more time at the library than in front of the TV, then they are dooming their children to poverty. Being broke is a state of finances. Being poor is a state of *mind.* It is poor *thinking* which causes poverty, and government schools are the academies of ignorance. They are programming the masses to fail, and they are doing so on purpose.

But if the poor cannot yet afford private schools, what can they do?

Homeschool, of course. Even single mothers on welfare can afford to homeschool.

You are a strong supporter of homeschooling. Why?

First of all, it is the *right* of the parents. Even though the motto of UNICEF is *"Every child is our child,"* and even though Hillary Rodham Clinton believes that *"There is no such thing as other people's children,"* children are *not* the property of the State.

Secondly, homeschoolers consistently test in the 85th percentile—at a *tenth* of the cost of government schools. How the NEA can bitch about homeschooling with those results just astounds me.

Until America demands a separation of school and state, the private schools must operate at a severe disadvantage. Even though they do a better job at less than half the cost, parents are still forced to first fund the government schools. Those parents who cannot afford private schools have largely turned to homeschooling because it's affordable and it's effective.

An immigrant family from Honduras moved to Riverton, Wyoming about 15 years ago. Their homeschooled daughter just won the National Spelling Bee. In fact, homeschoolers have won it sixteen times in the past twenty years. It's wonderfully embarrassing! (laughs)

Columnist Vin Suprynowicz put it well. He once wrote that every experiment needs a control group. Regarding gun ownership and the daily bearing of arms, Vermont and Alaska are the control group for D.C. and New York City.

For the government schools, the control group is the homeschoolers. "Amateur" housewives are—regardless of their race, income, and even educational level—teaching their children better than the "professionals." By the 7th Grade, homeschoolers are two years ahead, and the NEA and AFT are going bat guano over this.

The homeschooling movement has saved a large remnant of children from the zombie academies and their dangerous environments. These several million children are the seed corn of the future—seed corn which *otherwise* would have been consumed, leaving us to starve years ago.

What about homeschoolers' lack of socialization?

Oh, you mean their lack of odd clothes, tatoos, and body piercings? That they don't act like prison inmates? (laughs) That "lack of socialization" is a myth. Homeschoolers are highly involved in many things, such as scouting, church, sports, field trips, camping, gymnastics, etc. They're not missing out, and university studies have proven that.

Although there are no easy answers, the one unimpeachable fact is that *parents* generally know what's best for their own children. The only disagreement will come from those who want to cleave children from their families and grind out every spark of individual thought. I would rather see children taught to be Socialists by their homeschooling parents, than children taught to be *laissez-faire* capitalists by government schools. Although either case is pretty far-fetched, that's how deep my conviction on this goes.

What do you consider the most outrageous thing about government schools?

That every school system today has its own "Dr. Mengele" ready and eager to forcibly prescribe some very sophisticated and dangerous brain-chemical altering drugs, such as Ritalin or Prozac. Pot would be less harmful. Not even prison inmates are drugged at the 30% rate of our schoolchildren.

Many so-called "ADD" or "hyperactive" children are simply bored and frustrated by their cud-chewing environment. I know I was! I believe that the current biointrusions on our schoolchildren will someday be looked upon with the horror that we now view ancient bloodletting.

Here is a statistic the NEA won't tell you: Over 90% of all infamous killer kids were taking, or had been recently taking, some form of government prescribed brain-chemical altering drug. Kip Kinkel had been on Prozac, for example. Guns are *not* the problem. Damaged kids are the problem, and it is the government school system which is doing the damage. Has anybody ever noticed that mass shootings never seem to occur in private or parochial schools?

What about the rights of parents who wish to keep their children in the current school system?

You're mixing what are actually two separate issues. If some parents desire Prussian-style education, then that's their right. They can start up a private school under that format if they wish. Nobody is stopping them.

However, no parent has the right to force childless strangers at gunpoint to pay for schools, Prussian or not.

When you say "at gunpoint" are you speaking of taxes?

Well of *course*! Quit paying taxes and obese, D-student, pistol-packing agents of the State will eventually show up at your door. If you resist, they will evict you. Resist eviction, and they will kill you. Don't you know that all taxes are implicitly collected by threat of a gun? Pay or die. This is a cold, hard fact that Americans refuse to face. But, Tom, no purpose of government is so important as to justify making citizens homeless or dead.

No tax collector has ever put a gun to my head to collect my taxes.

I don't dispute that. However, you've been trained by the government to pay without a fuss—so, you

do. (laughs) But haven't you ever resented some use of your tax dollars that you wish you could opt out of? Some U.S. military operation overseas, perhaps?

Only about three or four times a day.

Well, the cost of government is public knowledge. Why didn't you calculate what percentage it constituted of your income taxes and refuse to pay it on explicitly moral grounds? Even if it amounted to only $14?

My share of it wouldn't likely be worth the trouble.

The trouble of calculating the amount, or the trouble of standing up for your belief?

Probably both.

Well, then you help make my point for me. We suffer under a large central government which nips away at us one bite at a time, and we're too cowed to even quantify the injury, much less protest!

What if *nobody* were required to pay taxes? Who would pay then?

If we truly *desired* what we were paying for in taxes, then no coercion would really be necessary? In the free-market, we pay for a movie rather than sneaking in. We pay for a dinner rather than sneaking out. Why can't government compete for its resources like everybody else? Because folks don't like what the government is selling! (laughs)

No, taxes are a form of robbery to fund something that the victim would not purchase voluntarily. And to top it off, the thief proclaims that he is robbing you for your own good! I stand by our right to be governed solely by our informed consent. That is at the heart of libertarian politics.

This tired, old notion that nothing would get done but for government and taxes is horseshit. People want roads and schools and they will find some way to pay for them in the private sector.

I don't want to force anybody to be free, yet many Americans would force me to be a slave on their Washington, D.C. plantation—if they could. It reeks of closed-shop unionism. Join or else. They should have the decency to let others live their *own* adult lives as they see fit.

Such rugged individualism comes easy for a man of your race and upbringing, but it hardly seems appropriate for those disadvantaged members of our society.

Well, men of my "race and upbringing" are at the helm of the socialist ship of state, so why didn't I go *that* direction?

Still, you can't deny that libertarianism makes much more sense for a white, wealthy entrepreneur than for a crippled minority.

Oh, which crippled minority do you mean?

I don't follow you.

Well, do you mean a crippled mi-

nority who has maintained his personal dignity and *works* for an honest living, or a crippled minority who blames the world for his condition and *votes* for his government check?

Uh, well...

Right. You see, it has nothing to do with race, education, or handicap. It has everything to do with *character*.

I know several wealthy, white businessmen so venal and conniving that I would not take their personal check. Conversely, I know a black woman in Sheridan with MS who founded what is now a thriving Internet biz and is one of the most honorable and industrious people I know.

Those with the mentality of a master or slave or thief—whatever their race or condition—*need* a socialist state. Those who value private property and hard work—whatever their race or condition—only wish to be left alone, and Wyoming is America's haven for them. They're long overdue for a haven. Today, they have one! We've proven that over the past two and a half years.

And we're not through yet. Freedom is always unfinished business.

Thank you again Governor Preston for this second interview. It's always interesting.

And for me, too. We're still waiting for you to visit us in Wyoming.

It's looking more and more inviting all the time.

* * * * * * *

For about 16,000 Wyoming Democrats in the southern counties, the January education initiatives were the last straw. Politically neutered, they had no choice but to pack up and leave for more hospitable states such as Washington, Colorado, and Oregon.

They were more than replaced by the 22,000 libertarians who eagerly moved to the nation's sole beacon of liberty. During what was clearly a very deep national depression, only Wyoming had any vitality and promise.

Meanwhile, the NEA and the AFT spend $14,000,000 in their propaganda campaign to derail Wyoming school privatization. If the public schools are abolished, children won't learn to read or perform simple math, the teachers' unions bellow. *"They're barely learning math or reading in the public schools now!"* was the countering opinion of most Wyomingites, who saw through the hysterical charges and threats.

Cheyenne, Wyoming   19 April 2017

Preston glances up at the sound of Tom Parks entering his office with a rictus of grief on his face. He's never seen his assistant and friend so shocked.

"Tom, what's wrong? Is it *Molly*?" asks Preston softly.

"No, sir, my wife's fine." He collects himself for a several seconds and then says, "Governor, we just got word from Washington."

Preston frowns. "Oh, hell. What have they done *now*?"

Tom's eyes tear up as he says, "Phil Miles has been found dead."

"*What?*"

"Yes, sir, I'm sorry. At the National Arboretum, where he went to see the azaleas in bloom. An alleged suicide, but it looks like he was VF'ed. Vince Fostered. Even the *Post* is describing the scene as 'suspicious.'"

Swearing under his breath, Preston stands briskly and leans on his desk. He shakes his head and says, "They finally caught on to him Tom. I told him not to contact us for a while, but they caught on to him and killed him. On the anniversary of Concord and Lexington, as a big *'Fuck You!'* Bastards!"

He sighs deeply and sits back down, deflated. "Tom, the privatization of our schools has just suffered its first battlefield KIA. We *must* see this thing though, for our children. And for Phillip Roland Miles. He believed so much in what we are doing, and"—Preston falters—"and he didn't even *live* here!"

The Governor drops his grieving head in his hands and sobs.

* * * * * * *

Preston slid into a black funk for nearly two weeks. Only when James, Jr. announced that his girlfriend Katherine had accepted his marriage proposal did Preston snap out of it. Katherine, a concert stage classical guitarist was already so much part of the Preston family that James and Juliette had considered her like a second daughter for nearly a year. Hanna adored her like a big sister. James, Jr.'s engagement was the only bright spot in his dad's life for months, until the August election.

Douglas, Wyoming   June 2017
Local Laissez-Faire Party members welcome their newest member, Douglas Bleth, formerly the SAC of the Casper FBI Field Office. Bleth retired early from the Bureau at a drastic cut in pension benefits because he *"could no longer in good conscience remain employed by an organization with such a history of violating not only its own internal policy and guidelines, but the Bill of Rights and the US Constitution."* The obvious murder of Phillip Miles, emblematic of Washington's insane lust for power, had been the last straw for Douglas Bleth.

Governor Preston sends him a warm note of congratulations, commending him for demonstrating *"superb ethics and a deep love of country."*

Wyoming Special Election   August 2017
On the ballot are three proposed amendments:

"Constitutional Amendment A: To repeal the following language from Article 21, section 23:

> *The following article [sections] shall be irrevocable without the consent of the United States and the people of this state:"*

"Constitutional Amendment B: To repeal Article 21, section 28:

> *The legislature shall make laws for the establishment and maintenance of systems of public schools which shall be open to all children of the state and free from sectarian control."*

"and Article 7, section 1:

> *The legislature shall provide for the establishment and maintenance of a complete and uniform system of public instruction, embracing free elementary schools of every needed kind and grade, a university with such technical and professional departments as the public good may require and the means of the state allow, and such other institutions as may be necessary."*

"Constitutional Amendment C:

> *Neither shall the state, nor any county, city or town, assess, levy, impose, or collect any sales or ad valorem tax on any homestead real estate or improvements thereof."*

C passes by an 84% majority. B passes by a 57% majority. A passes by a 62% majority. The voters of Wyoming choose to privatize education.

* * * * * * *

The only freedom which deserves the name is that of pursuing our own good, in our own way, so long as we do not attempt to deprive others of theirs, or impede their efforts to obtain it.
—John Stuart Mill

Cheyenne, Wyoming
Federal District Court   September 2017

Several organizations, such as the NEA, AFT, and other public school teachers' unions, sued the State of Wyoming. If victorious they would be entitled to, under the *Equal Access to Justice Act* of 1980, recovery of all legal expenses because they allegedly advanced a policy inherent to public interest legislation on behalf of a significant class of persons. Such is known as the *"private attorney general"* concept.

This had been expected by Preston's team.

After outlining the history of private education in America, its unlawful and unconstitutional usurpation by state and federal government, and the manifest failure of government schools to adequately educate the children of America, the Wyoming Solicitor General concludes his oral argument.

"There have been historical problems with irrevocable clauses in constitutions. First of all, such have a history of simply being ignored. The federalists ignored Article XIII, Section 1 of the Articles of Confederation which declared the Union to be perpetual and stipulated that any changes must be ratified by all 13 states. In The Federalist #40, *Madison argued that it was ridiculous for 12 states to be stymied by Rhode Island's adherence to the Articles, and* 'dismiss[ed] it without further observation.'

"Secondly, the clause does not specify what is 'consent of the United States' *Does it require a simple majority of Congress? A two-thirds majority? Must the President consent? Hence, the clause is void for vagueness.*

"Thirdly, the clause refers to the United States, a government which conceivably may not function or even exist in the future. Hence, the clause is prima facie conditionally revocable.

"Lastly, the clause itself is inherently contradictory with other language in the document. If the Wyoming constitution may be, according to Article 20, amended by the people, then the people may amend the entire

constitution, including Article 21. *This must be so because the people have the inherent right and power to inaugurate a totally new constitution invalidating the previous one. The US Constitution accomplished precisely this when it invalidated the Articles of Confederation of 1781. Article 21, section 23 violates the ultimately subordinate nature of constitutions to their creators, the people.*

"*In summary, the State of Wyoming believes, and is supported by a majority of the voters, the clause of Article 21, section 23 to be void and with no force or effect. As a matter of constitutional hygiene, some may believe it preferable to repeal the language outright rather than ignore it. This does not change the fact that although the people may indeed, for the public good, delegate some of their authority and selectively restrain themselves with a constitution, they cannot 'throw away the key' of alteration as future events may prescribe that constitution's revision or abolishment. This is hardly novel legal theory. Such is the history of not only our nation and of the states, but of nations throughout time. Article 1, Section 1 of the Wyoming Constitution is abundantly clear on this point:*"

> All power is inherent in the people, and all free governments are founded on their authority, and instituted for their peace, safety and happiness; for the advancement of these ends they have at all times an inalienable and indefeasible right to alter, reform or abolish the government in such manner they may think proper.

"*Last month the people of Wyoming decided the issue. They want a separation of school and state, which had been the original order of things when the United States of America was founded.*

"*The Article 21 sections following section 23 remain, of course, subject to revision or repeal only through the amendment process described in Article 20.*"

2017 USA economic news

A full-blown tax revolt has erupted across America. It was first brought on by young workers resisting the doubled FICA to keep the Social Security system afloat for retiring Baby Boomers, and then was picked up by most other workers.

Retirees assert that their benefits cannot be reduced because they had made plans to rely on them (even though this was originally discouraged back in the 1930s). Workers rightly counter that FICA rates are ruinous and that they cannot afford to house and feed their own families.

The Government, caught in the middle by generations of congressional weakness, cannot directly favor either side.

Debts are *always* paid, if not by the borrower, then by the lender. Though the Baby Boomers did not quite understand it at the time, they had "lent" trillions in Social Security from 1962 to 2015 to be "repaid" by their children and grandchildren.

Their progeny, however, increasingly refuse the "debt."

Thus, the "lenders" must pay since the "borrowers" will not.

The Government has only one solution—the one government's have always resorted to. Inflate the currency into worthless oblivion. It's the only way to force lenders into paying off the Social Security debt.

Yes, Baby Boomers will get their SS checks for the "full" amount. Purchasing power, however, will be another story. Not that any of it should come as a surprise. This tragic script was knowable long in advance. Any debt unpayable by the borrower must be, through default, paid by the lender. Sensible Americans back in the 1980s figured this out, and simply refused to join the racket. They were called "tax protesters."

By 2017, millions of workers had turned into Irwin Schiff, the famous tax protestor.

> *Until they become conscious they will never rebel, and until after they have rebelled they cannot become conscious.*
> —George Orwell, *1984*

Dumped by foreigners and domestically inflated beyond recognition, this is how the intrinsically worthless Federal Reserve Note finally rushed headlong to its long-overdue demise. Whether or not the FRN would take America with it was yet a question to be answered.

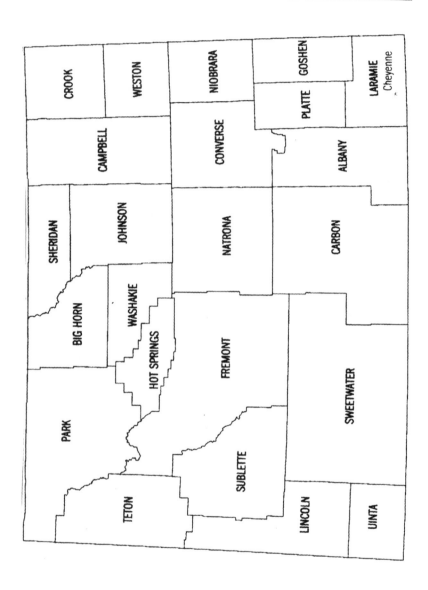

❖ 2018

Tuscon, Arizona   March 2018

After months of investigation by Arizona Attorney General, FBI Special Agent Michael "Feathers" Tipton is arrested for fabricating evidence and witness tampering. The Bureau's Office of Professional Responsibility (OPR) bitterly complains that Tipton is a victim of a vindictive sting operation brought on by allegations of a citizen's rights advocacy group.

Wyoming   Friday, 1 June 2018

The bells of Wyoming public schools ring for the last time. Come September only private education will exist. The Preston administration did not deign to wait for green lights all the way to the US Supreme Court, but enacted privatization with only a Federal District Court favorable ruling. The matter had been instantly appealed to the 10th Circuit, and the Wyoming AG ignored an injunction to delay privatization until the appellate ruling. The people, legislature, and supreme court of Wyoming had spoken. If a state cherishes its internal prerogatives, then it must exercise them.

The NEA *et al* were furious but could not persuade the Government to step in with force against such solidarity. Officials in Washington discounted the Wyoming school privatization as a sterile fluke which no other state had the interest or temerity in duplicating. It was Wyoming's first real constitutional challenge of federalism. D.C. blinked and the entire country knew it. The public school divestiture went ahead as scheduled back in 2016.

Nearly 20% of the the public school teachers had not been rehired. The axe had fallen on those who could not effectively teach, or were univerally disliked by students and parents. The purification process of the free-market had begun. It came as a shock to many life-long government employees.

*   *   *   *   *   *   *

I would like people to understand, "Your rights, you will not need them." Rights do not make you free; only by acting free can you become free....

But to fight for the establishment of rights or for recognition of rights by one's government involves tacit subordination to the state.... Thus, the passage of concealed carry permit laws in the United States is an admission that the right to keep and bear arms no longer exists in this country.

...The fundamental question is not what rights do I have, but why may anyone exercise coercive authority over me in the first place? It is coercion, not freedom, which must be justified. If coercion is not legitimate, there is no need for "rights." Arguing "rights" is arguing from an acknowledged and accepted subordinate —unfree—position.

So, your rights, you do not need them! They cannot and will not help you, because no government wishes to recognize them..., and it is fine with the state if you spend your life attempting to compel the state to acknowledge and respect their existence. The question is whether you will act free or how you will use your freedom....

— Jeffery Snyder, Interview by Carlo Stagnaro, 2/8/2001
www.lewrockwell.com/orig2/stagnaro2.html

Wyoming life   2018

Wyoming was bursting with new business activity (beginning with the construction industry for the 40,000+ relocators), which had hugely benefitted from the intrastate digital gold currency. Exchanged via encrypted files on a statewide ethernet, Wyoming was fast creating an insular economy with its own e-currency (called the *Oro*, Spanish for "gold" and a pun on the *Euro*). The *Oro* reduced economic leakage and dependency on the clearly failing FRN "dollar." Being fully backed by gold, the *Oro* was valued at $1/100^{th}$ of an ounce .999 pure. Spot gold is now $3,400, so it takes $34 to equal ₩1.

As in the 1800s, an ounce of gold (a $20 Double Eagle) would buy a nice suit or a good rifle. Today, nothing has really changed. ₩100 (*i.e.,* the same ounce of gold) still buys a nice suit or a good rifle. The relationship between gold and manufactured goods was historically stable because as gold mining became more efficient, so did manufacturing. The equilibrium has remained constant over 150 years, which is the whole point of honest money. Prices are information, and a stable monetary yardstick is required for accurate price information. Only the fiat currencies devalue. As Milton Friedman once wrote, *"Only government can take perfectly good paper, cover it with perfectly good ink, and make the combination worthless."*

The ₩ prices are cerebrally manageable and harkened memories of the late-1960s. A glass of house red is ₩1. A decent firearm, ₩100. A new pickup, ₩6,250. A nice 3/2 home goes for about ₩25,000. These prices seemed "right" to most people, versus the high $ prices due to inflation.

More and more local businesses accepted the *Oro* online (in a system similar to the old PayPal), and at POS smart cards (purchased anonymously, as the prepaid phone cards had been). Wyomingites who still got paid in FRN "dollars" usually converted them to *Oros* as quickly as they could, but given the insular nature of the ₩ it was harder and harder to find other locals willing to sell ₩ for $. (Most newcomers converted their shrinking FRNs to bullion before their move.) Many people predicted that the ₩ would totally crowd out the $ within five years. Gold/₩ and ₩/gold conversions are charged a 0.5% fee, and every county seat has a "₩ Exchange Center." (There are no fees for ₩/₩ transactions.) The *OroCorp* gold was secured throughout Wyoming amongst several secret alpine vaults.

Besides smart cards there were also ₩ bills, beautifully printed on sheets of rhodium Mylar. The durable synthetic material shines like gold in the light. The obverse side has denomination-different holographic scenes of outdoor Wyoming life, while the reverse is the "business" side of the bill with a twenty digit bar code serial number (verifiable on the *OroCorp* website) and many other security features. It was deemed by international currency experts as the most counterfeit-proof bill in existence.

Many Wyoming children know of no other currency, and thought only in *Oros*. Not since the 1920s had youngsters grown up with gold money.

The *Oros* are considered so attractive that out-of-state tourists often smuggle out ₩1 bills as souvenirs. Since the bills are issued with a redemption life of only two years, these thousands of eventually invalid ₩1 bills present a profit windfall for *OroCorp*.

Many people originally protested any expiration of the ₩ bills, and it took quite an educational program to explain the difference between money (gold bullion) and currency (₩ bills). While money was certainly tradeable on a daily basis, currency was more convenient. However, when people began to think of currency as *identical* to money, fewer people routinely redeemed their currency "claim tokens" for gold. This has always successfully tempted the gold warehousers ("banks") into issuing more claim tokens than they could honor all at once. Hence, a regularly expiring currency is essential to help prevent this historical fraud.

Also, when currency is hoarded its velocity decreases, which affects the economy. Taken to an extreme over time (*e.g.*, between 1929-1933 when the M3 shrunk dramatically and gold and silver coin could not make up the gap) this can cause a depression. Currency is meant to be *traded*, widely and often. Wyomingites had first to learn that currency is an information system backed by money (*i.e.,* gold or silver) used to deploy human effort. Currency is a product providing a *service*, and as such should have a finite lifespan.

So, the ₩ was made to expire after two years. The month and year of each bill's expiration was clearly printed on both sides, and people carefully checked all bills before accepting them. Wallets were often arranged with the oldest bills in front. Some people refused to accept soon-dead bills, but this was considered bad form if they had over two months of remaining life. However, to get stuck with a "Zorro" (zero + *Oro*) was the object of much joshing.

Sometimes tourists could be convinced to buy them, but usually the careless holder ate the loss. In order not to become surprised by Zorros, they were generally swapped three months out for new ones at the ₩ Exchange Centers.

All this scrutiny and activity seemed like a waste to outsiders, but Wyomingites understood it was an intentional reminder that currency is never money, but only its temporarily tradeable substitute. In this way, Wyomingites never lost sight of what money was—gold bullion coin.

Some Wyomingites wanted the *Oro* backed also by silver, but a bimetallic monetary standard had caused nothing but grief for America. Instead, 40% and 90% US silver coins, as well as .999 ounce generic rounds, found their own free-market price equilibrium with the ₩.

Sometimes, if the customer agreed, ₩ change was made in 90% silver dimes as ₩1 (the price of a cheeseburger) was too large for many transactions. It takes 13.82361 90% dimes to equal an ounce of .999 silver, and the 2018 silver:gold ratio is 22:1. Thus, 304 90% silver dimes equals an ounce of gold, or ₩100. Or, roughly three silver dimes for an ₩1.

A consortium was rumored to be considering the creation of the *Plata*, a silver-backed version of the *Oro*. When *OroCorp*'s CEO was asked about his opinion, he said, *"Why would I mind? Wyoming's a free country!"*

OroCorp had studied the feasibility of coinage down to an ₩ cent (which would buy a piece of bubble gum), but rejected it as cost ineffective. *Oro* smart cards served <₩1 transactions much better.

Federal Reserve officials publicly ignore the Wyoming *Oros* (for fear of igniting a blaze of imitation), but privately they fume. They'd tried to pressure the SEC and other regulatory agencies into shutting down the system as illegal banking, but this was thwarted by the participants' encryption as well as the Wyoming government's noncooperation.

The IRS was furious about the massive income tax evasion inherent to the *Oro* economy, but was as unsuccessful in penetrating the *Oro* database as it was impaneling sympathetic juries. The IRS soon gave up in bitter defeat.

Wyoming General Election   November 2018

The last batch of organized Tier 5 libertarian relocators (originally planned to maintain the previous four years of political gains) had turned out to be unnecessary. Libertarians were pouring into Wyoming without needing to be organized. The results from 2014 were the watershed. Most of the hard work had been done, and the state had proven herself the only real lifeboat.

James Preston was easily reelected, along with the libertarian county governments. Even the Democratic base of Sweetwater, Carbon, and Albany was evaporating like snow in June.

❖ 2019

When the Cambrian measures were forming,
They promised perpetual peace.
They swore, if we gave up our weapons,
That the wars of the tribes would cease.
But when we disarmed, They enslaved us,
And delivered us bound to our foe,
And the Gods of the Copybook Headings,
Said: "Stick to the devil you know."
— Kipling, 1919

The White House   January 2019

President Connor opens a smart leather folder and begins to scan his PDB (Presidential Daily Brief). After he reads the paragraph on Wyoming, he turns to his Chief of Staff and says, "If I had any doubt that those people are nuts, I don't any more. This year they plan on,"—Connor returns to his PDB—"banning civil forfeitures, approving medical marijuana and hemp crops, eliminating drug sentences, breaking the Wyoming bar association, and convening independent grand juries to investigate federal officials."

"Yes, sir, and that's just what we know about so far," confirms Sowers. "There's also a rumor of a poll tax, but we haven't confirmed that yet."

President Connor sits there, his head a bobbing cork in a sea of quiet fury. "So, having their own damn schools, money, and airline wasn't enough? They have to push us even further! Well, the patience of this administration is not endless! I'm tired of the least populated state in the Union thumbing its nose at us! Just like Rhode Island back in the 1780s, not sending delegates to the Philadelphia Convention, rejecting the Constitution by popular vote, and then boycotting the Union until 1790."

"But Rhode Island eventually *did* join, Mr. President."

Connor's gaze is unfocused off into the distance. "Yeah, they joined all right . . . after an incredible amount of pressure."

Wyoming General Session   February 2019

President Connor's intel was correct. The legislature approved several bills regarding drug decriminalization, which were signed into law by Gov. Preston. But even more stunning was the following:

> *RESOLVED, that the House and Senate of the State of Wyoming, seeking to reinstitute the original right of counsel under the Sixth Amendment to the Constitution for the United States of America, hereby declares that a criminal or civil defendant in a Wyoming state, county, or municipal proceeding has the right to choose any lay person as counsel for both assistance and representation, and no license of lay persons shall be required for their practice of law.*

The Wyoming Bar Association issued a blistering response, claiming that the very system of justice was threatened by swarms of self-styled "counselors" who would not only make a mockery of the courts but would also jeopardize their clients. The Bar claimed that many innocent people would be convicted due to uneducated and inexperienced representation, and thus immediately challenged the bill in supreme court.

The Bar did not, however, address the obvious counterargument: that it was the *defendant's* life and property on the line, and thus up to him to choose his own counsel, bar-certified or not. If certified attorneys were so much better than laymen, then they'd have nothing to worry about in this new free market, would they?

* * * * * * *

Officials from the NEA taunted the ABA with, "If you attorneys had better protected us teachers, then this wouldn't have happened to *you!*"

* * * * * * *

By summer most of the national trade schools and colleges offered lawyering associates degrees in Wyoming. Courses included, Fourth Amendment Issues, Discovery, Rules of Evidence, Direct and Cross Examination, Closing Arguments, Jury Nullification, and so forth. Thousands of applicants swamped the first semester. Many of them were not planning on a career, but simply wanted to be able to competently represent themselves, or a friend or family member in court if ever necessary.

It was considered within the broad realm of self-defense.

* * * * * * *

Very quickly, many poor/mediocre bar-certified attorneys were squeezed out of practice by hundreds of brilliant laymen who always wanted to practice law but couldn't afford an expensive accredited law university.

One Rawlins city prosecutor lost his case to a layman. He later moaned, "I graduate with honors from the University of Chicago, have been practicing law for twelve years, and I get beat by some woman from *DeVry* in her very first trial!"

Washington, D.C.   May 2019

Congress passes the *Safe Streets and Neighborhoods Act* which requires all *"assault weapons"* (which had supposedly been *NFA* registered under the *Dangerous Weapons Act* of 2007) to be turned in for a $500 compensation. Owners have 90 days to comply, or face a mandatory 10-year prison term with all of their firearms confiscated.

The Government immediately authorizes a study to help recognize in advance Americans likely to resist the *SSNA*. The study analyzes the psychological profiles of those who helped the Jews during the Holocaust. It finds that they shared three characteristics:

❶   Had a spirit of adventure
❷   Intensely identified with a parent of high moral standard
❸   Did *not* identify closely with social groups (non-team player)

All FBI field agents are given an abridged copy of the study to better target possibly dissident gun owners.

* * * * * * *

There is much mewling about the harsh terms of the *SSNA*, but since far too many gun owners had foolishly registered their battle carbines and rifles (or lived in states without private sale transactions, which made ownership transparent to the databases), little could be done. There was no local sanctuary, no place to go, nowhere to hide.

Except in Wyoming.

Wyoming   Summer 2019

Several million gun owners take their summer vacation in the Cowboy State to sell their soon banned rifles, like London children relocated to the countryside during the Blitz. Huge purchasing depots are set up off the Interstates just inside the Wyoming borders at Evanston, Cheyenne, Sundance, and Ranchester. Sellers are encouraged to also bring any related cases, shooting gear, magazines, accessories, ammo, and reloading equipment.

countryside during the Blitz. Huge purchasing depots are set up off the Interstates just inside the Wyoming borders at Evanston, Cheyenne, Sundance, and Ranchester. Sellers are encouraged to also bring any related cases, shooting gear, magazines, accessories, ammo, and reloading equipment.

I-25 south of Cheyenne is backed up for twelve miles. The Colorado State Patrol and the ATF erected a northbound lane checkpoint to ensnare front range Denverites eager to offload their rifles before the ban. A similar checkpoint is operated by the UHP and ATF on I-80 outside of Salt Lake City. Nebraska wanted checkpoints, but didn't have the resources.

Idaho, Montana, and South Dakota do not demean themselves with such checkpoints.

The smart travelers know to put their locked cased guns in the *trunk*, refuse to answer questions or consent to vehicular searches, and arrive via secondary routes. These folks make it to Wyoming. Other travelers do not. They are charged with illegal gun trafficking and have their firearms confiscated (as well as their cars under civil forfeiture laws).

Once in Wyoming, there is a final hurdle to clear. Because federal law prohibits the interstate private sale of guns, these out-of-staters are asked to sign a statement that they are *"present in Wyoming with the intention of making a home here."* Under USC Title 18 provisions this gives them Wyoming residency with respect to the federal gun laws regulating transfers.

For all, the trip is arduous. They have to pack up their prized possessions, make it through a law enforcement gauntlet, and then muster up the final will to actually make the sale. As they bitterly sell their HK91s and FALs and M14s—as they weepingly relinquish the WW2 and Korea M1 Garands of their deceased warrior fathers—they are consoled by the assurance that these cherished instruments of war, sacrifice, and liberty will never end up in a federal smelter or hydraulic press.

Most take cash, but many accept *OroCorp* account credits in ₩, hoping to someday return for good. Nearly 60,000 stay behind—political refugees happily living armed in tents, campers, and RVs—all vowing to sell their homes back in "Occupied Territory."

Cheyenne, Wyoming   August 2019

"Governor, that report you asked for is ready. The one on the forced urbanization of the rural West."

Preston smiles tiredly. "Oh, right. Thanks. I can't say I've been looking forward to reading this, but we must stay informed of our antagonists' intentions."

* * * * * * *

"RURAL CLEANSING"

[Do the] *"Wild Earth" and the "Wildlands Project" advocate the end of industrial civilization? Most assuredly. Everything civilized must go!*
   — John Davis, Editor of *Wild Earth*, 1992

Isn't it the only hope for the planet that the industrialized civilizations collapse? Isn't it our responsibility to bring that about?
   — Maurice Strong, interview with Jim Johnston for the *British Columbia Report*, 18 May 1992, Vol.3/#37/p.22

(The liberal cultural revolution) is not willing to live and let live... Cheyenne, Wyoming, can tolerate the existence of New York City and Los Angeles, but L.A. and New York City can't abide knowing that, out there on the steppes and in the mountains of the Great American Desert, the other America is leading an existence that fits its own particular circumstances, customs, and preferences.
   — Chilton Williamson, Jr., "Democracy and the Art of Handloading," *Chronicles*, Feb 2001

rural cleansing — to remove farm and ranch land from production by spurious ecological or environmental decree

Endangered Species Act (ESA) — legislation which protects plants and animals over human beings

toad throwing — using the US Dept. of Fish & Wildlife to harass a neighbor by sneaking an "Endangered Species" critter onto his property

God Squad — the Endangered Species Committee, a panel made up of seven cabinet-level officials convened to weigh the economic and social costs against risks of extinction, with override power of ESA provisions

   After two generations of a largely successful war on the American people, the US Government (USG) is now targeting the last holdouts: rural citizens. Having won the battles of economics, finance, politics, travel, privacy, communication, and education, the two final hills for the USG to conquer are the family farm and the country ranch.

   Where else is an American beyond daily police control? Where else is an American outside the 24 hour surveillance of omniscient databanks and ubiquitous cameras? Where else is an American generally free to do whatever he pleases? Where else can an American achieve physical self-sufficiency in food, shelter, and energy, and thus slough off the inherent bondage of the modern interdependent society? Where else can an American easily avoid the mindless pablum of television? Where else can an American raise his family as he sees fit, thus transmitting generational software (*i.e.,* values, morals, work ethic, etc.) in spite of government and media programming efforts?

> *There's nothing like the opportunity for children when they're being raised, learning to be around cattle and do chores, to be around wood and land and iron at a young age, learning to work. That's probably the biggest reason that we stay in the ranching business.*
>
> *That's why I want my grandkids around. ...It's pretty hard for a government agent to pull the wool over someone's eyes that's ever had to deal with fire and rain and wind and snow and all the other elements. My kids started working right at my side fighting fires, moving cattle at 11 or 12 years old....*
>
> *You don't just feed cows or chickens; you have to feed 'em right or they don't produce, and that's a discipline that's learned, that's what they learn very young. Not like a bunch of bureaucrats who live in an imaginary, abstract world. We have to live in the real world. If we don't adhere to and work with nature, we get cold pretty danged fast. Someone who works for the government because they've got a degree might get away with ignoring the truth, but anyone in the ranching business, we haven't been here for four generations because we ignored the truth and didn't work with nature.*

—from *The Ballad of Carl Drega* (2002), p. 169

The rural American, especially those on their own family farm and ranch, is the USG's final, and most threatening, enemy. The city folk have long since been co-opted, and even the libertarian holdouts are implicitly at government's mercy due to the fragility of urban life. Cut off electricity, food, or water for any extended period and Ayn Rand herself would have quickly caved from her 6th floor 34th Street Manhattan apartment.

The country folk, however, have yet to be conquered. They are the most threatening. What other Americans can thumb their nose at government and urban socialism and say, *"No thanks! We don't need you!"* Those outside of the tax/welfare circuitry are enemies to socialism because they have no vested interest in the redistribution/regulatory scheme. An urban "black marketeer" is bad enough in the eyes of government, but those engaged in the *rural* underground (*i.e.,* free) economy are many times more of a threat because of their lifestyle's self-sufficiency and privacy.

Since is it not cost-effective to monitor rural Americans individually, and since it cannot be done collectively, the solution is to urbanize them. From farm to public housing, from ranch to brick tenement, the USG must herd these mustangs off their land and into the city corrals where all broken horses belong. Obviously, they will not go willingly or quietly. So, the USG must "yank the rug out from under them." The "rug" is the land itself. This actually began during the early 1960s:

> In 1962, the Committee for Economic Development comprised approximately seventy-five of the nation's most powerful corporate executives. They represented not only the food industry but also oil and gas, insurance, investment and retail industries. Almost all groups that stood to gain from [farm] consolidation were represented on that committee. Their report ("An Adaptive Program for Agriculture") outlined a plan to eliminate farmers and farms. It was detailed and well thought out.
>
> ...[A]s early as 1964, congressmen were being told by industry giants like Pillsbury, Swift, General Foods, and Campbell Soup that the biggest problem in agriculture was too many farmers.
>
> — Joel Dyer, *Harvest of Rage: Why Oklahoma Is Only the Beginning* (1996)

Noting that farm children who went off to college rarely returned to the family farm, programs were instituted to send farm kids to college. As expected, they did not return. After a generation, a handful of agro-conglomerates had generally driven America's small farmers off their land by paying them less for their produce than the cost of growing it, thus throwing farmers into the welcoming clutches of bankers. Once mortgages had been assumed, foreclosures were only a matter of time given the artificial boom/bust cycles of the Federal Reserve. The Department of Agriculture helpfully supplied its Form A0109 farmland census data to the corporate raiders.

In 2019 you can count on *one hand* the number of multinational companies who control the world's grain supply. Three companies control over 80% of America's beef-packing market. Less than ten corporations control nearly all of our packaged food. The desired consolidation of America's farms into "agribusiness" had been achieved. It's been done only once before in history: during Stalin's reign with the 1930s "dekulakization" of independent small farmers and agricultural collectivization.

Farmers have gone from a majority to a minority to a curiosity. Since 1991, their leading cause of violent death is no longer accidents, but suicide.

By the 1980s, however, a mini-revolution in food and farming was flourishing: organic fruits, vegetables, and meats. In the nation's latest population migration, people were forsaking the madness of the cities and seeking small acreages of paradise in the country—especially in the West. By the late

1990s, the land rights movement (comprised of ranchers, farmers, and other rural folk) had become a major thorn in the globalists' hide.

What we're seeing in 2019 is a multi-pronged attack using the Endangered Species Act, the UN's "Rewilding" and "Biosphere Reserves" and "World Heritage" and "anti-desertification" programs, etc. You'll notice that the federal land grab under environmental pretense is a *western* phenomenon, perpetrated by Eastern Socialists. These are people who shriek at our mining, logging, hunting, fishing, and cattle grazing, yet who have long ago covered their own states with asphalt and concrete. What rampant hypocrisy!

One possible legal defense

We must challenge the *jurisdiction* of these land regulations. The two relevant clauses in the Constitution are:

> *To exercise exclusive legislation in all cases whatsoever,....over all places purchased by the consent of the legislature of the state in which the same shall be for the erection of forts, magazines, arsenals, dockyards, and other needful buildings;...*
> — Article I, Section 8, Clause 17 of the Constitution

> *The Congress shall have power to dispose of and make all needful rules and regulations respecting the territory or other property belonging to the United States [government];...*
> — Article IV, Section 3, Clause 2 of the Constitution

Fully one-third of America's land mass is being policed by the feds as if such were *"the territory or other property belonging to the United States"* government under Article IV, Section 3, Clause 2 of the Constitution. We're talking 28% of Montana, 49% of Wyoming, 50% of California, 63% of Idaho, 68% of Utah, and 87% of Nevada!

However, for the USG to regulate the use or disposal of property, the USG must be the *owner* of that property. It does not own the West.

IV:3:2 of the Constitution refers to *"territory,"* which is what the West was before statehood. Formerly owned by Great Britain, the *"Western territory"* was ceded to the Union after the Revolutionary War and was under the jurisdiction of the USG until western statehood. (See *The Federalist* #7 and #43.) Also under US jurisdiction after the War was the *"district of Vermont"* which was recognized as an independent republic (as were Texas and Hawaii) until becoming the 14th state in 1791.

The *"Western territory"* was carved up into singular territories in the 1860's. Idaho was a *"territory"* from 1863 until 1890. Montana was a *"terri-*

tory" from 1864 until 1889. Wyoming was a *"territory"* from 1868 until 1890. Arizona was a *"territory"* until 1912. When a *"territory"* becomes a state, it is no longer under the federal jurisdiction of IV:3:2. Once the western territories became states, all that land previously controlled by the feds should have legally gone to the states. The fact that the USG does not abide by this was the basis for several lawsuits by both individuals and states (*e.g.*, *U.S. v. Haught* in federal district court in Phoenix). The original 13 colonies got to *keep* their land when they became states, and under the "equal footing" doctrine so should the rest of the states.

If a state, by consent of its legislature, wishes to sell some of its land to the USG, it may—and that federal property is then under the exclusive jurisdiction of Congress under I:8:17 of the Constitution. But unless and until a state sells land to the USG, it still belongs to the state.

So, there are only two ways the feds may lawfully exercise criminal jurisdiction over USA property: **1)** If it is part of a US territory or protectorate (before becoming a state), or **2)** if it is property sold by a state to the USG. Look at IV:3:2 this way: chronologically in between *"territory"* and *"property"* is one of the 50 states. Forcing the USG to recognize this without having to resort to arms is the present and future dilemma of the American West.

> *The people of the West are being pushed to the limit. The surprise is not that they are finally talking about taking up arms to defend their way of life...but that they have waited so long.*
> — Vin Suprynowicz, *The Ballad of Carl Drega* (2002), p. 138

> *War is an ugly thing, but not the ugliest of things; the decayed and degraded state of moral and patriotic feeling which thinks that nothing is worth war is much worse. A man who has nothing for which he is willing to fight; nothing he cares more about than his own personal safety; is a miserable creature who has no chance of being free unless made and kept so by the exertions of better men than himself.*
> — John Stuart Mill

Casper, Wyoming   Fall 2019
"Grampa Bill, I heard on TV that our refusal to turn in our battle rifles is Whiskey Rebellion 2. That our actions are calling for federal intervention."

* * * * * * *

> *...It is remarkable how little changed in the nature of conflict and the parameters of political discourse during three decades of Revolutionary upheaval (i.e., between 1765 and 1795). There is lit-*

tle of substance to distinguish the rhetoric, perspectives, ideology, or methods of Tories and British bureaucrats in the earlier period from those of the friends of [federal government] *order thirty years later. There is an ideological identity between many of the suspicions, fears, diagnoses, and prescriptions for the cure of political ill-health in the writings of Thomas Hutchinson, James Otis, George Grenville, and Lord North in the years preceding the Revolution, and those of George Washington, Alexander Hamilton, Fisher Ames, and other Federalists after the war.* (at 227)
— Thomas P. Slaughter, *The Whiskey Rebellion* (1986)

In 1790, Treasury Secretary Alexander Hamilton urged a federal excise tax on the domestic production of spirits.   The grain farmers in western Pennsylvania, a rough and independent lot, didn't much care for this. It hurt their livelihood, and the feds had been little help in stopping the Indian raids. Being on the frontier of the new nation and far from reach of the young federal government, the whiskey-making farmers not only refused to pay the excise tax, they began to assault federal tax collectors who unwisely strayed too far from Philadelphia (the US capital at the time). Then, they coerced federal judges not to preside over excise tax cases. By August 1794, unrest had spread to twenty counties in four states.

Increasingly concerned, Washington and Hamilton decided that it was time for action. They formed a 12,950 man army, marched into western Pennsylvania and quelled the rebellion (although the leaders escaped into the mountains). Their supply line stretched to breaking, Hamilton authorized the impressment of civilian property. Crops and livestock were stolen, and fences were torn down for firewood.

1,500 soldiers under General Daniel Morgan (the famed guerrilla leader who so brilliantly harassed the British during the Revolutionary War) were left behind in Pittsburgh to maintain order until the spring of 1795. They frequently looted and destroyed private property, and roughed up civilians. Through this terror the federal government amply demonstrated its authority and quelled the tax revolt.

* * * * * * *

Bill Russell, now eighty-one years old, says, "Similar events, but different."

"How so?" asks the sixteen year-old.

"The Whiskey Rebellion of 1794 was basically a regional tax revolt. Our situation involves much, much more than that. The federal government is making noises of a military invasion to conquer a peaceful state which refuses to self-disarm in obedience to the *Emerson ruling and the resulting*

Dangerous Weapons Act of 2007 and *Safe Streets and Neighborhoods Act.* In order to disarm us of the most effective hand weapon ever created—the self-loading battle rifle—Washington, D.C. blithely proposes genocide under the guise of Civil War 2."

"But they promise not to confiscate handguns and hunting long guns. All we have to do is give up our AR15s, AKs, M1s, M14s, and FALs."

Russell chuckles. "Yeah, while they keep *theirs,* and more. It's like promising to leave an animal alone after he's been declawed. Oh, but he's allowed to keep his teeth? It's his very claws which keep him safe from predators. To assent to his declawing is suicide. Animals know this and won't permit it. You're forgetting that we've already given up our BARs, M2s, and M16s because of the *National Firearms Act of 1934.* Only time will tell if Wyomingites and Westerners have the survival sense of the average critter."

"What should we do?"

"Our choice is simple: Should we fight *with* our battle rifles, or without them? Do we have a better chance of freedom with them, or without them? Let me put it this way: my elk rifle doesn't protect my elk rifle; my *FAL* protects my elk rifle. Firearms are tools—specific tools for specific tasks. Can liberty be protected solely by hunting weapons? That would be like building a house with a Leatherman multitool—theoretically possible, but very arduous, and therefore never attempted."

"But doesn't our keeping battle rifles invite federal response?"

"No, not at all. There's a faulty hidden premise there."

"Which is what, Grampa?"

"That if self-loading, magazine-fed rifles had not been invented, we would be safe from unilateral disarmament."

"I don't understand."

"Okay. Imagine it's 1919 instead of 2019, and only bolt-action rifles exist. They were the battle rifles of their day. What tyrannical government of 1919 allowed their civilian possession? None. First, they registered and confiscated the Mauser M98 and Lee-Enfield, and then they worked their way through the hunting rifles and shotguns. We're seeing the same progression today, only the feds had to start much later because until 1934 we enjoyed unrestricted ownership of cannons, mortars, and machine guns—and all, somehow, without a crime wave.

"No, the government cannot allow its subjects to be as well armed as their enforcers. That's straight out of Tyranny 101. As Chairman Mao used to say, 'All political power comes from the barrel of a gun.' An armed citizenry means a *balance* of political power *vis-à-vis* the federal government. That was the entire *point* of the 2nd Amendment, which was fully explained in *The Federalist.* The whole purpose of our disarmament is the creation of an unchallengeable police state.

"So, no, my FAL is not a red cape to the federal bull. *Any* gun is. Congress is harping on military-pattern rifles only because they're the most effective remaining firearms at keeping tyranny in check, so it's logical strategy to confiscate them before hunting rifles."

Grandson grins. "So we're not gonna disarm, right?"

Russell lovingly places a weathered hand on the young man's shoulder. "I would bet on it, Son. I wouldn't bet on it."

"Good! They'd come after your FAL that Mr. Krassny used to own."

"That'd be some trophy, wouldn't it? After all the trouble he stirred up for them!" Russell says. "Hey, have I showed it to you lately? I just had some new optics mounted. Can't use the iron sights anymore with my old eyes."

"Awesome! Can we go out back and shoot it?"

"Sure thing, son. You know what you have to do, right?"

Grandson intones, "Load mags, pick up brass, and clean the rifle after."

Russell smiles. "You got it. What a deal, eh? Oh, and I'll bring along something you've never seen."

"What's that?"

"Harold Krassny's war-issue Colt .45."

"*No!*"

"Indeed. When his P-51 got shot down over Occupied Europe, he killed three Germans with it getting back to Allied lines. He gave it to me just before he died back in 2008. When I'm gone, I want you to have them."

"*No way!*"

Russell laughs. "Yep, you. I'd have given them to your father, but we both know he wouldn't appreciate them. He thinks Harold was a cold-blooded murderer responsible by example for over 200 deaths. Carl never understood what it takes to maintain our liberty, but you *do*. Grandson, I want *you* to have the FAL and the Colt, but only if you promise me something."

Grandson is instantly solemn. "Yes, sir, anything."

With great severity Russell says, "These are not just pieces of steel. They're not even just guns. They are sacred relics, son. They were owned by a true American patriot who fought and died for his country. You must promise me right here and now that you will *never*, under any circumstances, surrender them to some gun confiscation squad. Not out of fear, not out of weakness, not out of despair will you ever give them up and dishonor your grandfather and Mr. Krassny. And when you can no longer bear them because of age or infirmity, you will choose a worthy successor. Promise me."

The young man rapidly blinks his tears away. "I promise, Grampa. I will never give them up. They will have to pry them from my dead hands."

It's now Bill Russell's turn to blink away the tears.

* * * * * * *

A patriot must always be ready to defend his country against his government.
— Edward Abbey

Wyoming news   Fall 2019

The Wyoming State Shooting Association (WSSA), a pro-freedom gun organization which sponsors many excellent competitive events, reaches 10,000 members—an historic first. With the help of the WSSA, the state now enjoys nearly as many annual shooting competitions as Switzerland.

The Fuel Cell Energy Corporation, which has led the way for hydrogen production from coal, opens a strip mine in the Powder River Basin of Campbell County. The famous coal seam is enormous: 100' thick, 5 miles wide, and over 50 miles long—enough to last the world for 200 years. Early successful reclamations of strip mines have calmed much of the original environmentalist concern, though residual (and largely unfounded) hysteria remains.

Sergeant First Class Michael Poole of Camp Guernsey demonstrates incomparable style and decorum when he asks Governor Preston for his daughter's hand in marriage. James and Juliette both adore the clean-cut NCO, who wants someday to manage the Preston ranch and have many children with Hanna (who also dreams of a large family).

The Oval Office   Fall 2019

Chief of Staff Bill Sowers is meeting with Connor to update him on the nation's conformity with the *Safe Streets and Neighborhoods Act* and the initial stages of the UN's "Rewilding" program.

"And predictably, sir, compliance is lowest in the South and rural West. Since many of those states do not require gun registration or ownership permits, we have to extrapolate numbers based on ATF Form 4473s.

"Showing practically zero compliance is, of course, Wyoming. In fact, the ATF considers compliance to be less than zero."

Connor frowns. "*Less* than zero? How is *that* possible?"

"Because the few assault weapons that *have* been turned in weren't even worth the $500 compensation. One example was a Chinese-made SKS fused together by rust after being pulled from a pond. *SSNA* did not specify that the guns had to be in working order."

Connor's face grows red as he repeatedly clenches his jaw. "Bill, those people having been rubbing our noses in shit for five years now on the gun control issue. Now, they're making a mockery of our buy-back program designed to save lives!"

Sowers clears his throat and says, "Well, Mr. President, considering that Wyoming has the lowest crime in the country, they probably don't think the *SSNA* makes much sense out there."

Connor glares at Sowers for an eternal second.

"Just trying to understand their mindset, sir," Sowers offers.

"Yeah, well, who *can?* Those people are flat-out *nuts.* I'll bet their compliance with the UN's rewilding directives is also poor to nonexistent."

Sowers reluctantly replies, "Yes, sir, I'm afraid so. The UN has received absolutely none of its requested data on biosphere corridors. Its World Heritage signs at Yellowstone and Devil's Tower are stolen just as soon as they're replaced. UN personnel report that they are rarely served food in local restaurants, are refused lodging, and have their tires slashed almost daily. Several have been beaten. Most of them won't return without armed escorts."

"Armed escorts for UN people snooping around Wyoming?" reflects the President. "Yeah, *that* would really cause some shit out there! The Smurfs are lucky they haven't been shot at already."

Sowers nods in agreement. "Yes, sir, Preston's administration has really sounded the bell on the UN program. They even published that 'Rural Cleansing' report which—"

"—has gotten the entire West up in arms, yes, I know," finishes Connor. "The timing for another sagebrush rebellion couldn't be worse with next year's general election. Many Congressmen are getting skittish."

Sowers raises his eyebrows, remembering something. "Oh, while we're on the subject of congressmen, I have a copy of a Wyoming report on legislative reform that is being widely circulated. It makes for some, uh, well, interesting reading. Those people seem to be only just getting started."

* * * * * * *

President Connor is a voracious reader, and takes the report[1] to his study after the work day. As much though he loathes reading hard-core libertarian material, he vowed never to be caught surprised by anything the Wyoming crowd came up with.

* * * * * * *

President Connor puts down "Revising Democracy" and rubs his tired eyes. *Just when I thought they'd run out of daffy ideas!* He can tell that he will not easily fall asleep tonight. Thoughts of how to put Wyoming back in its place are already swimming through his mind.

---

1   "Revising Democracy" is reproduced in the Appendix at pages 433-444.

❖ **2020**

Secession is not a singular event. It consists of several smaller and sequential secessions. The first is a secession of the mind from the dominant culture. This is the most important secession, as all else stems from it. Next comes the cultural secession itself, which over time will grow into an economic secession. An internal nation must first develop economic self-sufficiency before political action.

The trouble with much of the talk of political secession since the 1990s is that no area of the country has "paid the dues" of all the lesser secessions described above. Political secessions are a de jure *recognition of a venerable and seasoned* de facto *secession.*

For example, the Confederate States of America had culturally and economically seceded from the U.S.A. years before their 1861 resolutions announced the political act. Taiwan was fully independent from mainland Communist China in everything but name. When Taiwan finally announced her de jure *independence in 2008 (just before the Olympics, when China dared not respond militarily), she was merely completing the final 1% of secession. Taiwan had been practicing 99% of secession since the 1950s.*

An ongoing example is the cultural, social, and economic Reconquista *of the Southwest. Texas, New Mexico, Arizona, and California are becoming the wealthiest portion of Mexico. And political power, that faithful caboose, is following right along. By 2030, the Hispanics will control those states in all aspects but name.*

The lessons of history are clear for any internal nation of the U.S.A. which desires to secede. Secession must first be lived *in the hearts and minds and bank accounts of the disenchanted. Such people must create a separate country in every area but political before the political paradigm can ever be realized. Once they do, political recognition is inevitable, and will largely feel anticlimactic when it eventually happens, just as a couple must feel on their wedding night after having lived together for many years.*

The world is geographically finite, and the scramble for blocks of land will soon resemble a frantic game of musical chairs. Internal and external immigration is rapidly shifting voting patterns to the left. The razor thin margin of the Florida results in the 2000 election clearly demonstrated this. Find a palatable area and "sit down" quickly, else you'll be left standing.

— James Wayne Preston, *Journals*

Cheyenne Sentinel   January 2020

Yesterday the legislature voted to dismantle the state's drivers licensing and vehicle registration system by 1 January 2021. Several national insurance companies are reportedly interested in establishing new offices to specifically serve the unique Wyoming market.

The Senate leader was quoted as explaining:

"Just because you travel in a motorized conveyance doesn't transform that right into a privilege. That has been a great American myth. Therefore, we will eliminate all vehicle registration fees and taxes, and replace the lost revenue with an increased sales taxes on gasoline, diesel, and tires. The proportionality and severity of road use is paid for by such taxation. Even electric cars will pay for the roads through their tires. Once this new system is operational, your cars will no longer be subject to any inspection, registration, or taxation.

"Similarly, individuals have a right to propel themselves down the road without any prior restraint or licensing. The great history of our English common law is that people are by default free to do as they wish, unless some action is proven to be a tort. Wyoming will be the first state to eliminate its driver licensing system, which has become over time a *de facto* National ID Card and database. A free people cannot be required to acquire and possess such 'papers' on their persons, always ready to be inspected by police.

"Also, Wyoming will no longer coerce people into insuring themselves against risks they *voluntarily* assume. Any drivers concerned about risk have the right to purchase private insurance for protection against being injured by those without assets or insurance. Those who choose *not* to purchase insurance personally assume all risk. In the absence of a state-issued drivers license, the insurance companies will no doubt begin to issue their own 'Certificate of Driving Competency' based on standards and testing of their own design. This is the most logical and equitable system, for it is the insurance companies with the greatest vested interest in driver competence and safety. However, the unseemly state and corporate partnership of the universal licensing and insurance scheme will end in Wyoming."

The White House   January 2020

Connor shouts, "No more *driver's licenses*? It's *unAmerican!*"

Chief of staff Sowers remarks, "Well, the licensing program *is* within the states' bailiwick, sir. Wyoming probably has the right to eliminate it."

"Not *and* keep receiving their highway funds!" snaps the President. "Look, otherwise I couldn't give a shit, but our future 'AmeriCard' is cut off at the knees because it's *based* on state driver's licenses! Goddamn it, I've *had* it with those people. They've been increasingly rebellious for the past five years, and this drivers license stunt is the last fucking straw!"

Sowers knows to keep his mouth shut and ride out the storm.
"Get me the Attorney General," orders Connor.

* * * * * * *

An idea that is not dangerous is unworthy of being called an idea at all.
— Elbert Hubbard

Wyoming   January 2020
Governor Preston discusses driver's licenses on his radio show:

"Some heartfelt concerns have been raised about deregulating the driver licensing system, so let me address those this evening.

"First, we all already know how to drive. A laminated plastic license is evidence of that, not the cause. None of us will forget how to drive safely when we longer have little cards in our wallets and purses.

"Regarding future drivers, the insurance companies will no doubt insist on training and testing far more rigorous than the current standards. Exams will include adverse weather driving, which no state requires. So, a privatized system will increase driver compentency, not diminish it.

"Some people have been very alarmed at the prospect of cars being driven without license plates, which they claim will enhance crime through anonymity. This will not likely be so. One, criminals can already remove or switch plates before a crime. Two, the 'getaway factor' is insignificant when you consider that 70% of Wyoming adults are daily armed. We don't need a policeman on every corner, because the citizenry at large is its own police force. There is no place for criminals to escape to, assuming that they manage to successfully commit a violent crime and not get shot."

* * * * * * *

Eliminating a part of American life which seemed grafted onto the national DNA was difficult at first, but folks gradually saw the light. Wyoming would thus avoid the dreaded "AmeriCard" and its police state databases.

Meanwhile, the federal trumpeting of indignation was deafening. A dozen threats were made: how Wyomingites would no longer be able to board commercial aircraft, get a passport, buy a hunting license, or cash a check, etc. Preston's team calmly and handily deal with each of the desperate claims, always ending their denunciation with:

Big Brother stops with Wyoming! No "1984" in The Equality State!

Denver, Colorado   February 2020

The 10th Circuit Court of Appeals issues an injunction against the State of Wyoming, prohibiting the dissolution of its drivers licensing system which is *"an essential component of national security."*

Cheyenne, Wyoming   March 2020

Tom Parks slams down his phone and rushes into Preston's office. "Sir, I've just heard that US Marshals are on their way here to arrest you on charges of conspiracy to violate federal laws."

The Governor stands up briskly as he grabs the phone. "I knew this would come. Tom, no US Marshal is to set foot inside this building. We planned for this eventuality, so you know what to do. Get to it. I'll call Colonel Mallory of the WHP."

Within minutes the Governor's Mansion is surrounded by Cheyenne Police and Wyoming Highway Patrol, who prevent entry to the US Marshals. After a mutual drawing of weapons, the outnumbered feds bitterly return to their cars, vowing to successfully serve their warrant another time.

* * * * * * *

The White House

After his eruption from hearing the news, Connor calms visibly, as if he's made a decision. "I want a meeting with the Joint Chiefs next week. Subject: Wyoming's insurrection and its military resolution. Have someone from Fort Bragg there, too."

"*Sir?*" asks Chief of Staff Sowers, his eyebrows raised. "That hasn't been resorted to since the 1794 Whiskey Rebellion."

Connor flashes a leer of triumph. "It *worked* though, didn't it?"

Casper, Wyoming   19 April 2020

Hanna Preston loved studying the American Revolution as a girl and knew all the battles and personalities by heart. She considered the shots fired on Lexington Green the true birth of the nation, not the 4th of July. So, nobody was surprised when she expressed her fervent desire to be married 245 years to the day after the events on Battle Road. It was also a tribute to a man her father deeply admired, who fell for his country three years ago.

There was still the arrest warrant for Preston, and Hanna was worried that the feds would see her wedding day as the perfect opportunity to serve it. Preston assured his daughter that the Justice Department would not be so telegenically stupid as to raid a wedding party and prove to America what brutes they were. Hanna was sufficiently comforted by this.

The ceremony was a large though simple affair, conducted on the family ranch by the riverbank. The theme was Western, and Hanna's beautiful 1890s style dress—handmade by Juliette—drew gasps from the crowd. Six-shooters were all but required of the male guests. The wedding vows, written by Michael and Hanna Poole brought tears to all. After the reception, the bride and groom quite literally rode off on horseback into the sunset for a mountain cabin wedding night. Nobody thought it corny.

Fort Bragg, North Carolina
US Army Special Ops Command HQ   19 April 2020

On the southeastern side of the sprawling army base is a multi-story red brick fortress. It houses SOCOM and the Special Forces Command (SFC). Computer-controlled turnstiles and armed guards keep unwanted people out, assuming they survived the trek across 200yds of blazing hot parking lot.

SFC has over 10,000 personnel under its worldwide command, though with only 120 staff members. SFC is lean and no-B.S. It has been quite busy since March. As Special Forces are usually deployed overseas, CONUS[1] ops are rare. Especially ones as large as this. If the planning staff have any reservations about tasking troops against civilians, they don't speak of it. Orders came down from the top, and they do their jobs as military professionals.

D-Day for Operation Defend Constitution is Tuesday, 11 August.

A low whistle is heard from a Master Sergeant known as one of the best military historians of the SFC. "Is anyone aware of what happened on that date?" he asks the room.

After several moments of furrowed brows, he answers his own question. "The final day of the battle of Thermopylae, 480 BC. When the Persians killed King Leonidas and his 300 Spartans. *Exactly* 2,500 years ago."

While nobody says anything to this, their countenances are grim. Random poignant glances can be caught if one is alert.

Cheyenne, Wyoming   April 2020

"Sir, one of our people at Camp Guernsey just heard something weird from a buddy down at Fort Carson in Colorado."

Governor Preston reads the brief in just seconds. "I don't like the sound of this, Tom. It confirms some other rumors I've been hearing from the Corps network. I'm going to give you some contact names out East. Here's what I want you to—"

---

1   CONtinental US

Fort Bragg, North Carolina
US Army Special Ops Command HQ   **May 2020**

General Adison reviews the final version of Operation Defend Constitution, and grunts. "Well, done, Colonel. Prepare a draft for the President."

Wyoming   **Thursday, 14 May 2020**

On his weekly radio show, Governor Preston occasionally likes to mention his favorite bumper sticker seen recently. They are always funny or piquant, or both. The Wyoming militiamen, however, understand that the one-liners are codes ordering some level of preparedness. Preston hasn't spoken one in many months, so when his show opened with a teaser for the rare segment, tens of thousands of men across the state listened with rapt attention.

About mid-through the two-hour show, just before a commercial break, Governor Preston says, "And now time for the best bumper sticker I've seen lately. You'll love this one, folks. Humpty Dumpty was pushed."

Faces tightened all across Wyoming. It was the most serious alert yet given. It meant "Action likely within 90 days." The militiamen protocol was clear. Rezeroing of rifles. Range practice of 1,000rds per month. Heightened training of team tactics. Physical fitness levels increased by 10%. Resolution of all important personal and family business. Verify six-month supply of foodstuffs and necessary goods. Confirm 100 gallons of extra fuel for every vehicle. Review retreat codes and destinations. Revisit cache sites.

Humpty Dumpty was pushed.

Prepare for war.

The Oval Office   **Wednesday, 17 June 2020**

President Connor has not spoken with James Preston since their first meeting in January 2015 at the Governors' Conference. Neither felt any affinity for the other, but matters had come to a head. Connor would rather avoid the national publicity of domestic military action, but that required the cooperation of Preston, his staff, and much of Wyoming. Such was unlikely.

Connor has a call placed to Preston. Without preamble he says, "Governor Preston, you have exhausted the Government's patience and restraint."

"Actually, Mr. President, it's the other way around," Preston says evenly, "but I take your point."

Momentarily derailed by Preston's carefree resolve, Connor continues, "Sir, you have evaded being placed in federal custody, and you have conspired with others in your administration to violate numerous federal laws. You have fomented in Wyoming an armed insurrection against the lawful and constitutional order."

"I and most of my fellow Wyomingites wholeheartedly disagree, sir. It is the *Government* which has broken its solemn pact with America. Since you brought up the Constitution, please explain to me how your administration, or any other, has guaranteed the States under Article 4, Section 4 a *republican* form of government. When has our supposed agency, the Federal Government, abided by the letter of the 2nd Amendment or the spirit of the 10th? What we now have is a *national* form of government, which was not the expressed object of the Constitution. Our Bill of Rights in tatters, and we in Wyoming will no longer stand for it."

President Connor is gripping the phone so hard his knuckles are white. With extreme effort he manages not to lose his temper. "Governor, you are speaking of legal issues which can be decided only by the courts."

Preston chuckles. "You mean the *federal* courts, don't you? Federal institutions arbiting federal authority. Speed freaks managing the pharmacy. Everyone sees through the façade by now, Mr. President. The game is over."

Connor takes a laborious breath and says, "Governor, I'm not going to argue the Constitution with you. Wyoming is in a state of insurrection, and I am empowered to suppress it with federal troops. Now, I will give you one last chance. We know that your militiamen have stepped up their training in anticipation of armed rebellion. For the sake of your people and of our nation, do not continue down this road to a civil war which you cannot win. Governor, you must instruct your citizens to lay down their arms."

"*Molôn labé!*"

With that, the line goes dead.

The phone still in his hand, President Connor turns to the room with a befuddled expression. He evidently does not know his Greek history.

National Security Advisor Bruner does know. He explains, "Sir, it's from a battle in 480 BC. Thermopylae was a suicidal holding action at a mountain pass to delay the Persians until the Greek navy could mobilize. Even though the Spartans were wiped out, their sacrifice rallied the Greeks to later prevail with renewed vigor. Xerxes abandoned his conquest of Greece, thus preserving the cradle of Western civilization and saving Europe."

Connor smirks. "So, Preston fancies himself the head of some modern-day Sparta? Saving America from the federal hordes, eh?"

Bruner replies, "He probably *does* imagine a vague parallel, yes, sir."

The President begins to pace next to his desk, which was always a sign of anger. "Well, what does 'mo-lawn lah-bay' mean?"

Bruner coughs. "The phrase means 'come and take them.'"

Connor frowns. "Come and *take* them?"

"Yes, sir. Their guns. If you *can*. It's a challenge—not a surrender."

Connor stops pacing. The change on his face terrifies all present. It was later described as *"an icy, demonic calm."*

The President nods his head grimly and says, "A challenge, eh? Fine. Challenge accepted."

Cheyenne, Wyoming   Thursday, 18 June 2020
"And now, for my latest favorite bumper sticker," announces Preston over the air. "He who laughs last thinks slowest."

Action likely within 60 days.

Fort Carson, Colorado   July 2020
A team from the SFC at Bragg arrives to brief commanders of the 10th Special Forces Group. Their Second Battalion would be instrumental in next month's operation.

Cheyenne, Wyoming   Thursday, 16 July 2020
"Oh, I saw a really good one in traffic yesterday," says Preston over the microphone.

He can imagine all of Wyoming waiting, breathlessly. At times he was amazed that the feds hadn't cracked the code, but then he calms himself with the assurance that militiamen knots consist of men who have known each other for years. Many have been friends since childhood. Newcomers were not automatically part of the inner cadre. They had to be invited, and that only happened after months of training, observation, and background checks.

Several FBI and ATF agents had been discovered posing as bona fide libertarian gun owners in order to infiltrate the militia. Preston's nickname for them was "mushrooms." Kept in the dark and fed shit. Often they were sent to separate and distant training missions in the grasslands.

Preston blinks his eyes and clears his head. "Yeah, I really laughed when I saw this one," he chuckles. "Ask me about my vow of silence."

Action likely within 30 days.

Denver, Colorado   August 2020
The mayor of the Mile High City shakes hands all around. "Thank you for coming, gentlemen. I assure you Denver's complete cooperation. It's about time the President took action up there. We've been losing many of our productive citizens to Wyoming for years. Businesses, too."

A US Army brigadier general nods. "We completely understand, Mr. Mayor. We appreciate your part in restoring constitutional order to the West."

Cheyenne, Wyoming   Thursday, 6 August 2020
"The word 'gullible' is not in the dictionary," Preston says over the air.

Action likely within 7 days.

* * * * * * *

A nation preserved with liberty trampled underfoot is much worse than a nation in fragments but with the spirit of liberty still alive.
— Private John H. Haley, 7th Maine Regiment (1860s)

The Oval Office   Monday morning, 10 August 2020

"Sir, I have Major General Adison of Special Forces Command on secure video link from Fort Bragg."

Connor nods firmly at the image of his SFC two-star. "Good morning, General Adison. What is the status of Operation Defend Constitution?"

"On schedule, Mr. President. H-Hour is 0545 MST tomorrow. Delta is handling the Cheyenne DA[2]. For OPSEC[3] we will use Fort Collins, Colorado as FOB[4] versus any Wyoming base. Delta will helo infil by MH-6N Little Birds courtesy of 160th SOAR, supported by 3rd Battalion, 10th Special Forces Group ODAs[5] in MH-60G Pave Hawks from the Colorado ANG.

"Three Cheyenne ODAs are tasked for the Governor's Mansion on Central Avenue, the Barrett State Office Building, and the Capitol Building. A fourth ODA will helo infil south of Casper to Governor Preston's ranch to support Delta there. All four ODA commanders have liaisoned with their FBI counterparts to handoff prisoners for arrest and facilities for search. Casper and Cheyenne FBI SWAT will be standing by if needed. An ODB[6] will set up in the Capitol with secure comm to SOCCE.

"Second Battalion, 10th SFG is less than three hours down the highway at Fort Carson. Although they will have to drive through Colorado Springs and Denver, it will be after midnight on a weekday. Their cover will be a training mission in the Roosevelt National Forest. The 2/10th will stage 8 miles south of the Wyoming state line on Highway 85 by 0300 in order to relieve Delta and the Cheyenne ODAs by H+30 Minutes. Their road time to Cheyenne will be no more than 20 minutes.

"3rd Battalion, 19th SFG will provide support from Draper, Utah. The 3/19th will be on station near Evanston, Wyoming for a possible eastern I-80 barricade, though I don't expect that'll become necessary. The bordering states' ANGs[7] will contain the Wyoming perimeter."

The President is pleased. He enjoys working with military professionals. Such a change from his years on the Hill. "Excellent, General, excellent! I have your Time and Phase Deployment Schedule right in front of me and I will study it today before I rejoin you by video from the Situation Room to-

---

2   Direct Action, a Special Forces mission involving a short, intense raid to seize, capture, recover, or destroy specific hostile personnel, equipment, or facilities.
3   Operation Security
4   Forward Operating Base
5   Operational Detachment Alphas (previously called "A-Teams") are highly trained and versatile 12-man SF teams led by a captain.
6   Operational Detachment Bravo, an SF Company HQ unit controlling multiple ODAs in the field.
7   Army National Guards

morrow morning at 0300. Director Klein will also be in the FBIHQ's SIOC room at 0300 to coordinate his field agents during Operation Defend Constitution. Meanwhile, my staff will keep in touch with you today as necessary. Good day, General Adison, and thank you."

Wyoming   Monday morning, 10 August 2020

Nearly 50,000 militiamen pagers go off simultaneously. The numerical code means "Action likely within 24 hours." It is the second highest alert. For communications redundancy, the alert code is echoed on TV, radio, and the Net. Men from 17 to 55 years of age don their gear and grab their rifles.

Bill Russel's grandson, now of militia age, hefts the Krassny FAL and slings it. On his hip is the WW2 vet's Colt 1911A1. The young man feels as though he has instantly matured another year. Months of training have prepared him to defend his liberty, his family, his state. He isn't alone. Many of his friends and most of his kin will also be at their staging points. They are all in it together, and the young man has never felt more proud. His grandfather hands him a Thermos full of hot coffee, and hugs him. "Rely on your knot, let them rely on you, and you four men will do just fine."

A private page is sent to a special team known as "The Gardeners." They are in charge of harvesting, at exactly the same time, all Wyoming "mushrooms." It's salad time.

The Oval Office

Moments after the SF general logged off, Connor's secretary buzzes the intercom and says, "Mr. President, I have the Governors of Idaho and Montana both holding in conference call. Line seven, sir."

Connor picks up the phone with executive briskness and stabs the blinking "7" button. "This is the President. Good morning Governor Dewey; good morning Governor Troxel."

"Good morning, Mr. President," the governors intone in unison.

With salutations out of the way, Connor gets right to it. "Gentlemen, tomorrow morning I will formally declare Wyoming in a state of insurrection. Its citizenry is openly and wantonly flouting federal law and Census 2020, as well as United Nations rewilding directives—all with the direct assent and support of the Wyoming government. Governor Preston was personally instructed by me to ensure his state's compliance with several congressional gun control acts, but he categorically refused to intercede with his law enforcement or guard forces. Therefore, I am federalizing the national guards of Wyoming's contiguous states to augment the military action by US Special Forces required to effect the arrest of Governor Preston, his staff, and several members of the legislature. I have already heard from the governors of Colorado, Nebraska, and South Dakota. They are acting to seal their borders with Wyoming tomorrow by 0530 MST."

Montana Governor Troxel says, "Sir, we're quite aware of the situation in Wyoming. Governor Dewey and I are calling to inform you that we've mobilized our state guards for stationing at the Wyoming border."

President Connor beams. "Excellent, gentlemen, excellent! Since time is of the essence, I have to move on Cheyenne at dawn. You both will be ready then, I take it?"

This time Idaho Governor Dewey speaks. "Actually, Mr. President, our guard troops will be in position within a few hours."

The President is puzzled. "But the Army won't be ready to act any earlier than dawn, and your ANGs are to coordinate with General Adison and his forces."

Dewey replies, "Sir, we won't be coordinating with General Adison."

Troxel chimes in, "That's correct, Mr. President."

Connor stares at the phone in amazement. "But coordination is necessary for the Cheyenne mission. We must—"

"Sir, the Idaho and Montana guards," says Governor Troxel "are not mobilizing for the Cheyenne mission."

"*What?* But Chey—"

Troxel cuts him off with, "Mr. President, we have just learned that the Wyoming state capital has been relocated to the Cody area until further notice. Governor Preston and his staff are already there, and enjoy full continuity of government. The Wyoming guard is establishing an internal main line of resistance from South Pass to Shoshoni, thus sealing off southern access to the Big Horn basin. Their guard is also staging on I-25 from Ranchester to Kaycee to prevent eastern access to the basin."

The Oval Office is tomb quiet, stunned.

National Security Advisor Bruner then quietly remarks to the Chairman of the JCS, "If Wyoming were a chessboard, I'd say Preston just castled."

Homeland Security Director Thaddeus Desmond overhears this and glares at Bruner.

Connor says, "This is wonderful intel, but how—"

"We know because Governor Preston requested our help in preserving the Republic, Mr. President," Dewey explains. "We have mobilized our state guards to *protect* Wyoming's western and northern flanks, not to invade our neighbor or support your unlawful military operation."

The President is speechless for several seconds before he erupts. "So, the poison of rebellion has spread outside Wyoming! This is *treasonous!*" Connor yells. "You are both *traitors!* Traitors to your *country!*"

"Sir, the Federal Government has violated its constitutional compact with the 50 states, especially in regards to the Bill of Rights. Under treaty law, this nullifies the compact, and any state may therefore act independently as a fully restored sovereign if it so desires. Wyoming evidently so desires, and we will aid her. You may have picked a fight with Governor Preston, but he will not have to fight alone."

"Are you both *insane?*" Connor shouts. "Do you honestly believe that three states with a total of three million people can hold off the might of the United States military?"

Governor Troxel says, "For now, yes sir. And three million people may not seem like a lot, but you're talking about America's Switzerland. Wyoming is, as we speak, fielding 50,000 trained militiamen, all with 7.62 battle rifles, and fully supported by their hitherto National Guard. You really should reconsider military action, Mr. President. Whether the US won or lost, it wouldn't be worth it. The British learned that the hard way with thirteen colonies, and you sure don't want to go down in history as the 21st century's King George. Good day, Mr. President."

The line goes dead with Connor's mouth still hanging open. He turns to Sowers and barks, "Get me General Adison again."

"Yes, sir, right away."

Wyoming

Wyoming steels herself for a federal invasion, her streets swelling with armed citizens packing their .308 battle rifles, 220 rounds of ammunition, water, bivvy shelter, and three days of provisions. Since most had stored their gear in their cars and trucks, transforming themselves into militiamen takes only minutes.

The Oval Office

"Mr. President," Chief of Staff Sowers says, "I have General Adison back on video link."

Connor turns to the screen and says, "General Adison, I am aborting Operation Defend Constitution. You are to stand down immediately."

Adison is stone faced. "Operation aborted, Mr. President, I understand. Our intel just informed me that the Wyoming ANG are sealing off the Big Horn basin. Also, their entire citizens' militia is mobilizing. Our OPSEC was extremely tight, sir, but somehow word must have leaked to Governor Preston's staff."

"Thank you, but we know all this, General," huffs Connor. "We're still not done here. On my authority commence with Operation Restore Liberty. The 7th Infantry Division and 3rd Armored Cav Regiment in conjunction with the 101st Airborne are to occupy Wyoming and neutralize its ANG. Militiamen are to be arrested for rebellion and detained for trial. Activate the tasked air wings for support. How soon can you move in?"

If General Adison is taken aback by the escalation, he doesn't let on. "Since those units are already on alert, just 24 hours behind the previously scheduled operation, Mr. President. H-Hour will be 0545 Mountain Standard Time, Wednesday, 12 August. We'll roll this up in a week, Mr. President."

"Excellent, General. See to it."

Wyoming   Tuesday, 11 August 2020

As the militiamen and guard forces were instructed to maintain readiness for the next 72 hours, the entire state remains coiled for defense.

All "mushrooms" have been picked, and are in cold storage.

The Pentagon   Tuesday, 11 August 2020

The inner halls of E-Ring bustle with uniforms, scurrying with nervous signals of the US military brain to its many extremities.

The White House   Wednesday, 12 August 2020

National Security Advisor Bruner arrives at his office at 7:00AM, ready to brief the President on tomorrow's operation. Reporters have gotten wind of all the military activity and are beginning to ask questions. Press Secretary George Bishop will have his hands full "denying" the well-placed rumors that President Connor was preparing for action against North Korea.

Bruner feels his wireless PDA vibrate. The Caller ID reads UNA. Unavailable. Nonetheless, few people have his private number so he answers it. Such an early call had to be important.

An unfamiliar voice says, "Have you opened this morning's couriered package yet?" And then disconnects.

Bruner frowns as he opens the small sealed parcel on his desk. Inside is a CD marked with a Sharpie pen, "From Wyoming to the President."

Bruner hurriedly makes his way to the Oval Office. Already present are the Homeland Security Director Thaddeus Desmond, Chief of Staff Sowers, the JCS Chairman, and several aides.

Bruner holds up the CD and says, "I just received this. It seems to have come from Cheyenne. It could be related to tomorrow's operation."

Connor exasperates, "Well what the hell are you waiting for?"

"Yes, sir," Bruner says as he inserts the disk into his running laptop. After a few seconds a media manager window opens with the query:

Play .mpg video file "Jigs Casey" now?

As Bruner clicks the Yes icon, Connor says over his shoulder, "And just who in the hell is *Jigs Casey*?"

At the same time the JCS Chairman's wireless PDA chirps, so he steps a few feet away to answer it.

The mpeg stream begins. It is a 1980s clip from comedian Steven Wright, a Boston comic known for his offbeat material and monotone delivery. He's on a large stage with a maroon curtain behind him. On a stool is a glass of water which he sips while previous laughter dies out. He gingerly places the glass back on the stool and stares out at the audience. After a deliciously pregnant pause, Wright drones into his next bit:

> *I got a phone call the other day. "This is Mr. Haynes, your student loan director. We lent you $17,000 years ago and haven't received a penny of it back. So, we were kinda wondering what you did with the money."*
>
> *"Mr. Haynes, I won't lie to you. I gave the money to my friend Jigs Casey . . . And he built a nuclear device . . . And I'd really appreciate it if you never call me again."*

As Connor and his staff gape at each other in astonished confusion, the JCS Chairman, now on a secure NSA phone, says, "Mr. President, you need to hear this, right now. I'm on the line with Lockheed Martin's Pentagon liaison. LM is upgrading Mk650 Evader MaRVs[8] of the Peacekeeper IIs we fielded in 2010 after the Chinese invasion of Taiwan. They discovered a problem with one of the missiles. Three of its re-entry vehicles are empty."

"*Empty?!*" shouts Connor.

"Yes, sir—without their nuclear warheads."

"*What?!*"

"Three W87 fission warheads," the CJCS intones. "Two-stage implosion. 300 kilotons each. That's fifteen times Hiroshima. Assuming a 1000' foot airburst, blast radius is 8 miles. Ground burst, the blast radius is only 1.5 miles but still sufficient to remove central Washington from the map."

The National Security Advisor exclaims, "*Three* nuclear warheads missing? *How?*"

"The LM liaison says they were removed while in their silos, not during or after transport," the CJCS replies. "It would have *absolutely* required the active collusion of base personnel. This was an inside job."

"What do these re-entry vehicles look like?" demands Connor. "How large a vehicle was needed to transport them?"

The CJCS says, "The RVs are matte black cones about 22 inches in base diameter, six feet in height, weighing 700 pounds. The outer layer is a carbon fiber phenolic resin heatshield. These are intact. What's missing are their aluminum substructures which are sheathed in a graphite-epoxy composite to contain the warheads. They weigh about 380 pounds apiece."

---

8   Maneuverable Re-entry Vehicles, which can be, unlike mere MIRVs, steered to penetrate ABM defenses during a second strike retaliatory role.

"So, the warheads could have been removed from their RVs and then transported in a single trip by any automobile," observes Bruner.

The CJCS nods. "Affirmative."

Connor, never famous for his grasp of 21st century military detail, asks his National Security Advisor, "Where are the Peacekeeper IIs based?"

Resignedly, Bruner says, "In converted Minuteman silos in the northwest wing of F.E. Warren Air Force Base. Cheyenne."

After several seconds of stark silence, Chief of Staff Sowers deftly articulates the predominant mood.

"Oh, *fuck.*"

President Connor collapses into his high-backed leather chair. Shaking his head he sighs, "Looks like there are two nuclear powers in America."

The NSA asks the CJCS, "General, what kind of time line are we looking at here? How long ago could these warheads have been stolen?"

After a brief flurry of conversation with the Lockheed Martin liaison, the CJCS replies, "He says that it *had* to have been since their last semiannual inspection, which was four months ago."

Connor shakes his head. "Four months! Carried by *donkeys* they could be *anywhere* by now, even in some U Street basement two miles from here!"

The Oval Office was never more quiet as each man visualized himself within the blast radius.

Something occurs to Connor. "Four months ago! That was just after Justice sent the US Marshals to arrest Preston. And then that smug bastard tells me to 'come and take them.' No wonder he was so damn sure of himself! He already had his nukes by then!"

"Mr. President, we don't know that for certain right now," says Bruner.

Doris, the presidential secretary, buzzes the intercom. "Sir, General Adison on video for this morning's conference."

President Connor collects himself briefly and then says, "General, I'm very sorry to say that something has come up which compromises Operation Restore Liberty. You are to abort."

The General's jaw clenches in frustration. "*Abort? Sir?*"

"You heard me, General Adison. Abort."

"But Mr. President, the men are *ready.* We can't 'cry wolf' with them twice in two days. Sir, what's happened?"

News of the missing nukes hasn't yet spread, so Connor keeps his poker face intact. "General, we'll get into it later, but the timing to proceed has soured. Please convey my thanks to your people for their superb preparation, but I have no choice but to abort at this time."

After the video link is cut, Connor turns to his NSA and says, "Contact the NEST Team at McCarren airport in Las Vegas. Put them in touch with the liaison at Lockheed Martin. And get me Director Klein. Find my nukes!"

* * * * * * *

The next day, National Security Advisor Bruner receives a second DVD, this one postmarked from Alexandria, Virginia. It contains just two files, a readme.txt and a self-encrypted file. The text file reads:

> *"The Union is a Union of States founded upon Compact. How is it to be supposed that when different parties enter into a compact for certain purposes either can disregard one provision of it and expect others to observe the rest?... A bargain broken on one side is broken on all sides."*   (Daniel Webster, Capon Springs Speech, 1851)

> Dear Mr. Bruner,

> An individual unconnected with and unknowledgeable of the encrypted contents of the second file will soon contact you with the passphrase (which we will anonymously communicate to him).

> You will know this person by an email with the subject line:

> *Cessante causa, cessat effectus.*

> After you have decrypted the enclosed file, President Connor may be inclined to grant the individual's wishes. He should do so, for the nation's sake.

Bruner clears the mental cobwebs of his university Latin.
Cessante causa, cessat effectus.
When the cause ceases, the effect ceases.
Bruner quickly emails his contact at the National Security Agency. The NSA at Ft. Meade, Maryland would have to crack this file, and fast.

one week later

Wyoming is still at battle stations. Guard forces have sealed off the Big Horn Basin with the cooperation of Montana and Idaho ANGs. Tourist traffic is prevented from entering the state. Yellowstone National Park, normally very busy during the summer, is empty of visitors.

The official story is terrorist threat of anthrax, though few people buy it. None in the media do, either, after a source within the Pentagon leaks the rumor that right-wing terrorists have hidden a stolen nuke in the Tetons.

The 7th Infantry Division and 3rd Armored Cav Regiment are kept on full alert for occupation after the nukes are found, however, extensive overflights of Wyoming with highly sensitive radiation detection equipment fail to locate the warheads.

NEST Teams scour the Beltway area, without success. That any of the warheads can be flown, driven, or Metroed into D.C. did not reassure Connor's administration. Several cabinet heads resign the same week for "health" or "family" reasons and quietly move away. President Connor spends most of his time at Camp David, or flying on Air Force One.

* * * * * * *

Not a single member of the Preston administration cooperate with the FBI. All refuse by email under the 5th Amendment to answer any questions.

two weeks later

The FBI and USAF Military Police polygraph test hundreds of Warren AFB personnel without finding a single culprit.

Alive, anyway.

Six *deceased* suspects from the Peacekeeper II maintenance section, however, were identified. Apparently, they had all been on an elk hunting trip near Pinedale, Wyoming when their Ford Excursion slid on an icy hairpin curve and fell off a 240' cliff. The SUV exploded on impact and was thoroughly consumed by fire. There were no survivors.

three weeks later

The FBI exhumed the six bodies and shipped them in a guarded refrigerated truck to their Crime Lab. DNA comparisons with military records did not match. Furthermore, all six bodies had tattoos on the soles of their right feet—indicative of medical school cadavers who had, while alive, sold their bodies to science for the going rate of $1,000.

All six Air Force personnel were single. They had simply disappeared. Phone and email records of their friends or family showed no contact, and all were uniformly shocked and outraged to be questioned by the FBI.

This did not burnish the Bureau's tarnished reputation.

four weeks later

All Peacekeeper IIs and Minutemen ICBMs are removed from Warren AFB and transferred to Minot and Grand Forks AFBs in North Dakota. Malmstrom AFB in semi-rogue Montana will lose its ICBMs in 2021.

* * * * * * *

The expected email is from the Wyoming Attorney General. It reads:

Dear Mr. Bruner,

I have recently been anonymously instructed by post that I am to email you the below series of characters in order to assist you in negotiations between the Federal Government and Wyoming.

> I do not understand how paragraphs of typographical gibberish will accomplish that, though I nevertheless have complied. This done, I will wait to hear from you.
> We have a crisis to resolve, one of several generations in the making. I hope that we settle our drama without bloodshed, in order to prevent what would surely be a costly and needless tragedy: America's Civil War 2.

Bruner cuts and pastes the several thousand metacharacter block into the DVD's encrypted passphrase window. After a few seconds, it is accepted and text appears on the screen. The first three lines are serial numbers, and Bruner already knows that they will match those of the missing Mk650 Evader MaRV 300kT nuclear warheads. The rest reads:

> President Connor has until 1 November to peacefully, honorably, and irrevocably conclude negotiations with the people of Wyoming, returning to them their liberties usurped by the Federal Government.

> We will diligently monitor Washington, D.C.'s abidance by this long overdue arrangement, and have no compunction of issuing you all a "reminder" whenever events deem necessary.

> The age of Tyranny in America will now begin to draw to a close, regardless of the Government's lack of reasonableness or integrity.

> We speak softly, but carry three very big sticks.

The Oval Office   September 2020

The anonymous, yet credible, threat sends shockwaves throughout the White House. President Connor convenes an emergency meeting in the Situation Room. Less than a dozen people are present.

Connor begins. "Let's recap what we know or can reasonably infer. One, that three active 300kT nuclear devices are in the hands of persons sympathetic to Wyoming. Two, that such persons likely have the ability to successfully position and detonate these nukes. Three, that they have the will to do so if we refuse to deescalate pressure on Wyoming. Four, that over a month of effort to locate these persons and recover our warheads has been fruitless. Five, that recovery is unlikely by their November 1st deadline."

"But that's still five months away! We're sure to find them by then!" exclaims Homeland Security Director Desmond.

"Extrapolating from what *trend* of current success?" challenges National Security Advisor Bruner. "We have come up with nothing but the identity of the six airmen responsible for the theft, and they have literally disappeared. Even if we *do* find them and persuade them to talk, any information they give us will likely be unavailing. We all know how tightly their operation's been run."

FBI Director Klein says, "I'm inclined to agree, Bill. We've not been able to backtrack the email packet route. The couriered DVD had no prints, and was fraudulently sent on the DNC's account. Dead ends all around."

"Whoever hired those Air Force people should have killed them after taking delivery," opines Bruner.

"Maybe those six are very deeply trusted," offers Sowers.

"But why leave *any* loose ends? Why not just *off* them?"

"Because of their goddamned *principles,* that's why!" snaps Desmond. "'No initiation of force' and all that. Their 'zero aggression' scruples prevent human loose ends to be snipped. They even reimbursed that medical school for the cadavers they stole! Mailed them $6,000 in cash and explained that no receipt was necessary. Of all the fucking nerve!"

Sowers says, "Why can't we simply go to the American people and inform them of Preston's nuclear blackmail? The country would seal off Wyoming and starve it into surrender."

The CIA Director retorts, "Because we have absolutely no *proof* that Governor Preston or his staff are involved, that's why! The FBI, NSA, and the Agency have tried to link the DVD and email to Wyoming, but can't. This anonymous intermediary keeps Preston off the hook. He can claim that the warhead thefts were an inside military affair by disgruntled airmen sympathetic to Wyoming's situation, and how could we prove otherwise?"

"I agree," says the CJCS. "Preston's got the best of both worlds: nuclear blackmail *and* bulletproof deniability. If we move on him, before or after any detonation, we'd have to prove our case to the American people. Preston could counter that the *Government* set off the nuclear blasts to blame on Wyoming. Polls show that nearly four of five citizens actually believe that Clinton's administration was involved in the Oklahoma City bombing."

"Yeah, thanks to Krassny's dissemination of laptop data," sneers Klein.

"Topic drift, gentlemen," says Sowers. "Let's get back to the nukes. They could take out Langley or Ft. Meade, or *both*, before they ever wiped out D.C. Hell, if the CIA and NSA got fried, much of the public would *cheer*."

After hearing from all in the room, President Connor speaks his mind.

"Look, here's the big picture. Persons unknown have the nukes and are capable of using them. We haven't found them yet, and probably won't in time. So, the only real question is this: is keeping Wyoming *more* important than losing the CIA and the NSA and all of D.C. by November 1st?"

Heads nod over the obvious choice. Connor could be quite persuasive when his emotions had cooled.

"Time can be on *our* side. We should negotiate in apparent good faith until November. If we don't find the nukes by then, we acceed to Wyoming's wishes. They can't keep them hidden forever, and they're the only trump cards Preston has. Once we find the nukes, and that may take months or even years, we can then deal with Wyoming in any way we see fit. Warren AFB's missiles have been removed, so Wyoming can't pull the same trick twice. Time's only against us until November. After then, it's against Wyoming. Let's cut these wackos loose. They've been nothing but trouble for the past five years. We'll deal with them when they're in a position of weakness, not strength. The wheel will turn, gentlemen. It always does."

The Oval Office   December 2020

Think of it this way, Mr. President. Wyoming is only asking for what the 13 original states enjoyed two hundred years ago was the Wyoming Secretary of State's opening comment to Melvin Connor and his cabinet heads.

After a series of extremely discreet and often rancorous talks with the Preston administration, President Connor bitterly allowed Wyoming to pursue a Taiwanesque course of muted *de facto* secession. The terms are not to be publicized, but it will prove easy enough to "connect the dots."

Its Army and Air National Guards will be transferred to full state control. Warren AFB and Camp Guernsey are to be phased out within two years, as well the Naval Petroleum Reserve Number 3 at Teapot Dome. All BLM and National Forest land will be transferred to Wyoming. Yellowstone and Devil's Tower will remain National Parks, though to be removed from the UN's World Antiquities Heritage jurisdiction.

All federal warrants for Wyoming persons, including Governor Preston and his staff, are vacated. All federal law enforcement field offices in Wyoming will be closed, leaving only an FBI liaison presence in Cheyenne. Wyoming agrees to assist the Government only in interstate criminal matters of violence, theft, or fraud.

Travel in and out of Wyoming will not be hindered. International flights will be allowed directly to the new large airport being constructed just northeast of Casper, though passengers must still go through US Customs and Immigration. (It was that, or force the Government to place checkpoints outside all Wyoming border crossings.)

Wyoming will remain in the Union, although under a strict "hands off" policy. Her internal affairs, including oil and gas drilling, mining, manufacturing, education, individual rights, banking, and system of government, will not be interfered with. Hemp crops, firearms, ammunition, R-12 Freon, and the like are not to be sold out of state, though enforcement of this provision seemed nearly impossible given the open borders. The feds will likely have to heavily patrol the six contiguous states for Wyoming contraband.

Not that Connor believes Wyoming's independent course could continue for more than a year, since the nukes would surely be found by then. But, as his single term under the 22nd Amendment will end on 20 January 2021, that is his successor's problem—who was stupefied when informed of the Wyoming accords. His first emotional inclination was to publicly disavow them in January and occupy Wyoming, but the threat of three 300kT nuclear warheads—current address unknown—made him "see the light."

Better that than to "feel the heat" of 1,000,000° Centigrade.

Pretty soon I'll no longer be the "First Prisoner," Connor muses.

Montana and Idaho are beginning to clamor for the same deal that Wyoming got, causing Connor to wonder if all three states each got a nuke. *What a mess! Not even a Republican president deserves this!*

Governor Preston did not negotiate directly with Connor's staff, but sent a note after the stormy talks finally concluded with a signed agreement. It contained only a quote. The words were nearly 219 years old, spoken by Thomas Jefferson during his first inaugural address to calm Federalist New England—horrified by Jefferson's election—which agitated to secede from the Union. Connor inexplicably finds himself rereading the quote almost daily.

> *"If there be any among us who wish to dissolve the Union or to change its republican form, let them stand undisturbed, as monuments of the safety with which error of opinion may be tolerated where reason is left free to combat it."*

President Melvin Connor refolds the heavy bond paper and pockets the furry edged note. He looks again at his desktop calender. January 20th is just six weeks away. *This job is way overrated!*, he concludes.

No president ever more anxiously awaited his retirement.

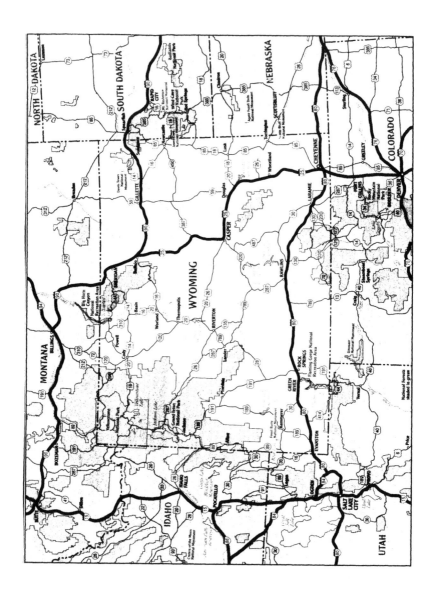

❖ 2021

Wyoming life   2021

The discomfort of regulatory pressure, like back pain, is never fully realized until it is relieved. With nearly all federal restrictions deactivated, the subcurrent of government-induced stress evaporates, causing business and social life to burst with vitality. People are free to live their lives without fear, and it is a heady experience—one not felt for over a hundred years.

Montana, Idaho, and South Dakota begin to institute Prestonesque reforms. They have to, or else lose their best people to Wyoming. Colorado, Utah, and Arizona were also feeling similar pressure. The libertarian ripples from the Wyoming stone were affecting the entire American West. Time would tell if a Western stone would send ripples across the American pond.

Sheridan, Wyoming   Summer 2021

Inside, the café is jammed with people so Kristi Ryan steps outdoors to the wood-decked patio. Being a sunny day, it is crowded also, but she searches for an empty chair. Having lived in Europe for many years, Kristi likes the continental fashion of sitting with strangers when space is tight.

She spots a two-top table with a man sitting alone sipping coffee and casually reading the paper. There's no place setting opposite him. He's well-dressed in a tan blazer and navy blue Oxford shirt. No wedding ring, but he doesn't appear to be sizing up skirts as a womanizer would do.

She walks up and says, "Excuse me, but would you mind if I shared your table? It's awfully crowded this time of day."

He looks up pleasantly, smiles and kindly waves his hand at the empty chair. "Not at all, miss. Please do."

He actually rises from his chair as she sits down.

"I hope I'm not interrupting your reading," she ventures.

"No, of course not. I'm glad for the company."

She smiles, relaxing. After she orders they make small talk for a while. He is an engineering consultant; she manages a retail clothing store. As they chat she finds herself liking him. He hasn't made a move on her, and he doesn't stare down her blouse. Seems to have some class. Matthew Walling has an easy way about him, and she really likes his deep chuckle.

Her espresso arrives and she takes a luxuriously long sip.

"*Mmmmm.* They don't make it this good in Montana."

"Montana?"

"Yeah, I just drove back from visiting my sister in Billings."

"Oh, she lives there?"

A dark mood shadows her lovely face. "Well, sort of."

Seeing his questioning look of concern, the dam breaks. "Lisa was arrested three months ago on federal charges of money laundering because she only accepted cash at her home business. She just got convicted last week. Her trial was a sham! Five years for refusing to have a bank account and give up her privacy! And she's the widowed mom of a two-year old."

Walling frowns. "What a raw deal! And how was it the *government's* business if she took cash instead of checks? The feds are so paranoid."

Kristi smiles. It's always refreshing to meet a stranger who understands, though this is becoming quite common. "Paranoid is right! You should have seen the federal judge. You'd have thought he was working for the prosecutor! I heard later that defense attorneys call him 'The Aussie.' None of my sister's motions or objections were allowed."

"'The Aussie?'"

"Yeah, for his kangaroo court. The DEA and FBI and ATF love him."

He nods his head, but his eyes begin to glaze over.

Oh, damn, now I've gone and bored him!

Just when she is about to really berate herself, he says, "This was in Federal District Court in Billings?"

Relieved, she says, "That's right."

"What was the judge's name?"

"Mott. Judge Clarence P. Mott."

She catches the faintest of smirks on his face. "Why, do you *know* him? Are you from Billings?"

"Nope, never heard of him. And I'm not from Billings, either. Actually, I just moved to Wyoming. I'm still getting used to no license plates on cars out here, and how everybody packs a pistol. What a marvelous state!"

"Oh, you just moved here? From where?" she asks, genuinely interested. Such a nice man, and so handsome, too. He has a calm authority about him. He makes her feel safe. She would like to know him better.

"From the east coast. A place called Durants Neck. North Carolina."

"Then welcome to Wyoming, Matthew. I hope you like it here."

"Thanks, Kristi," he says, smiling. "I think I already do."

The End

WYOMING REPORT

November 2002

INTRODUCTION

This Wyoming Report is the result of a leisurely five year feasibility study beginning in August 1997. Its purpose was threefold:

❶ To bring into sharper focus the concept before us.

❷ To identify any states which could serve such a concept.

❸ To recommend the most suitable state for implementation.

This we have done. First, some background material.

DIAGNOSIS

Where liberty dwells, there be my country.
— Benjamin Franklin

'Tis the same to him who wears a shoe, as if the whole earth were covered with leather.
— Ralph Waldo Emerson

The above two quotations hint sufficiently at the gist.

After authoring *Hologram of Liberty—The Constitution's Shocking Alliance with Big Government*, Kenneth W. Royce came to ten conclusions regarding the predicament of Liberty:

❶   At least 50% of Americans do not *want* to live free and responsible lives, and will resist any political attempts to be made responsible.

❷   Our political masters fully understand and encourage this, as it constitutes a powerful vested interest for both ruler and ruled.

❸   Even if ❶ and ❷ were not true, America is experiencing an accelerated philosophical, political, religious, and racial polarization. This was amply evidenced by the 2000 Elections.

❹   *"There's small choice in rotten apples."* — Shakespeare
The two-party system was designed, and is maintained, to prevent the emergence of any victorious 3rd party. Only billionaire candidates (*e.g.,* Perot, DuPont) have the horsepower to reach the general public.

❺   America has become (at least) two *de facto* separate countries, and she is now much too populous and diverse to govern as one nation. Many Americans are beginning to publicly discuss the likely (though desperate and vaguely distasteful) solution of secession.

❻   Translation of the above: Libertarians cannot possibly retake the entire USA through a political/philosophical renaissance. Even if the contrived 3rd party obstacles were removed, no majority of voters will slough off their socialist/fascist proclivities, even if all of them were required to read *Atlas Shrugged*.

❼   Conclusion: While Libertarians cannot retake their country, it *is* possible that they can "liberate" several counties, or even an entire state *if* they will geographically concentrate themselves under the mutual goal of a political *reconquista*.

❽   There are many examples of a certain class of people descending upon an area (usually a city) resulting in their substantial control of that area's moral tenor and social climate. Some examples:

Wealthy Liberals	Aspen, Boulder, Ketchum, Jackson
Homosexuals	San Francisco
White Separatists	Northern Idaho
Mormons	Utah, southern Idaho
Christians	Tulsa, Colorado Springs
New Agers	Crestone (CO), Cave Junction (OR)

❾   Moral: Freedom is relative. If you are free where you live, then you are *free*, period. Wouldn't you rather live in a *laissez-faire* county or state with no undue interference in your life, than in a nation which is nothing more than a vast gilded cage?

❿   Although there is currently no libertarian enclave, there *could* be if a sufficient number of determined folks relocated and *made* one. All that is necessary is a plan, place, and subsequent action.

     This Report will suggest plan, place, and action. But first, let us review how we came to be oppressed in America.

A REVIEW OF FEDERAL TYRANNY

The economic, political, and regulatory tyranny of the USG over the States and the People was achieved over a period of time spanning 200 years, comprising several succinct and hierarchial stages. As we will see, it was as carefully ordered and completed as any complicated gourmet recipe, which rules out accidental (yet constant) accretions throughout history.

The **first** stage was to institute a new central government with ascendant powers (both immediate and nascent) over the original 13 States. The unchallengeable authority of the *"United States"* over the States was gradually, albeit inexorably, knitted together by a series of key Supreme Court rulings, such as **Marbury v. Madison** (1803: Supreme Court has sole authority to decide constitutionality of USG's actions), **McCulloch v. Maryland** (1819: Congress has *"implied powers"*), **Gibbons v. Ogden** (1824: the term *"commerce"* stretched to mean that ultra-inclusive *"intercourse"*), and many others. Judicial building blocks for our prison.

This judicial infrastructure constructed, the **second** tier was social conditioning (so that the public would accept the next stage). In a classic Hegelian tactic of thesis/antithesis/synthesis, dissatisfaction was created with private banking, gold and silver money, and the lack of an income tax on the "fat cats." This was done from 1890-1913 by a series of contrived events (*e.g.,* artificial bank panics and recessions), which were fanned into roaring flames by key congressmen and media megaphones. By 1913, the public were ready, if not insistent, for sweeping changes in banking, currency, and tax law. As H.L. Mencken so keenly observed:

> The whole aim of practical politics is to keep the populace alarmed (and hence clamorous to be led to safety) by menacing it with an endless series of hobgoblins, **all of them imaginary.**

A concurrent and continuing form of social conditioning was/is the usurpation of local education by a "public school" system, wherein America traded McGuffey's Readers for John Dewey's "progressive education." The result has been the most harebrained, ignorant populace in Western history.

The **third** stage was economic and financial. As Mayer Auselm Rothschild so aptly remarked:

> Permit me to issue and control the money of a nation, and I care not who makes its laws.

In order to make war (foreign and domestic) it was paramount that the USG enjoyed funding independent of popular control. Such is the *sine qua non* of modern oppressive governments. To accomplish this requires three separate mechanisms: a central bank to monetize public debt, legal tender legislation, and a personal (not merely corporate or business) income tax based on payroll withholding. Two great monetary pumps work in tandem: one to inject intrinsically worthless "currency" into the economy, and the other to pump out "excess" liquidity by wage withholding. Naturally, the Supreme Court has done its duty in defending the so-called "Federal Reserve System," its "Federal Reserve Notes," and the "Internal Revenue Service."

The **fourth** stage was a dramatic increase in military personnel, technology, and equipment. WWII was clearly the watershed event here. Incredible advances in weaponry, aviation, communications, computer technology, encryption, and logistics were made during and after that global conflagration—followed by the "military/industrial complex" and the complete federalization of the state guards.

The **fifth** stage was intensive regulation to deproperty and disarm the citizenry. With almost total judicial sanction, Congress and the President have spewed forth laws, regulations, and executive orders encompassing nearly every activity and purchase. Such are, according to de Tocqueville, a form of social conditioning which *"compresses"* the people. Accompanying this was the militarization of state and local police (a tactic used to great effectiveness by the Nazis).

The **sixth** stage was, and is, active confiscation of people and property. The USG has the money and muscle, supported by the courts, to begin to really throw its weight around. And what can the people effectively do in response? Cut off federal funding? Challenge the FBI or IRS in court? Engage in combat with the US Army? All of these would be futile acts. We have been slyly led to a comfortably padded *corner*, from which there is little easy escape.

What we need is a wall to push *from*.

A UNIQUE PLAN FOR LIBERTY

The exit can usually be found at the entrance.

If you become lost, retrace your steps and leave where you came in. If you have become enslaved (however comfortably and agreeably), simply retrace tyranny's steps. You may indeed find that you can leave via the same door through which oppression entered.

This is far too simple for most would-be revolutionaries, who prefer to blow a hole in the wall to escape. While the situation may one day require this kind of a dramatic solution, most Americans probably would not sympathize with such violence. Since we have determined that at least bland national support is critical to our success, we must very slowly and carefully slough off our restraints in nearly identical order to their imposition (*i.e.*, education, health, money). Hence, our exit will be found at the entrance.

Just as our oppression did not occur overnight, neither will our Liberty. We must win back our freedom through the same mechanism by which we originally lost it—by "gradualism." To steal a man's bread, one doesn't dare grab the entire loaf. It's done one *slice* at a time. We lost our lives one slice at a time because we did not go to war over slices, even though they have eventually totalled nearly the entire loaf.

It is proper to take alarm at the first experiment of our liberties. We hold this prudent jealousy to be the first duty of citizens, and one of the noblest characteristics of the late Revolution. The freemen...did not wait til usurped power had strengthened itself by exercise, and entangled the question in [legalistic] precedents. **They saw all the consequences in the principle, and avoided the consequences by denying the principle.**
— James Madison

Similarly, we will steal *back* our lives one slice at a time, as the USG also will not declare martial law over slices. By the time the USG realizes just how much of the loaf we've retaken, it will have lost too much of this previous advantage as we become emboldened with our success and newly protective of our recently won freedoms.

The platform for this retaking of our liberties will be one of the states, of which we have gained executive, legislative, and judicial control through a bloodless *coup* of election.

How is it possible to sweep a state's election? By choosing a sparsely populated state of staunch conservatives, and then convincing sufficient numbers of liberty-loving folks to move there. It's a simple matter of mathematics. After several years of a quiet mass relocation, we could finally swing an election *our* way. Remember, libertarians are, and always will be, far outnumbered in national elections—so why should we keep trying to win presidential and congressional elections?

With a libertarian governor and state legislators, we could at last begin to bring home our stolen freedoms from Washington, D.C. We could at last implement a true free-market economy and become the model for other states. We could finally create a society based on individual rights of property and conscience.

We could enjoy, finally, an oasis of reason and responsibility where honor, integrity, and intelligence are at the helm.

We could have—at long last—a *home*.

OUR STATE'S CRITERIA

Given the unprecedented nature of our plan's virtual *coup d'état*, combined with the geographical, political, and economic requirements of our target state, we initially doubted that even one state would offer anything remotely favorable to our needs.

We were quite surprised, however, that *six* states made it to the "semifinals" and three to the "finals." The hands-down winner was the same state which the concept's author had chosen as the likely best choice. Below are our criteria for the target state, and the progressive elimination of all contenders but one. (Figures are from the 1990 Census, the latest available in 1997 when this Report began. 2000 Census figures relecting a 9% population increase do not alter in any way our conclusions.)

Total Population   (must be < 1,000,000)
Given that our plan absolutely requires a sparse population, this is the most important criterion for choosing our state.

Also included are the next five least populated states, even though they number over 1M people.

Wyoming	453,588
Alaska	550,043
Vermont	562,758
North Dakota	638,800
Delaware	666,163
South Dakota	696,004
Montana	799,065
Rhode Island	1,003,464
Idaho	1,006,749
New Hampshire	1,109,252
Nevada	1,201,833
Maine	1,227,928

Population Density   (must be < 35/mile^2)
There is ample evidence of philosophical and political mass psychosis when population density levels are great. Using the states' political recognition of the right to own and carry guns as a benchmark, the

most densely populated states typically have the worst civil rights records regarding the 2nd Amendment.

For example, here are the ten worst and best RKBA states:

DC	9,949		
NJ	1,042	VT	61
IL	206	ID	12
HI	173	KY	93
MA	768	LA	97
NY	381	WY	5
CA	191	MT	6
CT	678	AZ	32
MN	55	AK	1
MD	489	MS	55
RI	960	GA	112

with DC	**1,393** people/mile²	**47** people/mile²
w/o DC	**494** people/mile²	

The 10 best gunowning states have an average population density of only 47 people/mile². The 10 worst states (including D.C.) have a density of 1,393, and if D.C. is excluded their density is still 494, which is over *10 times* that of the 10 best states. We suggest that there is a very high correlation of low population density to reason, responsibility, and political sanity.

The national average in 1990 was 70/mile². Thus, the Committee requires a state with half or less than the national average, *i.e.*, 35 or less people per square mile.

State in bold also have a population less than 1M (we include Idaho). There are only 14 states with densities less than half the national average, and all are in the West or MidWest:

Alaska	1
Wyoming	5
Montana	6
South Dakota	9
North Dakota	9
Nevada	11
Idaho	12
New Mexico	12
Nebraska	21
Utah	21
Kansas	30
Oregon	30
Arizona	32
Colorado	32

We mention the case of Vermont at 61 people/mile² as a distant possibility, given its third smallest population of just 562,758.

Water/Land Ratio   (must be > 0.66%)

The national average is 0.66%, so we will use this as our standard. All of the above six states in bold meet this criterion:

Alaska	13.10%
Vermont	3.81%
North Dakota	2.42%
South Dakota	1.59%
Montana	1.00%
Idaho	0.98%
Wyoming	0.73%

Water/Population Ratio   (> 0.50 acres/person)

Water is life, and water rights issues will be key in the early half of this century. The national average of water acres/person is 0.65, though that figure is a bit high because of our huge Great Lakes. The Committee considers 0.50 water acres/person to be an acceptable minimum. Six of our top 7 states make the grade:

Alaska	100.12 water acres/person
North Dakota	1.71 water acres/person
Montana	1.19 water acres/person
South Dakota	1.13 water acres/person
Wyoming	1.00 water acres/person
Idaho	0.52 water acres/person
Vermont	0.42 water acres/person

Alaska is the last outdoors paradise in America, however, living there is arduous. The Dakotas, Montana, and Wyoming are quite wet at 1.00-1.71 water acres/person. Idaho squeaks by at 0.52.

Alas, Vermont (already on "probation" because of her high population density) drops out due to low water acreage/person, even though her water/land ratio is a very high 3.81%. Even if we kept Vermont in the running, she would be eliminated later because of her high Democratic voting history (half the counties voted for Gore in 2000).

Contiguous States ("brushfire quotient")

The Committee requires, for relative tax and business climate advantages, that our state border at least 4 other states. Also, such contiguousness will likely enhance the brushfire nature of our political actions.

It is advantageous, though not absolutely necessary, that our state border at least one Canadian province for increased opportunity of imports (legal or not).

Idaho	6 (plus 1 Canadian province)
Wyoming	6
South Dakota	6
Montana	4 (plus 2 Canadian provinces)
North Dakota	3 (plus 2 Canadian provinces)
Alaska	0 (plus 2 Canadian provinces)

Because of her remoteness from the "lower 48" we must remove Alaska from our consideration. While Alaska remains high on any pioneering survivalist's list, we conclude that she is far too isolated to stave off any US invasion or blockade.

Topographical Defensibility

Since the Committee believes US military action to be a likely eventual threat, we must consider topographical defensibility. For example, flat Poland has been overrun numerous times by Russia and/or Germany, yet mountainous Switzerland survived WWII without invasion by Hitler.

At this juncture, we must eliminate mountain-free North and South Dakota, which had remained in very solid running with Montana, Wyoming, and Idaho (the only remaining states).

Idaho offers the most topographical defensibility (*e.g.,* the Bitterroot Range), followed by Montana (*i.e.,* the western half).

Although Wyoming is generally a plains state (hence its name derived from the Delaware Indian term *Mecheweami-ing*, which means "on the great plain"), about 25% of her surface is mountainous. Wyoming also has a mean elevation of 6,700', the second highest after Colorado.

U.S. Land Ownership   (must be < 50%)

This affects not only freedom, but property prices.

Montana	27.7%
Wyoming	48.8%
Idaho	62.6%

Political Tenor

Wyoming is more conservative than even Idaho or Montana, with *zero* counties voting for Gore in 2000 (a testimony matched only by Utah and Nebraska). Two-thirds of Wyoming votes Republican, and the state has an entrenched Libertarian Party. (The only liberal enclaves are Jackson, Rock Springs, Laramie, and Cheyenne.) The allowed open carrying of firearms is fairly common throughout the state. Wyoming tied with Montana at 92% for RKBA in *Boston's Gun Bible.*

Idaho is population top-heavy in/around Boise, however, this metro area is not yet as liberal as the Hollywood playground/haven of Ketchum/Sun Valley (the "Aspen" of Idaho). Idaho is very much a libertarian state, which rated 97% (2nd Place) for RKBA in *Boston's Gun Bible.* Northern Idaho (above I-90) attracts many privacy-seeking folks.

Montana has remained an astonishingly "uppity" state to this day. She and Nevada were the only states to openly flout the egregious 55mph national speed limit with speeding tickets of only $5. In the mid-1990s daytime highway speed limits were "Reasonable and Prudent"—which transformed the state's highways into a *de facto* autobahn. Open carry of weapons and no open container laws (shades of Louisiana) combine to create an extremely libertarian climate (with a Boston T. Party RKBA score of 92%). The only liberal enclaves of note are Billings and Helena.

Business Climate

Wyoming is the winner, with excellent incorporation laws and lack of income (personal and corporate), gross receipts, and inventory taxes. Sales tax is just 4%, and fuel tax is only 9¢/gallon. Low property taxes. Aggressively seeks new business.

Social Acceptance

Northern Idaho has somewhat of a reputation for racist behavior, although this has been greatly overblown by the liberal media. (The Aryan Nations has only a few hundred members.)

Montanans and Wyomingans "live and let live," although they do not gracefully brook urbanites who whine that "it isn't like back home."

Election Sweep Possibility

Wyoming offers a near perfect opportunity for our scenario. Every four years (2006, 2010, 2014, etc.) are elected: the House, half the Sentate, the Governor, the Secretary of State, State Treasurer, State Auditor, Superintendent of Public Instruction, some Supreme Court Justices, and all county officials (clerks, treasurers, assessors, coroners, attorneys, sheriffs, DAs, and JPs).

Self-Sufficiency

Energy

Wyoming is the undisputed champion with huge coal production (1st in USA) and bountiful oil and natural gas (6th in USA). 95% of power is generated by low-sulphur coal, and the 5% is produced by the state's 10 hydro-electric plants. Electricity and natural gas prices are among the nation's lowest.

Food

Wyoming is very strong in cattle and sheep, sugar beets, barley, dry beans, beef, corn, and wheat. Wyoming has the largest antelope population, and has ample elk, deer, and fish.

Raw Materials

Over half of Wyoming's economy is based on trona, bentonite, gemstones, wool, hay, and timber.

Industry

More than 5M tourists visit Wyoming each year, spending over $1B. Minerals bring in $3.2B, and agriculture $1.5B.

OUR RECOMMENDATION: WYOMING

After much research and consideration, the Committee is unanimous in our strong recommendation that Wyoming be chosen for our plan. In fact, Wyoming appears nearly tailor-made for our needs. The few disadvantages are either inevitable given our criteria, fairly insignificant in a relative sense, or will be mostly minimized with a successful long-term implementation of our plan.

Wyoming pros:

Smallest population, 2nd lowest population density, ample water, 6 contiguous states, near ideal political conditions, superb business climate, friendly and conservative people, bountiful energy and raw materials, self-sufficient agriculture.

Wyoming cons:

Mediocre topographical defensibility, little commercial air service, variously harsh weather (wind and cold), small manufacturing base, lack of border with Canada, lack of coastline.

If Montana and Idaho were as sparsely populated as Wyoming, then the selection would have more difficult, however, *ceteris paribus*, Wyoming would have nevertheless remained our first choice. Montana and Idaho were strong runners-up, although they are both under fairly intensive colonization by the liberal yuppy/"infopreneur" class.

Wyoming, however, does not attract such people and has remained the most undiscovered state in the lower 48. Life and earning a living are more difficult, which has served to repel the daintier types.

Finally, Wyoming is a remarkably homogenous state regarding voting issues. Although a fiercely independent people, Wyomingites truly "pull together" for their special land. This Committee is confident that they can eagerly be led for dramatic change. Montana and Idaho, however, are more dichotic (though not to the extent of Colorado or Arizona), which would likely thwart our political agenda if attempted there.

In closing, we suggest that a unique fate seems to have preserved Wyoming for us and our kindred spirits, in a similar fashion that the USA retrospectively once served as a haven for the world's oppressed. As a rather eerie aside, this Committee has noted a recent surge of libertarian interest in Wyoming as a preferable state for the *laissez-faire* diaspora. (Also note the emergence of the NH-oriented Free State Project.) We take this to mean that we are definitely "on to something":

> [A] *fundamental scientific rule...: If the time comes for a fundamental innovation, a breakthrough discovery or invention will be made several times, at different places, and by persons working independently from one another.*
> — Stefan T. Possony, *Psyops*

We are very confident, however, that our plan is clearly the earliest, most extensive, and most ambitious of anything in its class. We believe that only a dramatic and concerted effort will achieve our desired results, and that our vision is, quite simply, one whose time has come.

(RE)TAKING LIBERTIES

Just as there was a specific formula for tyranny comprising several stages, there can be such for Liberty. As we will likely have only one chance at this it must be very carefully planned, and then executed with great courage and determination.

Counties

2006 and 2010 county "dress rehearsals" of the statewide effort in 2014 is absolutely vital. Twelve of the 23 counties have less than 15,000 people.

(Note: The "R#" is Republican %, and emboldened headings are actual figures, not estimates. Counties are listed in order of # of reg. voters, not gross population. 2002 is used for reg. voters, as it was a general election year. The estimated primary voters % is a 12-year average of 75%.)

Conservative counties less than 9,000 people:

	2000 pop.	2002 regist. voters	est. (75%) actual voters	FSPers with 25% local support
R82 Niobrara	2,407	1,559 / 65%	1,169	586
R73 Hot Springs	4,882	2,744 / 56%	2,058	1,030
R74 Crook	5,887	3,372 / 57%	2,529	1,266
R74 Weston	6,644	3,514 / 53%	2,636	1,319
R82 Sublette	5,920	3,589 / 61%	2,692	1,347
R84 Johnson	7,075	4,237 / 60%	3,178	1,590
R73 Washakie	8,269	4,478 / 54%	3,359	1,681
R60 Platte	8,807	4,631 / 53%	3,473	1,738
				10,557

Preliminary analysis indicates that as few as 10,557 current Wyomingans (or 10,557 FSPers with 25% local voter support) could politically control all eight of these counties.

Conservative counties between 11,000 and 18,000 people:

	2000 pop.	2002 regist. voters	est. (75%) actual voters	FSPers with 25% local support
R78 Big Horn	11,461	5,680 / 50%	4,260	2,131
R73 Converse	12,052	5,779 / 48%	4,334	2,168
R63 Goshen	12,538	6,202 / 49%	4,652	2,327
R64 Lincoln	14,573	7,590 / 52%	5,693	2,848
R48 Teton	18,251	11,802 / 65%	8,852	4,427
				13,901

Preliminary analysis indicates that as few as 13,901 current Wyomingans (or 13,901 FSPers with 25% local voter support) could politically control all five of these counties.

Controlling the 13 least populated counties

As few as 10,557 could politically control the 8 least populated counties, which means a geographical *third* of Wyoming. Only 586 could "own" Niobrara county. But here is the most amazing thing: as few as 24,458 current Wyomingans (or 24,458 FSPers with 25% local voter support) could politically control the 13 least populated counties, which geographically means *over half* of Wyoming. These 13 counties total an area the size of New York state! This kind of astounding political leverage exists no where else in the USA.

If we win in November 2014, then those of us who still live out of state will want to start packing and come to their new home. Even if we do not win the entire state, we will have won some counties for ourselves, and then can work for total victory in 2018.

Using political parties

The most important question is which party to field our gubernatorial candidate, Republican or a third party? A Republican nominee would clearly garner more votes than a third party figure and thus have the better chance of winning. However, he/she must first win the Republican Party's (RP) nomination. The difficulty of that cannot be measured presently. If the RP by 2014 has steered significantly towards a libertarian course, then our chances would be greatly increased, and we could possibly elect our own candidate in the primary election.

Or, the Libertarian Party (LP) could have made, by that time, large gains in voter popularity. If so, we would seriously consider an LP vehicle for our political goals.

We suggest a two-pronged approach: shifting the Wyoming Republican Party towards libertarianism, while enlarging the state's LP in order to command at least 10% of the general vote (instead of its 1-3% today). In this fashion, voters can choose from Freedom Party A or Freedom Party B.

State electoral considerations

Every four years (*e.g.*, 2006, 2010, 2014, etc.) the entire Wyoming state government is up for grabs. Their Senate rotates in halves, so even the upper house can be swept out of office every two elections.

In 1996, Wyoming had 488,190 people, of whom 343,300 (70.3%) were voting age. Some 240,711 were registered voters for the general election, and of these 215,844 (a very high 90%) voted. A simple majority of those was just 107,923 voters.

Think about that: just 107,923 people voting for Liberty in 1996 could have grasped the political reins of the entire state of Wyoming, and that was in the year of its *highest* voter turnout. In an *average* turnout year, just 94,954 people could have done it.

Approximately 70% of the population is of voting age. Averaging voter registration/turnout figures from 1978 to 1996:

% reg. primary	% vote primary	% primary votes of eligible voters	% primary votes of population
62.6%	64.8%	40.6%	28.4%

% reg. general	% vote general	% general votes of eligible voters	% general votes of population
69.3%	80.1%	55.5%	38.9%

Worst-case scenario   (194,251 relocator voters)

Using these percentages and a state population of 500,000 with 350,000 eligible voters, let us assume a "black sky" scenario wherein not a single native Wyomingite votes for our candidates. This would require that we move in 194,251 new *eligible* voters (not merely people) to gain a simple majority (*i.e.*, 55.5% of 350,000/2, + 1). This is as infeasible as it is unlikely. Even if we could convince 194,251 adults (and their children) to relocate (which is unlikely), such would increase Wyoming's population by over 40% in far too short a time to house them (much less absorb them into the job and business markets).

Thus, we must win over a large portion of the existing electorate in order to reduce the required number of our relocators. Besides, we are not trying to transform Wyoming into something that it's not.

Low middle-case scenario   (117,521 relocator voters)

The current political climate (based on registered voters) is 57% Republican, 31% Democrat, and 12% Other (including Libertarian Party and Natural Law Party).

"Other" is at least 5% in all counties, and up to 20% (Albany) and 28% (Teton), and is a significant/growing "wild card."

Assuming 350,000 eligible voters and an historic average of 55.5% actually voting in the general election (*i.e.*, 194,250), the normal voting pattern would be:

Republican	Democrat	Other
110,723	60,218	23,310

For our "gray sky" scenario, let us assume that we co-opt the following percentage of existing voters from their parties:

Republican	Democrat	Other
25%	10%	20%
27,681	6,022	4,662

for a total of **38,365** of original voters on our side, leaving a balance of 155,885 against us. So, 155,886 (155,885 + 1) minus the 38,365 already for us means we would need to relocate **117,521** new voters. Thus, with mild (*i.e.,* 19.8%) indigenous political support, our relocation is reduced by 76,730 voters, or 40%.

Obviously, these figures rely upon an average 55.5% (80.1% votes cast times the 69.3% registered) voter turnout of native registered voters (including our converts), versus a *100%* voter turnout of relocated voters in efficient locations through prepositioning.

Upper middle-case scenario   (71,289 relocator voters)

For our "cloudy blue sky" scenario, let us assume that we co-opt the following percentage of existing voters from their parties:

Republican	Democrat	Other
40%	15%	35%
44,289	9,033	8,159

for a total of **61,481** of original voters on our side, leaving a balance of 132,769 against us. So, 132,770 (132,769 + 1) minus the 61,481 already for us means we would need to relocate 71,289 new voters. Thus, with very good (*i.e.,* 31.6%) indigenous political support, our relocation is reduced by 122,961 voters, or 63%.

Taking an average of black vs. cloudy blue sky relocation numbers gives us 132,770, which is just a bit more dire than gray sky.

Best-case scenario   (40,790 relocator voters)

For our "blue sky" scenario, let us assume that we co-opt the following percentage of existing voters from their parties:

Republican	Democrat	Other
50%	20%	40%
53,362	12,044	9,324

for a total of **76,730** of original voters on our side, leaving a balance of 117,520 against us. So, 117,521 (117,520 + 1) minus the 76,730 already for us means we would need to relocate 40,790 new voters to round out the excellent (*i.e.,* 39.5%) indigenous political support.

An overview

Every indigenous Wyoming voter we swing to our side reduces by *two* the number of new voters whom we must import.

It should seem obvious to any reader that it is easier to educate and convert one native voter than it is to achieve *two* relocators.

Granted, we cannot expect to win elections solely through native conversion, however such will go far in reducing the burden of relocation.

Political education and conversion
Republicans
Since 57% of Wyomingites are registered Republicans, and since Republicans are closer to our political philosophy than are Democrats, we must focus most of our efforts on them.

"Other"
Next, we should focus on those registered "Other" as such are Libertarian, Natural Law, and Independent—all of whom exhibit the highest degree of individual thought. Although their total numbers are small (only 12%), we can expect a high conversion percentage. In fact, from those 23,310 voters we can almost get the same number of converts as from 60,218 Democrats.

Democrats
Lastly, the Democrats represent the worst conversion ratio, thus we should only try to persuade the swing voters and libertarian fringe of the DP. (The Mondale/Clinton/Gore crowd—70% of DP total—however, are hopelessly swaddled in ignorance.)

Phase 1   County relocation/integration
Establishing legal residence in a state does not mean that one must reside there year-round. For example, George Bush, The Elder had merely a hotel room in Houston and successfully passed himself off as a Texas citizen for 1992 voting purposes.

Since Wyoming has no personal or corporate income tax, becoming a Wyoming citizen has huge tax advantages for those in one of the 41 income tax states.

Nearly 6 million tourists enjoy Wyoming each year, with over half of them traveling there in the summer (usually to visit Yellowstone National Park). It would be a simple matter for prospective relocators (especially "infopreneurs") to check out Wyoming, pick a town, choose a sponsor (for address purposes), and change driver's licenses—all while on summer vacation.

There are already hundreds of registered Libertarian voters in Wyoming, and our plan is to ask them to "sponsor" some fellow libertarians from out-of-state. Guest house, spare bedroom, RV spot, tent space, whatever—all they have to do is lend their address to a kindred soul for driver's license purposes (as a mere P.O. Box will not legally suffice). We suspect that such local sponsorship will meet up to 25% of our needs.

At the same time, we will establish in each of the target counties very large mobile home and RV parks for those who cannot find a local sponsor. These "County Colonies" will suffice legally as a bona fide address for new Wyomingites, and will be filled sequentially by county, from the lowest population up, so that we may gain political control of as many counties as possible. Also, they will be filled up only after independent relocators and local sponsorships have been exhausted, so as not to telegraph our political intentions until the last minute.

Phase 2   Winning statewide 2014 election

We must give Wyomingites (and also Americans) initial *hope* through a dramatic victory at the polls. A liberty-minded governor and congress must totally sweep the elections in 2014. As this study proves, such is eminently possible with resolute action by a sufficient number of libertarians and conservatives.

To vote in Wyoming, one must have been a resident there for only 30 days. To maximize the element of surprise, Tier 3a Relocators will establish residency and register to vote (automatically through their new drivers licenses) no earlier than 60 days prior 4 November 2014.

Phase 3   First 40 days of general session

The governor must sustain that confidence with a boldly enacted platform locking out further federal tyranny (without causing the USG to overreact). A holding action, if you will.

During this period, Wyoming should brace herself for a great wave of tourism and relocation.

Phase 4   Creating our culture

Gun ownership and training (especially regarding military-pattern rifles) will be greatly encouraged by the administration. A libertarian society is unsustainable without a prevalent citizens' militia (which was notably lacking in the "Galt's Gulch" of Rand's *Atlas Shrugged*). What is missing from the classic libertarian model is a sort of martial ardor which inevitably comes from the universal daily bearing of arms by a free people. In Wyoming, many will seek to become a *rifleman*, as only riflemen have historically remained free.

Conversely, a mere armed camp cannot endure as a society without a political philosophy which clearly respects individual rights of property and conscience. Tomorrow's Wyoming will offer something never before seen in human history —not even in 18th century USA: a defensible, libertarian, militia society backed by the entire wherewithal of the state government and its officers.

Other significant freedoms we will protect are alternative health practices and parental control of schooling (*e.g.,* homeschooling, private schools, etc.) on a free-market basis.

Phase 5   Challenging the USG

The Governor's power consolidated with overwhelming support of the Wyoming people, we shall begin to bring home from Washington, D.C. calculated slices of our lost freedom. At the same time, we will increase Wyoming's self-sufficiency, grow strong, and prove our libertarian case by example.

This will culminate within our Governor's second term in our *de facto* secession from the coercive Union of vassal states. At first, it will be vital *not* to declare ourselves in secession, just as Taiwan has not overtly claimed independence from Red China.

Phase 6   Defending Wyoming from the USG

Nevertheless, our actions will be fiercely resisted by the USG, which will likely eventually declare Wyoming in *"insurrection."* We will be told to "lay down our arms." Our reply will echo one made some 2,500 years ago—that of Spartan King Leonidas when Xerxes I of Persia demanded it at Thermopylae:

> *Molôn labé!*   *Come and take them (if you can)!*

And that will probably begin the Second American Revolution. Washington, D.C. will have started it back in 1789 with their basely ulterior constitutional system, and the American West will end it with that image of true Liberty penned by Thomas Jefferson in his eternal Declaration of Independence.

ACTION TIMING

We recommend that Phase 1 be commenced in Wyoming at the earliest possibility, preferably no later than July 2002. We recommend that Phase 1a be targeted for the county elections of November 2006,

Phase 2a for the county elections of November 2010, and Phase 3a for the general election of 4 November 2014.

Relocator hierarchy

Tier 1a Relocators   (have moved to WY by August 2006)
These new Wyomingans will be the vanguard of our plan, which will be tested in 2-5 counties in the 2006 elections. They include those who will run for public office, plus key computing, administrative, and support personnel. Tier 1a Relocators will have actual Wyoming domiciles, jobs, and businesses for months or years before the 2006 elections, and will have fully integrated themselves with their localities.

Tier 1b Relocators   (have moved to WY by summer 2008)
Similar to Tier 1a Relocators, but for the 2008 HD and SD elections.

Tier 2a Relocators   (have moved to WY by summer 2010)
Similar to Tier 1a Relocators, but for the 3-6 county 2010 elections.

Tier 2b Relocators   (have moved to WY by summer 2012)
Similar to Tier 1b Relocators, but for the 2012 HD and SD elections.

Tier 3a Relocators   (become residents by 9/2014)
These are our final "surprise" voters, who establish residency 60-31 days prior the 4 November 2014 election. They will be locally sponsored to the fullest extent possible before resorting to the County Colonies.

Tier 3b Relocators   (have moved to WY by summer 2016)
Similar to Tier 1b Relocators, but for the 2016 HD and SD elections.

Tier 4 Relocators   (become residents after 11/2016)
These are people who have foreknowledge of our plan and have committed to relocate after a successful state election.

Tier 5 Relocators   (relocate before the 2018 election)
These are not "insiders" but new Wyomingites won over by our election and administration. We will need many thousands to "pack" the state prior to the subsequent general election of 2018 to stave off any defeat. Tier 5 relocators are key to *maintaining* political power after 2018 with second terms for our state government.

On this point, we must also point out that our plan in no small way depends upon a particular national economic and political climate—one which we did not (prior 9/11 and the *USA PATRIOT* Act) believe will likely manifest as early as 2010. Trend analysis indicates that 2014 is the far more probable year of criteria convergence (or, as astrophysicists say, "singularity"), with several macro-issues (such as Social Security crisis, unemployment, inflation, soaring crime, racial tensions, rising energy costs, persistent terrorism, lack of public confidence in government, etc.) peaking at about that time.

Many events, however, could dramatically accelerate our time table: premature domestic economic collapse (which we forecast by 2006), an electoral crisis of similar magnitude to the Bush/Gore election of 2000, spasmodic secessionist pressures, serious and persistent civil disturbances, or a regional war (*e.g.,* the Middle East, Korea, or Taiwan).

The terrorist attack of 9/11 is in retrospect such an event, and the Committee is now considering condensing our plan in order to "strike while the iron is hot."

As Phase 2a is merely a repeat of 1a in other counties, it may be possible to combine the two Phases in 2006 if the relocation numbers allow. Such a powerful start of 5-11 counties (vs. just 2-5) will provide us with a flexibility needed to weather unforeseen events, especially how such relate to post-9/11 and its regulatory/economic/social fallout.

Wyoming Legislature 2006-2016

Phase	1a	1b	2a	2b	3a	3b
	2006	2008	2010	2012	2014	2016
Senate Districts	1	2,18, 20,22	3,16,19 23	26,28 30	15,17, 21,24, 25,29	4,10
running total	1	5	9	12	17	19
running % of 30	3%	16.7%	30.0%	40.0%	56.7%	63.3%

	2006	2008	2010	2012	2014	2016
House Districts	2,20 27,40	1,26, 27,28, 30,50	4,6,21, 24,25, 51,54	3,5,22, 29,31, 32,34, 38,52	14,16, 19,23, 33,36, 37,55, 56,57	15,35,58
running total	4	10	17	26	37	40
running % of 60	6.7%	16.7%	28.3%	43.3%	61.7%	66.7%

SO, WHAT DO WE CALL THIS THING?

We should identify and classify along historical models the dynamics of Wyoming's governmental change. To wit: What will we have accomplished in 2014? A Revolution? A Civil War? A *Pronunciamiento*? A Putsch? A Liberation? An Insurgency? A *Coup*?

The answer is not merely semantic relief, but will illustrate more clearly the obstacles we must overcome.

DIAGNOSIS

The different varieties of upheavals are all distinct from each other, yet often share common characteristics.

Type	Actors	Goal
Revolution	masses	altered poli-socio structures
Civil War	divided national military	control of government
Pronunciamiento	military leader & officer corps	control of military
Putsch	military unit	internal military regime
Liberation	foreign military	new allied government
Insurgency	ethnic or political mitosis	rival autonomous state
Coup d'état	infiltrators	displace govt from state seize power w/i present system

For example, of the seven upheavals, at least three employ some elements of the domestic military forces as primary actors. This is not desireable for our purposes. Furthermore, the violence inherent to a Revolution, Civil Liberation, or Insurgency strikes them from candidacy.

This leaves one form of governmental change most similar to our plan: a *coup d'état*. The object of a *coup* is to seize power within the present political infrastructure by displacing government from the state.

A rigged election (with a nonviolent aftermath) has long served as one peaceful means of a *coup*.

Assassinations have also been catalysts for *coup*s. JFK's assassination in November 1963 has often been bitterly refered to as a *coup* which directly benefited the military and CIA by installing as President the pro-Vietnam War Lyndon Johnson.

HOW TO BAKE A *COUP*

The seminal work on how to actually plan and execute a successful *coup d'état* is Edward Luttwak's *Coup d'état*, which was published in 1979. We shall quote from it extensively:

> ...[T]he coup d' état *is now the normal mode of political change in most member states of the United Nations.*
> ...[During 1963 to 1978] there have been some hundred and twenty military coups, whereas only five guerrilla movements have come to power—and three of these followed the Portuguese coup in 1974. The function of the guerrilla movement has reverted to what it originally was—that of paving the way for and supporting the regular army: it holds the stirrup so that others may get into the saddle.
> ...[C]oups...are still the only form of political change that can be envisaged at the present time.
> — foreword to *Coup d' État*, Edward Luttwak (1979), p. 11

The coup is a much more democratic affair (than a revolution). *It can be conducted from the "outside" and it operates in that area outside the government but within the state which is formed by the permanent and professional civil service, the armed forces and police. The aim is to detach the permanent employees of the state from the political leadership, and this cannot usually take place if the two are linked by political, ethnic or traditional loyalties.* (at 20)

A coup consists of the infiltration of a small but critical segment of the state apparatus, which is then used to displace the government from its control of the remainder. (at 27)

If we were revolutionaries, wanting to change the structure of society (through warfare), *our aim would be to destroy the power of the political forces, and the long and often bloody process of revolutionary attrition can achieve this.* **Our purpose is, however, quite different: we want to seize power within the system,** *and we shall stay in power if we embody some new status quo supported by those very forces which a revolution may seek to destroy. Should we want to achieve a fundamental social change we can do so after we have become the government. This is perhaps a more efficient method (and certainly a less painful one) than that of classic revolution.*

Though we will try to avoid all conflict with the "political" forces, some of them will almost certainly try to oppose a coup. But this opposition will largely subside when we have substituted our new status quo for the old one, and can enforce it by our control of the state bureaucracy and security forces. This period of transition, which comes after we have emerged into the open and before we

are vested with the authority of the state, is the most critical phase of the coup. (at 58)
— Edward Luttwak, *Coup d' État* (1979)

Preconditions of the *Coup*

A) Political participation confined to a small fraction of the population (Little/no dialogue between government and people.)

B) Target state must be substantially independent from foreign powers

C) Target state must have a political center

Factors which weaken developed countries:

A) Severe and prolonged economic crisis, with widespread unemployment and/or hyperinflation

B) A long, unsuccessful war or a major defeat (military or diplomatic)

C) Chronic instability under a democratic system

Example: 1958 France (IVth Republic)

SECESSION

...Whenever any form of government becomes destructive to these ends (of liberty) *it is the right of the people to alter or abolish it...*
— American Declaration of Independence, 1776

*Most damaging of all was the fact that while an early draft of the Constitution had specified that "the Union shall be perpetual," **the phrase had been dropped prior to adoption of a final document.***
— Daniel Lazare; *The Frozen Republic*, p. 104

State after state made it clear that they were joining the Union *voluntarily*, without relinquishing their sovereignty. For example, Virginia's ratification resolution specified *"that the powers granted under the Constitution being derived from the People...may be resumed by them whensoever the same shall be perverted to their injury or oppression."* Madison had to admit, in *The Federalist* #39, that *"each State, in ratifying the Constitution, is considered as a sovereign body independent of all others, and only to be bound by its voluntary act."*

The early history of secession in America

There have been three successful secession movements in America. One was the Declaration of Independence and the founding of the Articles [of Confederation]. The second was the U.S. Consitution itself, whereby the states seceded from their original compact (the Articles). The third was the Confederate secession, that was successful, but militarily overturned.
— from an Internet thread on secession, 27 November 2000

A state's nullification of acts it considered unconstitutional or unlawful is an expedient to protect its rights within the Union. Nullification was not solely a Southern act. Massachusetts nullified the fugitive slave law and threatened to secede before complying with a Supreme Court ruling.

A state's secession is a forced necessity to protect its rights which can no longer be maintained within the Union. Secession was not originally or solely a Southern idea. It was the New England states which, on several occasions, seriously discussed leaving the Union.

In 1794, Senators Rufus King (N.Y., also a 1787 Philadelphia delegate) and Oliver Ellsworth (Conn.) approached Senator John Taylor (Va.) to discuss a peaceful dissolving of the Union because *"the southern and eastern people thought quite differently."*

After the 1800 election of Thomas Jefferson as President, which horrified the federalists, New England threatened to secede. (Alexander Hamilton's influence barely prevented New York from going along, which foiled the plan.) Jefferson's attack on the federalist judiciary, however, kept the secession coals smoldering.

> *If there be any among us who wish to dissolve the Union or to change its republican form, let them stand undisturbed, as monuments of the safety with which error of opinion may be tolerated where reason is left free to combat it.*
> — Thomas Jefferson, 1801, from his first inargural address

The coals flared up over the 1803 Louisiana Purchase, which enlarged the sphere of the South, as well as Jeffersonian appeal. Massachusetts Senator Timothy Pickering claimed that the northern confederacy would be *"exempt from the corrupt and corrupting influence and oppression of the aristocratic democrats of the South."*

> *The principles of our Revolution [of 1776] point to the remedy—a separation, for the people of the East cannot reconcile their habits, views, and interests with those of the South and West.*
> — Timothy Pickering, leader of the New England secessionists, in an 1803 letter to George Cabot

The Eastern states must and will dissolve the Union and form a separate government.
   — Senator James Hillhouse, 1803

Again, Hamilton was against secession. In what was to be his last letter, written to Theodore Sedgwick (one of the leading Massachusetts Federalists) the night before his 11 July 1804 duel with Vice President Aaron Burr, Hamilton wrote, *"Dismemberment of our Empire will be a clear sacrifice of great positive advantages, without any counterbalancing good.... [Secession would provide] no relief to our real disease; which is DEMOCRACY."*

Jefferson's Trade Embargo and Madison's War of 1812

The ruinous effect on New England of Jefferson's 1808 trade embargo with Britain and France kept Eastern resentment alive until the next catalyst, the War of 1812 and President Madison's Virginian policies. Hence, the Hartford Convention in January 1815 (convened by the "Essex Junto"). The British had already landed 4,100 troops and sacked Washington, D.C., causing President Madison and the First Lady to flee to Virginia.

There are not two hostile nations upon earth whose views of the principles and polity of a perfect commonwealth, and of men and measures, are more discordant than those of these two great divisions.
   — from a pro-secessionist Northern manifesto, just prior the War of 1812

[The 1789 Union was] *the **means** of securing the safety, liberty, and welfare of the confederacy* [of 1781], ***and not itself an end to which these should be sacrificed.***
   — John Randolph in 1814

While the New Englanders were discussing regional secession in Hartford, Major General Andrew Jackson routed the British invasion of New Orleans. News of Jackson's victory rescued Madison's administration and doomed the New England secessionist movement.

In no instance was it ever supposed that the states, which had joined the Union from their sovereign capacity, could not choose to quit the Union from that same sovereign capacity. The irony to appreciate here is that for the first twenty years of our constitutional history, it was the *creators* of that very constitution—the Federalists—who simmered with secession.

The moral? If the Federalists of 1794 to 1815—which included several personalities present at the Philadelphia Convention of 1787—saw no constitutional barriers to secession, *then how can anybody else?*

Leading up to the War Between the States

It depends on the state itself to retain or abolish the principle of representation, because it depends on itself whether it will continue as a member of the Union. To deny this right would be inconsistent with the principle on which all our political systems are founded, which is, that the people have in all cases, a right to determine how they will be governed.

This right must be considered as an ingredient in the original composition of the general government, which, though not expressed, was mutually understood...

The secession of a state from the Union depends on the will of the people of such state. The people alone as we have already seen, hold the power to alter their constitution. (p.296)

...But in any manner by which a secession is to take place, nothing is more certain than that the act should be deliberate, clear, and unequivocal. (p.302)

— William Rawle, *View of the Constitution* (1825)

If the Union was formed by the accession of States then the Union may be dissolved by the secession of States.

— Daniel Webster, 15 February 1833, U.S. Senate

The name of our federation is not Consolidated States, but United States. A number of States held together by coercion, or the point of the bayonet, would not be a Union. Union is necessarily voluntary—the act of choice, free association.

Nor can this voluntary system be changed to one of force without the destruction of "The Union."... A Union of States necessarily implies separate sovereignties, voluntarily acting together. And to bruise these distinct sovereignties into one mass of power is, simply, to destroy the Union—to overthrow our system of government.

— C.C. Burr (editor), *The Federal Government: Its True Nature and Character* (1840)

Any people whatever have a right to abolish the existing government and form a new one that suits them better.

— Abraham Lincoln, *Congressional Records*, 1847

The Union is a Union of States founded upon Compact. How is it to be supposed that when different parties enter into a compact for certain purposes either can disregard one provision of it and expect

*others to observe the rest? If the Northern States willfully and delib-
erately refuse to carry out their part of the Constitution, the South
would be no longer bound to keep the compact. A bargain broken
on one side is broken on all sides.*
>   — Daniel Webster, Capon Springs Speech, 1851

The South secedes

*If the Declaration of Independence justified the secession of
3,000,000 colonists in 1776, I do not see why the Constitution ratified by the same men should not justify the secession of 5,000,000
of the Southerners from the Federal Union in 1861.*

*...when a section of our Union resolves to go out, we shall resist
any coercive acts to keep it in. We hope never to live in a Republic
where one section is pinned to the other section by bayonets.*
>   — Horace Greeley, *New York Tribune*

*A nation preserved with liberty trampled underfoot is much worse
than a nation in fragments but with the spirit of liberty still alive.*
>   — Private John H. Haley, 7th Maine Regiment (1860s)

*Then, Senators, we recur to the compact which binds us together;
we recur to the principles upon which our government was founded;
and when you deny them, and when you deny to us the right to withdraw from a government, which, thus perverted, threatens to be destructive of our rights, we but tread in the path of our fathers when
we proclaim our independence, and take the hazard. This is done,
not in hostility to others—not to injure any section of the country—not
even for our own pecuniary benefit; but from the high and solemn
motive of defending and protecting the rights we inherited, and
which it is our duty to transmit unshorn to our children.*
>   — Jefferson Davis,
>   21 January 1861 Farewell Address to the US Senate

*It is joyous in the midst of perilous times to look around upon a peo-
ple united in heart, where one purpose of high resolve animates and
actuates the whole; where the sacrifices to be made are not
weighed in the balance against honor and right and liberty and
equality. Obstacles may retard, but they cannot long prevent, the
progress of a movement sanctified by its justice and sustained by a
virtuous people. Reverently let us invoke the God of our fathers to
guide and protect us in our efforts to perpetuate the principles which
by His blessing they were able to vindicate, establish, and transmit
to their posterity. With the continuance of His favor ever gratefully
acknowledged, we may hopefully look forward to success, to peace,
and to prosperity.*
>   — Jefferson Davis,
>   18 February 1861 Inaugural Address as CSA President

This country, with its institutions, belongs to the people who inhabit it. Whenever they shall grow weary of the existing government, they can exercise their constitutional right of amending it or their revolutionary right to dismember it or overthrow it.
 — Abraham Lincoln, 4 April 1861, first inaugural address

Had [President] Buchanan in 1860 sent an armed force to prevent the nullification of the Fugitive Slave Law, as Andrew Jackson threatened to do in 1833, there would have been a secession of fifteen Northern States instead of thirteen Southern States.
Had the Democrats won out in 1860 the Northern States would have been the seceding States, not the Southern.
 — George Lunt (Massachusetts), *Origin of the Late War*

All we ask is to be left alone.
 — Jefferson Davis
 President of the Confederate States of America, 1861

Modern secessionist sentiment

It very well may come to secession. Canada will likely lead the way, as she is much less cohesive a nation than America. Quebec came within a gnat's breath of seceding in 1995, and we expect it to do so within a few years, probably followed by B.C. Talk of secession shouldn't terrify you. Nations generally fizzle out after 200 years, and America is experiencing a vast polarization of politics to make disunion almost guaranteed.

We are no longer a workably homogeneous people. We are on the verge of a political revolution fought between the working class and the welfare class. Inner city gangs, formerly deadly enemies, are now making compacts. Informational entrepreneurs are abandoning the cities and fleeing to the countryside. Their tax base shrinking and their welfare roles rising, big cities must bleed their states for taxes. Such states (*e.g.,* N.Y. and California) are now losing productive people (taxpayers) to more free states (*e.g.,* Arizona, Colorado, and Idaho).

An *unprecedented* shift of demographics is now occurring. When the states realize that they can't stem the flow, they'll cry to Uncle Sam to equalize matters. Congress will comply—taxing us all so heavily that it really won't matter *where* we live. A war will begin between those who *work* for a living and those who *vote* for it. When the productive class realizes that all the political remedies have long been handed over to the Federal Government; that they are inexorably bound up as galley slaves for the socialist ship of State and its welfare drones—*that's* when the last resort of secession will be seriously contemplated.

Any government that is the exclusive judge to the limits of its own power is in effect a tyranny.
— *The South Was Right!* (1995), p. 233

Given the growing appreciation of the need for personal restraint and for institutional means for obtaining agreement amidst great social and politcal conflict, secession has become especially relevant to the present situation in the Western world—marked as it is by growing ethnic and cultural crises and social fragmentation. It is perhaps time to reconsider secession as a potential remedy—and as a return to the fundamentals of popular control.
— H. Lee Cheek, Jr., Prof. of Poli. Sci., Lee University
    Taking Secession Seriously: A Primer (2001)

Secession arises from individual rights.
— David Gordon, *Secession, State & Liberty*

Come, my friends, 'tis not too late to seek a newer world.
— Lord Alfred Tennyson

Like a marriage that has gone bad, I believe there are enough irreconcilable differences between those who want to control and those who want to be left alone that divorce is the only peaceable alternative.
— Walter Williams, *It's Time To Part Company*, 9/13/2000

When one contemplates the political discourse over the next few years, disunion is a slam dunk. Does anyone really think that Tom Delay, Dick Armey and Jesse Helms are going to find common ground with David Bonior, Hillary Clinton and Barney Frank? They don't belong in the same country, let alone the same legislature. Why not separate them before someone really gets hurt?
— Peter Applebombe, *If At First You Don't Secede...*
    26 November 2000, *New York Times*

Compact Theory must be explored as a legitimate constitutional doctrine for the very reason that James Madison supported it to the degree he did [in the Virginia Resolutions of 1798]. Madison, commonly known as the "Father of the Constitution," drafted the Virginia Plan, which became the body of the Constitution. He also proposed the amendments which became the Bill of Rights. In this sense he holds the position of ultimate arbitrator of constitutional questions. He clearly pointed out in the Virginia Resolutions that if a federal law violated the rights of a state without redress, then that state could nullify the law. If the federal government were to persist in its violating of that state's rights, then the logical continuation of the compact theory is that the state may eventually secede from (quit) the Union. It only makes sense that a governing entity such a state may leave a larger governing body it has voluntarily joined..., if that association is harmful to it.

The 10th Amendment guarantees certain powers to the states. This amendment recognized that a state did not give up its sovereignty entirely just by joining the Union. Only if a state had given up all rights to self-determination would it be logical to argue that they must continue in a Union where that continuance is harmful to the state.

The best evidence of the legality of secession is that the states were asked to ratify the new Constitution in 1787 and the Bill of Rights in 1791. Ratification, defined as "to approve," allows the option of not approving. North Carolina and Rhode Island stayed out of the Union for several years after its creation. These two states felt that participation would be detrimental to their welfare. Since a state had the option of declining participation in the Union based on its fear of harm from such participation, it follows logically that if a state joined the Union and conditions later became harmful, then a state must retain the right to end that participation and leave the Union. Arguments to the contrary put one in the seemingly untenable position of supporting the idea that "an organization voluntarily joined cannot be voluntarily departed." Now, this may be the way things are done in the Mafia, but it should not be the rule in a democracy.

There is, in fact, constitutional doctrine to support secession. The Constitution does not discuss secession, so preventing it is not a delegated power of the federal government. Nor is secession prohibited, by the document, to the states. It is, then, a power reserved to the states or to the people. This reflects the wording of the "reserved powers clause" of the 10th Amendment... (at 73)

— Chuck Shiver; *The Rape of the American Constitution*

Those who make peaceful revolution impossible will make violent revolution inevitable.
— John F. Kennedy

An opinion can be argued with; a conviction is best shot.
— Lawrence of Arabia

When you come to a fork in the road, take it.
— Yogi Berra

Successful secessions in history

1139: Portugal from Spain
It took four civil wars, but Portugal finally broke free.

1776: U.S.A. from Britain
In a 1775 address to Parliament ("Conciliation with the Colonies), Edmund Burke stated that to force the colonies back under British law was wrong because *"...you impair the object by your very endeavors to preserve it. The thing you fought for is not the thing which you recover, but depreciated, sunk, wasted, and consumed in the contest."*

1836: Texas from Mexico

1839: Guatemala from the U. States of Central America

1861: Southern States from the U.S.A.
Although the South was forcibly rejoined to the Union after War, the secession was itself initially successful. Had the South not fired on Fort Sumter (the last remaining Federal garrison in the South, which had only one week of rations left), and instead continued to blockade, the Civil War might have been averted. However, the cannon fire of 12 April 1861 was to the North a "Pearl Harbor" event.

1862: West Virginia from Virginia
West Virginians refused to secede from the Union with Virginia, declared their independence from both Virginia and the Confederacy in 1862, and became the 35th United State in 1863.

Here's the kicker: the Confederacy let them go in peace.

1903: Panama from Colombia

1905: Norway from Sweden
Norway declared its independence after 91 years of union with Sweden, and Sweden wisely let her go without war. (Incidentally, the Northern and Southern states had been together only 84 years when Dixie seceded.)

1949: Ireland from Great Britain

1965: Singapore from Malaysia

1965: Rhodesia from Great Britain
The Unilateral Declaration of Independence (UDI) lasted until 1980 when Rhodesia was abandoned by the "free world" to the eventual Communist dictatorship of Robert Mugabe.

1967: Biafra from Nigeria

PLAYBOY INTERVIEW:

JAMES PRESTON

a candid conversation with Wyoming's new Laissez-Faire Party Governor

A third-generation Wyoming native, James Wayne Preston hails from one of the Cowboy State's oldest and wealthiest families. Expecting a career as a military aviator, he graduated from the U.S. Naval Academy to fly Marine attack helicopters. A combat veteran of the first Gulf War (where he won a Purple Heart and Silver Star), he was honorably discharged as a Captain and joined father Benjamin Preston with the family businesses.

His entrepreneurial talents quickly blossomed as he formed several ancillary enterprises, most notably his ranching software firm.

Raised in a Republican household, James Preston was always interested in free-market philosophy and economics, and grew to embrace a more libertarian creed. Major influences in this thinking were Ayn Rand, Henry Hazlitt, Bastiat, Robert Heinlein, and Lysander Spooner.

Though originally uninterested in professional politics, James Preston felt increasingly drawn to the governor's mansion due to the exhortations of many friends and colleagues.

As the apparent culmination of a decade-long libertarian migration, Wyoming, a rugged and conservative western state, recently elected the rugged and arch-conservative Preston as America's first Laissez-Faire Party governor. His administration, with the enthusiastic support of the libertarian

legislature, has enacted the most dramatic state reforms in history.

More surprisingly to most observers, it seems to be working. Violent crime (previously very low) has all but vanished. GDP is rising at a phenomenal 1% per month, and the state is leeching the nation of top business and computer talent.

James Preston is married to Juliette Kramer, a highly regarded defense attorney specializing in Bill of Rights abuse cases. They have two teenage children, James, Jr. and Hanna, whom they homeschool. They live near Casper, on a 160 acre horse ranch.

In a series of intellectually electric conversations with PLAYBOY's *interviewer, Thomas Phalk, Mr. Preston spoke about a wide variety of topics, such as jury nullification, Christianity vs. libertarianism, evolution, drugs, abortion, guns, Ayn Rand, and his Wyoming agenda. His opinions were startling, fiercely-held, and well-delivered with cheerful seriousness. He answered every question without evasion, however, his replies were often very challenging.*

Brassy. Intelligent. Opinionated. Sincere. Provocative. Vigorous. Articulate. Wealthy. Candid.

James Wayne Preston is a man whose worldview is uncommon, yet oddly compelling.

You'll either love it or hate it.

Governor Preston, we're very pleased that you agreed to be interviewed by PLAYBOY. Thank you for joining us.
Thank you, Tom. I've always enjoyed the frank nature of your interviews. Not that I'm a subscriber... (laughs)

What do you hope to accomplish for Wyoming as Governor?
To help usher Wyoming into a new era of very limited and highly responsible *laissez-faire* government. To do that, I have to gradually become the weakest governor of the 50 States. The other States all have some degree of intrusive government, so if Wyoming doesn't suit you, you have 49 choices of bondage. Free people, however, needed *someplace* to live, and many of us finally decided to make that place Wyoming.

In what areas do you believe government has overstepped its bounds?
A shorter list would be the inverse: in what areas has government *remained* in bounds? (laughs) You name it, Tom, government is improperly and unlawfully involved in many things that are not government's affair. Health, education, child care, business operations, gun rights, property rights, jury rights, and privacy, to name just a few.

Turning to politics, how does the Laissez-Faire Party differ from libertarianism or Objectivism?
In the matter of free enterprise, not at all. LFPers are, however, more deeply involved in the gun culture than are Libertarians and Objectivists,

who often pay philosophical lip service to the RKBA—the Right To Keep and Bear Arms. How anyone can claim to be a gun enthusiast or RKBA supporter and live in New York City eludes me. LFPers, on the other hand, simply *love* to shoot. We're "gunnuts" and proud of it! We wouldn't dream of living anyplace where we couldn't shoot, and shoot often. True mariners don't live in Kansas.
Also, Ayn Rand had more faith in the institution of government than we do, as we flirt quite a bit with anarcho-capitalist ideas.

Anarcho-capitalism holds that all government functions could be performed by the private-sector, is that right?
Yes, spot on. There is only one political continuum, and it is *not* "right wing" and "left wing." It is No Government versus Total Government. Anarcho-capitalism is not anarchy. Anarchy means "without a leader," but it incorrectly connotes lawlessness and chaos. Anarcho-capitalism has law and order, but enforced by armed citizens and private security agencies.

What if an accused refuses to recognize the authority of any private security agency?
That is certainly his prerogative, but in doing so he places himself *outside* the law's protection and is thus fair game.

You mean the rest of society can go gunning for him?
You bet. By forfeiting a fair trial, he takes his chances on the run. Actually, the scenario isn't all too different

from today, if you think about it. But, hey, you're talking about the child of an embryo. We're a generation or two from the first experiment in anarcho-capitalism. By the way, a very interesting book on the matter is Neal Stephenson's *The Diamond Age*.

Would such a society actually work?

Well, we won't know until we try it and see, will we? The trouble with limited government is that it's never *stayed* limited. Perhaps no government at all is the answer...when we're ready for it.

Wyoming is now the most "gun-toting" state in the Union. Is a state-wide fascination with firearms really necessary?

You bet. A gun is simply a tool used to prevent aggression. For some-gunowners it is merely a means to that end, and that's fine. However, many other gunowners have discovered the historical, cultural, mechanical, and aesthetic wonder of firearms. I certainly did! The gun culture is part of our history, and is vital for our future. It is healthy, enjoyable, and helps to preserve our rights and sustain our heritage.

Nevertheless, in today's savage society, aren't additional gun control laws required to maintain law and order?

What, you mean the first 20,000 laws didn't work? (laughs) One definition of insanity is repetition of action with the expectation of different results. Anti-2nd Amendment laws have never reduced crime, yet that is the rationale for every new bill.

Oh, and to which "savage society" are you referring? Los Angeles? New York City? Detroit? We're not savage in Wyoming. An armed society is a polite society. We're both. We have the least crime in the nation.

And since criminals by definition don't abide by laws, let's call "gun control" for what it *really* is—victim disarmament. No, Tom—we don't need any more victim disarmament laws. We don't need any more victims, we need more *victors*. All those unconstitutional laws need to be repealed, just as we did in Wyoming. It's the only state where street criminals are outnumbered by armed citizens, and that's exactly the way it *should* be! We will continue to nourish our gun culture until it once again becomes second nature to us.

But the Supreme Court ruled in *Emerson v. U.S.* that the 2nd Amendment is not inviolable, and that the right to bear arms can be regulated if the government has a compelling interest.

Yes, and the Court utterly ignored those vital four words *"shall not be infringed"*—words which appear in no other Bill of Rights amendment. It was a cowardly, despicable omission.

In 1857 the Supreme Court ruled in *Dred Scott* that black Americans were not citizens within the meaning and protection of the Constitution. Eventually, they condescended to effectively overrule themselves. Perhaps someday that will occur with *Emerson*. But until then, we in Wyoming maintain that *"shall not be infringed"* means just that, and we will take the language at its word. Besides, it's a sad case for freedom if you have to wait for 5 Justices to figure out what any Laramie 4th grader knows.

Aren't you concerned with a federal response to Wyoming's nullification of U.S. gun laws?

Those laws once effectively disarmed peaceable Americans because of their leverage over the random individual. That leverage no longer exists in Wyoming, as we are a united front against further violations of our 2nd Amendment right to own and carry arms.

The ATF quickly figured that out and left Wyoming months ago. There was no point in their staying. Even if their goon squads encountered no citizen resistance, no gun case could ever be successfully prosecuted. Too many fully informed jurors out there! We will not send our neighbor to 20 years in the federal pen as a *felon* because a piece of wood or metal on his gun was ¼" too long or too short. That's over with!

Today, Wyoming is the most armed and safest place on the planet. We have all but eradicated street crime. So, the feds have left us alone. They sort of *have* to. (laughs) To pick a fight with us over *Emerson* at this point would be ridiculously spiteful and counterproductive.

Federal agents are actually leaving Wyoming?

Yes, they are. Many Wyomingites have thoroughly shunned federal agents and their families. Only five cities in Wyoming have more than 25,000 people, so it's difficult for federal agents to hide in our state.

A hobby of our high-schoolers is to locate their personal cars and regularly shoe-polish them with "FBI" or "ATF" or "IRS" or "DEA." The feds really hate this, although I can't understand why if they're truly proud of their work. For example, there are a dozen FBI agents in downtown Lander next to Ruffian's Ice Cream Bar who are livid about being "outed" by the so-called "Fremont County Map to your Local Feds." (laughs) All their home addresses were listed. What a *dozen* FBI agents are doing in a small, remote Wyoming town of 9,000 people is anybody's guess.

Still, federal law enforcement agents have a job to do.

Not if it means violating our Bill of Rights. They can't do that and stay unknown and unchallenged for long in Wyoming. While the ATF agent is out looking to imprison gunowners for some nonviolent technical offense his wife has no friends in town and few businesses will deal with them. After a few months of this, the wife will say, *"We're not staying here any longer"* and they transfer. As Jeff Foxworthy used to say, *"If she ain't happy...you ain't happy."* Word is circulating throughout the federal agencies that Wyoming is socially inhospitable, so they try not to get transferred there.

Ostracism and shunning are very powerful. When the wife is used as a stick to beat the man, it gets his attention like nothing else can.

That seems cruel to the wife.

Nobody forced her to marry and breed with a guy who has chosen to oppress his countrymen under the false color of law. Now, I will grant you that ostracism is unfair to the children, who had no choice in their parents. Perhaps, however, it will dissuade them from joining the ATF.

Your program in Wyoming is very aggressive and dramatic. How is it going over with the locals there?

Well, I admit that our program took many Wyomingites by surprise, even the conservatives. Most have quickly understood what we are trying to accomplish and now back the agenda very strongly—especially after experiencing the results for themselves.

Our relatively small liberal population, however, was quite shocked. I guess they didn't believe that I meant what I said during my campaign, or if elected that I'd actually back it up with action. I think they're still in shock.

I will be the first to admit that Wyoming is not and will not be for everybody. No state is. I'll also tell you that Wyoming will not be a cheery choice for those who demand government solutions to personal issues. If you don't like it, then move to or stay in California. There are many states wherein government supremacists may assuage their private conscience at public expense. Wyoming is not one of them.

You feel strongly about the jury nullification of disagreeable laws. How does this work?

Jurors have a 1,000 year-old right to judge both the facts and the *law*. The primary purpose of a jury trial is to simultaneously put the *law* on trial as much as the accused. The jury is

actually the *fourth* branch of government, which nullifies bad law when the legislature refuses its repeal. Our legislature proposed a constitutional Fully Informed Jury Amendment, and the people ratified it in April. Wyoming is the second state to do so, after South Dakota.

But that's a prelude for eventual anarchy.

If your premise assumes an inherently anarchist people, then maybe. However, Americans are anything but anarchist. High-spirited and shallow perhaps, but not anarchist. As much personal responsibility that's been bred from us, it still remains a significant part of our programming.

What we've forgotten, or more likely never knew, is that the *we* are the fountainhead of the law, who merely delegate our authority to government. Delegate, not relinquish. When government is ineffective or corrupt, then the people must repossess the law until they may once again delegate it back to good government.

In your speeches and writings you often harken to that theme of courage. Why?

Bravery pays the only principle, but cowardice *always* pays the interest as well. It's cheaper to be brave. Not to mention more honorable.

For example, the British were cowards until 1940 when they were forced to be brave. Churchill slapped them into clarity. But until then, Britain and Europe paid a *lot* of compound interest. So did we, on their behalf.

In your mind, what is courage and why is there so little of it today?

Well, courage is not the absence of fear. It is the *subjugation* of fear. For example, a 300 pound, maniacal knife-wielding man with murder in his eyes is certainly something to be afraid of. If you can run away and live, do so. There is no dishonor in that, and any good martial arts *sensei* will agree.

If, on the other hand, you *cannot* run away and live—if you are all that stands between him and your family—then you must be brave. You must fight him. The Brits finally faced up to Hitler and fought him. Only after the Battle of Britain did the American people decide that the English might be worth saving after all.

There are many types of courage other than physical, such as moral courage, social courage, and financial courage. The parent courage of them all is courage to *self*, which is the courage to act by that which you know or believe to be right.

Can you give some examples of these?

Sure. Moral courage would be sending an anonymous letter to the editor against closed-shop unionism. Social courage would be signing your name to it. Financial courage would be jeopardizing your own business by not selling to unionized companies. Physical courage would be defending your life and property against marauding union thugs.

There is a progression involved, but, as you can see, all stem from courage to self.

It is very rare for a person to truly and consistently exhibit courage in all *four* facets, that is, moral, social, financial, and physical. Generally, the courageous are so in just one or two facets. For example, Ayn Rand showed great moral and social courage by writing and speaking as she did, but very little financial courage regarding the income taxes with which she disagreed philosophically, yet continued to not only pay, but *over*pay for fear of an audit. There are people who would risk their fortune to defend what they believe is right, yet run from a fistfight. There also are people who would fight to the death in defense of themselves and their family, yet are too timid to speak up in public.

My point is that the courageous are also very often somehow cowards outside their own sphere, and those viewed as cowards can be courageous *inside* their own sphere.

Who has provided inspiration to you for courage?

Wow, there have been so *many*. I'll have to limit myself to those who exhibited four-faceted courage. Sir Thomas More certainly did. The stageplay and movie *A Man For All Seasons* is one of my favorites.

In my view, the most courageous man was Jesus Christ. At Golgatha, He had lost His property, family, and even His disciples. He even thought He had lost God the Father. Yet He never stumbled in His courage to self.

Why do you say that?

Well, after the disciple Peter sliced off the high priest's servant's right ear in the Garden of Gethsemane in Matthew 26, He chastised Peter,

Thinkest thou that I cannot now pray to my Father, and He shall presently give me more than twelve legions of angels? But how then shall the scriptures be fulfilled, that it must be?

What He was saying was, *"I don't have to go through with this if I choose not to."* You see, even when he apparently could have avoided the Redeemer's sacrifice without recrimination from the Father, Jesus remained courageous to self, and then demonstrated incomparable physical courage on the cross.

This is hardly a proper example, as the story of the crucifixion and resurrection has not been satisfactorily corroborated according to many historians.

Many other historians and scholars disagree, and quite a few of them were originally atheist. For example, applying biographical testing is very enlightening. Such looks at the number of manuscript copies of the original, and the time period between the original and the copies when none of the originals still exists. Take the manuscript copies of the writings of Caesar, Plato, Aristotle, and Tacitus, for example. We have only one to ten copies of them each, all written no sooner than *1,000* years after the originals. Nevertheless, the copies are held by scholars to be accurate. Regarding the books of the New Testament which were written between 40-90 A.D., the earliest

manuscript copies date only 40-50 years after the originals and more than 13,000 copies exist. If, by virtue of biographical testing, we may rely upon the genuineness of the purported works of Caesar, Plato, Aristotle, and Tacitus, then the veracity of the New Testament is even more assured. It was written by living witnesses and players, and would have been repudiated by other living witnesses if false.

So, you believe that Jesus Christ was the Son of God, who died on the cross and was resurrected after three days?

I certainly do. But that's just me. What's compelling is that people of early 1st century Israel believed it. They were *there.* Their faith and actions are the most compelling proof of the deity of Jesus.

Nearly all religions agree that Jesus was a moral man and a good teacher, so why is any further attribution necessary? Why can't we simply accept Jesus as that, and dispense with the troublesome and dubious claim of Godhood?

C.S. Lewis, who lived many of his earlier years as an atheist, addressed that precise issue best. Jesus declared himself not "a" Son of God, but *the* Son of God. Not "a" Christ, but *the* Christ. In John 14:6 He said, *"I am the way, the truth, and the life: no man cometh unto the Father, but by me."* That's an extraordinary claim.

As a claim, it was either true or false. If false, then Jesus either knew or did not know that it was false. If he knew, then he was a liar. If he did not know, then he was a lunatic. If Jesus was a liar or a lunatic, then he *cannot* be regarded as a "good man" or a "moral teacher." He is either Lord, or he was full of lies or insanity—meaning, a bad man. Logically there is no in between.

Nothing substantiates that Jesus was either legend, liar, and lunatic. That leaves only one alternative: His claim was *true,* and He is the Lord. What we do about it is up to us. That is the most concise case I can make for the deity of Jesus.

The world will admit that He was good, because He *was* and they have to give him at least *that.* However, the world refuses to proclaim Him the Lord, because doing so would conversely acknowledge that they are *not* the Lord. They just can't "go there," regardless of compelling evidence.

What if it was just a fairy tale supported by mass delusion?

The lives of the disciples and early Christian leaders is most telling. After the crucifixion, the disciples were scared men, running for their lives. Their leader had been publicly executed. They did not expect Jesus to rise from the dead, even though He had said that He would. Yet days later, this same group of men became bold and evangelical. Thomas no longer doubted and Peter shed his cowardice for courage.

What had happened? The resurrection. They, as well as hundreds of others, had seen and spoke with a living Jesus.

Couldn't they have made up the resurrection story?

No. It would have been at once disproven by the Romans or by the Jewish leaders by producing a body. It would have been in their interest to do so, for it would've ended the radical movement they'd tried to suppress.

What if the *disciples* had taken the body and hidden it?

To what end? To continue preaching a message they *knew* was a *lie*? All but *one* of them died martyrs' deaths. Andrew, Jude, Peter, Philip, and Simon were all crucified. Barnabas, James (the brother of Jesus), and Matthias were stoned. Bartholomew and James (the Less) were beaten. Luke was hung on an olive tree. Mark was dragged through the streets by his feet and then burned. Matthew and James (son of Zebedee) were killed by the sword. Paul was beheaded. Thomas was thrust through by a spear, and Thaddaeus was killed by arrows. Only John died of natural causes.

People simply do not allow themselves to be killed, much less in such violence, for preaching something they *know* to be a lie. Therefore, they could not have stolen Jesus's body —which was under Roman guard, mind you—in order to prop up some gigantic farce. It simply isn't logical.

As fantastic as the resurrection may seem, it is the only scenario which fits all the facts and accounts for the post-crucifixion evangelical zeal of the disciples and early Christians.

But even still, what if you're wrong?

If the Christian is proven wrong, then what has he lost? An otherwise bawdy, hollow, and pointless life? Hedonism for the pure sake of hedonism? He's lost nothing. A Christian needs no cosmic back up plan.

But, if the *atheist* is proven wrong, then he has lost everything. He had no back up plan. He was a trapeze artist without a net. Perhaps there is no life after death and perhaps there are no supernatural consequences for earthly actions, but that's not the way to *bet*.

Ah, Pascal's wager.

Perhaps, but I did not accept Jesus because of that. The Gospel rang true to me, and still does even through times of doubt and confusion.

If you could make Christianity the official religion of Wyoming, would you do so?

Absolutely *not*! My gosh, what a question!

Well, why not, if Christianity is best for mankind?

Not if it is forcibly imposed on people! God wants our free will and He hawks His wares, so to speak, in the free market of religions. Our will is the only thing we have that's truly ours. He wants us to *choose* Him for Himself. The real question is not whether God exists, but if so—would you want to *know* Him?

But why does there have to even be a Creator? Evolution is sufficient to explain the universe.

(laughs) That takes *more* faith than believing in a Creator! Look, why do we still have the ape, but not the "ape-man"—a supposedly higher form of ape? According to evolutionary theory of natural selection, the mere ape would have been weeded out long ago. Inferior transitional specimens are not supposed to survive within the same environment as their superiors. The ape wasn't weeded out because the "ape-man" never existed. *Ramapithecus, Australopithecus, Java Man, Neanderthal Man, Cro-Magnon Man, Peking Man, Nebraska Man,* and *Piltdown Man*—all them have been proven either man or ape or even pig, but never a transitional "ape-man."

That's why we see systemic gaps in the fossil records. They mirror the same gaps in the modern world.

Just because an "ape-man" hasn't been found doesn't mean that it never existed.

That's correct as far as it goes, but evolutionists argue that it *did* exist even though they cannot find a single example of one.

Look, even the simplest organisms are too complex to have arrived by sheer evolution. Take the so-called "simple cell." It contains DNA, required for cellular reproduction. So, the DNA had to be there *first.* And where did this sophisticated informational storage and retrieval system come from? Sir Francis Crick, who discovered the DNA molecule in 1956, stated that not even in 3 billion years of evolution could it have come by accident. Since he was an atheist, he could only postulate that advanced beings from outer space put it here. I'm curious if he ever wondered about *their* origin. If ETs themselves were a product of natural selection, and if they created our DNA (or gave us of some of theirs), doesn't their own advanced nature *magnify* the incredility of Darwin's theory? It forces evolutionists to climb an even *steeper* hill of proof to explain an even *more* sophisticated life form than us. Crick's ET hypothesis of human DNA, concocted to slice the Gordian Knot of irreducible complexity, actually destroys Darwinism.

Try as they might, evolutionists have never been able to offer any theory less outlandish, less fantastic than creationism. *They* are the real men of faith, not the deists.

Take the human eye, for example. *Why* would it have evolved? Remember, every transitional stage of evolution must have an *immediate* advantage to the species which engenders its retention by natural selection. So, why the pupil without a lens? Or, if the lens came first, then why the lens without a pupil? Evolutionists can't entertain such dilemmas. Oh, and don't forget the cornea, which is a pre-lens. Or the aqueous humour, the liquid-filled body behind the cornea. Or the iris muscle which controls pupil size like a camera shutter. Or the eyelids and eyelashes and eyebrows to protect the eye camera. All of these components came into sequential parallel being? It's absurd.

And I haven't even gotten into the retina, optic nerve, and the entire visual nervous system of the brain. Why would an eye develop without a visual cortex to make use of the information? And without the eye's information, why would a visual nervous system have developed at all?

If you take any combination of interrelated systems, or even system components, you will see that none of them would have had any evolutionary *reason* for existing before the other, much less on its own. Even Darwin admitted that trying to recon-

cile the eye with natural selection made him ill. Finally, if you consider the parallel evolution of the eye in the squid (a molluscs), the vertebrates, and the arthropods, the notion of the eye being produced multiple times amongst different *phyla* by modern synthetic theory literally makes scientists' heads swim.

Assuming that all of the above isn't too incredible, then the Darwinist must also accept the notion that an early visual system evolved into one so sophisticated that we still cannot reproduce it today. The best photographic film we have is 1,000 times less sensitive. Our eye's resolution is so good that it can see a lighted candle a mile away in the dark—about one second of angle. Its acuity can distinguish between over 10 million colors.

In short, life, any or all of it, is just too complex, and too obviously designed to be the product of modern synthetic theory. According to Romans 1:18-20, we can deduce the invisible through the visible, the metaphysical through the physical, and we are "without excuse" if we refuse to do so. Do you think it any accident that mankind since Egypt's First Dynasty has tried to understand his existence within theistic paradigms? We cannot help but do so, any more than water cannot help but run downhill.

We may understandably differ in our deisms, but we cannot be excused for our atheism. We can think a thousand things about God, except that He does not exist. The universe is far, far too wondrous to deny its engineer. All of creation screams "Creator!" and none of us can claim deafness.

Well, assuming a Creator, why can't life exist without any spiritual finale? You die, and that's it.

A one-act play, huh? (laughs) Well, if that third choice were available, you would still have the yoke of this world, which includes gravity, misfortune, general ignorance, stupidity, sickness, famine, and death. Furthermore, it would necessarily preclude any afterlife, which means that there is no reward or punishment for deeds done on Earth.

Immoral men of considerable strength could argue that a moral code would not be in *their* self-interest. Such would constrain them from rape, pillage, and plunder—which serves only *weaker* men, who deserve to be plundered under the Darwinesque rules of "might makes right." Absent some sort of justice in the afterlife, immorality has a point. (laughs)

Such a world would be nothing more than an endless series of warlords and clans. Mankind lived that way for centuries, and finally clawed its way out of it via the Enlightenment of the Renaissance. In other words, by the rule of equitable law in the protection of life and property.

Morality—assuming it could have ever come into being on its own —would instantly be reduced, first, to a mere construct, and then after a very brief interval of time morality would vanish. C.S. Lewis, again, proved that in *The Abolition of Man*. Hence, this third alternative could not exist for any significant period of time—certainly not for thousands of years.

Ayn Rand made a valiant *secular* attempt to justify a moral code outside of metaphysical implications, but failed. Although her argument that morality is in one's best self-interest was compelling, it had to remain woefully inadequate.

Why?

Because when the Apostle Paul wrote in Romans chapter two about the law being written in our hearts, he wasn't kidding. If it hadn't been in our hearts in the first place, we'd have never come up with it on our own. This was something that Miss Rand sadly never could grasp.

Humans attempt to be moral because deep down they believe that they *should*. We are inherently cognizant of our dark nature. While we'd all prefer to wallow around in the muck, we know, or at least sense, consequences to that. There is a gnawing fear—never fully extinguished—that evil *will* be punished, if not in this life, then afterwards.

PLAYBOY interviewed Ayn Rand about 50 years ago.

Yes, I've read it. It was excellent. She was a seminal thinker and a mighty champion for individual rights. However, she died a bitter and lonely woman, which suggests that Objectivism was lacking. Her work is a fine place to *begin*, but not to end.

Miss Rand was a devout atheist who viewed all religion as hostile to individual liberty. How do you reconcile Christianity with your libertarian beliefs?

There is really nothing to reconcile, Tom. For example, the Ten Commandments address offenses of three different natures: religious, moral, and criminal. Several commandments are of a religious nature regarding polytheism, idolatry, blasphemy, and the Sabbath day. The atheist libertarian would consider these irrelevant to his life, and is not affected by practicing Christians, especially since all "blue laws" have been repealed.

Other commandments deal with moral behavior, such as honoring one's parents, and forbidding adultery and envy. These make good sense, and promote decency. Again, no tort could be claimed by the atheist.

The rest prohibit crimes of violence or property, such as theft, murder, and perjury. Not even the atheist libertarian would argue with those.

There is no initiation of force to become a Christian. I do not see any paradox in being a Christian libertarian, who chooses to also abide by other laws which are moral and religious. Being a Christian in no way interferes with being a libertarian. In the secular realm, the Ten Commandments tell us to obey our marriage vows, honor our parents, earn our *own* stuff instead of coveting our neighbors', be truthful witnesses, and not commit crimes of violence or property. All that is in accord with libertarian principles.

How do you justify the Crusades and Spanish Inquisition, then?

I don't. There have been many outrageous and unlawful acts committed in the name of God, which cannot be justified anywhere in the Bible. Lord Ellenborough once wrote, *"The greater the truth, the greater the libel."* Man has the infinite capacity to mess things up, and man has twisted and perverted the Gospel of Jesus for political purposes.

The standard for Christian behavior is not a priest or the church. It is Jesus. He is the standard by which to weigh Christianity, and Jesus never forced anybody to accept Him.

But aren't Christian principles opposed to capitalism? I mean, the Bible talks about money being root of all evil and rich men not being able to get into heaven.

Let's quote accurately. I Timothy 6:9 said that the rich fall into temptation and a snare, and into many foolish and hurtful lusts, which drown men in destruction and perdition. In the next verse, Apostle Paul said that the *love* of money is the root of all evil, meaning the evils just described. Paul was speaking of the love of wealth luring Christians away from the faith. There is nothing inherently wrong with riches. It is only when riches begin to rule your life that riches become a problem, and this is recognized even in the secular realm.

Jesus addressed this issue in Matthew 19 when he counseled the rich young ruler who sought eternal life to sell his possessions and give the proceeds to the poor. *Then* he would have treasure in heaven. One could think of it as divesting from a failing bank and rolling over the balance into a new bank which was sound. Eternally sound. (laughs)

Was Jesus implicitly demanding this of *all* wealthy people? No. He merely recognized the one remaining blockage in *that* young man's life, his inordinate preoccupation with his possessions—his trust in riches over God. This same story was nearly identically told also in Mark 10 and Luke

18. When the wealthy young man went away in great sadness, Jesus remarked to His disciples, *"A rich man shall hardly enter into the kingdom of heaven. It is easier for a camel to go through the eye of a needle than for a rich man to enter into the kingdom of God."* Jesus did not say, or even imply, that it was impossible—just that it was very difficult because the wealthy are inherently quite loath to drop their faith in riches for God.

But if a camel obviously can't go through the eye of a needle, isn't that saying the same thing as impossible?

No, not if you consider what the "needle's eye" meant in ancient Jewish life. It was slang for the very narrow opening in large gates within the city walls. It was for foot traffic. A camel *could* get through, but only if it were kneeling down and unloaded. The allegory is perfect. A rich man *could*, with difficulty, enter the kingdom of heaven, unloaded and kneeling. Meaning, free of his past faith in the world's system, and humble to God.

However, don't take any of this to mean that it is wrong to seek wealth, invest profitably, or own successful businesses. Jesus made this quite clear in the parable of the talents found at Matthew 25:14. The moral is clear: we are not to allow wealth to usurp higher matters. This is sound policy even if limited to the secular realm. How many rich people place honor and integrity over money? Very few.

What would be your Christian view on drugs?

I believe that God created them, and for a reason. For example, it's no accident that so many things so easily ferment into alcohol, and the ability of mankind to "take the edge off" throughout history hasn't been all bad. Jesus had no compunction of turning water into wine, after all.

Cannabis, peyote, mushrooms, etc. are all natural substances, hence I don't believe that they are inherently iniquitous. Many Christians would disagree, but not necessarily because they want to dictate the lives of others. Rather, they are deeply concerned about the widespread injurious effects of drugs and alcohol on society, and rightly so. However, what they must appreciate is that drug addiction is first a spiritual and psychological problem—an issue of *demand*—and *not* an issue of supply to be forbidden by government in a costly and hypocritical social war. Millions of people would never use drugs even if they were legal and free of charge.

So, as both as a Christian and libertarian, I can't see responsible drug use as evil. People have a right to control their own diets. However, there's a vast difference between being drunk and being a drunkard. Whatever we do, we become— eventually. That's human nature. So, beware that nothing in your life— drugs, food, sex, music, gambling, TV, etc.—goes from recreation to harmful addiction.

Isn't there a schism between Christians and libertarians on the matter of abortion?

Generally, yes. It's a profound subject. Are you sure you want to explore it in detail?

Why not? That's what provocative interviews are for.

All right, but let's keep it simple.

Fine. How?

Let's talk about the easiest and largest issue: women participating in consensual sex who have at their informed disposal *many* ways *not* to become pregnant, including abstinence. *This* is is real issue of abortion.

OK, agreed.

Consenting adults know exactly where babies come from, and abortion is resorted to in well over 80% of the time as nothing more than postcoital birth control. Often, abortion is the *only* form of birth control. In over half the cases, not even condoms or spermicides had been used, much less the Pill. Abortion is being used—not as the last resort, but the *only* resort—and that is disgraceful.

Worse still is that at least 43% of abortions are *repeat* abortions. Even if abortion was truly a last resort, how many times can a woman morally repeat it? Didn't she learn anything from her *first* abortion?

Are you sure about the figures?

Yes, quite sure. In a 1987 survey by researchers with the Alan Guttmacher Institute, which is overtly *pro-choice*, the #1 reason why 76% mothers choose to terminate their unborn child is their concern "about how having a baby could change her life." In fact, the first eight reasons were all about the inconvenience involved.

If a woman chooses to have sex, she risks becoming pregnant. With such a pregnancy comes responsibility. How could it *not*? By voluntarily engaging in sexual behavior, she has voluntarily accepted the risk of co-creating with a man a separate human life. If the consequences of that pregnancy are too onerous, then she should have considered that *before* sex, not after. There is no "Rewind" button in life. That's why actions always have consequences.

Let's say that a man lying in a vegetative coma had at least a 95% chance of fully recovering and living a normal life, and that the recovery would begin in several minutes at the soonest and eight months at the latest. Would it *then* be moral or legal to remove him from life-support before that time? Of course not. Yet precisely the same thing is being done 1½ million times a year to unborn babies, generally out of convenience. Three out ten conceptions end in the destruction of the fetus. It's a gargantuan phenomenon.

The argument about women having the right to control their own bodies and destinies falls flat if it's *really* about avoiding the consequences of their own bad choices. Libertarian ethics correctly prize personal responsibility as the corollary to personal liberty, except, ironically, in this *one* particular matter. The existence of this exception really should give libertarians pause.

Also, the double standard against fathers is outrageous.

What double standard?

That men are—as they should be —held responsible for fathering a child, yet *they* don't have the option of preventing or demanding an abortion. A woman, however, can kill a man's baby as his sperm falls into the "abandoned property" category, or she can force him to support it. Men have no choice either way. Men are financial partners, but not *moral* partners? How is this not a double standard? If men enjoyed a similar situation, the feminist uproar would be deafening.

Choose *one.* If women indeed own their bodies and can abort their baby without the father's consent, then they should accept the responsibility of raising their children on their own. That is the flip side of ownership.

Or, if their developing baby is a unique human life which cannot be aborted by the mother for her sheer convenience, then the father is required to support it. But choose one.

You cited the shopworn figure of 1.5 million annual abortions. Doesn't that avoid the problem of 1.5 million unwanted babies? Who would raise all those children forced into existence by your moralism? Who would pay for them? The state? The pro-lifers?

Gee, how about their *parents*, Tom! Cannot society demand that its members demonstrate some personal responsibility for their actions? "Forced into existence by *my* moralism?" Millions of men and women regularly engage in—for the sake of sheer recreation—risky behavior fraught with a myriad of serious consequences, but pro-lifers are a bunch of up-tight prudes who would dare to legislate morality?

By the way, one of the main pro-choice arguments in the 1970s was that legalized abortion on demand would reduce the number of welfare babies. Just the opposite has hap-pened, because what you subsidize you encourage, and what you tax you discourage. Those same pro-choice liberals have politically guaranteed a continuing welfare class by *rewarding* unwed mothers through AFDC and other programs. Every fatherless baby increases the government benefits of the welfare mother, so why *should* she abort them?

Look, your question is based on an inversion of what's really going on here. 1.5 million humans are forced into existence each year because of irresponsibility. They are killed before they can even become children.

So, in your view, a fetus is a baby?

Expecting mothers seem to think so, don't they? When have you ever heard a pregnant woman say, "Ooh, I just felt my fetus move"?

Let's put it another way: an obviously pregnant woman is attacked on the street and miscarries. Does everyone say, "What is she so upset about? It was just a *fetus*!" Of course not—everyone understands that an unborn baby has been lost. "Fetus" was a medical term. Now it's a political one, as the abortionists cannot bring themselves to say the B-word—"baby."

It's ironic to hear a libertarian espouse a Catholic view on abortion.

Well, *can* one truly have a "view" on abortion? Isn't the only real pertinent question: When does human life begin? Meaning, when does a developing human being have the right of moral and legal protection? Remember, human life is *pleomorphic.* All of us are constantly developing and changing, so the matter isn't as cut and dried as one may think. So, considering that, when does human life begin? At the first cellular mitosis? After its first fetal heart beat? When brain waves are detected? After 6 months? After being born when it gets a name change from fetus to baby? After it is weaned? When it shows self-knowledge? When it can walk? When it can speak? When it becomes materially self-sufficient? *When?*

Pick one, if you can. But in doing so you're allowing the mother to exterminate its life *before* that point. Many so-called "pro-choice" advocates claim that any unborn baby is fair game. I really cannot see how a baby just minutes from being born is somehow inferior to a baby which had only just travelled down the birth canal. The argument is not logical because a born baby is no more "viable" in a self-sufficient sense than an unborn baby. The whole "post-birth viability" argument is a sham.

It allows for partial birth abortion —so-called D&E—a grotesque legal technicality often used to avoid a charge of infanticide. That's where a late-term baby—sometimes just moments from taking its first breath of air —is delivered feet first until only the head remains in its mother. Then —without any anesthesia—its brains are sucked out with a vacuum hose through a hole carved in the back of its head. The soft little skull collapses and the now-dead baby is then removed. How any mother can actually *watch* this happen I cannot fathom. A live, squirming baby killed with its head still inside the mother? It's something straight out of Dachau.

Perhaps that's why many mothers choose general, versus local, anesthesia during the procedure—because they *cannot* watch it. Well, if it's too horrific to *watch*, then perhaps it's because it's too horrific to *do*.

The most shocking thing about partial birth abortions is that, according to a leading practitioner, 80% of them are purely *elective* and not needed to save the mothers' life or health. Because of the late stage of pregnancy, she has *already* accepted the risk of carrying to term or near-term and going through delivery, so the argument of health risks is inherently disingenuous. In fact, to perform a partial-birth abortion, the birthing is already in full swing and must be stopped to commit the abortion. This is where *Roe v. Wade* has brought us. A "casual brutality born of nihilism" as Robert Bork described in *Slouching Towards Gomorrah.*

Even the original plaintiff in that case has changed her mind. Elizabeth Campbell is now pro-life.

Aren't you overstating the alleged danger of abortion?

I doubt it. In a superb essay[1] Jeff Snyder observed that abortion on demand is emblematic of our culture's facility in *not seeing persons.* American Indians were not persons, nor Japanese-Americans during WWII, nor Iraqis, nor unborn children. The goal of the totalitarian State is to *take*, for any reason, simply because the State desires it. The purpose of abortion rights is to *take* the life of a mother's unborn baby, for any reason, simply because she desires it. All the abortion case law about reasons for

1   www.nationofcowards.net/writings/RightRightforOurTime.html

"health" is hollow legal formalism given that any normal pregnancy involves *some* risk to the mother's health. Being able to terminate the life of one's child is the ultimate in parental power, and the lowest form of irresponsibility.

Snyder made the brilliant point that abortion is the perfect analogue of the ideal relation sought between the state and its subjects (who have happily assented to a role of infantile dependency), and thus abortion rights have logically become *the* litmus test for government leadership.

That is utterly harrowing to contemplate. Pro-choice Libertarians really need to mull that over.

Still, you must admit the entrenched political support for abortion.

Yes, and to me that entrenched —no, *rabid*—support is very curious. Senate confirmation hearings cannot hold their bladder for more than nine seconds before they begin prying from the nominee his position on *Roe v. Wade*. Every other consideration is secondary. A Democratic presidential candidate will get the longest and most earnest applause on any issue by promising to protect abortion on demand. I noticed this back in 2000 watching Al Gore's speeches.

Why is that? Abortion rights have nothing to do with the economy, or foreign policy, or the environment, or education, or national defense. Why is this puny issue so utterly determinative of political office? Because a politician who has no qualms about allowing mothers to murder their unborn babies simply for convenience sake will not be queasy about orches-trating, for State purposes, the deaths of other "non-persons," foreign or domestic. Support abortion on demand, especially partial-birth abortions, and *no* killing is unconscionable or too grisly. Political committal to *Roe v. Wade* is sort of like the secret handshake for the Club of Genocide.

My point is this: we are being conditioned to accept increasingly barbaric practices. It's the conditioning part of all this that deeply concerns me. Nazi Germany went through the same process, whereby extermination of the Jews from 1943-on was made possible by accepting their sterilization in 1933. Very few Germans in 1933 would have agreed with outright genocide. Similarly, Gloria Steinem herself may have been shocked in 1973 with partial birth abortions. Germany, the land of Bach and Schiller, reached genocide in just 10 years down the Nazi path. Forty years of *Roe v. Wade* has gotten us flirting with genocide ourselves.

Genocide? That's a very strong claim.

There was a "philosopher" from Princeton by the name of Peter Singer. He and his fellow bioethnicists declared that a "person" in the legal sense is a human being capable of "sustained consciousness." Meaning, babies, coma victims, and the senile are not "persons" and have no rights. They can be killed. Singer said that you should have up to *one year* to kill your baby. He originally quoted 28 days, but then upped it to a year. As monstrous as this is, such an opinion is a predictable extrapolation from the non-person argument of unborn babies. The philosophical trail of abortion leads to infanticide—just as prolifers warned in the 1970s.

Taking Singer even further, why limit personhood to merely "sustained consciousness"? Why not define personhood as "sustained self-support"? That way we could kill off any children and poverty-prone adults we wished. This is the next logical step from Singer, and it's already being seriously discussed in academic journals.

Euthanasia will be next. Hillary Clinton's Health Reform Task Force made the chilling observation back in 1993 that most of a person's health care costs are incurred in the last six months of life. You can almost hear the future licking of chops over the power to decide which of the elderly are "too costly to maintain" and whose life is "not worth living." Over half of Americans are over sixty. They might beware a *Logan's Run* society on the horizon.

Through legal positivism, people can actually cease to be persons. Attempting to redefine what it means to be a human being is inherently *very* dangerous. Personhood arguments based on sentience or self-support will lead to unexpected and shocking conclusions.

Are there any historical examples of that?

You bet. Nazi Germany's sterilization program came from the United States, by the Germans' own admission. Indiana had been sterilizing "mental defectives" since 1907. By 1934, seventeen states including California had coercive sterilization laws. The eugenics movement was becoming American public policy. The Supreme Court upheld forced sterilizations with Oliver Wendell Holmes decreeing that *"three generations of imbeciles is enough."* A major proponent of all this from 1932-on was Margaret Sanger, an ardent eugenicist who later founded Planned Parenthood. They sort of skipped over this in her website bio. Read her *Birth Control Review* for all sorts of interesting ideas and plans—stuff that sounds like transcripts from the Nazi Wannsee Conference of 1942 where they concocted the Final Solution.

Look, the reason why I am morally opposed to abortion as a form of purely elective birth control is that any postconception demarcation of personhood is artificial. A 3-month old fetus, 6-month old fetus, partial-birth, before the umbilical cord is cut, or a 12 month baby—it's all artificial, not to mention self-serving. It basically says, *"We can kill you until you grow old enough to physically defend yourself."* And, as any good libertarian will tell you, any law based on an artificial demarcation is inherently flawed, such as the drinking age or the voting age or the age of majority.

So, you really believe that life begins at conception?

Well it certainly can't begin any earlier! (laughs) And, no, it can't begin any later than fertilization. That's not an artificial demarcation, that's the most compelling scientific case. And if libertarians prize science as they claim to, then they should reevaluate their "pro-choice" position.

An ovum or spermatozoon is mere tissue, but a *fertilized* ovum is not. It has 46 human chromosomes, as do you and I. That amount of genetic information has been compared by Nobel Laureate biophysicist Dr. Francis Crick to about 1,000 volumes of the *Encyclopædia Britannica.* The fertilized egg is not an organ *of* the mother, but an *organism within* its mother—a unique and developing human life with potential, not merely a "potential life."

But recriminalizing abortion would cause a return of the back-alley abortionists, killing thousands of women each year.

As Ann Coulter pointed out years ago in her book *Slander: Liberal Lies About the American Right*, that supposition requires women to make good on their threat to: (1) refuse to use birth control, and (2) when they get pregnant, engage in unsafe and illegal abortion procedures—which is a stretch if you think about it. The argument basically threatens a two-tiered irresponsibility on the part of women —political extortion of the blackest hue.

Besides, you asked about my *moral* belief on abortion. I've explained it in some detail. I haven't yet explained what I would propose to *do* about it. Although I believe abortion, as convenient postcoital birth control, to be morally wrong, I would not seek to apply criminal penalties.

But why not, if abortion kills what you believe to be legal persons?

Because, if you think it through, the enforcement apparatus eventually required would be monstrous. For example, the feds would at some point have to test women for pregnancy at

all border crossings, just in case they were leaving the country for an abortion. Also, any natural miscarriages—which happen fairly frequently—would necessarily be investigated as possible homicides. That would be horrific.

Still, wouldn't that allow parties to abortions to go unpunished?

Unpunished criminally, but not unpunished morally.

I don't follow.

Well, I've never met a woman who had, for purely matters of convenience, an abortion who was fully at ease with herself over it. Similarly, I've never heard of an abortionist who seemed genuinely proud of it.

You may be overstating the case there.

Perhaps, but I doubt it. Me thinks the pro-choicers protest too much. It's like the quote *"Nobody speaks of God more than the atheist."* Deep down, I don't believe that even the very strident "pro-choice" activists are truly unconflicted about abortion. I've spoken to many such women who would not have a convenience-based abortion themselves.

We're not talking about a tumor here. Abortion kills a defenseless and developing human life with its own unique DNA, and there is no way around that. Not by calling it a "fetus" and not by calling it a "consciousless non-person." If an abortion must be performed, then how about for some truly compelling reason such as the mother's health, versus *"Damn it, I'm pregnant again!"*

What I'm saying is that the moral consequence of abortion affects those involved, even if they would not admit it. The corresponding guilt and grief will have to suffice. In a way, the wrong likely contains its own punishment. As such, it obviates any requirement for criminalization and its attendant enforcement apparatus. For example, one high-profile abortionist in Texas killed herself years ago. I think that after performing several *thousand* abortions, the enormity of it all finally caught up with her.

What if there is no corresponding guilt and grief? What if there is no moral punishment?

Then the pro-choicers and abortionists have nothing to worry about, do they? And thus, nothing to protest about, either. But they *do* worry; they *do* protest. Even the blandest of pro-life statements made from moral, and not political grounds, send them into a frenzy. Why? Because even if abortion on demand is left alone politically, to criticize it on purely moral grounds strikes a nerve. As well it should. The nerve is there for a reason. However pro-choicers try with semantic arguments, the nerve refuses to be anesthetized.

Even though my politics do not threaten abortion, my moral views on abortion will be reviled just as if I had the unilateral power to overturn *Roe v. Wade.* I will not criminalize the issue. I will leave the consequences of abortion to those involved, but I will never gloss over the inherent evil. It is a needless, ugly stain on our nation.

So, abortion is not a political issue for you?

No. As a state governor, what could I *do* about it anyway? Executive and legislative politics will not overturn *Roe v. Wade.* It's been decided as a *judicial* matter, and democratic pressures are quite inert there. To even ask presidential and senatorial candidates their position is fairly pointless. Short of appointing pro-life Supreme Court Justices—which is highly unlikely these days—what could they do about it? To question *congressmen* on the matter is just idiotic, as the House does not confirm Supreme Court nominations.

In short, the whole matter has been overly politicized, and should have probably been left to the States. Such would have greatly depressurized the issue, and with 50 publics and 50 legislatures addressing it we might have discovered a truly wise solution.

But that would mean some states would have outlawed abortion.

Yes, but many would not. If a Phoenix woman had to fly to L.A. for an abortion, then the cost and inconvenience may encourage more responsibility in the future.

Look, I would not criminalize abortion, but I won't excuse it, either. Furthermore, there should not be a single penny of taxpayer money to fund abortions. For "pro-choice" advocates to insist on government funding I find ghastly. 93% of all abortions are publicly funded through Medicaid and other programs, and they're amazed that the pro-lifers are so upset? That their tax dollars are subsidizing elective murder? They've a right to be upset. Abortion must be defunded publicly. At once.

What about drugs, prostitution, and homosexuality? Wouldn't Christians outlaw what libertarians consider victimless crimes?

Perhaps some would, but I personally would not. I think that both Christians and libertarians have some points to consider here.

The thing I'd suggest to my fellow Christians is that not criminalizing certain behavior for adults does not necessarily mean or imply *condoning* that behavior. Laws, principles, and preferences are not synonymous. Not all pleasure is necessarily a sin, and not all sin is necessarily a crime.

Morality and criminality are related, but they are not the same. They do not perfectly overlap, as many Christians seem to think.

A moral code includes, as a *subset*, the criminal code because not everything immoral can or should be made criminal, as I explained with abortion. Absent their initiation of force, people must be allowed to go to heaven, or hell, in their own way. To dissuade such behavior, Christians should—as in the case of abortion——employ moral arguments.

What would you suggest to your fellow libertarians?

That there is something more important than the freedom to do what one wants, and that is the freedom to do what one *ought*. Just because one has the personal liberty to do something does not necessarily mean that it *should* be done. The "ought" is, by the way, an *inner* and voluntary compulsion—not a coercive third-party one. I'm talking about *self*-government.

Let me explain it with a Scripture. Paul in I Corinthians 6:12 wrote, *"All things are permissible for me, but not all things are profitable."* Libertarians should contemplate that more often. Not all permissible things are profitable, meaning some things take more than they give—leaving the person with a net loss. Those engaged in drugs, prostitution, and homosexuality generally have shorter life expectancies. More suicides, too. They certainly suffer more illness and despair. That is statistical fact. In short, these things permissible under libertarian principles are not profitable, and thus fall outside of that which we *ought* to be doing.

Libertarianism is an excellent *inter*personal code. In fact, the whole tenet of interpersonal libertarianism was encapsulated in the so-called Golden Rule by Jesus during his Sermon on the Mount in Matthew 7:12.

However, libertarianism lacks much as an *intra*personal code. Libertarian ethics maintain that something is immoral solely if it involves fraud or initiation of force. While this definition certainly encompasses the *criminal* code, it omits much as a *moral* code. As fervently as libertarians may argue for the individual's implicit freedom to shoot up heroin with homosexual prostitutes —let's face it, nobody would actually raise their own children in such an environment! Nobody *aspires* to such a life. Just because certain behavior is properly excluded from the criminal code does not mean that it conversely deserves to be embraced, much less extolled.

Well, if noncriminal immoral behavior should not be legislated against, then why even discuss it? It's going to occur whether some people like it or not.

That's not quite the given you think it is. Think of it this way. While it's not against the law to be a jerk, it certainly isn't profitable. He misses out on the fine ladies and the good jobs. He isn't invited to parties. He may even die a bachelor, thus not transmitting his crude genes.

My point is this: In any society, there are many forms of disapproval. P.J. O'Rourke once wrote about a Stockholm taxi ride where he was cut off. The cabbie scolded the offending driver, *"Tsk-tsk."* No kidding. Laws are merely the highest form of disapproval, and these are codifications of certain mores. Social opprobrium is expressed in many ways, from frowns to outright shunning and excommunication. Extralegal sanctions can be very effective.

Shame and stigma work, *while* they work. Meaning, if a mild form of opprobrium begins to fail, then stronger measures will appear alluring. This is why Robert Bork was tempted by censorship. When shame evaporates, laws step in to fill the vacuum. If libertarians would not *pooh-pooh* or dismiss the idea of decency, then they might not have to worry so much about increasing numbers of laws on morality. Where values are strong, laws are unnecessary. Where values are weak, many laws are worthless because they cannot be enforced.

In Boulder I recently saw a greasy, thoroughly pierced, young punk proudly sporting a T-shirt which read, *"I don't give a fuck what you fucking think!"* This was at the mall, with reading-age children present. Does anyone mean to tell me that *that* was the purpose of the 1st Amendment? If one intentionally behaves in public with the goal to shock and infuriate, then perhaps one should suffer its effect.

Libertarians may have a qualm about that, given their noninitiation of force ethos.

No doubt. But that doesn't mean that we should surrender our streets to vermin. Here's the paradox: Society cannot create or maintain decency through laws, however, we cannot allow the triumph of indecency, either. That punk at the mall should have been shouted and booed out of the building by the rest of the patrons. Short of giving him a good thrashing, severe social opprobrium is the only answer I can think of. Do this regularly and we won't have to stomach such offensiveness any longer. I'd have done it myself, but I knew that I'd have had little support.

So, you're recommending public disapproval, yet you did nothing about the mall punk yourself? Isn't that hypocritical?

You've missed something here. If public disapproval is mild in method—such as booing—then *many* people have to collectively dispense that disapproval for it to be effective. If, however, the disapproval is harsh and physical, then only one man is needed. Recall the ending scene of *Dangerous Liasons* where the entire opera hall shouted down Glenn Close? If the movie had had just one more scene, it would have been of her moving from London. She had been banned. That was just as effective as one guy kicking her out of town. To get a dollar's worth of effectiveness, a hundred people must chip in a penny apiece, or ten people a dime, or one man the entire buck.

I *would* have initiated or joined in the booing the punk out of the mall —I'd have chipped in my penny or dime—*if* a supportive atmosphere had existed, but it didn't. Everyone was skittering away from this punk. I was on my own, so I would have had to spend the full dollar. Had I said *anything* to him he would have just used his favorite word on me in front of my wife, and I'd have squashed him like the cockroach he was.

Here's the irony: *he* would have had legal protection, not me. Somehow, that's insane. After decades of tolerance for depravity, we have boxed ourselves into a very smelly corner. One man *cannot* do anything—even though he knows he could, and a dozen people *will* not do anything—even though they know they should. As the band *Rush* sang in *A Farewell to Kings*, *"Will they read of us with sadness, for the seeds that we let grow?"*

Getting back to the original thread of discussion, drugs, prostitution, pornography, promiscuity, and homosexuality are not healthy things, and *will*—if left unchecked by social opprobrium—curdle and destroy a society. Is this not obvious? Libertarians must face some things.

Such as?

That there are social realities more poignant than economic ones.

That a free society cannot dispense with civic virtue and public morality. That decadence will lead to depravity, and vulgarity to obscenity. That free market exchanges of depravity will degenerate the entire culture. That industries made from the same will result in eventual social destruction. That a healthy community is more than a simple conglomeration of hedonists. That unconstrained personal expression is not the *sine qua non* of liberty. That libertarianism cannot become a suicide pact for decent public order. That even though *you* may not partake in pornography, homosexuality, or drugs—you will be greatly affected by those who *do*. That we foolishly ignore these "negative externalities" only at our own peril.

Montesquieu was right when he insisted that the primary prerequisite of any democracy was public virtue.

Now sound like a Stoic.

(laughs) So I'm the Zeno of Wyoming, eh? I think of it as simple realism. Even secular scholars are understanding these things. Robert Bork wrote in *Slouching Towards Gomorrah* that *"Unconstrained human nature will seek degeneracy often enough to create a disorderly, hedonistic, and dangerous society."*

Libertarians could stand to embrace a bit of Stoicism, actually. It would help to balance their predominant Epicureanism.

If you don't approve of drugs, prostitution, pornography, homosexuality, then don't partake of them—leaving others free to do so. Just like an offensive TV program—don't watch.

That's like saying *"If you don't like the smog, don't breathe."* You're ignoring their pervasive nature. Madonna can isolate herself from the Amish, but 12 year-old Amish girls can't isolate themselves from Madonna. And the Amish have a right to be upset about that. Culture is the social air we *all* must breathe, and the pollution has become toxic. You've the right to foul your own nest, but not the public air. We used to completely understand this. In my father's day, when he went out in public he could expect others to be well-dressed and polite. Others could expect that of him. One didn't assume the right to foul the public experience. Having a lousy day? Fine, keep it to yourself. You had no right to soil the day of a perfect stranger, and vice versa.

Seems impossibly quaint today, eh? Politely ask some kid to turn down his boombox or quit slapping his skateboard around while you're on the phone, and he'll promptly tell you to *"Fuck off!"* How did we get to this point? *Penuria hominem.* A shortage of men—through subsidized fatherlessness —but that's another topic.

Look, a high skank quotient indicates that society's soon demise. We know this from history. It's something that many atheist libertarians don't want to discuss. They cannot offer one example of a brazenly bacchanalian society simultaneously enjoying law and order. There is an indisputable correlation between indecency and crime. Go to any sleazy part of town anywhere in the world and see if you feel safe. The very idea is absurd. *"Come inside for the live-*

sex show! Oh, sir, you dropped your wallet!"

There is a correlation, if not causality, between good ethics and decency, and that's something atheist libertarians should not ignore. Christians should not be castigated by libertarians for calling something degenerate and socially destructive, any more than libertarians should be chastised by Christians for refusing to employ criminal sanctions on what is truly noncriminal behavior. They are much more in agreement than they realize, if they'd only ponder the issue from each other's perspective.

Christians confuse a criminal code to fully envelop the moral code, while libertarians confuse a moral code to fully envelop the criminal code. That is the most simple way I can put it.

Hmmm. Interesting. Please elaborate on that.

OK, let me explain it another way. Imagine a circle. It contains all offensive behavior, from public profanity to murder. But, there are several levels of offensiveness. The circle comprises three rings. The outer ring is merely rude behavior, which is randomly punished by mild disapproval in the form of folkways. The next ring is indecent behavior, which is generally punished by robust disapproval in the form of mores. The inner circle is criminal behavior, which is universally punished by stringent disapproval—laws.

Christians would mistakenly outlaw rude and indecent behavior, causing the criminal code to fully envelop the moral code. This surrogate enforcement through the police is a symptom of a lazy and cowardly people. I know many Christians and some of them are just plain weak and gutless —people who would first call the police over a loud party or a barking dog next door rather than simply go talk to their neighbor.

Many libertarians, on the other hand, mistakenly believe that if something is not criminal, then it can't be immoral because there was no coercion. I think that this, too, is a cop-out. I know many devout libertarians and many of them hide behind their politics because they simply don't have the courage to call decadence for what it obviously is.

Both envision overlapping moral and criminal codes, but in different ways. The Christian enlarges the criminal code to the full area of the moral code, whereas the libertarian shrinks the moral code to the area of the criminal code. Both views are fundamentally flawed and eventually unworkable.

Carried to their respective extremes, the first would eventually outlaw premarital handshaking, while the second would eventually allow copulation in the streets. There can and must be some middle case which is at least tolerable—if not comfortable—to both Christians and libertarians. And we need to forge that synthesis very soon, else we'll both be swept off the cultural map.

But you are still morally opposed to victimless crimes, aren't you?

Of course! That term "victimless crimes" is only half true. The so-called victimless crimes have no direct criminal victim, but it is silly to

imagine that they have no harmful effect at all. The indirect victim has been decent society—all in the name of "tolerance." G.K. Chesterton wrote, *"Tolerance is the virtue of those who don't believe in anything."* Florence King said it best: *"'Sensitivity' makes cowards of us all."*

But decency can not be legislated.

Right, and that's the paradox: Laws cannot force people to be kind and decent. Decency must be taught by parents, and rewarded by society. But today society instead scoffs at decency. Turn in somebody's wallet full of cash and you're an idiot.

I once found a used video called *Federal Follies* which had three US Government training films from the 1960s. This video was sold to mock the utter seriousness of these films. Granted, the films are incomparably corny today, but that's because manners and chaste behavior have become corny.

One 1966 Navy film titled "Blondes Prefer Gentlemen" showed two guys at a dinner party, a slob and a gentleman. The gentleman knew to R.S.V.P., to be courteous, to help a lady with her chair, how to use the butter knife, etc. He got the girl, whereas the slob did not. One thing that surprised me was that the slob of 1966—portrayed in the most boorish light then possible—is not, by today's standards, all that remarkable. The slob of 1966 is a fairly normal guy 50 fifty years later. That alarms me.

And another thing, what is unhealthy or abnormal about a man and women both losing their virginity to each other on their wedding night, and simultaneously co-discovering something rapturous and sacred for themselves? I mean, imagine the benefits: no sexual jealousy over past lovers, no chlamydia, no syphilis, no gonorrhea, no herpes, no genital warts, no AIDS, no past abortions, no guilt, no psychic damage. Just pure and innocent lovemaking. What could be wrong with that? But the world, including PLAYBOY magazine, sneers at such a notion and pulls it down into the mud.

We are sawing off the limb upon which we sit, just because we like the sound. It is truly madness. And, we're about out of limbs.

But these aren't the 1950s.

True, but have we really progressed and advanced as a society? Are people truly more contented? More joyful? More moral? Less criminal? Where have 60 years of rampant extramarital sex gotten us? Are women really happier today than they were in the '50s? I wouldn't bet on it.

You're a fascinating paradox of a man, Governor. A Christian who would decriminalize drugs, but a libertarian morally opposed to abortion. It seems both camps would be displeased with you.

(laughs) Actually, neither camp is all that displeased. Although I didn't consciously try to design a workable synthesis of Christian and libertarian beliefs, my views have apparently helped to form a coalition.

How do propose to solve the dilemma of a necessary public morality without such being enforced by laws?

The best idea I've heard is through the proliferation of voluntary communities owning private property, each with their own type of covenant restricting or prohibiting what they see as harmful behaviors. Such is libertarian in notion and in practice. If a particular covenant is disagreeable to you, then you don't have to live there or visit. In time, we would see drug-free communities—religious and secular—bisexual potsmoker communities, etc. Every individual would have a choice of many different communities which reflected one's personal morals. Each lifestyle community would compete for members. Folks would judge the tree by the fruit, and I suspect that communities embracing harmful behaviors will putrefy and fizzle out. Even if they didn't, their pathology would remain contained, which is the next best thing.

But that's discrimination.

Yes, it certainly is. That's the whole point. People have the *right* to be biased—or even prejudiced. It's called the free market. Only government does not have the right to discriminate. Can a woman turn down a marriage proposal? Of course. Is that bias? Sure. What's wrong with it? Nothing. Bias and discrimination are a part of human life. However, if left alone, things sort themselves out.

Sheer bigotry for the sake of bigotry would quickly become economically costly, if not socially costly. For example, a black family has an honest, successful hardware store but Buford Bigot won't buy from "niggers." Not only does he lose out by being forced to drive 30 miles to the next town for his supplies—folks in town begin to shun Buford Bigot. If, however, the whole *town* are bigots, then other towns will shun that town. In a truly free market, people will pay full fare for their prejudice and bigotry. Those who don't wake up and grow up will stay poor, alone, and bitter.

Both Democrats and Republicans are concerned that the Laissez-Faire Party will alter national elections. Is that likely?

(laughing) I really don't see what they have to worry about. Most Americans are satisfied with their gilded bondage and will continue to elect new jailers every four years. That is precisely why we had to concentrate on a particular state. Wyoming happened to be almost reserved for us, it seems.

We made room for government supremacists—they have the rest of the country. Why can't they make room for us in Wyoming? Their hysteria about the Laissez-Faire Party victory in 2014 speaks volumes. They will not rest until *everybody* is under bureaucratic decree.

Hey, Tom, do you know what is the biggest fear of liberals? That somewhere, somehow, somebody... is...*happy.* (laughing)

Can Wyoming retain such a provincial *Gemeinschaft*?

Yes. Several hundred thousand Wyomingites earnestly desire it. To understand us one must understand how 6th century Irish monasteries on the fringe of civilization kept alive Christianity and classical learning during Europe's Dark Ages. The seeds of the Enlightenment and the Renaissance were protected until the European soil was once again ready 500 years later.

America is quickly embracing a subpagan culture and is sliding into her own Dark Ages, and Wyoming will be someday likened to that tiny monastery of Skellig Michael. Precursors were gated communities and the home-schooling movement of the late 20th century. Wyoming was the logical extension of splintered attempts to create small islands of decency, civility, and common sense amidst a raging sea of depravity, larceny, and lunacy. We are endeavoring to form a center which *will* hold.

Will that center hold?

Only time will tell, but I believe so, yes. We fully understand what we are about, we have all the natural resources required, we are well armed, and we are training to defend ourselves. The nation wants to go to hell in a handbasket? Fine. Just don't expect us to join the journey, willingly or by force.

Governor, we at PLAYBOY appreciate the interview.

It was my pleasure, Tom, thank *you.* Come out to visit Wyoming sometime and see what all the fuss is about!

I just might do that Governor, thanks.

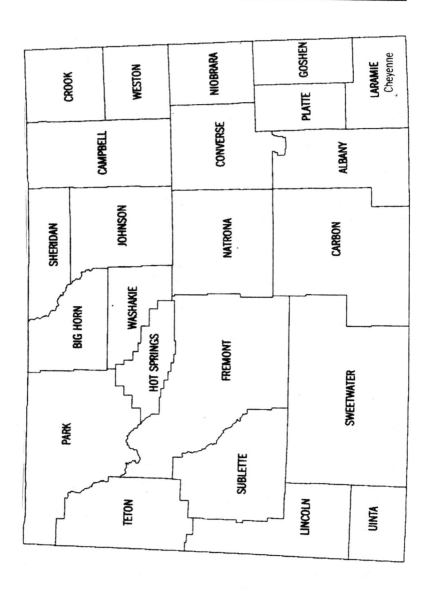

REVISING DEMOCRACY
by the
Wyoming Reform Council

The human saga is an ongoing experiment. With the goal of constant improvement, we intentionally try different things and hopefully learn from our mistakes. This is especially necessary in the field of politics. Within the continuum of anarchy to autocracy there are several major choices of political systems. In America we have roughly settled on a democratic republic. Although democracy in general is our tradition, we have not very widely experimented with different forms of it. Our failure to do so has allowed systemic defects to surface rather poignantly (*e.g.,* the 2000 presidential election), which in turn is causing some to challenge the very notion of democracy itself.

Are the American people fit to rule themselves? This has been the question for over 200 years, and we are beginning to doubt ourselves.

Therefore, we must objectively review our political infrastructure. If we can, for a moment, dispassionately suspend our civic mythology and work to diagnose the gridlock, unfairness, and inefficiency in our political *corpus*, we may be able to operate in time to save the patient. However, if we do not, the patient (already terminally ill) will die within a generation (two at most), taking the nation with it.

So, for your consideration, we outline several current issues which reduce the fairness and effectiveness of our democratic institutions. Please consider them carefully.

Must state legislatures have *two* houses?
Isn't one enough? It has been for Nebraska since 1937!

Much of the states' constitutions and political structures were borrowed, if not copied outright, from the US Constitution. Given the genealogy of the federal government from the Articles of Confederation and the Philadelphia constitutional convention of 1787, the one-state/one-vote of the US Senate was a predictable and unavoidable expedient for the states' ratification of the Constitution.

But is a bicameral legislature truly required for the *states*? Evidently not, as other states have done just fine with just one legislative body. Ask yourself this: If two houses are better than one, then would *three* houses be better than two? Hardly. In this case, two are not better than one. Sometimes, two is simply one too many.

Not only can one body of legislators function very well by itself, not only is an entire tier of unnecessary government removed, but a unicameral house will eliminate that corrupt and secretive organ of needless gridlock: the conference committee, which is run exclusively by kept men who kill any legislation which threatens their power.

In a unicameral legislature, everything is done in broad daylight. Representatives can no longer hide behind a committee's closed doors; they must visibly stand on their votes. No more shuttling bills back and forth between two houses, with each trip ratcheting up the dollar amount.

Why must your legislators be from your home district?

You may know of a candidate from another legislative district who is preferable to the candidates in your district. Since you are a Wyomingite voting for a *state* legislator, why must you be constrained to choose from within your district? Isn't it more fair that state legislators should be, just like the governor, elected by the state voters as a whole?

How can Reps be free to vote their conscience?

By we the People *electing* them based on their conscience.

This is not possible today with legislative districts and partisan primaries. When party candidates must claw their way to the nomination through caucuses and primaries, all you get are finalists skilled at little more than back-room politics. At the same time, fine candidates with strong public support are rejected for not placating their party bosses.

So instead of being able to vote for "the best of the bunch" you must choose between "the lesser of two evils." Because of this, voter turnout has been falling for forty years! We have a better idea.

Our solution to the above problems
How about a choice from amongst up to *80* state Reps?

Today's congressional elections are total Win/Lose propositions. Generally, two candidates face off; one wins and the other loses. If the winner gets 501 votes and the loser 499, it means that 499 diligent voters got absolutely nothing for their efforts, merely because two votes went the other way. And the winner claims he was voted in by "the people." No, by only 50.1% of "the people." (Hardly a mandate.)

In any election, up to 49.9% of a district's voters have no say at the Capitol; up to nearly half are *not* represented. It's unfair, frustrating and wasteful. Little wonder that only 55% of the eligible voters vote in Wyoming elections (and only 25% in national elections).

There's small choice in rotten apples.
　—Shakespeare

How about this instead:

❶　The 30 Senate Districts and 60 House Districts are abolished. (No more complex and expensive redrawing of districts every 10 years!) The Wyoming legislature is then streamlined into a unicameral house.

❷　A legislative candidate would first require the petition signatures (sigs) of at least 5,000 registered voters from across the state. These 5,000 sigs would: A) assure that Representative (Rep) a seat in the legislature, and B) allow the Rep entrance in the general election to increase his constituency (and thus his voting weight). The 400,000 eligible Wyoming voters means a maximum potential of 80 Reps, though this number would likely never be reached because voter registration and turnout is never 100%, and nearly all Reps would have more support than the 5,000 voter minimum.

Let's say that 50 Reps have received at least the required 5,000 sigs.

❸　A general election is then held. Understand that the 50 Reps have already made it to the legislature with their 5,000+ sigs—the election is held only to give those Reps a chance to *increase* their overall voter support. The voters who have petitioned for a particular Rep *have already voted.* This election is only for those voters who have not *yet* endorsed any particular Rep. (Actually, the petitioning could even be foregone with a general voting for one's candidate.)

❹　The results of the general election are published. Of those 50 Reps, let's say their voting support ranges from the minimum 5,000 to a high of 30,000. That means that the top Rep has six times more voting weight in the legislature than a Rep with only 5,000 sigs/votes.

❺　Once Reps begin their single 4 year term in January, their respective voters may switch loyalties on a semiannual basis. That way, no Rep could con the voters just to get elected. If a Rep begins to ignore the wishes of his/her voters, they can "change horses" and drain that Rep's voting influence. An incumbent's power is *exactly* proportional to his/her approval. Approval *grows,* power *grows.* Approval *wanes,* power *wanes.*

A Rep whose intraterm support goes *below* the 5,000 minimum for two consecutive quarters (or four times within his term) is ousted, and his residual supporters move to other incumbents. A Rep must have the mandate of at least 5,000 voters to achieve *and hold* office. See how equitable this would be? No more waiting out bad state Senators for four years and bad Congressman for two. For once in history, lawmakers would be accountable and responsive on a near daily basis to their bosses, the voters.

Summary

Every cohesive group of 5,000 or more could have their *own* Rep in the legislature. Voters in different counties with common issues and views could enjoy common state representation. Johnson and Sublette County Libertarians could have their own Rep. Teton County environmentalists could have theirs. The petroleum workers theirs. Minority viewpoints would finally have a palpable voice. And the voting *weight* of each Rep would exactly mirror his numerical voter *support*. Reps with more voter support would justifiably have a proportionately stronger influence in the legislature. Elections under this scenario wouldn't be Winner/Loser affairs with as little as 50.1% of the voters electing the legislature, and the other 49.9% griping about it. No more costly recounts and frustrating legal challenges. That sort of thing split our country in two back in 2000.

These elections would be *Winner/Winner.* You'd no longer have to limit your choice of Rep to just a mere handful in the primaries—you could choose from up to *80!* No more "lesser of two evils"—finally you could choose "the best of the bunch."

Now *that's* freedom of choice. That's *representation!*

"With up to 80 candidates all running for state office, wouldn't campaigning be too expensive and confusing?"

No, not necessarily. The initial campaigning could be done through a state website. Office seekers pay a nonrefundable fee to become listed and from there try to elicit the needed 5,000 signatures. Each petitioner would have an identical number of pages and mpeg video time to describe themselves, and their views could all be compared in a matrix.

Voters would cast their petition signatures electronically. With modern public key (asymmetric) encryption, your vote will be absolutely protected from tampering. The process is not only safe, but simple.

The website would *not* show a running tally of how many sigs each had, so as to encourage voters to choose out of principle versus from assured winners. It also will prevent the candidates from learning where they stand, and by "keeping them in the dark" they will have little choice but to remain true to their stated views. (Polling fosters expediency, and thus should be discouraged, if not made illegal.) Finally, the sheer suspense will create and hold much more public interest in the electoral process.

Voters cast one unrecallable petition signature. The computer software will ask *three* times: *"You are about to cast your one and only vote for _____. Are you sure of your choice? Yes or No?"* By clicking "Yes" three times, the silly Floridian farce of "I didn't know" is avoided.

In the event a voter's candidate does not receive the 5,000 sig minimum, he is *not* allowed to vote in the general election. Either way, he has already voted. This is to encourage committed decisions amongst the electorate, and to discourage the truly kooky. (*I.e.,* go *too* far out on a limb with your views, and perhaps not even 1 voter in 80 will join you.) Sure, a voter could prefer to vote in November rather than to petition, but this means that his menu of Reps has been decided by those with more resolve (who petitioned early). Also, the fewer the petitioners, the smaller the menu. So, there are pros and cons to petitioning.

"But some voters will not be represented!" some would cry. Well, what else is new? Today, up to **49.9%** of the voters are not represented when they pick a losing candidate in a tight race. Our plan is much more fair and inclusive. Voters may choose from up to 80 Reps, so at least one of them should be tolerable for even the random maverick.

However, if you pick a candidate who cannot garner even 4,999 other supporters *from across the entire state*, then your political views are so far out of the mainstream that they are not entitled to legislative weight. While the larger fringes will be represented (for the first time in history), the "fringe of the fringe" cannot—nor do they deserve to be.

Even if we had a legislature with 400,000 Reps (which is what 100% representation would require), not everyone's views could win. Today, each Wyoming Senate District covers 20,000 voters, and each House District 10,000 voters. Because of the Win/Lose nature of today's elections, up to nearly 10,000 and 5,000 voters in those districts have no representation. "All or nothing" gambling is fine for Las Vegas casinos, but it has no place in a modern democracy for choosing legislators.

Our plan offers real choice. With minimum voter blocks of 5,000 we believe that over 95% of voters will have actual legislative representation. This has never occurred in the history of democracy. Will the fringe be able to push through their agendas? No, but whatever *portion* of their agenda that is more reasonable can be coalesced with other Reps for passage.

Once the previous example of 50 Reps have achieved their 5,000+ sigs, a televised pageant is held the night before election day. Each Rep gets equal time (say, 2 minutes apiece) to answer questions and address the Wyoming voters at home (who are marking their impressions on a scoresheet with such categories as: Candor, Intelligence, Resolve, Personality, etc.). Even with commercial breaks, the pageant would take only two hours. Production costs are paid by the state fund which collected the $10,000 website application fees from all the applicants.

The next day, voters who have not petitioned go to the polls to cast their vote for one of the 50 Reps (or even for one of the original website candidates, although such would be rare). The end result is that 19 out of 20 voters will see his candidate serving in the legislature.

Barring the total elimination of legislators and turning the lawmaking power over to the popular vote (which is technologically feasible, though politically quite impractical), this bold reform is our best chance for a true and fair democracy. You will see huge opposition from lawyers and politicians, for it spells the end of their immoral and inefficient reign.

> *We find the worst atrocities always occur at the end of the war. And this is the end of the war. It is over and you just have to keep out of the way of the dying dinosaur's tail...*
> — Steve Kubby, American Medical Marijuana Assc.

> *Greater than the tread of mighty armies is an idea whose time has come.*
> — Victor Hugo

> *Ideas won't keep. Something must be done about them.*
> — Alfred North Whitehead

Part 2 of this Report discusses an even more controversial matter: the secret ballot and its inevitable path to tyranny.

NO MORE SECRET BALLOT

This is the key to history. Terrific energy is expended—civilizations are built up—excellent institutions devised; but each time something goes wrong. Some fatal flaw always brings back the selfish and cruel people to the top and it all slides back into misery and ruin.
    —C.S. Lewis, *Mere Christianity*, p.39

Whether the State can loose and bind
    In Heaven as well as on Earth:
If it be wiser to kill mankind
    Before or after the birth—
These are matters of high concern
    Where State-kept schoolmen are;
But Holy State (we have lived to learn)
    Endeth in Holy War.

Whether The People be led by The Lord,
    Or lured by the loudest throat;
If it be quicker to die by the sword
    Or cheaper to die by the vote—
These are things we have dealt with once,
    (And they will not rise from their grave)
For Holy People, however it runs,
    Endeth in wholly Slave.

What so ever, for any cause,
    Seeketh to take or give
Power above or beyond the Laws,
    Suffer it not to live!

Holy State or Holy King—
    Or Holy People's Will—
Have no truck with the senseless thing.
    Order the guns and kill!
    Saying—after—me:—

Once there was The People—Terror gave it birth;
Once there was The People and it made a Hell of Earth
Earth arose and crushed it. Listen, O ye slain!
Once there was The People—it shall never be again!
    — Rudyard Kipling, *MacDonough's Song*

Those who expect to reap the blessings of freedom, must, like men, undergo the fatigues of supporting it.
    — Thomas Paine, *The Crisis*, IV, (12 September 1777)

We believe that voting secrecy is an unnecessary evil. Stripping that veil is a vital component of a long overdue redesign of our democratic system. It would infuse a new and necessary responsibility for the actions of voters.

The secret ballot fosters secret government and its irresponsible dominion. When any atrocious government act occurs, all parties involved (though guilty) are allowed to falsely claim their innocence.

The enforcers say, *"We were ordered to pull the trigger!"*

The politicians say, *"We didn't pull the trigger!"*

The people say, *"We knew nothing of this!"*

After an avalanche, every snowflake pleads "Not Guilty."

To top it off, judges confer "sovereign immunity" upon such killers as FBI sniper Lon Horiuchi of Ruby Ridge. And everyone gets away with it because there is no assignable responsibility—no real chain of command. Well, if a democracy is a "government of, for, and by the people" then it is actually quite easy to assign responsibility. Enforcers are hired by particular bureaucrats, who are empowered by particular politicians, who are elected by particular voters. Everyone involved has a name, and the republic has a right to know who they are! If the voters were to be made *personally* responsible for the actions of their agents, then the voters would elect better people. It would simply be in their best self-interest.

The earliest and most eloquent case for eliminating voter secrecy was made in 1870 by jurist Lysander Spooner in his *No Treason*:

A man is none the less a slave because he is allowed to choose a new master once in a term of years...
The right of absolute and irresponsible dominion is the right of property, and the right of property is the right of absolute, irresponsible dominion. The two are identical; the one necessarily implying the other. Neither can exist without the other. If, therefore, Congress have that absolute and irresponsible law-making power, which the [U.S.] Constitution—according to their interpretation of it— gives them [in 1:6:2], **it can only be because they own us as property.** If they own us as property, they are our masters, and their will is our law. If they do not own us as property, they are not our masters, **and their will,...is of no authority over us.**
But these men who claim and exercise this absolute and irresponsible dominion over us, dare not to be consistent, and claim either to be our masters, or to own us as property. They say that they are only our servants, agents, attorneys, and representatives. But this declaration involves an absurdity, a contradiction. No man can be my servant, agent, attorney, or representative, and be, at the same time, uncontrollable by me, **and irresponsible to me for his acts.**

For still another reason they are neither our servants, agents, attorneys, nor representatives. And that reason is, that we do not make ourselves responsible for their acts. If a man is my servant, agent, or attorney, I necessarily make myself responsible for all his acts done within the limits of the power I have intrusted to him.... But no individual who may be injured in his person or property, by acts of Congress, can come to the individual electors, and hold them responsible for these acts of their so-called agents or representatives.

If, then, nobody is individually responsible for the acts of Congress, the members of Congress are nobody's agents. And if they are nobody's agents, they are themselves individually responsible for their own acts, and for the acts of all whom they employ. And the authority they are exercising is simply their own individual authority; and, by the law of nature—the highest of all laws —anybody injured by their acts, anybody who is deprived by them of his property or his liberty, has the same right to hold them individually responsible, that he has to hold any other trespasser individually responsible. He has the same right to resist them, and their agents, that he has to resist any other trespassers.

— Lysander Spooner, *No Treason*, Essay VI (1870)

We have a "limited liability" US Government just like "limited liability" corporations. The American legal encyclopædia *Corpus Juris Secundum* (19:XVIII, Sections 883-4) defines the United States Government as a foreign corporation with respect to the states. Corporate stockholders (voters) have no liability for the acts of their managers (Congressmen), who are themselves rarely legally responsible for corporate injuries to the public.

Our "democracy" operates with even more irresponsibility. The government cannot be sued unless it so consents, and its corporate managers (Congressmen) cannot be held accountable outside their boardroom. The corporate charter (Constitution) says so in I:6:2!

Spooner continues in Essays VIII and XIX:

A tacit understanding between A, B, and C, that they will, by ballot, depute D as their agent, to deprive me of my property, liberty, or life, cannot at all authorize D to do so. He is none the less a robber, tyrant, and murderer, because he claims to act as their agent, than he would be if he avowedly acted on his own responsibility alone.

...[The voters'] ballots are given in secret, and therefore in a way to avoid any personal responsibility for the acts of their agents.

No body of men can be said to authorize a man to act as their agent, to the injury of a third person, unless they do it in so open and authentic a manner as to make themselves personally responsible for his acts...   Therefore these pretended agents cannot legitimately claim to be really agents.

Men honestly engaged in attempting to establish justice in the world have no occasion thus to act in secret; or to appoint agents to do acts for which they (the principals) are not willing to be responsible.

The secret ballot makes a secret government; and a secret government is a secret band of robbers and murderers. Open despotism is better than this. *The single despot stands out in the face of all men, and says: I am the State: My will is law: I am your master: I take responsibility for my acts: The only arbiter I acknowledge is the sword: If any one denies my right, let him try conclusions with me.*

But a secret government is...a government of assassins. *Under it, a man knows not who his tyrants are, until they have struck, and perhaps not [even] then.*

This is the kind of government we have; and it is the only one we are likely to have, until men are ready to say: We will consent to no Constitution, except such a one as we are neither ashamed nor afraid to sign; and we will authorize no government to do anything in our name which we are not willing to be personally responsible for. (Essay VIII, *No Treason*)

The lesson taught by all these facts is this: As long as mankind...are such dupes and cowards as to pay for being cheated, plundered, enslaved, and murdered—...soldiers, can be hired to keep them in subjection. But when they refuse any longer to pay for being thus cheated, plundered, enslaved, and murdered, they will cease to have cheats, and usurpers, and robbers, and murderers and blood-money loan-mongers for masters. (Essay XIX, *No Treason*)

Whatever program the voters demand through their Reps, it's only *those* voters who benefit from and *pay* for that program. For example, take capital punishment. Those against it would pay for a murderer's life imprisonment. And, they would fund an insurance pool on each lifer to compensate any future victims in case the murderer escapes. Conversely, those in favor of capital punishment agree to be randomly chosen to "pull the switch" and would fund an insurance pool in case innocent persons were executed.

The whole point is to make voters *personally responsible* for their own actions and for those of their Reps, instead of distributing (in secret) the consequences of their poor choices across the state. Every enforcer is hired by some official, who is appointed by some elected officer, who is voted in by the people. It's about time we all learned what is being committed (however indirectly and unknowingly) in our name, and own up to it.

The answer is usually simple. Accepting the question is difficult.
    —Jeff Cooper, *The Gargantuan Gunsite Gossip 2* (2001), 144

A final word about democratic representation

Even by eliminating legislative districts to elect a reformed unicameral house, the democratic process remains inherently unfair.

In affirming that a man may not be taxed unless he has directly or indirectly given his consent, it affirms that he may refuse to be so taxed; and to refuse to be taxed is to cut all connection with the state. Perhaps it will be said that his consent is not a specific, but a general (implicit) one, and that the citizen is understood to have assented to everything his representative may do when he voted for him. But suppose he did not vote for him, and on the contrary did all in his power to get elected someone holding opposite views— what then? The reply will probably be that, by taking part in an election, he tacitly agreed to abide by the decision of the majority. And how if he did not vote at all? Why, then he cannot justly complain of any tax, seeing that he made no protest against its imposition. So, curiously enough, it seems that he gave his consent in whatever way he acted—whether he said yes, whether he said not, or whether he remained neuter! A rather awkward doctrine, this.

— Herbert Spencer, *Social Statics* (1850), Chapter XIX

Democracy is "consent of the governed" but true liberty requires the *unanimous* consent of the governed. This is called the free market. However, until the state apparatus is pared down to its bare essentials, democracy will remain, as Winston Churchill described, "the worst form of government, except for all the others."

What can we, personally, do to encourage the return of liberty?

- Decide which is more important—security or freedom. Money or freedom. Everything else you ever do will hinge on this.

- Know and understand the Bill of Rights; don't just memorize it; know what it means in real-life situations. Understand that the Bill of Rights isn't a Chinese menu; you can't just pick the parts you like or the groups you want to protect.

- Decide that you are not going to be a victim—that you are not going to passively accept the conditions of the police state. Resistance is risky, but as the Jewish partisans of World War II learned, those who resist have a chance; those who don't are defeated already.

- Decide that you are not going to be a collaborator, either. Don't work for police state agencies. Don't send your children to government schools if you can possibly avoid it. Think twice before you support ruthlessness perpetrated in the name of law and order, or before you call for more laws or regulations.

- Realize that governments fear mindset more than weaponry. If you have the tools but aren't prepared to fight, the tyrant won't fear you.

- Protest injustice and bureaucratic outrage— whether small or large—and not just on Internet newsgroups. Protest to the editor, the postmaster, the chief of police—whoever is responsible or who can help right the wrong.

- Don't purchase items made in police states or countries that use slave labor. If you order merchandise, make a point of asking its origin, and tell the vendor why you are refusing to buy an item that is the product of tyranny.

- Read historic and modern works on the philosophy of liberty. Understand the meaning and causes of events.

- Study and teach our children the principles of freedom.

- Do not vote for or contribute to politicians whose votes violate the Bill of Rights—no matter now much their rhetoric proclaims otherwise.

- Support *only* those politicians or organizations that take a no-compromise stance on liberty. "Compromise" that always moves us in the direction of tyranny and never in the direction of liberty is not genuine compromise; it is slow death.

- Do not obey morally unlawful orders.

- Gently educate those neighbors and friends who are receptive; don't harangue those who aren't—but do be ready on the day your most oblivious or statist neighbor finally feels the lash of arbitrary government power.

- Develop an inner conviction of being a free human being.

- **Live by what you *value* and not by what you fear.**

(From *The State vs. The People*, by Claire Wolfe and Aaron Zelman—jpfo.org)

❖ ENCRYPTION

After dinner with Governor Preston, Tom Parks opened up his large, sturdy briefcase and took out the powerful laptop computer inside. For many years he had religiously encrypted every data file, leaving absolutely no plaintext on his hard drive. He even scanned in all his paperwork, encrypted those files, and then shredded the paper before incinerating it in his fireplace.

Although Parks was not a criminal in the classic sense regarding property or violence, the Government had made potential criminals out of *everyone* with its unconstitutional laws, regulations, and executive orders against cash and privacy. He recognized the world for the extremely perilous place that it was, and employed very thorough measures to limit his risk of prosecution and conviction over some arcane regulation used to control American citizens under the guise of the so-called "War Against Terrorism." Encrypting his data and destroying paper evidence of his peaceable activities severely limited the "information is power" equation being used against him.

A long time ago Parks had very carefully set up his PGP key pair used for his private files. He preferred versions between 5.0 and 6.5 which offer his choice of algorithms: RSA or Diffie-Hellman (used in earlier versions of PGP). Since this key pair was generally for his own private use (*i.e.,* the public key would not be published), he did not use his name for the name of the key pair, but merely, for example, the letter "a." The "a" key could be for private correspondence, "b" for business correspondence, "c" for published work, "d" for emails to family, "e" for email to friends, etc.

This would also later provide him potential "plausible deniability" that he personally had ever generated the keys, as no name or email address had been given during key generation.

For the key pair size, he chose the largest then available: 2048-bits. Although many PGP users chose only 512- or 1024-bit key pairs, it makes no sense to opt for anything *less* than the maximum allowed by the software. While a longer key takes longer to generate (just like a long padlock key to cut from a blank), once generated it is just as fast to use as a shorter key (again, like padlock keys in real life). Furthermore, in a counter-intuitive way, each additional bit length *doubled* the "keyspace" (all the possible passphrase permutations, and hence computer cracking time)) of the key:

[Y]ou have to keep in mind the nature of digital numbers. Each bit in a binary key is like a fork in the road that a codebreaker must negotiate in order to get to the destination of the correct combination of ones and zeros. Every fork [i.e., every bit] presents a random choice between the correct turn and the wrong turn; a 128-bit key means that you have to guess the correct way to turn 128 times in a row. To make the course twice as difficult, you simply have to add one more fork; then you've created twice as many possible paths to negotiate, but still only one that is correct. But to make the course half as difficult, you don't divide the number of forks by two, but simply remove one.

— Steven Levy; *Crypto: How the Code Rebels Beat the Government—Saving Privacy in the Digital Age* (2001), pp. 57-8

So, a 2048-bit key pair isn't 2 times as hard to crack as a 1024-bit, it is 2^{1024} times more difficult. That 2^{1024} is, by the way, a very, *very* large number. It is roughly 1.8 times 10 to the 308th power.

This concept works even more powerfully regarding passphrase length since the element of permutation is not base-2, but a minimum of 26. The character length of the passphrase is the exponent. Assuming the user employed only lower case letters (a-z = 26), each additional letter increases exponentially the keyspace:

2 lower case letters	26^2 = 676
3 lower case letters	26^3 = 17,576
4 lower case letters	26^4 = 456,976
5 lower case letters	26^5 = 11,881,376
6 lower case letters	26^6 = 308,915,776
7 lower case letters	26^7 = 8,031,810,176
8 lower case letters	26^8 = 208,827,064,576

Meaning, each additional character here increases keyspace by 26 times. Although 208,827,064,576 seems like a very large number to us humans, it isn't to a modern computer. With a machine trying 500 million combinations per second (or, 500MIPS, which is computational child's play), that 26^8 keyspace can be cracked in 3.5 minutes on average, and 7 minutes at the very most.

A 7-character password (*i.e.*, 26^7 or 8,031,810,176 keyspace) would be cracked 26 times more easily: in just *16 seconds*.

While long passphrases are essential, why limit the base number to only 26 when there are many other characters available on the standard keyboard? For example, using a combination of upper and lower case letters (a-z, A-Z), the base is now 52 (26 +26).

Using a combination of upper and lower case letters *and numerals* (a-z, A-Z, 0-9), the base is now 62 (26 +26 +10).

Better still is using a combination of upper and lower case letters and numerals *and metacharacters* (a-z, A-Z, 0-9, plus !@#$%, etc.), the base is now *95* (26 +26 +10 +33). (Note: In case you're counting the metacharacters out of curiosity, the space key is the 33rd.) This means that an 8-character password from these 95 characters (*e.g.,* Joyful#8) provides 95^8 possible password combinations, which is a *31,769 times larger* keyspace than the mere 26^8 (208,827,064,576) combinations using only 8 lower case letters! Such would take our computer 77-154 days (versus 7 minutes) to crack.

A hacker trying to crack what he knew was an 8-character a passphrase would first try all the numerical permutations (10^8), then lower case (26^8), then upper case (26^8), then lower and numerical (36^8), then upper and numerical (36^8), then lower and upper (52^8), and finally numerical/lower/upper (62^8). If he had no success then the knew that the passphrase had at least one metacharacter, which made brute force hacking impractical due to the 95^8 size keyspace (which is 30 times larger than without any metacharacters).

Tom Parks knew all of this, of course. Passphrases are conceived, have a particular length, are stored, and then used. Each step offers its own vulnerability, which Parks had been very conscientious to minimize, if not nearly eliminate altogether.

Conception

Although the best passphrase would be a very long string of totally random characters from the 256 ASCII characters (these are accessed by holding ALT key while entering a number from 0033 to 0255, such as ALT+0163 producing £), such would be impossible to remember and would have to be stored somewhere convenient to the user (which simultaneously makes it much easier for a hacker to discover).

So, a passphrase must be something that the user can easily and perfectly recall (see Storage), without having to say it aloud (see Usage). However, it must also not be a phrase easily discerned or guessed by any third party (especially those who best know you.) One idea is to use an obscure (but memorable) line from a movie, and insert some numerals and/or metacharacters. For example, the classic line from *Sierra Madre* is, *"Badges? I don't gotta show you no stinkin' badges!"* Since this might remind you of the arrogance of totalitarianism, and thus George Orwell's famous work, you could insert "1984": *Badges? I don't gotta show you no stinkin' badges1984!* This would be a nearly impossible passphrase (55 characters) to guess or discern, yet easily remembered and quickly entered.

Length

You need a *minimum* of 8 characters amongst the 95 characters available on the standard keyboard (a-z, A-Z, 0-9, !@#$%^&*, etc.). If the software supports it, 30+ characters are far superior. The above sample passphrase contains 55 characters, which is 95^{55} possible combinations—or 5.95 followed by 108 zeros. That 55 character passphrase is 8.97×10^{92} times tougher to crack than the mere 8 character passphrase discussed earlier.

Our 500MIPS computer would need 3.78^{92} *years* to crack it.

Storage

The most secure form of storage is the user's memory without any written or social backup copies. Anything less is begging for trouble.

As the factoring aspects of decryption are sufficiently daunting (in that thousands of years of computer time are necessary) the *human* element becomes the weakest link. For example, there is no point in a 4096-bit key pair coupled with a 100-character passphrase using the 256 ASCII characters if you stupidly write down the passphrase in your DayTimer.

Usage

If somebody watches or videos your passphrase keystrokes, or hears you mumble it to yourself, or uses Tempest technology to read your screen at a distance, then all is for naught. Even if you avoid direct surveillance, there is still the indirect surveillance of "keysniffing" programs and devices. (More on this shortly.)

Hence, Parks chose a 64-character passphrase (something his father once told him in confidence as a boy) with numbers and metacharacters (including an Alt metacharacter for good measure, which increased the base number from 95 to 256). A 256^{64} length passphrase (1.34 followed by 154 zeros) could not be cracked through a "brute force" dictionary attack. It could never be guessed. And as he never wrote it down or spoke it aloud, it remained safe in his memory. The first three elements of passphrase security —Conception, Length, and Storage—had been well executed.

The name of "a" was chosen for the key pair. Once the passphrase had been entered, the PGP chewed on the key pair generation for many minutes. What it was looking for were two very large prime numbers which when multiplied together would produce a number 2048-bits long.

To factor a 2048-bit key into its parent primes is, for all practical purposes, impossible. (It was already impossible at "only" 1024-bits. A 2048-bit key is 1.8×10^{308} times more difficult than *that*.) The process is called *discrete logarithm* and has been known for 2,000 years (beginning with Eratosthenes of Alexandria) as an *exceedingly* difficult computational task, requiring about a million million quadrillion (*i.e.,* 10^{27}) more operations than used to generate the product in the first place. It is basically a *one-way* function which can be done but not "undone." Mathematicians call them *time deterministic trap-door polynomials*.

Mathematicians Whit Diffie and Marty Hellman figured out how to use this phenomenon to realize their dream of public key encryption. The problem of classic *single* key encryption is that since the key both encrypts and *decrypts,* it requires a secure channel (*i.e.,* prior arrangement) to exchange the key. But if you *have* a secure channel to do so, then why not simply exchange the message then—without encrypting it? Secure channels were possible when A and B lived in close proximity to each other, but in the modern digital age this is rarely the case. Commerce is only as wide as communication and money. With digital money, communication (*i.e.,* information) has *become* the money. The intrinsic value issue aside, money really has always been just *information.* Fractional equilibrium.

Since strangers across the ocean cannot easily or quickly establish a secure channel to exchange a key, Whit Diffie understood that some sort of *public* key encryption was vital for digital commerce. The answer was to split the single key in two, one public and one secret. A key *pair* would be generated, one half of which (the "public" key) could be transmitted in the clear (as it's useless for decryption). The other half of the key (the "secret" key) is kept by the owner. Whatever one key encrypts, only the *other* key may decrypt. This is called asymmetrical encryption. Thus, if I have your public key, I can encrypt messages which *only you* can decrypt (since only you have the secret key and the passphrase). In fact, I could not even use your public key to decrypt that message which I had just encrypted. It is this one-way function which makes the public key useless to a hacker.

Let's explain it in a different way. In single, or symmetrical, key encryption it is the *sender* who performs the encryption, not the recipient. However, in public, or asymmetrical, key encryption the *recipient* is involved in the encryption process (by generating for the sender the public key from the parent primes). In effect, this public key (provided by the recipient) acts as line noise which changes plaintext into cyphertext. Since only the recipient has the secret key (the only thing that can strip away the noise), and since the public key is useless in stripping away the noise (it's like a rock thrown in the water to cloud things up, but it cannot conversely make the water clear—hence the one-way function), public key encryption successfully thwarts the main rule of encryption (*i.e.,* that key delivery remain secure).

Returning to Parks's encryption tradecraft, he recognized the urgency of protecting the two keyring files.

Leaving such in the clear on a computer makes a hacker's job much easier. The *public* keyring contains all those public keys you had collected over the years, and thus spilling the beans as to whom you have been sending encrypted files. Leaving it in the clear makes your network of friends and colleagues easily known. (This is vital information that you should protect.) The *secret* keyring contains all your secret keys, which can be used against you as proof that you had encrypted a particular file. Also, anybody with your secret key can sign bogus public key certificates in your name. Finally, allowing access to your secret key makes decryption *theoretically* possible (although certainly not easy), versus utterly impossible without it.

Parks protected the keyring pair by encrypting the files pubring.pgp and secring.pgp with PGP's IDEA single key encryption (using a unique passphrase). Thus, the keyrings and their keys are absolutely unavailable to any outsider. Next, he renamed these encrypted pubring.asc and secring.asc files as a pair of DOS help files (which did not exist for the corresponding arcane .exe files): interlnk.hlp and intersvr.hlp. (He would remember that the intersvr.hlp file was the secret keyring file because of the "s" in svr.) He then changed the timestamp of these two files to 3/10/93 6:00:00AM to precisely match the timestamp of the DOS 6.0 system files.

Since these two DOS help files were written on the hard drive *after* the original DOS files had been, a clever investigator might notice that interlnk.hlp and intersvr.hlp were in cluster blocks far separate from the ones containing the other DOS files. This would strike him as unusual and thus cause him to question the date/time stamp of interlnk.hlp and intersvr.hlp. He would then look at them with a hex editor (which directly reads the disk without need of an operating system) which would reveal interlnk.hlp and intersvr.hlp to actually be PGP files. (Nevertheless, without cracking them he wouldn't know *what* they contained. Even if he suspected encrypted keyrings, he would not be able to open them, much less use the keys.)

What one could do is copy alphabetically by filename the entire DOS subdirectory (which now, for the moment, include interlnk.hlp and intersvr.hlp) into a new subdirectory called dos2, shred the original dos subdirectory, then rename subdirectory dos2 as dos. This would place interlnk.hlp and intersvr.hlp alphabetically within the other files on the drive itself, and not alphabetically by mere virtue of OS directory sorting.

While this was quite clever, it still left the encrypted PGP keyring files on the hard drive, and if an investigator examined the entire drive with a hex editor he could still peel back the DOS name camouflage (not that he could, however, easily crack the encryption).

The best thing to do was not keep interlnk.hlp and intersvr.hlp on the hard drive at all. That way, if his laptop were ever lost or seized, there would be absolutely *no* way his encrypted files could be cracked (without the use of the NSA's rumored quantum computer).

So, Parks made several DOS system disks on floppies, each containing the entire DOS subdirectory (including interlnk.hlp and intersvr.hlp). To any casual snooper, these floppies would look like DOS disks (*i.e.,* boring!). Physical separation by floppy increased security significantly. These he sprinkled about generously, including giving one to his trusted attorney for safekeeping. He even hid some on the Internet.

Lastly, after making sure that the DOS camouflaged PGP keyring files would properly open and operate, Parks shredded the original files pub-ring.pgp and secring.pgp from his hard drive. Just for good measure, he shredded the randseed.bin file used to seed the PRNG (pseudorandom number generator) for that session. (More on "shredding" shortly.)

Parks was justifiably confident that his keys were well protected through a combination of encryption and disguise.

Now, he had to protect his passphrase. This was most important. Although Parks had conceived a long and difficult passphrase (*i.e.* with a keyspace of 95^{64}) and stored it only in his memory, he still needed to *use* it safely. This took a bit of ingenuity, as the FBI had a very clever technique which had worked many times in the past. His passphrase *could* theoretically be caught by a "keysniffer" (which the feds had perfected in many forms since the mid-1990s). To install such a program or device on Parks's computers required a surreptitious entry to his home and office, and such had been legally permissible since March 2002 by the "sneak and peek" warrants authorized by the blatantly unconstitutional *USA PATRIOT* Act of 2001.

As a practicing attorney, Parks well understood this, too. So, to thwart keysniffing techniques, he linked his palmtop computer to the larger computer (home, office, or laptop), and entered the necessary passphrase into the larger computer's RAM clipboard. Hence, the larger computer never had any passphrase keystrokes entered in it at all. Furthermore, since his palmtop was always on his person, it could not be surreptitiously compromised with a keysniffing program or device. Also, the LCD screen of the palmtop (versus a CRT monitor) foiled Tempest attacks or Van Eck phreaking (which reads another's CRT from a distance without the owner's knowledge[1]).

Finally, Parks kept his laptop as a "stand alone" machine which he never connected to the Internet. This kept it totally free of viruses and cookies. (Computer hygiene was, after all, similar to sexual hygiene.) It also made impossible for a hacker to get into his laptop online (which happens more often than one may presume).

All of the above was merely to *setup* his PGP procedure and files. To actually use them, Parks did the following.

After booting up, Parks would insert the floppy with the DOS files, copy the two DOS camouflaged files (interlnk.hlp and intersvr.hlp) to a temporary working directory as pubring.asc and secring.asc. Then, he would decrypt the two keyring files and access them as needed—always using his linked palmtop to transfer passphrases. Once the session had ended, Parks

---

1   For an excellent (and hilarious) discussion of Tempest and Van Eck phreaking, see pp.350-365 of Neal Stephenson's superb novel, *Cryptonomicon.*

would securely shred the both the camouflaged and decrypted keyring pairs, and then delete the empty working directory.

Merely "deleting" a file doesn't delete it all; it only allows the file to be later overwritten if no unwritten disk space remains. This is why one may easily restore files long after they've been "deleted." (Col. Ollie North did not know this.) Few computer users understand how difficult it is to *securely* shred data from the magnetic memory of floppy disks and hard drives.

Computers are simply a megalopolis of magnetic switches which read either ON (a "1") or OFF (a "0"). Each switch is called a "bit" and there are 8-bits to a byte (which is 2^8 or 256 possible permutations making up just one character). A 100-gigabyte drive stores 800 billion bits of binary information.

On a drive or diskette, disk platters serve as the magnetic medium, the surface of which consists of what are called magnetic domains. These act individually like microscopic magnets with positive and negative poles. To save what the read/write head recognizes as just 1-bit of information requires *millions* of magnetic domains, sort of like strands of carpet. Let's say 10,000,000, for example. Imagine a dense carpet with 10 strands per inch. To contain 10 million strands (*i.e.,* magnetic domains) for just 1-bit of binary information means a room-sized carpet about 26 feet per side.

Remember, this is only for *one* bit. To store just one character would require 8-bits, or a carpet 74 feet square. A square *mile* of this carpet would store about 375K of data (which is about 75,000 words of an average 5-character length). A 100G hard drive would be the equivalent of 16.3 *miles* on each side. Now, just imagine that city-sized carpet shrunk down to the size of a cigarette pack, which is how small a 100G laptop hard drive is these days.

When writing to the disk platter, the read/write head passes over the surface and flips the magnetic domains towards one direction, just like a vacuum cleaner does to carpet. By creating, altering, and deleting files, magnetic domains are overwritten (*i.e.,* revacuumed) many times.

What is now important to understand is that *each* time the read/write head passes over the magnetic domains, it does so with *imperfect* overlap. For example, let's say that you smoothed a carpet in one direction (writing data on it, so to speak), and then sloppily vacuumed it in the *opposite* direction. Anybody could see that old information (*i.e.,* from the original smoothening) remained in the medium even after deletion (*i.e.,* from the vacuuming).

Even if you had *carefully* vacuumed, some strands would either have been missed, or stubbornly kept their orientation (*i.e.,* polarity) from the original smoothening (data). Just *one* magnetic domain (*i.e.,* one strand of carpet) retaining previous polarity is old information which had not been securely deleted. If enough magnetic domains exist with recoverable old information, then chunks of possibly sensitive data could be pieced together.

This is precisely what government agencies rely upon to retrieve data deleted beyond software recovery methods. By employing hardware techniques such as magnetic force scanning tunneling microscopy (STM), they may analyze a particular disk sector's magnetic domains for old "layers" which have not successfully been "revacuumed" through overwriting. The Federal Government even has a specific laboratory in Linthicum, Maryland called the Defense Computer Forensics Lab (www.dcfl.gov) dedicated to retrieving data regardless of hard drive or diskette condition.

They are extremely good at their work.

Thus, the trick to deletion overwriting is to make sure that *every* strand of carpet is vacuumed, and in a random series of particular passes to totally clear the magnetic orientation of the old layers. There are several methods of overwriting. (The DoD 5220-22.M standard is quite fast and moderately effective, but should not be relied upon for shredding sensitive data. That the Government doesn't trust it for Top Secret data speaks volumes.)

The current standard was devised by Dr. Peter Gutmann of the University of Auckland back in the mid-1990s, and this is the default method in Sami Tolvanen's widely acclaimed Eraser program (www.tolvanen.com). Eraser uses Gutmann's 27 deterministic passes (the order of which is shuffled by the Tiger hash function) preceded and followed by 4 passes of random data (created by the ISAAC pseudorandom number generator), totalling 35 passes. This should overwrite all data despite drive encoding. Eraser installs (as "Erase") in the Windows Explorer File command structure and is supremely simple to use. Click and shred.

Tolvanen's Eraser first overwrites the cluster tips (or "slack space"). One must understand that the space allocated to a file is larger than the file itself. Let's say that you save a 59K-sized file. In doing so, your computer's file system sets aside a 64K-sized block of clusters, which leaves 5K of slack space (cluster tip). It's sort of like how a plate is always larger than the meal on it. Normally, this 5K of cluster tip would not be compromising since it had not been written to and is simply empty disk space. However, this is the exception because files are frequently overwritten, which always alters their size. (For example, you could append that file with 3K of additional work, changing it into a 62K-sized file.)

Although files usually *grow* in size through each work session, sometimes they *shrink*—and here is where unshredded cluster tips can get you into trouble. Let's say that your final version of that originally 59K-sized file got thinned down to 40K. That old 19K of data still exists on your hard drive, even though it is no longer accessible through its parent file! It resides in the cluster tip of the 64K block, overwritten *only* if and when there is no other free disk space. Depending on one's computer use, it could take months or even years for this 19K of plaintext data to be overwritten—or never at all. Therefore, it is vital that the shredding process (both for individual files and for un-used disk space) overwrite all file cluster tips.

Most free space overwriting programs do *not* overwrite cluster tips! This is because although cluster tips may indeed be empty of data, they are necessarily allocated to their particular files and thus *not* listed by the computer's file system as actually being part of the disk's free space. Only a high-quality shredder program such as Eraser accounts for this and shreds all empty cluster tips still attached to their files.

So, once his session has ended, Parks encrypts his data files, and se-curely shreds the originals (as well as pubring.pgp and secring.pgp, which had been decrypted from pubring.asc and secring.asc). He also shreds the randseed.bin file used to seed the encryption process (which, if left on the drive, could ease the task of finding one's previous or next session keys). Then he renames pubring.asc and secring.asc back to interlnk.hlp and in-tersvc.hlp. Next, he "Erases" the contents of the Recycle Bin, if any. Then, he shuts down Windows and reboots in DOS (which has far fewer applica-tions open, and thus offers more cluster tips available for overwriting). From DOS he overwrites the entire unused disk space (which includes cluster tips still attached to files)[2]. Next he defrags his disk with Norton, and then again-overwrites the free space (which is differently organized after defragging).

Only *then* does he turn off the computer.

All this is a rather large inconvenience, obviously. Parks believes the security to be well worth the trouble. Any high-level security (physical, finan-cial, legal, computer, etc.) is accomplished only through *layers*, and Parks's combined efforts likely make any data recovery next to impossible from a practical standpoint. While *nothing* is *theoretically* impossible given suffi-cient time, determination, and resources, many things are basically impossi-ble from a *practical* standpoint.

Meaning, the incredibly huge effort required to divine plaintext from his laptop (assuming such were possible) would be *far* in excess of its value. And that is precisely the *point*. Security is never absolute—merely relative.

If all freedom-lovers consistently adopted similarly stringent mea-sures, then their data could not be easily used against them, if at all. We are in a war for our freedom, and it's time we thought defensively at every level.

---

2   If your computer does not have sufficient RAM, Windows will create virtual memory on disk in the form of a swap or paging file, which cannot be reliably shredded during a Windows session. (Ideally, you should have enough RAM whereby you may set to 0K the virtual memory option in Control Panel.) Shred from DOS this swap file, as it contains plaintext data! Windows 9x and ME usually store it at C:\win-dows\win386.swp. (Windows NT/2000 overwrites theirs automatically upon shutdown.)

❖ WYOMING QUICK FACTS

Land area
Land area ranking	9th (97,818 square miles)
Forest area	16% (9.8 million acres) of state total
Ownership	48% Federal Government
	42% private property
	6% state land
	4% Indian trust land
Farms and ranches	9,100, averaging 3,802 acres (2nd highest)

Topography
Highest point	13,804' (Gannet Peak)
Lowest point	3,100' (Belle Fourche River; Crook County)
Mean elevation	6,700' (second only to Colorado)
Annual precipitation	14.5 inches (from 5" to 45" locally)

Wyoming is *not* as dry as one may think!

Wyoming's 714 square miles of surface water is 87% of Idaho's, and 97% as much as Arizona's and Colorado's *combined*.

Wyoming is a fisherman's paradise with 15,846 miles of streams and 297,633 acres of lakes. The 3,400 lakes, ponds, and reservoirs support 90 varieties of fish (42 are game fish). Cutthroat Trout is the state fish.

Wyoming statehood
10 July 1890 as the 44th State (now with 23 counties).

2000 Population
Population	493,782
Population ranking	50th (Alaska's has 550,043)
Population density	5.0 per square mile (49th after Alaska's 1.0)

Wyoming firsts and largests
Highest national production of coal, bentonite, and gemstones.
Largest global reserve of trona.
Largest antelope population on the continent.
Largest single elk herd in the world.
First government in the world to grant women suffrage (1869).
First all-women jury in the world (1870; Laramie).
First National Park (1872; Yellowstone).
First county public library system (1886).
First National Forest (1891; Shoshone).
Largest National Forest (Teton) in the 48 States.
First woman statewide elected official (1894; Estelle Reel Meyer).
First National Monument (1906; Devil's Tower).
First American town governed entirely by women (1920; Jackson).
First woman governor in the U.S.A. (1925-27; Nellie Tayloe Ross).
Largest/oldest outdoor rodeo in the world (Cheyenne Frontier Days).

Wyoming Economy
Minerals ($3.2B), agriculture ($1.5B), and tourism ($1.0B).
Wyoming is 1st in the nation for production of coal, bentonite, and gemstones; 2nd in wool; 3rd in sheep and lamb; 5th in crude oil and natural gas; 8th in sugar beets; 9th in barley; and 10th in dry beans.
Other top ag products are beef, corn, hay, timber, and wheat.
More than five million tourists visit each year, spending over $1B.

Wyoming business climate
No personal income tax.
No corporate income tax.
No gross receipts tax.
No inventory tax.
4% retail sales tax.
Only 9¢ gallon fuel tax.
Low property taxes.
Favorable inheritance and unemployment taxes.
Excellent business laws (corporations, LLCs, trusts, etc.)

Wyoming energy
95% generated by locally-mined low-sulphur coal. The other 5% is produced by the state's 10 hydroelectric plants.
Electricity and natural gas prices are among the nation's lowest.

www.javelinpress.com

NOTE: Javelin Press is enjoying rapid growth, which may affect our address or pricing. Please verify both from our website *before* you send your order!

Prices each copy:	**Retail**	**<40%>**	**<44%>**	**<50%>**
You & The Police! 5½"x8½" 168 pp. 2/2005	1-5 copies **$16**	6-37 **$10**	38-75 **$8.80**	case of 76 or more **$8**
Bulletproof Privacy 5½"x8½" 160 pp. 1/1997	1-5 copies **$16**	6-39 **$10**	40-79 **$8.80**	case of 80 or more **$8**
Hologram of Liberty 5½"x8½" 262 pp. 8/1997	1-5 copies **$20**	6-19 **$12**	20-39 **$11**	case of 40 or more **$10**
Boston on Surviving Y2K 5½"x8½" 352 pp. 11/1998	1-5 copies **$11**	6-17 **$10**	18-35 **$9**	case of 36 or more **$8**
Boston's Gun Bible 5½"x8½" 848 pp. 4/2002	1-2 copies **$33**	3-7 **$19.80**	8-15 **$18.48**	case 16 or more **$17.50**
Molôn Labé! 5½"x8½" 454 pp. 1/2004	1-5 copies **$27**	6-13 **$16.20**	14-27 **$15.12**	case 28 or more **$13.50**
Safari Dreams 5½"x8½" 220+pp. 1/2008	1-5 copies **$26**	(see website after Jan 2008 for discount details)		

Mix titles for *any* quantity discount. This is easiest done as ¼ case per title:
¼ case of: **Y&P!** 19   **BP** 20   **HoL** 10   **BoSY** 9   **BGB** 4   **ML!** 7

Shipping and Handling are *not* included! Add below:
non-case S&H for *Boston's Gun Bible   Molôn Labé!*:
First Class (or UPS for less-than-case) add: $6 for first copy, $2 each additional copy.

non-case S&H within USA for other titles (*i.e., Y&P!, BP, HoL, BoSY, SD*):
First Class (or UPS for larger orders) add: $5 for first copy, $1 each additional copy.

CASE orders (straight or mixed) UPS Ground: $30 west of the Miss.; $40 east.

Overpayment will be refunded in cash with order. Underpayment will delay order!
If you have questions on discounts or S&H, email us through our website.

These forms of payment *only:*
Cash (Preferred. Cash orders receive signed copies when available.)
payee blank M.O.s (Which makes them more easily negotiable.)
credit cards (Many of our distributors take them. See our website.)

Unless prior agreement has been made, *we do not accept and will return* checks, C.O.D.s, filled-in M.O.s, or any other form of tender. Prices and terms are subject to change without notice (check our website first). Please send paid orders to:

by Kenneth Royce (Boston T. Party)

You & The Police!   (revised for 2005)

The definitive guide to your rights and tactics during police confrontations. When can you *refuse* to answer questions or consent to searches?   Don't lose your liberty through ignorance! This 2005 edition covers the *USA PATRIOT Act* and much more.

168 pp. softcover (2005) $16 + $5 s&h (cash, please)

Bulletproof Privacy
How to Live Hidden, Happy, and Free!

Explains precisely how to lay low and be left alone by the snoops, government agents and bureaucrats. Boston shares many of his own unique methods. Now in its 10th printing!

160 pp. softcover (1997) $16 + $5 s&h (cash, please)

Hologram of Liberty
The Constitution's Shocking Alliance
with Big Government

The Convention of 1787 was the most brilliant and subtle *coup d'état* in history. The nationalist framers *designed* a strong government, guaranteed through purposely ambiguous verbiage. Many readers say this is Boston's best book. A jaw-dropper.

262 pp. softcover (1997) $20 + $5 s&h (cash, please)

Boston on Surviving Y2K
And Other Lovely Disasters

Even though Y2K was Y2¿Qué? this title remains highly useful for all preparedness planning. **Now on sale for 50% off!** (It's the same book as The Military Book Club's *Surviving Doomsday*.)

352 pp. softcover (1998) only $11 + $5 s&h (cash, please)

Boston's Gun Bible   (new text for 2006)

A rousing how-to/*why*-to on our modern gun ownership. Firearms are *"liberty's teeth"* and it's time we remembered it. No other general gun book is more thorough or useful! Indispensable!

848 pp. softcover (2002-2006) $33 + $6 s&h (cash, please)

Molôn Labé!   (a novel)

If you liked *Unintended Consequences* by John Ross and Ayn Rand's *Atlas Shrugged*, then Boston's novel will be a favorite. It dramatically outlines an innovative recipe for Liberty which could actually work! A thinking book for people of action; an action book for people of thought. It's getting people moving to Wyoming!

454 pp. softcover (2004) $27 + $6 s&h (cash, please)
limited edition hardcover $44 + $6 (while supplies last)

Safari Dreams   (new for 2008!)
A Practical Guide To Your Hunt In Africa

Possibly the most useful "one book" for making your first safari. Thoroughly covers: rifles, calibers, bullets, insurance, health, packing and planning, trip prep, airlines, choosing your PH, shot placement, and being in the bush. Don't go to Africa without it!

220+ pp. softcover (Jan 2008) $26 + $5 s&h (cash, please)

www.javelinpress.com
www.freestatewyoming.org

www.javelinpress.com

NOTE: Javelin Press is enjoying rapid growth, which may affect our address or pricing. Please verify both from our website *before* you send your order!

Prices each copy:	Retail	<40%>	<44%>	<50%>
You & The Police! 5½"x8½" 168 pp. 2/2005	1-5 copies **$16**	6-37 **$10**	38-75 **$8.80**	case of 76 or more **$8**
Bulletproof Privacy 5½"x8½" 160 pp. 1/1997	1-5 copies **$16**	6-39 **$10**	40-79 **$8.80**	case of 80 or more **$8**
Hologram of Liberty 5½"x8½" 262 pp. 8/1997	1-5 copies **$20**	6-19 **$12**	20-39 **$11**	case of 40 or more **$10**
Boston on Surviving Y2K 5½"x8½" 352 pp. 11/1998	1-5 copies **$11**	6-17 **$10**	18-35 **$9**	case of 36 or more **$8**
Boston's Gun Bible 5½"x8½" 848 pp. 4/2002	1-2 copies **$33**	3-7 **$19.80**	8-15 **$18.48**	case 16 or more **$17.50**
Molôn Labé! 5½"x8½" 454 pp. 1/2004	1-5 copies **$27**	6-13 **$16.20**	14-27 **$15.12**	case 28 or more **$13.50**
Safari Dreams 5½"x8½" 220+pp. 1/2008	1-5 copies **$26**	(see website after Jan 2008 for discount details)		

Mix titles for *any* quantity discount. This is easiest done as ¼ case per title:
¼ case of: **Y&P!** 19   **BP** 20   **HoL** 10   **BoSY** 9   **BGB** 4   **ML!** 7

Shipping and Handling are *not* included!   Add below:

non-case S&H for *Boston's Gun Bible   Molôn Labé!* **:**
First Class (or UPS for less-than-case) add: $6 for first copy, $2 each additional copy.

non-case S&H within USA for other titles (*i.e., Y&P!, BP, HoL, BoSY, SD*):
First Class (or UPS for larger orders) add: $5 for first copy, $1 each additional copy.

CASE orders (straight or mixed) UPS Ground: $30 west of the Miss.; $40 east.

Overpayment will be refunded in cash with order. Underpayment will delay order!
If you have questions on discounts or S&H, email us through our website.

These forms of payment *only:*

Cash (Preferred. Cash orders receive signed copies when available.)
payee blank M.O.s (Which makes them more easily negotiable.)
credit cards (Many of our distributors take them. See our website.)

Unless prior agreement has been made, *we do not accept and will return* checks, C.O.D.s, filled-in M.O.s, or any other form of tender. Prices and terms are subject to change without notice (check our website first). Please send paid orders to:

by Kenneth Royce (Boston T. Party)

You & The Police!   (revised for 2005)
The definitive guide to your rights and tactics during police confrontations. When can you *refuse* to answer questions or consent to searches?   Don't lose your liberty through ignorance! This 2005 edition covers the *USA PATRIOT Act* and much more.
   168 pp. softcover (2005) $16 + $5 s&h (cash, please)

Bulletproof Privacy
How to Live Hidden, Happy, and Free!
Explains precisely how to lay low and be left alone by the snoops, government agents and bureaucrats. Boston shares many of his own unique methods. Now in its 10th printing!
   160 pp. softcover (1997) $16 + $5 s&h (cash, please)

Hologram of Liberty
The Constitution's Shocking Alliance
with Big Government
The Convention of 1787 was the most brilliant and subtle *coup d'état* in history. The nationalist framers *designed* a strong government, guaranteed through purposely ambiguous verbiage. Many readers say this is Boston's best book. A jaw-dropper.
   262 pp. softcover (1997) $20 + $5 s&h (cash, please)

Boston on Surviving Y2K
And Other Lovely Disasters
Even though Y2K was Y2¿Qué? this title remains highly useful for all preparedness planning. **Now on sale for 50% off!** (It's the same book as The Military Book Club's *Surviving Doomsday*.)
   352 pp. softcover (1998) only $11 + $5 s&h (cash, please)

Boston's Gun Bible   (new text for 2006)
A rousing how-to/*why*-to on our modern gun ownership. Firearms are *"liberty's teeth"* and it's time we remembered it. No other general gun book is more thorough or useful! Indispensable!
   848 pp. softcover (2002-2006) $33 + $6 s&h (cash, please)

Molôn Labé!   (a novel)
If you liked *Unintended Consequences* by John Ross and Ayn Rand's *Atlas Shrugged*, then Boston's novel will be a favorite. It dramatically outlines an innovative recipe for Liberty which could actually work! A thinking book for people of action; an action book for people of thought. It's getting people moving to Wyoming!
   454 pp. softcover (2004) $27 + $6 s&h (cash, please)
   limited edition hardcover $44 + $6 (while supplies last)

Safari Dreams   (new for 2008!)
A Practical Guide To Your Hunt In Africa
Possibly the most useful "one book" for making your first safari. Thoroughly covers: rifles, calibers, bullets, insurance, health, packing and planning, trip prep, airlines, choosing your PH, shot placement, and being in the bush. Don't go to Africa without it!
   220+ pp. softcover (Jan 2008) $26 + $5 s&h (cash, please)

www.javelinpress.com
www.freestatewyoming.org

www.javelinpress.com

NOTE: Javelin Press is enjoying rapid growth, which may affect our address or pricing. Please verify both from our website *before* you send your order!

Prices each copy:	**Retail**	**<40%>**	**<44%>**	**<50%>**
You & The Police! 5½"x8½" 168 pp. 2/2005	1-5 copies **$16**	6-37 **$10**	38-75 **$8.80**	*case of 76 or more* **$8**
Bulletproof Privacy 5½"x8½" 160 pp. 1/1997	1-5 copies **$16**	6-39 **$10**	40-79 **$8.80**	*case of 80 or more* **$8**
Hologram of Liberty 5½"x8½" 262 pp. 8/1997	1-5 copies **$20**	6-19 **$12**	20-39 **$11**	*case of 40 or more* **$10**
Boston on Surviving Y2K 5½"x8½" 352 pp. 11/1998	1-5 copies **$11**	6-17 **$10**	18-35 **$9**	*case of 36 or more* **$8**
Boston's Gun Bible 5½"x8½" 848 pp. 4/2002	1-2 copies **$33**	3-7 **$19.80**	8-15 **$18.48**	*case 16 or more* **$17.50**
Molôn Labé! 5½"x8½" 454 pp. 1/2004	1-5 copies **$27**	6-13 **$16.20**	14-27 **$15.12**	*case 28 or more* **$13.50**
Safari Dreams 5½"x8½" 220+pp. 1/2008	1-5 copies **$26**	(see website after Jan 2008 for discount details)		

Mix titles for *any* quantity discount. This is easiest done as ¼ case per title:
¼ case of: **Y&P!** 19   **BP** 20   **HoL** 10   **BoSY** 9   **BGB** 4   **ML!** 7

Shipping and Handling are *not* included!   Add below:

non-case S&H for   *Boston's Gun Bible   Molôn Labé!*:
First Class (or UPS for less-than-case) add: $6 for first copy, $2 each additional copy.

non-case S&H within USA for other titles (*i.e., Y&P!, BP, HoL, BoSY, SD*):
First Class (or UPS for larger orders) add: $5 for first copy, $1 each additional copy.

CASE orders (straight or mixed) UPS Ground: $30 west of the Miss.; $40 east.

Overpayment will be refunded in cash with order. Underpayment will delay order! If you have questions on discounts or S&H, email us through our website.

These forms of payment *only:*

Cash (Preferred. Cash orders receive signed copies when available.)
payee blank M.O.s (Which makes them more easily negotiable.)
credit cards (Many of our distributors take them. See our website.)

Unless prior agreement has been made, *we do not accept and will return* checks, C.O.D.s, filled-in M.O.s, or any other form of tender. Prices and terms are subject to change without notice (check our website first). Please send paid orders to:

by Kenneth Royce (Boston T. Party)

You & The Police!   (revised for 2005)

The definitive guide to your rights and tactics during police confrontations. When can you *refuse* to answer questions or consent to searches?   Don't lose your liberty through ignorance! This 2005 edition covers the *USA PATRIOT Act* and much more.

168 pp. softcover (2005) $16 + $5 s&h (cash, please)

Bulletproof Privacy

How to Live Hidden, Happy, and Free!

Explains precisely how to lay low and be left alone by the snoops, government agents and bureaucrats. Boston shares many of his own unique methods. Now in its 10th printing!

160 pp. softcover (1997) $16 + $5 s&h (cash, please)

Hologram of Liberty

The Constitution's Shocking Alliance
with Big Government

The Convention of 1787 was the most brilliant and subtle *coup d'état* in history. The nationalist framers *designed* a strong government, guaranteed through purposely ambiguous verbiage. Many readers say this is Boston's best book. A jaw-dropper.

262 pp. softcover (1997) $20 + $5 s&h (cash, please)

Boston on Surviving Y2K

And Other Lovely Disasters

Even though Y2K was Y2¿Qué? this title remains highly useful for all preparedness planning. **Now on sale for 50% off!** (It's the same book as The Military Book Club's *Surviving Doomsday*.)

352 pp. softcover (1998) only $11 + $5 s&h (cash, please)

Boston's Gun Bible   (new text for 2006)

A rousing how-to/*why*-to on our modern gun ownership. Firearms are *"liberty's teeth"* and it's time we remembered it. No other general gun book is more thorough or useful! Indispensable!

848 pp. softcover (2002-2006) $33 + $6 s&h (cash, please)

Molôn Labé!   (a novel)

If you liked *Unintended Consequences* by John Ross and Ayn Rand's *Atlas Shrugged*, then Boston's novel will be a favorite. It dramatically outlines an innovative recipe for Liberty which could actually work! A thinking book for people of action; an action book for people of thought. It's getting people moving to Wyoming!

454 pp. softcover (2004) $27 + $6 s&h (cash, please)
limited edition hardcover $44 + $6 (while supplies last)

Safari Dreams   (new for 2008!)

A Practical Guide To Your Hunt In Africa

Possibly the most useful "one book" for making your first safari. Thoroughly covers: rifles, calibers, bullets, insurance, health, packing and planning, trip prep, airlines, choosing your PH, shot placement, and being in the bush. Don't go to Africa without it!

220+ pp. softcover (Jan 2008) $26 + $5 s&h (cash, please)

www.javelinpress.com
www.freestatewyoming.org